Also by Charles L. Westbrook

Nonfiction

***The Talisman of the United States, The Mysterious Street Lines of Washington, DC** (1990)*
***The Talisman of Jerusalem** (1991)*
***The Talisman of Rome** (1991)*

THE

KABALYON KEY

A Novel

From the Winston Family Chronicles

Charles Westbrook

Manufactured and printed in the United States of America
BOOK AND COVER DESIGN BY CHARLES WESTBROOK

TheKabalyonKey.com   KabalyonKey.com

1. Winston, James (Fiction) 2. Washington, DC (Fiction) 3. Vatican (Fiction) 4. Edinburgh (Fiction) 5. Paris (Fiction) 6. Jerusalem (Fiction) 7. American history (Fiction) 8. Religion (Fiction) 9. Mystery (Fiction) 10. Sociology (Fiction)

This book is a work of fiction. All of the characters, names, businesses, companies, institutions, incidents, events, and dialogue in this book are fictitious. They are drawn from the author's imagination and are not to be considered as real. Any resemblance to actual events or persons, living or dead, is purely coincidental and unintentional except for those people and events described in a historical context.

PUBLISHED BY CATHEDRALL PRESS
A division of Encycloware
PO Box 3964
Greenville, North Carolina 27836

CathedrallPress.com
encycloware.com

Library of Congress Cataloging -in- Publication Date July 2009 PRE000002239
Westbrook, Charles
The Kabalyon Key / Charles Westbrook. — Ist ed.
ISBN 978-0-9626554-1-8
ISBN 0-9626554-1-4   (paperback: Limited Illustrated Edition)
The Kabalyon Key Trade Mark and Copyright 2004, 2005, 2006, 2007, 2008, 2009

FIRST EDITION: JULY 2009

10 9 8 7 6 5 4 3 2 1

Each generation leaves its mark on the world.

Dedicated to all of those who search for
the light of religious freedom.

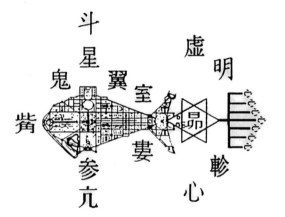

"On the study of history … at best hypothetical, say, as a novel." Jakob Burckhardt

(a) FINDINGS - Congress makes the following findings:

(1) The right to freedom of religion undergirds the very origin and existence of the United States. Many of our Nation's founders fled religious persecution abroad, cherishing in their hearts and minds the ideal of religious freedom. They established in law, as a fundamental right and as a pillar of our Nation, the right to freedom of religion. From its birth to this day, the United States has prized this legacy of religious freedom and honored this heritage by standing for religious freedom and offering refuge to those suffering religious persecution. International Religious Freedom Act, 1998

This book is a hiding place where I can lose myself for a time.

"I have seen the fnords."

What if our sole purpose in life is to see God?

September 22, 2004 - The Day of the Equinox
"Out of the Mouths of Babes."

I sat in a McDonald's this morning, next to a glass window painted over with the golden arches. I was working on my laptop, writing a novel titled *The Kabalyon Key* which deals with the mysteries of *the presence* of God's love and how people sometimes do not see it. A little girl I had never met before, no more than four- or five-years-old, wearing a *bright* blue travel-light T-shirt from L. L. Bea*m*, walked up to me and asked,
"Why are you working on the computer—here?"
I told her, "I had to get some work done."
She said, "I love you."
I asked, "What?"
She said, "I love you."
Steganographic. *Hidden in plain sight*. God speaks through tiny miracles. God spoke to me today.

"And Jesus said, 'I praise you, Father, Lord of heaven and earth, because you have hidden these things from the wise and learned, and revealed them through our angels—the little children.' " Luke 10:21.

***

This book is a labyrinth which can be read in every direction and gives intimation of, and points to, its Author. A special thanks to Lea, Mitch, Mike, Rick, and Susan.

Real learning takes place when people are exposed to new ideas which allow them to delve into the subject for themselves.

"All that I am sure of is that I do not know." Socrates

"Our intense need to understand will always be a powerful stumbling block to our attempts to reach God in simple love ... and must always be overcome. For if you do not overcome this need to understand, it will undermine your quest. It will replace the darkness which you have pierced to reach God with clear images of something which, however good, however beautiful, however Godlike, is not God." *The Cloud of Unknowing*

THE
KABALYON KEY

Et in Arcadia ego
THE LIPS OF WISDOM ARE SEALED,
EXCEPT TO THE EARS OF UNDERSTANDING
True Transmutation is a Mental Art
You and I are One

Cosmographica

Yet if Paradise did exist in this earth of ours, many a man among those who are keen to know and enquire into all kinds of subjects, would think he could not be too quick in getting there: for if there be some who to procure silk for the miserable gains of commerce, hesitate not to travel to the uttermost ends of the earth, how should they hesitate to go where they would gain a sight of Paradise itself?

Illustration from a woodcut found in Basil Valentine's *Azoth Philosophorum (Philosophy of the Secret Fire, the Great Secret of Alchemy)* revealing the mandala map used to alter consciousness. Valentine was a fifteenth-century German monk of the Order of Saint Benedict. A hermaphrodite stands upon a winged fire-breathing dragon. The dragon stands upon a winged globe with a triangle and square from Euclid's geometry of the square of the four and the triangle of the three inscribed at the center. In the enclosed space of an egg is the double-headed hermaphrodite (a Shiva Ardhanareeswara, a Harihara, and the Platonic symbol of the Soul - thymos, eros, and logos), a male on its right and a female on its left. The word "rebis" is on its breast. In its right male hand *it* (the homo-faber) holds a compass. The left female hand holds the set square. Above its head is the symbol of Mercury. On the male side are the symbols for Mars, Venus, and the Sun. On the female side are the symbols for Jupiter, Saturn, and the Moon. This illustration can also be found in *The Illustrated History of Freemasonry*, Moses W. Redding. Redding & Co., New York: 1892.

Historical Notes and Facts

Over one thousand new viruses attack computers connected to the World Wide Web each month. Computer hackers are hired by businesses and governments to advise them on computer security.

Nikola Tesla transmitted low frequency signals tuned to the Earth's natural resonance frequencies. Tesla was implemental in the discovery of alternating current.

The *Kybalion* is a real book, available in the public domain. The word *kabalyon* is encrypted within the Bible.

Thomas Jefferson listed the *Cabala, Mysteries of State* (1691) among the books in his personal library cataloged under the subheading of Politics. Also included in his library were *Philo de temporibus, Edifies anciennes de Rome par Desgodetz* (1779), *Architecture del Alberti* (1565), *Chamber's Chinese Designs* (1757), and *Ruins of Balbec (The Sun City of Solomon) Otherwise Heliopolis in Coelosyria* (1757).

It is known from early records that the temple complex commissioned by Roman Emperor Hadrian for *Colonia Aelia Capitolina*, now modern-day Jerusalem, was designed by the same architects responsible for the temple complex at Baalbek in Lebanon.

James Turner Barclay purchased the house and grounds of Thomas Jefferson's estate, Monticello, with the exception of the family graveyard, from the heirs of Jefferson in 1833. General John Hartwell Cocke, Barclay's neighbor and a friend of Jefferson's, who received a letter from Joseph Cobell concerning keys placed in Jefferson's coffin, tried unsuccessfully to buy the estate before Barclay's purchase. Barclay cut down trees and dug up the grounds surrounding the house at Monticello under the pretense of establishing a silkworm farm. He dismantled parts of the house, which he left in ruins. Six years later, after selling the property to Commodore Uriah Levy, Barclay and his family embarked on a topographic archeological expedition to Palestine. Barclay wrote a history of Jerusalem titled *City of the Great King; Jerusalem: As It Was, As It Is, and As It Is To Be*, which was published in 1858 after he returned to the United States. Commodore Levy bequeathed Monticello to the United States Government at his death in 1862. Between 1833 and 1878, the graveyard at Monticello was periodically looted by souvenir hunters. The obelisk erected over Jefferson's grave was reportedly replaced twice. During the Civil War, the state of Virginia took control of Monticello. In 1864, Monticello was purchased by one of the founders of the Confederate Secret Service, Benjamin Franklin Ficklin, but it would be stripped from him under Reconstruction. In 1879, the Federal Government auctioned off Monticello to Levy's nephew, one of the richest men in the United Sates, who sold Monticello to the Thomas Jefferson Foundation in 1923.

Devil's Tower, an extinct volcano, is a holy site for the Dakota Plains Indians who carry out a twenty-eight day Sundance initiation each year at the time of the summer solstice. Devil's Tower was the first National Monument in the United States.

Arthur's Seat, an extinct volcano, is a holy site associated with the Beltane Fires Festival, which corresponds to the vernal equinox. The Queen of England's summer residence, the Palace of Holyrood House, is next to Arthur's Seat. Holyrood derives its name from a Celtic reference to the Cross of Jesus. Arthur's Seat is in the shape of a lion.

As of 2008, the Sea King was no longer the helicopter used by the White House.

St. Peter's Basilica, whose dome dominates the Roman skyline, is aligned by way of the street patterns to the celestial equinox and the solstice.

In 1760, two teenagers, Dabney Carr and Thomas Jefferson, met while attending Rev. James Maury's *Classical School for Boys.* On weekends they climbed to the top a bare hill on the Shadwell plantation, which Jefferson later named Monticello, to study the classics under a great oak tree. Years later, Carr and Jefferson became two of the principal Virginian revolutionaries that charted the course for a new nation.

At auction in Amsterdam in 1789, Thomas Jefferson purchased a copy of Theodor de Bry's 1619 edition of *Grand Voyages to the Americas, designed to promote the 'rightful' claim of Protestants to settle America.* On the cover is a picture of Theodor de Bry, a noted Frankfurt publisher and engraver of illustrations of alchemical and Rosicrucian works by Michael Maier and Robert Fludd, holding a **compass** in one hand and **skull** in the other, two enlightened symbols of knowledge.

The first volume of de Bry's edition contained Thomas Harriot's *Briefe and true report of the new found land of Virginia, a report on Sir Walter Raleigh's 1585 expedition by Harriot, the first European mathematician to visit America.* Included were engravings of John White's drawings related to idol worship and the design of an Indian lodge. Most historians believe that Jefferson used Harriot's report from de Bry's edition as his guide in writing his enlightened treatise *Notes on the State of Virginia, of 1785.* Included in de Bry's volume was a folded map of the West Indies, of unknown origin, and the first published, accurate engraving of Christopher Columbus.

Christopher Columbus discovered the Bahamas on his first voyage in 1492 and spent twelve days there before sailing on to Cuba and Hispaniola. It is uncertain where he sighted his first landfall. It is traditionally accepted that the historic event occurred on San Salvador, formerly Watling Island, at the extreme southeastern end of the Bahamas. It is believed that Columbus navigated across the Atlantic using either dead reckoning or the more accurate method of sailing down a latitude line. A dead reckoning course would have placed his landfall in the southern Bahamas. The more accurate method of latitude sailing would have placed his landfall near North Eleuthera, south of the Great Abcro near the current 77 degree longitude. On his second voyage, Columbus measured his latitude position using solstice observations at Discovery Bay in Jamaica near the same longitude. On his fourth voyage, he explored the coast of what is now Panama and sailed as far south as the mouth of the Columbia Bay, the southern position of the 77 degree longitude. He then sailed north to Cuba and was stranded for one year on the north coast of Jamaica where he observed a lunar eclipse at St. Ann's Bay which allowed him to determine his longitudinal position. He recalculated his latitude to be 19°, which is within one degree of the correct number.

The first project funded by the Constitutional Government of the United States was the creation of a city plan for Washington, D.C. That project was overseen by then Secretary of State, Thomas Jefferson. Major Pierre Charles L'Enfant *did not* design the city plan for Washington, D.C. On April 15, 1790, one year to the day before the cornerstone for the District was anointed in Masonic ceremonies, Congress ordered Jefferson to create a new uniform system of coinage, weights, and measures for the country. Like an ancient practitioner of dactylomancy, Jefferson devised a method based upon the motion of a pendulum stationed at the 38 degree latitude. He considered the motion of the Earth the constant and standard around which all other things should be measured.

   He wrote: "There exists not in nature, as far as has been hitherto observed, a single subject or species of subject accessible to man which presents one constant and uniform dimension.

   The globe of the earth itself, indeed, might be considered as invariable in all its dimensions, and that its circumference would furnish an invariable measure; but no one of its circles, great or small, is accessible to a measurement through all its parts, and the various trials to measure definite portions of them have been of such various result as to show there is no dependence on that operation for certainty.

   Matter, then, by its mere extension, furnishing nothing invariable; its motion is the only remaining resource.

The motion of the earth round its axis, though not absolutely uniform and invariable, may be considered as such for every human purpose. It is measured obviously, but unequally, by the departure of a given meridian from the sun and its return to it, constituting a solar day. Throwing together the inequalities of solar days, a mean interval, or day, has been found and divided by very general consent into 86,400 equal parts.

A pendulum, vibrating freely in small and equal arcs may be so adjusted in its length as, by its vibrations, to make this division of the earth's motion into 86,400 equal parts, called seconds of mean time.

Such a pendulum, then, becomes itself a measure of determinate length, to which all others may be referred to as to a standard." (**Plan for Establishing Uniformity** etc.,1790.)

Jefferson later changed his system under the advice of a principal player in the French Revolution, Charles Maurice de Talleyrand-Périgord, the Bishop of Autun.

"Almighty God hath created the mind free ... All attempts to influence it by temporal punishments or burthens ... are a departure from the plan of the Holy Author of our religion ... No man shall be compelled to frequent or support any religious worship or ministry or shall otherwise suffer on account of his religious opinions or belief, but all men shall be free to profess and by argument to maintain, their opinions in matters of religion. I know but one code of morality for men whether acting singly or collectively." – These quotes appear on the panel of the northwest interior wall of the Jefferson Memorial. Excerpted from two sources: first, "A Bill for Establishing Religious Freedom, 1777," the last sentence beginning "I know but one..." is taken from a letter to James Madison, August 28, 1789.

Birdwatching is the second-largest hobby, next to gardening, in North America. There are approximately sixty-five million birders in the United States, who spend at least eight hours every week in the field observing birds.

According to ex-Jesuit priest Dr. Malachi Martin, the author of *The Keys of This Blood* and *Windswept House,* "Black Rites" have been performed at the Vatican. Both *FRONTLINE* (PBS) and *60 Minutes* (CBS) have aired reports on "God's Banker" about the Vatican's involvement with the Italian "black" Freemasonry lodge, Propaganda Due, a "state within a state."

Thirty-five percent of Americans have been marked with at least one tattoo.

Three days before the transit of Venus in June of 2004, a former President of the United States died. In the 300 days following the transit of Venus, a Pope died and was entombed at St. Peter's. A future king with a Scottish lineage and the Supreme Governor of the Church of England was remarried. The *Global Icon* was moved to a new location within the Louvre.

The photophone, first tested in Washington, D.C., is the forerunner of modern fiber optic communications.

The largest ongoing engineering project in the United States is America's farms. The second is the American highway system. North Carolina has the largest state-maintained highway network in the United States.

The English Royal family owns approximately 6,600 million acres of land, one sixth of all the land on Earth. In the United States, the Federal Government is the largest land owner.

In 1790, on the return trip from Peking, A. E. van Braam Houckgeest, a Dutch-American tradesman, presented a porcelain plate service to Martha Washington. Each plate features the initials "MW" in the center of a golden sun surrounded by a closed chain of elliptical links with the names of the fifteen states that comprised the United States alongside a thin ouroboros serpent (Ananta-Sesha nāga) biting its tail. A banner underneath the sun contained the Latin motto "DECUS *ET TUTAMEN AB ILLO*" — A Glory and Defense from It. The ouroboros (a symbolic hermeneutic circle) was a popular icon during the American Revolution, a symbol of eternal life and indivisible knowledge.

According to x-ray analysis by the Louvre's research laboratory, the *Global Icon* - the symbol of the Ideal, better known as the *Mona Lisa,* or the black widowed *Femmes Fatale,* the female personification of Death and the alluring woman in art and literature, like the bibical Lilith in the garden or Salome who dances the seven veils and holds the Baptist's head on a silver platter - has been painted over at least three times. There is no documented evidence that it was painted by Leonardo da Vinci. In 1987, archeologists discovered a 1700 year-old mosaic of a woman's face on the floor of a Roman temple in Sepphoris in Galilee, the traditional birthplace of the Virgin Mary. The mosaic has since been called "The Mona Lisa of Roman Palestine."

Dr. Carl Jung believed that humanity and nature share a common consciousness, as did Plato, Thomas Jefferson, Albert Einstein, Joseph Campbell, G. W. F. Hegel, Immanuel Kant, Friedrich Schelling, Sir Isaac Newton, Emanuel Swedenborg, Frederick Law Olmsted, Ralph Waldo Emerson, as well as Yeshu ha-Notzri, better known as Jesus of Nazareth.

The Crown Point Lodge, the tavern of Colonel Shadrack Allen, in Pitt County, North Carolina was visited by President George Washington on his Southern Tour in 1791 during the planning of Washington, DC. The Crown Point Lodge was considered a training lodge for the early craft of Freemasonry in North Carolina. Charles Westbrook grew up near the site of the old lodge. He acquired part of the library of Colonel Allen in 1976 as a gift from a friend.

Washington, D.C., as well as other cities and landscapes, may have been designed to form the images presented in this book. These images are the copyrighted artistic expression and intellectual property of Charles L. Westbrook.

"Those who labour in the earth are the chosen people of God."

Thomas Jefferson, Notes on the State of Virginia

"Where is to be found Theology more orthodox or Phylosophy more profound than in the Introduction to the Shast[r]a? 'God is one, creator of all, Universal Sphere, without beginning, without End. God Governs all the Creation by a General Providence, resulting from his eternal designs. — Search not the Essence and the nature of the Eternal, who is one; Your [Jefferson's] research will be vain and presumptuous. It is enough that, day by day, and night by night, You adore his Power, his Wisdom and his Goodness, in his Works."

John Adams to Thomas Jefferson, December 25, 1813

Aum...brel...la

In the middle of a sun-scorched desert, the thirsty shepherd and his flock approached the flowering acacia, its gnarled and twisted branches reaching toward heaven.
Flickering shards of sunlight filtered past its leaves. He heard the sound of birds.

Prologue

He directed his coffin to be made on yesterday morning: Had **all his keys** put under his head. He had frequently declared that he did not wish to live any longer than the 4th July; & was not afraid to meet death. The night before last he said I resign myself to my God. – *Joseph Cabell* to John Cocke, 4 July 1826.

CHARLOTTESVILLE, VIRGINIA — APRIL, 1878

Cloaked in the black of night, a pulsing glow through the glass globe of a lantern fitfully illuminated the darkness.

Two sweat-drenched U. S. Army privates in red shirts and dirt-covered blue trousers held up by Y-back suspenders clambered atop a loose earthen mound tracked with ankle-deep footprints that spiraled to an opened grave.

One private blew out a match he had used to relight the dying wick of the kerosene lantern he clenched in his hand. The other private slumped in exhaustion, clutching the sturdy oak handle of a shovel plunged vertically into the ground.

"The light went dead, sir. I'm sorry." The private holding the lantern waved his hand in front of his face to chase away the sooty stench of the flame.

"Don't let it happen again," a raspy voice called out from the bottom of the grave.

"How does it look, sir?" The private aimed the lantern over the edge of the opened pit.

"Very well preserved," replied an officer in a naval uniform. Hunching forward, he examined the condition of a closed, lead-lined cedar casket. He hastily brushed away clumps of loam covering its lid, revealing a finely carved circular crest of two scrolled letters surrounded by the words:

REBELLION TO TYRANTS IS OBEDIENCE TO GOD

"I'm going to pry it open," the officer explained, wedging the blade of a chisel into a seam where the lid joined to the inner leaden coffin. A loud *crackle* pealed the air as he broke the soldered seal. He dropped his tools and anchored the ends of his fingers under the edge of the lid. "Hold that light steady."

The heavy wooden lid *creaked* as he lifted and shoved it to one side.

"Goddamn, look at him." The officer glared at the secretive smirk on the face of the hallowed corpse sleeping with the earth.

A night owl screeched, *"Who ... Who ... Who do you see?"*

The eyes of both privates widened as they knelt down to get a closer look.

"Immortal demigod, it's the Devil himself." One of the privates bowed his head and swiped his hand in front of his face and chest in the sign of the cross. "He's the spit and image of his portraits. He could have been buried just yesterday!"

"Petrified," the officer remarked. "It must be the soil."

"There it is, sir." The other private gestured with a firm handhold on the swaying lantern. "It's tucked under his left hand, exactly where Major Ficklin's report on the Burrowsville preacher claimed it would be."

Sweeping, light-filled shadows rippled back and forth across the grave.

"I see it." The officer leaned forward and gingerly tugged on a red, leather-bound book. "He's got one hell of a grip on this thing."

The officer pried the book free with a forceful jerk. The book flew open and ancient pages, barely clinging to the binding, separated into a falling blanket over the corpse.

"Move the light this way," the officer cried. "Some of the pages fell out—"

"There, sir." The private wielding the lantern spotted a brittle, worm-eaten page lying outside the casket.

The other private pulled the shovel from the ground and pointed with the handle. "Another page is over there."

"I think I have them all." The officer shuffled the detached pages back into the sticky, mildew-slickened cover of the book.

"Don't forget the keys," the private holding the shovel reminded. "General Cocke's letter we found at Bremo said the keys were hidden under his head."

 The officer groped under a velvet pillow supporting the corpse's head. "I feel something." He retrieved a wadded up leather chord tied to two brass keys and bundled around a sculptured walnut-size clay figure of a human skull. He eyed the Cross of Saint Andrew carved on the back of the skull. "A Scottish token ... I've got them," he affirmed, slipping the items into his coat pocket.

Suddenly, a bull-throated voice bellowed out of the darkness, "Is that the book?"

"Yes, it is, sir." The officer peered up through the harsh wash cast from a lantern brandished before the bearded face of a gangly gentleman wearing a gray towncoat and matching coachman top hat.

"Hand it to me," the man in the gray coat directed in a pragmatic tone. He held out his opened hand.

The officer carefully passed the book to him.

"Un-*believ*-able." The man's voice clipped with impatience as his deep-set eyes pored over the cover of the deteriorating book. "And to think that Barclay spent nearly three years searching for this." The tips of his fingers traced over two Greek letters hand-tooled into the binding. "This will do. Close the casket, man. And cover his grave. We have what we came here for. I will not be accused of sacrilege. We are not common grave robbers."

"Yes, sir." The officer dropped to one knee, slid the lid shut, and the smiling face of the corpse obscured into darkness. Next to the pillow lay an undetected, single sheet of curled and yellowed parchment. Faintly penned words and numbers read:

ECOSSAIS - AGNUS DEI PALFRENIERI - CAMVLODVNVM - A HOLY HEAD - ARARAT - SAINT JOHN
Pietàn - Dun Breataìinn - Eden Cumbrian Halfdam - Gibeah to the Tomb of Amos - Brandon to Henricopolis
The Ancient Field – Shahanshah – Tagzig – Sandalyon – Arianism – Dogo-deiwos
Eochaid-Lugus – Logos – Dominus Hibernae - Cavandish - Fokas - Kefallonia - Greenville – Drake
*MedUSA's Child - A Trojan Horse - **A Deadly Fraud is This***
Poggiobonizio - Kashi - Caravaggio - Shadwell - Kells - Poplar Forest - Chadwick - Lego - Colle - Highland
Oak Hill - Chard - Pisa
Edinburgh - key of letters 8 3 1 6 9 4 7 2 5 / 2 9 18 4 6 3 7 5 / 3 Paris - Ephesus
Washington - key of lines 1 5 7 8 7 9 6 3 4 / 8 3 6 1 4 7 2 5 9 / 1 Rome - Ammann
*D. Carr - Aristotle - **Σοφια** - Apollo - Mars - Jupiter - Minerva - **Θεοτόκος** - Plato - J. Maury*
Honi soit qui mal Y pense

The private dropped the shovel and pulled with a two-fisted handgrip as he assisted the officer up from the grave. "I thought our orders were to remove the body?"

"Only from the Mazzei grave. You heard him. Cover it up," the officer commanded, stepping surefootedly onto solid ground.

The private grabbed the shovel and scattered freshly turned earth over the coffin in the wearisome *tap, tap, tap ... tap, tap, tap ...* of a Devil's tattoo.

The man in the gray coat held tightly to the book. Treading over a soggy humus of decaying leaves, he stepped past a small pile of bricks and tiles stacked at the end of another opened grave. A sprig of hemlock *snapped* under his foot. He sat down on the remains of a broad, fragmented marble slab next to a battered, six-foot-tall granite obelisk, which rested on top of temporary wooden rollers. He lifted his lantern above his head. "Hold this lamp," he instructed.

The officer moved closer to the misshapen obelisk and grasped the lantern. The shadows shifted. A few of the worn, lichen-stained words carved on one side of the obelisk, like a hidden message, were barely visible in the flickering light.

... Author of the Declaration ...
Statute
... for Religious Freedom ...

The man with the book turned to a page still clinging to the binding. "This is as fascinating as his copies of the *Lex, Rex*, the *Mabinogion*, the *De Re Rustica*, the *Vastu Shastra*, and the *Cyropaedia*. It's a map of some sort ... for the *Domesday*—a language of symbols—a philosophy of the ages. We think only in signs." He unfolded a bookmark formed from a dog-eared, Continental sixty dollar bill, imprinted with an emblem of a tilted terrestrial sphere encircled by a motto from the book of Psalms, *DEUS REGNAT EXULTET TERRA*. "God reigns, let the Earth rejoice," he translated, placing the fragile treasure back into the book. "Now, hand me the keys," he ordered.

"Here, take them." The officer pulled a leather cord dangling two keys from his pocket and dropped them into the man's waiting palm. He peeped over the man's shoulder at the strange symbols and faded illustrations scribed on the opened pages. "What do you see, Mr. Peirce?"

"I see ... our destiny." His fingers curled around the keys.

One Year Later

Thus saith the Lord God: 'Behold, I lay in Zion for a foundation a stone, a tried stone, a precious corner stone, a sure foundation: he that believeth shall not make haste.' – Isaiah 28:16 -17. The stone which the builders refused has become the head stone of the corner. – Psalm 118: 22.

Stones. Massive stones, hewn and unhewn marble blocks stacked on top of one another, surrounded two Army officers like a temporary fort in defense from an unseen evil. Behind them towered an enormous stone block wall, outlined by the amber glow of the alpha-dawning beauty of morning. The officers were dressed in uniforms of plain, dark blue trousers and single-breasted sack coats with five convex gilt buttons down the front. A gold laurel and a palm wreath encircling a silver castle on the front of their forage caps identified them as U. S. Army Engineers. The insignia on their general staff shoulder straps ranked one officer as a captain and the other as a first lieutenant.

The rickety cadence of iron-edged, wooden wheels turning on bent axles filled the air as an open carriage pulled by a team of high-stepping, snorting horses rolled up and stopped. The coachman sat motionless. The passenger, a man with a serious face framed behind a graying mustache that merged with his sideburns, energetically jumped to the ground. He tucked the sleeve of his coat under the cuff of the rider's glove protecting his left hand. His fingers brushed over a row of spiderweb patterned gold buttons beneath a circular patch depicting a golden square and compass. The insignia on his collar marked his rank as a Lieutenant Colonel. He peered in the direction of the junior officers and approached the encampment in a stiff-legged stride.

"Good morning, sir," they said in unison, standing to attention.

"Is everything ready?" the colonel asked. "I want to inspect the outer casing."

The captain nodded, patting a bulky, brown leather haversack hanging from his shoulder.

"Yes, sir." The lieutenant motioned. "This way, to the lift."

The three blue figures disappeared into the darkness as they merged with the shadow cast by the stone wall that loomed before them. Their knee boots *clapped* across twenty-inch-wide, solid oak planks that served as a walkway over the mudholes at the base of the wall. They stepped onto a metal gantry that supported a cumbersome wooden lift suspended from cables, connected to block and tackle that extended straight into the air.

"Go!" the captain shouted, rotating his forearm. With a lopsided jolt, the lift, bit by bit, crept upwards. High above them could be heard the loud *clicking* and *clacking* of ropes pulling and metal gears grinding against metal gears.

"We are leaving hallowed ground," the colonel murmured in a New England accent. His eyes shifted from side to side in the shadowy ambience as he inspected the repairs to the seams between the white marble blocks. "It's well built now." He gazed upward at the approaching edge of the wall. "With its new foundation, it should support the weight of the world."

Emerging from the shadow into the somber sunlight, the three officers were greeted by the sight of a seventy-foot-tall balance crane arching over the other side of the wall. The rigging on the crane's hoist resembled the mast and boom of a tall ship with the sails removed.

"A *Sororium Tigillum*, the Sister's Gibbet." The colonel tugged at his glove as he studied the crane.

"How's your hand?" the captain inquired.

"I have a strong hand. The wound is healing."

With another quick jolt and a pendulum sway, the unsteady lift came to a halt. Cautiously they crossed over to a wooden catwalk that wrapped over the top of the fifteen-foot-wide wall. Slipping on grains of sand scattered across the catwalk, the colonel grabbed the lieutenant's arm and caught his balance.

"Be careful. Watch your step," the lieutenant warned.

"Christ!" the colonel barked. "You need to keep this place clean." He held up his empty fist and stomped his foot. "There could be an accident."

The lieutenant snapped to attention.

The colonel locked his eyes directly with the lieutenant's. "This will not be the site of someone's grave. There will be no accidents!"

"Yes, sir," the lieutenant acknowledged in a thick Scottish brogue. "Don't get festered, sir. It will not happen again."

"To the transit, sir," the captain suggested.

The officers paraded forward. One by one, birds perched along the edge of the wall glided into the air in a V-shaped pattern, as though pushed away by an invisible force that enveloped the three officers.

"Sir, the theodolite has been set up over the newly laid stone from the *river*." The lieutenant pointed to a three-legged surveyor's transit erected over a one-foot-square stone block standing between two wooden instrument boxes. "It's at the northwest corner. It's sighting the marker that replaced the first obelisk on the main line."

"The plumb line. Is it true?" the colonel asked as they approached the transit. "It must be true." He eyed the brass bob suspended from the precision geared theodolite, its taut string ever-so-slightly vibrating as it hovered into place over a four-inch-square hollow cutout for a Lewis key.

"It's as accurate as science will allow," the lieutenant replied.

The colonel stopped short, his arms bent at the elbows with his hands resting on his waist. He keenly serpentined rearward, his face rubbernecking upward. "Plato's Heaven. Not a cloud in the sky. We're blessed. It's a perfect day for this," he boomed.

"It's the only day this year," the lieutenant remarked.

"Correct, we need to get this right." The colonel cocked his head and sighted at the transit over the stone. "Is it aligned in the right direction? Are you sure it's polar?"

"Yes, sir," the lieutenant replied. "I've followed the shadow method, equal altitudes, as well as Polaris observations. I've rechecked it twelve times. It's an optical illusion. The walls are not straight. Nothing looks straight from this height." He stooped down and raised the lid from one of the boxes. "I see myself." He grinned at his reflection in the mirrored finish of a ten-inch-diameter, gourd-shaped, brass orb securely resting inside the felt-lined box.

"The Helmholtz resonator," the colonel marveled. "Does it work?"

Cupping the resonator in his hands, the lieutenant lifted it from the box. "Listen," he shared. "It's a deep, hollow, moaning sound." He positioned it into a beveled indention at the base of the stone.

The colonel pulled at his trousers, crouched down, and placed his ear to the opening at the end of the long neck of the resonator. "Mother Earth … I hear it. The singing siren over the spindle of necessity. It's like the constant hum from a nautilus shell." He stood up and held out his hand. "Your compass, Lieutenant."

The lieutenant unfastened the buttons of his coat, reached inside, and retrieved a military pocket compass attached to a tarnished chain that hung from his neck. He unclipped it and flipped open the cover engraved with Oriental markings and symbols. "Here, sir."

The colonel held the compass close to his face, mesmerized by its hurling needle. "The bone of Haroeri. A seaman's secret. A paradoxal compass of the wise. This still amazes me. It's the only compass I've ever seen that does this." He positioned the compass on a ceramic cradle connected to a brass pedestal directly beneath the theodolite. The words *Alvan Clark and Sons of Cambridgeport, Mass.* were etched into the pedestal.

"It's like an astrolabe for the sun and moon. Set it to the plus on the rose," the lieutenant instructed, "then rotate the outer ring to locate the lunar nodes."

The colonel leaned forward, stretched his neck, and sighted through the scope with one eye closed and one arm crossed behind his back. His eye fixed on the fine-wired X of the lens centered on a hand-size, gold-painted ball perched at the top of a rusty metal pole. "The crosshairs are on the marker," he muttered. "Good job, Lieutenant."

Standing erect, the colonel pulled a crumpled scrap of paper from his pocket and referenced a list of notes, numbers, and calculations.

Decus et tutamen ab illo - *Book of Loagaeth* - *Anthemius On Burning-glasses*
National Academy of Sciences notes – Lazzaroni readings - 4/15/1862 – C. H. Davis
1. Massebah Tumoulus - Peregrinus deviation - 7 degrees 50 min. - Thomas Holme maps
2. URSE – Shiva – Selene – Kocbah to *Mizar* – Polaris according to Kabalyon
3. 5 /15 degrees 40 min - *HA=LST - a –l* = (Jnought)^2 * ((k * d * r)/(2*Z)) - Spectral density
4. Virgula divina – Air Loom – Mag. Decl.. 10W 3 degrees, 56 min. – Monoceros – Full Moon Venus rising – Arago – Hero of Alexandria – Jyotirlingam -- *Shi'ur Qomah*
5. 1 degree 7 min. – Rodrigues rotation formula, counterclockwise space transformation – Sept 18 morning - Sattvik 7.83 Hz =nv/2L U. S. Coast Survey – C. S. Peirce – Ref. Michelson
6. Potential barrier – Point where the height of energy barrier is precisely equal to the total energy, and kinetic energy is zero. Golden string – Collapse of wave function to rebuild new wave – Boltzmann constant – The Unconscious Influence – Ref. notes from chronoscope paper by *Dr. B. Brown Williams*, professor of electrical-psychology Greenville, North Carolina
7. Hippodamian grid – Harrisburgh Obelisk – John Ballendine – Simeon DeWitt – Old Scotch Tom – Yorktown – Otter Town – Aligned to Dr. Maule's 1725 survey of Beth - El from Somerset – Acquired from Maj. Gen Foster and Gen Potter's raid on Washington and Tarboro

He skillfully rotated the theodolite to a new bearing, then sighted. "I can see the mast on their dome." He referenced his notes, angled the scope toward the ground, and sighted again. "It's centered on his stone—our Zoheleth." He reset the scope, degree by degree, raising the altitude. "It's sited on Levy's statue. I see the eyes of the Father holding the Declaration."

"Everything's lined up," the captain said, recording the observations in an oversized, green-marbled ledger he had retrieved from his haversack. Handwritten notes and calculations crowded its margins. The title block at the top of the page read: U.S. ARMY CORPS OF ENGINEERS.

The colonel checked the scrap of paper one last time. He increased the altitude, rotated the scope west, then cupped his eye to the lens. "The error is as wide as the District. The moon is not at perigee. Newcomb was right. The lunar tables were wrong. It's nearing its transit position with Alcyone. The star of the individual and her six sisters, the daughters of Atlas, at the hub of the Logos. Venus should be rising. Eighteen days 'til the start of the eclipses of the sun and moon."

High above the three officers, a full moon hovered in the western sky.

"The eye of the Gorgon's head is in the crosshairs," the colonel judged, still spying through the scope across the sea of the moon. "It's converging on the crater." He rotated the scope nearly 180 degrees while lowering its angle. "I see the Gillis Marker on the old meridian. It's dead center. An excellent job, Lieutenant."

The captain approached the transit, bent down, and opened the other wooden box. The hinged box unfolded in four directions to reveal a brass clock, leveled to match the plumb line of the theodolite. Smeared letters stenciled on the inside of the box read: PROPERTY OF AG BELL – COLONIAL BEACH.

"The time?" the colonel asked.

"Three minutes away from the calculations, sir," the captain replied.

The lieutenant picked up an unfurled wig-wag flag at his feet. His arms outstretched, he signaled it above his head.

The colonel realigned the hairline marks inscribed on the rotating baseplate of the scope, then squinted through the eyepiece. Adjusting the focus, he spotted the close-up, wavy image of a man's face smiling through a window just over a mile away. "I see old Pierpont." The colonel smiled in recognition. He repositioned the mirror on a heliotrope attached to one side of the transit. Sunlight reflected off the mirror in a hundred, brilliant, silvery spikes.

The man in the window held up a pocket watch, pointed to it, then stepped to one side. As he did, the light of the sun refracted through the window's beveled glass.

"The crosshairs are perfectly aligned to the circular marks etched into the glass over his chapel," the colonel noted.

"One minute, sir!" shouted the captain.

The colonel fine-tuned the scope to a sharper image. The light intensified, widening into a spectrum of colors that bent through the lens. "Newton has done a great job with his math," he whispered.

"Thirty seconds!"

A quick flicker and the light glowed steadily through the eyepiece. The colonel recoiled from the scope, his eyes squeezed shut. "It's bright. Damn, it's bright!" He flipped a circular brass ring into position over the end of the eyepiece. The ring held a one-inch-diameter optical filter made of rose-colored gemstone. A numbered laboratory label attached to one side of the filter read: Optical-Calcite #47 Property of the Smithsonian. He sighted again through the scope. "The sun's in the circle. Time?"

"6:35," the captain reported, "with an atmospheric refraction correction, sir."

"The father rises with the sun. Their calculations are *correct*," the colonel acknowledged.

"The moon is overhead. It's beginning to wane." The lieutenant's eyes narrowed as he surveyed the sky. "I see the shadow bands in the luminous soniferous aether wind. Something's moving. Is it a shooting star or Petit's other moon?"

"Now!" the captain shouted, his concentration synchronized with the clock.

The colonel toggled the brass ring away from the eyepiece as he sighted. He rotated the scope one degree and seven minutes, then raised the altitude with a steady hand. "Yes, yes ... I see the bird's tail feathers." He smiled in awe. "God's eyes, it's perfect! Good job, Lieutenant." He detached the filter from the brass ring and dropped it into a gray felt pouch that hung from a knotted cord tied to his belt.

The lieutenant and the captain exchanged satisfied smiles.

"Captain, Lieutenant," the colonel addressed them.

They stood at attention, their faces dipping in golden waves cast from the pulsating mantle of the rising sun.

"This quoin will be the chief cornerstone," the colonel ordered. "It must not be disturbed. All measurements must be calculated from this stone. Everything must be built to a *zero tolerance*."

The colonel gaped up at a flagpole attached to the top of the crane. An outdated Centennial flag with thirty-seven stars *flapped* in the breeze. "The flags of our fathers." He spoke in a solemn tone, "This is our resolve. It is built upon a sure foundation. One hundred years. Gentlemen, what we are doing here must endure!"

塔

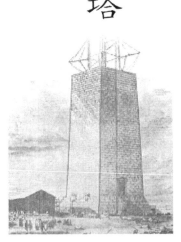

Eight Years Later

CALCUTTA, WEST BENGALI, HINDUSTAN

"Where the hell is the little weasel?" the captain muttered, staring into the bustling mosaic of human bodies parading before the entrance to the Jatayu Hotel. He heard a resonating *whirring chirp*. A bent and bony snake charmer holding a pungi flute to his lips was sitting crosslegged next to a potted fern, trying to coax a king cobra from a hole in a wicker basket full of venomous vipers.

"You are an Englishman." A shadow of a man draped in a ragged robe emerged from the faceless crowd. He pointed with his trembling hand at the captain's dusty red uniform. "Are you worthy? Did you drink—"

"He is a crazy beggar, Captain," Koffa's familiar voice called out from the crowd. "Bad *kárma*. An untouchable, not born of Purusha. Do not give him anything, or you will lose your virtue. Leave him to Bhowanee."

"You're late, Koffa." The captain glared at the wily, brown-skinned Thuggee garbed in a loose-fitting, white kurta, a grimy maroon waistcoat, with a black turban coiled atop his head. He turned back toward the barefooted stranger. The outcaste had vanished.

"The crowds, Captain. There are a million people in the streets of Kalikatta. We have plenty of time. The shop is just down the street, near the Oxford Mission. The manager will be waiting. *First*," Koffa reminded with an upturned palm, "*my payment*. No paper, only silver rupees as we agreed."

The captain pulled a leather pouch from his pocket.

"Is it all there?"

"Don't get me festered, Koffa. I'm not wasting time counting money. I trust you. Don't you trust me?" The captain tossed the pouch into the smuggler's waiting hands. "It's heavy."

"Follow me," Koffa said, tucking the pouch into the pocket of his waistcoat. He led the captain deep into Calcutta's southern millwork of bazaar-filled streets. "Ganga Niyama," Koffa translated the Hindu script on a street sign. "This way." He hustled the captain down a narrow and deserted alleyway mired with puddles of tainted water. "There is his establishment." He pointed to a weathered placard over a red wooden door left ponderously ajar on the front of a rundown, stuccoed building.

A JOHN COMPANY ☠ CALCUTTA CITY EXPORTS

On a stone bench beside the door, an old woman with her head covered with a blue odhani sat sobbing as she cradled a dead child wrapped in a yellow blanket.

"Her grandson died from the malaria," Koffa said. "Sometimes it is hard to let go." He pushed the door open. "Go inside and have a seat. The manager will be waiting."

The captain stepped through the shadowed doorway. The door slammed shut, and he found himself in the pitch-black of a strange room. Without warning, a strong hand gripped his arm and wrenched it behind his back. "What the—" The captain's Adam's apple jumped in his throat at the sting from the sharp edge of a cold blade.

"Listen carefully. Do not speak or move until I tell you to," a man with a cultured Oxford accent ordered. "Surrender your sidearm."

The captain drew his Beaumont-Adams service revolver from his shoulder holster and dropped it at his feet.

"I am going to ask you some questions, sir. Answer truthfully or it will be the death of you. Do you understand?"

"Yes."

"Who sent you?"

"Warren. General Charles Warren."

"Warren. Another one," the man groaned. "How do you know Warren?"

"I worked with him in Palestine at Gibeah."

"Palestine?"

"Yes, I'm a three-legged surveyor. We were searching for treasure."

"Are you English?"

"No. Scottish, from Edinburgh. I'm a friend of James Fergusson."

The man withdrew his dagger and released the captain's arm.

The captain stood perfectly still, his muscles tense. He heard the strike of a match and the room illuminated from the single flame of a lantern.

"So, you are the officer Koffa told me about. I am Mohandas Freer, the manager of this fine shop. I cater to the connoisseurs of Indian aesthetics." He waved his jagged-edged blade of Damascus steel in front of the captain's face. "Why are you here?"

"Like you don't know?" the captain answered smugly to the brutish Bengali in a gray sherwani jacket and a red fez topped with a white feather. "To see the *map* to the treasure of Brahma, Shiva, and Vishnu."

"*Na-Ma-Si-Va-Ya*—the faces of God. You could easily go to the Hindu temple down the street and recite a mantra from the Vedas, or visit a vihara and meditate with a traveling Brahmin vipra from Benares to learn about *that* treasure."

"I wish to discover my own way."

"Your own way." Freer laid his dagger on a table and stepped before a long, black veil covering a doorway. "Mokska-Patamu, the dangerous quest ... the Great Game of the emperors and the immortals." He thoughtfully stroked his well-manicured goatee. "How old are you? Remember ... watchful of your thoughts. Truthfully."

"Thirty-seven." The captain eyed the Y-shaped cross carved on the dagger's ivory handle as he flicked the back his middle finger across his neck and wiped away a drop of blood.

"Do you seek this treasure for yourself?"

"No."

"Do you seek it for Warren?"

"No."

"So ... for whom do you seek this treasure?"

"My children and my children's children."

Freer lifted his lantern and pulled the veil to one side. "Come with me, Captain." He led the captain into a backroom and approached a small square table draped with a dingy cloth. A bundled linen sheet, stained in hues of red, purple, and brown, was piled high at its center. Freer tied the lantern to the end of a rope suspended from a wooden beam arching over the table.

The captain peered through the dim light at the wallshelves filled with rolls of silk cloth, canvas bags stuffed with tea, and shipping boxes labeled: David Sassoon & Co.

He detected the hypnotic scent of opium. An ornately carved jade pipe lay on a shelf next to a statuette of the goddess Isi mounting a seven-headed vâhana while holding a boy with almond-shaped eyes. On the facing wall hung a circular mandala bounding the monstrous head of Makara attached to the body of a golden fish. He looked toward the end of the room at a large stone effigy of Maitreya, the future Buddha, with a broken hand and a foot missing, sitting on the floor below two framed color portraits of Queen Victoria and Baron Clive of India.

"Many have come before you in search of *this* treasure." Freer gestured with his hands toward the table. "Look!" He slowly lifted the stained sheet. "And wonder …"

The captain's eyes narrowed. "Jesus …" He squenched his noise from a foul stench. Three bearded human heads with their eyes gouged out lay in a green-brown soup of liquid muck that filled a large silver platter.

"Your predecessors," Freer chuckled. "The Three Excellencies—a Frenchman, a Spaniard, and an Italian. Brahma built our world from the heads of careless men such as these who *thought* they could discover their own way." With one hand, Freer lifted one of the heads high into the air by its blood-matted hair. "Mother's milk …" Lumps of wiggling maggots leached out from its severed neck onto the platter. "Are you certain you are prepared for this quest?"

"No," the captain answered calmly. "That's why I need a map."

Freer plunked the head back to the platter. Decaying flesh slid off bone. "You are a curious man, Captain. You know all the right answers." *Tap*— Freer knuckle-rapped the table. "Alright, I'll show it to you." He placed the platter with its contents on a nearby shelf, then returned to the table. With both hands, he snatched the tablecloth like an artful magician, swirling it upside down and back onto the table.

The captain stepped closer. "A map …"

"Yes, Captain … hidden in plain sight." Freer unleashed the rope tied to the beam and lowered the lamp toward the map. "I acquired this rare find from the discarded papers of Sir Henry Rowlinson on the Hangseseshwari temple to the goddess Kali— the skull collector who rules over the seven sacred villages of Saptagram. This map is as old as the first Magadha dynasties. Follow these symbols," he instructed, as he smoothed down the creases in the cloth. "To the west … to the rock inscriptions of Chandra Varma at Bankura, along the Road of the Weeping Panther, then north to Panchanpur between the Valley of the Lion and the Cobra … to the caves beneath this skull-shaped mountain by the Holy Sarasvati River. This is the path to Bodhyagaya."

The captain retrieved a brass pocket compass from a leather pouch attached to his belt. He flipped it open, bent forward, and aligned it to the map. "A well-marked road. It leads to …" He paused. "I've seen this before. On the stele Dieulafoy discovered near the Chogha Zanbil ziggurat in Khuzestan. A cross … a figure of some sort—"

Slam— The table shook as Freer dropped the palm of his hand over the figure on the map. "One more question, sir." His eyes were fixed on the symbols engraved on the cover of the captain's pocket compass. "Truthfully … *Who are you?*"

The captain squarely met Freer's gaze in the subdued light from the lantern's flame. "Andrew Alexander Winston."

One Hundred Years Later

HOLY TRINITY PREPARATORY SCHOOL, GEORGETOWN, MARYLAND

The glass-paneled door of the classroom swung open. A nun in a blue habit, with a Y–shaped paternoster rosary marked with gauds of knotty rudraksha seeds and bone *clattering* at her waist, entered the room clutching a purple file folder labeled: *RSCJ.* Her radiant white coiffed hood spread out over her head like bird wings, as she stepped behind a podium in front of a wide, slate-green chalkboard. ACCELERATED CLASS FOR ADVANCED LEARNERS was scrolled in bold letters across the top of the board, partially screened by an overhanging, retractable wall map of the world. A wooden plaque inscribed with the words, **Use one's God-given gifts to become the very best person possible**, hung high above the map. Directly above the plaque, the sweeping second hand on a circular clock passed twelve and the minute hand *clicked* to 9:18.

"Good morning, Sister Rosalyn," the mixed class of 4th, 5th, and 6th graders greeted in unison.

"Good morning, my little lambs," Sister Rosalyn Pierina acknowledged. She pinched the black plastic-framed reading glasses hanging from her neck and held them to her eyes while thumbing through papers from her folder. "Today I want to illustrate a lesson on the power of prayer. Please, move your chairs closer. Place them in a semi-circle around me, so everyone can see." She waved her arms in a circular motion. "Gather 'round. Front row and center."

The class of twelve students, all dressed in school uniforms of matching colors, dragged their chairs across the floor and rearranged them into the shape of a crescent moon around Sister Rosalyn.

"In a newspaper article, I read the following story about an American photographer who covered the war in Korea." Sister Rosalyn glanced back and forth between the papers in her hand and the young faces before her. "According to the newspaper, this photographer was taking photographs while walking through a field of dead American soldiers. Hundreds of young men lay bloodied and lifeless in a frozen field of ice and snow. The photographer wondered how such a good God could let something so horrible happen. So the photographer began to question the existence of God."

"Surely the man would not doubt the existence of God," a young girl commented in disbelief.

"This man did," Sister Rosalyn stressed. "So the photographer prayed to God to help him overcome his doubts. 'If you really exist, show me a sign,' the photographer pleaded as he prayed before the field of the dead." Sister Rosalyn lifted her eyes to her young audience. "That's what we do, if we have doubts. We must pray to God for an answer. What do you think God did?" she prompted.

"I don't know," said a young boy, shaking his head.

Sister Rosalyn gave the boy a bucktoothed smile. "When the photographer developed his film, he discovered that he had accidentally taken a photograph of the *ground.* To his amazement, he saw a strange shape formed by a mudhole in the middle of a slush of blue-white snow. He held the photograph up to the light and gazed at it. When he closed his eyes, he saw an afterimage of a circle of light outlining a familiar face."

"Whose face did he see?" a young girl asked.

Sister Rosalyn smiled again. "The experience made the man a believer. The face he saw was the face of God. God had shown himself and answered the man's prayer. Sometimes, all we have to do is ask." She withdrew a xeroxed copy of a photograph from her folder. "The seeds of knowledge come by way of the eye." She lifted her rosary from her side and serenely closed her eyes. " 'Lord, I do seek your face. Do not hide it from me.' " She opened her eyes. "This is a miracle picture. Children, I want you to look at this photograph for thirty seconds," she instructed. "Then close your eyes and lean your head back, and tell me what you see." She passed the photo to the boy in front of her.

Each child in turn examined the *linga* of black and white splotches.

"What do you see, Freddy Holbrook?" the sister asked a red-headed, freckled-faced boy.

"I don't see anything," Freddy said sourly. He handed it to the boy next to him.

"What about you, Raymond McCartney? What do you see?" Sister Rosalyn asked again.

Raymond opened his eyes wide, then squeezed them shut. He hesitated. "I don't see anything either." He shook his head and sighed. "Maybe a J and a heart?"

"Hand it to me, hand it to me," the girl sitting next to him demanded. She snatched the photocopy from Raymond's hand.

"And what do you see, Jane Elizabeth Walker?" Sister Rosalyn asked with a stern expression.

Jane Elizabeth glanced directly at the pinto photo. She closed her eyes and tilted her head upward, as if preparing to pray. "I don't see anything," she admitted in a pouting whine. She reluctantly passed it to the boy next to her.

"And you, James Winston. What do you see?" the sister questioned, her eyes riveted on the boy.

James, the youngest in the class, gazed at the copy of the photograph, burning what he saw into his mind's eye. His eyes blinked, then closed. A confident smile spread across his face.

"I see the face of God, *hidden in plain sight*."

He opened his probing blue eyes and stared at the Pal Cross engraved on a circular gold pendant attached to the front of Sister Rosalyn's habit.

Seven Years Ago

CAPRAROLA, NORTHERN LATIUM, ITALY

A wrinkled-faced bishop endowed in black with a scarlet sash around his hips stood alone on the balcony of the Royal Stairs of the Villa Farnese. His brow creased as his eyes wandered over the colorful landscapes, grotesques, and emblems embellishing the walls of the central colonnaded courtyard.

"Welcome, Archbishop Bracciolini," a voice echoed. "It is an honor to be visited by the secretary of the Vatican's Congregation for the Doctrine of the Faith." A cheerful, bald-headed Benedictine monk stumbled over the hem of his gray habit as he hurried up the wide marble stairway. "*Scusi,* Archbishop. I am running late. I am Monsignor Flavius Luni. I am your guide. Is this your first time to the villa?"

"Once before," Bracciolini replied with downturned eyes at the awkward monk, "when I was younger."

"This beautiful villa was commissioned in 1559 by Cardinal Alessandro Farnese, a nephew of Pope Paul III." Luni fidgeted with the sleeve of his habit. "It was built by the architect Giacomo Barozzi da Vignola on the foundations of an old fortress, the reason for its pentagonal shape. Vignola was one of the architects of the Jesuit Church of the Gesu in Rome. He is noted for his single point perspective technique. As you know, Cardinal Farnese authorized the founding of the Jesuits."

"*Sì.*" Bracciolini nodded.

"During the High Renaissance, the Farneses were a very influential family in Caprarola. Our city was once a center of Christian Kaballic teaching."

"Monsignor Luni, I am *only* interested in the Room of Maps. I need to compare the zodiac on the sky map to the illuminations from this codex unearthed during the excavation of the Temple of Asclepius in Aydin, Turkey." Bracciolini held out a red, leather-bound book gripped in his six-fingered hand, its cover embossed with the image of a woman cradling two children.

"This way, Archbishop." Luni led Bracciolini up the spiraling stairway to the fifth floor loggia and approached a large set of grilled doors. "We keep this room locked during the winter." He groped through the pocket of his habit and retrieved a ring of keys. "The key." The keys slipped through his fingers, falling onto the foot of the archbishop. "*Scusi.*" Luni bowed down as though to kiss the archbishop's feet and picked them up.

Bracciolini smirked in disapproval.

"The key that locks this room, also unlocks." Luni tested a key in the keyhole of the rusty lock. "But sometimes you have to turn it the other way." *Clunk—* He pushed open the heavy door and ushered his guest into an immense room, its walls covered in maps of the world, its vaulted ceiling frescoed with a zodiac of the heavens. "The Sala del Mappamondo is an artistic marvel. These map friezes where created by Orazio Trigini de' Marii, a Renaissance specialist in cosmography and geography, and Giovanni Antonio Vanosino, a church expert on chorography and topography."

"Topography?" Bracciolini questioned.

"*Sì,* the surveying of cities," Luni replied as he pointed to the ceiling. "Some believe this sky map was modified at some later date with the addition of Jupiter, derived from a cartoon by Michelangelo."

Bracciolini looked up at the mythical figures that formed the ornate zodiac. "The healing powers of the starry sky." His eyes settled on the unusual depiction of Capricorn. "Two goats." He opened his book to a marked page.

"Like the damaged map at the Sala Bologna at the Vatican, this sky map is said to represent the visible sky on a specific date." Luni pointed. "Its zodiacal signs are strangely out of place. The disordering allows the positioning of four signs to a larger scale, which renders this zodiac pointless for astronomy or an astrology horoscope. Notice the centering of Ophiuchus and the cross-vaulted pairing of Capricorn and Libra at the southwest end of the room. The scene contains elements from the myths of Capella and Capricorn. The supreme deity on the *ground* is shown as an infant, nursing under a she-goat Capricorn—the sign of late December, the birth of the new sun, and Emperor Augustus. Some say this image is a pun on Cardinal Farnese's nurturing patronage to Caprarola, which means goat hill. Others say it signifies the union of pax Rome with pax *christi* to form the perfected Christian Commonweath."

"Libra … a *fire* on her altar. A Hindu or Zorastrian calendar perhaps … health, justice, liberty. A crossed-vaulted pairing … the solstice." Bracciolini's eyes traveled the ceiling, then downward to a wall map of the two Americas illuminated in gold. "The place." He read the name on a portrait in a false niche over the map. "Colombo."

"There are seven geographic maps of the world on the walls," Luni explained. "The niches contain the portraits of noted explorers. The two maps on the northern wall emphasize the holy cities of Jerusalem and Rome. Notice the allegorical scenes of the Jewish high priest holding the round temple sheltering a menorah on the map of Jerusalem, and the seven hills above the terrestrial globe on the map of Rome."

Bracciolini turned a page in the codex to a drawing of a woman cradling a child below the symbol of a menorah combined with the Magen David. "A virgin … Virgo." He looked up, searching the ceiling for the constellation. "Aries, *der Januar*, Taurus, *der Feber*, Sagittarius …? *Nein*—" He shook his head. "It is not correct."

♓ ♈ ♉ ♐ ♑ ♒ ♌ ♊ ♋ ♍ ♎ ♏

"Remember, the signs are out of sequence, Archbishop. The zodiac in this sky map begins with Pisces rather than Aries. The corresponding months have to be read in the following order: 12, 1, 2, 9, 10, 11, 5, 3, 4, 6, 7, and 8. This results in a shift of the sign of Virgo into the fall of the year. Some believe the relocation of Virgo on this sky map signifies the Fourth Eclogue of Virgil which prophesies the return of a virgin who would give birth to a child who would bring forth a Golden Age of Truth."

"*Ja*, Ashvin." Bracciolini nodded. "*Novus Ordo Seclorum*, a Virgin, the protector."

"The proper zodiacal order for the three signs following Taurus are Gemini, Cancer, and Leo. But on this sky map they read from left to right." Luni arched his arm, moving it from sign to sign. "Leo … Gemini … Cancer. This suggests a deliberate decision to emphasize Gemini. Just as Capricorn and Libra are paired, Gemini and Aries are also paired at the opposite ends of the vault."

"Gemini—*airborne* in the clouds—a Solstice," Bracciolini noted. "Aries—*treading water*—an Equinox. Blood of the Lamb." He turned the page to a figuration of a three-headed shepherd embracing a lamb. "Poemandres—one flock, one shepherd, one church." He eyed the drawing at the bottom of the page, a woman holding two children. "Siblings." He stared upward to the ceiling. "Gemini, a biform … Twins."

Day 1
Zero Tolerance

We assert a posture of zero-tolerance for any "white man's shaman" who rises from within our own communities to "authorize" the expropriation of our ceremonial ways by non-Indians; all such "plastic medicine men" are enemies of the Lakota, Dakota and Nakota people. (Part five of the Declaration of War Against Exploiters of Lakota Spirituality, passed at the Dakota Summit V, a gathering of US and Canadian Lakota, Dakota, and Nakota Nations, consisting of about 500 representatives from 40 different tribes and bands of the Lakota, unanimously passed on June 10, 1993

THE EARTH TREMBLED under his feet, as a young man adjusted the earpiece from his i-Pod. Swaying his body in a slow spin, he closed his eyes and sang off-key to the voice of Louis Armstrong singing, "It Was a Wonderful World."

"I see trees …"

Midsummer in Paris is like no other time of the year. Because of the city's latitudinal location, the sun always sets late in the day in summer, sometimes lingering as late as 9:18 P.M. in this "City of Light" that never sleeps.

The time was twenty-five minutes before 9:18 A.M. As with every morning except Tuesdays, a long line of visitors began to form at the entrance to the Crystal Pyramid. Faces from every corner of the globe gathered around the seven public fountains in the Louvre's Grand Plaza.

An elderly African woman, wrapped in the Grecian folds of a pale yellow shawl, read from her guidebook, her head bent over as though in contemplative prayer.

An East Indian couple and their child waited patiently. The young mother fleetly fanned herself with a rouge-colored booklet, as her husband cradled their frightened fledgling who was too young to understand the significance of the place.

Draped in pastel green chiffon, an Italian madame with an elegant sense of fashion sat casually at the edge of a fountain. Cross-legged, she seesawed one foot dangling a stiletto while twirling a sky-blue silk-lace parasol over her shoulder, her swanlike neck angling her face toward the warmth of the morning sun.

A dreamy-eyed, middle-aged Japanese gentleman wearing dark-rimmed glasses held a black denim knapsack labeled *Northface* in his left hand and an old, 23.5 mm *Canon* camera in his right. He gazed up at the cornices of the buildings that surrounded him. His head owlishly pivoted as he leisurely inspected the fifty-two statues of painters, mathematicians, and philosophers that guarded like a pantheon of Greek gods over the entrance to a sacred space.

A deaf couple spoke to each other in sign language, sharing secrets that no one could hear.

"Coo-coo-ca-roo. Peace to you," a snow-white dove cooed its singsong and took flight above the Crystal Pyramid that loomed before the daily drama.

THE SEVENTY-SEVEN-FOOT-TALL, Egyptian-style structure consisted of a network of cables that supported six hundred and seventy-eight panels of diamond-shaped crystal glass. Serving as the modernist emblem of the Louvre, the Crystal Pyramid had been created by the Chinese-American architect and former Harvard professor Itoh Ming Pei. In Chinese the name Itoh Ming means "to inscribe brightly."

Pei and his firm had done just that, with an impressive list of architectural wonders which covered the globe, including the East Wing of the National Gallery in Washington, D.C., the John F. Kennedy Library in Boston, the Portland Museum of Art in Portland, Maine, the National Center for Atmospheric Research in Boulder, Colorado, and the Rock and Roll Hall of Fame in Cleveland, Ohio.

"ALL THESE STRANGERS making plans … thinkin' things they got to do. What they need to think is … I LUV—" The young man opened his eyes to see the lady who had been standing behind him, smiling at him. Appearing somewhat red-faced, he smiled back. "Hello. I wasn't aware you were standing there," said the twenty-year-old college student who had forged to the head of the line. He removed his earpiece, turned off his i-Pod, and placed it into his camera bag. "I'm Mike Archer. It's my first time here. I'm from the States. I live in Kitty Hawk, North Carolina." He pointed to the airplane logo on the front of his Carolina blue T-shirt. "I've been in Paris for two days." Mike eyed the man standing next to the lady. The middle-aged couple were dressed in *bright,* matching, khaki-colored, travel-light clothing from L. L. Bea*m*.

"Kitty Hawk," remarked the lady's husband, "Kill Devil Hills. The first powered airplane. Ezekiel's Machine. The Wright Brothers, the birdmen."

"Yes. The home of the first flight," Mike said proudly. "First, man saw the birds, then the Wright Brothers came."

"No, I believe the first flight happened in Spain. The first glider was flown by the Islamic astronomer Abbas Ibn Firnas," the husband corrected with a smile. "And the French might say, first man saw the birds, and then the Montgolfier brothers came—"

"G'day," the man's wife interrupted. "I'm Mary and this is John." She motioned to her husband. "We're from the Godzone—New Zealand, Queenstown. I'm originally from Canberra. I grew up on Arthur Circle near Collins Park. John's an airplane pilot—one of the Flying Angels. I raise tropical fish. I specialize in ribboned seadragons, the *Haliichthys taeniophorus Gray,* the old Rainbow Serpents once worshiped by the aboriginals of Australia. They are a rare species, very hard to find. They blend right in with their surroundings. We've toured much of Southern Europe over the past two months." She began to describe the course of their recent travels. "We started in Morocco, then crossed Gibralter to Spain. We've spent time in Madrid, Barcelona, and Nice. It's quite nice in Nice. We toured the King's château at Amboise, then visited Chartres, where we walked the labyrinth in the Cathedral of the Assumption of the Virgin and saw the Virgin's Holy Tunic. They say the Ark of the Covenant is hidden at Chartres Cathedral. And now we're touring Paris for the next four days. It's our first time here also. We're very excited to be visiting the Louvre."

"I can't wait!" Mike said excitedly. "I've been planning this day for three years. I'm an art major, with a minor in photography. I have an interest in old paintings, especially the works from the Renaissance. Modern photography is rooted in the iconic techniques developed by the Renaissance painters," he explained as he studied the camera hanging around her husband's neck. "I see you have a camera. Do you want me to take your picture?"

"No time," John replied. He pointed to the entrance.

At that moment, the guard changed the sign to *ENTRÉE DE LA COUR NAPOLÉON.* Without any instructions to do so, without any pushing after their patient wait, the long line of international visitors began their procession into the Crystal Pyramid.

Inside the entrance, four guards supervised a security station. On a long metal table sat an x-ray machine manufactured by **Rapid-I-Scan Security Products,** a California company that had cashed in on the increased global fears associated with terrorism. Rapid-I-Scan offered a wide array of turnkey systems for their customers worldwide, such as airports, courthouses, mail rooms, schools, prisons, churches, embassies, palaces, and museums. The trademark on the machine, a fish-eye, included the company slogan:

To See Beyond the Surface of Things

Mike noticed the sudden change on the faces of everyone standing in line, proper and expressionless. A nervous-looking man with fear in his eyes was ordered to stand aside and spread-eagle, outstretched in the pose of Leonardo da Vinci's *Vitruvian Man,* while a guard traced the pentagram outline of his body with a magnetic wand.

"Please empty the contents from your bags and pockets into the trays." Another guard handed Mike a shoebox-size plastic tray.

Mike heeded the guard's instructions and placed the tray into the two-foot-square opening at the front of the x-ray machine. He passed through a security archway. A third guard directed him to turn in a full circle as an air mist from the archway's trace analyzer hissed like a snake, sensing for explosives.

"Next." The guard motioned Mike forward.

Mike watched with concern as the guard at the end of the table manhandled his $4,000 digital camera. "Be careful with that—" He instinctively raised his hand to ask permission to speak.

The guard glanced at Mike as he inspected the optical toy. He noticed a name tag: *J.J. Archer.* He nodded his approval and placed it in a tray.

After hastily securing his camera, Mike scampered aboard an escalator to the below-ground lobby. In a steady descent, he scouted out the voluminous geometric-space.

This has been my dream. His eyes narrowed, studying the glass pyramid above him. *Look at this thing. It's designed like a necker.* He bowed his head over the railing and noted the crisscross diamond-shaped shadows spread over the marble floor below. *The light shines in from every direction. There're sundogs and rainbows dancing on the floor. Where's the nearest ticket counter?* He surveyed the spacious lobby. *Ah ... there it is.* He dashed to the ticket window. "A day pass, please."

"Twenty Euros," said a balding gentleman peeping over the rims of his gold, pince-nez glasses. "Do you need a visitor's guide? Or maybe an audio guide?"

"No. Just a day pass." Mike scooped a handful of coins from the side pocket of his camera bag and slapped them onto the counter. All but one of his coins were Italian one-Euros with the bas-relief of Leonardo's *Vitruvian Man. Ten Euro cents, the* Birth of Venus *by Botticelli,* Mike recognized the image on the single coin. *Hmm ... Renaissance Humanism.*

"One moment, *Monsieur.*" The ticket agent counted, "... *dix-huit, dix-neuf, vingt.*"

In a Devil's tattoo, Mike drummed his fingertips on top of the counter in a rhythmic *tap-tap-tap-tap, tap-tap-tap-tap.* Annoyed, he slumped to one side, checking his Timex Expedition wristwatch, while the agent bureaucratically processed the receipt. *I do not have time for all this. I need to get there before a crowd forms.*

"Here is your ticket, *Monsieur.*"

"Mer-see," Mike said, thanking him in a poorly mimicked French accent. He snatched the pass from the countertop, beelined to the south sortie to the Denon Wing, and waved the pass at an inattentive attendant who halfheartedly guarded the entrance.

Peering through half-closed eyes, the attendant nodded his approval, and Mike, wide-eyed, walked into the chambered heart of the cultural maze.

"Signs mark the way," Mike muttered to himself, noticing a cardboard poster of the famous face with the hypnotic Medusa stare and enigmatic smile above a two-inch-wide, red arrow that pointed down a corridor. But Mike knew where he was going. He had planned his route months in advance. His path was highlighted in his DK *Eyewitness* guidebook by a *bright* yellow-orange line from a magic marker.

"Down the First Floor corridor, pass the Greek and Roman antiquities." He flashed a split-second glance at the pages of the guidebook, followed by a wondering stare down the corridor. *Okay. This way.* His heart raced in anticipation.

"Where am I?" *Here I am. Oh, turn right, up the stairs.* "Ah ... the Armless Wonder, number 399." He retrieved his camera from his bag. *The Hellenistic Lux Ferre*—the Venus de Milo. Snapping photos, he stalked around the half nude goddess.

Okay. Mike checked his guidebook. *Through the next room and up the stairs.* Two steps at a time, he sprinted up the wide Daru Stairway, then stopped and marveled at the sight before him. A marble statue, resembling an angel that had descended from heaven, rested peacefully on the landing beneath the domed oculus in the roof. "The Nike!" *The Winged Victory of Samothrace. It's beautiful.* He took another photo.

"Left ... Right ... Which way?" Mike proceeded up another flight of stairs, then down a wide hall. "Now left," he watchfully whispered the navigation, "down this corridor and to the left."

As Mike encountered the museum's collection of Renaissance art, his pace slowed. His gaze traveled the walls. "The Poussin Room. Paradise ... I *am* in Arcadia." His heart soared. "Cortone's *L'Adoration des Mages* ... Reni's *David with the Head of Goliath* ... Raphael's *St. George and the Dragon* ... Luini's *Salome Receiving the Head of St. John* ... A Botticelli ... *Venus and the Graces Presenting Gifts to a Young Woman.* Jesus!" *Is that a Golden Ratio?*

He stepped before a painting precisely recessed in a golden, decorative frame. "*The Saint Veronica* by Costa ... *The Mandylion,*" he recognized. He aimed his camera and quickly took a photo of a painting of a primitive photo. *The true image, the holy icon not made by hand. God, wouldn't it be cool if I could take a photo of Jesus,* he reflected wishfully.

Continuing forward, he rounded a corner and entered the famous *Grande Galerie* of the Denon Wing. The walls, covered with paintings and portraits from Italy, unfolded before him like two patchwork quilts of breathtaking colors. The gilded, ornate ceiling shimmered with hundreds of framed frescos of the gods coming down from the heavens to greet humanity. The vast gallery, which stretched out over a quarter-of-a-mile, appeared endless.

It's the perfect place to get lost, Mike thought.

"The Leonardos ..." He lingered before a group of paintings. *There's the pinecone staff ... and Hebrew letters.* His eyes panned from religious landscapes to portraits. *Bacchus, Madonna of the Rocks,* the *Saint Anne,* and the *Portrait of an Unknown Woman.* "Ah ... *Saint John* with the hand sign of heaven and Earth." He counted, *One, two, three, four, five ... I thought there were six. I'll come back to these later.*

Clap-tap, clap-tap. Mike heard footsteps accompanied by muffled voices, as the gallery filled with the first congregation of sightseers, all heading in the same direction. Accelerating his pace, he advanced toward his destination. *I want to take my photos while no one is around, to get the best angles. I need to get there first.* With great expectations, he entered the newly renovated Salle des États gallery.

IN THE YEAR 2000, the celebration year of the Millennium, a Japanese television network funded 6.1 million dollars for the renovation of the Louvre's Salle des États gallery to house the museum's most precious piece of art. On April 6, 2005, following a brief period of curatorial maintenance and analysis, the masterpiece attributed to Leonardo da Vinci and nicknamed the *Global Icon* was securely displayed in a climate-controlled container behind bulletproof, nonreflective glass. It hung at a new vantage point below a lightwell, designed to capture the natural lighting of the sun.

The painting's provenance could be described as truly bizarre and certainly dubious at best. Unsigned, undated, and unidentified, there was no documented evidence that proved Leonardo had been the artist. A whole mythology had been created to explain its origin. The first record of the painting appeared in the 1660 cataloging of the works of art in the collection at Fontainebleau, the residence of King Louis XIV, The Sun King and the God-given, whose motto was *L'État, c'est moi,* meaning "I am the state." In 1911, the painting was stolen from the Louvre, after which it mysteriously resurfaced in Florence three years later. The press coverage of the theft had made the painting world famous. Before then, only a few French and English families of nobility had cared about its existence.

As though to elevate art to a new level of importance as a voice for human reason, this *Global Icon,* which spoke no words, would serve as an international diplomat. Starting in 1963, the painting functioned as a political tool for France's cultural diplomacy.

Called "The Year of the Silent Revolution," 1963 was a year in which the world changed hands. Robert Frost died that year and a fork in the road began. The top films at the box office were Otto Preminger's *The Cardinal,* Alfred Hitchcock's *The Birds,* and Stanley Kubrick's *Dr. Strangelove, Or: How I Learned to Stop Worrying and Love the Bomb.* "Please Please Me" was the number one song on the charts in England, by an up and coming rock and roll group called the Beatles. The current world war was a Cold War. *Dr. No,* the first James Bond film, was shown in American theaters. The first episode of *Doctor Who* was broadcast in the United Kingdom. Two hundred thousand Freedom Marchers lead by Martin Luther King, Jr. descended on Washington, D.C. to protest discrimination in an attempt to acquire the human rights guaranteed to them by the Bill of Rights and the United States Constitution. The CIA's Domestic Operations Division was created. Six members of the Organization of the Secret Army were sentenced to death for conspiring to assassinate Charles de Gaulle. The three superpowers—the United States, the Soviet Union, and Great Britain—signed a nuclear test ban treaty. The sprawling beltline highway system encircling Washington, D.C. was finished that year. Morris L. West published *The Shoes of the Fisherman.* Hannah Arendt published *Eichmann in Jerusalem: A Report on the Banality of Evil.* A volcanic eruption near Iceland formed the Surtsey Island. The Arecibo Observatory offically began operation and NASA launched the world's first geostationary satellite. The Russian Valentina Tereshkova became the first female cosmonaut. T. A. Mathews and A. R. Sandage discovered quasars, which raised the possibility of communication via radio signals from distant stars. Dr. Michael DeBakey first used a Left Ventricular Assist Device to take over the circulation of a patient's heart during surgery, ending the long held dispute on where the human soul resided.

Pope John XXIII, a Rosicrucian Freemason, who had stated, "I want to throw open the windows of the Church so that we can see out and the people can see in," died that summer after the formation of Vatican II. Elected as the first "modern Pope," Pope Paul VI promulgated the documents of the Council of Vatican II, the chief among them *Gaudium et Spes* and *Dignitatis Humanae.* Vatican II changed the Church with new humanist doctrines related to Western ethical thinking within a *free society.* New views on religious freedom were adopted which were in harmony with the First Amendment of the U. S. Constitution as a civil right, supporting the belief that an individual endowed with reason and free will is responsible for the decisions that effect his eternal destiny. In a *free society* no one else can make those decisions for an individual. Belief and truth reside in the human consciousness and *the landscape of the individual spirit* as the *foundation* of human dignity.

In the fall of that year, the first Catholic U. S. president, John F. Kennedy, was reportedly assassinated in Dallas, Texas. Sworn in as the next president, Lyndon Johnson continued the war in the former French colony of Vietnam. The conflict divided the country as 58,020 American soldiers lost their lives in a war that become known as the "wound that would not heal."

Nine months earlier, the French Republic lent the *Global Icon* to the president of the United States and the American people. One and a half million curious visitors viewed the painting in two special exhibits at the National Gallery in Washington, D.C. and the Metropolitan Museum in New York. President Kennedy and the First Lady personally welcomed the painting in Washington. Two and a half million more visitors viewed it in 1974 when it traveled to Tokyo and Moscow. The painting had now become the Louvre's primary drawing card and marketing tool. It had become a part of humanity's collective consciousness. Presidents and kings come and go. Popes and other religious gurus live and die. But the *Global Icon* endures with a soul of its own. There are nearly 260,000 works of art in the Louvre. The *Global Icon* is the *omphalos* of that art, a centerpiece that draws six million human souls on a cultural pilgrimage each year from the four corners of the world.

"I DID IT!" Mike exclaimed with breathless excitement. *No one is here yet.* Spellbound, he stood studying the painting, bathed in a veil of morning sunlight that washed the gallery. *A perfect composition ... seated ... balanced ... divided into thirds with opposition ... a pyramidal central space against a mountainous landscape. The chest. The key and a lock of hair in her hand over Mom's book.*

Primed with long hours of planning and preparation, Mike moved into action and retrieved a selenium cell exposure meter from his bag. He checked a reading as he raced across the room, his eyes darting back and forth at the illuminated features in the painting—the Hekate-like face, the hands, the tiny city, and the scrolling across the arm. With the uneasy feeling of being watched, he glanced up at the security cameras spying from the ceiling. He reached for his digital Nikon. Instinctively adjusting the settings, he engaged the built-in infrared polarized enhancement feature, then framed his subject through the eyepiece. Electronic shutter-*clicks* filled the gallery. The blinking clock in the corner of his first photo series recorded: 9:14 AM

A four-inch-wide wooden railing kept Mike twelve feet away from the bulletproof and acidproof glass box protecting the precious work of art like an inaccessible Devi. But his camera's Clear-Crystal Zen zoom lens, with an optical *zero tolerance*, allowed him to focus through the nonreflective glass and capture vivid close-ups, right down to the finest lines of the painting's signature craquelure.

Within minutes, a throng of tourists filled the gallery and shutters from other cameras started *snapping* at the elusive face. Then, in a shared moment of puzzled surprise, someone in the gallery spoke out loud, followed by a rapid succession of voices falling like dominos.

"Oh, my God! Look!"

"What is that?"

"It's changing!"

"What is that?"

"It's different somehow."

"It's not the same."

"What's happening?"

"What is that?"

"Is the painting—"

"Mother of God! What is that?"

"Yes, *who* is that?"

Mike barely noticed the cacophony of voices babbling around him in a swirl of confusion. He blocked them out, as in a trance, his mind focused on optical details. Then, suddenly, he began to comprehend what he saw through the lens.

"What the hell?" Mike lowered his camera away from the *rilievo schiacciato*. His eyes widened in amazement at the spectacle unfolding in front of him. *Lift the veil,* he thought. *Form does not follow function.* Hearing the piercing shrills of whistles blowing, he glanced to one side at three guards entering the gallery.

As though rendered deaf, the crowd ignored the birdcalls from the guards.

"Back. Back."

"Move back!"

"Stay back!" The guards shouted as they pushed the onlookers away from the semicircular railing that protected the painting.

Awe-struck, the guards halted and froze. Every face in the room was transfixed on the *Global Icon.*

One of the guards regained his composure and began leading the other two in their instructions, "This way, please. This way."

"This way."

"Move, this way."

Aware that he might lose a once-in-a-lifetime photo-op, Mike secretly flipped the rapid advance switch on his camera and began shooting a montage of infrareds at seven-frames-per-second.

A guard tapped Mike on his shoulder. "Come with me, *Monsieur.*"

Mike and the other visitors were hurriedly escorted from the gallery. The oversized gilded double doors, the only entrance to the Salle des États, *slammed* shut. Two guards stationed themselves in front of the doors. One guard whispered frantically into a shoulder microphone with his eyes darting back and forth at the crowd. The other guard rapidly jotted something down in a green notepad. The *Grand Galerie* reverberated from a flood of questioning voices.

"I can't believe it."

"Did you see that?"

"Did you see what I saw?"

"Unbelievable. It's absolutely unbelievable!"

What's going on? Mike grappled in confusion, trying to understand what was happening.

The *clap-tap, clap-tap, clap-tap, clap-tap* of approaching shoes echoing off the parquet floor shifted Mike's attention to the eastern end of the gallery. A menacing wall of blue suits, consisting of nine guards blocking any exit to the east, trooped toward him.

Clap-tap, clap-tap, clap-tap, clap-tap ... Ten or more guards advanced from the western end of the gallery.

The bewildered visitors now found themselves encircled by security staff of the Louvre. A man, in a light brown suit with a bright yellow badge pinned to his lapel, began to address his captive audience. "*Excusez-moi* ... May I have your attention, please?" the man's voice rose above the clamor in the firm monotone sound of authority. "Your attention, *please.*"

The questioning voices immediately subsided.

Mike spied past the guards and spotted a few bewildered tourists being led out of the east end of the gallery.

"Everyone, please remain in the gallery. **Do not leave,**" the man in the brown suit instructed. "We need to speak to everyone present. Remain calm. Everything is under control. Please cooperate with our security people." He motioned to the guards. "And those of you with video or film, we will have to confiscate your cameras."

***

Day 2
Gophers

A Gopher is a term for a computer system predating the World Wide Web that organizes and distributes files on interconnected servers. The first Gopher was created at the University of Minnesota and named after the school's mascot. Two computer terminals, known as Veronica (true image) and Jughead, allowed the user to search global indexes of resources stored in Gopher systems.

TWO SHADOWY FIGURES holding heavy Mag-lites, probed their way into the dark entrance of a freshly re-excavated earthen tunnel. The swaying pendulum beams from their flashlights played deceptive tricks, casting elusive images which the two silhouettes appeared to be chasing.

"I hear water dripping. Is it safe?" asked the tall, heavyset man with full, sagging jowls. "Earth is falling all around us." He bent forward as if in penitence before prayer and squeezed through the narrow passage. "There's barely room in here to spread my shoulders. Hmm ..." He wiped his lip and brushed away grains of sand from the wiggling, racoon-gray mustache fanning out beneath his nose.

"This is the new part of the tunneling. It's not as sound as the rest of the maze. But, it is holding up. It *will* hold up. Do not worry," the thin, olive-skinned man with Moorish features assured, his voice echoing like a chirping bird in the cramped space. "*Ala tool*, stay close," he invited with a sweet, soil-smudged smile. He pointed with his Mag-lite, carving out a channel of luminance through the pitch-black of the precarious passageway. "It is just as I described. Only a few more meters."

Abruptly, they stopped before a wall of table-size stones blocking the tunnel.

"Dottora, *hera* it is. Let me throw my light on it." The thin man aimed his Mag-lite at a grouping of geometric symbols scored into the rough-hewn surface of a single marble block. The jagged inscription appeared suspended at the middle of a spiderweb network of hairline cracks that doglegged outward through the limestone blocks that bordered it. "See, it's beyond a doubt the same markings found on the pottery."

"*In Hoc Signo Vinces* ... the *yoni*," the Doctor whispered in awe, moving his face closer to better see in the shifting light. "Re-mark-able," he marveled, scanning the symbols with his piercing blue eyes. "Yes, Mohamad, I agree. This is a truly remarkable discovery. It must have taken a lot of effort to find this site."

"Oh, *la*—no, Dottora, it was not that difficult. This tunnel is a re-excavation of a previous tunnel, which leads directly to the stone wall. There are dozens of pre-existing tunnels down *hera*. Every one snaking back upon itself then back upon another. Back to this spot. Back—to the *Wall*. Everything begins and ends with these markings. The world stops *hera*."

Mesmerized, the Doctor rubbed his hand over the symbols.

"Do you recognize them?" Mohamad asked. "Are they from the first century?"

"Yes, I believe they are," the Doctor said simply, adjusting the beam from his flashlight to better observe their depth and width. He stared as though he could see right through the symbols. "I'm almost certain of it."

"That means the original tunnels are at least that old," Mohamad remarked.

"But, these inscriptions are different. These slashes ... they may not be the same as the others." The Doctor methodically touched the markings like a blind man reading Braille, following the slashes in a downward motion. "Curious. Very curious."

Crackle

The Doctor stepped back. "I feel something under my foot. Mohamad, here! Shine your torch at the base of the wall."

Mohamad leaned forward and held his light on a human skull with its temple bashed in, lodged under a pile of collapsed masonry. "Looks like someone hit it with a rock." He pulled it from the rubble.

"Don't pick it up!" the Doctor instructed too late.

"Sorry." Blank-faced, Mohamad dropped it, and the skull shattered at his feet.

"Jesus!" The Doctor bent down to collect the pieces. "Damnation, man. What the devil is this?" He wiped away a chalky sediment, revealing a finished stone floor at the wall's footing. "There are markings here."

"They are channels carved deep into the stone floor," Mohamad said.

"I think these channels are key slots where the marble stone was slid into place," the Doctor suggested with quick analysis.

"Or where it was slid out of place." Mohamad wondered, "Is it a door?"

"The Gate to Hell," the Doctor muttered. "Here. Hold my torch while I take some photos." He removed a digital *Canon* camera from his *Northface* hip-pack.

For the next few minutes, the camera's Zeon flashes illuminated the darkness.

"Something's wrong," the Doctor noticed. "The lens is out of focus—it's blurred." He stopped his photography and turned his face toward Mohamad. A jittering swell of dust began to fall from the ceiling. United by a state of uneasy awareness, they stared directly into each other's bulging eyes.

Mohamad fumbled with the flashlights. "*Hera.*" He handed one back to the Doctor, then lifted a warning finger to his lips. "Shhh." He cupped his ear toward the symbols on the wall. "*Estanna …*" His worried eyes shifting, he knelt down and placed the tips of his fingers into the channels. He sensed a dampened vibration. "*Moya*, the stone is weeping. Quickly, sir, we must leave," he advised in an anxious tone.

"But I need to take detailed photos of this wall," the Doctor protested.

"The photos you have taken will have to do. *Ala tool,* this way," Mohamad urged. "We have very little time! *Rooh! Al ann,* now!"

Crumbling pieces of earth and debris from all four sides began caving into the crawlway. Within seconds, the thin air filled with a sweeping haze of Roman earth. The two men evaporated into the darkness.

"Hurry." Mohamad grabbed the Doctor's shirt sleeve and pulled him in a rapid retreat. "Stay close to me." Both men were now coughing heavily in an effort to breathe the thickening, toxic mix of earth and stale air. "Ahk—" Mohamad hacked. Fear set in as he lowered to a crouching position. "We will suffocate if we do not get out soon." *Did I turn the right way?* He halted. "I cannot see through all of this!" *Jog my memory.* "Which way?"

The Doctor drew a ragged breath. "Baphomet!" he scorned. "Seal the reason from my soul! What kind of mess have you gotten me into?"

"*Ya'aburnee!*" Mohamad shouted. "Move quickly, *lif yassar*, Dottora, this way!" His heart hammered. "*La* … no …" He paused. "*Ala tool!*"

"God will guide us." The Doctor fell to his knees and dropped his flashlight. The light went dead. A stinging mix of dust and tears leached into his eyes. He heaved. A muddy mixture of mucus drained from his nose. He stuck out his tongue and used the hairs from his mustache to strain the grit from his mouth. His face paled. With a tight grip on his camera, he crawled forward.

"Cover your mouth. Keep the dirt out of your eyes," Mohamad said, sucking in air through the loose tail of his shirt he held over his face. "Careful—"

"Cha—haakt." The Doctor released a strangling cough.

"*Hennak!*" Mohamad pointed with the beam from his Mag-lite while pulling the Doctor up with his other hand. His eyes sharpened. "*Hennak!* There is a light!"

A feeble glow, like a lighthouse cutting through a dense fog, beckoned.

"*Alhamdulillah,*" Mohamad praised. "Toward the light, Dottora. Toward the light. Step into the light!" *Feet ... do your thing.* He scrambled.

"Move aside Mo-ha-mad," the Doctor struggled to speak. "I'll go first."

The two grubby *gophers,* resembling shadows emerging from darkness into radiance, stepped out of a five-foot-tall crack in another stone wall. They found themselves standing in a voluminous twenty-foot-wide corridor with a fifteen-foot-high arched stone ceiling. Suddenly, the ground and everything around them shook with a split-second *rumble—*

Then, an unearthly *silence.*

In a cautious about-face, they stared back at the opening from which they had made their escape. A billowing cloud, as from a tiny atomic explosion, mushroomed from the crack and dusted them with a fine residue of rusty-red sediments. Their eyes shone white on their powdered faces.

"An earth—quake," Mohamad's voice strained as he spat dirt. "It was only a minor tremor, perhaps an aftershock."

"Ahh—ck." The Doctor cleared his throat and the color crept back into his face. He wiped his eyes and glared at the crack in the wall. "Bugger," he grumbled. "This upheaval was major enough to collapse that tunnel." He pulled at his matted hair. "Why, man alive, all this effort lost!"

"But we know the location of the markings," Mohamad reassured. "We have the coordinates, down to the longitude and latitude."

"You're right. We can come back to these digs later. For now, I need to compare these photos. What is the quickest way out of here?"

"*Ala Tool.* Follow me."

The Doctor raised his camera to his face and lightly blew across its lens. "Look at all this filth—God, I pray my camera is not damaged."

Dusting off their clothes and kicking the sediment from their shoes, the two haphazard explorers strolled down the poorly lit corridor.

"*Hera* it is." Mohamad approached the bottom of a narrow flight of chipped and battered stone stairs. "Be careful, Dottora. The center of every step is very slippery."

"Undoubtedly worn from the thousands of pilgrims who have come before us," the Doctor surmised. Ascending the stairway, perspiration beaded off his brow from the sudden change in air temperature. He approached a rust-stained iron door at the top of the stairs, lit from above by a bald lightbulb at the center of a corroded, wire-caged electrical fixture. "Shoo—" He waved away a death's-head hawkmoth attracted to the light. "They're bad luck." He jiggled the doorhandle. "It's locked."

"*Wahad da ghee ga.* I have a key." Mohamad stepped forward and fumbled through his pants pockets. "*Hera* they are." He dangled a metal ring of *jingling* keys. Sampling each one in the lock, he searched for the weight of the tripping tumblers. *Clunk*— Metal rubbed against metal. "*Asmodeus of Solomon*, open says-a-me," Mohamad commanded as he grasped the handle and swung the heavy door outward. Its hinges *squealed* like fingernails across a chalkboard.

Crossing the threshold, the two muddled apparitions blended into a spill of shadows beneath an archway. Stepping from the shadows, they raised their hands to shield their half-closed eyes from the intense rays of the morning sun until their pupils adjusted. Their new field of vision encompassed an immense excavation site. Huge blocks of stone were roped off and marked by dozens of red plastic surveyor's flags *flapping* in the breeze. Beyond the excavations sprawled the outskirts of a Middle Eastern city. Hundreds of stone and stucco buildings, with two-foot-diameter satellite dishes perched atop their terra-cotta tiled roofs, loomed in the distance.

"It reminds me of my home at Habitat," the Doctor commented.

Signaling to the Doctor, Mohamad gestured with his grimy hand to the area before them. "This is the southern excavation site. Look, the southwest corner is still standing. Follow me. This way, to the Western Wall."

The two men walked briskly on a cobblestone path littered with rubble until they came to a narrow street angling between rows of buildings. They zigzagged through a high-walled alleyway, then turned a corner and found themselves at the edge of a spacious plaza filled with hundreds of people.

Entering the plaza, the Doctor eyed a ceramic plaque on the corner of a building:

Ha'kotel Ha'ma'ra'vi

For the Jewish religion, this plaza is the center of the world.

———

Seest thou these great buildings?
There shall not be left one stone upon another, that shall not be thrown down. – Mark 13:2

THE HISTORY OF THE HA-KOTEL and the Temple Mount is an amalgam of fact and fiction, a merging of historical legends and religious fables concerning Solomon's Temple and its destruction by the Babylonians. In addition, there are the treasure stories, such as the one alluded to in the text of the Copper Scroll discovered in 1952 at Khirbet Qumran on the northwestern shores of the Dead Sea. The seven-foot-long scroll is engraved with an unusual reverse script resembling Greek letters that describe *topographical* features surrounding Jerusalem. Many researchers denounce the scroll as a hoax. Others believe the scroll's script reveals the hiding places of sixty-six caches of Temple treasure, with one cache supposedly buried deep within the Solomonic Temple complex. Some treasure hunters even claim this cache contains the fabled Lost Ark of the Covenant.

However, the facts supporting this pseudo-history of the Temple Mount are few. Such theories, relegated to the realm of legend and myth, have failed to hold up under scrutiny. Contrary to the religious beliefs and customs still adhered to by many, no hard archeological evidence exists to prove any of these legends as fact. The new wave of historical scholars, known as the minimalists of the Copenhagen School, shed new light on the accuracy of past archeological studies of the Holy Lands based upon biblical myths. The Old Testament stories were not a true history, a true *truth*, but a work of historical fiction. Those stories had been created as propaganda to promote a social-political agenda to unite tribal communities under early Hellenistic and Roman rule in the region known as Palestine. The kingdoms of David and Solomon were mere fairy kingdoms, and so were their temples.

The accepted history suggests King Herod rebuilt the temple in the first century B.C. Herod reportedly placed golden needles around the edges of the roof of his temple to ward off the birds and keep the temple clean from their droppings. But, the Temple Mount's association with Herod fell apart under the weight of new evidence that indicated the structure originated under the rule of the Roman Emperor Hadrian.

On this hallowed site, Hadrian built a temple dedicated to the Roman cult of *Jupiter Capitolinus* which replaced the old Central Asian temple to Caesar Augustus at the city of Pergamos, once the location of the Greek world's second largest library and a haven for Hellenistic philosophers and artists. Hadrian named his new temple city, *Colonia Aelia Capitolina*, and consecrated it at the exact location considered at that time to be the geographic hub of the known world, the near-center of the Eurasian-African land mass. Other shrines in his temple-city honored the deities Bacchus, Serapis the Christ, Venus Astarte, and Dioscuri. In 325 A.D., Eusebius, an early Greek apologist, church historian, and father of the Nicean Creed, recorded that Hadrian's shrine to Aphrodite, the goddess of love, was located at the traditional site of Jesus's tomb. According to Jerome, another early Christian historian, Hadrian erected a statue of Jupiter over the holy ground of the resurrection and a marble statue to Venus, the *Lux Ferre*, at the place of the crucifixion.

What is certain, is that in the year 333 A.D., the Roman Emperor Constantine transformed Hadrian's abandoned temples, as well as the rest of the *Aelia Capitolina*, into his vision of the new Christian Center for the Roman Empire. Constantine's grand scheme transferred the geocentric religious seat of the Catholic Church from its old below-ground catacombs at Rome to his new shrines and churches at Jerusalem. Constantine dedicated his New Jerusalem in honor of his mother, Helena, a woman of reported British or Scottish nobility.

The Vatican is considered the religious nerve center for the Roman Catholic religion today, with various Catholic organizations specifically formed to bring about peaceful coexistence between Catholics and other faiths in Jerusalem. One such organization is the Sisters of Sion, whose iconic logo is a menorah and a fish. However, there are still a few hardliners within the Roman Catholic Church who see Jerusalem as *their* city, and *their* city *alone*, specifically redesigned by Constantine for *their* religion. The crusaders of the eleventh and twelfth centuries were a verification of this long-held belief, as the Roman Catholic Church and certain European monarchs inspired various attempts to reclaim Jerusalem from the Muslims, the Turks, or whoever occupied *their* holy sites.

Today, all of the above-ground structures on the Temple Mount are Islamic in origin. The Dome of the Rock, the Al-Aqsa Mosque, and the Dome of the Chain were all built upon Hadrian's abandoned temple, in order to rid the Muslim world of Greco-Roman religious influence. After all, the Muslims had their own geocentric holy site at Mecca, the location of the Mosque of the Haram and Ha Ka'ba near the twenty-third parallel. Often called "the above-ground maze" by certain groups within the Catholic Church, it is the holiest of Islamic cities, aligned to the four directions of the compass and the hills around Mecca.

Even devout Muslims, who see religion and the state as twin principles of the same entity, contend that the Temple Mount is solely a Muslim creation. According to an official statement by the director of the Al-Aqsa Mosque, "There are no Jewish remains on the Temple Mound. There never were Jewish antiquities here." In relation to the Temple Mount, everything archeologically Hadrian, Christian, and Jewish resides deep below ground, under the temple platform.

With the occupation by the British in 1948 and the subsequent colonization of Zionist immigrants into the region, the Temple Mount regained its legendary status as the heart of the Holy City created by David for the Jewish people. Still, much of the Old City was controlled by the Jordanians and the Muslims. The Zionists were barred from the Temple Mount and the Ha-Kotel. Then, in 1967, the Six-Day War reclaimed the Old City for the Zionists, and the Ha-Kotel became accessible to all nations.

"LOOK, NOTHING HAS CHANGED. There is no damage. No one has noticed the tremor," Mohamad observed, as they debouched onto the stone plaza. "The entire city is built on rubble. There is a fault line that runs down the Hinnom Valley. One day this city will surely be destroyed by a big quake. Dottora, my auto is this way."

Careening through the bustling crowd, the Doctor eyed a Haredi rabbi with an unshorn beard and coiled sidelocks, his head covered with a royal-blue yarmulke.

Reaching out his arm bound with a protective phylactery, the rabbi reverently touched the cyclopean retaining wall of stone ashlars, the Wailing Wall—the *El-Mabka*, the Place of Weeping. It is here, according to folklore, that the angel Raphael descended to Earth and tapped the ground with a rod, causing a reddish healing water to spring forth into the Pool of Bethesda, the Sheep's Pool. Jewish tradition teaches that the *infinite presence* of the god *Yahweh*, the ancient Canaanite cupbearer, resides behind the Wailing Wall, making it the holiest structure in Jerusalem.

The Doctor pulled a handkerchief from his pocket and wiped the sticky sweat from his brow as he hurried through the plaza. He heard the *murmuring* chants of people praying in harmony with the birds *chirping* from their perches nested between the spaces in the Wall. He noticed an elderly beggar woman wearing a tattered, *bright* blue travel-light poncho from L. L. Bea*m*. Meandering peacefully, she scattered bread crumbs from a wicker handbasket on the pavement for the hundreds of black, gray, and white swallows. The Doctor squinted, staring up at a huge circle of birds swooping in the thermals, casting quickening shadows that flittered above the bowed heads of the faithful praying before the Wall. He glanced down at his feet shuffling over the stone pavement.

It's in plain sight, the Doctor pondered. *They are attracted by the* **shape** *of the Temple. It's an aviary for the birds. There are more birds here than humans. But there are no bird droppings anywhere. Look at all these people standing above where we were tunneling. They are all praying directly beneath a bird's nest. The birds—Yes, the birds. They already know!* He hastened forward. "We need to get back to the Institute," he shouted to Mohamad, who steadily paced ahead of him. "I can download these photos at my office and compare them to the others."

———

TWENTY MINUTES LATER, the Doctor and Mohamad drove up in a rusty four-door Fiat to the gated entrance of a building complex. A carved granite sign next to the gates read:

PASSIA
Palestinian Academic Society for the Study of International Affairs
18, Hatem Al-Ta'i Street - Wadi Al-Joz

The PASSIA is a regional think tank. Its offices are situated due north of the Temple Mount, at the heart of Jerusalem's district of international influence.

Leaving their car in the parking lot, they walked to the rear entrance of the building complex. The Doctor inserted his security pass into a slot in a brushed aluminum panel engraved with the words: **Rapid-I-Scan**. Magnetic seals in the door released with a *thud*. He held the door open for Mohamad and followed, letting the steel door *slam* shut behind them.

An attendant standing next to an x-ray machine gawked at the two ghostly figures as they entered the rear lobby. "A devil's storm must be brewing today," he commented, assuming a sandstorm was responsible for the layers of grime covering their clothing. "Please, insert your belongings into the plastic tray for inspection." He watched as they filled the tray and slid it into the x-ray machine. "Step through the archway." He motioned.

Approaching the arch, the Doctor's eyes veered up to the fish-eye logo above the name: **Rapid-I-Scan**.

Retrieving their belongings, they walked toward the middle of a mandala-like pattern formed from the contrasting hues of cyan in the glazed Egyptian floor tiles. Their bodies seemed to disappear and reappear as they strolled through the darkened lobby. A glowing television monitor flickered in one corner, broadcasting an urgent news report from Channel 47, Al Jazeera TV, a station owned by the Millennium Radio Group of Boston.

In front of a tragic scene of tumbled buildings engulfed in flames, a grim-faced reporter held a microphone to his lips. "The quake occurred at 9:18 this morning and was felt as far away as Mecca," the talking head informed.

"Man alive!" the Doctor exclaimed below his breath, with a comprehensive stare at television. "Things are progressing faster than I anticipated. We have much work to do. Let's go, Mohamad."

They quickened to the lobby elevator and entered. Absentmindedly, the Doctor pushed the illuminated number 3 on the control panel.

"*Khamsa*—" Reacting to the Doctor's mistake, Mohamad pushed L5. "We are going to your office, sir, not the Department of Regional Religious Affairs." He shrugged his shoulders and leaned against the wall.

Within seconds, a bell rang and the doors slid open directly across the hall from the Doctor's office. The Doctor pulled a key from his pocket, stepped four paces forward, and unlocked the door.

"I will have to download the photos from the memory stick," the Doctor said impatiently. His hand fumbled for the light switch.

A buzzing *hum* reverberated through the room.

Mohamad batted his eyes from the harsh fluorescent lights hidden behind the milk-white plexiglass covering the ceiling. He heard water *trickling* from a recirculating feng shui tabletop fountain sitting at one corner of the Doctor's cluttered desk.

The drab institutional-gray office was buried five levels underground. Rows of bookshelves lined one wall. Banged-up, miltary-green file cabinets climbing floor to ceiling lined another wall. In the absence of windows, a five-foot-wide panoramic photograph of Jerusalem as seen from the Mount of Olives provided a vicarious view above the computer table behind the Doctor's desk. On the table sat a laptop next to a framed pantone copy of Mantegna's *Descent into Limbo,* an etching of Jesus descending into Hell after his crucifixion.

"My photo files of the clay ceramics are in this computer," the Doctor explained as he activated the laptop. He ejected a photo memory card, the size of a stick of gum, from his camera and inserted it into the laptop's digital media slot. With a few rapid taps on his mouse pad, a folder labeled APSARA PAINTINGS AND CLASSIC ICONS OF FERTILITY CULTS appeared on the screen. He opened the folder to a group of illustrations. "The watchful gazes of domen deities—the oculus and hand motifs. Drawings of the Virgen Niño from the Catacomb of Priscilla, the ancient American Staff God, and the all-seeing Eye Idol from the Birak Eye Temple. These aren't it." He opened a subfolder titled SCARAB SEALS. "A Hyksos Serpent and

Lion resurrection talisman from Canaan … a triad fertility seal … the Hakate snake goddess from Knossos. No—" The Doctor opened another folder. The screen filled with a collage of photos of fifth-century Grecian vases covered with illustrations of Greek gods painted by an unknown artist called the Pan Painter.

"He's got a big *wahid.*" Mohamad gawked at the photo of the sexually aroused, goat-headed god chasing the Arcadian shepherd before a phallic herm.

"The watering system," the Doctor chuckled, "Osiris's lost member. It's Pan or Nodens, the Celtic Zeus, a fertility woodland god, an expression of the celestial king Cepheus chasing his queen Cassiopeia." He opened another folder labeled THE SEALS. "Here it is." Photos of pottery markings filled the screen. He typed on the keyboard and accessed the photos stored on the memory card.

Mohamad leaned closer to inspect the side-by-side photos. After a long moment he remarked, "Look, those are nearly identical." He scratched the back of his head. "But I have never seen these other markings. They are different somehow."

"You are looking at the original photographs taken in 1984. Much of the world lives with its eyes wide shut. What the public sees is often doctored a bit. Do you know about this symbol, Mohamad? Its history?"

"Only what I have been told."

With that, the Doctor began to tell a tale.

"Very few people know the whole story," the Doctor divulged, addressing Mohamad face-to-face. "In 1990, Ludwig Schneider, the editor-in-chief of *Israel Today,* became friends with a Greek Orthodox monk who lived as a hermit in a remote part of the Old City of Jerusalem. This secretive monk showed Schneider a hidden cache of artifacts he had excavated from Mount Zion just before the start of the Six-Day War. These artifacts consisted of ancient pottery shards, small stone pieces, and some unusual oil lamps. All were engraved with a never-before-seen religious symbol."

The Doctor stared back at the computer. Using a pen as a pointer, he motioned to the screen. "This symbol consists of a seven-branched candelabrum, the Jewish menorah, on top, a Star of David commanding the center, with a fish-shaped loop at the bottom."

"The markings on the wall ..." Mohamad gawked at the photos.

"Yes, it's the same symbols we saw on the wall this morning," the Doctor recounted. "These symbols are extremely old. They are found in Proto-Canaanite and Old Negev inscriptions that predate the Hebrew. The menorah, the seven branched lamp of God, is said to symbolize the burning bush at Mount Sinai and the Tree of Life that once grew in the middle of the Garden of Eden, which we Kabbalists believe one day will stand again in the New Jerusalem as a symbol of God's enlightened presence in the middle of the Messianic city."

"A burning bush in the middle of the Messanic city?" Mohomad questioned.

"A vision of something greater than ourselves ... God appeared to Moses in a flaming bush that was not consumed by fire. The menorah is one of the most important ritual symbols in the Jewish Temple. Lit by the honored service candle of the *shamash* at the seeding season of the equinox, the menorah is a symbol of the enduring mystery of God's love. A depiction of the Jewish menorah can be found on the Arch of Titus in Rome, in a scene showing the holy treasures and the spoils of Jerusalem being carted away by the Romans. In that depiction, the menorah has no feet. It rests on an octagon shaped platform, a Vishnumandal containing eight images of deities, one in the form of a *sea dragon*—an early deity of the Romans."

"A dragon?" Mohamad barely breathed the question. "A deity of the Romans?"

Pointing to the next symbol in a crisscross motion, the Doctor lowered his pen. "The Magen David or Shield of David, also called the Star of Redemption, is in the shape of a crossing hexagram. In the New Testament, this is a symbol for the morning star and a sign of the coming of the Messiah. It is a symbol of *Yah*, the son of lights—the great radiance—and the protector of the twelve tribes, denoted by the twelve points of the star. The crossing triangles, forming a crystal shape, are said to symbolize the creative forces that drive everything in nature. One triangle points upward, positive and ascending, and the other downward, negative and descending. It's a symbol of the two opposing forces found in all things. As a religious symbol, it represents the Jewish hope for the coming of the Messiah. It's found on the flag of Israel and the Great Seal of the United States. This symbol is similar to the Christian symbols, *Alpha* and *Omega*, found at the end of the New Testament, or the *Christogram* of the Greek letters X and P used by the early church as a monogram for Christ and the center of the world."

"This symbol I know about." Mohamad nodded.

The Doctor made a looping motion with his pen to the lower part of the symbol. The pen's movement trailed shadowy afterimages across the screen. "This fish shape can be found cradled in the arms of the Egyptian cartouche for the *ka* mortuary priest. The same symbol appears in the art of the oldest Christian catacombs as a symbol of the victory of life over death. It is sometimes called the *Vesica Piscis*, the Vessel of the Fish, an important construction in sacred geometry and a symbol for the *womb of the universe*. It was considered a sign of Messianic hope, long before the Latin cross. For the early Christian church, the Greek word for fish, ICQUS, was a code word for the identity of the true Messiah."

"I see." Mohamad squinted at the screen. "I also know something of this already."

"But this fish shape on the wall is different from the marks we have in our earlier photos," the Doctor said, puzzled. "It's not really a fish shape, but a tear drop, with crisscrossed lines running at diagonals, as on a finely cut diamond. It reminds me of inscriptions I've seen on ocher brick seals discovered in the Blombos Cave on the southern coast of Africa—the oldest works of art in the world."

The Doctor pulled his eyes away from the screen and leveled Mohamad with a serious gaze. "Schneider persuaded the monk to show him where he had discovered the artifacts. The monk led him to a cave behind a rock adjacent to the Tomb of David, situated next to the Upper Room on Mount Zion, the legendary site of the Last Supper, where they carried out the rites of passage of the Great Fear Feast. Today, the entrance to that cave is sealed off with iron bars and secured under heavy lock and key. David's tomb is located on the lower floor of the Chapel of the Last Supper. The tomb contains a cenotaph from the time of the Crusades which is venerated by certain Jews. Excavations in 1951 revealed that this tomb rested over another building that may have been a synagogue belonging to an early Judeo-Christian community. The tomb has a niche in the wall facing east which some believers say will be the resting place for the *Aron Brit HaShem*, the Lost Ark of the Covenant—if it is ever found."

"The Lost Ark?" Mohamad questioned.

The Doctor faced away from Mohamad, rose to his feet, and selected a reference book from the bookcase. "Legend has it that a great secret is hidden behind the wall of that cave. It has been theorized that behind the cave wall at Mount Zion is sealed away part of the treasures from the Second Temple, including the Lost Ark. This theory is based on a description found in the Dead Sea Scrolls, discovered in 1947 and supposedly written by the Essenes—the Sons of Light."

"The Sons of Light?"

"Yes, Mohamad. Scholars have numerous opinions regarding authorship of the scrolls. The Dead Sea Scrolls were first considered a forgery, since their discovery coincided with the creation of the new Zionist state. But historians now consider them to be authentic. The carbon-14 dating of the parchments indicates their age from 168 B.C. to 233 A.D., a broad stretch of history. One scroll, called the Temple Scroll, contains detailed instructions for building and furnishing a temple."

"*Aish?* The Lost Ark?" Mohamad questioned again. "A lost scroll for building a temple?"

The Doctor placed the book on the table and opened it to a page of architectural drawings.

"Yes, the Lost Ark ... if you believe in such things. According to legend, the Ark, the embodiment of God's presence on Earth, was displayed in an inner courtyard, the blessed womb of the Temple of Solomon called the *Holy of Holies of the Earthly Sanctuary*—the sacred place where Heaven and Earth, the *Tiphereth* and *Malkuta*, meet. Within this temple, Yahweh's visible Divine Presence, the *Holy Shekinah Glory*—a brilliant beam of white light—would settle upon the Ark of the Covenant *on certain sacred days of the year* by way of a special opening in the wall that faced east. Other accounts have the *Shekinah Glory* falling upon the breastplate worn by a high priest within the temple. The breastplate was supposedly inscribed with the names of the twelve tribes of Israel and the words *Urim* and *Thummim*, meaning *light* and *perfection* or *light of perfection.* Also inscribed upon the breastplate was a third secret word, or *symbol*, which represented the *hidden name of God.* According to Lady Flavia Anderson's research on the ancient Jewish secrets, the *Urim* and *Thummim* were glass globes filled with water and sited to the sun to invoke a light for igniting a sacred fire. There were no cult images of Yahweh allowed within the Jewish temple. So it was only within the divine presence of the *Shekinah* beam of light that Yahweh could magically be revealed."

"Invoking a light of perfection?" Mohamad questioned. "A seal for the hidden name of God? And the Ark is the dwelling place?"

"The *Shekinah* is a very important symbol for the power of God. Thomas Jefferson suggested using an emblem of the *Skekinah* on the first seal of the United States to symbolize their settlement in the Promised Land. Listen to this." The Doctor opened another book from the shelf and held it at arm's length. Its pages shone like a ball of light in his hand. "According to the *Soncino Zohar,* God manifested His presence into the created world through the Divine Light, the *Shekinah,* the *Bahá* of the Lord." He glided the end of his forefinger over the text and read aloud,

'This light is the connecting link between the divine and the non-divine. God, the protector of Israel, is borne along by four *Hayyoth,* the Holy Beasts, constituting His throne.... Through this hierarchy an emanation of the Divine Presence is conveyed to earth, just as the prayer of human beings is conveyed up to heaven. The *Shekinah* originally rested on the *cosmic tabernacle,* the *Mishkan,* but ... it accompanies the wise. God's Throne, consisting of the *Hayyoth,* is the instrument of His providence on earth.'

The four *Hayyoth* are pictured as each having a face, respectively resembling a man, a lion, an ox, and an eagle. These faces correspond to the four constellations that mark the cardinal directions on a compass rose."

"The four directions on a compass rose?" Mohamad's brow creased.

The Doctor closed the book and returned it to the shelf. "The four cardinal points denote the universal dominion exercised by the *Holy Shekinah.* The scholars of the Spanish Safed schools of mysticism believed that the *Shekinah* appears only to certain inspired individuals as a sign of their divine purpose in life. Such examples are Moses and the burning bush, Saul's conversion after he witnessed 'a Light from heaven, above the brightness of the Sun,' or the *Shekinah* descending as a brilliant luminance within a pillar of smoke that guided the Israelites across the desert. Another incidence occurred on Mount Sinai where the Ten Commandments were given to the children of Israel. However, many Jews believe the *Shekinah* descends each Friday at sunset to transform each Jewish home during the Sabbath. The *Talmud* teaches that the *Shekinah*, the illumination which appears to the questing mystic, is everywhere. One only needs to focus his heart in order see it. Others believe that man cannot see God in His fullness. Man can only see the emanation of God as the *Shekinah*."

Drawing by Benson Lossing (1854). Thomas Jefferson proposed the first Seal of the United States, with the *Shekinah Glory* in the Clouds of Glory with the Israelites fleeing into the Sinai Desert on the reverse and the All Seeing Eye on the obverse.

"Dottora, I've heard this term used before, but in a different way."

"There are other interpretations of the *Shekinah*. In Hebrew the word means 'the dwelling of the Divine Presence of God's radiant spirit.' Yet, in traditional Jewish literature, this radiant spirit is viewed as the female aspect of God—the consort Asherah of Galilee, Saraswati who holds the Book, the *Malkhut-Shekinah*—the Bride of God, or *Shulamite* in the Song of Songs, where it is sometimes identified with King David. The Bride is seen as a form of the *creative presence* of the infinite God in the physical world, like Shiva's Shakti. According to the Kabbalah, evil came into our world once God became separated from his feminine counterpart. In this polarized view, the *Shekinah* is accepted as the Mother to us all just as God is our Father. It is believed that the *Shekinah* created the physical universe when She fell from grace and formed matter, which contains within itself the power to generate a divine illumination." The Doctor's eyes wandered up to the golden crescent atop the Dome of the Rock pictured in the panoramic above his desk. " 'And there appeared a great wonder in heaven; *a woman clothed with the sun*, and the moon under her feet, and upon her head a *crown with twelve stars*. And she being with child cried, travailing in birth, and pained to be delivered.' The *Shekinah*, the childbearing light, is thus the creative force within the universe."

Mohamad appeared confused. "*Ana ma fehempt*, the creative force?"

"The seed of the Tree that grows in the Garden within each man, actualized by the Awakening of the Serpent Power and the Sacred Marriage which restores the balance. The *Shekinah* is the Celestial Bride, with which we must unite in order to transform ourselves before we can rejoin with God. She is the *Holy Spirit*, called the liberating angel, an *angel of freedom*, which will take the soul of man back to its universal source, which is his creative source."

"So the *Shekinah* is like a female God … a harlot mother?"

"Yes, Mohamad. The female, the Enlightening Spirit and the giver of form into the world. A few followers of the mystical Kabbalah compare the *Shekinah* to the consort of Yahweh, like Adam's Eve, or Lilith, the bird woman—the handmaid who planted the tree in the garden. Another example is the Old Negev deity *Elat*, the feminine form of *El*, who guards above the tree in the garden of Gat. Or the ancient Canaanite and Egyptian goddess Hathor, who spills the stars of the Milky Way and rules over the 'Twin Sycamore Trees of Turquoise' that guard the eastern gate to heaven as spoken of in the *Book of the Dead*. The *Shekinah* is a female manifestation of God, which dwells not only above the Ark and in the Temple, but within every man. In this guise, the *Shekinah* is a symbolic light that represents the soul of man fallen from grace and seeking reunion with the Creator. It's similar to the Christian view of the Holy Ghost—the Father, the Son, and the Mother. In the Bible, the *Shekinah* is identified with eagles' emanations ... *alis aquiae* ... on eagles' wings. Ah—um," the Doctor cleared his throat, then recited a passage from the Bible. " 'You have seen what I did to the Egyptians, and how I bore you on eagles' wings and brought you to myself. And to the woman were given two wings of a great eagle, that she might fly into the wilderness, into her place, where she is nourished for a time, and times, and half a time.' "

"Eagles' wings?" Mohamad offered an uncertain look.

"The *Shekinah* is sometimes associated with the *Matrona*," the Doctor continued to explain, "the angels from Ezekiel's vision of the New Jerusalem which prophesied the return of the *Shekinah* to the Temple as the guardian of the 'way of the tree of life,' as found in the book of Genesis. The *Shekinah*, as a distinct entity, is a light that serves as an intermediary between God and man. It's been called the path to the origin of the *logos*, the First Cause of the cosmos, a *light* that signals the coming of the—"

"And this female entity of light rests atop the Ark of the Covenant?" Mohamad interrupted. "Wait a minute, Dottora. Are you saying the treasures of the Second Temple and the Ark of the Covenant are located behind the marks on that wall where we were standing this morning?"

"Baphomet! You are getting ahead of me, Mohamad." The Doctor shook his head. "The Ark of the Covenant and Solomon's lost treasures are only legends, pots of gold that people search for at the end of a rainbow."

Point and *click*. The Doctor addressed additional pictures. "As it turns out, that cave at Mount Zion was once the consecrated grotto and ritual baptismal pool of the first Nazarene, or Messianic church. It was a special place for anointing the sick with oil for healing. The thirty to forty artifacts discovered by the monk have been carbon dated to a time between the first and second centuries. Among these artifacts is a brick-shaped piece of local marble inscribed with the three symbols and words in ancient Aramaic, 'For the Oil of the Spirit,' which may date to the first century."

Point and *click*. A grainy photo of an object resembling a necklace appeared on the screen. "A ceremonial silver lamina, a thin metal plate with holes bored at both ends inscribed with similar symbols, but with additional text, was accidentally discovered in the Judean Desert outside Jerusalem in 1963. Many believe *it* also dates to the first century. A Catholic priest and archaeologist deciphered the Aramaic text to read, 'For the Oil of the Spirit.' He discovered that this inscription was nearly identical to a Bible verse found in James, chapter five."

Point and *click*. A close-up of the markings on the lamina expanded across the screen. "The priest believed the lamina, only three inches by one inch, was a talisman that identified its owner as a believer in *Mashiach*, the Messiah—the Anointed One. This talisman may have been used in early Judeo-Christian baptism rituals to confirm the forgiveness of their sins. The symbols on the talisman acted as a type of *key* that unlocks the door to the Kingdom of Heaven."

Point and *click*. The screen flickered and dimmed. The image faded. The internal speakers on the laptop spat static. *STA-KAT, SAT-KAT—*

"Man alive! What's wrong with this thing?" The Doctor rapped the side of the laptop with his hand, then jiggled a wire that fed into it. A close-up of the symbol from one of the photos reappeared. "Ah … That's much better. As the inscriptions have been tied together by a thread of commonality, the combined symbols on the pottery have since become known as the Messianic Seal—the Blood Sign … the Sigil of the Second Coming. This could be the *oldest* talismanic symbol of Christianity."

"So what does that have do with the Wall?" Mohamad wondered as he picked grit from under his fingernails.

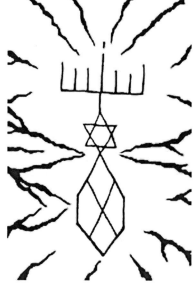

"It's not the Wall that's important," the Doctor replied. "It's the tunnels!"

Point and *click*. A map resembling a maze for the Minotaur expanded onto the screen.

"As you are aware, Mohamad, we are not the first to have tunneled beneath the Temple Mount or the surrounding area. Many have come before us. Below the Temple Mount is a vast, bewildering, labyrinthine network of tunnels and narrow passageways leading to crypts, grottoes, and galleries. There are forty-two catalogued conduits and passageways, and thirty-seven documented wells and cisterns. There is even a large central cave known as the Well of the Souls directly beneath the Dome of the Rock, as well as various other chambers associated with Solomon's Stables."

"It's a labyrinth for such." Mohamad nodded knowingly.

Point and *click*. Another map appeared. "Perhaps the oldest digs under the Temple Mount are the Tunnel of Hezekiah and the Siloam Channel. These serpentine tunnels were designed as aqueducts that ran to the Gihon Spring, a major source of pure water for the city since the early Bronze Age. According to biblical accounts, Hezekiah's Tunnel was built in preparation for the attack by the Assyrians. This water system was a tremendous engineering feat by any standard. At one time, critics of biblical history said openly that it was impossible that these tunnels were created before the first century B.C. Because of the engineering complexity of the project, many believe the system must have been designed by the Romans at a later date."

"*Aiwa*, I know about the older tunnels," Mohamad said.

Point and *click*. A detailed survey map popped into view. "Additional tunnels were later created by the Ashvins twin riders, the Knights Templar. The Templars were founded in the French city of Troyes, in the Champagne region north of Dijon and Lyon, once the major crossroads of learning in Europe. The order was established by Saint Bernard, the head of the Cistercian monks. These monks were heavily involved in deciphering newly discovered Hebrew texts. After the crusaders regained Jerusalem in 1104, the Templars spent the next nine years occupied with the demanding task of excavating a series of shafts under their quarters at the Temple Mount. No one knows for certain what they were looking for, or what they discovered."

"Probably searching for treasure," Mohamad commented.

Point and *click*. An animated map tracked horizontally across the screen, then stopped. "At the start of the nineteenth century, the Ottoman Empire began to crumble, which opened the door for Europeans to explore Jerusalem. It was the heyday of European exploration in the Levant. In 1818, the Austrian botanist, F. W. Sieber, who had earlier studied the ruins at Crete, was the first of these new explorers to map out Jerusalem. Eighteen years later, the Englishman Fredrick Catherwood used a 'camera lucida' to create panoramic drawings and the first accurate cartographic portrayal of the Old City. Catherwood later mapped the Mayan temples of Yucatán and must have been aware of the similarities. His explorations were followed in 1838 by the American biblical topographer, Edward Robinson. Robinson explored Egypt and Palestine, searching for archaeological evidence that might prove that the stories in the Old Testament described actual places. Some say Robinson searched for a lost treasure, and that he had been funded by certain wealthy Europeans."

Mohamad's eyes shifted with piqued curiosity. "A lost treasure ..."

"Before exploring in the Middle East, Robinson studied in Germany under the famous geographer, Carl Ritter," the Doctor informed, noticing Mohamad's excitement. "Ritter had ties to the Bethmann-Hollweg banking house in Frankfurt. That family intermarried with the Rothschild's, the original Bauer family. The descendants of these families later became major players in the Zionist settling of Palestine by way of the creation of the 1917 Balfour Declaration that was promoted by Sir Philip Sassoon, one of 'the Rothchilds of the Far East.' "

"These are the men who founded Israel?" Mohamad questioned. "But what about the treasure?"

"It is said Robinson did not find a treasure. But, he did discover the location of certain communities that seem to corroborate descriptions in the Bible. This led to the possibility that the Bible was historical and not a mythology, as promoted by the intellectual communities of that day. In his remapping of Palestine, Robinson renamed the old Arabic cities, giving them biblical names in an effort to validate the Old Testament. He was a clever archeologist. He dismissed much of the Catholic influence in Jerusalem, such as the *Via Dolorosa* and the Church of the Holy Sepulcher, as absurdities related to mysticism. Before Robinson, the geography of Palestine appeared problematic from a bibical context. In many ways the geography of the Holy Land we know today is the byproduct of the research of Robinson."

"Are you saying the Bible is historical?" Mohamad scratched the back of his neck.

"Of course not," the Doctor scoffed. "However, Robinson's findings inspired other topographical expeditions to Palestine. Between 1840 and 1841, Lieutenants Aldrich and Symonds of the British Royal Engineers performed the first British Military Survey of Palestine, with additional surveys plotted by the Swiss explorer Titus Tobler four years later. Those surveys were followed by a series of surveys between 1854 and 1865 by Dr. James T. Barclay, a follower of the Disciples for Christ, who once owned the home of Thomas Jefferson. Barclay's grandfather, Thomas Barclay, was a Quaker immigrant from Ireland. He established a bank in Philadelphia and was appointed the first American consul to France by President George Washington. The elder Barclay worked closely with Jefferson on diplomatic issues related to France. He was in charge of Jefferson's French accounts. He knew everything about the treasure trove that Jefferson brought back from Europe. The grandson, Dr. James Barclay, led two private expeditions to Palestine. He described his findings in his book, *City of the Great King; Jerusalem: As It Was, As It Is, and As It Is To Be.* He was the first to note the lunar stations on the Mounts of Olives. His book became the standard authority on Jerusalem for English and American scholars. It was a principal work that renewed Christian interest in the history of Jerusalem. Barclay also published perhaps the first accurate topographic map of this city, titled 'Jerusalem and Environs. From actual and minute survey made on the spot.' He was the first American to explore the tunnels beneath the Temple Mount. He was also responsible for discovering the Royal Cave next to the Temple Mount, better known as Zedekiah's Cave, where the treasures of Jerusalem were reportedly hidden during the sack of the city by the Roman Emperor Titus. Years later, the first Masonic rituals in Jerusalem were performed in that cave."

"The treasures of Jerusalem?" Mohamad's eyes widened. "Treasure hunters ... a topographic map?"

"Yes ... Queen Victoria and her son, Prince Edward Albert, sponsored further investigations of the region through the Palestine Exploration Fund formed in 1865 by Sir George Grove and Arthur Stanley. Two years later, the British Army Engineers mounted a special expedition to Jerusalem headed by three topographic engineers, Charles Wilson, Captain Andrew Winston, and Lieutenant Charles Warren. They were part of an English research organization known as the Ars Quator Coronatorum, the Four Crowns Research Lodge founded by nine British Freemasons. Their primary mission was to *map out the topography* of the city to the newly adopted Ordinance Survey standards. However, Lieutenant Warren, who was called the 'Mole,' is said to have harbored a hidden agenda. He had been sent to clear up doubtful questions concerning the biblical archaeology of the city, such as the true nature of the Holy Sepulcher, the *true direction of the walls* of the Temple Mount, and the precise location of various towers and tombs encircling the Old City. For three years, they excavated beneath the Noble Sanctuary and the surrounding city. During their explorations, they uncovered a fourteen-foot-wide, vaulted central access corridor connected to another tunnel that descended vertically for eighty feet through solid bedrock with a series of minor digs under the Temple Mount—"

"That is part of tunnels we explored this morning," Mohamad interrupted.

"I know," the Doctor acknowledged. "They also discovered other deep tunnels containing Templar artifacts, including a broken Templar sword, a seal, pieces of a lance, and a medieval spur marked with a Templar cross. These artifacts are now preserved by the Templar archivist for Scotland in Edinburgh. They are kept with dated letters from a certain Captain Montague Brownslow Parker who took part in a later excavation. It is from Parker's letters that we first learned about the markings we rediscovered on the wall this morning. His letters also describe a number of painted marks on the foundation stone of the southeast corner of the Temple Mount. Those marks were assumed to be Phoenician or old Hebrew characters. No one has yet succeeded in translating them."

Point and *click.* "Here is an illustration of the tunnels excavated by the Templars beneath the Temple Mount, taken from the British Army report of 1870. It also shows the extensive digs left by Warren's excavations. Warren's maps are the best picture we have today of the architecture of the Temple Mount. Those maps have intrigued many treasure hunters. Between 1909 and 1911, a Finnish theologian named Walter Juvelius believed he had found *coded* scriptural passages in the book of Ezekiel that suggested the location of the lost treasure of the Temple of Solomon. He conceived the idea of digging under the City of David, located on a ridge south of the Old City, possibly the original site of ancient Jerusalem."

"*Fayn?* I did not know this." Mohamad rubbed his nose with the back of his hand.

"Captain Parker, the well-to-do son of an English Duke, followed the advice of Juvelius and performed an unauthorized excavation of the cave floor beneath the Dome of the Rock in an attempt to find the Lost Ark." The Doctor pinched his nose and dried soil flaked off his mustache. "Father L. H. Vincent, a prominent archeologist associated with the Roman Catholic Ecole-Biblique et Archéologique Française of Jerusalem, joined the excavation. The Ecole-Biblique is the oldest archeological institute in Jerusalem. It was founded by a French Dominican priest who came up with the novel idea of quantifying biblical research on a scientific understanding of the region's *original geographical* context. Father Vincent documented Parker's topographic findings. He even published an account in his book, *The Underground Jerusalem*, a work consulted to this day by researchers of the First Temple period. Later, Vincent performed a survey of Jerusalem which detailed the *topography* related to the oldest known churches and monuments."

"The maps I followed for my tunneling came from Vincent's book."

"You did a good job, Mohamad. *Kowaies kateer.* Those maps were derived from Parker's research on the previous Templar excavations. Parker secretly dug in the cave known as the Well of the Souls, below the Foundation Stone of the Dome of the Rock, where hollow sounds had been detected in the floor. However, his exploration found nothing but bedrock. If the Ark was hidden under the Temple Mount, it eluded Parker. When his digs were discovered by the Ottoman authorities, the members of his expedition quickly fled the country."

"So, is there really a Lost Ark?" Mohamad asked.

Point and *click.* An image of an old newspaper clipping with the caption, **The Father of Israel**, tracked to the center of the screen. "Some very important people thought so. At the end of the twentieth century, Baron Edmond de Rothschild, better known as the Father of Yishuv to the Zionists, became interested in the Lost Ark. His family incorporated the Shield of David as part of their family crest. He was an international banker who lived in Paris. Some say his family's banks helped to fund the establishment of the United States with the assistance of Haym Solomon, a friend of George Washington. Solomon supposedly wrote the first draft of the American Constitution and was instrumental in the creation of the Great Seal of the United States. Baron Rothschild financed the excavations of the French-Jewish Egyptologist, Raymond Weill, in his search for the Lost Ark outside of the Temple Mount. Although the Lost Ark was not found, between 1913 and 1914 Weill did uncover the old City of Ophel. He also discovered the supposed burial place of King David in 1923. But more importantly, he discovered what could be the *oldest* known Levite seal for Jerusalem—a base-relief of a bird with outstretched wings."

Point and *click.* A photo of a first-day cover letter with seven commemorative Israeli L'malekh postage stamps, arranged in the shape of a dipper, appeared on the screen. "We now identify this bird image as the *L'malekh,* meaning 'belonging to the king of Judah.' Others interpret it as a solarization symbol for the winged soul, with the inscription meaning '*the property of God.*' "

"Like a ziz bird ... eagles' wings ... the *Shekinah?* Were we tunneling in the wrong spot?" Mohamad probed, gazing at the image on the stamps.

Point and *click.* Another newspaper clipping slid into position beside the cover letter. "Not according to the beliefs of some other tunnelers. In 1996, the Zionists tunneled along the Western Wall north of Wilson's Arch, at the old entrance to Hadrian's Temple. In recent years, this tunnel has been opened to tourists."

Point and *click.* Associated Press photos of the Ha-Kotel riots materialized next to the newspaper clipping. "Then in July of 1981, Arab officials discovered other unauthorized tunnels excavated by a rabbi named Getz, which created tension between Arabs and Jews over the control of the Temple Mount. Rabbi Getz was convinced the Lost Ark had been hidden in a chamber beneath the temple complex. Of course, the rabbi found no secret chambers or any evidence of a Lost Ark."

"A secret chamber," Mohamad wondered, "the key slots on the floor."

The Doctor knowingly smiled. Point and *click.* He referenced additional photos. "The last Palestinian uprising, in 1996, began in the wake of the opening of Jerusalem's Hasmonean Tunnel, which runs adjacent to the Haram al-Sharif, Islam's third holiest shrine. Arab discontent over that tunnel nearly started a Holy War."

"I remember that event," Mohamad recollected. "The control of the Temple Mount is considered important to the Jews, the Muslims, and the Palestinians."

"Yes, Mohamad. Even the Muslims and the Waqf, the Islamic Trust, have excavated beneath the Temple Mount. In 2000, they began construction on a fourth mosque over Solomon's Stables. Rumors circulated in the press claimed it was all a masquerade for PLO treasure hunters."

"*Aish,* the PLO ... looking for treasure?" Mohamad inquired skeptically.

Point and *click.* A photograph of the Vatican moved into position and overlapped all the other images on the screen. "Yes, but a few of these groups have tried to unite against the others."

"Backstabbers," Mohamad spat with disdain.

"Or possibly something else," the Doctor said with concern. "In October of 2000, the Reuters news service reported that the late Yasser Arafat had sent a personal appeal to the Pope to intervene and help resolve the crisis in the Middle East. The appeal by Arafat was revealed in a letter by Nemer Hammad, a top Palestinian official in Italy. According to Hammad, the Palestinians needed a prestigious person such as the Pope, who is perceived as being above politics, to mediate over the control of the Noble Sanctuary. However, the book of Daniel, chapter eleven, verse forty-five, makes an interesting prediction about the Temple Mount. 'And he shall plant the tabernacles of his palace between the seas in the glorious holy mountain; yet he shall come to his end, and none shall help him.' Some doomsayers believe the 'he' in this verse is a reference to the Antichrist, who will setup upon a *wing of the temple* an abomination that causes desolation."

Mohamad's eyes darted uneasily to one side. "*Shaitan*, the Antichrist?"

"The rider on the horse of desolation. The signs of the return." Point and *click*. The Doctor linked to a Google Earth satellite photo of Israel. "Jerusalem lies between two seas, the Mediterranean Sea and the Dead Sea," he pointed out. "The term *glorious holy mountain* surely refers to the Temple Mount. The doomsayers believe this Bible verse indicates the apparent end of time when the Pope will vacate Rome and seize Jerusalem to exercise control over the Glorious Holy Mountain of God. They believe that the installment of the Seat of Peter between the two seas is the explicit goal of Satan. A passage from the book of Isaiah is said to foreshadow this, 'For thou hast said in thine heart, I will ascend into heaven, I will exalt my throne above the stars of God; I will sit also upon the mount of the congregation, in the sides of the north. I will ascend above the heights of the clouds; I will be like the most High.' "

The Doctor pressed the *Escape* key. One by one, the images fizzled off the screen.

"It is hard to believe that someone did not discover something. There has to be something more important, something more than just those markings on the wall."

"Apparently, others feel the same as you. Who do you think has been flipping the bill on our tunneling? These markings are extremely important. Form does not always follow function, Mohamad. I need to get confirmation from a higher-up who has access to the original pottery. If he agrees, then we need to consider our next course of action."

"Surely we will continue our tunneling?" Mohamad rubbed his fingers together, anxiously polishing his thumbs.

"Maybe." The Doctor began typing an e-mail to his colleague. Raising one eyebrow, he wiggled his chubby fingers over the computer keyboard. A ripple of doubt stirred beneath the surface of his worried eyes as he glanced at the panoramic photo above his desk. "Maybe not," he whispered to himself. "There is another location … another Jerusalem."

Pecking at the keyboard, one finger at a time, he composed an encrypted e-mail and included the new photos as encrypted attachments. The outgoing message tag read:

To: professorJBMaisun@georgetown.eduu

***

Day 3
Mayday

Beltane or Beltaine, also known as May Day, or May Eve, celebrates the sacred union of the May goddess and the May god. During the first stirring of spring, the Maypole dance represents the unity of the Male and Female gods, with the pole itself being the god and the multicolored ribbons that encompass it, the goddess. The festivities are believed to welcome the Spring Maiden to the Bel fires for her first experience.

A FRENCH PROVINCIAL CLOCK, custom built for Thomas Jefferson in the shape of a golden disc between two, ten-inch-tall, onyx obelisks, sat at one end of the prestigious Resolute desk. Its tiny internal gears were turning and *ticking.* Its brass hands, coated with brown tarnish, toggled to 9:01.

In an unguarded moment, the President of the United States, Andrew Curtis Scott, stood with his back to his desk, his arms folded. A tear beaded from the corner of one eye, as he stared out the windows of the Oval Office. Droplets of morning dew clinging to the glass refracted a spectrum of faint halos across the ceiling. *We're all on our way to dying,* he lamented. *I miss you.*

President Scott's thoughts filled with images of his late wife, Mary, who had succumbed to a malignant cerebral tumor three months earlier. The weeks following her passing were a monotonous blur for Scott, as if acted out more from habit than a desire to live. He knew it had been his duty to his country that had pulled him through the ordeal. The Presidency had been his lodestone. He wondered how he would manage the rest of his life without her.

He turned from the windows and glanced at one corner of his desk, covered with cards and mementos from thousands of well-wishers. The nation had been somehow depolarized by his wife's tragedy, just as a family can be bonded by such an event and pulled together in a time of need. His eyes solemnly drifted over a copy of the *Washington Post* that lay on his desk. The headlines read: **President Won't Sign U. N. Pact … bonus Section E Congress Kills Filibuster, Signaling the End of Free Speech … Jesus Removed from Easter Display over Fear of Separation of Church and State … Artic Oil, Global Warming Opens Sea Routes … British Ex-Prime Minister Converts to Catholicism … Vatican Changes Rules for Electing Pope … Israel Test Robotic Snake … Turrell's Land Art Finished at Roden Crater … Solar Storm Slams Earth - Largest Solar Flares on Record Could Disrupt Power Grids and Communications Links.** Next to it, bold headlines from a copy of the Fort Meyer *Pentagram* reported: **Pentagon Cuts Boy Scouts from Bases to Resolve Claims Military Engages in Religious Discrimination** and **Wicca Pentagram finally allowed on VA Graves.**

"Congress is dysfunctional," Scott murmured. "Our faith in government is dying. Ah … the burdens of this office. The whole world stops here." *But tragedy always brings hope,* he assured himself. *There are no rainbows without some rain. The worst thing to be without is hope. If not for hope, our hearts would break. Hope is one of America's great guiding principles. That's the beauty of hope. It always moves forward. You should never take away a person's hope. It might be all they have.*

MANY POLITICIANS are unscrupulous and self-serving. In the trusting eyes of the public, President Scott was not. His presidency had been founded upon the matter of his character. In one speech he had told the American people, "The great values in life are inherent in our democracy, the rule of law, political debate, and freedom of speech and religious and personal belief. *Freedom.* The most powerful force in this world is the force of human freedom. True freedom is derived only through the actions of people and not from the directions of government—who in the *light of freedom*—is only the servant of the people. No government that represents *freedom* should ever ask what its people can do for it; rather it should ask, 'What can government do for the people which it serves?' The *soul* of our government is *freedom.*"

Although it was President Scott's final year in office, no one had yet labeled him a lameduck. A graduate of Rutgers, he was well admired by his fellow citizens and maintained an approval rating of eighty percent throughout his presidency. Even his opponents said that he could charm the birds out of the trees. In times of crisis, he had broken the rules and defied the odds to make the tarnished office he held respectable again. He was an endangered species of politics, a dedicated leader.

Yet, the uncertain times associated with international terrorism brought on by religious fanaticism toward America's global interests forced Scott to support new and broad-reaching changes in the law of the land. One such change included an Executive Order extending Section 215 of the USA Patriot Act, which forever gave the Government the authority to monitor and censor what people read. Another Executive Order gave Homeland Security the power to direct all actions over "faith-based" churches in the United States. Although America had entered a period of calm, terrorism and security had become the new watchwords for the Twenty-First Century. Scott had once proclaimed, "The work of securing our vast nation is not done. We are a nation in danger."

PRESIDENT SCOTT shifted his diligent gaze back to the bombproof polarized windows. From his vantage point he could see the sun reflecting off the pyramidal top of the Washington Monument, like a shimmering beacon of hope. His poignant memory of Mary deepened.

"Look at that sky, Jack. Not a dark cloud in sight. It's a beautiful day, except for that puff of smoke no bigger than a man's hand. Eight more months and then I'll pack it in. I'll sell the house in Georgetown and move to Utah. I'll write that book and cash in. It'll be a piece of fiction, a *roman à clef*, but I'll call it my memoirs. Or maybe I'll make a fortune when they sell the image of me as a ten-inch-high talking puppet." Scott grinned. "I want to retire at our ranch near Zion. Mary loved that park."

Jack Carter, the president's personal secretary, smiled thinly as he tucked reports titled, CLEAN WATER ACT AMENDMENT, IRAQ - NEW EDEN and WORLD DAMS, TRINITY FDR Orders 1902, into his briefcase.

"That's curious," Scott observed. "The red aircraft warning lights aren't blinking on the Washington Monument at this hour. Here she comes!"

At the rear of the White House, the president's helicopter, Marine One, descended into a circle of sea-green grass surrounded by thousands of roses, violets, amaranths, and lilies dancing in the downdraft of its blades. In the language of the presidential birds, Air Force One is the call sign for any fixed-wing aircraft that the president happens to be on at any given time. Any rotary-wing aircraft that the president occupies is referred to as Marine One. The call sign, Marine One, is derived from one of the experimental test helicopters equipped with tactical capabilities flown by Marine Helicopter Squadron One, known as the Fleet Angels, stationed out of Quantico. The current primary presidential helicopter is a Sikorsky VH-3D, also called the Sea King, which is stationed at hanger HMX-1 at Bolling Air Force Base at Anacostia. For security reasons, Marine One never flies alone. In a presidential shell game, a second identical helicopter is always in the sky at the same time to serve as a decoy to confuse any would-be attackers.

"Do we have everything, Jack?"

"Yes, sir. We'll cover this morning's briefing once we're on board."

Chu, chu chu, chu— BAM.

President Scott flinched.

"Whoa!" Jack yelled, ducking to one side. "What was that?"

The president swiped his eyes toward the window. "A little sparrow hit the glass."

"Only a bird ... God, I thought it was something else," Jack said, picking up papers he had dropped on the plush, sunbeam-yellow carpet.

"Those windows are not only bulletproof, they're *bird*proof as well," Scott chuckled. "I read where a researcher at Virginia Tech proved that sparrows navigate using polarized light. It must have been misdirected by a reflection in the window."

———

PARADING ACROSS THE GROUNDS of the White House with his personal secretary and a Secret Service escort in tow, the president approached Marine One.

"Hello, Mr. President," the copilot greeted, shaking the president's hand. "We're catching Air Force One at the rear runway at Plato for your scheduled meeting at Golden Lion."

"Andrews, Langley. That's fine—Oh, my God!" Scott fell to his knees, tripped by a rut in the ground a few feet away from the Sea King.

In a split second, four Secret Service agents encircled him, their sidearms drawn.

Catching hold of Jack's arm, Scott pulled himself up.

"Are you alright, Mr. President?" Jack asked with concern.

"I'm fine," Scott said shortly. "My mind's eye was still on the sparrow."

"It's a collapsed burrow, sir," Jack noted. "Those damn gophers are everywhere on the White House grounds."

"Good morning, Mr. President," said the flight attendant, as President Scott climbed the doorway-steps and entered Marine One. He handed the president a Florida orange for good luck. "Can I get you anything?"

"No," Scott replied. He tossed the orange out the doorway. "Well ... A cup of coffee, maybe ... a maple cream cappuccino. And yes it is. It's a beautiful morning."

"I think you hit a bird when you threw that fruit," the attendant said. The doorway ramp ascended, and the attendant secured its latches. "I think you hit two. Two birds with one orange. Good throw, Mr. President."

I thought it only hit the ground, Scott mused.

In the Sea King's cockpit, the copilot systematically studied the readout on the instrument panel. Flipping switches, he performed a quick test on the navigation. "7.8333 degrees off polar," he informed the pilot. "That can't be right." He pushed the reset button. "That's better. True north. Everything checks okay."

A FASTEN YOUR SEAT BELT sign flashed above the seats in the president's finely furnished cabin.

President Scott strapped himself in, as Jack sat down across from him. Scott pointed to the flashing sign.

"Oh, yes—sure." Jack rose up, fumbling for the buckle.

"It could save your life," Scott reminded with an indulgent smile.

Once secured, Jack opened his briefcase and sorted through his papers. The cabin *rumbled* as Marine One rose from the ground. The onboard PA system began playing U2's "A Beautiful Day."

"I know that song," Scott said, cocking his head to one side as he listened. He stared out the window at the outline of the twenty-foot-wide wingspan of the *Bird Effigy*, a sculpture hovering just above the ground in the First Lady's Gardens next to the White House.

"Christianity rocks ... That's from the band whose do-gooder frontman keeps pushing us to support some third-world cause," Jack noted. "He's everywhere. He's a global superhero. One day he'll be as popular as Jesus."

"Yes, Jack. He's not even an American. What is his name? He has a name that sounds like a clown. I once knew it, but it didn't matter then. I guess it doesn't matter now, since I can't remember it."

Jack searched through his papers for more important topics and began his briefing. Raising his voice above the roar of the Sea King's 3,000-horsepower engines, he began, "Sir, here are the morning files on the key events from yesterday—"

"Your coffee, sir." The attendant, holding a saucer and a *rattling* cup, politely interrupted the conversation to hand the president his cappuccino.

Scott inhaled the aroma steaming off the top and took a sip. He lowered the cup, his upper lip topped with a milk-froth mustache, and nodded for Jack to continue.

"Sir, we have alarming data from the Department of the Interior. Four minor earthquakes occurred at the same time in the continental United States last night—in New Madrid, Missouri; San Francisco, California; Charleston, South Carolina; and Hebgen Lake, Montana. Eruptions occurred at Mount St. Helens, Montserrat, Masaya Volcano Park, and the Italian island of Stromboli. The volcano near Colima, 430 miles northwest of Mexico City, also erupted. Minor quakes were felt all around the world, with a severe quake outside Tel Aviv at 9:18 A.M., their time. More that two thousand people have been displaced. Aftershocks were felt as far away as Jerusalem. There is a crack in the Knesset. Israel's legislature has temporarily vacated the building. I'm not certain how any of this has affected the setup in the Sinai or the underground stuff near the obsolete Negev reactor we're not supposed to talk about."

"State secrets ... Their textile factory. Contact the CIA, MI6, and the MFO in Rome—" Scott stopped short, glancing out the cabin window. "Look at *that* ..." He turned his head and stared Jack straight in the eyes.

The cabin shook with a gyrating *rattle* and *hum* vibration. The Sea King violently pitched to one side. The president's cappuccino flew into Jack's face.

In the cockpit, the copilot shouted over his headset, "Mayday! Mayday! This is Marine One!"

————

A BATTLE-SCARRED Vietnam veteran, wearing a *bright* sand-colored, travel-light vest from L. L Bea*m*, standing near the fountains of the gear-like, wheel-shaped WWII Memorial, would later recall how Marine One seemed pulled toward the gigantic vertical pillar of stones, as though ensnared by an invisible magnetic force. Like a scene from the Ray Harryhausen movie, *Earth vs the Flying Saucers,* the six-ton chopper clipped seven tiers away from the southwestern corner of the pyramidion top of the Washington Monument as easily as a knife slicing through butter. The echoing *boom* from the instantaneous crash was deafening. The flash from the explosion erupted like a Roman candle.

Because the Washington Monument is built of standing stones, one resting upon another without any internal support, the structure relies entirely on its vertical weight to maintain stability. A horizontal impact could have toppled the entire monument, but Marine One had gained enough altitude to prevent extensive damage to the structure.

Since it was before 10:00 A.M., no sightseers had gathered inside the monument's observation deck, which was partially torn away by the collision. Nearly all of the debris from the falling stones, the observation deck, and the remains of Marine One fell on the southwest side of the monument, within the perimeter of the monument's security wall and away from the early line of visitors waiting to acquire passes for the first morning elevator ride to the top. One news report would later call it a miracle that no one, except those onboard Marine One, were killed in the accident.

Within minutes, fire crews, park officials, military personnel, and a live television team from CNN with play-by-play coverage were at the scene. The circling helicopters gave the National Mall an Orwellian feeling, as government security personal were called upon to close off all the roads going in and out of Washington.

————

FOUR BLOCKS NORTHEAST of the crash site, at FBI Headquarters in the J. Edgar Hoover Building, a team of blazer-clad special agents with holstered Italian Berettas and Japanese cell phones clipped to their belts gathered before a wall of Chinese-manufactured monitors. They were scrutinizing video recordings taken from the various Park Service security cameras that maintain constant vigilance over the goings-on at the National Mall.

Clenching a glass of water, a man sat poker-faced at the head of the table in the middle of the room. His glassy eyes met the expressionless stares of the agents as he addressed them with a voice that pounded the air. "Looks like Hell got hungry again today, and the Washington Monument is where it fed. What do we know?"

"Sir, security is at the highest level throughout the District," an agent reported. "Everyone on the Hill and around the White House has been evacuated. Everything's secured and wrapped tight. We have beefed up our aerial reconnaissance. The sixteen-mile radius of restricted airspace around the Washington Monument has been extended to sixty miles. All the great birds have been called. There's a single Open Skies OC-135B Observation Aircraft and three EC-130 advanced communications equipped Compass Calls constantly flying over Washington as we speak. In addition, there's an F-15 Eagle and a T-38 Talon circling the city, along with a battle ready, E-8C Joint STAR, Surveillance Target Attack Radar System, just in case. The ISIS airship over Baltimore is being redirected to Washington." He pointed a remote control at the monitors at the end of the room. "Monitor 16 has a closed-circuit feed from a camera on an Unmanned Aerial Vehicle, a UAV Dragon Eye, which is maintaining a constant watch over the crash site. The city is guarded better than Fort Knox. The black box recorders from the Sea King have not been analyzed at this time. At the present, all we have to go on are the recordings from the Park Service."

"Everything on the Mall is monitored," another agent explained, leaning slump-shouldered with his palms resting on the edge of the table. "So is everything in Washington, for that matter. We have a panopticon society, an ideal prison. There are no camera shadows in Washington. Everyone is recorded. Hell! We're way past *Nineteen Eighty-Four*, with full-blown surveillance. We're on the verge of a THX—"

"These are all digital, high-definition recordings, sir," a third agent added. "It allows us to blow up the smallest details—license plates, name tags, body tattoos, people's faces—even the hairs on their faces. Biometric sensors, using CAD point-path software, identifies everyone in the streets and compares them to the face scan data bases of the FBI and Interpol. Everything is stored as digital *zeros* and *ones*. You'd be surprised how much information can be placed on the head of a pin."

"So, is this an incident or an accident?" the man at the end of the table, whom the three agents had been addressing, catechized. "Is this another Kennedy thing? Are we dealing with any religious extremists or rogue elements?" Wearing faded blue jeans, a sweatshirt with *BRAGG THE TIN MAN - 4:20 - REMEMBER KENT STATE* stenciled on the front, and a yellow security clearance ID tag clipped to his grass-stained collar, the man at the end of the table was obviously not an employee of the FBI.

"The recordings suggest an accident," another agent replied. "Carbon-based error maybe, or a malfunction with Marine One."

"REX 84 protocols are on hold. There's no hostile air environment with this one, sir," noted an agent sitting casually at the table. "There is absolutely no indication of a missile—nothing at all. In relation to a rogue element, it certainly looks like an act of God, unless you want to call God a terrorist. Everything is burned to a cinder. The only bodily remains are Scott's and Jack Carter's broken legs and severed heads."

An agent standing next to one of the monitors removed a retractable metal pointer from his shirt pocket. He pulled on its end to extend it and tapped the glass on the screen. *Tap, tap.* "This is a Key Hole-13 satellite replay of the area at the time of the crash. This fish-shaped area is the Mall at the nerve center of Washington. The Washington Monument is here," *Tap—* "below this circular area, the Ellipse." *Tap—* "This shadow we see moving is Marine One. It's off course. This other shadow bear-in-the-air is the decoy." *Tap—* "There. Stop the clock. Freeze-frame that," he instructed the other agent. "There, that flash. Marine One clipped the top of the monument. There are no other flashes. Nothing. Nothing at all. It's an accident," he concluded.

At the back of the room, agent Evans Blake stood cross-armed in a wooden pose before the wall of flickering monitors. The expression on his face appeared as exciting as pudding hardening, as he scrutinized the playback on monitor 7. He stepped forward, picked up a universal remote from the table, and pressed a button. All of the video recorders *click*ed to a stop and reset.

Blake confidently turned and addressed the man seated at the end of the table. "Sir, that's not exactly accurate," he spoke out of turn in a flat, neutral voice.

"What's not accurate, Blake?" Another agent interjected in an irritated tone.

"There's not a damn vapor trail or a flash from a primary explosion anywhere on those recordings."

Two of the agents in the room exchanged glances.

"You remember the last time, Blake," one of the agents reminded. "You got it wrong. You better be sure before you start offering analysis."

Blake glanced at the skeptical gaze of the man sitting at the end of the table.

Slam— The man in the sweatshirt forcefully dropped his hand to the table. "I'm not here for this! Get to the point!" He jerked back in his chair, resuming a concentrated control.

"Sir, the recording from the Washington Monument has a strange half-second dropout, some sort of electromagnetic pulse, which is not natural to the timing track," Blake explained calmly against the adversarial comments. "This dropout occurred precisely at 9:18 A.M., according to the clock timing sequence."

"What are you getting at, Evans?" another agent asked. "Are you suggesting a Black-Op in the CIA shot the thing down with one of their satellites? Hell, they're the only ones with that sort of technology."

The bloodshot eyes of the man wearing blue jeans showed signs of surprise. His mouth opened with muted words of concern.

"What I'm saying," Blake cut to the quick, "is that something out of the ordinary, some unusual electrical disturbance, affected this recording. This disturbance coincided with the time of the crash. We have a *commonality* here. I think it's worth investigating further. Perhaps the same phenomena that caused this disturbance affected the electrical components of Marine One," Blake stressed, looking directly at the man at the end of the table.

Click. Blake pressed the *Slow/Play* button on the remote. The monitors began replaying fifteen scenes synchronized in slow-motion, showing Marine One from takeoff until the fatal crash.

All eyes in the room converged on the video playbacks. The clock counters on all the monitors wound up in unison to 9:18 A.M., the time of impact. The replay on monitor number 7 skipped a frame, seen as a slight, almost imperceptible *flicker*.

The man in blue jeans lurched forward from his chair and fixed his worried eyes on agent Blake.

———

THIRTY MINUTES EARLIER and six time zones away, the Vice President of the United States, on a special diplomatic mission to the Vatican, stood poised outside the offices of the Pope. The vice president grasped a deep greenish-blue crystal dove, a gift from the people of the United States to the Holy See as an offering of peace.

AS A YOUNG REPUBLIC, the United States had maintained consular relations with the Catholic territory, known as the Papal States, from 1797 to 1870. The United States carried out diplomatic relations directly with the Pope in his capacity as head of the Papal States from 1848 to 1868, although not at the ambassadorial level.

After a military investigation discovered that higher-ups within the Vatican had been involved in the assassination of President Lincoln, the United States severed all diplomatic ties with the Holy See under a law passed by Congress in 1867. Their relationship further eroded with the loss of papal territories in 1870, during the period of European nation building. Then in November, 1983, Congress, without public hearings, quietly revoked the 1867 law. At that point in time, the two countries joined forces to overturn European communism and the socialist liberation theology promoted by certain Jesuits.

Prior to 1984, Presidents Kennedy, Nixon, Ford, Carter, and Reagan had designated personal envoys to the Holy See for discussions related to international humanitarian and political issues which bolstered bonds between the United States and the Vatican on areas of mutual international interest. The interaction between the two governments was best characterized as an active global partnership for human dignity. In the public eye, this collaboration promoted a common agenda of religious freedom and tolerance, justice, and global respect for the rule of law.

DEPUTY CHIEF OF MISSIONS in Rome, Dr. Tom Chedwick, stepped in front of the vice president. He gripped the handle of the ornate, double doors that led into the formal offices of the Pope. "Be careful, don't drop it," he cautioned, as the vice president approached.

"A crystal dove," the vice president said with a determined grin. "I wonder if he'll understand the symbolism behind our gift? He's old school. Do you think he'll support a U.N. policing of the Temple Mount and the West Bank?"

"The meaning looks clear to me. Picinelli's *Mondo simbolico* refers to Mary, the Mother of God, as the *colomba immacolatissima*, the most immaculate dove—the Immaculate Conception," Chedwick replied. "Saint Gregory of Nyssa said 'the soul becomes enlightened, when it takes the beautiful shape of a dove.' Such is peace. It's your job to convince him. Let's meet the queer fisherman of the First World."

With the wedge of awareness, Chedwick held open one of the doors, and the vice president entered into a richly adorned audience chamber. At the far end of the room, a benignly smiling Pope, wearing a Triple Tiara resembling a decorated pinecone, sat between four attendants. "Smile at Archbishop Bracciolini, the Pope's new secretary from Berlin," Chedwick advised the vice president in a low voice. "He was with the CDF.

As Chedwick stepped through the doorway, his cell phone chimed the first six notes from Francis Scott Key's "Star-Spangled Banner." He fished through his coat pocket, retrieved his phone, and covered his mouth as he answered.

At the same time, a man entered the room from another door to the papal office and whispered into the ear of one of the Pope's attendants.

Chedwick flipped his phone shut and firmly grabbed the vice president's left arm. "We have a situation," he calmly whispered into the ear of the vice president. "The President's on vacation."

The papal attendant whispered in the Pope's ear. Immediately the elderly pope arose and crossed the twelve feet of space that separated the two dignitaries. He clasped both of his trembling hands around the hands of the dumbfounded vice president, who still clenched the crystal dove. In half-broken English he consoled with a benevolent gaze from his jaundiced eyes, "Madam President, I am so sorry. May the grace of God be with you and your country."

Twenty minutes later, a convoy of pitch-black Mercedes limousines followed by an armed military escort of blurred blue lights and *screeching* sirens sped out of

Vatican City and down the Via del Terme Deciane. They raced through the gates of the Villa Domiziana, the U.S. Embassy to the Holy See in Rome.

In the United States, a shocked public watched a surreal news report simulcast over the nine major networks. Besieged by a gauntlet of reporters, video cameramen, and professional Italian paparazzi, a CNN anchorman posed calmly in front of the gates of the U.S. Embassy. The dome of the Vatican could be seen hovering on the horizon.

"Today, just minutes after shaking hands with the Pope, Vice President Jane Elizabeth Walker was sworn in as the next President of the United States."

***

Day 4
Ebola

The Ebola hemorrhagic virus is part of the negative single-stranded RNA family of viruses known as filoviruses. The incubation period for Ebola runs from two to twenty-one days, depending upon the strain. The mortality rate for those who are infected is seventy to ninety percent. The virus is known for its signature shape, a shepherd's crook.

RACING DOWN a two-lane blacktop stretching across the flat terrain south of Fountains Abbey in Yorkshire, the high intensity Angel Eye Halogen headlights from a Morgan Aero 8 reflected off the asphalt and *diffracted* through an encroaching morning fog. Staring through the roadster's dew-covered windshield, the driver sighted twenty-three, white, golf ball-size objects hovering on the edge of the horizon. As the Aero 8 sped forward, the objects shape-shifted into Epcot-like Kevlar-covered spheres from Disney World.

Slamming on the brakes, the driver stopped at a gate to a twenty-foot-high security fence that encircled twenty-three gigantic geodesic radomes looming over a group of white buildings. A sign above the gate read:

MENWITH HILL INTELLIGENCE FACILITY
NO DEMOCRACY IN HERE - YOU CAN SEE AND HEAR, BUT DO NOT SPEAK

"Good morning, Colonel Braxton," said one of the four armed guards stationed at the gate. Another guard approached and began dowsing underneath the car with a mirrored sensor attached to a long handle.

"I see you have new ride today," the guard commented, appreciating the sleek, aerodynamic lines of the Aero 8.

"My XK8 is in the shop," Colonel Braxton said impatiently. He handed a red, white, and blue ID card to the guard.

The guard swiped the card in a handheld scanner and waited patiently for confirmation. The scanner's digital readout streamed: CHECKING RAPID-I-SCAN CLEARANCE - LEVEL FOUR ... AUTHORIZED ... PLATE OF MUTTON

The other guard pulled the sensor from under the car and signaled his approval.

"Everything checks okay, sir. You are clear to go."

The motorized gate *rattled* as it rolled aside. Colonel Braxton pulled the gear shift, revved the engine, and drove into the heart of the facility, making a sharp left turn in the direction of the radomes.

———

LOCATED AT 54.0162 N, 1.6826 W, near Fewston, Menwith Hill Station is a sprawling, security complex that covers 560 acres above ground. Often called Britain's largest bird's nest, Menwith Hill serves as the principal NATO theater for ground segment node communications with high altitude intelligence satellites. It is the nerve center of the highly automated Global ECHELON, or "No Such Agency," surveillance network for processing Internet and PURPLE traffic collected through thirteen global monitoring stations which supports the sixteen member US Intelligence Community.

Menwith is jointly operated by the United Kingdom's Government Communications Headquarters and the United States' National Security Agency, the NSA, the world's largest intelligence-gathering operation. The facility was established in 1956 by the US Army Security Agency, the ASA, with command over Menwith transferred to the US Air Intelligence Agency in 2003.

"What hath God wrought?" Samuel Morse asked on May 24, 1844, quoting Numbers 23:23 in the first telegraphic message, sent over a copper wire from the old, below-ground Supreme Court chamber in the United States Capitol to his partner in Baltimore. That copper wire eventually evolved into the Transatlantic Cable, a 1,852 mile-long snake of coiled copper and super high bandwidth fiber-optics that joins two countries, two continents, and transcends both time and space.

The original Menwith complex had been strategically located to tap into the high bandwidth Transatlantic Trunk Line that linked the United States to Great Britain. This is an extension of the main landline running from London to New York, and then to Washington, D.C., Fort Meade, and Beltsville, MD. It is the primary line of communications for the World Wide Web, serving as the spinal column for the new "Global Consciousness."

In the early 1960s, Menwith Hill became the first communications site in the world to receive sophisticated "early-bird" IBM computers, which the NSA used to intercept worldwide telex messages. With the end of the Cold War, Menwith has shifted its mission to monitoring international messages, civilian telephone calls, and telecommunications between various governments, depending upon their political, military, or economic value. According to a *Time* magazine article, Menwith Hill has enough computer power through its IBM BlueGene/L and Silkworth Processing Systems to monitor all phone calls and e-mails transferred throughout the entire world within a twenty-six hour period.

The aboveground facilities at Menwith consist of five acres of secured buildings confined within a complex of radomes, vertical antenna masts, and satellite dishes, all pointing eastward. In 1984, British Telecom completed a twenty-five million dollar extension to Menwith known as Steeplebush. Within the Steeplebush compound for information absorption resides the primary monitoring facilities of Inter-Net National Computer Security, or INNCS, a branch of the NSA's Special Collection Service.

The INNCS facilities include the Global Maze Room, jokingly referred to as the Kitchen of the Belly-Busters, an electromagnetically-shielded, underground, concrete bunker. Within the Global Maze Room are 244 office-size cubicles where computer experts monitor the security of the World Wide Web and guard it against virus attacks. Approximately a thousand new viruses attack the Internet each month, with virus attacks increasing exponentially with the web's growth.

SITTING SQAURELY BEHIND HIS DESK in officle number 144, Belly-Buster Lieutenant Clarence "Chuck" Daily was running a routine statistical steganalysis of data transmitted over the major Internet arteries for the Washington, D.C. Silently eavesdropping, he leisurely intercepted all messages within Internet Relay Chat porn sites for suspect viruses in their video mpeg files.

Man, I love this job! There are more channels here than satellite TV. Clarence grinned, leaning back in his chair with his arms folded behind his head. He fixed his eyes on the movie playing in the upper right corner of his monitor.

He leaned forward and picked up a pen, unfolded a *London Times*, and peered at the checkerboard pattern of an unfinished, mandala-shaped crossword puzzle next to the horoscope on the back page. " 'Another name for an amphiptere.' Six letters down, begins with a D," the unsure cruciverbalist mumbled. "Ah … a sticky wicket." He reached for a cookie from a paper plate. "A drake—No, that's not enough letters." He bit into the chocolate-chip. "A draig … No, still not enough—"

Beep Beep— VIRUS DETECTED - 9:18 AM flashed onto monitor 7.

Clarence spied the screen from the corner of his eyes. "Wait a minute …" He spat cookie crumbs. "I think I found a little bugger. A little creepy crawler."

He switched on three additional monitors and started a background check on all files in the region. Typing from his central keyboard, he ran a quick scan-program and found nothing that confirmed the preexistence of the anomaly.

It's a new snake in the grass, Clarence acknowledged with the thrill of discovery. "Another sticky wicket … I guess I get to name you." He glimpsed the video mpeg file still playing on the monitor. "All right, how about Anaconda, the big snake," he murmured. *Seems appropriate to me.*

Clarence saved the infected file and checked the next, where he marked the data signature of the same anomaly. He saved that file and moved to another. Again, he detected the same anomaly. He found it in another file, and another, and another.

This is odd, he pondered. *I've never seen a new virus replicate this fast.*

He eyes darted from screen to screen. VIRUS DETECTED – LEVEL ONE – 9:22 AM flashed on all three monitors.

"Bloody damn!" *Is every data file in the Washington region infected?*

Clarence gophered his head up from his cubicle to get the attention of the walking supervisor. To his amazement, heads were popping up from every officle in the auditorium-sized room. Every face mirrored the same expression of concern, as they looked for assistance from the supervisor.

A clock at the far end of the room read 9:25 A.M.

———

FIVE HOURS LATER and five time zones away, the sun cast a different light. Above the White House, a flag fluttered at half-mast, a sign of distress and a symbol of mourning, as a new Marine One landed on the back lawn.

A Secret Service Agent standing in the shadows of the South Portico lifted the button microphone on his coat lapel to his lips. "Here comes the Dragon Lady."

As smooth as silk, President Jane Walker stepped from the Sea King wearing a stylish navy-blue Isabella Birde dress suit that fit like a crooked T. Her brown eyes fixed on the West Wing as she paraded straight to the south entrance to the White House. By her side were four Secret Service agents along with her personal secretary,

William Benning, a native South African, who held a firm six-fingered grip on a portable defibrillator in one hand and the Football in the other. He noticed Walker sidestepping a hole in the ground. "A gopher hole," he commented.

"I thought it was a snake in the grass," Walker acknowledged. "We need to get rid of these nasty pests. You're a snake-eater. That's a good job for you, Benning."

The culture conscious, long-legged Benning put on his dogface and nodded. His woolly dreadlocks dangled like serpents over the head of Med*usa*. "Look at all the dead birds." He kicked at a lifeless bird at his feet. "Scott could throw on target."

"They're a real nuisance," one of the agents complained. "We started having problems with sparrows about a week ago. At first, we thought it was caused by a poisonous gas attack from a terrorist. But the birds tested negative. They keep crashing into the trees and buildings around the White House. Don't touch 'em. They may be infected with the bird flu."

WILLIAM W. BENNING was the only member of the White House staff who was not Yankee White. He had immigrated to the United States twenty years earlier in order to attend Yale, one of America's dream colleges, where he was considered an ascending star in international law. Walker's well-to-do parents had sponsored Benning's college education, which lead to his close association with the Walker family. The *Washington Post* had called him "one of the country's future advisors and political strategist" and "a conduit to the White House." Shrewd and determined, he quickly became a junior member of the Council on Foreign Relations, the Trilateral Commission, and the Club of Rome, three of the world's leading Anglo-American and European think tanks and umbrella organizations. He had served as Walker's unofficial right-hand man since their college days at Yale, where they met, and later as her campaign manager in her run for the Senate. He knew everything about Walker, and Walker kept him on a tight leash.

———

FOUR SERIOUS-FACED GOVERNMENT ADVISORS with tiny American flags pinned upside down to their lapels filed into the redecorated Oval Office.

"Good morning, Madam President."

"Good morning, Madam President."

"Good morning, Madam President."

"Good morning, President Walker."

Walker appeared as though the weight of the world had been placed upon her shoulders as she sat on one of the king-size sofas at the center of the room. The somber Bordeaux tone of the sofa's rich goat leather seemed to emphasize her mood. She picked up a legal pad and a copy of the *Washington Post* from the coffee table and scanned the headlines: **Farewell to Scott, Walker Takes Charge … How Much is the White House Worth? 285 Million … 77,000 Dead in Peru from 7.7 Magnitude Earthquake … Three-Headed Snake from Secaurus, $250,000 on eBay … Rare White Buffalo Born on Wyoming Farm … UN Geoengineering Ice Sheet … Quick Actions May Stop Global H5N7 Bird Flu Pandemic … The New Roman High, Roman Air Polluted with Cocaine.** On the table, an unfolded copy of *USA Today* reported seven front page headlines: **Country Mourns Scott's Tragic Death … Marvel Comics Captain America Rises from the Dead … House Votes to Prevent Supreme Court's Authorization to Rule** on 'Under God' … **Anubis, God of Dead, Floats down Thames … First Detailed Map of Human Cortex Created at MIT … Cardinals Poised to Win the World Series, DC Metro Dragons Lose to the DC Cardinals … Bird Species Face Extinction - Songbirds are Dying Out … Cloned Cat breeds Illuminated Kittens.**

"We need to send these people some relief," Walker said. "We need to put on a show. We need to make these people think we are pulling for them. That always helps America. The world needs to see our country as a together nation, united and rallied around the flag."

Benning sat next to Walker. He tightened the tie behind his V-neck sweater, like Rodney Dangerfield looking for respect, then thumb polished the Pall Cross lapel pin attached to his blazer.

"Gentlemen, let's get down to business." Walker prompted, "What's the fallout from President Scott?"

"We're still investigating the matter. So far, it appears to be an act of God," one of the advisors responded wryly. "Everything is being coordinated through Homeland Security. The FBI, CIA, NSA, and military are working in unison."

Walker jotted down a few, barely legible, chicken-scratch notations.

"There'll be a state funeral two days from now, with full military honors," reported another advisor, pouring a glass of water. "The procession will start at the White House and end at the Capitol Rotunda. Scott's body will lie in state for one day. Following his daughter's wishes, he will be interred near the Hamilton family crypt at Rock Creek Cemetery."

"So, the transition is going smoothly?" Walker asked hopefully.

"Yes. There're no situations on the domestic front," an advisor replied in an upbeat tone as he settled into a comfortable chair.

"Fine," Walker responded. "Very good news to hear—"

"Wel—l, ah, to be honest, President Walker, there is one other thing," the short, mousey-looking official sitting across from the President interrupted in a timid voice.

Benning's head popped up like a jack-in-the-box. "And what's that, Dr. Ziegenfuss?"

Dr. Hinestine Ziegenfuss, an NSA advisor to the Office of the President, peered from behind his tortoiseshell glasses. He shuffled through papers from a folder sitting on his lap. "I have it here … somewhere." He halfheartedly smiled, exposing his nubby, nicotine-stained teeth. "President Walker, we are extremely concerned about a computer virus we discovered in the past twenty-four hours. We have confirmed reports from twenty-five other industrialized countries where infections have simultaneously taken place. This virus must have been synchronized in some way."

"How deep is the infection and what are the risks?" Walker probed.

"I'd say it's at about ten percent at this time. We feel that it can be contained without any threat to national or global security. However, we are concerned because so many countries are involved," Ziegenfuss warned delicately.

"So there's *nothing* to worry about?" Benning asked for reassurance.

"No … Not now," Ziegenfuss replied. "We have our best minds working on the problem to determine its full scope."

"All right then … let's finish our little turkey talk." Walker pushed forward. "Anything else on the domestic front?"

The group moved on to other issues. The morning briefing finished on schedule, and the four officials said their good-byes, leaving President Walker and Benning alone in the Oval Office.

Walker sat down for the first time behind her new French Provincial desk and kicked off her blue suede Lady Bird dress shoes. "These dogs are killing me," she sighed. "Any more gurus today? Who do we rub elbows with next?"

Benning checked his Beitling wristwatch, twisting the band on his bony wrist. He pulled on his sleeve, revealing four, one-inch-long, branding-scars embellishing his lower arm, the tribal marks of royalty. "Jane, you have a photo-op at 2:00 with the Brass Hats in FDR's Fish Room."

"The old warhorses," Walker responded. "Some Spartans who want to run the *show*. We would have a stratocracy, if they had their way. Those jack offs only love the smell of death. They keep barbarism alive through *force* and *fear*. It's turning into the basis of our government—a Culture of Fear."

"But there are broader economic and social issues to consider … consumption, GNP," Benning counseled. "There's a reason for all those golf courses. We are a nation forged in the crucible of war. The military-industrial complex is a multi-headed chimera that must be fed. We have to look like we're fighting evil. In our mean world, animals prevent the escalation of conflicts among themselves through the displays of *force* and *fear*. They are motivated by self-preservation and *survival*. It's in their shared interest to *cooperate* instead of fight. It's a win-win solution which maintains peaceful equilibrium. Likewise, our nation must present a display of force to the rest of the world. War is Peace. It's a non-zero-sum game we're playing. It's Hobbes's Leviathan, where the power to coerce is required to bring civilized *order* out of *chaos*. If America is going to be the world's savior, our government must be *feared*. It's nothing new. It's a Hamiltonian game. Alexander Hamilton held firm that liberty was ensured through civic order."

"But only animals let *fear* take control. We're not animals," Walker countered. "When I was younger I used to fly fish with my father at Webster Lake near our home in Massachusetts. The Nipmuc Indians have an interesting name for that lake." She absentmindedly scrolled her finger across the top of the desk. "They called it Chargoggagoggmanchauggagoggchaubunagungamaugg."

"A mouthful." Benning grinned. "The sixth Great Lake?"

"It's the longest place name in the United States. It means, 'you fish your side of the water, I fish my side of the water, nobody fishes the middle.' Serious minds do not waste time and energy playing games for a draw, and people are not equal under nature's laws. Wars may be the economic basis for a hierarchical society, but gung-ho neocon *fear mongering* and non-zero-sum-games *suppress* freedom, competition, and human progress. Our country has always strived to be its creative best. That means winners and losers."

Benning nodded smugly, then continued, "The Top-Drawers from the upper crust are scheduled later this afternoon, with some more orchestrated jawboning. Sandwiched between that is an appointment with Reverend Wichards at 4:30."

"Speak of the devil. Wichards, another virus attack," Walker harped, her eyes surveying the view of the Rose Garden. "He's another one of those backwoods evangelists preaching Adam was created first and that women were an afterthought."

"Could be," Benning snickered. "Evangelist is just an anagram for Evil's Agent. I don't care for him either." He picked up a quill pen fashioned from a Quetzal feather lying on the edge of her desk and swatted at a fly. "But, Wichards is overseeing Scott's funeral. He had ties with Scott. I'm sure he'll try to rally around the new flag bearer. He's always wielding his faith as a political tactic to make his empire bigger. You know he's best friends with Speaker of the House Bartram. He's an old Navy man. With John Bartram serving as temporary vice president, Wichards and his religion are just too close to the White House for my comfort."

FOR THE PAST TWENTY YEARS, Reverend William Wichards had held both the left and right ears of the Presidency, gaining for himself the title of "Pastor to the White House." Wichards began his calling in the remote hills of Eastern Tennessee, where he led a congregation of poisonous Snake Handlers within the Church of God with Signs Following. The practice of snake handling is based on a passage in the Gospel of Mark that says a sign of the true believer is the power to "take up serpents" without being harmed. Wichards had been bitten 666 times and claimed that "the sacrament of the Holy Ghost flowed through his veins." His loyal 'sign followers' professed him to be "the one man on Earth with immunity to the Serpent."

A man of pious persuasion, a doublethink-master at emphasizing some topics while downplaying others, Wichards quickly became the charismatic founder of a stadium-size, altarless megachurch in Fairfax, Virginia, where he preached a positive, seven-step Plate of Plenty theology using seductive, contemporary music and big screen computer generated graphics on a stage artfully crafted between the icons of a golden flame and a hypnotic, forty-foot-tall, tilted globe spinning between two towering Doric columns. Wichards also headed the "League of 10,000," a right-wing, extremely hostile, coalition of Christian evangelists and part of America's moral minority. His other noted entrepreneurial achievement included a two-billion dollar, tax-exempt global media empire, spearheaded by GodsGreat-GlobalChurch.nett, where Wichards had mastered the art of God-casting over the Internet. But his crowning glory was his coordination of the yearly get-together of the Christian Union of Brothers, also known as the "Watchers over the Promise," in which 190,000 men come to pray to their god in unison on a day of atonement and reconciliation on the National Mall. The event, under the banner of "Let Our Freedom Shine," consisted of an eighty-hour public reading marathon from the Holy Bible, leading up to the National Day of Prayer on the first Thursday in May. One newspaper report compared the event to the Muslim pilgrimage to the Ka'aba in Mecca.

"I don't look forward to trucking with a pitchman like Wichards." Walker barked. "He's a two-faced tub-thumper. He can't be trusted. How do we deal with such a zealot? He can talk your ear off with religious babble, but he doesn't know a thing about theology. Sometimes he's as crazy as a coot. His firebrand form of theocracy violates the First Amendment and our godless Constitution. There must be a way to paper over Wichards. The man's got too much power to be ignored. There's a lot of bad blood we have to deal with, Benning. If we're not careful, we'll find ourselves in the middle of a militant religious crusade." Through the reflections in the windows, she watched Benning step over to the Chippendale liquor cabinet.

Floomp. Benning pulled the cork from a bottle. "The presidency has always followed certain rules of religious etiquette. It would be a political faux pas not to be associated with Wichards. You'll have to pretend you're a praying person. We'll play a tit for tat and *wait* and *see* if he measures up to the new rules. If he doesn't pass our litmus test, we'll leave him preaching to his own choir." He lifted a glass of J&B Rare to his lips.

"Pour me one." Walker swiveled her chair around.

"What's bothering you?" Benning asked with concern.

"I'm as mad as a wet hen. I've got one hell of a headache, Benning. I think it's this damn room. It's like Hell's kitchen. I've always disliked oval rooms. I find them disorienting. I always get this uneasy feeling that the world is spinning around me." Mallet fisted, she pounded both hands knuckles down on the desktop. "I have to hold on to all four corners just to keep my ground. These oval rooms always seem to exist in that revered Palladian architecture that Jefferson loved so much—Renaissance Humanism." She sliced an angry glare at the Jefferson clock resting on a bookcase shelf, still *ticking* like *the presence* of another consciousness. Pulling at her coat sleeve, she checked her wristwatch-size heart-rate monitor: 123 bpm. She closed her eyes, clenched her jaw with a controlled breath, and forced her heart rate to slow. "I'm going to need a Tantric massage," she sighed as she opened her eyes. "It's my first day, and it's a hard job when you have to rule the roost. Everybody hates the CEOs. We're always the bad guys! It's even harder for a woman. I'm a square peg in a round hole. No one sees a mother hen as the cock of the walk. I have to be the toughest kid on the block. It makes my blood boil! Plus, my restless heart is prone to mistakes."

"Slow down, Jane," Benning said calmly. "Follow your own advice. Don't let *fear* take control. Things can always be *fixed* with some pills that can clear the landscape of your mind and blur the edge of your memory. You're the one in charge now. You're the Alpha Female. The new *gatekeeper* with your finger on the button. A person's character is tested by how they handle power. You're going to raise the bar for women in the world. They will soon discover what's good for the goose is good for the gander." He placed a half-full glass of Scotch on her desk and winked with an assuring smile. "You could shoot someone and get away with it."

Walker crossed her arms in a resigned shrug. "I think my first order of business as the new president will be to make things square. I'll redecorate; add a woman's touch to the Oval Office."

"There's a betting pool among the Old Fellows in Congress that your first order of business would be how to position the toilet seats," Benning said with an amused look on his face. "So, you're a Square Dealer and not a New Dealer?" Ice cubes *clanked* as he swirled his glass. "Is that a policy disclosure or a new spin?"

"Don't be ridiculous. I'm neither. I'm not even a Real Dealer. I'm a stickler for the rules, but I do not intend to follow Scott's legacy of lip service, or to maintain the *status quo* from the Old Guard." Walker spun her chair around again and glared out the windows of the Oval Office. "I'm not a dealer at all." She lifted her glass and knocked it back. "We are a united people with one constitution that binds us. I swore an oath and signed my name to preserve, protect, and defend the Constitution against all enemies of the people, both foreign and domestic. I intend to do that, Benning. This president makes no deals."

JANE ELIZABETH LEE WALKER presented herself as a modern politician with a moderate mix of liberal and conservative views. Her politics mirrored that of Scott's middle-of-the-road conservatism, a position required by anyone who occupied the White House. Yet her personal beliefs tilted left, toward those of her family, who funded many liberal causes and the emerging New Age religions.

A daughter of privilege, she was cradled in the lap of luxury. Her parents were politically well-connected graduates of Yale. Both sides of her family operated from old money and were deeply rooted in the Eastern Establishment from Boston to the Carolinas, with lineages that dated back long before the Founding Fathers.

In her youth, Walker had hoped for a military career, but she lacked the vigor. After attending Yale's School of Law long enough to become initiated into the Hegelian Order of the Skull and Bones—the Brotherhood of Death—the ambitious Boodle Girl enrolled in the Air Force Academy in Colorado Springs, America's leading bird school. She graduated at the top of her class with a single-minded determination to obtain four stars. But after a brief appointment at Bolling among the "Chief's Own," she was unable to continue active service due to a heart problem, an odd arrhythmia that required a pacemaker.

Fascinated with politics, the family business, she made use of her apron strings and attended the Georgetown University School of International Affairs. Within twelve short years her ruthless ambition carried her through the political maze at a surprising pace. She served one term as a popular, tough-as-nails Senator of New York before being tapped as President Scott's VP for seven years. Now she was the Commander-in-Chief, with sixty-three stars on the Seal.

The forty-one-year-old Walker had never married. Within hours of taking her oath of office, a British newspaper headline hailed her as "The New Virgin Queen." The moniker was far from accurate. As a product of her time, Walker had played all the games and had negotiated many affairs during her quick rise through politics.

One such exploit during her youth had nearly led to a scandal, but Walker's pushers and spinners, such as Benning, had managed to save her virginity in the public eye. It had started as a harmless dare at a party but escalated into an incident which helped to mold her character. A so-called friend acquainted her with the recreational powers of the silver spoon. Stimulated with a new self-awareness, she was flown to Amsterdam. Window space was rented in the Wallen, where she had her first experience at servicing the public. Photos were secretly taken, payoffs were hastily made, and the family pride was temporarily saved. To add insult to injury, the photos revealed Walker's strange obsession with keeping a diary of her life, by way of tattoos, which were strategically placed on her body. "Tramp stamps," she called them. The young harlot often joked to Benning, that half of her time in Washington politics had been spent "hiding the tats." Under her veneer was an illustrated woman whose past was as colored as the ceiling of the Sistine Chapel. Now perceived as a fashionable, prim and proper public servant, Jane Walker fully understood where to hide the dirty laundry, as well as her whips and chains.

Most of all, she knew her place as president. Weighed in the balance, she was aware of the workings of the long-held Anglo-American Pax administered by the shepherds from the Court of St. James that first made the United States the guardian over the old British Empire and now the international cop for global human rights and industrial progress. She fully understood that even the President of the United States was answerable to someone. Power is always shared. Jane Elizabeth Walker was now the fiftieth most powerful person in the world.

A MILE DUE WEST OF THE WHITE HOUSE in the Reiss Lecture Hall, Room 101, at Georgetown University, a Sulpician-Jesuit school empowered by the Holy See,

 1939

a balding professor in his late-seventies stood before a floor-to-ceiling screen displaying slides from a PowerPoint program as he addressed the glassy stares of a room full of graduate students. His featured lecture for the week was titled "Xanadu – The New Vision Quest: Engineering an Efficient Image of the Global Village—the Shape of Things to Come."

Click. He pressed the remote control in his hand. The screen swiped to a collage of photographs that a tourist might have taken at Disney World.

Dominating the center of the screen, a circular Fresnel bright spot from the projector shined directly on a pantone color photo of the Trylon and Perisphere buildings from the 1939 New York World's Fair. The 650-foot-tall, triangular, spear-shaped Trylon and the 180-foot-diameter, stucco-covered Perisphere towered at the hub of a spiderweb pattern of broad avenues branching away from the two structures. Next to the Perisphere stood a well-positioned sundial fountain and a 120-foot-tall statue of George Washington looming before a reflecting pool called the Lagoon of Nations. Notations at the bottom of the photo read: Depression—Icons of Hope— PROPAGANDA—Bernays—Air Loom—CIA Brainwashing—Democracy Married to American Business—Democracity—City of Tomorrow and the Singing Tower of Light—The Electrical View of Our World—Christianopolis—Era of the Golem—Robert Moses—Ethical Culture.

To the left of the central photo was a color cartoon of Elekton, the golden moto-man robot, from the hall of Electrical Living at the fair.

At the right of the photo, a black-and-white aerial photograph of the Mall in Washington, D.C. depicted the Capitol Building, the buildings lining the Mall, the Washington Monument, and the Lincoln Memorial. In the lower left corner, a color illustration showed people gathering at the dedication ceremony in the fair's United States Temple of Religion.

In the upper left corner, another black-and-white photo depicted the wheel-shaped *Unisphere* from the 1964 World's Fair, a metal sculpture which symbolizes the embodiment of "man's achievements on a shrinking globe in an expanding universe."

In the upper right-hand corner, a color photo insert of a painting of a trilon and a sphere by A.I. Rice titled *Within the Gates* was captioned:
Entrance to Heaven and the unseen Presence of God – OMM 0918 state-scantioned

In bold red letters, **AWARENESS TYPES: DEATH, LOCATION IN THE WORLD, CREATIVITY, ORDER OVER CHOAS, TIME – ATTRIBUTES OF CONSCIOUSNESS: ENERGY AND AWARENESS = SINGULARITY OF LIGHT SPITTING THE DARKNESS INTO A STATE OF BECOMING – 2028 - SPIRIUTAL MACHINE - ZERO POINT QUANTUM FIELD - AFTERLIFELOG - MARKETING OUR TECHNOLOGICAL SINGULARITY, FIND / GENI - BERKELEY-MIT-GEORGTOWN-PRINCETON-STANFORD-RAND-FORD-WALKER - OCEAN OF WISDOM BECOMES OMNUSCIENCE** was scrolled at the top of the screen followed by a quote by the former Soviet Premier Mikhail Gorbachev from his 1996 speech at the State of the World Forum. "We should ... help in the development of a Global Consciousness ... to change the world for the better."

"Le Monde de Demain," the professor lectured. "People, in the world of tomorrow, both time and space will be transcended as the concepts of *near* and *far* disappear. The vast global community of nations will be seen as a small village interconnected by two invisible and instantaneous lines of geocommunication, one grounded to the planet through the World Wide Web, and the other circling the heavens by way of satellite technology. These are the *Universalis methodus*—our vehicles for the global noosphere—the Global Soul—the Planetary Brain. The durable graphic language of the Internet, the new metaphor for God, will surpass mathematics as it becomes the dominant global language that binds humanity together into a transcendent reality. Automation will make physical labor obsolete as well as the traditional value we place on goods and services. The economic output of this nascent society will be the sharing of information and human knowledge. Both newly acquired intellectual knowledge and creative skills will become the primary virtual commodities purchased and sold within an efficient economy, whose design is based upon information absorption."

Finishing his lecture, the professor gathered his papers, turned his back to his audience, and announced in the voice of command, "Dismissed."

As the class vacated the auditorium, the professor retrieved five books from the podium, a cookbook titled *The Art of Making Bread at Home, Salvador Dali's Dream of Venus: The Surrealist Funhouse from the 1939 World's Fair, Collective Intelligence: Mankind's Emerging World in Cyberspace, New Thought: William James - The Religion of Healthy-Mindedness,* and *The Creation of Chaos: William James and the Stylistic Making of a Disorderly World.* He slid the books into his briefcase, unaware that an admiring student had walked up behind him.

Wearing a *bright* melon-colored, travel-light shirt from L. L Beam, the student cradled two red books and a notebook titled *GU, Theology 001 – The Problem of God* bookmarked with a slip of paper on which was written, "Streams of Consciousness – awareness of the awakening mind." The gold leaf on the binding of one of the books read: *Hope and Tragedy* by Dr. Jon Battista Maisun, Ph.D.

"Professor, would you please do me the honor of autographing your book?" The student presented what he presumed to be the class bible of required reading.

Startled, the professor cautiously turned toward the student hovering just outside the peripheral vision of his right eye. "Yes ... of course." He reached into the pocket of his gray tweed suit and pulled out a ballpoint pen with a little blue globe on the end, a souvenir he had acquired from the U.N. gift shop a week before. As he accepted the book, he eyed the author's name on the cover—H. G. Wells. "I am sorry." He politely handed the book back to the student. "This is about the other new world order."

"Oh, I'm always getting them confused." With a *mal fino* grip on the correct book, the student apologetically handed it to the professor. He tried to divert his attention away from the professor's yellow-marbled, cat-like, diseased left eye which sighted slightly to the left.

Smiling at the student, the professor signed in one quick swipe.

A.M. D.G. — The New Vision Quest — J. B. Maisun

BORN IN IZMIR, NEAR PERGAMON, Turkey, Jon Battista Maisun was a Rhodes Scholar with a doctorate in political science from Cambridge, a masters from The International School of Geneva and an undergraduate degree in sociology from Oxford with training in rhetoric from Stonyhurst, the renowned Jesuit prep school near Clitheroe, England. His early career included work on the formative stages of NATO and the OSS, the forerunner of the CIA and the NSA. An instructor at the National Defense University and a member of the Council of Foreign Relations, the Knights of Malta, and the Bilderberg Group, he was a player within the cabals of the geopolitical elite. His skills as a diplomat led to his appointment as a key international advisor for three U. S. ambassadors to the United Nations.

Still healthy, robust, and sharp-minded, Professor J. B. Maisun was considered "The Man" from the towers of Ivy League intellectualism. Journalists often referred to him as an "honored prophet" and "the American Rasputin," the country's leading authority on the history and workings of modern-day international diplomacy. His book, a bestseller within certain circles, was considered sacred literature by his graduate students, many of whom had advanced over the past fifteen years to hold the highest government positions in the land. Even the new president had been a student of Professor Maisun. His mentee, Jane Walker, had often sought Maisun's advice related to international diplomacy.

_____

MAISUN SPIED A CLOCK on the wall as he left the classroom. He held the back of his hand close to his face and checked his wristwatch. *Bloody Oxford time—I set it five minutes ahead.* He shook and rotated his wrist. *This gravity-driven kinetic watch never keeps accurate time. I'm running late.* An aggravating thought clouded his mind. *I need to stop by my office and get my mail before I leave campus.*

Exiting the building, he crossed the Hoya courtyard, entered the Leavey Center, and took the elevator to the seventh-floor. Opening the door to his well-maintained office, he immediately eyed a scaled-down copy of Hans Holbein's *The Ambassadors* hanging on the wall behind his desk.

Let me sharpen my mind with some mental aerobics. He approached the artwork, his right eye quivered rapidly back and forth, studying the images in the painting. *I see the longitude of the upside-down terrestrial sphere centered on Africa, the celestial globe, the sundial set at Good Friday, the inscriptions on the dagger and the book, the half-hidden crucifix, the dividers, the collar of the order of St. Michael, the astronomical instruments for finding longitude, and the other objects related to the seven arts of the* Quadrivium. He stepped to one side and viewed the painting from a different angle. "Hmm, the simulacra." *I can never discern that damn anamorphic skull.* "Ah … the limits of my vision." *That's strange … from this angle the crucifix would be on top of the skull.*

He turned away and zeroed in on the letter tray on the corner of his desk. Searching through his snailmail, he opened a green padded envelope from the National Audubon Society. A complimentary blood-red Audubon birdcall dangling on the end of a green, braided lanyard fell onto his desk. He removed a sleeve of glossy color brochures advertising three free books for only a $19.99 membership: *A Field Guide to Bird*

Songs, Creating A Backyard Bird Garden, and *Trail of the Money Bird.*

"Ripley's book? I trained with Ripley." Maisun skewed a smile as he tossed the brochures into file 13. *Someone looking for a donation,* he conjectured. *Besides, I do not care to speak the language of the birds.*

He picked up the birdcall, tucked it into his coat pocket, and sat down at his desk. He moved a book titled *Poems by Gerard Hopkins - "As kingfishers catch fire, dragonflies draw flames"* to one side. It rested on a dated copy of *The Scotman,* with the headline: **Mother-of-two, Jumps with Both Infants off Kinnoull Hill Tower.** Out of habit Maisun reached across his desk and lifted the silver ball of a Newton's Cradle and released it. He momentarily closed his eyes, meditating to the *tap ... tap... tap* of a Devil's tattoo. He took a deep breath, then booted up his Apple-Macintosh G9. *"You've got mail,"* a perky, synthesized, female voice sang from the speakers. The first e-mail heading read: Subject: "Kabalyon" From: JAW@PASSA.nett.

Maisun opened the e-mail. The screen instantly filled with scrambled characters and numbers. "A secure PGP e-mail," he mumbled to himself. "There's a photo attachment." He retrieved a dog-eared business card from his scuffed crocodile skin billfold and held it close to his face. The embossed front of the card read: MILLENNIUM RADIO GROUP. He flipped it over and read a small list of handwritten words and numbers. "Which one of these is for the e-mail? Yes … Here it is."

He typed A-B-R-A-X-A-S, and the characters slowly changed to a coherent message. He eagerly read the communication. *I think I see where you are going with this.* He clicked on the photo attachment and studied it. *I need to visually confirm the markings on our clay pots.*

He printed a color copy of the photo file, then opened an icon labeled WILLIAM'S VIRUS DETECT. The program accessed a world map. The industrialized countries were highlighted in red. Numbers scrolling at the bottom of the map counted back and forth: 12 percent, 13 percent, 14 percent, 12 percent.... Maisun nodded, closed the program, and deleted it along with the e-mail files. He then performed a hard drive security wipe to erase any residual data signatures from the e-mail and program files. He ejected the facsimile from his printer, creased it into four uneven folds, and inserted it into his billfold.

Folding his arms, he patiently waited for the security wipe to finish. *There is much work to do. Timing is critical. Only eight years. We need all of the codices to make this happen.*

Beep, beep— The G9 signaled, *"Task complete."*

Maisun switched off the computer and pushed a department key on the side panel of his desk phone. "Hello, Donovan. Yes … you, Wild Bill," he greeted, tucking the phone tightly to his ear. "I'm fine. How are you? … Look, I need to confirm my appointment at the observatory. … That's correct. … I will be attending the services. … Fine. I will be there by five."

He hung up, pulled a cell phone from his coat pocket, and dialed a number.

A voicemail answered, "Please leave your message at the tone."

Beep.

"Hello, William. The programming is working splendidly. Everything is on schedule."

———

FIVE TIME ZONES AWAY at Menwith Hill, Colonel Gerald Braxton, supervisor of the Global Maze Room, swept through a narrow lobby past a secretary sitting at a security station before a steel door.

"Colonel ...," she said openmouthed, reaching for the button on an intercom. "I'll see if he's in."

"This is urgent." With a bundle of folders tucked under his arm, Braxton swung open the door and charged into the office of the INNCS Global Commander.

"Sir, excuse my interruption. We detected a major infection this morning," Braxton reported in an apologetic tone. He stared at a man sitting at a desk whose face was hidden behind papers fanned out in his hands. "I think we have a serious problem." He dropped the folders filled with computer readouts onto the Commander's desk.

The Commander lowered the papers from his face, revealing steel gray eyes filled with concern. "How would you rate it?" he asked in an assertive, baritone voice.

"It's X-rated, sir. A Level One Fucker." Braxton opened one of the folders.

"It's source?"

"We do not believe it's from a pirate, since the virus is not stealing data or spying on anything. There are no signs of a skull and crossbones here, no signs of a two-way line of communication—at least, not yet. No one is getting rich off of this one. It could be just a game from an old-school hacker." Braxton shuffled through the readouts. "It's not from a Russian Mailman, since there is no evidence it came with someone's e-mail, nor does it act like a nefarious activity such as a spamming or a phishing scam from a routing black hole or zombie network. But we have confirmed that it's replicating to other machines. It's a Creeper. This suggests the vicious path of a network worm. You know the way these viruses can operate. Form does not always follow function. It could be accelerating toward a state of critical mass. It's one hell of a snake. I think this thing has a directive, sir."

"Information warfare?" the Commander ventured. "Do you think it's coming from a terrorist?"

"No. But I'm not certain."

"A custom trojan? An anklebiter? Does it carry any rootkits?"

"No," Braxton replied again, "but it could be a carrier."

"How long before it nukes?" the Commander questioned.

"I'd guess a month before we have a *pan*demic. Maybe—maybe a month before it could cause part of someone's system to go brain dead into a Stone Zero. I don't know what part of the system it will attack first. I'm not really sure about the speed of infection at this stage. It could be days. We're running tests as we speak."

"What are we calling it?"

"I have 244 names for this bloody thing. We're not crying wolf on this one, sir."

The Commander lifted his eyes to Braxton. "The Ebola!" he declared.

"Sir, I think we need to outsource this one. It requires special expertise," Braxton suggested in a worried tone, "perhaps some creative backdoor people."

The Commander pressed the button on his office pager and addressed his secretary in an outer room. "Mrs. Weatherington, relay a message to Susan Hamilton in Charleston. And make it a secure Clipper-Capstone communication by way of Sky-Link."

***

Day 5
Crack Climbers

Crack Climbing, known as chimney climbing, is the sport of mountain climbers who specialize in scaling fractures in mountain rocks. The fractures can be as thin as a hair or wide enough to hold a human body.

THE WORLD-CLASS CRACKS found at Devil's Tower in Cook County, Wyoming, are a magnet for mountain and crack climbers. Revered as a holy site by the Lakota Sioux and appreciated as a scenic wonder by local settlers, the forty-million-year-old monolith rises 1,267 feet above the waters of the meandering Belle Fourche, known locally as the Sun Dance River. The Tower is composed of phonolite, a type of igneous rock with a unique mineral composition of aegirine-augite, orthoclase, and sphene crystals. Once it lay hidden below the Earth's surface, but the erosion of time slowly stripped away the softer rock layers to reveal a huge, prehistoric volcanic plug.

In 1892, Wyoming Senator Francis Warren persuaded the U.S. General Land Office to create a timber reserve surrounding the Tower. Later, Senator Warren launched an unsuccessful campaign to turn the reserve into a national park.

In 1901, the clockmaker, explorer, and naturalist, John Muir published the book, *Our National Parks.* Another naturalist, Frederick Olmsted, Jr., who had redesigned the city plan for Washington, D.C., brought Muir's book to the attention of President Theodore Roosevelt. In the summer of 1903, Roosevelt visited Muir beneath the trees at Yosemite where they laid out the foundations for a National Park Service. Eventually, the Park Service assumed control of all national monuments, both natural and man-made, including the 1,347-acre reserve bordering Devil's Tower.

Congress passed the Antiquities Act in 1906, which empowered the President of the United States to grant National Monument status to any federally owned lands containing historic landmarks. On September 24 of that year, President Roosevelt invoked the Antiquities Act and designated Devil's Tower as the Nation's first national monument.

The name, Devil's Tower, was first affixed to the site in 1875 by a scientific team led by Colonel Richard I. Dodge. Colonel Dodge had been sent to the area to explore for gold, although his mission had been a blatant violation of Native American treaty rights. Dodge interpreted Devil's Tower as a literal translation of "Bad God's Tower," one of the Native names for the monolith.

Mateo Tepee, or Bear Lodge, has become the most common name used by Native Americans for the Tower today. Other names from different tribal languages include: Bear Lodge Butte, Grizzly Bear's Lodge, Penis Mountain, Mythic Owl Mountain, Grey Horn Butte, and Ghost Mountain. According to Kiowa Indian mythology, once upon a time, seven maidens were playing in the woods far from their home, where two monstrous bears chased after them. The girls found refuge by climbing a mountain that rose high into the heavens. As they ascended the mountain, they were magically transformed into seven special stars. The bears tried in vain to pursue the seven stars up the mountain, with their great struggle leaving claw marks in the rock face which became the outer cracks and grooves of Devil's Tower.

On July 4, 1893, amid the fanfare of two thousand spectators, William Rogers and Willard Ripley became the first recorded climbers to reach the summit. Since then, picnicking and climbing the Tower on Independence Day has become an annual event.

More than four thousand crack climbers ascend the Tower each year in a test of endurance on a firm rock for an excellent climb. In the summer, the temperature can reach as high as 107 degrees, forcing climbers to hide their heads in cracks to get relief from the unrelenting sun. Because the rock's surface can become too hot to touch, most climbers ascend by way of the shadowed northern approach. New bolts or fixed pitons are not permitted in the rock face to reduce physical impact on the Tower. Only replacement of existing climbing assist hardware is allowed.

To control the use of the site, the Park Service created a set of voluntary guidelines to limit climbing during the month of June out of respect to Native Americans, who hold a deep reverence for the mountain as a spiritual place of renewal.

In 1998, a group of crack climbers disputed the new restrictions. Their contention escalated into a court case. They were concerned that the guidelines were an infringement on religious liberties protected by the Establishment Clause of the First Amendment to the United States Constitution. In a decision that snaked around the letter of the law, the Court determined the Park Service had not violated the three-part test established by Lemon v. Kurtzman, 403 U.S. 602 in 1971.

"The Establishment Clause of the First Amendment states that 'Congress shall make no law respecting an establishment of religion...' The Courts of this country have long struggled with the type and extent of limitations on government action that these ten words impose. **At its most fundamental level, the United States Supreme Court has concluded that this provision was to prohibit the making of biased laws, 'which aid one religion, aid all religions, or prefer one religion over another.' Everson v. Board of Ed. of Ewing, 330 U.S. 1, 15 (1947).** Defining this prohibition on a case-by-case basis has proven a difficult endeavor, but the Court has developed a number of useful frameworks for conducting the analysis. ... **In Lemon v. Kurtzman, 403 U.S. 602 (1971), the court established a three-part test for delineating between proper and improper government actions. According to this test, a governmental action does not offend the Establishment Clause if it has a secular purpose, does not have the principal or primary effect of advancing or inhibiting religion, and does not foster an excessive entanglement with religion (Lemon, 403 U.S. at 612-13).**

Balanced in the analysis of the permissibility or impermissibility of the Government's actions is the ability of government to accommodate religious practices. The Supreme Court "has long recognized that the government may (and sometimes must) accommodate religious practices and that it may do so without violating the Establishment Clause" (Hobbie v. Unemployment Appeals Comm'n of Florida, 480 U.S. 136, 144 (1987)... The Supreme Court has said, "[a] law is not unconstitutional simply because it allows churches to advance religion, which is their very purpose. For a law to have forbidden 'effects' under Lemon, it must be fair to say that the government itself has advanced religion through its own activities or influence." Id. at 337. ... **Actions step beyond the bounds of reasonable accommodation when they force people to support a given religion...."**

———

Man is a rope, fastened between animal and superman – a rope over an abyss. A dangerous going-across, a dangerous wayfaring, a dangerous looking-back, a dangerous shuddering and staying still. – Nietzsche

AT THE EDGE of a two-acre clearing beside a dense patch of pine forest, a middle-aged Native American woman in a red denim shirt and jeans sat patiently on the hood of a mud-spattered, yellow, H1 ALPHA Hummer. A gold plastic badge pinned to her shirt pocket read: **Four Bears Casino.**

With devoted eyes, she watched two tiny figures climbing like geckos, inching their way up the northern approach of Devil's Tower. The corner of her lips curled upward as she observed the first of the two figures reach the summit and disappear from view behind the ledges and boulders. But her expression changed to concern as she eyed the strange motions of the second climber. "Something's wrong," she murmured.

As the second climber hoisted himself upward, one of the weathered bolts that secured his lifeline nudged away from the rock wall. He yanked again at his lifeline, taut and oscillating, and the bolt pulled free. In a chain reaction, seven more bolts unratcheted from the wall in a rapid *pop, pop, pop, pop, pop, pop, pop* that sounded like gunfire. Headfirst, the climber plummeted twenty feet, like a spinning, misguided yo-yo, thrown out from the wall and then back into it with a hard *slam.*

In the clearing below, the woman covered her mouth with her hand. Her face paled with shock. Her dark brown eyes focused on the climber dangling motionless in midair. Suddenly, the tiny figure began to move in quick jolts, like a fish caught on the end of a line. "Oh, my God, he's alive!" she exclaimed in a hushed breath. "Hang in there!"

"Dammit! My leg …" James Winston winced in pain. His body now hung in an awkward, nearly upside-down kinbaku position. He resembled a stillborn baby swaddled in its umbilical cord, entangled like the angel Shemhazai, the leader of the fallen Watchers and guardian of hidden treasure, suspended in repentance between heaven and Earth.

If only I could reach that ledge, I could reset the line and regain my bearings. Feeling lightheaded, he wrestled with the grim possibilities of his precarious situation. *But I'm in the toils with this damn rope wrapped around my leg. It's cutting off my circulation.* Every time Winston pulled on the rope, it tightened around his leg like a tourniquet over his popliteal artery. The beat of his heart pulsed through his throat and pounded at his temples, sending a blood-rushing dizziness to his head. His fingers clawed at a knot with no success. *It's gonna tear my leg off! I'm going to pass out from the pain. I need my knife to cut this Gordian knot.*

White-knuckled, Winston strengthened his grip on the lifeline and agilely pulled himself upright with one hand. Tight and lean, his biceps and delts bulged. He gritted his teeth and ignored the pain long enough to grab a penknife bearing a tarnished, winged US Air Force insignia from his pants pocket. He felt a searing ache in his leg that stabbed at his sciatic nerve. A split second weakness surged over the left side of his body. With a quick breath, he flipped open the notched blade with his thumb and gripped the knife in one hand. The well-honed blade shimmered like a miniature light saber from a Star Wars movie as sunlight diffracted around its edge.

His adrenalin surging, his fingers tightened on the rope, strengthened by the fear of dying. With a chant of willpower he urged himself forward, "I will exceed what I see ... I am unbound. Here—Cut, you snake!"

The old reliable blade took a moment, but the rope frayed then cut with a loud *smack*, and Winston was freed.

He set himself upright on the lifeline and secured his penknife in his pocket. Slowly, he seesawed his body in the metronomic sway of a circular Foucault pendulum movement that, inch-by-inch, carried him closer to a nearby ledge.

It's within arm's reach, he estimated. *If I can swing over to the wall, I can grab hold and work my way down to that ledge.* He shifted his body to one side. "Find the balance," he muttered. *I need to get into the swing of it.*

Unknown to Winston, his actions had caused the rope to abrade on a sharp rock above him, slowly cutting through the taut lifeline. One last swing and the rope *snapped*. A loud, tension-releasing, bullwhip *Pop...p...p* echoed from the Tower.

"Did he fall?" the woman gasped, watching from the clearing below.

Winston lost his breath. The world went dark. In a flash of light, he found himself hurled into a four-foot-wide crevice a few feet above the ledge. His bleeding fingers held tight to the wall. His feet felt glued to the rocks. He was wearing CleatBops, a specially designed rubber toe-cleated rock climbing shoe from Carnac. The CleatBops allowed him to cling to the cracks in the rocks like a bug on a wall.

I'm not going to die today. He squinted up at the formidable rock wall. *Where's the next tie-on?* He spotted where the various bolts and pitons had been torn away.

Down below, the woman breathed a sigh of relief as she observed Winston reappear, inching himself into view until he came to rest on a horizontal outcrop.

Winston sat with his knees cradled to his chest, his heart pounding. His nostrils flared as he caught his breath. *Holy Jesus! That was one blood rush to the head. I think I strained something.* He twisted his body and stretched his right shoulder where his muscles felt tight. All discomfort vanished, except for a slight tingling sensation as he unclenched his hands. His quivering fingers felt numb. *These cuts are not that bad, but I need to take care of them before they fester.* He wiped his bleeding hands across the square and dot logo on the front of his T-shirt. *I may be bloody, but I'm unbowed. Sometimes you have to play hurt. I guess I just got initiated into the Brotherhood of the Rope. I nearly lost it that time.* He leaned back against the rock wall and rubbed a jagged scar snaking up his forearm. *But it's not the first time, and it won't be the last.*

Winston looked up toward the top of the Tower and shouted, "Billy!" Cupping his hands to his mouth, he shouted again, "Billy...?" A desperate feeling of being abandoned at the end of the world settled in the pit of his stomach. *Dammit, where are you? I'm eighty feet from the top of your 'god of obstacles', and I'm stuck here!* he inwardly growled, his desperation turning to anger.

Suddenly, a merlin, an endangered prairie gyrfalcon, flew down from above and landed on a ledge a few feet away.

"Well, what do you want?" Winston's eyebrows arched. "Any winged wisdom?"

"*Chirp-chirp-chirp, chirp-chop, what, what,*" sounded the merlin. Its head darted in rapid forty-seven degree tilts. In a majestic swoop, it extended its wings and glided away. Its head still *tilted* to one side, gazing from one ubiquitous eye, the merlin gracefully descended in a floating concho-spiraling trajectory to the valley below.

Winston's eyes blinked, tracking the merlin's flight. *I see trees ...* He scanned the panorama of the vast *chöying* wilderness. The forest of scattered lodgepole pines resembled an army of warriors guarding Devil's Tower. In the distance, a network of roads extended into the wide-open plenums of space like a man-made spiderweb radiating into the extremities of nowhere. Absorbed in the world before him, he felt at peace as his mind and soul merged with the landscape in an all-encompassing state of nothingness. Then his deep sense of well-being dwindled to a different feeling, a fundamental and primal premonition that something unknown was waiting. He realized he was perched at the edge of a special place, like a seat at the center of the universe. Somehow he knew he had seen it all before.

CLINGING TO HIS THOUGHTS instead of a rope, as though the world had tightened around him, James Alexander Winston came to grief contemplating his thirty-seven years and the checkered past that had brought him to this rocky ledge.

Winston pulled a stick of "Freedent" gum and a plug of dried valerian root from his shirt pocket. He unwrapped the gum, coiled it around the root, and chewed it into his mouth. Reaching into his pocket, he retrieved the tarnished penknife and stared at it in the palm of his bloody hand. *My father gave me this. My childhood. This sudden quiet of place requires that I should face it.* He closed his eyes and was eased by a poignant memory, ghostly distorted images of tragedy and hope flickering through his consciousness like a good-bad dream.

He recalled the day his father left on an extended trip. He was a child, his eyes brimming with tears at the thought of his father's absence. *"Big boys don't cry,"* his father comforted. *"I'll be back in seven days. That's your lucky number. Always take note of that number. I have to do my service for God and country. Take this."* He handed him the penknife. *"It's my gift to you. Use it wisely. Make me proud. I might not always be around, Jimmy. But I give you my word, I will always be there for you. It's a promise. I keep my promises. I love you, Son. Love never dies."*

HIS FATHER, a descendant from an old Yorkshire family, was the noted British archeologist and linguistic anthropologist, John Alexander Winston. A graduate of the University of Edinburgh, a disciple of the archeologist Sir William Petrie, and a student of the American explorer Roy Chapman Andrews, his father taught as an adjunct professor at American University in Washington, D.C., whose school motto was *Pro deo et patria.*

James favored his father—tall, shadow-shaven with sideburns, and sun-bleached brown hair. He had his father's chiseled face, etched with fine-lined crow's feet that highlighted the sides of his piercing blue eyes when he squinted. His rugged looks appeared menacing and inviting at the same time. He resembled a no named cowboy from a spaghetti western, right down to a bobbing Adam's apple. But, it was from his mother that Winston had acquired his quick analytical mind.

His mother, Mary Zebedee Collins Winston, who also taught at American University, was an astronomer, mathematician, and amateur ornithologist. She had attended both Sarah Lawrence College and American University, where she had served as the editor-in-chief of *The Eagle*, the AU school paper. Birds were her passion. She was a disciple of the world-famous "birdman," Sidney Dillon Ripley. Ripley, the flamboyant curator of the Smithsonian Institute between 1961 and 1984, had been an original operative of the Office of Strategic Services, the forerunner of the CIA. Winston's mother had grown up in Dixon, Illinois, on Lincolnway. She often told the story of how as a child, she had been saved from drowning in the lake at Lowell Park by the handsome teenager who lived down the street.

His parents met while teaching at American University. After their marriage, they established themselves as a working couple in the areas of astro-archaeology and archaeoastronomy. Both were fascinated by the ground-breaking research of Maurice Leblanc, a turn-of-the-century French mystery writer and part-time archeologist. Leblanc may have been the first to suggest the idea of a correspondence between a constellation and a configuration in the landscape. His book, *La Contesse de Cagliostro*, contained a puzzle involving a "devil's treasure" associated with the seven stars, which formed the image of a Great Bear, that were connected with the seven Benedictine Abbeys of the Caux countryside in Normandy. Everything in Western civilization since the Dark Ages had been built upon the Benedictine plan.

The Winston family team was the first to discover that the Newgrange burial chamber had been aligned to the constellation Orion in the year 4567 B.C. Located north of Dublin, Ireland, Newgrange is considered the second oldest known megalithic structure to have an astronomical function. The location of Newgrange to the nearby burial mounds of Knowth and Dowth traces a pattern on the ground that mirrors the stars found in Orion. His mother had been fascinated by the ceremonial architecture of Newgrange, such as its roof boxes, which allowed the soul of the dead to escape the domed tomb. The roof boxes had been designed to focus and bend light into *knifelike slivers* that entered the womb of the burial chamber at sunrise during the winter solstice. Winston's mother had often said, "The light of God pierces the womb of Newgrange, the dome of stones, and something more."

She was so wise, he reminisced. His eyes blinked. Winston recalled a treasured moment when his mother instructed him on the workings of the constellations. The sky had paled into twilight, greeted by the sparks of fireflies, as they sat at the side of a sandbox next to the slide, the monkey bars, the roundabout, and the maypole swing in Rock Creek Park. His mother sketched the outline of a constellation in the sand, then pointed to the heavens and regaled her son with a story.

"*De profundis ad astra ... from the depths to the stars ... Look at the sky, Jimmy,*" she said sweetly, "*our holy ocean ... the Primum Mobile. It's older than the world.*" She guided his small hand with one finger extended and pointed to the constellations receding into an inky black. "*Bodies of Diamonds ... Virgo, Leo, Cancer, Gemini ... There is Cassiopeia in her chair. She is the key. See the outline of the rebel hunter, Caomai, with his bow? The oldest star chart. He battles the bull and predicts the seasons. At his heart is the Trapezium fish, a nebula waiting for a nova—from Rigel to Betelgeuse and its planet.*"

Winston smiled as he remembered how much he loved her stories about the stars.

"*Star chasers we are—one, two, three,*" she said, guiding his hand. "*The three stars in a row, Mintake, Ainilam, Ainitak, form his belt of pearls. Those stars have been called The Three Marys, The Three Kings, The Three Magi who followed the star of Bethlehem. The Bible said never 'loose the bands of Orion.' They guide the way to Ophiuchus. See that star to the lower right of them? There. Right there. The Dog Star, the soul of Isis. That's the star they follow. Everything has a pattern, Jimmy, even the infinity of the heavens. The heavens declare the glory.*" She stared upward with a slight tear in her eye. *"My God is full of stars."*

Lovingly, she held his hand and pointed to another twinkling stargroup. She recited in her gentle voice, " *'Our language is a virus that came from outer space.' Patterns out of the chaos. It's child's play. Patterns out of the chaos. The stars are the angels that guide us, Jimmy. Stars are the global constant. The world is set in motion by the stars. And there are always patterns, even in the chaos."*

WINSTON had proven himself to be a piece of work since he was two years old. He was born left-handed and stubbornly refused to learn to write with his right. An inquisitive child by nature, he could tear a clock apart and reassemble it in a new and different way. While attending the exclusive boarding school of Woodberry Forest, he showed promise as a mathematician, with talents that bordered that of an autistic savant. He won several national high school competitions sponsored by the Gifted and Talented Program of the National Security Agency. The NSA classified him as an 'Indigo Child,' an individual free spirit born with unique seeing capabilities. Tagged as a math prodigy, headhunters identified him as one of the best and brightest of the working herd. At seventeen, he was accepted by MIT into a fast-track program that assured him a Ph.D. within two years. Recruiters guaranteed him any job of his liking within his chosen field of Informatics, also known as Computer Artificial Intelligence. He was considered a budding genius in the areas of computer linguistics, message algorithms designed around IOA, and LISP programming of computer symbol manipulation and self-modifying code.

Unexpectedly, tragedy struck during his first year in college. His parents were murdered in an attempted robbery as they jogged one morning through Rock Creek Park. Their sudden death had shaken Winston's resolve. He dropped out of school and withdrew from life into state of deep depression. Despair spawned from loss can permeate a life and lead to desperate choices for a turbulent soul. He had reached the hellish limits of his nadir. Now Winston's demon wanted out.

With nothing to lose and left to his own devices, Winston chose a life of playing with chaos. Within a year, he had become a notorious underground computer hacker, known as Joe Wales. He taught himself how to bypass fire-walls, walk through backdoors, and formulate passwords to compromise private and public computer systems. He danced with chaos by creating the core routines for many of the world's most destructive computer viruses. At one point, he had infected an estimated 69,000 government terminals in forty countries. He was one of just a handful of hackers to compromise AMS, Microsoft, Sun, Oracle, Pacific Bell, and the North American Air Defense Command. He was the first cracker to achieve remote access to the archetypal ISO shellcodes used by the secured central hubs of headless Internet root servers. Winston had discovered that by rearranging the archetypes, he was able to destroy the instruction language which controlled the flow of traffic on the Internet.

FBI Hacker Hunters finally snared the outlaw in an Internet chat room while he played a Geocaching game with a fellow hacker, Eric Allmen, from the Cult of the Dead Crow. Winston found himself facing the classic Prisoner's Dilemma, a non-zero-sum-game studied by mathematicians and strategists. The game consists of three players: the Keeper who jails the Prisoner, the Prisoner, and a second prisoner called the Board. In the game, the Prisoner and the Board play against each other in various scenarios that affect their release from prison or their time spent in prison, depending on how they cooperate with the Keeper. The game is played out through strategic actions between the two prisoners, based upon their self interest or mutual interest. But in reality, the Prisoner's Dilemma is a win-lose game played between the Prisoner and the Keeper.

In Winston's dilemma, Allmen evaded prosecution by turning state's evidence against Winston. After pleading guilty to three charges of computer theft and creating and distributing computer viruses, the Boston Federal District Court sentenced Winston to eighteen years. In lieu of prison, the Government placed him under probationary arrest with the proviso that he work for a special unit within the NSA, who valued his talents as an asset that should not be locked away.

In a logrolling bargain, Winston was allowed to moonlight his services to private industry as a samurai. He understood his fate. Like every American, he was a prisoner of his government. But, he was a self-sufficient prisoner. His innate ability to *read the roads* of the information superhighway made him the prince of the cyberworld. It was an odd path he had chosen which bypassed the Fortune 500 game plan. In a time in which 20 billion dollars was spent annually on worldwide cybersecurity, he was more than fairly compensated for his expertise. He had groomed himself to be a modern-day soldier of fortune, and now found himself riding on a runaway gravy train. In the prime of his life, James Winston had acquired a diet of go-his-own-way financial independence. His life suited him, somehow. He had not grown up in a traditional home, and he was not the marrying kind.

REMEMBERING THE PAST soothed Winston, but it also opened up the dark places that harbored pain. *Regret cannot turn back the clock. The misdirected discretions of youth ... I was seeking a thrill from the discovery of forbidden knowledge. I had lost my bearings. My wings were broken. Tragedy led to my misfortune. My misfortune has led to my life's reward*, he concluded as the specter of his past faded from his mind's eye. *All my dreams fulfilled ... Self-pity is such a worthless emotion. Those were the salad days, my blessing in disguise.* He grasped the penknife. *It can be a million miles away, but your past is never dead and gone. The real ghosts are the memories of the dead that linger in our minds. People who walk out of our lives leave tracks. Death is all around us. Everything is connected. There are no accidents. Everything happens*, he held firm, staring at the penknife, *for a reason. There is always a bigger plan. Thanks Dad.* He secured his penknife in the zip pocket of his trekking pants, then gazed out at the haunting hues of a sky welded to jagged peaks on the northern horizon. *A person's worries can seem so small when you sit at the edge of a place such as this.*

Siva—crack—Saki

He spotted a spike of lightening in the distance, followed by a rumbling drumroll from Thor's axes striking the Earth. *Looks like things are goin' to fester.* Winston knew he had to reach the top. His eyes blinked as he sharpened his focus on the atmospheric colors of a rainbow arching over the approaching clouds. *There's something in their movement*, he pondered. A radiant spectrum outlining a vertical sun pillar floated in the upper atmosphere, signaling the path of the chameleon that reawakens the sleeper. *That cloud resembles a white snow bunny. Odd shapes in the clouds ... Where do they come from? Constellations out of stars. Patterns. Promises. My life saved.* He glanced at his bloody hands. *No rainbows without some rain.*

As though the heavens had mysteriously lowered a Jacob's ladder to save him, a rope suddenly dangled above his head in a beckoning, spiraling spin.

The rope of the Dhyanis. Winston pulled a smile. *I'm not forgotten after all.*

He pushed himself up shakily and regained his inner balance. He spit out his gum, then wrapped the rope around his hand and gave it a quick yank. Hand over hand, Winston nimbly belayed himself toward the heavens, like a spider inching up a single, almost invisible filament that would serve as the future support for a latticed web.

LIMPING UP AND OVER a few rocky ledges, Winston found himself at the summit of the timeless volcano. The distant horizon had vaulted away from sight, giving him the feeling that he had become one with the sky. The high mesa stretching out before him resembled a dry desert covered in patches of green and brown, needle-skinned prickly pears. *Where is he?* Winston's shirt clung to his chest as he turned into a breeze carrying the sharp scent of sagebrush.

In a clearing at the eastern edge of the tower sat a Native American wearing a worn, black Stetson with his long white hair bound in a ponytail. The man sat cross-legged on the ground with his eyes closed and his palms down in a near vajrasana posture of a small pyramidal mound. He was comfortably bundled up in a travel-light blanket from L. L. Bea*m*, embroidered with *bright*-colored symbols in red, blue, yellow, and green. Two backpacks, resting on a coiled pile of rope used to hoist them to the top of the Tower, lay on either side of him. The numbers **7** and **12** were stenciled in red on each pack. Directly in front of the man stood twelve, two-foot-high stones positioned in a circle approximately twenty feet in diameter. At the center of the circle, next to a cracked and weathered buffalo skull, a pile of blue-green stones supported a three-foot-high, vertical post of porous hazel wood.

Winston stepped closer and quietly observed the man. A four-inch-long gorget, made of polished, osseous-white eagle bone tied to a strip of leather cord, hung from the man's neck. The gorget was etched with the symbols of a fish and a bird's feather. The man, whose face was barely wrinkled for his age, beaconed with a wide toothy smile as he nodded his head back and forth in rhythm to Fleetwood Mac playing through the headphones attached to his i-Pod. Winston faintly heard the steady woodpecker drumbeat of "The City" from *Mystery to Me.*

"You look like an ostentatious old peacock meditating on that medicine wheel," Winston shouted.

The man pulled the headphones down around his neck and turned off his i-Pod. "Unci Maka—the Sacred Hoop—my Wheel of Life," he said, holding his right hand at the heart of his chest. "My body and mind are harnessed together. I am surfing, catching waves. I'm *dream weaving* through a hundred opened eyes, that I might see the world through my mind, and yours. I seek the formless realm of the Pure Land, my pivot point in the turning world. I see through darkness with a cat's-eye view. The world is not as it appears. Dark is not darkness. You must gaze at the world in order to do the *dream weaving.* If you gaze at the movement of a shadow of a rock, through your dreaming weaving, you might discover that even a shadow has light. I see visions with open eyes. I am *awake!* It is all a dream and I am a part of it all. I'm watching the Immovable Watcher. I am overcoming. I am killing time. Time is dead. It is only a flash between two eternities. Only when the clock stops can I come to life and discover myself, when past and future are joined within the eternal now. I am being or becoming—I exist in both time and endless time. I am here to *learn* and *share*. I am a seeker. All of us are seekers. I'm always searching for the core of my inner consciousness." He widened his toothy grin, revealing a gold tooth reflecting a radiant ray from the morning sun.

"You need a new consciousness, leaving me hanging back there," Winston harped in an angry tone. "Where were you, Billy? I could have been killed!"

"I thought you liked hanging loose," Billy responded calmly.

Winston massaged his left shoulder and gave the old sage a stern look. "Yeah. Every which way but— Didn't you hear me when I called out for you?"

"Yes," Billy replied, "but I was busy talking."

"Talking? There's no one here," Winston noted.

"I was talking to God," Billy said.

Winston cocked his head and eyeballed the medicine wheel, the sacred tool of the rhabdomancer.

"When you call out for help, you are seeking a strength beyond yourself. It is a good thing. But, James, you are too quick to anger. You have only ascended the Second Mountain. I know you have been remembering. You are haunted by your past and your spirit is in need of healing. But, you have more anger than sorrow. You are wounded beyond your hands. Tragedy triggers pity. Self-pity is your enemy and the source of your misery. Ah … such self-suffering you have. But wisdom can be born from suffering. James, you are not that important. You must silence the voice of your ego. The silencing of your ego allows you to hear your inner heart—which brings you closer to your soul." Billy shook his head. "Your ego is loud enough to block out the subtle whispers of your heart. Listen beyond your pity. Pity comes from *fear*. What you fear is not your loss. What you fear *most* is *death*. To fear death is to resist your life, which misinterprets Nature. We are all beings on the way to dying. The Earth belongs to the living. You are dying within yourself. You are over thinking. *Forget*. Time purges all things. What matters most is the marrow of your life. You need to discover your cosmic center, the place of your soul. Only then can you discover your heavenly origins. Everything you do, everything you say, every part of your life, is misdirected unless you *know of* and *understand* your cosmic center. Unchain your heart. Bind your wounds and release yourself. Become bound for Glory."

"But, Billy …," Winston stammered.

"Silence!" Billy snapped. "The wise man is silent. Wake up and stand still in *your* silence. Silence brings sanctity. Anger, lust, envy, and false pride will be moral defects if you are not sanctified. Every day, you need three minutes of silence. Only then can you see that the Immortal Man is *Silence*. Settle down and free yourself from your mental chatter. Become conscious of everything around you. Look beyond the physical world. Look within yourself. This is the awakening. Count to zero, and close your eyes and dream…. *Focus*. Learn to listen. *Seek the angelic whispers*. There is a glorious reality in the sounds of dreams. Dreams are not created. Of all things that are, the most ancient is God, for he is uncreated. If you want to talk to God, simply shut up and listen. Try to hear the bird songs," Billy said with a mystic parlance as he calmly closed his eyes. "Every day, surround yourself with the songs of the birds. They are *singing* every morning. They are singing *unimaginable* things."

Even high at the top of Devil's Tower, the *chirp-chop, chirp-chop* cadence of the birds could be heard echoing from their nests in the walls of the tower.

"James, your vision of ancestral remembering is certainly strong. It is a good thing. It is good to honor those who came before us and paved the way. Self-remembering is the first step. But what you remember, as with what you see, you must *share*. If you see something and do not share it, you will have lost the reason for seeing it. A life such as yours, which can see the surprises in this world, needs to share them."

Billy held his hand to his closed eyes and extended two fingers. "There are other worlds beyond the one we *think* we see. Even those with the eyes of an eagle can be blind. But, you do not need the sharp eyes of an eagle to see. What we see is what we are. If what you see is good, then you are good. Many take the limits of their own field of vision as the limits of the world. But you can see beyond it. I see something in you which you do not. Bear witness to your buried power. Do not tune Him out. Wrestle with your reality. The world is only what we perceive it to be. Follow the arrow from your eye. Always look before and after. Push yourself beyond your limits. Become detached from the folly of your fellowman and unfold the wings of your perception. You, James, have the ability to *see* and *stop the world*. This is your calling. Your sight will bring you *power*. Continue to practice what I have taught you and you can exceed what you see. Free yourself so you can face the unknown. You are unbound!"

"I'm not certain about that," Winston blurted. "I feel like I live in chains."

"Good. The first step toward freedom is the realization that you *cannot* live in chains. James, you are a one-of-a-kind creation. There never has been and never will be another person like you. Use what talents you possess. The woods would be very silent if no birds sang except those that sang the best. There is a reason why birds always sing after a storm. The birds fly over the rainbow, from black holes to time warps. They fly upon a ribbon of light. Light … from the Living Flame." Billy inhaled a deep breath, his eyes barely opened, squinting.

He's starting to dream weave. Winston observed Billy's trancelike expression.

"*Aum … brel … la …* The breath of life begins in the lungs and ends with the lips. Listen. There is a reason why a Buddhist monk lights a candle when he prays. Light is the outcome of a consuming flame. The burning only makes it brighter. From our birth until our passing, we live in the Light. Each of us is a being of light and *bringer* of light—internally illuminated splendor. Light touches all aspects of our being. It is the underpinning of the *All* and all that is constant. Light is the radiance of truth. The man who seeks *truth* finds *light*. Before the void of life's uncertainties the sacred tree is not dead. It still sings with the sun. There is life in its branches. Be aware. Use the knife of your dissecting mind and you will see it. Everything is pushed by Light. Light is like another language. To know another language is to have a second soul—a soul which flies with the birds above the Earth and across the firmament of the heavens. You need to learn to speak—the language of the birds."

Winston stared at the old man who had been a surrogate father and a source of strength to him over the past two years. *Black holes and time warps … He's talking in riddles again. What's he getting at this time?* Winston wondered. *Light … singing with the sun … language of the birds …?* "Billy, I don't understand."

Billy peered from behind the wide brim of his Stetson with a solemn expression on his face. His clear, coffee-brown eyes, like Albert Einstein's, were weary but full of life. He gazed into Winston's studious blue eyes and guided in a teacher's voice. "Swiftness of mind. Sever your head from your body and open your awareness beyond your thoughts. You must think without thinking. If you can think without thinking, no explanation is necessary. I am *only* an example. You need to listen to what I say and watch what I do. There is a difference between what you want to hear and what you need to hear. You are still a child because you think that way." Billy lowered his eyes. "Don't bandage your head before it gets hurt. You need to visit the place where the fishes swim. Knowledge is more than knowing facts. Think about what you know. Answer the questions you have within yourself. Those are the only questions that matter. He who thinks he knows everything, understands nothing. You must learn what is right, not what is easy. Advice is easy." He shook his head.

"I'm only trying to learn," Winston said. "So I should stop listening?"

"One repays a teacher badly if he remains only a pupil. James, what I know is not limited to me. I am not your only teacher. Nature is your mentor. Hear Her echo and respond to it. Persuade Her and discover the Ideal of Holy. Look around. You are a man inside a Bigger Man. You are a being-in-the-world. Be able. Awareness is doing. Become your own teacher. Birth your own creation. Open the door for yourself, so you will know what is. Look clearly into your own world. The ultimate mystery of being is the mystery of *your* being. The only questions you need to ask yourself are: Where did you come from? Why are you here? Where are you going?" Billy knowingly grinned. "Who the devil are you? Oh … you have much to learn. You achieve knowledge by comparing the two sides of life. Dark and Light … Death and Life … Love and Sorrow. Compare the two sides. Find the balance. Exercise your mind. If you can change your mind, you can change your life. If you can speak your mind, you can see your life. Perfect knowledge only happens through your self-realization. How else will you learn, if you do not learn on your own?"

Billy fixed his eyes on the medicine wheel and resumed his cryptic words of wisdom. "You must confront your inner demon to defeat the one outside," he expressed with certainty in his voice. "Fight the wild gander. Truth only comes when the 'I' is dissolved. Gaze upon yourself from an unaccustomed place. Eye yourself, so you can learn to deny yourself. Only then will all your restless desires be gone. Trust your instincts. It's a part of being brave. Sometimes you have to be brave. You have to admit you are flawed. You have to have the courage to rebuild your temple—and start over again. You must save your own self, James. It is not the responsibility of others. With courage in your convictions, do not compromise. Have faith. Faith is something given, not achieved. Life is a leap of faith, and a balance of faith, in yourself. It is the impossible victory over yourself. Remember, every man searches for himself, but very few ever find themselves. No bird soars too high, if he soars with his own wings. Such is the flight of the bird of freedom. Freedom is at your fingertips. But fear can steal it from you. Do not become paralyzed by fear. Do not be afraid to take it."

"But, Billy—" Winston hung his head and stammered again.

"Silence … I fully understand the discomfort of your spirit. The sounds of life can be burdensome. Turn down the volume." Billy motioned with one hand down, his fingertips touching the ground, and the opened palm of his other hand cradling upward toward the middle of his chest. A metal band inscribed with the name of an MIA from the Vietnam War slipped down on his wrist. "Silence is the beginning of peace. Silence is your pursuit. Silence requires patience. Take time. Time brings all things to Light. Stand still and watch a rose unfold. Patience can be a virtue. Never idle, but do not hurry. Give pause. Seek guidance from others who do the same. Learn to *listen*. There is a cadence, a heartbeat, and a tone in everything you hear. Direct your attention to the sounds around you and the holes between the sounds. *The silence....* Strengthen your awareness and you can be in two places at once. Once, all of life spoke the same language—a language of silence."

Winston thoughtfully stared at the ground.

"It is good to remain silent concerning things of which you cannot speak, but do not hide yourself in secrets." Billy observed Winston's silence. "You need to speak so you can connect. Say hello to everyone you meet and break the silence. Permit yourself to be exposed to someone else by acknowledging their existence. Smile with them. Look for the things that make us human. You will discover yourself through your relationships with others. If you seek peace, you must remember that we belong to each other. There is a wider wisdom, deep within ourselves. Everything you need you have already. Follow your *passion*. Look honestly into your own heart, and you will fear nothing as you find the hearts of others. A whole mirror-world is within us. It is a cognitive world. And it is full of frightening things. *Stop that world* and everything around you will change. Break away from the conventions that bind your perceptions so you can reinvent yourself. Learn from your silence. In times of quiet, we are alone with ourselves and with God. It is an uneasy magic. The process is laborious and painful. Some people wonder when their God will come." He paused. "Truth always resides above reason. God—is already here." Billy smiled. "Those who place themselves at the top of a pecking order in relation to God, do not know what God is. Be careful where you bow your head. Do not mistake a theater for a temple, or a circus for a sanctuary. Do not cling to the false beliefs. Not every spoken word is sound, my friend. Where secrets and mysteries begin, vice and roguery are not far behind. Like a dreamcatcher, our world is crisscrossed by a web spun by Spider Grandmother to catch the unseen light. It is a huge net which holds all kinds of fish. Do not become entangled in it. By the time you recogonize an evil, it is always too late. Beware of the forked tongue of the man whose belly does not move when he laughs. Beware of those with the high-sounding names as you recognize your chosen path. But do not put your judgment in front of you first. Stay sober, with humility. Remember, you are your brother's keeper. Love all, trust a few, do wrong to none."

Watch what I do ... What's he doing? Winston observed.

"Be aware that there is always a right time and right place." Billy lifted his head. "Each of us has our time in the sun. Pay attention. Vision is the art of seeing the invisible. Examine things with care. God is in the details. I know it is hard to conquer anything with unforgiving verticals, especially the earth above ground. But when we are forced to stop, it is time to acquire a new vision. A time to determine what direction to take. A time to find the best approach up the Devil's tower."

With a controlled breath, Billy closed his eyes and aligned his face toward the *center* of the medicine wheel. "Keep a memory of this moment," he advised, holding his hands together with the tips of his thumbs touching. A *vibrant glow* from a narrow *teja* of light passed over the middle of his face. "Reach for twilight … I am moving toward it." He placed his hand to his chest with his index finger pointing upward. "Of the seven sacred rites, the first you must learn to master is the Keeping of the Soul."

BILLY, a half-breed Lakota of the Great Sioux Nation and a descendant of the Ghost Dancer, Wovoka, was referring to the seven rites of spiritual passage within the Lakota religion. These being: the Keeping of the Soul, the *Nagi Gluhapi Na Nagi Gluxkapi*; the Rite of Purification, the *Inipi;* Crying for a Vision Quest, the *Hanblecheyapi*; the Sun Dance, the *Wiwanyag Wachipi*; the Making of Relatives, the *Hunkapi*; the Preparing for Womanhood, the *Ishna Ta Awi Cha Lowan*; and the Throwing of the Ball, the *Tapa Wanka Yap.*

Billy opened his eyes filled with a dark luminance. "The soul is the lamp whose light is steady, for it burns in a shelter where there are no winds. It cannot be extinguished." His eyes fixed straight ahead. "It is from the darkness of Raven that light came into the world. At the interior of every shadow is a spirit of light. No one can own the spirit of another. It is impossible to violate your nature. Whatever they have taken from you, this can never be taken from you. You must hold your lamp before the wind. But do not step away from the shadows. *Engage* the shadows. Raven is a trickster. You cannot trust the shadows. The shapes of the shadows are not clear. The shapes of the shadows are not solid. Shadows never stand still long enough for us to discern a true shape. A shadow is always a shadow of something else. A shadow only becomes visible by way of light. A shadow is a sign of *the presence* of light. All of this is a light of truth. *Always* search for the *light* from your lamp. To find your lamp, you need to see yourself in the hearts of all beings. To hold your lamp, you will need to see both the *dark* and the *light* of life. To achieve that, you must follow the winding path of the snake and become a warrior of change. Change does not always mean you move forward. Inward, James. Who am I?" Closed fisted, Billy tapped at the heart of his chest. "I am the one that I am! Inward change. The *inward* light."

Billy's was as motionless as the rock tower upon which he sat. His eyes glowed as he stared at the *center* of the medicine wheel. "The self-centered warrior has to grow in unselfishness. Learn to change… The cautious warrior must grow in courage. Learn to change…. The reckless warrior must grow in carefulness. Learn to change…. The timid warrior must grow in confidence. Learn to change…. The self-belittling warrior must grow in self-love. Learn to change…. The dominating warrior must grow in sensitivity. Learn to change…. The critical warrior must grow in tolerance. Learn to change…. The power-hungry warrior must grow in kindness and gentleness. Learn to change…. The pleasure-seeking warrior must grow in compassion for those who suffer. Learn to change…. And, the God-ignoring warrior must become a God-adoring soul," he drilled. "Learn to change, my friend."

Billy abruptly faced away from the circle of stones and looked up at Winston. "Your life, like a match, requires a force to ignite. Use your *will,* the inner kernel of every being. *Will* is *power. Will* is the force which manifests your wants and needs into a reality. Nothing is more useful than the narrowness of thought combined with the energy of *will.* Use your unbending *will* to seek out your wisdom, strength, and piety. Discover yourself in your chain of being, through the Keeping of the Soul."

What did he do …? Winston diverted his attention to the medicine wheel, his eyes blinking. In a three-second, rapid eye scan he recognized the functionality of the pattern formed by the stones. Four branches of fresh juniper positioned on the ground divided the area of the circle into equal quadrants. As though to prove to himself, or to Billy, that he could solve the mysteries of time from the circadian movement of a shadow, he surmised that the post at the cross-axis of the mandala served as a gnomon for a sundial. "I see by the shadow from that poor man's compass that it's 9:18 A.M."

Billy closed his eyes and shook his head in disbelief. *When will you learn?*

Winston tilted his head to one side as the advance of a rhythmic *chopping*, like a rushing train approached from a distance. "Yeah, I'm beginning to hear the sounds of the birds," he wisecracked.

A cyclonic cloud of wind and dust enveloped the area around the two companions, as a Sikorsky Sea King rose up over the southern slope of the escarpment.

"The dragonfly!" Billy called out with concern. He sprang to his feet, his legs spread apart and fists clenched in a fearless warrior pose, and faced the approaching helicopter which appeared to materialize out of nowhere. The expression on his face calmed, as he drew up through his feet the energy from the earth above ground.

Winston aligned his eye to the optic axis of his OMEGA GPS wristwatch. Its seven-segment polarized LCD flashed: 9:19 AM. Pointing to the Sea King, he tried to shout above the whizzing roar of the man-made bird. "They've been tracking me!"

Billy held tight to his flapping blanket. He cupped his other hand behind his ear. Winston pointed to his watch. Billy shook his head to acknowledge that he understood. He stepped closer and began to decipher the sounds coming from Winston's lips.

"It's a Code Yellow. Big Brother's calling. They've come to get me. Let's go!"

The helicopter flew close enough to obtain a face-to-face visual.

"To the chopper?" Billy shouted, pointing to the hovering Sea King.

"No!" Winston pointed to the ground. "To Bear Lodge!" He pressed a button on his wristwatch, and the LCD stopped flashing. In a dash, he grabbed the pack marked with the number 7. He glanced up, his eyes settling on a woman's face smiling down at him from the forward window of the helicopter. He froze in his steps and smiled. *Another ghost from the past.* Securing the pack to his back, he gave her a thumbs-up.

She motioned a thumbs-up back to him.

Winston scrambled to the edge of the summit and away from the whirling force of the Sea King. He bent down, plucked a tuft of dry grass from the ground, and tossed the broken blades into the air to test the wind. With a determined grin, Winston took a flying leap off the northern approach of Devil's Tower. "*L'appelle d'vide!*" He greeted the call of the void.

Billy snatched his Stetson off his head and haphazardly stuffed it and his blanket into the side pockets of the other pack. Pulling the pack over his shoulders, he swiped his eyes up at the hovering Sea King. He flashed a wide, toothy grin at the woman and gave her a thumbs-up as well. Then, like a bent arrow shot from a bow, Billy sprinted to the edge of the Tower and leapt into midair in pursuit of Winston.

"Geronimo!" Billy bellowed.

The Sea King swayed forty-seven degrees to one side and flew away from the summit.

At the base of Devil's Tower, Margaret Eagledove sat on the hood of the yellow

Hummer, gazing up into the darkening, midmorning sky. Her head slowly rotated, tracking the unsynchronized birdmen falling off air and descending from the towering monolith. Their parachutes were visibly marked with the numbers **7** and **12**, billowing above their outstretched arms and legs in the pose of the *Vitruvian Man.*

"Show-offs. They'd better get here before the park rangers." Margaret jumped off the hood and grabbed a pair of Bushnell Instant Replay butterfly binoculars from the dash. "James, you *devil,*" she groaned, watching his wild-eyed expression with the help of 77 mm magnification. She pressed RECORD on the binoculars as Winston's face moved out of her line of sight and Billy's toothy grin shifted into focus. A gold tooth sparkled. "You sonofabitch—" she fumed. *You're going to kill yourself with these foolish antics, Mr. Flying Eagledove.*

Winston hit the ground in a running motion a few feet from the center of the clearing. He pulled on the lines, tugged at the silk, and secured his parachute.

Right on the mark, Margaret thought.

Approaching the Hummer with his gear tucked under his arm, Winston smiled and offered Margaret a quick wave. He pulled a navy-blue baseball cap from his pack, adorned with a two-inch-wide American Flag embroidered on the front, and covered his head. "Kicking it freestyle!" He slapped her a high-five. "That was one hell of a BASE jump!" He threw his gear in the rear of the Hummer, then opened the driver's side door and reached for a set of polarized aviator sunglasses resting on the dash.

"Hang 'em high … Are you, okay?" Margaret asked with concern.

"Yeah." Winston smiled, shielding his eyes with the glasses. "We're making tracks back to my place. Something's festered. I have a situation."

Margaret's attention turned skyward, her head slowly panning, glued to Billy's haphazard descent.

Falling like a wounded bird, Billy hit the ground in a hard roll. His parachute folded in the wind as it just missed the trees.

"Yahoo!" Billy yelled. He staggered as he picked himself up and began securing his gear. "Buffalo Woman," he panted, addressing his wife by her honored name, "come here and help me with this thing!"

———

THE RADIO BLASTED "Jim Dandy to the Rescue!" as the SUV swayed and bounced along an eroded, serpentine logging road running next to a low, riprap fence that marked Winston's territory north of Keyhole State Park. Turning tires kicked up a cloud of dust, as Winston steered onto the gravel-strewn driveway riddled with potholes that led to Bear Lodge.

Billy's Stetson crushed in as his head bumped against the low roof of the Hummer.

"Slow down!" Margaret yelled.

Winston spied the NSA insignia on the side of the Sea King nested in a broad field next to the front lawn. He braked to a jerking stop. The radio cut short and urged a sputtering, "Go, Jim—"

"Billy, you take the Hummer. I could be a while," Winston reckoned.

Billy removed his crumpled hat, remolded it into a dome shape, and placed it back on his head. "I believe you are about to experience a journey of the soul. This will be your first pilgrimage." He grabbed Winston's arm. "Home and journey, James. These are the two lasting gifts we give to our children. One is the roots of our family tree.

The other is the wings of a bird to fly from it. Fly safely, my friend," he counseled.

Winston absentmindedly nodded and stepped to the rear of the Hummer, his eyes riveted on the helicopter.

Billy followed close behind. He reached into the cargo bed and handed Winston his belongings. The expression in Billy's eyes deepened. "When I was a young hunter, I became lost in the canyons of the Black Hills following the path of the Great Black Elk. I journeyed for many days without water. And I hungered. I became weak and delirious with visions of demons and spirits hiding in the colored cracks of the canyon walls. I soon passed out from the heat of the sun. When I awoke, I found myself under the shade of a Great Tree. Everyone finds shade from a Great Tree as they journey through the seven circuits of life. I found mine, or it found me, here at Mateo Tepee, where the first of my people had the vision. The shade from your Great Tree is somewhere else. Only you will see it. Only will you understand it. Only you will believe in it."

"I got it, shady trees," Winston muttered.

"Go forth and declare yourself. Go before the others and become a leader. Take part in your life's great adventure. Remember … to follow your own best path. Walk in Beauty. Small steps … small steps, James. Small steps can overcome the mistakes we make unceasingly. Stalk yourself. There is no quick path through the forest of the seven circuits for he who starts the quest for the source of his being. It is a route of many roads leading from nowhere to nothing. Consider the end. Live like you were dying. Do not lose sight of the path you are on, or you will be as a bird with no wind to carry him aloft. Always test the wind before you fly. The wind blows wherever it pleases. Only the birds have learned to master the spirit of the wind because they know it is always there to catch them. Stay true to yourself; never be ashamed of doing what is right. Your heart knows what is right. Once you decide on what you think is right, stay the path. It was meant to be. Believe in yourself, but do not be vain. The only limits you have are those you put on yourself. There is dignity and sanctity to life. Remember to respect your flesh. Act as a warrior, with tolerance and respect. Your body is like the Bear Lodge. It is the house of your soul."

"I understand, Billy. Thanks for the encouragement. You take care of Margaret. Watch after Bear Lodge for me. I'll see you when I get back."

Billy grasped Winston's arm with both hands. "Remember that there are seven directions, north, south, east, west, above, below, and *self*. Seek the four guardians. Life is a mystery. The longest journey is the journey inward, where you will face many questions. But the answers are sometimes outside yourself. There are places you know about which you have never seen. Everything is in *plain sight*. Place your hands on the ground and touch the earth. Embrace it. Feel it. Ground yourself to it. You walk upon God's greatest secret everyday. Love the world—this Earth—and it will love and nurture you in return. Now, go where eagles dare. Be! Fly with the eye of an eagle. They are free to soar. The spirit eagle is the First Cause, who dropped its egg into the chaos which is our world. It is the guardian of the highest of the three realms. Wakinyan, the spirit eagle protects us," Billy explained. "The spirit eagle instructs us—'Hands off, *this world belongs to God.*' " He nodded. "It shall come to pass."

"Yeah, Billy, whatever." Self-absorbed, Winston half-smiled and stepped away.

"Stop your rapping, let's go," Margaret shouted from the car window.

"Alright." Billy climbed into the Hummer.

"Great Trees," she chided. "*I found you passed out in the mountains.*"

"I remember." Billy smiled, gripped the wheel, and turned the ignition key. The radio squawked. *STA-KA—STA-KA*— Simon and Garfunkel were singing, "America." He eyed Winston as he drove away and whispered to himself, "*E pluribus Unum.* There is a reason why God put you in my way. Out of many, you are the One."

Winston stood with his eyes locked on the man and the woman exiting the Sea King as its propellers slowly *whirred* to a stop. The woman held one hand over her head to keep her hair out of her face. Ambling through an ankle-high field of pulsating, wheat-green grass shimmering a buttercup yellow, she held up her other hand and waved.

Winston's Adam's apple jumped in his throat.

"Hello, Cowboy," Susan greeted with a tight smile, her lips an inviting, sweet pink.

"Hello, again, Susan," Winston spoke above the staccato *whump-whump-whump* of the Sea King. "How's my bosom buddy?" In a downward gaze, he gave her his devil-may-care look. "I got your Christmas card."

"I'm fine, James. I didn't get yours. Did it get lost in the mail?"

The expression on Winston's face revealed nothing, his eyes turning.

"So, how's the High Plains Drifter from Wyoming?" She bit down on her lower lip and tipped her head slightly, half-circling around him like a stalking tigress inhaling a whiff of danger.

"It's been a dizzy day." Winston slowly turned his head to keep up with his eyes. "I had some trouble holding on."

"I see you're still palling around with Billy. You look a little battered and bruised, but you're aging well. Been training for the Eiger?"

"It's the anti-aging century," he replied. "I still work out. But not like you." Winston could tell she was still into body shaping. He shifted his feet. "I forgot to send it."

"How quickly we forget." Susan rolled her eyes. She confidently squared her shoulders, folded her arms, and gazed away.

Still unforgiven, Winston thought.

SUSAN HAMILTON was a clever, seductive siren and a bit of a tomboy, athletic, lean, and toned. Her auburn, shoulder-length hair highlighted the glow of her alabaster skin and mysterious blue-green eyes that often changed colors with her moods. A former agent with the FBI and the Epidemic Intelligence Service, with a Masters in marine biology from Cal Tech, she was an intriguing combination of smart and sexy.

"James, we're here to stomp out another fire," she stated hastily. "The Commander just pulled me from an investigation of a possible terrorist attack from some 'rock snot' toxic algae that's killing birds along the beaches around Charleston. I called it in as a negative threat. Algae growth patterns have naturally increased with the recent temperature changes in the Gulf Stream. I guess they figured we worked well together the last time." She motioned to the man approaching from the Sea King. "This is CIA liaison, Dr. William Strange Bains, one of the handlers from the SCS out of Laurel. He has been cleared by the Commander to tag along."

Captain Obvious ... Winston gawked at the hairpiece that tilted like a wooly tarantula about to crawl off the top of Bains's head. *Another CIA face guy dressed in a business suit.* He sized up Bains's bookish appearance. *This shadow spook even has a little briefcase.* "Dr. Bains, Welcome to the Badlands."

"Good morning, Jefferson," Bains addressed Winston by his INNCS code name as they shook hands. "I previously supervised SCS operations at The Point." With a nervous tic that twisted his face into a grimace, he scanned Winston's attire. *He's not at all what I imagined. He looks more like he belongs on the cover of* Field and Stream *than* PC Age. "I see you wear the hacker's emblem."

"The Glider," Winston smiled, "the Game of Life."

Bains clamped his jaw shut and stood with a quiet confidence, protectively cradling his briefcase to his chest. "Wonderful view ... This big wooden birdhouse must be Monticello?" He took in the panorama of the 12,000 square-foot log cabin sprawling horizontally below the tips of the tall vertical lines of blue-green, overlapping conifers. *None of this is quite like I imagined.*

"Not quite, Doctor. It's not on the World Heritage List of structures worthy of being preserved at all costs. I call it Bear Lodge, my million dollar baby. It's got no mailbox or house number. It's the place where I come to live off the grid," Winston said with a carefree smile. "I lived in an apartment once, but living with someone on top of you is not really living. Now, I'm yupscaled. It's my slice of heaven out on the frontier. It's home. So, what's the story?"

"Jefferson, we had a *situation* at Steeplebush yesterday morning which requires your immediate assistance," Bains spoke in a crisp, businesslike voice. "This is a no-choice decision. So far, the Four Horsemen—Rousseau, the Big Lug Hume, Emerson, and Marx have also been called in. We're calling this operation Project Capricorn. I have preliminary files on a data disk I think you need to review."

"Alright. Let's check it out in my media center," Winston suggested.

As they approached the front entrance to Bear Lodge, Susan updated Winston on the history of the computer virus and the severity of the situation. Bains paraded a few paces behind them, pondering the architectural features of the Bear Lodge complex. Losing his footing, he fell to his knees and bumped his chin on his briefcase.

"What are all these holes?" Bains asked in an aggravated tone. "Prairie dogs?" Regaining his footing, he pulled at the knot in his tie and repositioned his hairpiece.

"They're from the gophers." Winston glanced at the hole in the ground. "They're hard to see because of the patches of goat head weeds. That stuff's next to impossible to remove from the landscape. The gophers are nasty pests, but my friend, Billy, has a big-eyed, stuffed horn-owl, a Minerva that sees the vista. It works like a charm in keeping them and the wolves away from the main house."

Approaching the front door, Bains lingered to read the inscription on a plaque hanging above the doorway next to a copper birdfeeder. He winked his left eye.

Bear Lodge
Ilingu - Stop your walking, traveler, and enter this sacred temple
***Nature is a living system, so sacred that those who use it profanely
will surely lose it; and to lose nature is to lose ourselves. (TAO)***

Winston pushed the handle and opened the unlocked door.
Stepping into the foyer, Bains inspected his new surroundings. He noticed a two-

by-three-square-foot, stone bas-relief of the *Vitruvian Man* attached to wall behind an altar table. *Renaissance Humanism,* Bains equated. "It looks like a scarecrow guarding the entrance to the house."

"A warning to the birds and their prying eyes. It's an artwork my father owned. He was a fan of Leonardo. He once said there was a map hidden in the *Last Supper.*" Winston dropped his gear on the floor and emptied his pockets into a fruit bowl on the altar table. He filled it with spare change, a ring of keys, a torn two-dollar bill, and his penknife. "Margaret left me some landspam." He sorted through a neatly stacked bundle and removed a green, padded envelope from the National Audubon Society. "Something different ..." He opened it and retrieved his complimentary, bloodred Audubon birdcall, dangling on the end of a braided green lanyard. He dropped it into the fruit bowl, tossed the brochure-filled envelope to the table, kicked off his Carnacs, and stepped into a pair of quick-lace Salomon running shoes. "This way, Doctor."

Winston led his guests down an unlit hallway. Its walls were lined with tribal masks from Africa, Tibet, and Mexico.

"You have a lot of faces, Jefferson." Bains counted. "Seven."

"I keep it random. My faces of the fallen. It's the Hall of Lies," Winston said honestly. "A collection from my father's travels. The last one's a mummy mask from Lake Moeris in Egypt. Seven's my lucky number."

Bains stopped before a glass globe display case situated in a lighted niche in the hallway. "What's this?" He peered at a cracked, wooden disc, the size of a silver dollar, inside the globe.

"It's a family heirloom—an item that got me interested in cryptography and mathematics. It's an old key-disc from a Bazeries cipher machine created by Thomas Jefferson. It was part of a bundle of wooden key-discs which rotated on a metal spindle. The outside edge of each disc was hand carved with a random alphabet, with the correct order of the discs on the spindle serving as a cipher key. Jefferson created it to encrypt his private correspondence. Everyone was trying to hack into his mail and learn his secrets. Jefferson was a big advocate of cryptographic freedom."

"A rare find." Bains's eyes were glued to the disc. "How did you obtain it?"

"My father gave it to me. He told me he got it from the great-great-granddaughter of Dr. John Patterson, a mathematician who taught at the University of Pennsylvania. Patterson was once considered our country's leading mathematician. He was a friend of Benjamin Franklin and Jefferson. He helped found the Franklin Institute. My mother was a Celestial Circle member of the Franklin Institute."

From the hallway, they entered the library. The rustic space soared thirty feet high into a cathedral ceiling. The pine-planked floor, stained in a warm amber and held in place by protruding cast-iron nails, gripped at the soles of their shoes. In one corner, a spiral stairway climbed to a catwalk that accessed the book-lined walls on the second floor. A four-foot-diameter globe made of deep, sapphire blue crystal stood next to the stairway. Looming in a fierce posture, a towering, twelve-foot-tall, stuffed polar bear wearing a beaver-skin cap guarded the globe. Three doors exited the library: an entrance on the east wall, a narrow door on the north wall, and a back door on the west wall. Above the archways of two of the doors hung framed plaques with etchings of the Chinese trigrams for "power" and "happiness." A fieldstone fireplace dominated the middle of the southern wall of floor-to-ceiling windows.

"My Pergamos," Winston said warmly. "This is my living room." He removed his baseball cap and pitched it across the room. It landed on the tip of one of the buffalo horns of a bronze replica of James Earle Fraser's *Calling the Buffalo* and swung back-and-forth like a flag in a breeze.

"Skookum … I'm impressed," Bains said smoothly. "Luxury living, this place is fit for a king. And what's that, the throne?" He gawked at an oversized, green recliner at the center of the great space.

"That's my VDC." Winston stood behind his curiosity seat. "It's a device for hacking my head. I call it the Chair of Buddha. The throne's beside the sacred scrolls in the room behind that door." He pointed to the narrow door in the north wall.

Bains wagged his head and stepped away to admire the books on the shelves.

THE VDC was Winston's personal Virtual DiaGnostic Corner, or Twilight Sleep Counselor. The chair resembled a Lazy-Boy recliner that had been custom fitted to Winston's six-foot-two physique. Developed in Seoul, Korea by the gadget masters of 3-Stars Electronics and marketed globally by California-based **Rapid-I-Scan**, the $30,000 VDC was designed around the sciences of kinesiology and iridology to help people with sleep disorders, although the technology had been dubbed the new "virtual love machine" by certain Internet user groups. Others called it an adaptation of the "God Helmet," a skullcap apparatus created from the early studies in NeuroMagnetics by the Canadian neuropsychologist, Dr. Michael Persinger, which enhances and records the binaural brain-beat-resonance phenomenon. According to Dr. Persinger's research, the lobes of the brain behave like a resonator, automatically responding to low intensity magnetic fields derived from solar flares, seismic activity, radio and microwave transmissions, electrical devices, and other external sources. The human brain is naturally hardwired to receive signals from what Dr. Persigner called the "Grand Organizing Design" — G.O.D.

The chair utilizes thirty-two miniature neurofeedback inducers located at key meridian points on the human body which test for levels of muscular relaxation. Subsonic data riding on a 4-13 Hz tone hidden within the white noise of background music is delivered through earphones, producing a specific EMF, an electro-magnetic field of left and right brain stimulation. The audio neurofeedback therapy from a VDC allows the user to reach new levels of Alpha sleep consciousness. In practice, thirty minutes on the VDC is equal to eight hours of natural sleep.

As with many computer hackers, Winston had trouble sleeping. He had acquired an odd form of insomnia known as "28-awake." Perhaps it had been one too many jolts from the caffeinated sodas over the years, or the tragedy from the sudden loss of his immediate family, but sleep deprivation had become Winston's Achilles' heel. He claimed he did not sleep for fear of waking up, but because he considered sleep a waste of valuable time. One of Winston's favorite sayings was, "I slam, therefore I am." Crash and burn had been his lifestyle for eight years as a rogue hacker.

The VDC now allowed Winston to monitor the deepest levels of his sleep and form an unconscious left and right brain wave stasis. It helped him to relax from his over-thinking and realign his physical well-being to a greater level of normalcy. But like a junkie in need of a fix, Winston required downtime on the VDC at least once a month to maintain his proper balance.

"HACKING YOUR HEAD?" Susan plopped down in the oversized recliner. "I've never sat in a VDC before. I suppose you don't end up with a lobotomy scar with a thing like this."

She leaned back and surveyed the lofty ceiling held up by heavy pine timbers locked together with oak treenails. A nineteenth-century, twelve-foot-tall, wall tapestry of a Mercator projection of the world hung from the rafters. A two-foot-tall carved wooden statue of an eagle with a fish in its talons perched on the rafters above the tapestry. Directly overhead, a feathered dreamcatcher dangled from the end of a brightly-lit chandelier made of deer antlers. She nudged herself up into the chair, her head sinking deep into the pillowed headrest. Her throat clenched as she suddenly heard a female voice from a set of hidden speakers: "Say *Aum*. Relax. Breathe. Count to zero. Close yours eyes. You are *awake*." The speakers spat static. *STA-KAT STA-KAT.*

"I have a session in the VDC every few days," Winston explained as he quickly fell back into his old comfort zone with Susan, "it's like a morning bath in the Ganges. There is a big difference between going to sleep at night and passing out at the end of the day. It's my Achilles' heel. If I don't get enough sleep, I end up with an impaired glucose tolerance. Then I can't think straight, and I start seeing things."

"I remember your crazy sleeping habits," Susan commented. "The lack of sleep can affect the biochemistry in the processing of vision. But, they have medications for that. Sometimes it can be corrected with a proper diet."

"A VDC is better than some medicated Edge Effect or even counting sheep. It can open the ears of your mind. On a clear day, my VDC can pick up a VOR broadcast from Khabarovsk. With the VDC, I can even solve problems while I sleep. Efficient sleep, there's nothing like it. I wake up feeling like a new person."

"Some hypnopædia sleep-learning for the busy life ..." Susan's eyes wandered toward the Mercator projection and honed in on the carved eagle. "Maybe sleep refreshes the body, but it rarely sets the soul at rest."

"There is a brain-circuit training procedure I follow when I use the VDC," Winston said. "I massage my face with Spikenard oil and chew on some dried valerian root that Billy gave me—followed by eight cups of nard tea and a magnesium supplement. It takes *a lot* to get me relaxed. Then I let the VDC massage the body meridians along my spine while listening to a Hemi-Sync CD of peaceful music. I try to empty my mind of any internal dialogue and concentrate on something that I want to dream about. I use the VDC as a type of consciousness encoder. It's like a Buddhist Samadhi experience, a non-dual state of consciousness, where I start living in a *Turiya* dream and take a holiday from myself. Billy compares it to dream weaving—a process he follows in interpreting symbolism found in dreams. Dream symbols are thought to represent internal ideas and feelings—the language of the mind. Everything we think about has a double meaning. Lately, I've been practicing by concentrating on that world map hanging from the rafters."

"Dream weaving?" Susan's eyes narrowed "Dream symbols? Translation, please?"

"Billy practices it in preparation for a vision quest in the Lakota rite of passage." Winston answered. "Dream weaving might be compared to a hallucinatory event generated in the brain by building certain visual and auditory circuits that allow you to better understand the world around you." Winston slightly touched the center of his forehead. "It's an exercise in Cartesian dualism which promotes a separation of the physical body from the mind. Billy's like a Hindu Mahavir, or Rishi seer, with his religious circuits prewired into his brain."

"Billy's just a cockeyed idealist. Religious circuits … a Samadhi experience … Cartesian dualism of the mind and the body. James, I bet you have a book by Shirley MacLaine tucked away on those bookshelves."

"They're called religious circuits because they're often associated with mystical events," Winston elaborated. "During intense meditation, some people claim to have experienced visions of God, like the prophet Moses hearing a voice from a burning bush. When I was in elementary school, a teacher once tried to show me the meditation. It's a normal state of mind for Billy. He doesn't require stimulus from psychoactive substances such as psilocybin, peyote, LSD, or some prescription medication. He dream weaves while gazing at flashing lights—like the sunlight flickering through the leaves in the trees. He's described consensual hallucinations where he sees lines of light raging in the memory non-space of his mind. It reminds me of the deep-hacking experiences I've had on the Internet. He can even see sounds and smell colors. Seers like Billy are highly attuned to the world around them."

"People who see sounds and smell colors can have miswired circuits in their brains. Sounds like complex epilepsy," Susan diagnosed, "or a psychosis. A flickering light can trigger a seizure. Some epileptics opt to forego surgery and take drugs to stop their visions. They have a problem with frontal lobe atrophy. Billy might have synesthesia, where sensations from one part of the body are felt somewhere else. Perhaps he's cross-circuited." Susan rose from her reclining position. Her elbow brushed against the items haphazardly stacked on a bamboo table. She glanced at an open deck of Tarot cards surrounded by an assortment of music, data, and game CDs: "Core Rulebooks," "Spyro," "Realm and Conquest," "Halo7," "Dead or Alive 7," and "Dragon Lance." DVDs lay at one end of the table: *Birth of a Nation*, *The Man who would be King*, *21*, *The Lone Ranger and Tonto*, *The Matrix*, *Johnny Carson – Karnac the Magnificent – Best from the Tonight Show*, *Wagon Train*, *Star Trek – Episodes: Omega Glory & Paradise Syndrome*, *Bonanza*, and *77 Sunset Strip – Episodes 1-13*. "You're still addicted to video games," she scoffed.

"I'm training my eyes," Winston replied, his eyes on Susan.

"She noticed five empty cans of carb-free cola surrounding a loaded Beaumont-Adams service revolver and a paperweight statuette of Lord Nataraja-Shiva, the dancing Creator-Destroyer, with one foot balanced atop the demon-dwarf Apasmara. The statuette held down a bundle of newspaper clippings, including an article from *Behavioral Psychology* which reported that caffeine, the world's most popular drug, helped to focus one's current train of thought, but hindered short-term memory when the thoughts were unrelated. Beside the clippings sat a pile of periodicals: *Advanced Imaging*, *British Archaeological Reports*, *OSIRIS*, *Molecular Brain Research*, *The Hacking Quarterly*, *The Zardoz List*, *Backpacker*, *MEGA Foundation Journal*, *Phenomena*, and *Wired*. Seven books were stacked on the table: a first edition of *Catcher in the Rye*, *Gödel, Escher, Bach: an Eternal Golden Braid*, *The Mind's I: Fantasies and Reflections on Self and Soul*,

Lakota Spirituality, Neurotheology: Virtual Religion in the 21st Century, Neuromancer, and the tearful eyes from the cover of *The Great Gatsby.* An article cut from the *Physical Review Letters,* titled "Ori's Time Travel Curve," which had been twisted and taped into the shape of a Möbius strip unfolding into another dimension, lay on top of a book titled, *Philosophical Perspectives On Computer-mediated Communication.* An unfolded letter from the Wilderness Society, two tickets to the DEFCON convention, and a pair of backlighted magnifying glasses used by coin collectors surrounded the periodicals. At the other end of the table lay an issue of

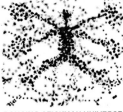

Astronomer magazine, opened to a dated article, "Morphogenetic Field Resonance: Seeing Problems as Patterns, the Emergent Structures - Smithsonian Astronomer Discovers an Image of a *Stickman* Aligned to the Earth's Polar Axis when Mapping the Universe.' "

"Have you ever considered caffeine rehab?" She gawked at the cluttered table. "Have you read all of this?" *No wonder your eyes are always blinking.*

DANCING STICKMAN UNIVERSE

"Ah—hmm," Bains cleared his throat, eavesdropping from the far corner of the library. *He's not just a hacker ... he's wired.* Bains shifted his attention to the books on a nearby shelf. *Every subject imaginable.* He scanned a few of the titles: *Revised edition of John Webster's Elements of Natural Philosophy and Astronomy, The Cathedral and the Bazaar, Lectures on natural phenomena: Newton's System of Philosophy.* He winked at a fish-eyed CCTV lens spying from the center of a knothole above a group of DVDs on the shelf. He read their titles: *Pan's Labyrinth, Enemy of the State, Shadow Conspiracy, Clear and Present Danger, Three Days of the Condor, The Magnificent Seven, Mr. Smith Goes to Washington, Dr. No, The Net, Raiders of the Lost Ark, North by Northwest, Independence Day,* and *Two Mules for Sister Sara.*

"It's one of my deadly sins," Winston replied to Susan, "my drug of choice. Caffeine withdrawal can be a real headache. It's hard to go cold turkey. Plus, it puts me in the zone."

"Excuses." Susan picked up one of the CDs and read the title aloud, "Wolfgang Amadeus Mozart's *Maurerische Trauermusik.* Preparing for the president's funeral?"

"Mozart's the man." He took the CD from Susan's hand and placed it back on the table. "It's part of a project I've been toying with, concerning the neurological activities of eye-brain coordination."

"What's this?" She snapped up a photograph of a multicolored wave pattern.

"It's a copy of my brain fingerprint," Winston replied. "I'm testing the brain-computer-interface of the VDC to see if it can read a person's mind. Eventually the sensor setup should allow me to probe into a person's awareness and observe their intentions. The FBI is using this technology. People can lie about anything, but their brain always tells the truth. As in a game of poker, everyone has a tell, a subtle signal that gives them away."

She gave him a curious look and tossed the photo back to the table.

"Susan, look at this." Winston pulled a slip of paper from the pile of materials and waved it in front of her face. "Whaddya see?"

"It's a drawing of a cube," she said matter-of-factly.

"Yes, but it's a drawing of a Necker Cube—a snake-in-the-box. In 1832, the Swiss crystallographer, L. A. Necker, discovered a certain ambiguous aspect of a wire-frame cube when depicted as an orthographic projection. The projection loses its perspective cues, which help the brain identify the cube's orientation in three-dimensional space. Study it for a moment." Winston laid the drawing on the table.

Susan gazed down at the drawing. "Necker? There's a Caribbean island by that name. Who is that Virgin man who lives there? Wow … The image flip-flopped, back and forth. It's jumping off the paper. From one cube image to the next cube image. Then back to the first," she said, astonished.

"That's right, it's an optical illusion," Winston said. "The Necker Cube represents a changing reality. Geometric shapes seen by the eye represent a reality, but not necessarily a true reality. Knowing the difference between perceiving things and seeing things is crucial for understanding your reality. You have to think outside the box. Appearances can be deceiving."

"I measure my reality with a yardstick," Susan said, "scientific-based, verifiable discovery. If you can measure something, then it must be real."

"But what is real?" Winston asked. "The mind is the slayer of the real. You cannot rely solely on your senses. The mind has to discern what is true, not your eyes. The eye sees everything in two dimensions, like film in a camera. The brain turns our world into 3-D. Everything we see around us can flip-flop and shape-shift into something else instantaneously. Our perception of the world depends upon our own personal perspective, how we see things in our mind. How do you lay a yardstick on that? Reality is not something we experience, but rather something we make. You should read Poincaré's *Science and Hypothesis* on the characteristics of time and space representation. Your mind can often instantaneously see the true shape of things and solve a problem before you can consciously think it through. When you try to think things through, you're always swimming in a mix of ideas, which includes the wrong answers. Your first thoughts and instincts are more likely to lead to the truth."

"I'll need to do more research to translate all of that," Susan said, flustered. "I'll be sure to purchase that study next time I'm in a bookstore. TMI, James. You're over-explaining things again. You need to follow the KISS principle."

"The KISS principle?" Winston smiled eagerly. "We might need to practice."

"I'm referring to Occam's Razor, James. Keep-It-Simple-Stupid. The simplest explanation is always the best."

"Yeah, but the simplest explanation is not always the most accurate. Occam's Razor can lead you away from discovery. The only way of discovering the limits of the possible is to venture into the impossible. Sometimes the best solution is the most difficult solution." Winston sat down in his VDC. "Susan it's all about breaking away from the conventions that bind your perceptions. My VDC serves as an interdimensional portal, or gateway, to the cerebral. It's a wicked device for hacking cyberspace using enticing, subliminal messages, where sounds are supplanted on top of sounds. I've been studying the new high-definition video technology as an avenue for creating seductive subliminal messages, by placing digital images within digital images. Hidden digital watermarks can be weaved between the binary code of the *zeros* and *ones* in digital picture files. It's an old, *steganographic* technique of hiding something in plain sight."

"Steganographic," she questioned, "a secret writing technique?"

"It's one of the first widely used forms of secure communications. Renaissance artisans even applied the technique to these old French playing cards." Winston pulled a card from the Tarot deck. "I think the idea was later promoted by Francis Bacon as a way of securing private correspondence—like using lemon juice as invisible ink. They now use steganography on paper money—"

"Yes, I know about all that," Susan cut him off. "Remember, I work for the NSA—DARPA's into this kind of stuff ... their brain machine project—" She snatched the Traitor card from Winston's hand and dropped it faced-up to the top of the deck.

"Right," Winston said. "It's like their S-quad electromagnetic mind-altering technology. I once used this technique to send hidden data to a fellow hacker. We called it our Secret-Speak. There are three different mediums for hiding data—text, audio, and images. You'd be surprised what people are really seeing on the Internet. I can easily hide a simple 8-bit *stego* black and white image inside a 32-bit color *cover* digital image, sight unseen. You can hide the whole Declaration of Independence in a single Web bug image. But the mind can see it. The brain can see what's true. Everything is absorbed by the unconscious eye. I'm testing how it might be applied to 3-D image-based rendering Talisman graphic technology. Can you imagine how this could be used in a video game? Using polarized stereoscopic glasses to watch complicated 3-D structures—artificial realities built around hidden symbols that can control the mind."

"James, hidden messages in media are as outdated as vinyl LPs." Susan critiqued with a sigh. "So you are toying with mind control by way of visual stimulation. Subliminals in the looking glass ... selective advertising working its way into our nervous systems. Or some political artistic agitprop. I think the media dragon's nine major networks may be way ahead of you on this one. Ten, if you count the BBC. Some say there's a hidden face in the Paramount logo. Even the Pentagon has spent a hundred million dollars on a psychological MKULTRA warfare operation in order to influence foreign media with pro-American messages. Subliminals have been around for ages. James, you're thinking too much. You need more than these books to keep you company. The bookworm can sometimes come back and bite you."

"Is that a proposition?" Winston asked slyly.

"James, you need to get yourself a pet. Maybe a loveable, little beagle to match those sad puppy dog eyes."

Unamused, Winston shook his head. He covered his face with a mask, the kind that men wear sometimes. He frowned. "Quit looking at me like I'm crazy," he said peevishly. "Susan, I think this is stuff you need to know. We're living in the age of visual stimulation and thought manipulation. The twentieth century is a century of icons. It's an image-based society—an Age of Pattern. Our whole modern world is filled with virtual realities that allow us to escape the limits of everyday experiences through different altered states of consciousness. Everyone is immersed in an artificially simulated world filled with hidden messages, be it advertising or politics. Messages are posted on just about everything. Everyone is starting to become characters in someone else's predesigned world. It's Plato's cave."

"Plato's cave?" She looked puzzled. "Translation?"

"Plato divided all things into two worlds, a physical world of belief, illusion, and ignorance and a metaphysical world of wisdom, understanding, and reason. It's seeing the world divided between idealism and materialism. Plato believed there was an invisible reality that lies behind the world of appearances. In the *Republic*, he wrote a parable known as 'the allegory of the cave.' In the story, human beings were chained to each other in a cave, where they could see only the shadows of the real world on the cave walls, like the predesigned world you see on TV. In their prison of comfort, they believed the shapes of the shadows were the real world. It's all they could see. They were living inside someone else's skull—someone's predesigned world. But outside the doorway of the cave was the true reality, where the sun shined bright. One day, a brave individual turned around, saw the light, and broke free of his chains. He left the cave dwellers to investigate that other world. When he returned to his prison to report on what he had seen, no one believed what he told them. It was beyond the scope of their understanding. They were still chained, living their lives beneath the shadows on the wall, trapped by the subliminals that made their shadow world more attractive."

"OOSOOM … out of sight, out of mind … the fables of Chicken Little and Peter and Wolf," Susan compared, "or the movies *The Island* and *Logan's Run*."

"Yeah, like the sky was falling, the individual who had seen the light began to teach everyone about another world." Winston lifted his long frame from the VDC. Standing square, he cocked his head slightly, crooked one arm taut above his head and stretched like a cat, and then added, "He shared himself with his fellowman like it was his moral duty. And slowly, one by one, they ignored the shadows and stepped into the light. If you know of the existence of a subliminal message, it cannot control you."

"How's that?" she prompted.

"Images are fundamental to the operation of the human mind. There are certain images, known as negative or taboo images that can almost *stop the world* in relation to how the mind operates. I read about this study in which researchers at Mason University's Krasnow Institute presented a group of test subjects with hundreds of pictures that included taboo images or **fnords** mixed with photos of well-known art, landscapes, and architecture. The test subjects were instructed to search the photos for a particular target image. An irrelevant, emotionally disturbing taboo picture—a subliminal image—preceded the target by every two to eight items. The closer the negative pictures were to the target image, the more frequently the subject failed to spot the target. Their brains actually failed to process what they saw immediately after the taboo image—a type of temporary blindness. A taboo image has an almost magical capability to block out the truth. The researchers dubbed this phenomenon 'emotion-induced blindness.' They believe a mental bottleneck for information processing is caused by certain types of negative visual stimuli, which captures human attention and jams up the processing in the brain, so subsequent good information can't get through. Certain images can almost shut down the brain."

"The trauma of seeing an image can shut down the brain," Susan repeated skeptically, "and make you lose your memory?"

"Yeah. Can you tell me what you where doing on September 10, 2001?"

Susan stood blankfaced.

"To get around this emotion-induced blindness, I believe you have to reprogram your preconceptions of the taboo image. You have to *see* the **fnords**. If we know everything there is to know about a taboo image, the brain will ignore it. It no longer appears as taboo, and the negative image loses its power over you. Your brain will not be interested in the subliminal anymore. You will be *free* of it. It's like learning to lose a *demon* inside your *psyche*."

"So, the shadows in Plato's Cave are taboo images," Susan summarized. "They block out the light."

"It depends on how we see the world. You are your brain." Winston turned on the CD player and the in-house stereo began booming the Eagles singing "One Of These Nights." The cover of the open CD case lying on the table pictured a winged buffalo skull. Winston mouthed the lyrics as he led Susan to the back door. "Feel that resonance from those bass-reflex speakers. They're the best."

Bains wrenched from the loud music. He wandered to the north door that Winston had pointed to earlier, nudged it open, and curiously peeked inside. The closet-sized room contained a vitreous china Crane Designer 192 and a Sureflush model number 31372. Five small piles of toilet-read including *Kull - The Shadow Kingdom*, *Time*, *People*, *USA Today*, *Outside*, and *Sit & Solve Lateral Thinking Puzzles* surrounded the "throne." At the top of one pile, the feature story on a *Sports Illustrated* read: **Capital City Adores the Washington Mystics**. On another pile, the cover of a *Wildfowl* depicted a photo of an eagle under the headline, "Becoming Hard to See." Imprints of two-dollar bills covered the roll of paper hanging on the wall. Looking from behind the door, Bains curled an S.E.G, a hacker's abbreviation for a "shit eating grin."

"You're lagging behind, Doctor. This way," Winston directed.

As though to deify himself, a gilded frame showcasing a vibrant cross-section of a PET scan of Winston's brain hung above the back door.

Something new, I see," Susan remarked as she passed under the bright-colored photograph. She read the small plaque at the bottom of the picture frame. "*Quo habitat felicitas nil intret mali* ...Where happiness dwells ..."

"It's a photo of my worm-infested brain," Winston remarked. "It's the best computer I've ever played with."

"Nice shot." *A fitting image.* "I always wondered what your other self looked like." Susan paused to observe the varying hues of blues, yellows, greens, and reds patterned throughout the scan. "You're a little aroused in the visual cortex of the occipital lobe. Look at the size of that pineal." She winked.

"It's serotonin enriched. Look at it closer." Winston pointed. "Tickle my brain. I bet you can't guess what I'm thinking."

Susan shook her head as she walked past him through the back door.

Winston scanned her shapely, athletic figure. His eyes blinked as they moved from her ankles to her head, drinking up everything in between. *She's every woman. A dancer's body.*

"I feel your determinative energy," Susan uttered in a soft whisper. "Don't over think things, Gandhi." She rolled her eyes at Winston with an alluring smile.

"It's my animal magnetism." Winston grinned slyly. "I see your eyes are green today. Good guess."

He's still got that urdhvarata, she thought, *and the bluest eyes I've ever seen.*

Bains quickened his pace to catch up. He glanced up at the brain scan with a questioning look before joining Susan and Winston. They huddled in a walk-in closet, containing only a copy of the painting *Descent Into Limbo* by Andrea Mantegna that hung on the rear wall.

"Somewhat cramped, isn't it, Jefferson?" Bains hugged his briefcase and nudged himself in beside Susan. His face paled, feeling straightjacketed-claustrophobic. "So where is your media center?"

"It's right here," Winston replied as he flipped the light switch.

The overhead light in the tiny space blinked, the floor began to slowly descend, and the open doorway to the library exchanged views with a sliding steel door.

"We're now twelve feet below ground. Where happiness dwells, evil will not enter." Winston's voice activated the door in front of him to reveal the well-lit interior of a thirty-by-twenty bunker. "Welcome to the Cave of Brahmâ."

Banks of computers, electrical testing equipment, and other PC toys and smart stuff gizmos lined the walls of the Cave of Brahmâ. A well-equipped test bench was covered in a disarray of wired experiments and electronic projects. In the middle of the room sat a ten-foot-diameter, double-layered, inflatable, clear, hard plastic ball, which nearly touched the ceiling. Tangled wires were attached to it, like a haphazardly decorated Christmas tree.

"So this is the media room. It appears you're prepared for the fallout." Bains marveled at Winston's lair. "I see you are on top of the digital decade. Impressive. This must have cost a pretty penny. Do the people at Microsoft know about this?"

"Not yet," Winston replied with a slight smile. "It's my Sanctum Sanctorum, the place where I care for my inner geek—the techie deep within each of us. It's where I come to spark the Muse. Let me share the secrets of the tomb. The facility is cut into the bedrock to help shield it," he explained his private hideaway. "The walls are encased with half-inch, double-layered steel-plate with a magnetic core sandwiched between the steel layers to prevent outside monitoring. This place blocks out all the noise. There is one central ground communications line with its own IP address and a secondary communication line connected to Sky-Link by way of a satellite dish."

"What is that thingamajig? Fuller's dome?" Bains gaped at the strange pink translucent plastic-bubble wraped around an internal carbon-fiber spherical frame. "It resembles the New Year's Eve ball they drop at Time's Square."

"World-first Fisher-Priced technology." Winston smiled proudly. "That's my sacred relic—a play toy. It looks dymaxium, but it's a Zorb that I've modified into a hyersphere of fifth dimesion time-space."

"What's a Zorb?" Susan asked.

"It's a human-size, geodesic, hamster ball. You get inside of it and roll around like a busy hamster."

"A hamster in a ball," Bains repeated.

"It's like a job, Dr. Bains." *Flump, flump.* Winston patted the side of the Zorb. "A dream job. Its design is based on the geometric drawings found encoded in the backward script of Leonardo da Vinci's notebooks."

"From Da Vinci?" Bains questioned.

"Leonardo was the great note taker who studied the nature of light and water. He had pages of backward scribble in his notebooks filled with ideas reflected right out of the back of his mind, like bringing Brahmâ to form. This Zorb is connected to the VDC upstairs through a bank of computers using the low-heat diamond light processors. They push optical data to a holographic headset by way of an IBM micro-parallel-curved resonating waveguide circuit." He pointed to a schematic on the bench next to a CD labled: *Red Giant Software - Trapcode: Horizon, Starglow, Shine, Lux, Sound Keys.* "It's part of my experiment in neurofeedback psychotechnology. Any precieved flow from an optical array means the perciever is moving forward or backward in free fall. Holding the flow steady stops the free fall. It's an incredible isolation chamber for relaxation. Being suspended in free fall inside a rotating globe is truly mind spinning.

"Some more yogatronics for the technoshaman," Susan quipped.

"I've redesigned it with extra pentacross supports and an internal spherical 3-D sterographic Schlegel projector." Winston pushed with both hands on the Zorb. "When I'm finished, I'll have a traveling VDC unit, which I plan to roll off the top of Devil's Tower," he joked, tapping his finger to his forehead.

"So, you're a dare*devil, I see,*" Bains bantered.

"Well, I'm not a devil," Winston said, "just someone who enjoys a life that's lived. Life's happier when you don't take it so seriously. A measure of pleasure is the treasure I pleasure. Let's take a look at this virus."

Bains opened his briefcase, retrieved a CD containing a sample of an infected data file from a folder marked with an NSA logo, and handed it to Winston.

Winston eyed the rainbow refracting through its plastic surface. *A flood of information,* he thought.

"We're calling it Ebola," Susan added. "You need to run it on an isolated PC."

"Sounds deadly," Winston wisecracked with an anticipatory grin. He booted up a laptop on the worktable and inserted the CD.

"There are treasures to be found, me mate!" a voice from the computer welcomed as a purple and gold Jolly Roger waved across the screen.

"Let's open the portal." Winston typed **R-E-B-U-S-7-7-7**.

A 3-D replica of Winston's head emerged through a digital rain of numbers and spoke, "Keep a weather-eye open! Oho! Blaze away!"

"My animated Avatar. It's all simulated." Winston reached across the table and pried the lid from a can of mixed nuts, a medicinal blend of honey roasted almonds, cashews, and Spanish peanuts next to a bowl filled with carrot chips. He pinched a few nuts and popped them into his mouth. "Food from the Earth … Care for some?"

"No thank you," Bains replied.

"How about a carrot chip? The besties … they're good for your vision."

"An itty-bitty piece." Susan picked from the bowl and bit into a slice of carrot.

Winston opened the data file labeled EBOLA. The screen filled with lines of computer code. His eyes blinked as he formulated his thoughts, one line of code at a time. "I can see how this might fester. It's obviously a DES matrix of some sort. And it's multilayered." He popped another nut into his mouth. "It might even be an IDEA matrix, they're more efficient than a mere DES."

"We know that," Bains barked impatiently. "We've figured that out already."

"If it's DES, it should be breakable through Differential Cryptanalysis," Winston muttered. "The Data Encryption Standard is just a spin-off from IBM's old, 128 bit Lucifer cipher. But this could be a Serpent-1 cipher with 4500 gates … Hey." His eyes blinked. "There's a backdoor to this thing."

"We know that also. We figured that out as well." Bains paused. "We're now trying to define the backdoor."

"Marx and Emerson are working on it at Fort Meade," Susan remarked.

"It looks like a version of a standard SATAN backdoor, in my eye," Winston uttered with prehensile perception. "Yeah. We're definitely going to need the stuff at Fort Meade to walk through this backdoor." He reached for a half-empty can of diet cola and took a sip. "Hmm ... It's a bit flat."

"That's why we are here, to take you back to Meade," Bains affirmed.

"So, how far has this thing spread?" Winston asked as he ejected the CD.

"Findings indicate that any unsecured computer connected to a landline during the past six days is infected at some level." Bains took the CD from Winston's hand.

"How about those connected to Sky-Link?" Winston asked.

"They're clean," Susan replied. "We're now using Sky-Link for secure communications. The think tanks and prime facilities at Langley, the Pentagon, Bolling, Fort McNair, Suitland and the seven Blue Genes are secure."

"Computers touch us in everything we do. Every society on the planet would come to a screeching halt if all the computers were shut down," Bains stressed with concern shadowing his face. "So we designed Sky-Link and USSPACECOM Vision 2020 to function independently from the World Wide Web. It's part of our 'eyes in the sky' that blankets the globe. Those satellites are protected by the military as U. S. territory. All transmissions through Sky-Link pass through the Sugar Grove Communications Facilities which use the quantum cryptography perfected at Site Y at Los Alamos. Quantum cryptography transmits data by way of photons. You can't hack photons. *Light transmissions* are secure. Everything is secure when it's pushed by light. On top of that, we encrypt everything through Golden Clipper-Capstone chip technology. Clipper-Capstone is used to secure communications between the White House and the Pentagon. But with the recent solar flare activities, we are concerned about the reliability of Sky-Link on the day-side of the Earth. From its conception, Sky-Link was isolated just in case the Web was ever shut down by a killer virus, such as the *Great Worm* of 1988. It appears that day has arrived. If we drop the ball, the world could go to Hell in a handbasket."

"You look worried, Dr. Bains. Worrying can be a destructive habit," Winston said. "The Internet is the most stable machine ever assembled by man. It's never been shut down. I know we can figure this out—"

"James, we need to get going," Susan interrupted.

"Right. Let me get my things. But, I need to check something in my other lab before we leave."

"Another lab?" Bains asked.

"Yes. Come see."

Winston ushered them into the elevator and they ascended back to the library.

"The lab is just outside." Winston pointed to the library windows that overlooked the backyard of Bear Lodge.

Bains stepped to the windows. At the far end of a five-acre clearing, he noticed an object that resembled a seventy-foot-high dinosaur bone protruding from the ground, next to a garden of thirty-six glass paneled solar collectors mushrooming toward the sun. "You're energy independent. What the *hell* is that, next to all the solar collectors?" Bains asked, puzzled.

"Everyone could be independent. Especially since everything is pushed by light,"

Winston replied with a smile. "I'm light harvesting. It's one of those new efficient Israeli systems created for the desert. Someday NASA is going to use this technology to solar power interstellar spacecraft from the moon."

Susan peeked out the window to see what Bains was talking about. "It's a miniature version of Devil's Tower."

"Yes and no ... just a little microcosm," Winston responded. "It's my bit of artistic expressionism. It's a replica of the Einsteinturm in Potsdam at Telegraph Hill. I call it the Mendelsohn Synagogue. It's my key to the universe."

"A what? A private chapel?" Bains questioned. "I thought you said another lab. That looks like a towering, concrete boulder in the middle of a solar farm."

"It's in the eye of the beholder. Form does not always follow function," Winston said. "One could argue whether it makes sense to define any building in terms of architectural style. The Einsteinturm is often called the main example of Architectural Expressionism. The Einstein Tower was the first important building designed by the famous architect, Erich Mendelsohn. It's a solar observatory, like a medicine wheel. But it totally resembles something else. It's where they tested the relative motion of the Earth to luminiferous aether. Until the Second World War, it was the most prominent research institution of its kind in Europe."

Winston pointed to his Mendelsohn Synagogue. "My copy of the observatory is formed out of concrete and steel. At the top of the building is a movable, domed

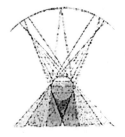

$I = (Jnought)^2 \cdot (k \cdot \partial \cdot r)/(2 \cdot Z)$
Arago White Spot
discovered by Leonardo

fiberglass roof. Inside is a rotating floor that supports a digitally enhanced twelve-inch refracting telescope." He headed for the main entrance of the library. "Excuse me. I'll be back in a moment. I need to set the light aberration autoalignment on the telescope and reset the `syslogd` daemon to run a scheduled task on my computers. There's a special event I want to record this week. I'm doing some halo hunting with a spectroscope. I'm testing one of Einstein's theories on the bending of light as it passes a massive object in space. I'm calling it my Huygens-Grimaldi experiment."

"A Huygens what? Bending light?" Bains asked, "What type of an experiment is that?"

"It's an experiment my mother always wanted to try." Winston stopped in his tracks and picked up a sketch from the pile of papers near his VDC. "Christiaan Huygens is the guy who invented the balance spring which makes pocket watches accurate." He handed the sketch to Bains. "Take a look at this. The Cartesian geometry required to find the focal point for my experiment was drawn by Leonardo in the late 1400's in his study on the effects of shadows on spheres."

"I don't know what to make of it," Bains remarked. "It could be a ball of ice cream on an ice cream cone."

"Well, since we have a bright sunny day, let me show you a trick." Winston opened a drawer from beneath the table and retrieved a kitchen match. He pulled the briefcase from Bains's arms, passed it to Susan, and handed the match to Bains. "Hold this match in the sunlight." He led Bains to the windows.

Winston pulled a rare, gold-plated buffalo nickel from his pocket and began flipping it in and out between his fingers, as though warming up before playing a piano. He pinched it between the tips of his index finger and thumb, barely touching its tiny gear-like reeding. Angling the face of the nickel at arms length, he carefully positioned it between the globed end of the kitchen match and the light of the sun. He stretched his arm further. "I need a long light path. Hold it steady, Doctor."

"A gold nickel?" Bains questioned. "What are you doing?"

Susan watched with quiet interest.

"It's my personal challenge coin. I'm looking for a spot of light at the center of a black hole. Be still. Keep it steady, Doctor," Winston instructed, his voice edgy with a spark of anticipation. "Just a little dot." Winston's eyed the profile of the Indian's face on the nickel. "Oh … Billy," he whispered, "everything is pushed by light."

Suddenly, the tip of the match burst into a blue and orange flame.

"How did you do that?" Reflections from the flame flickered in Susan's eyes.

"Diffraction," Winston replied. "It's not as mysterious as it seems. It's a law of physics. Light bends around the edges of the nickel and is refocused, as with a magnifying glass or a Fresnel lens effect. It's the mixing of photons traveling in a light wave, like *the winding path of a snake*. They concentrate into a small spot of *pure* white light into a type of shadowgram. Isaac Newton discovered that when he looked at a distant candle flame while holding a pin near his eye, he could observe a candle static in the diffraction pattern of light at the sides of the pin. It's the same principle used in the military's new light cloaking technology. If my calculations are correct, I should observe the same thing during the upcoming eclipse of the sun. I'm going to measure an astronomical first contact and try to catch a few Baily's Beads."

Tight lipped, Bains shook the match to extinguish the flame. "You're a real magician. It's a nice parlor trick. Does it always work?"

"Nothing is foolproof, Doctor. Stare too hard and you'll *bust a blood vessel*."

Winston left Susan and Bains alone in the library.

"I've read his dossier," Bains said. "Is he really as good as they say? Is he the best of these hacking gearheaded geeks? His maverick, Zen-like attitude goes against the grain somehow. He seems a bit too eclectic to me. He doesn't seem focused enough in any one area. He's a wonk with too many irons in the fire. Plus, he has a bad resume."

"That's his secret, Dr. Bains. He's a modern Renaissance man. A real polymath. He's carpe diem, second to none. He has that uncanny sixth sense that allows him to seize the day." She smiled and added, "This man jumps off mountains."

"I know he's a barnstorming brainstormer with a devil's eye for details, but I still don't care for his aerobatics." Bains shook his head in disapproval. "He's a highflyer with too many techno-attachments. He's blinking into snap judgments. You need proper information to draw valid conclusions. He's thinking without thinking. He reminds me of Narcissus, in love with the reflections of his own ideas."

"You need him, Dr. Bains." She handed Bains his briefcase. "He's the g-factor of the Backdoor Group."

Unaware of the wayward compliments, Winston stepped back into the library. "That takes care of that," he said pleasantly. "Let me get my things. Then we'll go pave a New Road."

Day 6
Grief

The display of grief makes more demands than grief itself. – Lucius Annaeus Seneca

NESTLED IN THE HEARTLAND of America, a family of four began gathering around the television to share in the nation's grief. The television flickered. A ghost-image of the Washington Monument before the Capitol Building faded on and off the screen.

An announcer's voice *crackled* and *sputtered.* "This is a special report. Due to the live coverag—of the funer—of Presiden—Andr—Curtis Scott, *One Life to Live* will be preempted in many areas of the country."

Brad Middleton, a sixteen-year-old young man from Wichita, Kansas, walked into the living room and sat down beside his mother on the sofa. "Hey, Mom. Is it on yet?"

"It's starting," she replied as she gently petted Chester, the well-behaved family cat curled in her lap.

"Hi, Dear," Brad's father said sweetly, as he entered the room with Carol, Brad's younger sister. He noticed the flickering screen. "What's wrong with the TV? Change the channel to CNN. We'll get better reception on cable." He glanced at his son. "Brad, what's that hanging around your neck?"

"It's my free, Audubon birdcall. I got it in the mail yesterday." Brad twirled the bloodred birdcall on the end of a lanyard for everyone to see.

"Look! It's starting." Brad's mother pointed with the remote in her hand at the talking head that appeared on the screen.

"Dan," Washington correspondent Chet Armstrong addressed his co-anchor, "today's ceremonies follow the standard established for all presidential funerals since the assassination of Abraham Lincoln. This somber occasion is the nation's remembrance of a president who helped the broken government of the dis-United States bounce back from the edge of extreme pessimism. Three days ago, America trembled from the tragic death of a president. The eyes of the world are weeping today in mourning. There is no language spoken or unspoken, or skillful combination of words or thoughts, that can adequately express the loss this nation feels. Here in Washington, before the grace of God, goes President Andrew Curtis Scott."

"That's true, Chet," CNN documentary historian Dan Newman agreed. "He was not a philosopher-king or a warrior-prince. President Scott was a man of courage, candor, and honesty. He was man you could trust." Newman shuffled through the papers in his hand and began a discourse of factoids. "The funeral begins in front of the White House, across from the Zero Milestone. The procession will begin precisely at 12:18 P.M. That's 9:18 A.M. on the West Coast. Security in the city is at an extremely high level today. The police are equipped with pepper spray and pellet guns. The dark-suits-with-ear-buds are situated throughout the city."

"Dan, there is Black Jackie, the riderless horse, following the caisson, supported by a full military escort from every branch of the Armed Services. Behind them can be seen the Washington Monument roped off and guarded by security personnel."

"Look at the beautiful horse," Carol said. "The boots are on backwards!"

Tat, tat ... tap ... tat, tat ... tap, a drum sounded a Devil's tattoo to the cadence of wooden wheels turning on sturdy axles, as the caisson rolled forward. The military escort in full-dress marched in unison. Veterans standing by the curb instinctively placed their hands over their hearts as the flag-draped coffin approached them.

"Chet, the procession is starting its long approach to the Capitol Building, where the casket will lay in state before being interred tomorrow at Rock Creek Cemetery."

"Dan, the procession is now passing the U.S. Treasury Building."

"Yes, Chet. The Treasury Building was designed by the South Carolinian architect, Robert Mills, a close friend of Thomas Jefferson. Mills was also responsible for creating the first design for the Washington Monument. In fact, it was Jefferson who proposed to Mills the use of an obelisk in the design."

"That's true, Dan. Even the White House and the Capitol Building are the products of Jefferson's architectural vision for the city he founded."

"Chet, there at the corner of Pennsylvania Avenue and 12th Street is the Franklin statue, by the sculptor Jacques Jouvenal. This brings to mind one of Franklin's most famous quotes on American liberty. 'They that can give up essential liberty to obtain a little temporary safety deserve neither liberty nor safety.' President Scott often used that quote in his speeches to point out how lackadaisical Americans had become toward their expected freedoms. Scott once said, and I quote, 'The complacency of its citizens is the biggest threat to our Nation's security.' "

"Yes, Dan. Franklin, the kite flyer who held the *key* to the spark of nature, was a principal player in the founding of our country. He was the 'first of the first' American philosopher, a scientist, a writer, a noted Freemason, and an American Deist. In relation to his Deist beliefs, Franklin once wrote,

'Here is my creed. I believe in one God, Creator of the universe. That he governs it by his providence. That he ought to be worshipped. That the most acceptable service we render to him is doing good to his other children. That the soul of Man is immortal, and will be treated with justice in another life respecting its conduct in this. These I take to be the fundamental points in all sound religion.'

Many of the founding fathers, including the humanist Jefferson, were associated with Deism. Deism was a religious movement born out of the European Enlightenment and promoted by early Freemasons. One of the *key* Deist principles is the belief in Isaac Newton's view of God as a watchmaker who set the universe in motion, but left man to his own devices to govern his destiny by following the laws of nature."

"Chet, I suppose it might be classified as a religion of science for the Enlightenment."

"Yes, Dan, you could easily say that. Deism was deeply connected to the study of the natural sciences. In fact, the natural sciences and advanced mathematics taught in America's public schools today are considered the core curriculum for the Deism promoted by our Founding Fathers such as Jefferson."

"True, Chet. But Deism was more than the mere promotion of the natural sciences. Many of the first republican forms of government were designed around the political views of Deism. Social Deists believed that a government could be created that served as a symbolic artificial watchmaker and the ultimate sovereign over the life of man."

"Yes, Dan. America today, in many ways, is truly the Deist government envisioned by Thomas Jefferson and the Founding Fathers—"

"Chet, the procession is now passing the Ronald Reagan Building and the International Convention Center. Look at the people in the streets. Thousands have come to witness this event as they endure one of Washington's grueling heat waves."

Fluttering *Chirp-chop, Chirp-chop, Chirp-chop* sounds came from a section within the crowd gathered under the poplar trees lining Pennsylvania Avenue.

"Listen to that, Chet. Like a requiem for the dead, there are a hundred or so bystanders sounding bird calls."

"Dan, I understand the Audubon Society recently performed a successful fund-raising campaign by giving away fourteen million birdcalls to the American people."

Chirp-chop— Brad held out his bloodred birdcall and twisted the painted birchwood cylinder against the vertical pewter shaft. *Chirp-chop, chirp-chop*—

"Dan, there is Freedom Plaza, Washington's only paved public square. The unusual design in its pavement is a bas-relief of the map of Washington, D.C., attributed to Pierre L'Enfant. Of course, this map is not the true plan used in the layout of the city. Historians agree the city plan for Washington was drawn by Major Andrew Ellicott on orders from Thomas Jefferson. The plan for Washington is *not* L'Enfant's design."

"That's correct, Chet. The city plan is essentially Jefferson's design."

"I understand L'Enfant's grave is located in Arlington Cemetery, near President Kennedy's grave and the Eternal Flame. Kennedy, of course, is remembered as the king of Camelot … our King Arthur."

"Yes, Chet. L'Enfant is buried near Kennedy's grave, although his grave marker is somewhat ironic. His memorial also has a bas-relief map. However, it is a copy of the Ellicott-Jefferson plan, and not the one attributed to L'Enfant," the anchorman chuckled. "His grave marker is next to the Curtis-Lee House, a mansion built for George Washington's grandson, George Washington Parker Curtis. Later, it was the home of Robert E. Lee, who was a captain in the U. S. Army Corps of Engineers. Its eastern portico of Doric columns was modeled after the facade of the celebrated Temple of Hera, known as Juno to the Romans. The Temple of Hera was once thought to be a Temple to Athena, the goddess of the Greek Gnostics at Paestum—an ancient temple located near Naples, Italy. The Curtis-Lee House is in direct alignment with the Eternal Flame at President Kennedy's grave and the Lincoln Memorial, the memorials to the two presidents who were shot in the head."

"It's nearly lunchtime," Brad's mother announced, as she left the sofa for the kitchen. "I'm going to get the casserole out from last night, if anyone is hungry."

"Maybe later, Mom." Brad petted the gray tabby, his eyes glued to the television.

"Dan, the procession is now making its way past the Federal Triangle. These buildings are the brainchild of Andrew Mellon, the highly successful financier and industrialist who served as Secretary of the Treasury from 1921 to 1932. Mellon worked with the distinguished Board of Architectural Consultants from Chicago, who developed the design guidelines for the site."

"Chet, there is the J. Edgar Hoover FBI building across the street from the Department of Justice. For years the FBI, originally started by a relative of Napoleon Bonaparte, was headed by the flamboyant J. Edgar Hoover. The position made Hoover one of the most powerful men in America."

"Such men are not forgotten, Dan. I understand there is a memorial room to Hoover in the Temple of the Scottish Rite at the corner of 16th and S Streets.

"The procession is now moving past the National Archives. Chet, this is where the nation's Holy Writ penned on lambskin—the Declaration of Independence, the Bill of Rights, and the United States Constitution—are stored away from public access."

"Dan, each day the cherished contracts that allow the federal government to exist as the sovereign power over the people are exhibited before the public eye. But at night they are stored in one of the world's most secure vaults, located twenty feet below ground."

"Chet, across the street from the National Archives is the Navy Memorial. Its pavement depicts a bas-relief polar coordinate map of the world—"

"Dan, the procession is now passing the Zodiac Fountain, a work also funded by Mellon. This is one of fifty-four such zodiacs found throughout the District."

"Yes, Chet, Pennsylvania Avenue is a symbolic microcosm that mirrors both astronomy and geography through its various memorials and architecture."

"Dan, they are now passing the East Building of the National Gallery of Art, designed by I. M. Pei. Pei also designed the famous Crystal Pyramid at the entrance to the Louvre. Adjoining the East Building is the National Gallery of Art. The National Gallery was funded through a fifteen-million-dollar donation from Andrew Mellon. Between 1930 and 1931, Mellon acquired twenty-one paintings from the Hermitage Museum in Saint Petersburg, Russia. These included rare works by Jan van Eyck, Botticelli, Titian, Raphael, Anthony van Dyck, and Rembrandt. Today the National Gallery is one of the world's leading art museums. It contains two of the seven paintings by Leonardo da Vinci held in the United States. The most famous is the *Ginevra de'Benci,* code named 'Bird,' which was purchased by the National Gallery for five million dollars in 1967—"

"Maybe not, Chet. A few art experts do not consider the owl-faced, Lilith-looking woman among the junipers to be a true Leonardo—"

"Look, Dan. Across the Mall from the National Gallery is the new American Indian Museum. It was built upon one of the last open spaces on the National Mall. It's a fascinating work of architecture, which follows the occult expressionism of the Mendelsohn design, where form does not always follow function."

"Yes, Chet. The building resembles the Einsteinturm Observatory at Potsdam on Telegraph Hill, in Germany. The American Indian Museum's exterior east court pavement is marked and aligned to the solar equinox and the day the building was founded, which also denotes the start of *Yom Kippur* and its Temple ceremony of the two emissary goats. There's a totem pole at the front entrance, where falls of running water placidly subdue the mind. The museum has a domed roof open to the sky, like the original Capitol Building. Several of the museums and monuments surrounding the Mall include this Palladian design … or is it Vitruvian? In either case, it's Renaissance Humanism."

"Chet, one eye-catching architectural feature of the American Indian Museum is the eight glass prisms encased in a window in the south wall. Each prism is sited to the sun for a particular time of day and season. They catch the sun's rays and reflect a spectacular, rainbow spectrum of dissected light onto the interior of the domed Potomac room. This light show changes every day, and is best seen between 11:00 A.M. and 2:00 P.M. Elevators leading to the exhibition areas feature various bird motifs that refer to the cardinal directions. The whole building emulates a solar clock."

"Dan, I did not know the American Indians dealt with prisms."

"Yes, Dan. It doesn't really fit, now does it? However, most religions share a reverence for light."

"Chet, I believe the Newtonian Deists dealt with prisms in their reverence to light.

Chirp-chop, chirp-chop— Brad twisted again on his complimentary bird call. "Dad, the guys are meeting at the park for a game." He sprang up from the sofa and stepped toward the door. "Can I borrow the car?"

"Sure," his father replied, still watching the television. "It may need some gas. Gas prices are through the roof. We're having problems in the Middle East again."

"Can I catch a ride to Betty's house?" Carol asked.

"Yeah." Brad grabbed his *bright*-green baseball cap, embroidered with an 'I in the triangle' travel-light logo of L. L. Bea*m*, from the hall coat rack.

Omega Walkways

"Chet, the procession is now making its way onto the Capitol Grounds. The public park that surrounds the Capitol was created in 1874 by Frederick Law Olmsted, the 'Wizard of Central Park.' Olmsted, a self-proclaimed, antireligious and pronature extremist, created many of America's great public parks. He designed the National Arboretum, the brick grotto on the Capitol Grounds as well as the unique walkway which encircles the Capitol in the horseshoe-shape of the Greek letter *Omega*."

"Yes, Dan. Olmsted was the *Alpha* and *Omega* of American landscape architecture. I believe he was also the architect of Rock Creek Park, which is due north of the White House."

"That's true, Chet. He was only eclipsed by his son, Rick Olmsted, who redesigned much of Washington, D.C. at the turn of the twentieth century. The younger Olmsted worked with the Senate Park Commission in the replanning of Washington and the Mall. This was a far-reaching redesign of the District of Columbia, which included the reshaping of the *entire topography* of the region through a series of protective parks and roadways that extend as far south as Mount Vernon."

"Dan, the eight-hundred pound coffin is being carried up the steps of the western portico of the Capitol. This is where President Scott once echoed his voice across the Mall as he took his oath of office before the temple of American law, with the statue of the Goddess of Freedom in the dress of Alcibiades standing atop its tholos."

"Yes, Chet, the coffin will lay beneath the mural on the interior dome of the Capitol, which was painted by the former Vatican artist, Constantino Brumidi, often called the Michelangelo of the Capitol. He once worked on the restoration of Raphael's famous fresco, *The School of Athens*. Brumidi created two frescos on the interior of the Capitol Rotunda. The first is *History* and the other is the *Apotheosis of*

Washington, which means the *deification* of Washington."

Brad's father stared at the television, as the camera slowly panned upward past the false *chiaroscuro* bas-relief around the drum formed from the contrasting shades of dark and light for tricking the eye. It paused on the depiction of the Aztec Sun Stone with carvings representing the four cycles of creation and destruction bounding the skull face of the god Tonatiuh, the Fifth Sun of Burning Water. The camera then zoomed 180 feet upward to the frescoed concave surface of the vibrating interior 'eye' of the dome. Looming overhead like a modern adaptation of the Lascaux initiation cave paintings, a goat-faced George Washington sat majestically draped in royal purple atop a rainbow, with his left arm raised, holding a sword beneath a bright, round, yellow sun. His right hand gestured to an open book. Encircling him, a cloud of angels draped in robes shaped in the form of Hebrew letters symbolized the coven of the original states. In fanfare, four of the angels held an unfurled banner, revealing the words, *E Pluribus Unum*. Mythological scenes of gods and mortals mingled together filled the outer ring of the fresco. Each scene symbolized aspects of the American way of life: Mercury, the god of commerce, carried his snake-entwined caduceus and a bag of gold; Ceres, the goddess of agriculture, held a horn of plenty; Minerva, the goddess of science, stood beside a robed priest wielding a compass, teaching Franklin, Fulton, and Morse; Neptune, the god of the sea, aimed his trident, leading Venus, goddess of love, as she pulled the Transatlantic cable; and the Roman Bellona-like, sword-wielding, angry Goddess of Freedom, assisted by a fierce eagle, trampled the powers of Tyranny.

On the screen a priest stood before the coffin and offered a short invocation, "With faith in Almighty God we receive the body of this man of noble purpose." His voice reverberated within the circular stone chamber. "We pray to God, the giver of Light, to deliver His servant and *set him free*. We pray for all who grieve today for Andrew Curtis Scott, that they may be heard by God and know the consolation of His Love."

"Dan, as the coffin rests at the axis of the Rotunda, surrounded by murals such as the *Landing of Christopher Columbus* and the *Baptism of Pocahontas*, mourners will be allowed to file past it and pay their final respects to the former president. It is estimated that 24,000 people will view the casket within the next twenty-four hours. Let us observe three minutes of silence."

For the next three minutes, the camera focused on the flag-draped coffin, resting upon a catafalque skirted with a black pall. The only sounds heard were the shuffling shoes of the first mourners echoing off the stone floor of the Rotunda.

"Here is a rundown of today's historic event by the numbers. Twenty-five heads-of-state are attending the funeral," Armstrong read from papers in his hand. "One hundred and eighty foreign ministers and ambassadors are present. There will be a fifty-one-gun salute at various military bases around the country at dusk. This military salute will coincide with a rare astronomical occurrence known as the transit of Venus. Four million citizens have made a pilgrimage to Washington, D.C. to witness the funeral. It is estimated that one hundred million Americans are watching the broadcast on television."

Brad's father checked his watch. *I have to take the other car to the shop then get ready for tonight's barbecue. I'm going to be late.* He hurriedly left the room holding the remote, leaving Chester alone on the sofa.

According to the Austrian physicist, Erwin Schrödinger, a cat left alone for an hour in a room with a diabolical electronic device and secured against direct interference with the device, had a fifty-percent chance of dying. Three hours later, having defied the odds with his nine lives, Chester sat purring like an electric shaver, his piercing eyes watching the mourners slowly parade past the spotlighted casket draped with an American flag.

"This concludes today's coverage of the funeral of President Andrew Curtis Scott. Tomorrow morning we will continue as the president is interred at Rock Creek Cemetery. Thank you for watching this special event from CNN, where our tongues are all about the news. This is Dan Newman."

"And Chet Armstrong. God bless America."

Chester arched his back, stretched, and padded lazily in a circle before jumping off the sofa and exiting through a side door.

———

AT 4:18 P.M. Mountain Standard Time, the observatory room at Winston's Mendelsohn Synagogue appeared as dark as night except for the twinkling glow of switches from a bank of computers on a far wall.

Suddenly, one of the monitors illuminated with the numbers on a clock face counting down. The room lit up with a sporadic *hum,* as perimeter fluorescent track lights, one by one, flashed to life.

Resting on its axis at the middle of the room, a refracting telescope angled skyward. Slow-speed, electric motors began *whirring* as they rotated the canon-size telescope into position.

Words scrolled across the computer monitor in rapid succession: WEATHER CHECK ... NO PRECIPITATION ... CONFIRMATION ... PROCEED.

The domed atrium circumvolved and precisely aligned itself to the one-foot-diameter glass at the end of the telescope. A three-foot-wide shutter in the roof slowly retracted, revealing the yellow-blue glow of the evening sky.

The monitor then displayed a video image of the sun. Hellish pulsing hues of immense red and yellow magnetic loops and flux ropes splaying into space surrounded an orb of millions of dark, swirling, vibrating sunspots.

At one corner of the monitor, a prompt read: RECORDING IMAGES NOW.

———

PROFESSOR MAISUN trotted up the cobblestone walkway to the lone structure at the top of Observatory Hill. He squinted at the late sun reflecting golden off the windows of the white building. *Two wings and a dome ... a miniature Capitol Building*, he compared. *It reminds me of the Griffith.*

Outside the front entrance, beneath a brass sign reading, Heyden Observatory, The Laboratory of Entomology and Biodiversity, an attendant sat in a metal folding chair studiously thumbing through a book. He puckered his lips, whistling below his breath the notes to "Dixie." As the professor approached, the attendant courteously jumped to his feet. *Another one from the old-boys network*, he thought, pulling at a red thread tied around his wrist.

"My invitation." Maisun handed the attendant a letter. "I hope I'm not too late."

"No, they haven't started yet," the attendant politely replied.

Maisun pulled on the sleeve of his coat and unbuttoned the cuff of his purple shirt. He slipped his watchband above his wrist and held his arm out for the attendant to see.

The attendant noted the numbers tattooed on Maisun's wrist: 8 3 1 6 9 4 7 2 5.

"Let me mark you off." He placed his book on the chair, picked up a clipboard with a pen chained to it, and checked a short list of names under the heading GRIGORI-JASONS-CIRCUIT-PAPERCLIP-SIAI-EGG-COBRA. "The rest of the luminaries are inside. Have a good evening." He held the door for Maisun to enter. "Watch your step. They're waiting in the observatory upstairs," he informed, as Maisun disappeared through the threshold.

The attendant opened his book, and continued reading. The title on the cover read: *My Pet Goat*, by A. Pike, Supreme Pontiff.

Maisun navigated up a narrow stairway that led to a set of steel doors. He opened them and entered the main observatory. A colloquium of twelve other highbrows was hobnobbing in a huddle around a widescreen monitor displaying the omnipotent open-eye of the Engraved Hourglass Nebula. Behind them loomed a twelve-inch-diameter refracting equatorial telescope aimed through the open atrium.

"Lo and behold, I see the Grey Eminence is here," an officer in a full dress naval uniform greeted. "What do you think of our observatory?"

"It's not the largest I have ever seen," Maisun answered soberly, trying to appear dignified as he took in the confined domed-covered space through his good eye.

"But this building has a bold history. It was completed in 1844. It's the third observatory ever built in America. It was used in 1846 to determine the latitude and longitude of Washington, D.C., the second such calculation for the nation's capital. You know the whole world is measured from those coordinates?"

"Yes, I know," Maisun said.

"How, How, Professor," a well-dressed gentleman with a cleft lip interrupted. "It's a rare privilege. I saw you on TV this afternoon. You were attending the ceremonies."

"Watch your back, Maisun," the officer whispered before he stepped away, "Ahithophel Belias is a bastard—"

"How, How," Maisun acknowledged the well-dressed gentleman. "Yes, and I will attend the services tomorrow. I consider it this evening's early-bird special."

"It's out with the old and in with the new," the gentleman responded rhetorically. "It's a time for renewal, don't you think? What is your opinion of the new president?"

"Scott's ideology is not something we could have tolerated much longer. His accident fits in well with our plans. But, I see nothing new with Walker." Maisun's marbled left eye shifted to one side. "Presidents are mere window-dressing. Puppets and clowns for the pony show. Voting, candidates, black donkeys and white elephants, or some Retro vs. Metro idiocy. It's the blame-game ballyhoo of our circus sideshow. It's all designed to give a feeling of empowerment to those who do not have the power. It's how we pacify the untouchables in the American caste society."

"True," the gentleman agreed. "Everyone is marked by a stigma."

Maisun's right eye slowly shifted, glaring straight at the gentleman. "We still have a pseudo-republic," he spoke bluntly, "the workers, the citizens, and the philosopher kings. As in any republic, it's the philosophers who rule. This is the Q.E.D. We are a group of foreign interests who play together nicely in the same sandbox. As you know, much of this country is owned by foreign interests. One percent of the population owns ninety percent of the wealth. Ask any of the Big Boys on Wall Street—small investors need not apply. We slew and cut up the Americas over a hundred years ago, and we hold our hand over the European lion. It's the Iron Law of Oligarchy. We are the janissary that stands atop the food chain," he bragged. "We are the *echelon*—the 'eye' above the pyramidal heap of a surrendered humanity. Trust me. Trust the brain trust. It is not a vanilla world. It is a BDSM lifestyle that is our cornerstone. We are a brotherhood of *masters*, and the rest are our *submissives*. They'll never bite the hand that feeds them."

"Lambs to the slaughter." The gentleman smiled, then flattered, "In a world of the blind, the one-eyed man is king."

"These rank-and-file boeotians," Maisun said with an upturned nose. "Their freedom is a slavery acquired through the mundane suffering of their ordinary lives, as they run an amazing rat race through our maze of beautiful images. The human organism is a quickly conditionable system. They sacrifice the prime of their life for a pocketwatch when they turn sixty-five. Lives controlled by a clock—these lost souls are simply cogs in our grand machine which spins their world."

"AGOATU," the gentleman blurted. "There are degrees to human freedom. Theirs is an Arcadia of habitual lives, living without. But, the weak and sluggish are happy in their servitude within the Artificial Paradise."

"We train them by dazzling them with our entertainment," Maisun bolstered. "We do our best to make sure this Generation Y does not exceed an eighth-grade mentality. Intellectual miniaturization … Everything must be written with little words and short phrases. Their Lilliputian minds can only absorb so much." He tapped the side of his forehead with his finger. "Ignorance is Strength. We make ignorance a true bliss for the masses. Through our social cloning, they spend their lives of leisure sitting in front of a blue screen, watching someone else's vision and rooting for someone else's team. They think the real world is the wasteland of reality TV." He sniggered. "Their children pray to the Mickey Mouse, the purple dinosaur, and the Potter boy. It's all part of the new psycho-social curricula of the public schools sanctioned by our government to stamp out likeminded kidgets. It's the Hundredth Monkey Principle— socialize the idea. Train a few and the rest will quickly follow. Abraham Lincoln said, 'The philosophy of the schoolroom in one generation is the philosophy of the government in the next.' We *must indoctrinate* them while they are young to ensure that no child's soul is left behind. They're all chasing the Joneses and betting on the lottery—instead of investing in themselves. This Great Unwashed! They labor in the *shadows*, while we bask in the *light*."

"They are a Lost Generation," the gentleman grunted a laugh. "Join or die—America is *Gilligan's Island*, a petri dish experiment. Capitalism for the few, socialism for the masses. We make money their struggle."

"Such a waste of human existence. But they willingly sacrifice their lives. It is their submission by consent, which allows us to touch their inner fears and guide them with our higher truth. They are a perfect feudal slave force." Maisun shrugged his shoulders. "Our membership may be declining, but we control the information. Out of the 190 million wage slaves in America, *half* of them are functionally illiterate—and we want to keep it that way. We do not want them to *think*. It is how we illuminate the existence of the democratic values so we can manipulate this system of government."

"Oligarchy rules by foisting democratic catchwords—the placebo effect," the gentleman agreed. "The sweet *suggestive* slogans—Soft Power by way of the **fnord** candy. It's how we shape their patriotism and initiate them to *believe* through an unbending faith in our doctrine of unquestioned assumptions."

"No one can shield himself from our influence. Not even ourselves," Maisun warned. "A snake can take a lion's eye out. We must be careful. Control is a delicate thing. There is an art to persuasion and consent. It requires faith in *the Image*. Through the media, our Ministry of Truth, we direct everyone and everything—every aspect of society. Mass persuasion via the ten-second sound bite and the loaded language ... the thought-terminating cliché. It is a powerful opiate for the people which keeps them unaware. We could re-engineer the whole surface of the planet and no one would notice. Ninety percent of the population is medicated. They now absorb an average of six hours of sex and violence from our programming everyday, followed by a daily dose of antidepressants. It's how they come into their *being*."

"Zombie drugs robbing them of their free will," the gentleman commented.

"We have a nation under therapy. They all want a milkman to deliver a hodge-podge of bottled answers. They look for guidance from the teletrash of a multi-millionaire, prim and proper, talk-show host, who tells them what to read and provides them with step-by-step plans on how to raise their families. We dictate their reality. What we *allow* them to see and hear is all they know. In America, people believe what they are *told*. They do what they are *told*, like some medieval society following the religious symbolism created by cathedral builders. These foolish changelings are *so* gullible. *Mundus vult decipi* ... the world wants to be deceived. We could tell them that the harlot Magdalene was the new Christ, and they would believe it. They read butchered, abbreviated, illustrated versions of the Bible, designed for high school graduates who cannot read. They have wrestlers, comics, and rock stars preaching to them on how to become saved, if only they make a proper donation. Faith embracing pop culture ... you would think they would know that God is bigger than that."

"The blind lead the blind ... Christian entrepreneurs and preaching charlatans eager for notoriety. They are *afraid* not to keep up with the technical revolution. Fear is a powerful bridle. It's how we censor *that* book and shape our godless society," the gentleman said with a hollow laugh. "Although 'weaving spiders' are not allowed, I attended a powwow at the Grove just last month in San Francisco, where one of the lakeside chats dealt with how science should stomp out the Christian religion before it's too late. But as one of their elite pointed out, 'They are doing it for us.' "

"The legs of Christ are broken," Maisun chuckled. "In our godless society all physical activity is quickly shifting into the virtual world. Soon every aspect of life will be tapped into the XYZ of the Global Consciousness, our Planetary Mind. In this new sophisticated age, everyone will be exercising with their thumbs and fingers. It is the most effective way for us to maintain control. By the year 2050, they will all be jacked-in by way of a Delgado bio-chip implanted in their skulls, allowing them to connect directly to the World Wide Web simply by thinking. With the SPASUR fence and DARPA's Air Loom GWEN system in place, we will soon be able to fully control their minds—and the images in their minds. Imagine ... One day, everyone will be watching or listening to their electronic laser devices pioneered at Blackburn, then suddenly they will hear the *static* of the cyclotron resonance from the *omphalos* and the dangers from the individual will become a thing of the past, as we become one like-mind. Everyone will be *perfectly attuned* to the workings of our Divine Machine. What is happening to America is not simply a chance situation. It is our total transformation of society. We are transcending biology. We are going to change what it means to be human."

"Paradise-engineering—It's for our betterment." The gentleman tried to grin. "A safe, pre-determined outcome. They should thank us for allowing them to breath."

Maisun paused in deep thought, gazing down at the unmoving, checkered pattern in the tile floor as though studying a chessboard. He refocused his attention back to the man's question, his right eye widening as it met his colleague's. "Throughout the wayward eras of Hamiltonian, Jeffersonian, Jacksonian, and Wilsonian policy making, there has always been a captain that steers this nation's ship. The *power* behind the throne remains *invisible*. Sir, I make no bones about it. The presidency is many men, and all of them are unelected. They are chosen for their positions by those of whom we do not speak. The number of their legion is 322, and each of them is born and bred a Babylonian Bonesman, whose bones are as hollow as that of the birds."

"The skull collectors," the gentleman murmured, lowering his eyes, "the butchers."

"The lion tamers and the snake charmers," Maisun sneered. "We are governed through a backdoor deal, where the left doesn't know—or care—what the right is doing. It's the *key* to our success. I cannot even begin to imagine an executive branch being placed into the hands of one individual. It has always been this way. Very little ever changes. It never does in a society where people do not care about the system that governs them. Sir, this government was founded on three rules. ... First, the government may not injure, or, through inaction, allow its citizens to come to harm. They must *feel* safe. They must have *hope*. President Scott said it in every speech. Hope, hope, hope. Jesus is coming," Maisun chuckled. "Second, the government must obey the laws given to it by its citizens, except where such laws conflict with the first rule. It has to satisfy their irrational emotions and their nagging needs—the 'consumer is king.' Of course, the government is the only one allowed to interpret the law," Maisun added. "And third ... the government must protect its *own* existence, as long as such protection does not conflict with the first or second rules. Thus the reason this government spies on its citizens. As long as these three rules *appear* to be followed, this government will continue to operate under the *status quo*. Our *carte blanche* is assured. Plus, the military has been in our pockets since the September coup. We have ridden the back of the Goat since 1901."

"But you should never second-guess a woman," the gentleman warned. "I know she is one of *his* daughters, but this woman has a bad heart. Some consider Walker a loose cannon. I think we need to watch her like a hawk."

"Don't be absurd. I assure you she is no different from any other president. There are no more heroes, kinglets, or even queens. She may not be Snow White. I know she dances with the seven dwarves. But she is not a Manchurian candidate either. She wears no purple hearts, bronze stars, or good conduct medals. It is true that she is just a fledgling. However, she is bipartisan. She has been groomed. I groomed her. As with all presidents, she serves as a *prop.* Her every word is calibrated for effect. Actors and liars have always made the best presidents," Maisun said proudly.

"And self-serving, mendacious lawyers," the man coolly added.

"Speak for yourself, sir. She will support our cause." *I've seen the photos. She can put on a show,* Maisun thought. "There is another side of her that you do not understand. It runs in her blood. She is the perfect Alice for our Wonderland of white rabbits, fish footmen, mad hatters, and holy kings and queens of hearts—"

"How, How, Professor," greeted a priest dressed in a well-pressed, charcoal-gray suit with a white collar around his neck. *Tap*— He clicked his heels together, squared his stance, and raised his looped thumb and forefinger of his hand over his right eye. His fingers seem to frame a purplish, dime-size, star-shaped hemangioma on his forehead. He gripped Maisun's shoulders and lightly kissed him on the left cheek. "Dare to kiss a snake?" he whispered in Maisun's ear.

"How, How, Father," Maisun responded, stepping back and raising his looped fingers to his good eye. He spied a gold button, engraved with a Y-shaped Furca cross, pinned to the priest's lapel. *Cain and Abel, I see another future manipulator.* He held the priest's shoulders and returned the greeting with a kiss. "How is your brother in Rome? I saw him a year ago. I understand he is ailing?"

"He is doing fine. I am certain he will continue his work until he dies. It is hard to cook his goose. He is such a strong-willed individual. But his days are numbered," the priest said in smooth tone. "He soon will be at death's door. The camorra within the priesthood will be changing. For now, the rudder is still in his hands."

The conversations in the room were suddenly interrupted.

"Gentlemen, your attention please," echoed the firm voice of a man standing near the computer monitor. "We take our desires to reality because we believe in the reality of our desires," he welcomed with a maxim. "We see the world present-at-hand."

"How, How!" the congregation hailed in unison.

"This afternoon's special event is the transit of Venus," the man at the monitor introduced, "the observed passage of that planet across the disc of the sun." He stepped away from the monitor and typed on a keyboard next to the finely-balanced telescope resting on a precision gear box. Like a hundred *chakra* awakening, a painful, ear-piercing *squawk* assaulted everyone in the room, as hard metallic wheels and gears began to turn in unison, aligning the telescope with the sun.

The squeaking wheels want some grease, Maisun admonished wryly.

"Venus, the immortal sister of Earth, is known to us by various names," the man explained. "The Greeks called Venus, Phosphoros or Lucifer, the brightest object in the morning sky, the *Lux Ferre*—the *light of freedom.* It was Milton's rebellious angel. The Greeks called it Hesperos when it was seen as the most radiant object in the evening sky. The Aztecs called it Quetzalcoatl, the winged serpent, who brings forth the power of life." He pointed to a flickering image of the sun on the monitor as he adjusted a dial to stabilize the picture. "Venus is a true paradox in the heavens. No other planet comes closer to Earth, but Venus's vaporous veil of clouds will not allow our telescopes to see its true surface. It greets us every day, but remains hidden."

GALACTIC TABLE

He stepped before a chalkboard below a spiderweb-patterned, seven-ringed, spiraling mandala of the galactic version of the periodic table hanging on the wall and pointed to a diagram that illustrated the orbit of Venus. Photos of the Pioneer, Venera, Vega, and Magellan spacecrafts were taped to the top of the chalkboard above scribbled notes: 81 known transits = 100%, June (Descending Node2) = 44 = 54.3 %, December (Ascending Node3) = 37 = 45.7 %. 1435, 1648, 1778 Venus in Moon's shadow. Conjunction Dec. 23, 2007 – clocking the Second Coming

"As we are all aware, the four-year ecliptic cycle of Venus produces the path of a pentacle which can be traced in the evening sky." The man pointed back and forth to the chalkboard. "For four years, Venus appears as the *stella matutina,* the morning star, near the time of the winter solstice. Then for the next four years, it will appear as the evening star at the time of the summer solstice. Our Olympic games are tied to the cycle of Venus. Babylonian texts written in 1600 B.C. describe the motions of Venus in conjunction with all of their historical events. Venus is the marker of history and discovery. It is the marker for the great Phoenix cycles. When the explorer, Captain James Cook, sailed to the South Pacific, he observed a transit of Venus to determine the true size of the solar system—the great yardstick, the *Holy Grail* of astronomy— the distance between the sun and Earth—the sacred space between the fire and the crucible. That measurement was used to test the clocks that the Englishman, John Harrison, had constructed to calculate longitude at sea. The observation of this transit was the first major study carried out by the American Philosophical Society, started by Benjamin Franklin in order to pursue 'all philosophical experiments that let Light into the Nature of Things.' Even Thomas Jefferson understood the importance of this alignment with the sun. He ordered Lewis and Clark to observe the transit of Venus on their transcontinental expedition. Our country is founded upon it!"

The heels of his shoes *clapped* across the tile floor as he approached a table scattered with books and pamphlets. He picked up a copy of the *The Great Conjunction: The Symbols of a College, the Death of a King and the Maze on the Hill* by the London Psychgeographical Association and brandished it in his hand. "What we will witness this afternoon happens only once in one hundred years or so. Once in a lifetime for those whose lives are synced to this unique event." He dropped the pamphlet on top of Velikovsky's *World's in Collision* and returned his attention to the monitor. "This event happens in pairs with two transits occurring eight years apart. Those eight years, the *divine period* proclaimed by prophets and recorded in the annals of history, is the time in which the world changes hands and is made new."

"Gentlemen," the man proclaimed in a forceful voice, "let us watch as Lucifer, our *Lux Ferre*, becomes Hesperos! Like an invisible seed-grain in germination, Lucifer will step in front of the sun for just a few minutes, as it tries to block out the divine light of the unforgivable fire, just as it has tried for eons upon eons. It never succeeds in its attempt. It needs help!"

"Come this way, Professor; let us go rub some elbows." The priest led Maison toward the group of wide-eyed men encircling the monitor. "Pay close attention." He motioned Maisun closer. "You do not want to miss anything. Since the first days of Hellsfire, this is something we have all dreamed about, but we didn't know what to say about it, or what to do about it. The stars now favor our plans with the death of a king during the conjunction of Venus. We are ready to enter our millennial Golden Age of Pergamon. They are preparing the altars at Nazca, Berlin, and Birobidzhan. The Wall and the edifices to the Beast and the divine *Osor-Api* have been finished. The Great Tribulation has begun." He softy recited a verse from the book of Revelation. "And I saw an angel standing in the sun; and he cried with a loud voice, saying to all the fowls that fly in the midst of heaven, Come and gather yourselves together unto the supper of the great God; That ye may eat the flesh of kings, and the flesh of captains, and the flesh of mighty men, and the flesh of horses, and of them that sit on them, and the flesh of all men, both free and bond, both small and great. And all the fowls were filled with their flesh."

"*Oremus*," whispered one of the men. "*Phaëton ... Ave Satani.*"

For the next hour, the compeers watched in wonder as a small, almost invisible, black dot placed itself between humanity and the life-giving light of the sun.

I stand here with power mongers, these wannabes, these Caesars who follow the stars, Maisun thought derisively. *They need to read their Shakespeare. 'Men at some time are masters of their fates; The fault, dear Brutus, is not in our stars, but in ourselves, that we are underlings.' But, the wheels are in motion. Stealth is crucial to our success.*

_____

PROFESSOR MAISUN exited the Heyden Observatory and approached a stretched limo waiting in the parking lot.

"Where to, sir?" the driver asked. He leaned forward and turned off the Sirius radio wailing "Venus" by Frankie Avalon. The digital clock on the radio lit up—8:39 PM.

"To the Temple," Maisun directed.

Twenty-three minutes later, the limo turned a corner on S Street and parked next to a solemn neo-classical building guarded by two mammoth stone sphinxes.

"This will not take long," Maisun directed the driver as he stepped from the limo. He approached the rear service entrance, removed an ID card from his billfold in his breast pocket, and inserted it into the metal slot of a security panel on the wall. Red LED letters flashed: RAPID-I-SCAN – APPROVED – ENTER.

Maisun pushed on the heavy bronze door, stepped into the ornately decorated interior of carved and polished stone, and stopped as the door *slammed* shut behind him. He placed the ID card back into his billfold, removed the folded facsimile, and slipped it into his coat pocket.

His footsteps echoed off the black and white checkerboard marble floor as he passed a memorial stained-glass window depicting the rays of the sun falling from the words FIAT LUX. He proceeded down a long hallway paneled with exotic wood that terminated at an elevator. He entered, pressed L4 on the lighted panel, and began a slow descent. He glared at an antique lithograph of the Lord's Prayer framed on the wall. He read the words from the prayer intermingled between architectural symbols.

In Earth as it is in Heaven. He smiled. *If only they knew.*

The elevator doors parted, and Maisun proceeded into a long, dimly-lit room. Instinctively, he walked through a maze of bookcases, cabinets, and wooden card-indexes, turn after turn, imitating a well-trained rat, until he reached a gray-steel door with a tiny mezuzah fixed to the frame. He glanced up at the inscription on the plaque above the door as he removed his shoes and socks.

KEEPERS OF THE CAULDRON - LET NO ONE ENTER WHO DOES NOT KNOW GEOMETRICS
Geo-measure, twenty-three and a half degrees, he thought, pulling a ring of keys from his pocket. He slid each key back and forth until he found the one engraved with the words: KEY TO THE NEW YORK WORLD'S FAIR.

"*Het-Ka-Ptah, Dubhe,*" Maisun muttered as he firmly inserted the key into a deadbolt. His fingers tightened, exerting a solid pressure as it turned. A green light on the door's security panel *blinked.* He pushed on the cold steel handle and entered.

As the overhead lighting automatically flickered on, Maisun found himself standing in a Beit Genizah room, approximately ten-feet square. The walls were cut from limestone that glittered in the harsh light. Directly in front of him stood a shrine made from a rough hewn block of metallic-black magnetite covered in blue linen. A Bible, turned to a page containing the Lost Word, lay on the altar in front of three, scallop shaped, burnished clay pots stained with ocher. The pots respectivfully sat before a pure gold statuette of the Elamite deity Inhushinak cradling a ram, a clay water vase modeled into the bearded head of Jupiter-Serapis, and a toothless human skull. Two-foot-high, spiraled bronze columns guarded the Bible on its right and left. Above the altar hung a picture frame, concealed by a purple velvet drape.

Maisun retrieved the facsimile, entangled with an olive-green lanyard dangling a bloodred birdcall, from his coat pocket. He separated the two and coiled the lanyard onto the altar. He held the photo in front of his face, moving it back and forth, as he compared it to the outer markings on the clay pots.

Yes, they are. They are the same, he agreed, slipping the photograph back into his pocket. He paced across the room and opened the lid to a decoratively, carved, lime-mortared ossuary resting atop a mahogany table. The ossuary contained three metal safe deposit boxes. He removed one, carried it to the altar, and opened it. Carefully lifting a clay pot from the altar, he cradled it in one hand and stared into the bowl at a painted image of a cross-armed man with keys in his hands encircled by script spiraling out to the rim. *It's a remarkable object,* he admired, tightly clenching the tips of his fingers into four of the twelve dimpled grooves around one side of the rim. He placed the pot in the felt-lined metal box, closed the lid, and locked it by rolling the thumbwheels on its combination lock.

Motionless and resolute, Maisun looked up at the covered frame on the wall. He reached out and gently pulled away the drape. Stone-faced, he closed his left eye and bowed his head humbly before it with a reverent stare from his one good eye.

"*I Tego Arcana Dei,*" he tongue tippingly whispered. He bowed his head again. His eye fixed on the open page of the Bible. *Truth ... the* Kabalyon, he thought.

He draped the picture and left the room with the safe deposit box, leaving the birdcall, like a votive offering, on the altar.

Day 7
eNigmaS

Enigma: Puzzling, mysterious, half-remembered dreams, a German cipher machine.

THIRTY-THREE MILES NORTHEAST of Washington, D.C., the facilities of the NSA and the American branch of INNCS reside in an over-glassed, electromagnetically shielded, Black Cube Building at the heart of an eighty-six-acre, heavily armed compound within the Fort Meade Army Base. It is a city in itself, a place that army personnel at Fort Meade call the "Throne of the Mother of Secrecy," the "Palace of the Overlord," the "Lion's Eye," and the "Hub of All Things Covert."

The National Security Agency was founded at 12:01 on the morning of November 4, 1952 by President "Give 'em Hell" Harry Truman, a Freemason who had put a sign on his desk that read: **THE BUCK STOPS HERE.** Truman signed a memorandum that established the NSA from the work of pioneering cryptologists who broke Japanese and German coded messages in WWII, such as the German Enigma. That signature invoked far-reaching changes for American society. Since then, the NSA has employed the world's leading experts on cryptology and electronic communication systems. The Agency had been instrumental in the creation of flexible storage technology and the first large-scale, solid-state computers. The whole Digital Age of integrated circuits, CDs, DVDs, HDTV, MPEG, JPG, TIFF, hard drive storage, and the World Wide Web is a byproduct of NSA research.

Since the early 1960s, the most advanced computers in the world have been used by the NSA. At present, the NSA is experimenting with 3-D optical DNA-based nanocomputers, simulating an artificial intelligence that can think at the speed of light, twenty times faster than any current commercial computer. With a 75 billion dollar annual budget and nearly 25,000 employees, the NSA is capable of blanket-coverage information absorption throughout all of the United States. It achieves this coverage as a result of its SIGINT mission, which uses artificial intelligence technology to screen communications for specific *keywords* brought to the attention of NSA cryptologists.

The NSA constantly monitors all communications in the United States, at both the transmitting and receiving ends, through tempest attacks, or CPU snooping, which can detect electromagnetic signals emitted by a computer terminal using an RF wideband receiver and a COVISP-1 compromising video emanations processor circuit. It is said that any computer turned on in a person's home has the capability of transmitting sound reflected off the glass of the monitor back through the computer, with the signal being transmitted by way of a fiber optic telephone connection. The theory behind such an odd form of communication had been proven in 1880 by Alexander Graham Bell and his associate, Charles Tainter, in an experiment in Washington, D. C., with a device they called the photophone.

———

WINSTON tugged on his baseball cap as he accompanied Susan and Dr. Bains down the wide C-Wing corridor of the Black Cube Building. Approaching a T-intersection, he peered up at the anamorphic reflection of a security archway in a convex-domed mirror hanging from the ceiling.

"After you." Bains turned the corner and motioned Winston and Susan through the archway, as a scanner checked for their sixteen-digit personal IDs concealed in the subdermal biosensor-chips implanted in their arms.

Winston could be tracked via satellite through a software program known as PROMIS. Everyone working at the NSA had been tagged like livestock. As with everyone in the United States, all electronic aspects of Winston's life, such as e-mails sent and received, television watched, credit cards used, and phone calls made were stored on the DARPA's petascale-data base AfterLifeLog Matrix System located at both Fort Meade and Menwith Hill's underground Global ID Registry. Records stored within the AfterLifeLog Matrix are claimed to be more secure than the Mormon Church's record vaults at Granite Mountain in Utah.

"I know this RFID technology is supposed to protect against ID theft, but I hate this damn thing. It's always itching," Winston complained, as a radio beam from the scanner touched his arm. The security arch *buzzed,* clearing him for entry. The security station monitor recorded: ARRIVAL - JEFFERSON - 9:18 PM.

A kind-faced receptionist wearing a *bright* tangerine-colored, travel-light, knit shirt from L. L. Bea*m*, sat at the desk next to the security arch. Her complimentary Audubon birdcall dangled at the end of a braided, green lanyard around her neck.

"Hello." Winston smiled at the receptionist.

"Please sign this." She handed him a pen and a sheaf of papers held together with a paperclip.

He swiped his signature on the first document: *T.J. James Winston.*

"Now this," she instructed.

He signed another.

"And here." She pointed to the dotted line.

Winston repeated the bureaucratic ritual twelve times.

"Pin this to your shirt." The receptionist handed each of them an ID tag with a holographic photo. Susan's ID was imprinted with her code name: SALOME. Winston's read: JEFFERSON.

Bains led them to a door next to the reception area. "Jefferson, you and Salomé wait here while I get an update. Things are running slow. It's bag burning day. New security codes are being distributed throughout ECHELON. They are having problems with the Cowboy Dictionary computer. I also need to make sure everyone else has arrived." Bains input a code, T-E-G-R-O-F-G-L-Y-C-O-N, through a keypad on the wall and a *thud* sounded. He opened the door to a conference room.

Low-level fluorescent plexiglass panels in the ceiling evenly lit the room's cold blue, acoustical-insulated walls. A sixteen-foot-long, oval, glass-top table surrounded by cushioned office chairs commanded its center. A television hung from the ceiling in one corner. On the back wall hung a circular plaque of the NSA Seal, depicting an eagle with a silver skeleton *key* in its talons. Above the seal, inscribed in two-inch-high gold letters, was the motto of signal intelligence: "GET IT, KNOW IT, USE IT."

Susan sat down in a chair.

Winston tossed his cap on the table, walked over to the television, and switched it on. A video of a speech by President Dwight Eisenhower began playing.

"... we have been compelled to create a permanent armaments industry of vast proportions. Added to this, three and a half million men and women are directly engaged in the defense establishment. We annually spend on military security more than the net income of all United States corporations...." *STA-KA ... STA-NAK* ... "In the councils of government, we must guard against the acquisition of unwarranted influence, whether sought or unsought, by the military-industrial complex. The potential for the disastrous rise of misplaced power exists and *will* persist. We must *never* let the weight of this combination endanger our liberties or our democratic processes."

"Winston flipped through the channels to CNN. "Let's listen to the trusty voices and watch Scott's funeral while we're waiting."

"I think you're thinning on the top," Susan noticed. "You need a haircut."

Winston brushed his hand over the back of his head and slumped in a chair.

"Chet, the casket is now being taken to the hearse waiting outside the east portico to the Capitol Building. From here the procession will make its way north to Rock Creek Cemetery."

"Look, Dan. There is Reverend William Wichards exiting the Capitol with the late President's daughter. The marble statue behind them is the goddess Ceres, the patron of the Greek mystery religions. Reverend Wichards will be conducting the graveside service. And there is the Secretary of State, accompanying President Walker. Also with the president is Dr. J. B. Maisun, the noted international political advisor and professor at Georgetown University. The current buzz in Washington is that President Walker will be appointing Dr. Maisun as the new United Nations Ambassador."

"Chet, the procession is now passing Union Station. That impressive statue at the front of Union Station is of Christopher Columbus, the District's namesake. There are several memorials to Columbus in Washington. Union Station was designed by the Chicago architect Daniel Burnham, who, in his day, was considered the world's greatest architect. Burnham used St. Mark's Basilica in Venice as his model for the facade of Union Station. St. Mark's stands before St. Mark's Square, a paved plaza with dimensions said to have been derived from the Temple of Solomon—"

"Dan, our aerial view from the government's sky-cam helicopter shows the long parade of limousines en route to Rock Creek Cemetery. Look, there is a large crowd of mourners lining North Capitol Street. This is an incredible sight."

"Chet, the funeral will include a private service at St. Paul's Episcopal Church on the cemetery grounds. Cameras are not allowed in Rock Creek Cemetery today. The services are expected to end after the military discharges a volley at 2:45 this afternoon—"

"So, for now, we will be turning our broadcast back to our regular coverage. Thank you for watching today's special event from CNN, where our tongues are all about the news. This is Dan Newman."

"And Chet Armstrong. God bless America."

Winston lumbered up and turned off the television. The speakers spat static. *STA-KAT, STA-KAT.* He scanned the conference table. A single, folded, brochure lay face-down at the middle of the table. He sat down again and slowly dragged the brochure across the table with the tips of his fingers, until he could read the words on the back cover: NSA ONGOING MISSION STATEMENT. "Have you read this?"

"No," Susan replied.

"Listen to what this says about the 'Holy Hammer.' " Winston read aloud a description of the NSA seal.

"In 1965, Lieutenant General Marshall S. Carter, Director of the NSA, ordered a seal to be designed to represent the NSA. The approved insignia contains much symbolism. The white, semicircle border displays the words National Security Agency across the top and United States of America across the bottom, separated on either side by a five-pointed silver star, a pentagram. The circular shape of the seal represents perpetuity and continuance, the symbol of eternity."

Susan's locked her eyes on the seal hanging on the wall. "Eternity? We'll never be out of a job."

Winston grinned and resumed reading.

"An American eagle with wings inverted on a blue field is the centerpiece. In heraldry, the eagle is considered a symbol of courage, supreme power, and authority. The eagle in the NSA insignia symbolizes the national scope of the Agency's mission. The eagle faces to the right, the direction of peace. Facing left symbolizes war.

The dexterous and sinister talons of the bird clutch a silver skeleton *key*. The *key* represents the *key* to security. It evolved from the emblem of Saint Peter the Apostle and his power to loose and to bind. It also symbolizes the mission to protect and gain access to all secrets.

The breast of the eagle boasts a chief, blue escutcheon, supported by paleways of thirteen pieces of red and white. The Escutcheon, or Shield, placed on the breast of the eagle, is an ancient mode of bearing. A description of the Escutcheon taken from that of the Great Seal of the United States explains that the Escutcheon is composed of the chief and pale, the two most honorable ordinaries, or common figures. The pieces represent the several states all joined in one solid compact *entity*, supporting a chief, which unites the whole and represents Congress."

"I didn't know all that," Susan said.

"We sound like an Indian tribe," Winston wisecracked. "I wonder if Bains is our pope at the NSA?"

"Let me see that brochure." Susan grabbed it from Winston's hand. Holding it close to her face to decode the fine print, she read aloud.

"The National Security Agency collects, processes, and disseminates foreign Signals Intelligence (SIGINT). The old adage that *knowledge is power* has perhaps never been truer than when applied to today's threats against our nation and the role SIGINT plays in combating them.

So knowledge *is* power," Susan added with a grin. "How many volumes are in your library, Mr. Jefferson?"

Winston smiled back.

Susan flipped through the pages of the mission statement, reading various sections that caught her eye.

"As the world becomes more and more technology-oriented, the Department of Information Assurance's (DIA) mission becomes increasingly challenging. ... DIA professionals go to great lengths to make certain that government systems remain impenetrable. This support spans from the highest levels of U.S. government to the individual war fighter in the field. NSA conducts one of the U.S. government's leading research and development programs. Many of the Agency's R&D projects have significantly advanced the states of the scientific and business worlds.

NSA employs the largest cadre of mathematicians in the United States and perhaps the world. Its mathematicians contribute directly to the two missions of the Agency by designing cipher systems that will protect the integrity of U.S. information systems by searching for weaknesses in adversaries' systems and codes.

Within the intelligence community are four intelligence gathering services. Human Intelligence (HUMINT) is primarily the responsibility of the CIA and DIA. Imagery Intelligence (IMINT) belongs to the NGA, the National Geospatial-Intelligence Agency. Military Intelligence and Measurement and Signature Intelligence (MASINT) is the responsibility of the DIA. Together, these complementary disciplines give our nation's leaders a greater understanding of the intentions of our enemies."

"We sound important," Winston said.

"We're not an ostrich with its head in the sand. How would the world survive without us?" Susan placed the brochure face-down at the middle of the table.

The door to the conference room opened and Bains entered. "The rest of the Backdoor Group is waiting for us in the Crack Chamber," he said firmly.

"I never cared for the name, Backdoor Group," Winston remarked, as they followed Bains out of the conference room. "We were going to call ourselves the Backstreet Boys, but that was taken. Who are the hackers here today?"

"Marx, Hegel, Rousseau, Emerson, Hume, and Kant," Bains answered woodenly. "Hegel has been working on it since we discovered it. He flew in from Menwith Hill on an X-43A scramjet last night."

MOST PEOPLE have one name, given at birth, which they keep for life. A name is uniquely personal. It is a powerful symbol of identification and a statement of one's self. As with the permanent mark of a tattoo, a name is a symbol of one's inner-self— an expression of one's soul—or the personality created during the first seven formative years of life. Those who have adopted a sobriquet belong to a select group of people who have *empowered themselves by choice*. The Black Bag Operation of twelve hacking misfits called upon by INNCS and the SCS to aid in times of crisis is known as the Backdoor Group, or the Men of Janus, after the Roman god-king who holds the keys to the Doors of the Solstices. The Backdoor Group consists of the following spoiled identities, code names derived from their geographic place of origin: Charles Forbin, known as Rousseau; Carl S. Spieldburg, known as Hegel; Abe Maslow, known as Schelling; Wilhelm Gattes, known as Marx; Joseph Smith, known as Plato; Robert Sinclair, known as Hume; Thomas Paine, known as Kant; Francis Barrett, known as Carlyle; Isaac Aslmov, known as Olsen; Stevie Jobbes, known as Emerson; Andrew Downing, known as Olmsted; and James Alexander Winston, known as Jefferson.

"YOUR FELLOW INMATES have been trying to find a *key* to the backdoor. We're currently at Code Yellow," Bains explained, leading them down a wide corridor to a set of steel doors. "I am in direct contact with the President's personal secretary. Once we reach Code Orange, the Executive Branch will become involved, and the operation will transfer to me, under the direction of Homeland Security. Salomé," Bains addressed Susan with a stern stare, "you stay with Jefferson and report directly to me on your progress."

Winston glanced at a "Peanuts" cartoon of Snoopy sleeping over his doghouse taped to one of the doors. His eyes tracked up at a plaque hanging above the doorway.

CRACK CHAMBER – ERIKSON ROOM 3603
(*Alter Ego – Sophomore's Dream* – The Other I – Light Up Your Silver Spoon)
Everything is an allegory, on top of an allegory, built into an allegory.
Welcome to the Enigma.

Bains swung open the doors. "Time is of the essence," he said, short of patience. "Now, tow the line."

All of the attending code-breaking misfits were sitting in front of a group of computer monitors, except for Marx. Marx slouched next to a table with one hand in his pants pocket and his other holding a cup of coffee with steam spiraling off the top. He was wearing a tie-dye shirt with the slogan, **Free Mitnick - If You Really Want To Foul Things Up, You Need A Computer**, silk-screened across the front. He and Jefferson immediately began a mano a mano, jostling for a position of authority.

"*The United States of America* is the anagram," Marx prompted in a deep, growling voice that sounded like furniture being dragged across a hardwood floor. "So what's the password?" he demanded, his bugling eyes magnified behind his taped-up, Harry Potter glasses.

"Attaineth its cause, *freedom*," Jefferson replied, feeling like Karnac the Magnificent.

"Greetings, Jefferson. Welcome to the Puzzle Palace and our extraordinarily gifted group of comrades." Marx curled a S.E.G. "How's the old face on the nickel?"

"I'm a magnum force. Much better than the phone phreaks from the Eastern Block." Jefferson looked amused, feeling at home and in his element. "I see the heavyweights are here today."

"Birds of a feather flock together," Marx chuckled as he repositioned his glasses that were sliding off the end of his nose.

"So what's been thrown at the Aunt Sally?" Jefferson prompted.

Marx pulled up a chair. "Park your ass down and we'll show you the strawman."

"This virus is an absolute monster," Hegel groaned, his scraggly Einstein-haircut fanning above his shoulders as if electrically charged. He stuck his finger in his mouth and uncorked it with a *pop*.

"Fleur-de-lis!" Rousseau puckered his lips and curled his pencil-thin mustache. "I've been studying it all day—Jell-O Wrestling with it. It's worse than a resident memory Screaming Fist virus." He stood up and sashayed away from the table.

"I have a different ideology on this one," Hume added as he slowly rose from his chair. The Big Lug was wearing a black cutoff T-shirt with a Harley-Davidson skull and wings logo above the slogan "**A WAY OF LIFE**" displayed across his back. His appearance resembled a fierce giant. "Not a lot of anomalies. I think it's a bit flabby, a lot of useless *zeros* and *ones*." The big-bellied powerhouse stomped across the room with heavy treetrunk thumps in his steps. With his eight-inch long, braided goatee and massive size, he looked like a wrestler for the World Wrestling Federation.

"Yes, it transcends anything we have tried to hack before," Emerson noted. He placed a pencil in his shirt's plastic pocket protector, next to his i-Pod. His appearance was the opposite of Hume. Emerson was a thin man, clean shaven, with every hair on his head meticulously gelled into place.

"So, you'd say that it has its own individuality?" Jefferson responded.

"Oh, absolutely—Absolutely— " Hegel replied. *Pop.*

"D-uh … We performed a winnow procedure to purge any useless chaff." Marx began in an instructional tone. "After breaking it down into packets, we resequenced it to determine the design of the Ebola. It follows a DES matrix, with six separate data streams or segments." He hesitated for a second, as though he knew more than he wanted to say. "It's a hybrid, maybe working in tandem with an Akelarre IDEA cipher. Normally, a Date Encryption Standard matrix has two or three segments, but this virus is more complicated, almost Byzantine."

"The data flowing within each segment appears random," Emerson added. "But look at this." He pointed to a Perspecta Crystal Ball, a rotating optical computer display, at the end of the table. A 3-D depiction of the virus floated in mid-air inside a transparent plastic dome. "It is built upon a matrix ladder, or lattice, similar to the DES algorithm. It reminds me of a double Triple DES-DES variant, an angry Lucifer algorithm. But Marx is our expert on Lucifer, not me."

"The Ebola could be based upon a genetic algorithm, similar to the structure of human DNA," Marx started again, "the Holy Grail of biology. It even has a de Brujn-type sequence, which is the mathematical basis for non-interacting DNA segments. The DNA molecule has two segments in its double helix ladder. This virus has been designed with six interlocking segments."

"We've been able to remove one segment from the virus and run it through a compiler to get a screen readout." Hume pointed to monitor number 4. "It's taking just over twenty-four hours to do a stripping. Hooks Law says extension is directly proportional to force. It could take six to seven days to compile the whole thing."

"So we're working around a timetable," Jefferson remarked. "Seven, that's my lucky number."

"We've been able to locate the keyhole for its backdoor," Emerson added.

"The backdoor of this virus can be addressed with a standard SATAN protocol," Marx explained.

"Translation please?" Salomé started jotting down notes in a scribbled shorthand that resembled a Masonic code. "What's a SATAN protocol?"

"SATAN stands for Security Administrator Tool for Analyzing Networks." Jefferson answered.

"D-uh … Every good hacker has followed a SATAN routine at one time or another," Marx added. "It's the standard backdoor deluder protocol for the Internet."

"SATAN is a hacker's best friend, but the Internet's worst enemy," Hume said with his beefy arms folded. "All computer networks tied into the World Wide Web are opened to the backdoor protocol known as SATAN. The program is readily available in the public domain. The SATAN protocol is how a hacker can enter the World Wide Web and wreak all sorts of havoc."

"Dead to rights," Marx agreed. "SATAN allows us to attack any system."

"To keep SATAN from being able to address a main computer server, a group of separate computers known as Guardians are placed between the system and their link to the World Wide Web by way of the phone line," Jefferson said. "A group of these guardians form a firewall that protects against the entry of SATAN— "

"Now, here is the strange thing about this Ebola virus." *Click.* Marx tapped the glass on the monitor with the end of his pen. "Even though it contains a SATAN backdoor, we have found no backdoors in the firewalls of any systems we have tested which allows this virus to break in. So the Ebola is not entering any of the systems connected to the Internet by way of a standard backdoor routine such as SATAN. Furthermore, the backdoor for this virus appears to require a six-word entry *key*. This *key* may consist of six input places for words made up of numbers or characters, or a combination of both," Marx suggested. "At first we were not certain what this lock and key arrangement would do. Perhaps it could disable the virus. Perhaps it could even speed up the rate of infection or slow it down. Or even worse, it could turn on a sleeper bug within the virus. So we tested various password combinations on quarantined laptops to see what might happen—"

"Since there are six segments in the virus," Emerson interrupted, "I suspect that each keyword addresses each segment in some way. So, actually, we could be dealing with six backdoors."

"That's true," Marx acknowledged, then continued. "We ran tests by inputting various words or symbols at random. What we discovered was that every time we input a wrong word, the virus fork-bombed into other parts of the system, like a fast growing kudzu. The laptops quickly became DEADBEEF. It's a booby trap. We cannot just randomly input words until we find the right one. That could advance the virus directly into a plague."

"We have a backdoor protocol for testing every word and symbol known to man," Emerson said, waving a pen in his hand, "but we have to run them on separate computers. There are more possible word and symbol combinations than there are available quarantined computers. Somehow we need to narrow down our search for the correct keywords."

"It's a hairball," Hume added in frustration. "We've sailed in the cyber-doldrums." He folded a data sheet he had scribbled on, fashioned it into a flying-fish paper airplane, and tossed it across the room. "This Godzillagram barely floats on air."

Marx grabbed the flimsy paper *vimana* before it hit the floor, refolded it into a paper dragon airplane, then tossed it. "D-uh … It's a struggle that puts me in the deep sixes as well," he shrugged. "I've had a dingdong battle with it."

"Fleur-de-lis," Rousseau agreed. He grabbed the flying dragon in mid-flight, refolded it into the shape of a fish-eyed zeppelin, and attached a paper clip to one end. He tossed it high in the air to Jefferson. "It's weighted down with too many *zeros* and *ones* to make it fly."

Salomé held up her hands and crossed them in a T, for a timeout. "I'm confused," she said, baffled by the techno phraseology. She watched the fish-eyed zeppelin, resembling a twisted AIDS ribbon, spiraling in an ascent above the table.

"Let me throw in my five cents worth," Jefferson said, retrieving a gold-plated buffalo nickel from his pocket. "No more excuses, Rousseau." He thumb-flipped the nickel to Marx. It hit the table and spun around, defying gravity, like a miniature gyroscope. "Marx, you need new glasses. It's not that difficult to understand," He quickly snatched the paper fisheye in mid-flight and unfolded the data sheet, "just follow the old hacker's airplane rule, Build it Beautiful. It's easy if you fold your thoughts in a different way," he spoke confidently to Salomé. "This virus has six coded segments, each with its own separate lock." He pointed to the data sheet and refolded it into a dove-shaped origami washi bird. "What we need are six *keywords* to put into the locks to open the backdoors." He tossed the dove to Salomé. "If we're lucky, those *keywords* will turn the damn thing off. Now, does that clear up the fog?"

"I think I've got it." She caught the paper bird. "But where do we find these *keywords?*"

"Good question." Jefferson redirected his attention back to his fellow hackers. "So, how is this virus getting into the World Wide Web, if not by a SATAN backdoor?"

All of the other members of the Backdoor Group were holding challenge coins of various denominations in their fingers.

"Okay ... I don't see any wooden nickels," Jefferson acknowledged with a smile. "It's decided then. You take my challenge."

"It's better than drawing straws," Marx spoke up. "Yes, we take your challenge. We're going to let you be the gridmaster on this one, Jefferson."

"Alright, so what about the SATAN backdoor?" Jefferson pushed forward.

"I know this sounds crazy," Marx paused, "but I think the virus is riding on a separate modulated carrier wave that enters directly into the computer by way of the hard wire, regardless of the data being pushed through the wire. Hume discovered that any computer that has never been connected to the Internet does not have the virus. But as soon as it is connected to the phone line, it becomes infected."

"It's a type of plus-code modulation. This virus is leaping right over all the known firewalls," Hume said with concern. "It has a mind of its own."

"D-uh ... It's a complicated little SOB. The virus appears to be growing within the .EXE DOS files, like an old Jerusalem Virus. The degree of infection is somehow associated with the crystal clock cycle of the computer's main processor, which may be related to how fast the signal is being modulated off of a 7.83 Hz lowband carrier wave. PCs built around the Chinese 'Dragon Chip' and its 666.66 MHz processors have been hit hard. Those CPUs are used to operate the Chinese 'Soaring Dragon Servers' that connect much of the Web to the Far East. It covers over a quarter of the planet. This virus could shut down the Hong Kong Disneyland. I'm still trying to isolate a possible carrier wave on the phone lines. Now, if any of this holds water, the bigger question is this—Who is modulating the signal over the phone lines? We are the only ones in control of the main Transatlantic Trunk. And the virus is not coming from us. We have isolated our secured computers from any ground power and Internet connections so we can safely study the virus."

"Okay, let's get cracking." Jefferson approached monitor 4. "Let's put it under the magnifying glass and glean some information."

"It's gibberish encoded on gibberish," Hume described. "But, there's a pattern here, some leaky abstract. It could be a palindrome or a cab cannon maybe. It even

```
22.23,22.1,0,0,0,0.1,0,0,0.1,0,0,0.1,0,0,0.7,7,0,0,0.1,0,0,0.1,0,0,0,0.1,0,0,0,0.77,01,23
44.23,00.1,0,0,0,0.7,0,0,0.7,0,0,0,0.7,0,0,0.7,7,0,0,0.7,0,0,0.7,0,0,0,0.7,0,0,0,0.53,23,58
42.23,12.1,0,0,0,0.7,0,0,0.7,0,0,0,0.7,0,0,0.7,7,0,0,0.7,0,0,0.7,0,0,0,0.7,0,0,0,0.28,33,16
41.23,02.1,0,0,0,0.7,0,0,0.7,0,0,0,0.7,0,0,0.7,7,0,0,0.7,0,0,0.7,0,0,0,0.7,0,0,0,0.33,43,15
30.23,24.1,0,0,0,0.7,0,0,0.7,0,0,0,0.7,0,0,0.7,7,0,0,0.7,0,0,0.7,0,0,0,0.7,0,0,0,0.43,00,12
29.23,26.1,0,0,0,0.7,0,0,0.7,0,0,0,0.7,0,0,0.7,7,0,0,0.7,0,0,0.7,0,0,0,0.7,0,0,0,0.23,23,08
28.23,44.1,0,0,0,0.7,0,0,0.7,0,0,0,0.7,0,0,0.7,7,0,0,0.7,0,0,0.7,0,0,0,0.7,0,0,0,0.36,13,13
27.23,29.1,1,0,0,0.7,0,0,0.7,0,0,0,0.7,0,0,0.7,7,0,0,0.7,0,0,0.7,0,0,0,0.7,0,0,0,0.34,36,01
38.55,38.0,0.1,1,0.7,7,7,7,7,7,7,7,7,7,7,7,7,7,7,7,7,7,7,7,7,7,7,7,0,0,0.77,01,23
22.23,12.1,1,0,0,0,0.1,1,0,0,0,0,0,0,0.7,7,0,0,0,0,0,0,0,0,0,0,0,0,0.43,01,38
21.23,28.0,0.1,1,0,0.1,1,0,0,0,0,0,0,0.7,7,0,0,0,0,0,0,0,0,0,0,1,1,0,0,1,1.54,53,15
18.23,33.1,1,0,0.1,1,0,0.1,1,0,0,0,0,0,0,0.7,7,0,0,0,0,0,0,0,0,0,0,0,0.43,03,19
12.23,42.0,0,0,0,0,0,0,0,0,0,0,0,0,0,0.7,7,0,0,0,0,0,0,0,0,0,0,0,1,1.35,03,48
11.23,54.1,1,0,0.1,1,0,0.1,1,0,0.1,1,0,0,0.7,7,7,7,0,0,0,0,0.1,1,0,0.1,1,0,1,1,0,0.13,23,14
52.23,32.0,0,0,0,0,0,0,0,0,0,0,0,0,0.7,0,7,7,0,7,0,0,0,0,0,0,0,0,0,0,1,1,23,13,00
13.23,11.1,1,0,0,0,0,0,0,0,0,0,0,0,0.7,0,0,7,0,0,7,0,0,0,0,0,0,0,0,0,0,0,0.24,24,12
77.18,22.0,0,0,0,0,0,0,0,0,0,0,0,0,0.7,0,0,7,0,0,7,0,0,0,0,0,0,0,0,1,1,13,23,14
38.55,38.1,1,0,7,7,7,7,7,7,7,7,7,7,7,7,7,7,7,7,7,7,7,7,7,7,7,0,0,21,27,18
22.23,22.0,0,0,0,0,0,0,0,0,0,0,0,0,0.7,0,0,0,0,0,0,0,0.7,0,0,0,0,0,0,0,0,0.43,23,16
54.23,02.1,1,0,0,0,0.7,0,0,0,0,0,0,0.7,7,0,0,0,0,0,0,0.7,0,0,0,0,0,0,0,7,0,0,1,1,34,48,18
42.23,12.0,0,0,0,0,0,0.7,0,0,0,0,0,0,0,0,0.7,7,0,0,0,0,0,0,0.7,0,0,0,7,0,0,0,0,0.25,23,28
35.23,49.1,1,0,0,0,0,0.7,0,7,0,0,0,0,0,0.1,1,1,1,1,1,0,0,0,0,0,0,0.7,0,7,0,0,0,0,1,1,36,36,19
22.23,32.0,0,0.1,1,0,0,0,0.7,0,0,0,0,0,0.1,1,1,1,1,0,0,0,0,0,0.7,0,0,0,0,0,0,0,0,0.33,23,08
15.23,20.1,1,0,0,0,0,0.7,0,7,0,0,0,0,0,0.1,1,1,1,1,1,0,0,0,0,0.7,0,0,0,0,1,1,77,01,23
02.33,32.0,0,0,0,0,0.7,0,0,0,0,0,0,0.7,7,0,0,0,0,0,0,0.7,0,0,7,0,0,0,0,0.33,23,28
26.43,48.1,1,0,0,0.7,0,0,0,0,0.7,0,0,0,0,0.7,7,0,0,0,0,0,0,0.7,0,0,0,0,7,0,0,1,1,31,23,08
07.53,57.0,0,0,0.7,0,0,0,0,0,0.7,0,0,0,0.7,0,0,0,0,7,0,0,0,0,0,0.7,0,0,0,0,0.33,43,17
38.55,38.1,1,0,7,7,7,7,7,7,7,7,7,7,7,7,7,7,7,7,7,7,7,7,7,7,7,7,0,0,32,23,13
12.23,22.0,0,0,0,0,0,0,0,0,0,0,0,0,0.7,0,0,0,0.7,0,0,0,7,0,0,0,0,0,0,0,0,0,1,1,13,23,28
22.24,19.1,1,0,0,0,0,0,0,0,0,0,0,0,0.7,0,0,7,0,0,7,0,0,0,0,0,0,0,0,0,0,0,0.53,33,18
02.43,07.0,0,1,1,0,0.1,1,0,0.1,1,0,0,0,0.7,0,7,0,7,0,7,0,1,1,0,0.1,1,0,0.1,1,0,0,77,01,23
22.13,26.1,1,0,0.1,1,0,0.1,1,0,0,0.7,7,0,0,0.7,7,0,0,0,0,0.1,1,0,0,0,0,0,0,0,1,1,37,13,36
32.23,28.0,0,0,0,0,0,0,0,0,0,0,0,0,0.7,0,0,0,0,0.7,7,0,0,0,0,0,0,0.7,0,0,1,1,0,0.1,1,0,0,0,0,13,03,18
21.21,20.1,1,0,0,0.1,1,0,0,0,0,0.7,0,0,0,0,0.7,7,0,0,0,0,0,0,0,0,0.7,0,0,0,0,0,0,0,0,1,1,37,03,40
52.25,02.0,0,1,1,0,0,0,0,0,0,0.7,0,0,0,0,0,0.7,7,0,0,0,0,0,0,0,0.7,0,0,0,0,0,0,1,1,0,0,23,23,33
53.23,29.1,1,0,0.1,1,0,0,0.7,0,0,0,0,0,0,0,0.7,7,0,0,0,0,0,0,0,0.7,0,0.1,1,0,0,1,1,18,13,28
77.18,02.0,0,1,1,0,0.7,0,0,0,0,0,0,0,0.7,7,0,0,0,0,0,0,0,0.7,0,0,0,1,1,0,0,35,23,15
22.23,42.1,1,0,0.1,1,0,7,0,0,0,0,0,0,0,0.7,7,0,0,0,0,0,0,0,0,0.7,0,0,0,0,1,1,43,43,36
22.23,12.1,1,0,0,0,0.7,0,0,0,0,0,0,0,0,0.7,7,0,0,0,0,0,0,0,0,0.7,0,0,0,0,0.23,23,28
38.55,38.0,0,0,0,0.7,0,0,0,0,0,0,0,0,0,0.7,7,0,0,0,0,0,0,0,0,0,0.7,0,0,1,1,77,01,03
15.11,13.0,0,0,0.7,0,0,0,0,0,0,0,0,0,0,0,0.7,7,0,0,0,0,0,0,0,0,0,0.0,0.7,0,0,0,22,23,19
16.43,32.1,1,0.7,0,0,0,0,0,0,0,0,0,0,0,0.7,7,0,0,0,0,0,0,0,0,0,0,0.7,0,0,35,21,08
17.32,27.1,1,0,7,0,0.5,0,0,0,0,0,0,0,0,0.7,7,0,0,0,0,0,0,0,0,0,0,0,0.7,0,0,53,03,18
18.24,24.0,0,0,0.7,0,0.5,5,0,0,0,0,0,0,0.7,7,0,0,0,0,0,0,0,0,0,0,0,0.7,0,0,44,23,06
19.23,22.0,0,0,0.7,0,0.5,5,5,0,0,0,0,0,0,0.7,7,0,0,0,0,0,0,0,0,0,0,0,0.7,0,0,1,1,83,17
20.25,23.0,0,0,0.7,0,0.5,5,5,5,0,0,0,0,0,0.7,7,0,0,0,0,0,0,0,0,0,0,0,0.7,0,0,63,23,40
21.13,22.1,1,0,7,0,0.5,5,5,5,5,0,0,0,0,0.7,7,7,7,7,0,0,0,0,0,0,0,0,0,0,0.7,0,0,73,23,18
23.30,00.6,6,6,0,0,0.5,5,5,5,5,0,0,0,0.7,7,7,7,7,7,0,0,0,0,0,0,0,0,0,0,0.7,0,0,83,23,13
21.23,27.1,1,0,7,0,0.5,5,5,5,5,0,0,0,0,0.7,7,7,7,7,0,0,0,0,0,0,0,0,0,0.7,0,0,18,23,48
20.23,23.0,0,0,0.7,0,0.5,5,5,5,0,0,0,0,0,0.7,7,0,0,0,0,0,0,0,0,0,0,0.7,0,0,15,23,13
19.55,38.1,1,0,7,0,0.5,5,5,5,0,0,0,0,0,0.7,7,0,0,0,0,0,0,0,0,0,0,0.7,0,0,27,30,11
18.23,28.0,0,0,0.7,0,0.5,5,5,0,0,0,0,0,0,0.7,7,0,0,0,0,0,0,0,0,0,0,0,0.7,0,0,43,53,48
17.21,22.1,1,0,7,0,0.5,5,0,0,0,0,0,0,0,0.7,7,0,0,0,0,0,0,0,0,0,0,0,0.7,0,0,13,25,12
16.43,25.0,0,0,0.7,0,0.5,0,0,0,0,0,0,0,0,0.7,7,0,0,0,0,0,0,0,0,0,0,0,0.7,0,0,77,01,23
15.21,22.1,1,0,0,7,0,0.0,0,0,0,0,0,0,0,0.7,7,0,0,0,0,0,0,0,0,0,0,0,0.7,0,0,0,31,43,41
52.13,41.0,0,0,0,0.7,0,0,0,0,0,0,0,0,0,0.7,7,0,0,0,0,0,0,0,0,0,0,0,0.7,0,0,0,28,15,18
32.33,01.1,1,0,0,0,0.7,0,0,0,0,0,0,0,0,0.7,7,0,0,0,0,0,0,0,0,0,0,0,0.7,0,1,1,0,0,14,33,10
38.55,38.0,0,0,0,0,0.7,0,0,0,0,0,0,0,0,0.7,7,0,0,0,0,0,0,0,0,0,0,0,0.7,0,0,0,0,1,1,81,03,17
42.11,22.1,1,0,0,0,0,0.7,0,0,0,0,0,0,0,0.7,7,0,0,0,0,0,0,0,0,0,0,0.7,0,1,1,0,0,1,1,52,27,18
47.22,28.0,0,0.1,1,0,0,0,7,7,7,7,7,7,7,7,7,7,7,7,7,7,7,7,7,0,0,0,0,0,0,0,0,41,03,11
12.43,42.1,1,0,0.1,1,0,0,0,0,0,0,0,0,0.7,0,0,1,1,0,0.1,1,0,0.1,1,0,0,1,1,61,18,00
27.53,20.0,0,1,1,0,0.1,1,0,0,0,0,0,0,0,0.7,7,0,0,0,0,0,0,0,0,1,1,0,0.1,1,0,0,48,28,13
```

looks a little acrostic. Can you read the tea leaves?"

"What do we have?" Jefferson leaned forward in his chair to study the screen, his eyes blinking. "It's hard to see. This thing's in the way." He swung aside the hinged polarized screen filter covering the glass. "Marx, look! These numbers look like garbage with a dangling point, but I think they're keepage. The skyscrapers on the left and right of the readout have a numerical series. They remind me of a Bongard pattern recognition problem or a Vernam cipher."

"It looks like a sudoku puzzle to me," Salomé said. "What's a Vernam cipher?"

"A Vernam cipher is a scheme where the plaintext is combined with a key symbol," Emerson explained. "It's sometimes called an OTP, or a one-time pad. This type of cipher is used for perfect secrecy. But, it's not theoretically unbreakable. OTPs were used by the Soviets," he added, with a sideways glance at Marx. "That's old-school cryptography."

"And a Bongard problem?" Salomé asked.

"The basis of awareness," Marx grunted. "If you are presented with two sets of similar but different diagrams, the Bongard problem involves finding the common patterns between the two sets. It requires a discerning eye to solve the Bongard."

Jefferson's eyebrows arched inquisitively at the screen. "It's some sort of nondual substantial morphic form, like an Arecibo message from SETI. It could be self-referencing … maybe an Oracle Form." He unconsciously rolled a gold-plated nickel between his fingers as he conjured the readout. "Looks like it's surrounded by a bunch of ouroboros numbers."

"What are ouroboros numbers?" Salomé asked.

"It's known as the ouroboros snake," Kant spoke up, hiding behind a large monitor at the far end of the room. "They're binary numbers of 2^n bits—the ultimate magic numbers. They're the building blocks for all computer languages."

"I think these are coordinates—latitude and longitude perhaps," Jefferson conjectured, methodically inching his index finger up and down the columns. "This could be a cipher with plaintext coordinates mixed with a bunch of useless *zeros* and *ones*. It's a basic *steganographic* technique. This virus could be a carrier for a payload of data, like a memory bag-exchange. It's possible that every virus segment could be a carrier for a payload."

Marx nodded slightly. "Maybe, maybe," he repeated in an even tone.

"Fleur-de-lis," Rousseau said with a sigh of relief. "This was getting hard, until you popped up with that idea—I think you're right, Jefferson."

"Contact NGA and National Reconnaissance at Chantilly," Jefferson instructed. "Have them rain dance these two columns of numbers against all possible longitude and latitude combinations. Look for sequences that appear more than once—and any sort of **fnord** that might misdirect. Let's see what pours off the umbrella."

"Yes," Rousseau agreed. "Let's add an egg and cook out the *vital*."

"This will take a few minutes," Emerson said as he ran the numbers through a program to crosscheck for useable matches. He held the end of a pencil between his fingers, wiggled it in his mouth, and tapped in a nervous rhythm against the edge of his teeth. "Ouch!" He recoiled. "I've got a loose filling."

"D-uh … What do you make of it, Jefferson?" Marx asked, his eyes slanting to one side with a proud expression on this face.

"It has design." Jefferson replied, studying the readout. "It has purpose. But it's not hidden all that well. In many ways it's structured like a straightforward cipher, with the *key* built into the virus. It's similar to an old text cipher, based on typos. It's just lying there waiting to be found."

"Jefferson, Marx, look at this!" Emerson motioned to a monitor displaying a crosscheck readout. "One set of numbers on the left column and one set on the right repeat ... and they match up to a location."

"What is it?" Jefferson asked.

"Grid Latitude 38 degrees North, 53 minutes, 38 seconds. Longitude 77 degrees West, 01 minute, 23 seconds," Emerson replied.

"We need topographic survey maps and a GPS plot," Jefferson suggested.

"I'm running a GPS solution through an NGA link," Emerson said.

A digital, topographic map appeared on one of the monitors. A set of rapidly shifting crosshairs locked to the two coordinates.

"Got it!" Emerson exclaimed.

"Where is it?" Jefferson asked.

"It's thirty-two miles southwest of here," Emerson answered.

"And where is that?" Jefferson asked again.

Point and *click*. The map zoomed into the location of the locked crosshairs.

"I'd say just about where the president's helicopter went down," Emerson said.

A stunned silence filled the room, as the hacking philosophers stared at the intersecting crosshairs next to a *flashing* red dot on the computer monitor.

"We're investigating a computer virus, not the death of the president. Right?" Jefferson questioned.

Salomé nodded. "That's outside our jurisdiction."

"So, where exactly is this location?" Jefferson squinted at the screen.

"It's a field west of the Washington Monument," Emerson pinpointed.

Jefferson moved his face closer to the screen. "What's that?"

"What is what?" Marx fired back.

"That? The red dot on the map?" Jefferson pointed with his index finger to the *flashing* red dot."

"Let me look it up on the program legend," Emerson said. Point and *click*. A window appeared that defined the various objects on the digitized map. "According to the map legend, it's a GPS reference point."

"What the *hell* does that mean?" Hume wondered. "Why are the crosshairs next to a GPS reference point?"

"I'm going to tap into the Park Service video feed and see what it is," Emerson said. "Let's watch it on live TV." He addressed one of the miniature telescopic optic-eyes hidden in the balled tips of the flagpoles encircling the Washington Mounment.

Everyone gathered closer to Emerson's monitor.

"It's a stone marker of some sort," Emerson said. "Let me pull up a different angle." A feed from another webcam appeared on the screen. "There're words inscribed on it."

"What does it say?" Salomé asked.

"Images aren't clear," Marx complained. "Something's wrong with the feed—"

"The map legend says it's the Jefferson Stone," Emerson interjected.

Salomé darted her eyes at Jefferson.

Jefferson smiled back. "Look, I'm going to drive over there and bird-dog this thing. In the meantime, find me someone who knows more about what that GPS dot represents. Contact the people in charge of this area so I can get additional background information," he instructed. "We'll need clearance from someone to get to this area. It's probably Park Service territory. Double check with the guardians at Homeland to be safe."

"What are you looking for?" Her brow furrowed in confusion.

"I'm not sure," Jefferson answered, "but I think I'm looking for clues."

"Clues?" Salomé questioned. "Care to translate that?"

"Yeah, clues," Jefferson answered, his voice even, "*possibilities*. In the world of cryptography, there are two ways of coding information. One is a cipher where there is a substitution of letters or characters for other letters or characters to reveal a hidden message. All ciphers can be broken using enough computer power and enough time." He pointed to the monitor. "The latitudes and longitudes we extracted from this virus segment are an example of a cipher."

"Yes, I know that," Salomé said.

"The other way to code a message is by way of symbols or words that hold special meaning to only those who have knowledge of the original meaning of the coded word or symbol, like a Zancig Code. This gives a coded message a higher level of secrecy. It's the way spies communicate, cloaking ideas in perceptual forms. Where ciphers can be broken using computation, codes normally cannot. Codes require logical analysis and a search for *possible commonalties* using word or symbol association. There is usually some meaningful and related synchronicity beyond mere coincidence that allows codes to be broken. I don't think the Ebola is that cut-and-dry. I think the backdoor *key* to this virus is not based solely on a cipher, but rather on a coded message."

"A coded message ... that sounds *possible*." Marx nodded in agreement.

"It's part of the dichotomy between inductive and deductive thought," Jefferson explained. "I learned this years ago while creating learning algorithms for artificial computer intelligence using simple word and graphic association routines to simulate cognitive neural networks in computers—the so-called Strong AI, where a computer becomes a type of Absolute Mind with a separate consciousness—the Technological Singularity, the Holy Grail of Computer AI—"

"The techno-rapture for the nerds," Emerson chuckled, "Boltzmann graphic learning machines. Yes, it does sound *possible*. I could hitch my wagon to this star."

"In AI, symbols allow a computer to quickly grasp bundles of information," Jefferson said. "They serve as a universal language for a pattern of thought. Symbols guide action. It's a concept known as place-tracking—a form of contrast comparing used in critical thinking, as well as magical thinking. The mind is a symbol-processing system that associates images and structured patterns with metaphorical places. For example, we collect souvenirs to remind us of the places we have been. They serve as coded images—like code words—that remind us of a specific mental place that only we can remember and understand. The same is true with old photographs in personal remembering, which reveal the hidden shape of things in our past." He nodded at Salomé. "We can follow this same reasoning in reverse and have a place defined by a specific image, or set of images. Thus the place could serve as a *stimulus* for revealing a code word, with concealed images at the place serving as a reference for determining the coded meaning. In steganograhy, these concealed images placed in plain sight are known as *semagrams*. Semagrams can be contained in anything, such as seemingly harmless drawings, paintings, musical compositions, or photographs."

"D-uh ..."

"Computational semiotics and artificial intelligence related to computer memory is established by coordinating stored places with images of those places." Jefferson sliced an aggravated glance at Marx. "It uses the old mnemonic room system for remembering things around a central memory place. The commonality of the images helps to reference the place, and the place helps to reference the common meaning of the image. Usually, there is a central place that is called a *locus* or *domain*, which allows us to grasp the true meaning of the image using the place as a stimulus. All of Western thought is logocentric, meaning all words and semiotic images are tied together to a central *locus* of thought that serves as a compass for human understanding. Pattern recognition, the cuing of common patterns, is at the heart of human intelligence and human behavior. To read the coded meaning of a symbol, you need to look beyond its denotation and find its connotation. Images can be *signifiers* for *concepts*—*a canon of signs* or basic governing laws. The differences between semiotic images can sometimes reveal alternate levels of meaning for an image and hidden motivations, depending on social and cultural conditions."

"I see," Salomé said with a confused look. "I'm in a mental Pez. I need a thorough translation on all of this."

"For instance," Jefferson elaborated, "if we wish to recall the meaning of an image of an eagle, a signifier, we must place that image at a definite *locus*. Place an image of an eagle on a sign at the zoo, and you have one meaning. Put that same image on the presidential seal, and you have an entirely different meaning. An image that is properly united with a place determines its coded message. There's a protocol for transforming signifiers into messages. Coded messages are limited to MMLs, or Minimum Message Lengths. An MML is a formal information theory restatement of Occam's Razor." Jefferson puckered a kiss toward Salomé. "The symbols that generate the shortest overall message are most likely the ones used in translating a code. When you see an image, you naturally read something into it. What you read into it is your own independent code from your personal frame of reference. Your personal vision. Images can help to make us independent."

"D-uh … I'm not certain about that," Marx grunted.

"I think these coordinates reference a place, a *locus*." Jefferson began to lay out a plan for investigation. "And there is something at that location that serves as a reference image for a related *keyword,* or a type of *stego-key*, which unlocks the virus's backdoor. It could be a *rebus* word puzzle, where pictures or groups of pictures act as a golden thread that defines a hidden word or phrase—pointing to a *syntagm,* a new meaning, from ordered signifiers. Or maybe it's a Glass Bead Game, where you try to discover words and make connections related to a central theme for better understanding an idea. The image at the *locus* serves as the *key* to the lock—"

"Yes, pure processing-logic uses symbols in a logical series to produce new knowledge, a message," Hegel added in agreement. "A dialectical phenomenology, this virus could be a real test of our deductive abilities."

"So, it's a scavenger hunt," Salomé compared. "We're searching for semagrams."

"You could call it that, or some buzzword bingo," Jefferson chuckled, "or a tippit guessing game." He felt somehow charmed by the Ebola. "But in my eye, it's more like Geocaching with a new spin."

"A geo what?" Salomé questioned.

"It's a crazy GPS treasure hunting game—a modern take on a nineteenth-century garden game where clues for finding a treasure are hidden in an outdoor public place inside a waterproof container called a *letterbox*. I used to play virtual versions of Geocaching on the Internet, searching from site to site for letterboxes hidden on someone's web page. Hackers used the game to pass messages among themselves. It's all a guess on my part," Jefferson ventured, his voice uncertain. "But maybe this isn't simply a virus. Perhaps it's a type of Geocaching game generator. I remember a group of hackers chatting about this type of thing on the Internet once. There was this badass hacker known as the Snake—he used ouroboros numbers as a gateway into other computers. Gateway 28. This virus could be the work of the Snake. I don't know.... We could be starting on a wild-goose chase. But the best litmus test is to try things out. One thing's for sure, there's a continuation here. The data from this virus is leading us to this spot." *Click.* Jefferson tapped the glass on the monitor. "And this spot has my name on it. Someone is taunting us. It's referencing something. Someone is referencing something. And it's got to be more important that just a little, red, flashing dot!"

"Fleur-de-lis," Salomé whispered.

***

Day 8
Unmovable Mover
The Tower in the Garden

This stone that I have set up as a pillar (massebah) shall be God's house - Genesis 28:22
You shall not set up an Asherah—any kind of pole beside the altar of the Lord your God that you may
make—or erect massebah, for such the Lord your God detests. - Deuteronomy 16:21–22

WINSTON EYED THE CLOCK on the car dash. 5:49 AM. He looked out the window at the first light of day picking its way into a milky half-light. In the distance, the Washington Monument, like Aaron's rod, invoked a holy calm over the crash site.

Susan removed the key from the ignition as she hummed along to the radio playing Little Jimmy Dickens singing "May the Bird of Paradise Fly Up Your Nose."

"My mother used to take me to the Washington Monument when I was a kid," Winston recalled, still staring out the window.

Susan glanced through the windshield at the marble tower. She reached into her shoulder bag and grappled for her cell phone and a folded topographic map. "I think we have everything." She handed the map to Winston.

They stepped out of the pearl-black Suburban parked in a tow-away zone next to the John Ericsson Memorial, a gnarled and misshaped monument symbolizing a Yggdrasil Tree where the three destroyers of disharmony—the rhizophagic dragon *Niðhögg*, an ophiophagic eagle of the sky, and the goat *Heiðrún*—hide above and below the world of man.

Winston pointed to a NO PARKING sign next to a bright-red, octagonal STOP sign next to a leaky green fire hydrant. "Should you park here?"

"It's all right. The government plates will keep it from being towed." Susan locked the doors with the remote security sensor. *Flump.*

Winston gave Susan an inspective look. "You've got lipstick on your teeth."

She rolled her tongue over her teeth. "Now?"

Winston nodded a quick approval. "Nice smile."

They walked past three stone pagoda lanterns positioned at the edge of the Tidal Basin. Winston paused and inquisitively eyed the worn symbols on the lanterns. "My father used to collect inscriptions from stone markers like these," he commented. "He said they mark the sites of buried treasure."

Emerging from the shadows beneath an umbrella of trees, a heavyset, bearded park ranger in an olive-tan uniform with an arrowhead patch on his shoulder lumbered across the Elysium Field. He resembled Smoky Bear holding a flashlight. Around his neck hung his free, bloodred Audubon birdcall, dangling at the end of a braided green lanyard. "Are you the people from the NSA?" he asked as he approached.

"Yes, we are." Susan reached into her shoulder bag and removed her ID badge.

"It's kind of early for a private tour." The ranger noted the badge number, 918.

"You must be Ranger Nobles." She eyed the plastic name tag on his shirt pocket.

"Yeah, I'm Ray Nobles." He shook her hand.

"I'm Susan Hamilton. This is my associate, James Winston."

Nobles swiped a glance at Winston's worn trekking pants and faded baseball cap. *Not your run-of-the-mill ... He looks like he belongs at the Fish and Feather Expo for hunters instead of the NSA.* "You know, you look a lot like—"

"Hello. Yeah, I know." Winston grinned mischievously. "I'm not the enforcer, I'm the third president."

Susan smiled.

Ranger Nobles looked puzzled.

Winston immediately began dowsing his surrounds. "Ranger Nobles, I know it's early, but we want to look at the area within the crash site, especially this location." He held out the map and pointed. "We have a few nagging questions about this landmark. The map references it as the Jefferson Stone."

"That's right. It's the Jefferson Stone, a stone that denotes a marker placed there by Thomas Jefferson."

"Damn." Winston sliced a smile. "So, I put a marker there."

"You must have forgotten about that," Susan played with Winston's verbal volley.

"Let's take a look at this stone." Winston pushed forward.

"Sure, no problem," Nobles said, still puzzled. He slipped his flashlight into his belt holster. "Come this way."

The three strolled across a dew-covered field next to the crash site. They checked themselves through one of the security stations separating the temporary, man-size coils of razor wire fencing the Monument and stepped into the elongated, early-morning shadow cast by the giant broken stylus.

"It's a nice morning," Susan commented, feeling a pleasant breeze.

Nobles took a deep breath. "The humidity is low today and it's not too warm," he reported like a weatherman. "It's a perfect seventy-seven degrees."

"I see our clock is broken. Looks like a big yard sale." Winston observed the nearby field littered with fallen stones and debris. "It's a real mess."

"Yes," Nobles acknowledged. "We've been cleaning up. It's a slow process with all of the investigations. When I got a call this morning to meet with you cloak-and-dagger folks from the NSA, I figured it was about the accident."

"No," Winston corrected. "We're just data mining … looking for background information on the marker."

"I overheard some investigators talking yesterday." Nobles lowered his voice, his eyes shifting. "They said that the crash was an accident caused by an electrical malfunction. The Park Service is already talking about rebuilding the Monument—making it better, making it stronger." He looked up at the sky-clad obelisk. "Our monuments to the ego. Man always looks at the outward appearance of things. We forget to look at the heart. Deeds, not stones, are the true monuments of the great. George Washington was a Samson in the field and a Solomon in the council. In the eyes of many, he was a monument unto himself. The country's first archetypal hero—the father of his people, the patriot, the mythic revolutionary leader. He was seen as almost God-like by his adoring peers and as a demi-god by his detractors."

Winston noticed a score of dead birds littering the ground at the base of the Monument. "Did all these birds die from the crash?"

"No," Nobles replied. "The birds started flying into the Monument a few days ago, about the same time the Pentagon finished an underground telecommunication line running to the White House." He pointed to the nearby street construction. "They're missing their landing grid. They may be infected with the bird flu. Don't touch 'em."

"It's probably that toxic alga," Susan ventured. "Ranger Nobles, what can you tell us about the Jefferson Stone?"

Nobles cleared his throat as though preparing to give an official tour. "This whole area was a cattle yard before the Civil War. Lincoln's sons once kept pet goats inside the White House. They even tended sheep on the White House lawn—"

"Ranger Nobles, we're more interested in the Jefferson Stone than the general history of the area," Winston interrupted.

"Alright," Nobles said, his mouth still open. "It's a two-foot-square pillar made from Richmond granite. It was erected in November of 1888 on orders from the Office of Public Buildings and Grounds." He hesitated. "No … I'm sorry, I have a terrible memory. It was December 1889, maybe." He rubbed his forehead groping for details. "I bought all those vitamins pills that are supposed to help with memory, but I keep forgetting to take the little rascals," he chuckled. "This marker was installed by the Army Corps of Engineers. It was erected on the site of the original sandstone marker known as the Jefferson Stone, or Jefferson Pier—"

"Paper memory—I find it helps to write things down," Susan interrupted.

"My world's in a wire. Who needs to remember anything when a search engine can do it for you? The Akashic Records of the Internet 'memex' is our auxiliary brain," Winston joked. "So this marker, you say, is not the original marker?"

"If my memory serves me, the original marker was only a wooden post that Thomas Jefferson personally erected here in 1804 during his last term in office. He placed it here to mark the location for a zero degree of longitude for the newly founded country. A few months later, he had the wooden post replaced with a stone marker. In that same year, an additional stone obelisk, known as the Meridian Stone, was erected on Meridian Hill, just north of the White House."

The three gathered around the humble granite stone protruding from the ground. A yellow-billed cuckoo bird was perched on the eastern face of the stone, bobbing up and down in a friendly regurgitating motion.

"These birds are bad luck. Don't touch 'em." Nobles waved it away and pointed toward the White House. "The Meridian Stone was the first obelisk erected in the district. It's no longer on Meridian Hill. It was lost when they converted the top of the hill into a park, designed after the formal Renaissance water parks in France and Italy. It's now called Malcolm X Park. Around 1886, the government proposed moving the White House to that site. If my memory serves me, later, the local Freemasons planned to build the Temple of the Scottish Rite on that hill. I once read that they wanted to construct a replica of Rodin's *Gates of Hell* on Meridian Hill."

"Gates of Hell?" Winston questioned, remembering a book in his library. "That's one of Dante's nine regions of his *Inferno*, which symbolized a rite of passage of the damned to Hell. I've been studying Dante's cosmology. Dante's ideas are presented in his esoteric masterpiece, *La Divina Commedia*, where in the seventh gulf, a phoenix is used as a symbol of the souls of the damned."

"Me, too. I've studied cultural cosmologies for years," Nobles said. "It almost feels like a job. You're right. Dante is the man responsible for the Christian cosmological view of heaven and hell. What you're saying is interesting. In 1922, a statue of Dante Alighieri was placed in Meridian Hill Park. In that same year, a statue of Joan of Arc, the French heroine who spoke to the spirits of Saint Catherine and Saint Margaret, was placed directly on the main cross-axis of the park, near the old meridian marker." He pointed back to the Jefferson Stone. "The axis of this city respects the spirit of the place. Following specific instructions on celestial observations predetermined by President Jefferson, government surveyors formed an imaginary line between the Jefferson Stone and the Meridian Stone. This line passed right through the front and rear doors of the White House. The two stones served as *termini* for the demarcation of the first prime meridian of the United States."

"So there's more than one marker for the meridian?" Susan asked.

"Yes. I guess you could say there're really four markers on this meridian. It's an important line of longitude. If my memory serves me, sometime in June of 1923 the Commission of Fine Arts, in conjunction with the Shriners, erected a granite marker called the Zero Mile Stone next to the circular roadway, known as the Ellipse, south of the White House. It's near the national Christmas tree, the old Yew Tree of Immortality. You can see the Christmas tree from here. It's that pinecone-shaped Jolly Green Giant just beyond the Flaming Sword Memorial on the Ellipse." He pointed. "The Zero Mile Stone marks the location from which all U.S. highways are measured. There's a carving of the winged-helmet of Mercury on its north side, the guardian of roads. The Nation's first asphalt roads were laid down in Washington—"

"I thought the Prime Meridian was in Greenwich," Winston interrupted.

"It is. But the American meridian was established before the world settled on Greenwich as the Prime Meridian for the globe," Nobles clarified. "Back then, many countries had their own prime meridians. A prime meridian has always served as a means of organizing a society around the economic relationships of both time and distance. Congress felt that having our own prime meridian would aid in separating America from the economic control of Great Britain."

"I see," Winston acknowledged.

"If my memory serves me, Jefferson originally wanted to establish a National University at the site of the Jefferson Stone. His plan called for the building of a University Church at the middle of the Mall. The Jamestown colonists tried to do the same thing at Henricus, southeast of Richmond, the first English college in the New World. Henricus got wiped out by the Indians and later evolved into the College of William and Mary at Williamsburg. Jefferson's plans fell through when Congress declared that building such a university would be unconstitutional. With the aid of Freemason supporters such as the Capitol architects, Benjamin Latrobe and William Thornton, and the noted Virginians, Joseph Cabell and General Cocke of Bremo— Jefferson's plan evolved into his academic village and architectural masterpiece, the University of Virginia. It was built near Monticello, Jefferson's treasure house."

"Freemasons," Susan repeated.

"These men were part of Jefferson's private club," Nobles replied.

"Edgar Allan Poe attended that university," Winston remarked. "I remember reading 'The Cask of Amontillado' and 'The Gold Bug' when I was in the sixth grade. It got me interested in cryptography."

"I read 'The Gold Bug,' too," Nobles remembered. "It's about the search for a lost treasure. Let me see your map." He reached for the map in Winston's hand. "We're right here due south of this star shape over the White House—at the center of this eight fold path of roadways shaped like a two million-year-old spear point, man's first weapon." He patted the Park Service logo on his shirtsleeve, then pointed back to the map. "The early maps for the city designated this site as a memorial to George Washington. According to L'Enfant, the reported designer of the city, the founders originally wanted to build a pyramid at this location, something possibly as enormous as the Great Pyramid outside Cairo. Can you even begin to imagine such a thing in the middle of this city?" Nobles sideways-eyed the Monument. "In 1833, the Washington Monument Society was established from the earlier efforts of the Monument Association of 1812. They built the Monument over there, choosing an obelisk pointing to heaven instead of a pyramid. It was supposed to house Washington's crypt, but the location of the crypt was changed to the Capitol Building."

"George Washington is buried at the Capitol?" Susan questioned.

"No. His grave is at Mount Vernon, unless it was looted."

"Looted?" Susan questioned again.

"Grave robbers looted his family crypt after he was interred and stole away with Washington's head and some bones. But, legend says the grave robbers grabbed the wrong remains. No one knows for certain who is buried in Washington's tomb."

"Skull collectors," Winston murmured, arching his head upward at the tower of stones blocking out the morning blue. "It's gargantuan."

"Robert Mills is credited with its design, although Thomas Jefferson suggested the idea of an obelisk to Mills," Nobles said. "Jefferson called it the 'Lantern of Demosthenes,' the Dark Lantern, sometimes known as the 'Sword of Demosthenes.' It's said Jefferson came up with the idea in 1786, after he saw an obelisk in front of a temple at Lord Burlington's Palladian gardens at Cheswick."

"Who was Demosthenes?" Susan asked.

"He was a Greek orator who spoke with stones in his mouth to overcome a speech impediment," Nobles replied.

"Talking stones?" Winston questioned metaphorically. He angled his head up again at the marble monolith.

"A symbol for free speech, perhaps," Susan suggested.

"In a Greek legend, Demosthenes once held up a lantern in a futile attempt to find an honest man," Nobles explained. "Of course, George Washington always held a reputation as being an honest man. So Washington's association with the Lantern of Demosthenes is appropriate. It's a fitting symbol of Greek democracy. In ancient Athens, the civic heart of the city had an open-air plaza called the … ah … what was it called? It's on the tip-of-my-tongue. Ah … the Agora. It's like our National Mall. The Agora was bordered by the *Bouleutereion*, the council house of the representatives of the people; the *Metroon,* the shrine of the mother of the Gods; and a great altar to Zeus Agoraeos—the orator." Nobles pointed to the obelisk. "The monument we see here is totally different from the original design proposed by Mills. This obelisk was created by the Army Corps of Engineers. They followed a new design proposed by George P. Marsh who lived in Rome as an ambassador to Italy. He was a man of letters and is best known as America's first environmentalist. But he was also the American expert on the design of ancient Egyptian obelisks. He extensively studied the obelisks scattered throughout the city of Rome. The Army Corps of Engineers and the Washington Monument Society, headed up by the Freemason W. W. Corcoran, oversaw its completion. He was a local banker, one of

America's wealthiest citizens. The Washington Monument is made of nothing but stones, except for the nine-inch aluminum pyramid capstone at the tip. An inscription on the side of the capstone that faces the Capitol Building reads, *Laus Deo*. It's so sad that this engineering marvel has been damaged." Nobles shook his head.

"That's Latin," Susan said. "I studied Latin so I could interpret the scientific names for marine life. *Laus Deo* means Praise be to God."

"A lantern? That's a strange thing to call an obelisk." Winston eyed the gaping hole at the top of the Monument. "They cast shadows. They're gnomons."

"We at the Park Service are aware that it's a type of clock," Nobles agreed. "It took them nearly seventy years to finish building it. Construction was halted before the outbreak of the Civil War due to a lack of funds and fears that the Catholic Church was involved in its initial construction. The Civil War nearly halted the completion of the Capitol dome as well. For a while, the umbrella of Cartesian arches that formed the structural supports for the new iron dome stood incomplete. But Lincoln insisted that it be finished to cover the *eye* of the dome to keep the *light* out. The new dome stood as a symbol of the Iron Age of American industry. The Capitol Building was completely redesigned and expanded, starting around 1853, under the supervision of the Army Corps of Engineers. They finished it in 1865. It's been called one of the most ambitious architectural projects in American history. At one time, it was the grandest building in this city. Its design is attributed to architect Thomas Walter, but it's dome follows an earlier design proposed by Robert Mills. In the light of the Jefferson-Mills connection, it's possible Jefferson was responsible for the design of the new dome. Although, the dome's design probably originates from Michelangelo and St. Peter's in Rome."

"They stopped construction just before the Civil War?" Susan inquired.

"Yes. For many years after the Civil War, the Washington Monument remained an unfinished pillar of stones. It stood about as tall as the main tower of the Castle of the Smithsonian." Nobles pointed to the vine-covered, brick castle with its octagon-shaped towers and windows. "Construction ceased when an anti-Catholic, pro-American party, known as the Order of the Star-Spangled Banner, took control of the Monument. They were outraged after they learned that a certain stone, a gift from the Pope, was to be installed in the Monument. The pro-American party seized the Pope Stone and reportedly threw it into the Potomac River."

"A lot of fuss over a stone," Winston remarked.

"It was rumored that the Catholic Church had been involved in the initial design of the Monument, with engineers and artisans hired from Italy," Nobles continued to explain. "The Pope Stone was a *terminus* from the Temple of Concord, the site of the earlier Temple of *Juno Lucina Moneta*, at the base of Capitoline Hill in the Roman Forum. That temple rested atop the *arx*, the northern peak of the Capitoline Hill. Juno Lucina was the consort of Jupiter and the mother of Mars—the *Goddess of the Giver of Light*, procreation, the full moon, and the sacred marriage. It's said she tried to kill the infant Hercules with some snakes, but she only drove him insane."

"A Goddess of Light?" Susan questioned. "The full moon ... snakes?"

"Yes, in the second-century B.C., the Lucina was associated with the Latin word *Lux*. It is said that when a child was born, it was 'brought to Light,' coming into the world from the dark cave of its mother's womb—becoming enlightened."

"Plato's cave," Susan blurted. She laid her hand over her belly and stared up at the Monument. *Juno ... Pregnant Madonnas.*

Winston gave Susan a quick glance. *She'd make a great mother.*

"A lot has changed in America." Nobles shook his head. "In 1982, just before relations between the United States and the Holy See mended, a new Pope Stone was installed in the Monument. Its inscription reads, *A ROMA AMERICA.* It's one of the 193 memorial stones inside the Monument, many of which are Masonic. You know, one of the popes even held a Mass on the Mall in 1995. Another had a birthday party at the White House. The new Pope Stone was installed on the upper level, so it could be lying in that pile of rubble." He pointed to the debris littering the field.

"It looks like it's as tall as Devil's Tower from here," Winston said, looking up again at the obelisk. He felt *its presence.* "It reminds me of a Tarot card. I wonder why they built it so tall?"

"It's the second tallest memorial column in the United States, Mr. Winston."

"What's the tallest?" Susan asked.

"It's the San Jacinto Monument in La Porte, Texas," Nobles replied. "Although the tallest memorial in America is the Jefferson Gateway Arch in St. Louis."

"Yeah, everything's bigger in Texas," Winston wisecracked.

"There are two other obelisks associated with the Park Service. There is one in Jamestown and another at Bunker Hill," Nobles added. "There are obelisks scattered all over the globe. There is one in New York. One in Istanbul. One in Buenos Aires. There are two in London. The largest obelisks of the ancient world are located in Axum, Ethiopia."

"So the Jefferson Stone marks the original site for the Washington Monument?" Susan prompted.

"Oh, no. That's a myth recorded in a lot of history books." Nobles pointed to the location of the Jefferson Stone on the map. "Robert Mills used the Jefferson Stone as a surveying benchmark. Even the Washington Monument is referenced from this stone. The Washington Monument was intended for that exact spot over there, as a centerpiece for the public eye. Its cornerstone was laid in 1848." He pointed again to the Monument. "It's the single piece of architecture that dominates everything in Washington. Notice how the Capitol, the tallest building on the Mall, and the Smithsonian museums cradle our Beacon of Light. By law, no structure surrounding the Mall can be taller than the Capitol Building and the Washington Monument."

Nobles tracked his head past the broken circle of flags waving at half-mast then up at the Monument. He lapsed into a momentary silence, spotting a flock of geese migrating north in a V-shaped wedge formation. "Look at those geese. They always know where to go. They don't need a compass. They follow the stars. They're flying north and flying high. The signs are favorable. You know, the Romans once practiced arithmomancy. They believed the flight patterns of certain birds predicted the future. Can you imagine such a thing? Relying on the birds to determine one's destiny. They say some Chinese scientists can control the fight of pigeons with micro brain implants. They're goin' to do that to humans someday." With a brief shake of his head, he returned to the subject. "The whole Mall, our garden of knowledge of good and evil, embraces this monument. The creative endeavors of man surround it. The birds …," he said, still gazing at the geese. "Much of the Smithsonian along the Mall is the legacy of the secretary of the Smithsonian, the naturalist Dillon Ripley. He was known as the great *birdman*—a noted ornithologist. Ripley referred to the museums on the Mall as the sacred grove, our country's Agora … the *hortus in urbe.*"

"The garden in the city," Susan translated.

"The idea for a National Mall goes back to 1851 to the landscape gardener, Andrew Jackson Downing, He modeled it after the first public park in America at Hartford, Connecticut. He believed the Mall should serve as a public symbol for Democracy—the new savior of humanity," Nobles chuckled, "and just like the temples of Greece, the Mall during the Civil War was surrounded by brothels."

"My mother studied Ripley's works," Winston remembered aloud. "He was a spymaster with the OSS." Winston eyed a strange object circling in the sky. "What the *hell* is that?" He pointed. "Was that a big bird that just flew over?"

"That's a military Unmanned Aerial Vehicle, a UAV Dragon Eye with a computerized image guidance system. It's maintaining constant surveillance over the crash site and the heart of the Mall. They have increased Homeland Security to new levels since the crash."

"Computer guidance, I've read about those aircraft," Winston remarked. "Homeland Security always sounds German. I thought we won World War II."

"So the Jefferson Stone marks the center of the District of Columbia?" Susan queried, jotting something down in a pocket-size notepad.

"It was thought to be at one time. Look at the inscription." Nobles pointed to the weathered letters on the north face of the marker.

Position of Meridian Post erected April 10, 1793
and
Position of the Jefferson Stone pier erected
December 18, 1804
Recovered and Re-erected, Dec, 1, 1889
XXXXXXXX
District of Columbia

"See. The next to the last line was hastily chiseled away," Nobles awkwardly knelt down and traced his fingers over the bumpy X-shaped gouges in the stone. "If my memory serves me, that line of the inscription once read, 'Being the center point of the District of Columbia.' It never was the center for the District. The midpoint of the District is in the atrium of the Pan-American Union Building, over there." Nobles lumbered up and pointed toward a neoclassical building about four hundred yards away. He then pointed to the location of the Pan-American Building on the map in Winston's hand. "It houses the Organization of American States, one of the world's oldest regional organizations. At the middle of the building's atrium, next to the birdbath, is a statue of the Aztec god, Xochipilli. It's a crossed-legged statue, an Aztec version of a Buddha. Xochipilli, also called the Lord of the Soul, or the Lord of Consciousness, was a guide in Aztec religious rites involving a vision quest. In the District of Columbia, that crossed-legged statue is the X that marks the spot for the center of the District," Nobles chortled.

"You would think the Jefferson Stone would be the center," Susan said.

"True," Nobles agreed. "But, the Jefferson Stone was laid only to locate a prime meridian for the country. The meridian that runs through the White House is a point of reference around which the rest of the nation's geographic boundaries were measured. Washington, like ancient Thebes along the Nile, was intentionally located between the northern and southern states. Many of the first state boundaries and the later gridwork that tamed the land west of the Appalachians were referenced from this stone. It was the country's primary surveying benchmark—"

"In fact, it still is," a voice sang from behind them. "I'm Cecil Howard from the Maryland Department of Surveying. I'm the GPS expert you requested. I take it you're with the NSA?" Howard greeted, unaware he had startled them.

"Oh, hello … Yes, I'm Susan Hamilton and this is my colleague, James Winston." Susan pointed at Ranger Nobles, her eyes fixed on Howard. "And, this is Ranger Nobles. He's with the Park Service." She pointed at Winston, her eyes still locked on Howard.

"Hello, I'm James Winston," Winston introduced himself. His eyes darted at Susan then back to Howard, who was wearing a T-shirt with a Wizards logo of an eclipsing sun and moon and an eagle holding a ball outlined with longitudes. *American Idol … 'Let Me Be Your Teddy Bear' … This guy looks like the ghost of Elvis … slicked-back ducktail haircut … with long sideburns…. Kissin' cousins, he's a mirror image.*

Howard shook hands with Susan, then with Nobles and Winston.

"Yes, you're right," Nobles noted as he greeted Howard. "They still use the Jefferson Stone. They take GPS measurements off of it every six months or so."

"I see you're a Wizards fan. I follow the Mystics. Whaddya know about the Jefferson Stone?" Winston asked Howard.

"I overheard part of your conversation. The sound travels far when the tourists are not around," Howard replied, his upper lip curling to one side as he spoke. "This stone harbors a few of Jefferson's secrets. He was a man who never stopped. In his spare time, he was constantly inventing things that might serve the public. You know, he even reinvented the plow that feeds the world. Jefferson once said whether he retired to bed early or late, he always rose with the sun and the songs of the birds."

Songs of the birds, Winston mused. *Billy's bird language.*

"Jefferson worked closely with the city's first architects," Howard pointed out. "He influenced the initial design of the Capitol Building, trying to make it an *enlightened* space that was both symbolic and utilitarian. For example, Jefferson oversaw the design of the glass lantern that covers the *oculus* of the old Hall of Representatives to the right of the dome. You can see the lantern from here." Howard pointed toward the Capitol. "It's now called Statuary Hall, filled with statues of demigods. Jefferson started the first national church services in the House Hall which continued until after the Civil War. Every denomination was allowed to preach in that Hall—Baptists, Swedenborgs, Unitarians, and Catholics. The Speaker's podium was used as the preachers' pulpit."

"That's right," Nobles agreed. "*Vox populi*—the voice of the people."

"From my personal research, the whole city of Washington was part of Jefferson's vision to build a fourth Rome in the New World, after he returned from France with a secret sorbetiere machine," Howard asserted. "Washington, like Rome, is located between seven hills on a fork in the river. Jefferson gave birth to the thing from the very beginning. It's carved on Mount Rushmore. The face behind Washington is Jefferson. With the aid of his Italian friend, Filippo Mazzei, Jefferson retained skilled

Italian masons and sculptors to work on the Capitol Building. Jefferson was even responsible for naming this city the Capital, after the Capitolium—one of the seven holy hills in Rome."

"Seven holy hills," Susan repeated.

"Yes, ma'am. Lt. Montgomery Meigs of the Army Corps of Engineers, who oversaw the construction of the Washington aqueduct and the Capitol during the Civil War, shared the same vision. After the war, Meigs thought that Washington should be the capital of a new Holy Roman Empire. Ah ... the Civil War, Civil Rights. What is it with the American psyche? If we're not fighting another country, we're fighting among ourselves. It seems that our mentality is rooted in the American spirit of revolution, an internal terrorism that's become a celebrated part of our lives."

"The fast pace. Too much anger, maybe?" Winston remarked beneath his breath. "My friend, Billy, would say we all need just three minutes of silence."

"Italian masons built the Capitol Building—a fourth Rome?" Susan questioned.

"Jefferson admired the Italians and their architecture," Howard replied. "His friend, Mazzei, was a freethinker and a political activist in Europe. He influenced many of Jefferson's liberal views used in the wording of the Declaration of Independence. He was greatly influenced by Pico Dell Mirandol's *Oration on the Dignity of Man.* Some scholars call Mazzei the Godfather of the Declaration of Independence. It was Mazzei who originally came up with the idea that, 'all men are by nature equally free and independent, a quality essential to the formation of a liberal government.' Mazzei even founded the Constitutional Society that promoted a constitutional republic for the United States. He's been called the 'Gardener' of the American form of government. The Federalists accused Jefferson of being an infidel and a promoter of political despotism because of his association with radical freethinkers such as Mazzei, Thomas Paine, and Joel Barlow."

"Infidels and freethinkers, sounds like the Backdoor Group," Susan lowered her voice to Winston.

"Yeah, and we're standing at the crossroads of a government of despotism," Winston muttered back.

"The loggerheads, Jefferson and Hamilton, were always arguing over what direction the country should take," Howard characterized. "The Founding Fathers wanted to build the world anew. Hamilton and his Essex Junto followers, who supported a National Bank funded by foreign investors, saw America as a new imperial power. Jefferson envisioned America's vast, unexplored wilderness as an Arcadia of freedom. It was the start of a division in American politics that continues to this day. The Federalist versus the Anti-Federalists evolved into our Janus-faced two party system, the liberals versus the conservatives. Who knows what we'll call them a hundred years from now."

Winston looked at Susan. "Loggerheads we are."

She nodded with a tight Baekje-lipped smile.

Howard registered an uncertain look.

"I see you know your history," Nobles remarked.

"I try to. Thank you very much," Howard replied. "I have a minor in American history. But it's useless. It doesn't pay the bills."

"You know your history," Winston agreed. "But, what about the Jefferson Stone?"

Howard brushed away bird droppings from atop the granite marker and took a seat. "Don't … the bird flu," Nobles said.

"Jefferson always had a spectacular eye for real estate, having purchased the Louisiana Territory." Howard glanced at Nobles. "But I could never figure out why he placed the Capital in the middle of a God-forsaken swamp—like a *tabernacle* in the wilderness. Even today, the buildings of the Federal Triangle Complex depend on sump pumps to regulate the underground water so they won't collapse. It's built over the old sewage canal that once ran to the Captiol, like a channeled *yoni* leading to a *lingam*. So, I researched the history of Washington when I was in graduate school and discovered that Thomas Jefferson's father, Peter Jefferson, was one of Virginia's leading surveyors. In fact, Jefferson's whole family lineage was connected to various colonial surveyors and geomancers who laid down the roads leading to many of the courthouses and churchyards throughout Virginia and Maryland. It was considered a prestigious job in that era. George Washington grew up with the same type of family background. Nearly everyone in Washington's family tree was educated in the *art* of surveying. They were people who knew how to measure their place in the world."

"My great-great-grandfather was a surveyor," Winston commented.

"Geomancers," Susan mumbled while jotting down a note.

Howard fixed his eyes through a gap in the trees and focused on the Jefferson Memorial. "In 1751, Peter Jefferson, along with the surveyor Joshua Fry, who had grown up in Somersetshire, not far from Glastonbury in England, created the first accurate map of Virginia, known as the *Fry-Jefferson Map*. On that map, they set up new longitudes for Virginia that were referenced from a point of latitude at Currituck Inlet. Earlier in 1728, William Byrd, who was a patron of Thomas Jefferson's maternal grandfather, Isham Randolph, led a surveying party that established the boundary line between Virginia and the Carolinas which ran west of Currituck Inlet. Isham was one of the seven children of William and Mary Randolph, who have been called the Adam and Eve of Virginia. Byrd had been schooled in surveying and mathematics under the supervision of Charles Boyle, the Earl of Orrery."

"Adam and Eve—" Susan questioned.

"Orrery," Winston interrupted. "That's an astronomical device."

"It's part of the religious mind-set they had back then," Howard answered Susan. "Yeah, the orrery was the first mechanical model of the solar system that demonstrated the motion of the planets around the Sun. It was created by Boyle's clockmaker, George Graham. Graham made all kinds of devices for defining the true shape of the Earth and determining its true axis. He even made an instrument used by the astronomer James Bradley in the discovery of the aberration of light, which proved that the Earth was in motion and not the center of the universe."

"Aberration of light," Winston noted. "My Huygens-Grimaldi experiment."

"Byrd kept a diary on his survey written in an odd cipher of pseudonyms, in which the surveyors were identified by astronomical names such as Bootes, Orion, and Astrolabe," Howard revealed. "One landowner was referred to as Solomon's housewife. Byrd wrote two reports on the survey, *The History of the Dividing Line Betwixt Virginia and North Carolina*, and *The Secret History of the Line Betwixt Virginia and North Carolina*. Byrd called their survey a 'Journey to the Land of Eden.' He met with his surveyors at a parish church near the Brandon Plantation in

Virginia. They then traveled to Currituck Inlet to start the new boundary line. One of the surveyors was William Mayo. He was well known in England for his surveys of Barbados and maps of the Caribbean. He and Byrd later founded Richmond and Petersburg. Mayo became the leading surveyor for colonial Virginia. In 1737, he surveyed the upper Potomac. Peter Jefferson was a neighbor and friend of Mayo. Many believe it was Mayo who taught Peter Jefferson the skills of surveying."

"I didn't know all that," Nobles remarked.

"There's even more," Howard added. "The zero meridian used by Peter Jefferson for his new map for Virginia passed through Currituck Inlet. That meridian had earlier been measured by the English mathematician, Thomas Harriot. Harriot wrote about it in his *Briefe and true report of the new found land of Virginia*, a report on Walter Raleigh's 1585 expedition to Virginia. Thomas Jefferson owned a copy of this report. It's more than possible that Peter Jefferson and Mayo knew about Harriot's work as well. The zero meridian on the *Fry-Jefferson Map* runs directly over the large astrobleme of the Cape Charles meteor crater discovered in 1993 in the Chesapeake Bay. It continues north to where the Susquehanna River empties into the Chesapeake Bay near Havre de Grace, Maryland. The first meridian east of that zero meridian on the *Fry-Jefferson Map* ran through the middle of William Penn's Philadelphia. The first meridian west is the same meridian that Thomas Jefferson used to *reference* the location of this stone I'm sitting on. That meridian was seventy-seven degrees west of London on Peter Jefferson's map. The seventy-seventh degree meridian became important to navigation at sea and global commerce."

"How's that?" Winston asked.

"That meridian crosses Jamaica, passing west of Flamstead, Port Royal's Naval Lookout. Old Port Royal was a notorious haven for sea pirates. It was once governed by Admiral Edward Vernon. In 1762, the British established a meridian at the Naval Lookout from which the British clockmakers, John Robison and John Harrison, successfully fixed their nautical watches to determine an accurate longitude at sea. The global longitude system we have today is the outcome of that test. The *whole world* was mapped out from that meridian."

"Port Royal ... There's a type of logic known as *Logique Port-Royal*, from a seventeenth-century French textbook on logic," Winston remarked. "It's studied by computer programmers for creating language for artificial intelligence."

"Admiral Vernon," Nobles noted, "that's the man Mount Vernon is named after. Mount Vernon originally was owned by George Washington's brother, Lawrence, who married into the powerful family of Lord Fairfax. Lawrence served under Admiral Vernon as a captain aboard Vernon's flagship in the West Indies. After Lawrence died, George Washington inherited the estate."

"Yeah," Howard agreed. "But perhaps the most interesting thing on the *Fry-Jefferson* map is hidden in plain sight."

"So what is it?" Winston asked.

"It's a compass rose," Howard replied.

"A compass rose?" Susan questioned.

"Yeah. The compass rose printed on Peter Jefferson's map marks a fifteen minute zone of latitude that runs due west directly over the future location of the Mall and the heart of Washington, D.C. The compass rose marked the thirty-ninth parallel, an important line of latitude for navigation at sea."

"Why is that?" Susan asked.

"The pointer stars of the polar star group which point to Polaris, the North Star, never set below the horizon and are always visible starting at this latitude. This compass rose may have served as a point of future reference. Later in 1786, Jefferson published his famous *Notes on the State of Virginia* which included a map similar to his father's, only this map denoted both a longitude and latitude passing through present-day Washington. I believe the location of this city and the country's first prime meridian at

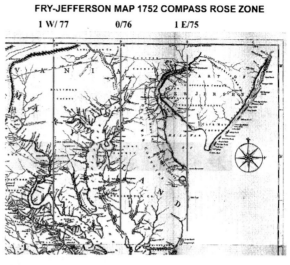

FRY-JEFFERSON MAP 1752 COMPASS ROSE ZONE

1 W/ 77   0/76   1 E/75

this spot were a form of homage by Jefferson to his father."

Father worship, Winston analyzed with a quick thought. *Father Time.* He glanced up again at the Washington Monument, then returned his attention to Howard. *Yeah, the wiser and older Elvis from the* Change of Habit. "So, are you saying that the location for this city was established before they started the American Revolution?"

"No, Mr. Winston," Howard countered. "I'm not suggesting any such thing. But the evidence presented on the *Fry-Jefferson Map of Virginia* does. And there're some other maps that lead to a similar conclusion."

"Other maps?" Winston questioned.

"Yes, for example, the L'Enfant and Jefferson-Ellicott maps of 1792 denote a zero degree longitude for Washington, suggesting that the city, from its conception, was intended to be located on a global prime meridian. On the L'Enfant map, Jefferson proposed a Roman itinerary Jupiter column be erected at the public square, now known as Lincoln Park, due east of the Capitol. The column was to serve as the first zero milestone for the country. Its proposed site was just shy of the current seventy-seventh degree meridian. They even hired a black freeman, Benjamin Banneker, to record the corresponding solar and lunar positions used in the initial survey—"

"That's right," Nobles interrupted. "A lot of history books claim that L'Enfant was fired by Jefferson for refusing to release his drawings to President Washington and that Banneker reproduced the plans from memory for Major Ellicott. But, L'Enfant's plans were looted from his home the night before he was fired," Nobles chuckled, "probably on orders from Jefferson, who knew the design already. Jefferson had already proposed a square shape for the district which followed the grid plan of Philadephia, the old *Nine Square* plan of New Haven, and the *Bloomsbury Square*— the 1695 Nicholson Plan for Annapolis. Ellicot laid down the borders before L'Enfant was ever hired. It takes a frame to make a thing whole. It ended with the frame. Banneker only aided in the survey of the district's forty boundary stones. But, he was skilled in astronomy. His father was a Dogon royal-priest from Ethiopia."

"Ethiopia," Susan repeated, "that's where you said they have the largest obelisks."

"Banneker may have been exposed to Dogon cosmology which follows the stars and claims that humanity was created from the belly of *Nommo,* a fish-man who descended from the heavens," Nobles said. "Their cosmology was a type of father worship. According to their cosmic-myth, *Lebe,* the oldest ancestor who represented speech and language, died and was buried in the earth. He was swallowed by *Nommo,* the master over speech. *Nommo* vomited up *Lebe* as a river serpent that carved out the topography of the land forming the Dogon cosmological world—their Garden of Paradise—overseen by certain Dogon rituals designed to invoke the spirits and bring proper balance into the world."

"Solar and lunar calculations ..." Susan jotted in her notepad. "A fish-man descending from the heavens ... Jesus." She shook her head.

"Balance into the world ... like Brahma awakening Vishnu to fight a demon. Dogon cosmology sounds similar to the Lakota's," Winston said. "And those maps, Mr. Howard?"

"Well, there is the earlier 1737 survey of the northern neck of Virginia by Lord Fairfax, and his young protégé, George Washington," Howard noted. "William Mayo directed that survey with Peter Jefferson's assistance. The map created from their survey is devoid of any lines of longitude, but lines of latitude are presented. The compass rose printed on that map denotes a fifteen minute zone aligned east-west with the latitude of Washington, D.C., as though someone knew in 1737 that this latitude would serve as a point of future reference. And then there is the 1606 map produced by Captain John Smith for the first Virginia Colony. It shows the location of present-day Washington squarely at the middle of the map, with an old Indian community known as Nactchtanch at that spot. It's as if the area around Washington was predetermined to serve as the future heart of the Virginia colony. Later, Virginia was divided and lands were appropriated to Lord Baltimore for his Catholic colony. The dividing line ran right down the middle of Virginia and subsequently through the middle of the future location of Washington."

"Are you implying that someone in England had plans for the site?"

"The maps seem to indicate preplanning, Mr. Winston," Howard stressed.

"So every state has its boundary referenced from this stone?" Susan questioned.

"Not exactly," Howard clarified. "In 1842, Congress ratified a bill that relocated the zero meridian so it would pass through the Capitol Building. This meridian was established around astronomical measurements taken at the newly-built observatory at Georgetown University, which is interesting, since the location of the Capitol on Jenkins Hill was originally the proposed site for Georgetown University. Early topographic maps suggest Jenkins Hill was an artificial mound. I read a report in the Library of Congress which stated it was the site of an American Indian temple. In fact, according to archeological studies, the area of Washington as far north as Rock Creek Park was the site of a well-organized Native American community."

"I read the same thing," Nobles said. "The Indians settled around Jenkins Hill because of its abundant water supply. Throughout history, settlements have always prospered along a fork in a river. George Washington scouted the area for natural springs before choosing that hill for the Capitol. I heard you can't dig a hole three feet in the ground around the Capitol Building without striking water."

"That's not the original site for the Capitol?" Susan challenged.

"Yes, it is," Howard said. "But before it was chosen, John Carroll, an American Jesuit bishop, had decided to build a college on that hill. His family owned much of the land in that area. The original patent for the hill in 1671 was for Maryland's Governor Thomas Notley's Cerne Abbey Manor. George Washington, who had been formally educated by the Jesuits in America, convinced John Carroll to change his mind. Some say the Capitol Building might have been built in Alexandria on Shuter's Hill, or maybe some other virgin site, if Carroll had not agreed to the change."

"Who were the Carrolls?" Susan asked Howard.

"They were a prominent Catholic family in the area. The Carroll's were related to the Calverts of Maryland. John Carroll studied at the English Jesuit college at St. Omer where he was groomed to become a priest. Many English and colonial Catholics were educated at that college. John Carroll became the first Catholic Bishop of Baltimore and the founder of Georgetown University."

"And the new meridian, Mr. Howard?" Winston asked.

"Later, Congress built an observatory due north of the Capitol Building on North Capitol Street. The new meridian was referenced from that observatory. A sandstone obelisk, called the Gillis Obelisk, was set up to mark the new meridian. Congress maintained this meridian for astronomical and geographical purposes. They adopted the British meridian for nautical purposes. Most of the western states were measured from this new meridian until around 1850. After that date, the meridian was moved again to the newly-built Naval Observatory on a hill in the area known as Foggy Bottom. It was located near Braddock's Rock at Easby's Point, a bedrock ledge, also known as the Key of All Keys. The new observatory was headed by Simon Newcomb, the first astronomer to confirm the measurement of the speed of light. He performed his tests between mirrors stationed at the base of the Washington Monument and the Signal Corps School at Fort Myer on the other side of the Potomac."

"Speed of light … Oh, Billy." Winston remembered, "Yeah, my mother mentioned that experiment once."

"The first international sea charts were also created at that observatory," Howard said." The charts were overseen by Matthew Maury, nicknamed the 'Pathfinder of the Seas.' Maury once stated that the oceans were 'a part of that exquisite machinery by which the harmonies of nature are preserved,' and offer 'evidences of design.' His grandfather, Reverend James Maury, was Thomas Jefferson's tutor in the classics."

"I've heard of Matthew Maury," Susan said. "He formulated the plan for laying the Transatlantic Cable along the Atlantic Ocean's Telegraphic Plateau."

"That cable is the backbone for global communications," Winston noted.

"Maury compiled the first textbook on oceanography, life from water," Susan remembered. "But, Key of All Keys?"

"Braddock's Rock was inscribed with an early surveying benchmark, the Key of All Keys, around which all of the plots of land of the first colonial estates in this area were measured," Howard replied. "It was named after General Braddock of the French and Indian War who camped his troops near that rock. Legend has it that a young Lt. Col. George Washington sat on that rock and dreamed up the future plan for the Capital. Braddock's Rock was later quarried and its stones used in the foundations for the Capitol Building and the White House. The quarry was filled in when the

Army Corps of Engineers modified the shoreline of the Potomac in the late nineteenth century. Sometimes we still have to confirm the old boundary lines to this benchmark. The remains of the rock can still be seen at the bottom of a brick-lined well located near the old Naval Hospital."

Howard stepped up to Winston and pointed to the map. "The old Naval Observatory is located here. You could say that many of the delineations in the United States, including county boundaries, state boundaries, and even personal property boundaries, were referenced from these three meridians that ran either through the White House, the Capitol Building, or the old Naval Observatory. These three lines of longitude set the bounds for all geographical and astronomical measurements in the United States. The country was literally built around these three lines of longitude."

"But what about Greenwich?" Winston pressed.

"If my memory serves me, in 1882, Congress passed a joint resolution authorizing the president to call an international conference to determine a prime meridian for reckoning longitude and regulating time throughout the world," Nobles interjected. "Two years later, forty-one delegates from twenty-five countries met at a conference held here in Washington."

"Since the 1300's, the Madeira Islands had served as the zero meridian for navigation," Howard added, "with many countries having separate national meridians. This created mismatches in the time zones marked on local maps used for trade and commerce. So, it was decided to adopt a single zero meridian to replace the numerous ones already in existence. Various sites were considered, such as the Great Pyramid, Jerusalem, Rome, Philadelphia, Copenhagen, Paris, Pisa, and Madrid. But since most countries were already using the Principal Transit Instrument at the Greenwich Observatory outside of London for nautical purposes, it was decided that the Greenwich Meridian should become the Prime Meridian. The Greenwich Observatory was built mainly for lunar observations, using the stars as background markers for lunar positions in order to create lunar tables for marine navigation."

"Pisa ... Why would someone choose Pisa?" Susan asked.

Howard continued without an answer. "In addition, all of the countries adopted a universal day. The universal day is a Mean Solar Day, measured at midnight at Greenwich. Greenwich Mean Time is counted on a twenty-four hour clock. A true Solar Day varies in length depending on where you are located on the planet."

Susan shook her head. *What does that have do with Pisa?*

"Of course the Greenwich Meridian follows closely to an ancient meridian created by the Romans," Howard remembered. "The Roman meridian was aligned to a Roman obelisk at Laystone a little north of London. The Romans adopted London as their main camp in the British Isles. London was originally a community created by the ancient Brits. It was called *Tri-Novantes* or New Troy."

"Laystone?" Nobles questioned. "Back in the mid-1600's, the grounds for the White House were part of an estate called Lay Stone. I believe it was adjacent to the estates of Jamaica and Port Royal. And there was another estate called New Troy over where the Capitol Building stands, created about the same time. The Lay Stone estate was owned by John Lewger. He oversaw the first Catholic colonization of Maryland for Lord Cecil Calvert, who created the 'Act of Toleration,' a law concerning religious freedom in the Maryland colony. And in relation to Rome, George Washington's great-great grandfather, Francis Pope, owned a tract of land just north of New Troy which was called Rome. They used to jokingly call him the Pope of Rome because he envisioned a city for this area modeled after Rome."

"Interesting, I didn't know that," Howard remarked.

Jamaica and Port Royal, a pirate's den, Winston thought. *Skull and Bones ... the Sodom and Gomorrah of the New World ... New Troy ... a Trojan horse ... the virus, Lay Stone, a Roman obelisk ... a fourth Rome at the center of Virginia and Maryland ... Virgin Mary.* He sliced another glance at the Washington Monument. *A Catholic law concerning religious freedom ...* His eyes darted to the Jefferson Stone. *Jefferson.*

Howard pointed in a northwest direction to the current Naval Observatory. "In 1893, the Observatory was moved to the present location on Massachusetts Avenue and the meridian used for astronomical purposes moved with it—"

Nobles interrupted, "I believe it was in 1927, maybe ... a tablet was installed with a cross-line to indicate the location of the new meridian. That meridian passes through the Vice President's Residence on the Naval Observatory grounds."

Howard nodded in agreement. "The line continues north over the grounds of the Episcopal National Cathedral and south over the old Holy Trinity Parish at the Jesuit Covenant of the Visitation."

"That's the oldest Catholic church in the District," Nobles added. "It was founded in the late 1700s, right after they started laying out the city plan for Washington."

"I know," Winston said. "That's where I attended elementary school."

"The meridian then passes over Arlington Cemetery," Howard pinpointed, "near the Eternal Flame, and on toward the George Washington Masonic Memorial in Alexandria on top of Shuter's Hill."

"The meridian seems to pay homage to a lot of religious institutions," Susan noted.

"Or perhaps these institutions are paying homage to the new meridian," Winston remarked, remembering the pin on Sister Rosalyn's habit.

"Shuter's Hill," Nobles recalled. "That's where Benjamin Dulany, the best friend of George Washington, built his home. It was Dulany who convinced Washington to become a Freemason. The Freemasons built a shrine to Washington on that hill in 1922, I think. It's modeled after Pharos, the ancient Lighthouse of Alexandria, one of the Seven Wonders of the World. I've visited the memorial. The Masons have an impressive library in that building. It's like a museum. They have a stone on display from the battlefield near the Milvian Bridge north of Rome, where Emperor Constantine first saw a vision of light. It was a key event in world history. It's where he reunited the Roman Empire and started the Roman Catholic Church. They even have a replica of the Ark of the Covenant on the top floor."

"Ark of the Covenant?" Susan questioned. "A lighthouse ... a vision of light—"

"But why is the Jefferson Stone noted as a GPS marker on this map?" Winston refocused on why they were there.

Howard looked down at the marker. "Every time we do a major survey in Maryland, the old maps eventually reference the Jefferson Stone. The first triangulation of the District in 1880 referenced the Jefferson Stone. It was carried out under the direction of Superintendent Charles Pierce and Subassistant C. H. Sinclair for the U.S. Coast Geodetic Survey. Pierce was a famous American philosopher and mathematician. He was a follower of German idealism and believed the world was composed of signs that acted as a mental guide for understanding the evolution of nature's laws in a true reality."

"Signs …," Susan said to Winston, "like keywords around the *locus.*"

"I've heard of Pierce," Winston remarked. "He formulated the logical Formal Concept Analysis for OODA—observe, orient, decide, and act—used in computer artificial intelligence routines."

"They triangulated the Statue of Freedom atop the Capitol to the Jefferson Stone as a key Datum." Howard tramped around the marker as he explained, "You see, every time the meridian was moved, this stone was still used as a benchmark. The stationary GPS satellites, the global birds that orbit the Earth, keep track of certain *key* Datum locations on the ground as a reference because their orbits change slightly in relation to the natural wobble of the planet. Some GPS course corrections are made from the location of this stone, as well the Meades Ranch marker in Kansas. I've set up a Java GPS on top of the Jefferson Stone many times to determine new course corrections. But, I doubt I could do a reading today with the recent solar flare activity."

"I read about the sunspots in the newspaper," Nobles commented.

"The GPS satellites reference the Greenwich Meridian in time and space by way of spherical triangulation to the current Naval Observatory's Atomic Master Clock," Howard continued. "The location of the Naval Observatory's atomic clock is benchmarked by GPS satellites to the Jefferson Stone. Everything is lined up by way of the global birds. And the global birds have an eye on this stone. Of course, a lot will change when they start using PARCS."

"What is PARCS?" Susan asked.

"It's the atomic clock they have planned for the International Space Station." Howard sat cross-armed on top of the Jefferson Stone. "The meridian that runs through the White House has left its mark on history. World Wars have been planned on top of this meridian. Peace treaties, such as the one signed in 1979 between Israel and Egypt over the Sinai, have been established on it. By way of this meridian, the whole world and every aspect of society are synchronized to this single spot." He smiled proudly. "The world stops here. This granite marker is the *omphalos* for the whole planet. It's the center for everything. It's the *unmovable mover.*"

"You have certainly offered a new level of importance to what otherwise looks like a meaningless granite marker," Susan said. "Any more questions, James?"

"No." Winston's eyes blinked as he cleared his mind.

"Thank you for coming here so early in the morning," Susan stated. "I think you have fully answered our questions."

"Yes—thank you, thank you very much." Winston shook Howard's hand.

"Don't … the bird flu." Nobles stepped away.

"I hope I haven't bored you," Howard said with an entertaining smile. "'Til we meet again, may God bless you. *Adios.*"

Susan accompanied Howard and Nobles away from the Jefferson Stone, leaving Winston alone beside the granite pillar.

Winston lingered a moment. He watched Susan still taking notes as she walked between the two experts. *He even walks like Elvis,* Winston mused.

"Coo, coo, what's going on? Who? Who-who-whoo? To the left, to the left."

Winston turned his attention to the Jefferson Stone. He noticed three silver-burgundy pigeons craning their necks and prancing around the marker as though doodlebugging a minuet. The birds bobbed their heads and cooed, waiting for the sun to rise into position so they could set their bearings and take flight. One pigeon flapped its wings excitedly, pecked at the dirt, and pulled a grub worm from the ground. It snapped its beak and quickly swallowed the fat morsel.

You little guys are alive and kickin'. Winston eyed the bird track petrosomatoglyphs in the sand, resembling an Oriental script following a crooked-zigzag Fibonacci spiral. *Japanese? No ... Chinese or Sanskrit,* he compared. *The Jefferson Stone is at the middle of a virtual notepad for the language of the birds. Satellites tracking the center for the world. I'm getting a little festered. I need to fix my bearings and try to understand what all of this means.*

"To the left, to the left, to the left."

Circumnavigating the locus, Winston checked out the nearby Washington real estate. To the east, the base of the damaged, marble-clad Pillar of Society obscured his view of the horizon. The morning sky glowed red, yellow, and orange. He eyed the dome of the Capitol, barely visible, looming around one side of the Monument in a warped illusion through swirls of steam rising up from the cast-iron gutters in the nearby streets. He heard the faint *rumble* of a subway train, like a furtive dragon stirring under the ground.

Hypnotic, he felt.

"To the left, to the left, to the left."

Facing south, he could see the domed Jefferson Memorial standing in the distance like the Roman Pantheon. He remembered the noble words from a speech by Franklin Roosevelt. "*Jefferson, the humanist, believed as we believe—in man. He believed as we believe that men are capable of their own government. And that no kings, no tyrants, no dictator can govern for them as well as they can govern for themselves.*"

Could Jefferson have imagined all this, way back then? Winston wondered.

"To the left, to the left, to the left."

He sighted west toward the World War II Memorial. *A plaza bounded by a temple of government on one side and a cemetery on the other.* Winston fixed his position. He gazed at the tree-lined reflecting pool, then looked beyond it to the Minervian temple where the Zeus-like statue of the billy-goat-bearded Father Abraham posed with his hands gesturing in sign language—the Greek letters for the *beginning* and the *end* above the facist symbols of Roman authority. *I see trees ... old oaks, solid and sound. Men who belong to the ages. That's where the people congregate to speak to their government ... all the way over there, on the other side of the Washington Monument.*

He remembered his father telling him about a hot August day in 1963. Under a nearly cloudless sky, his father stood with 250,000 other citizens before the steps of the Lincoln Memorial and listened to the enduring words of Martin Luther King, Jr. who quoted from the book of Isaiah, the Messianic dream of the American conscience. " 'And the *glory* of the Lord shall be revealed, and all flesh shall see it together,' " Winston murmured, as he turned and gaped up at the Washington Monument, " 'for the mouth of the Lord hath spoken.' "

"What's going on? Who? Who-who-whoo?"

The 'Lantern of Demosthenes,' the Dark Lantern ... a fitting symbol of democracy.

"Hmm … Egyptian." *The architects of the Mall certainly had a fascination with the temples of different gods,* Winston surmised. *Memorials built from someone else's ruins. The guardians ... Why choose these architectural symbols to honor? Why is this locus surrounded by temples?*

He turned north, toward the back door of the White House. He heard the out of tune calls of the cicadas, signaling the start of their seventeen-year life cycle. His eyes blinked as he wondered about the implications of the new presidency and the dark horizon that lay beyond. *Christmas trees. Yes, Jane. I still remember you.*

"What's going on? Who? Who-who-whoo?"

Susan giggled girlishly as she approached Winston from behind.

"James, did you realize Howard looked an awful lot like—"

"Yeah. I know." Winston held his eyes on the White House. "But the king is dead. There are no more kings in Washington. We have ourselves a new queen—"

Susan's cell phone *chimed.* A bell tolled from the tower of the Smithsonian castle. Startled pigeons took flight.

"Hello … Yes, I think we're finished here. … That's good news. Where? … Thanks." Susan snapped her phone shut and quickly jotted in her notepad. "This site has a strong footprint. The reception is really clear. James, they decoded another segment of the virus. It contains latitude and longitude coordinates as well."

"Where?" Winston asked.

Susan read from her notepad. "Latitude 48 degrees, 58 minutes, 33 seconds – Longitude 2 degrees, 27 minutes, 37 seconds."

"And where is that?" Winston asked again.

"Paris, France." Susan paused. "What do you make of this, James?"

"Unknown by means of more unknown … This might not be easy," Winston answered, his voice uncertain. "We didn't see any letterboxes sitting on that stone. Everything here is associated with prime meridians and obelisks."

"I agree. None of it makes any sense."

"We need to get to Paris. Nobles mentioned something about a prime meridian in Paris." Winston flashed an idea from a memory that served him. "Maybe there's a commonality associated with prime meridians."

———

The soul's impurity consists in bad judgments, and purification consists in producing in it right judgments, and the pure soul is one which has right judgments. – *Epictetus* (55-135 A.D.)

PROFESSOR MAISUN placed a legal-size envelope on the ticket counter and paid the agent with a folded twenty-dollar bill. He glanced at a sign above the window.

SPECIAL EXHIBITS: THE SNAKE CHARMERS
El Greco's *Laocoon* and William Blake's
The Great Red Dragon and the Woman Clothed in the Sun
On Exhibit Every Day of the Year

He spied the clock behind the counter. It was 9:18 A.M.

"This is a Daypass, sir," the agent explained. "It will allow you to tour three of the special exhibits. May I recommend the 'Madonna with Child - The Human Tradition of Cleaning from Christianity to Ivory Soap.' It's very popular."

"I only want to visit the BodyWorlds exhibit," Maisun urged.

"I've seen it. It's better than the exhibits at the Mütter." The agent opened a map, and marked with a pen, then handed the map to Maisun. "It's located on the ground floor. Here is your change." He dropped two dimes and a quarter into a metal tray.

"A collector's edition." Maisun eyed the dimes as he placed the coins in his pocket. He pulled anxiously on his sleeve and checked his wristwatch. *I'm going to be late.* "What's this?" He spied a stack of local event advertisements on the counter.

Washington D.C. Dragon Boat Festival
Thompson Boathouse, Rock Creek National Park
Saturday - Sunday, 28 - 29 May

He picked up the flyer, slipped it in his coat pocket, then grabbed his envelope.

Entering the museum's rotunda, Maisun stopped next to a marble fountain with a statue of Hermes standing on a severed head and holding a Y-shaped *kerykeion*, the magical wand of the Gnostics. "Hmm ... the god of signs." He palmed the coins from his pocket, sorted out the Mercury dime, and tossed it into the fountain.

Which way to the ground floor? He glanced at the brochure and then descended a wide marble stairway. *Beep, beep.* He stopped again on the landing to answer his cell phone. "Hello. ... Yes, William ..."

"I received your message, Professor," a whisper of a voice reported over the phone. "They are on their way. *He* has figured it out."

"Good, I am returning the pages from the codices to him today." Maisun fanned the envelope in his hand. "I will contact you later." He switched off the phone and proceeded through the garden café to the central galleries on the ground floor.

. A well-dressed, dog-faced attendant held duty beside a marble arched entry to a temporary exhibit hall. On loan from the Hirshhorn Museum, Salvador Dali's "Crâne de Zurbaran" hung like Darth Vader's diabolical mask of terror above the keystone in the archway. Maisun widened his eye as he approached an easy-to-read sign.

WELCOME
NO PHOTOGRAPHY OR VIDEO, OUT OF RESPECT FOR THE DEAD
BodyWorlds presented in conjunction with art from the International Necronautical Society.
We, the First Committee of the International Necronautical Society, declare the following: Death is a type of space, which can be mapped, entered, and eventually inhabited. Death is delightful. Death is dawn. That there is no beauty without death or its immanence. We shall sing to death's beauty.
Death is Enduring. Death is the Infinite. Death is the goal of Life.
We Live against the Space of Death.

Maisun checked his wristwatch again. *He's late.* Stepping forward, he presented his Daypass to the attendant and entered a dimly lit corridor.

"Nice cologne," the attendant remarked as he nodded for Maisun to enter.

Background music provided a surreal ambience as Maisun swayed his head to Sinatra singing Cole Porter's "I've Got You Under My Skin." He opened his brochure, held it close to his face, and widened his one good eye.

"Since its first exhibition in Mannheim in 1997, more than 23 million people have viewed BodyWorlds, making it the world's most successful touring museum exhibit. Your tour begins with the human skeleton, followed by a journey into the locomotive system and the digestive system. You will see nerve and vessel specimens and even observe the development of new life in a mother's womb. Your tour will provide you with a new insight into the structure of the human body."

The mood music changed to "A Touch of Grey" by the Grateful Dead. Maisun closed the brochure and slipped it into his pocket. He continued down the corridor and stopped before crossing a threshold into the world of the macabre. The darkened gallery before him was filled with freakish exhibits of twenty-three skinless, plastinated human bodies. The stiff figures of gray, white, and red bands of muscles, organs, and bone seemed frozen in time, like the mummified 5,000-year-old Iceman discovered in the Italian Alps.

Suddenly, a voice came out of nowhere, as if nowhere was where it belonged. "Pickled. Preserved. Saving ourselves for history. People as art. The concept is way beyond that of mere creative expression. Don't you think, Professor?" The man spoke in an icy, decisive voice as he approached Maisun from behind.

Like a scene from a Hollywood film noir, Maisun stiffened to attention and stared straight ahead at the looming shadow on the wall of *the man* who stood behind him. "Humans are the only creatures who hoard their dead. I suppose this is one way to live forever. But I would rather be remembered for my creative endeavors."

"We all yearn for immortality," the man said. "No one wants to pass away unheralded. We all wish to achieve an acceptable level of happiness and freely live out our fantasies, one slow, excruciating moment at a time. It's a common human desire we all share. All religions take advantage of that desire. How helpless we are, like netted birds, when we are caught by our desires."

"But, death is not the only way to immortality," Maisun commented.

The man moved closer. "Immortality is our obsession. We all want to find a way to live *forever*. Be it through the self-sufficient lives of our children or the long-lived lives of our deeds. Ah ... How we do hate the finality of *Death*," he said in a chilling tone, "the terror of our own nothingness. I understand the faithful Catholics of Mexico City have embraced the Yin. They venerate Saint Death, the Hindu Kali and the last of the four horsemen, as a skeleton dressed in a hooded robe, wearing a crown, and carrying a globe and a long scythe. These odd devotees of *La Santa Muerte*, their name for the skull-headed Grim Reaper, have taken death and personified it. They've made it into almost a god—an angel of God—their new messenger. Ah ... the Specter of Death ... the second darkest moment of our lives—the finial nadir of our existence. It is a preoccupation of the Buddhists. Karma and all of that ... or Hermes of our stone. Did you notice the little winged Messenger in the museum's rotunda?"

Maisun nodded, frowning. "Yes ... the water god."

"I understand there are four hundred shrines to Saint Death in the United States alone," the man recounted. "One is even here in Washington, D.C. And I had heard that Catholics had lost their direction in our country. Now half of the Catholic Churches in America have members with Spanish surnames. They are increasing their legion. Never underestimate the power of that church. No one gains authority in this world, except by way of the Vatican."

"I concur," Maisun affirmed.

"I *loathe* Death. We think we choose our direction through life with free will, but our lives are predetermined by Death. There is no such thing as life without limits. I read an article titled 'The Fable of the Dragon-Tyrant' in the *Journal of Medical Ethics*. In it, Death was metaphorically personified as a monstrous dragon who demands human sacrifices. The Dragon-Tyrant had existed forever. It was a fact of life. You cannot stop it. You cannot kill it."

"Death is eternal," Maisun agreed, "the primal mystery."

"Death is the ball and chain of our existence. It's the only certainty in life. We know we are going to die, so we do whatever it takes to keep on living. In many ways, man's world is built in honor to Death. Humanity lovingly holds out its arms, consumed by it. We spend our entire lives preparing for the Sacred Skull. We want our last five minutes of fame—our public face in the obituaries to appear proper."

"Our seasons in hell," Maisun said. "It is the price we have to pay. But suffering and death are the vehicles for our evolution. In Buddhism, death leads the Buddha on the path of a deeper truth which allows him to appreciate life. They believe you have to die many times before you realize you are alive."

"So, death is only temporary. You are a deep thinker, Maisun," the man said with an Archaic smile. "You make me think about the sharp-sighted praying mantis, the deep thinker of the insect world. These little camouflaged prophets and soothsayers are considered holy by some cultures. It is believed that if you become lost and you see a mantis that you should travel in the direction it is facing, and it will lead you home. People always follow the one who prays," the sciolist snickered. "The mantis is famous for its almost human mating habits. They say that the male praying mantis has to *die* in order to reproduce. As he copulates with a female, fast as lightning she bites his head off, devouring his brain and taking his memory, if he has any. The act of losing his head places him into a state of ecstasy. His headless body goes into convulsions as it continues to fertilize her eggs until she has eaten the rest of him. He wants to go on *living*. What a lucky way to die...." The man eyed Maisun. "Can you imagine such a thing—substituting a guillotine for Viagra in the bedroom?"

"No wonder they're praying," Maisun replied in disgust. "It would be a bloody mess. ... You're late, sir. I was beginning to wonder if you would show. I was unable to contact you. I assumed you were at Lubbers off Witch Point on the Abaco—"

"Oh, I'm sorry. I try to keep my whereabouts unknown. I stay there only when I visit the new Atlantis at Paradise. I was engaged in another oil deal. More *profits* ... I just flew in from my retreat at World Islands in Dubai—a group of man-made islands shaped like a Mercator map of the world. It's next to Palm Jumeirah, an island shaped like a *holy* palm tree. Those islands are architectural and engineering marvels. They are called 'the eighth wonder of the world.' I spent the night at Oxon Hill Manor. Did you know that World War II and the U. N. were sanctioned from that house?"

"Yes," Maisun smiled smugly.

"I always try to arrive five minutes early, but I was admiring the outdoor statuary gardens in front the Hirshhorn," the man explained. "There is a complete micro-cosmology in that garden with a pine tree next to *Six Dots over a Mountain* at its center and a massive, crane-like, steel and cable structure—the *Builder*—standing above a sunken world containing *The Visitation*, a *Lunar Bird*, and the *Prophet St. John* wielding his staff before our *Golden Sphere*. They even have statue by Rodin!"

"Rodin," Maisun questioned, "the Symbolist?"

"Yes, the creator of the *Gates of Hell* near Napoleon's Tomb. I stop by the Gates every time I stay at my retreat near the Bois de Boulogne. Rodin's *Burghers of Calais* is on exhibit at the Hirshhorn. One of those figures holds the key. There are many fascinating sculptures in that garden, such as the *Horse and Rider*. It reminds me of the wild pleasures of my daughter. Do you have any *children*, Professor?"

"No." Maisun glanced over his shoulder at the Boris Karloff expression on the man's taut, rawhide-leathery face, the result of years of sun worshiping. He spied the Y-shaped patterned, gold button pinned to the man's lapel.

"Ah … the younger generation." The man sighed. "Life has gotten even shorter in our digital age of planned obsolescence. Even when we preserve ourselves like digital data, a simple change in the hardware of society can leave us virtually useless as we age. We are always eclipsed by the views of the younger generation, who think they can fly by the seat of their pants. We are always circumvented by our own creations. Our children are always better than we were. We want them to be! It's Cope's Law. Our species evolves. It keeps getting better. It keeps getting taller and heavier. A whole lot heavier." The man released a sardonic laugh and patted his belly.

"How, How. Evolution," Maisun echoed agreement.

"*Ars moriedi,* the art of dying." The man motioned with his arms in stiff, animated gestures toward the skinless bodies frozen in front of him like department store mannequins. "Look at all of this. They've been stripped of their memory, their wrinkled skin of life. There are few things worse than touching dead skin," he hissed, sucking in air with his teeth clenched together. "Come this way Professor. Let's look at the mysteries that lie underneath the skin of this death warmed over."

The two men approached an exhibit of a skinless, headless body that had been fully plastinated. The body sat posed in front a computer monitor displaying a Quicktime video from a Jimmy Buffet concert. It held a plastinated, skinless mouse in its left hand. A plastinated, featherless parrot sat on its left shoulder. Staring up at the monitor from a silver platter in its lap lay a severed head. The head had been dissected in half, revealing a cross section of its plastinated brain. A group of school children paraded between Professor Maisun and the exhibit.

 "Oh, my God!" a young girl wearing *bright* purple, travel-light excursion shorts from L. L. Bea*m* said to her friend, who stood wide-eyed with disbelief. "A parrothead." She pointed with morbid curiosity.

"Don't touch," the teacher corrected the child's behavior.

As the children walked away, Maisun inwardly recoiled as he felt the man's hand resting on his left shoulder.

"Look …," the man chuckled coldly, "one of the headless hardwired by a mouse to a virtual world. Humanity seeking truth from the light of a computer monitor. It's the new image of our devotion—the noble savage staring at the ghost in the machine, filling up his *blank slate.* This new priest must be a computer pirate, the panoptic man who sees the world with one 'I' as he tries to hold on to his head. It's a fascinating idea. He's a lot like you, Maisun!"

"The power of the Global Consciousness," Maisun said.

"Yes, the power of consciousness," the man agreed as he stretched his neck and held his face within inches of the plastinated brain. "This head reminds me of someone I knew." He read from a small plastic sign, " 'The brain floats inside of the skull, where it is protected by a thin layer of fluid.' It's like an embryo floating in its mother's womb. They say our intellectual strengths and weaknesses depend in a large part on the pattern and distribution of our gray matter. Each person has a unique brain density. These curled up knots … No two memory maps of the brain are really the same." He tilted his head so he could observe the expression on Maisun's face. "This beautiful brain makes me think about Darwin's *Descent of Man*. Thirteen million years of man. How many Platonic cycles is that?"

Maisun shrugged indifferently.

"I can't hear you, Maisun. Speak up!"

"I'm not certain."

"You know, Darwin was not searching for our monkey ancestors. He was looking for a universal phenomenon that rests at the core of the human mind—the elegant design. He was searching for the animal mind, the violent hunter that is buried deep within us all by eons of evolution. He was performing a study of a descent into limbo," the man furled his lips and persisted with his philosophical explanation. "Did you know the ancients had the same brain material as we do? They simply engaged their minds on different topics, which we overlook in our modern world. In the fifteenth century, Leonardo da Vinci, the great necromancer who kissed the vulture and thought he could fly like the birds, produced realistic sketches of the dissected human body as he searched for the source of the *anima*—the human soul. In his day, there was a great debate as to where the soul resided. This was the great philosophical question of his age. Some believed the human soul was in the human heart—the chakra, the *anahata*. And when the heart stopped beating, the soul left the body." The man placed his right hand over his chest as if to pledge an allegiance.

Maisun unconsciously placed his hand over his heart.

"Others believed the soul resided in the human brain," the man added. "As far back as 6,500 B.C., the Catal Hüyük culture in Turkey drew giant bird images in their shrines to the bearded-vulture, as a *god-form*, who was responsible for removing the heads and skulls of the deceased in order to capture their souls. Their *bird images* evolved into that of the vulture-gods, the Great Soul Grabbers. Grabbing the soul was the central tenet within the ancient shaman birdman rites of passage. Such rites can be found all over the world. It brings to my mind the birdman cult of Easter Island, the most isolated island on Earth. The birdmen worshiped *Makemake,* the creator of humanity. They built a temple to *Makemake* next to an extinct volcano. In their yearly celebration to *Makemake*, the young warriors, in their rite of passage, swam through shark-infested waters to a pillar of stone standing before a small island to gather the sacred eggs of the sooty tern. The first initiate to acquire a bird egg became chief of the island for a year. It was truly an odd form of electing a new leader. Can you imagine such a process? Birds, bird eggs, seasonal cycles, and nature's laws controlling the direction of a society—and an understanding of the soul."

"No." Maisun blurted. "But such rites have shaped our modern society."

"The brain or the heart … Even the enlightened, soul-searching Thomas Jefferson wrote about the eternal consequences of man's struggle to reconcile the dichotomy of the head and the heart. Yes, as soul-searching, enlightened men, we use our brains today to discover our souls. The brain, the *locus* of our identity, is the natural point of departure of the soul at the time of death. Da Vinci, the quintessential Renaissance man, was a brain man. He studied countless corpses, trying to establish the location of the soul, as well as the energy that allowed the soul to govern the human body. Eventually, he determined what he thought were the exact coordinates of the *Buddhata*, the embryo of the soul, inside the brain—the God Spot. He considered this location the source of the creative consciousness—the *Tathagatagarbha Essence*—within the human mind. An *axis-mundi*, I wonder?"

Maisun nodded, his eyes locked on the plastinated brain.

"Neurobiologists tell us if the soul exists, it must reside in the limbic system, the seat of our primal emotions and memories—the part of the brain inherited from our earliest ancestors. It is the source of the *thinking* inner voice that governs our religious and mystic experiences—the source of our *personal* consciousness. The soul is a very *personal thing*. Karl Marx wrote that organized 'religion is the soul of a soulless environment,' where the soulless gather together in awe to their collective neurosis. Carl Jung once said that people will do anything, no matter how absurd, to avoid facing their own souls. You have to *think*, to discover your soul, Professor Maisun," the man proclaimed forcefully. "You have to break away from the old foolish, piscivorous faiths. You have to change your silly, know-nothing ways. You have to take a left turn in life to keep things convoluted … to keep things fragmented. You have to retrace the outline behind Da Vinci's *sfumato* to see the logic of the truth through a new Z to A way of looking at things. You have to break the cardinal rules, disobey the Ten Commandments, and embrace the seven deadly sins."

The man closed his dark and unfriendly eyes. "They say that when you die, you see a beautiful white light." His eyelids quivered as he spoke, " 'Hung be the heavens with black, yield day to night!' Only out of darkness comes the light. Darkness, our monstrous mystery," he said lovingly. "Our world is slowly losing its link with the dark. The electrical light pollution from our cities has blocked it out. Our society has lost its connection with the rhythmic patterns within nature. The modern world is no longer attuned to the daily cycles of *dark* and *light*. We read in black and white. But we do not think that way. Everything is gray. Especially as you grow old. Between the subtle shading and the absence of light, lie the nuances of illusion … our darkness. We need to redefine the dark to *see the light*. We need to hold the left hand of Darkness as our guide."

He reopened his eyes. "We need to find the guiding stars that dot the darkness, so that we can find ourselves. Each of us harbors a fugitive. The Devil is evil only if we wish to perceive her that way. So, what is the true nature of things?" He paused. "Is it the 'as above, so within' of some philosophical Yin-Yang?" he crowed. "No!" he snapped. "There is no *perfect* spiral in a seashell. The golden mean is not in everything. Fibonacci numbers do not govern nature. And *phi*, as a number, never was used by the Greeks. The order within mathematics cannot articulate the true mysteries of nature. We see order in nature and we call it evidence of God. But what we see is only the order our minds apply to nature. Deism is circumvented by Darwinism. God is not immutable. It is a blind watchmaker that has set our world in motion."

The man slowly snaked his body around and faced Maisun. "What is it that we truly gravitate toward?" he questioned in a stern voice, then answered. "It's a universe governed by the Black Hole in which we live. At the crux of it all, at the pivot of every vortex, is a Black Hole—like a dragon lurking in our souls, gnawing away at the Yggdrasil of the world, and then *spitting it out* in some new mangled and mutated form. This is the great burden of the beast. It is our *cancer*. It is the human analysis of ourselves and the world around us! The Greeks understood it in their Saturnian mythos. Hawking has proven it in his mathematics. What is a soul?" the Tartarean man catechized with a brutal tone in his voice. "Is it the pure white essence we are born with, which becomes tarnished as we venture through life? Or is it like an empty cup, which must be filled before we lose our lives? *Tabula Rasa.* The philosopher John Locke said we come into the world with a *blank slate.* How full is your cup, Professor?" the man asked forcefully.

Maisun remained reticent. His right eye twitched nervously.

"What is bothering you, Maisun? You look like the cat that just swallowed the canary," the man mocked with acidic laughter as he continued to monopolize the conversation. "This BodyWorlds exhibit far surpasses Leonardo's anatomical drawings, or even *Gray's Anatomy*, with its Vitruvian Man on the cover. Not even Picasso could dissect the reality of the human form as well as these plastinated bodies, don't you think?" He eyeballed the cross-section of the brain. "Leonardo was the first to preserve body parts with a solidification medium. He injected hot wax into the brain of an ox. Plastination is a superior preservation technique. Did you realize that creating a full-body plastinated man takes an average of 1500 hours and $90,000? A corpse's water and fat is replaced with liquid plastics. This process preserves the tissue structures, resulting in an authentic representation of the human body."

"I read all that in the brochure," Maisun said, a trace of impatience in his voice.

"Look at that specimen. He should have eaten less and exercised more," the man said sternly. "Perhaps he followed a high-protein diet and became overly acidified? He did not maintain his personal temple. He should have followed a raw food diet. Healthy food is *living food*—organic, unprocessed, and uncooked. Ah … I suppose it depends on which fad-diet book you read. *Dernier cri* ... The body is such a fragile thing. And so is human freedom. We need a diet book that feeds our souls."

Maisun stared repugnantly with his good eye at the brochure in his hand. His glassy left eye appeared to follow the ranting man.

"Although I cannot fly like a bird or see through walls with penetrating x-ray vision, I appreciate Nietzsche's views of the superman. Nietzsche said that God is dead. We all know that nobody died on the cross. Nietzsche believed the joy of life is only found in the life that is lived dangerously. The alchemist, Faust, concluded the same thing. 'Live life dangerously and you live it right!' Perhaps that is why we take such risks and do not maintain our temples." The man brought his hands together, interlocked his fingers in a tight grip, and bowed his head.

"A seven-legged ass," Maisun discounted, "I agree, no god died on the cross."

"There comes a time in our lives when we realize beyond all doubt that we are old…. At least older that we ever dreamed we would be. Such is the cross which the wealthy must bear. We live longer than everyone else—six to eight years longer than average. Growing old is a tiring odyssey for the soul. In countless ways, we search within ourselves for the Fountain of Youth. We detoxify our bodies and cleanse ourselves through the correct balance; be it by aromatherapy, chakras, or even reflexology. We rub Rogaine into our scalps. We numb our foreheads with Botox. We take pills to boost our memory or dope up with propranolol to help us to forget. We are about to enter an age of smart drugs that prevent all age-associated, cognitive decline. We can now flog our nerves to discipline our minds and increase our IQs through the 'Mozart Effect.' It is a new age for the neurosciences." The man touched his forehead with a quick tap of his index finger. "*True transmutation is a mental art.*

Yes—For every problem there is a solution. For every ailment we have a remedy. We can tinker with anything until it's made perfect. At my new clinic for neo-biology, we are working on memory drugs that allow us to play 'Jeopardy'—to know the answers before we know the questions. We can now think like the prophetic muses."

Maisun riveted his good eye to one side, following the man. His eyes goggled in opposite directions.

"I'm not stark raving *mad*, Maisun. Every good businessman hunts for the best deal, and I am a savvy predator, Professor. I have a selfish gene. While the rest of the world has enslaved themselves to the moral obligations of altruism, I have always invested in myself," the man blustered with an iron tone of self-assurance. "We have to constantly reinvent ourselves to be successful. The creative endeavor is man's way in the world. We hold the square and compass. We can redesign our world and redesign ourselves. Science and technology is where my faith lies. But … our world is not about the best and brightest, it's about being young. Just between you and me, I've had four facial threading plastic surgeries. I do wish to look my best." He sniggered again. "I inject myself with 'bioidentical' hormones. I bathe in lavender, basil, and nard. I take liquid colloidal minerals and curcumin with green tea mixed in water from Lake Drummond every day. It's part of my prescription for reform," he said boastfully, as he raked his hand through his thick, wavy, hair. "Did you know that gray hair may hold the *key* to the cure for cancer?"

"No." The balding Maisun glanced at the man's full head of hair which matched the bluish-gray discoloration of his skin. "I read that eating fish prevents cancer."

"A face-lift, a tummy-tuck … A little surgery can do wonders. I've had my whole body scanned with a nano-probe. I've even had my fingerprints erased to save my identity. Our ability to change ourselves is something that empowers us."

"I agree." Maisun opened his mouth and stretched his cheeks in a quick facial exercise. "I use metal aerobics to help me live longer. It improves my memory skills."

"Use-it-or-lose-it," the man chortled. "Did you know that the plastination technique has been advanced at my institute in Texas? We are studying VMAT2, the God Gene, if you believe in such a thing."

"No." Maisun gave the man a cockeyed, withering glance.

"It's an outgrowth of the old Methuselah project. Before now, all we could do was vitrify the brain with a cryoprotectant that saved it from decay. With the new green chemistry and the *correct electromagnetic field*, we have formulated a process that retains tissue structure with a biomaterial derived from the Klotho protein formed from a combined Sylphium and *Juniperus phoenicea* extract which can be reanimated through epigenetics by way of a vibrated healing energy used in material transformation—the life-sustaining *Chi*." His sharp eyes slanted to observe Maisun's single-eyed reaction. "Like the snake herb of Ophiuchus or the life-giving-blood from the right side of Medusa, certain elements have been found to interact with human cells under polarized light by way of specific electromagnetic RF frequencies, regenerating the correctly woven structure of our DNA."

"It sounds intriguing." Maisun nodded.

"We now control its language. He who controls that molecule rules the world."

"I thought it was who comtrolled the water," Maisun muttered.

"Extended life is within our reach. Thirty years from now, death may become a thing of the past. But, not everyone can be a winner, Professor. Life is a zero-sum game. You have to have some losers. The new technique requires a few life-sustaining stem cells from brain harvesting. A few thumb-sucking embryos may die." He smirked. "But like Jesus, a sacrifice is always required." His smile slid into a frown. "In our brave new world, some lives have more value than others."

"Yes, some lives do," Maisun agreed.

"I am my own man, Professor. They call me the Oracle of New Haven, a captain of industry who rules over the snakes of Manhattan. I am a *Nephilim* from the *Grigori* and the world is *my* oyster. My happiness is my highest good. I follow the Iron Rule, 'Do unto others as you wish, before they do it unto you.' I have always sat in the catbird seat. It's evolution. Our enlightened self-interest always positions the best of us at the top of the pecking order. Material acquisition … Who is in *this* world is not in a quest for gain. 'But what shall it profit a man, if he shall gain the whole world, and lose his own soul?' And what shall a man give in exchange for his soul? It is easy to be *preserved*," he decried, his words galvanized, glaring at the plastinated displays across the room. "*A tutto c'è rimedio, fuorchè alla morte.* Professor, I may prolong my life, but not for thirty years. Who will deliver me from this body of death? I want to be the captain of my soul … if for just one day." He burned a cold stare at the cross section of the plastinated brain. "If - only - we - knew - how - to - capture - the - soul." He punctuated every word with a shake of his six-fingered fist in front of his chest.

There was an uneasy *silence.*

"So, what have you learned about *the seal*?" the man probed in a stern tone.

"They discovered markings on a tunnel wall below the Temple six days ago. These markings match the ones on the clay pots held in our temple. It is obvious that this is an important location for what you are looking for." Maisun refolded the brochure and inserted it into his coat pocket.

"How do we gain access to this area?" the man asked sharply.

"Sir, people are working on that as we speak … but it will take time." Maisun held out the envelope. "Here are the pages from one of your codices. Your inside man is doing an excellent job. He has embedded the coordinates of the previous locations into his programming. If the plan should fail, he would be the perfect scapegoat."

"*My* inside man—" The man snatched the envelope from Maisun's hand. "Professor, do you think *we* are weak? Do you think we are weird? Remember…. You are a part of this, Maisun. Stop your thinking!" He leveled his lips close to Maisun's left ear and whispered a directive. "I know it's hard to warm up to a tepid thing. But we have a code of conduct we must follow. We have a proper protocol. People are being paid well, Professor. I expect results!"

The man stiffened, centered his black tie across his red shirt, and pulled on the lapel of his understated pinstriped business suit. He walked away from Maisun and disappeared into the shadows of an adjoining corridor. The museum's music system began playing Simon and Garfunkel's "Sound of Silence."

Good-bye Darkness, you obstinate man. Maisun felt relieved as he watched the ominous presence recede into the shadows. He turned away and contemplated with an oculus eye the cross section of the plastinated brain. *The Soul. A cup half empty? Or a cup half full? Knowledge was power.* He took umbrage. *I'm tired of being a cat's paw go-between.*

Day 9
A Concord Clock

As for me, my first passion, the passion of my youth, had been—not for its object, indeed, but for its determining cause—a clock! ... We all are of the citizens of the Sky. - Camille Flammarion

SUSAN AND WINSTON walked through the gangway that connected Pan Am flight 2074 to the Terminal B customs checkpoint at Charles de Gaulle International.

Heavy duty ... Winston spotted a stout man in an off-white lambskin blazer standing next to a security arch and a backscatter x-ray scanner. The man held tightly to a 3 X 5 color photograph, checking it against the passengers as they deplaned. His bulldog face, sporting a gray, Stalinesque mustache, held a sustained gaze on Susan as she approached. His eyes widened. Self-consciously, he straightened his tie and patted his head to smooth down his neatly trimmed Ceasar haircut.

"Hello, *Mademoiselle* Hamilton. I am Inspector Guillaume Ciacco Parott," the inspector greeted in the raspy voice of a chain-smoker. "I have been expecting you." He reached out to bring her hand to his lips in the age-old courtly gesture.

"*Bonjour*, Inspector. This is my associate, James Winston."

"Hello," Winston attempted to shake hands, but Parott maintained his grip on Susan. *This fat guy seems a little brutish,* Winston judged.

Parott offered Winston a brief, obligatory smile and gestured a quick okay with his other hand finger-pinching the photo. "*Enchante*, nice to meet you." His eyes peeked at Winston. *Dirty Harry,* he surmised. He quickly readdressed Susan. "*Mademoiselle* Hamilton, you are far more beautiful than your photograph," he cooed as he discreetly folded the photo and slipped it in his coat pocket. "It is an undeniable delight to meet you. Your smile is such a beautiful attire. It takes my breath away. I adore your hair. You could be a model. *Parlez-vous Français?*"

"*Merci.* Just a little," she replied with a slight smile.

She's not a model, Winston mused. *She's actual size.*

"Your plane was late," Parott said. "I have been waiting for over an *heure*."

"Our flight had to take a different route," Susan explained. "They told us navigation was interrupted by the recent solar flares." She stepped toward the lens of a biometric passport scanner and started to swipe her thumb to confirm her identity.

"It's not going to work for me," Winston said to Susan. "They need to read my digital implant or do a full hand-scan. I'm outside the biometric population. I was born without fingerprints. Only a small part of the population is born without fingerprints. It's my physical handicap, but my hacker's resource."

"We can forego security." Parott grabbed Susan's travel bag. "Everything has been arranged. Let me make your day. I have a car waiting to take you to your hotel."

As they walked through the lobby, the inspector began humming along to the background music playing a French version of "Day Tripper."

Winston heard a faint static skipping to the beat of the music. STA-KA, STA-KA. He spied the belly-billboard of a young pregnant woman wearing a cropped, body-hugging shirt revealing a jeweled ring pierced just above her navel and below a colorful butterfly tattoo. She stood beside a small boy in a *bright* yellow T-shirt depicting Pete's Dragon below the slogan **Disneyland Paris - World of Magic.**

The boy covered his eyes with both hands and stuck out his tongue. "You can't see me," he teased his mother.

"Peek-a-boo," she laughed joyfully with her son. "Peek-a-boo."

Winston felt lost in his navel-gazing. *Everyone's playin' hide-and-seek.*

The boy darted to a nearby window, entranced by an airplane leaving the runway. He held his nose flattened against the glass. "The big bird! I see myself!" He patted the glass with his small hands at the reflection of himself. "I'm happy. I see myself!"

Winston noted the smudges of the boy's barely visible fingerprints on the glass. *Steganographic,* he thought, spying the reflection of the boy and his mother in the window. "Inspector, who's the guide we'll be dealing with today?"

"Why, it is me, *monsieur.* I am a security liaison for the *Musée du Louvre.* I am also a city historian. I sometimes teach at La Sorbonne."

"Yes, the coordinates we're looking for are near the Louvre," Susan stated.

"*Oil, Oui.* Close, *Mademoiselle.* Very close."

———

TWENTY MINUTES LATER, Inspector Parott held a loose grip on the steering wheel of an unmarked blue Fiat as he and his two VIP passengers sped along the *Boulevard Périphérique,* the primary highway that loops Paris.

"*Via* car, it takes about half an hour to get to the heart of Paris from Charles de Gaulle," Parott raised his voice above a police radio *squawking* an annoying metallic crosstalk. "Have you been to Paris before?" He darted his face back and forth from the road to Susan, who sat beside him in the front seat.

She said nothing as she adjusted her seatbelt.

"And you, *Monsieur* Winston?"

"I was forged in the Crucible. I did survival training through the SCS at Paris Island, but that was hell." Winston rubbed his nose, noticing the smell of food permeating the cup holder-less car. "Yes, when I was younger. I was here with my father. He worked at the École du Louvre." He spied a pile of crumpled candy and sandwich wrappers lying on the floor of the backseat. *Gluttony,* he thought.

"Yes, *oui,* I've been here before." Susan said with a daunting gaze, observing the distant Paris skyline. "It's a beautiful city."

Reaching to turn down the radio, Parott veered the car into the other lane.

"The road—" Winston warned, as they sped within inches of another car.

"*Oil, Oui,* I agree. Since Baron Haussmann's renovation of the city's landscape during the Third Republic, Paris has become the most beautiful city on Earth," Parott remarked in a Francien dialect that punctuated the syllables. "I visited your country once—New York City. I saw the Statue of Liberty—our lady who bears the torch, the *light bearer,* like the Colossus of Rhodes. You know we gave you that statue." He spun his head around and gave Winston a quick glance.

"Yeah, I *know,*" Winston said irritably. "The road, man, watch the road."

The car careened and weaved as the inspector raced through eight lanes of traffic.

"The French *envy* your country, *monsieur,* with its many liberties. America is a place of such hope. Yours was the first 'new' nation to be founded upon ideas and principles set forth in your Constitution and Bill of Rights. The torch of American liberty burns like a wildfire over the landscape of the whole world. As long as your country adheres to those principles, *liberty* and *freedom* will persist. We admire such principles. Your country is truly blessed. Do you care for a snack?" Parott reached for a packet of peanut butter crackers sitting on the dashboard. He tore the package open with his front teeth and slid a cracker into his mouth.

"No, thank you," Susan politely declined.

"Hmm … the peanut butter is a delicious Marvel meal." Parott smacked his lips. "How about you, *monsieur*? Do you care for a cracker?" He crunched down on another cracker.

"No, thanks," Winston said. "Envy is one of the seven deadly sins," he spoke under his breath. "*Bon appétit*. Don't choke on the peanut butter."

"*Oui.* I understand, *monsieur*, they go better with ketchup, and so do freedom fries." He chewed quickly and swallowed. "*Excusez-moi,* please excuse my French cuisine," he chuckled. "It has been a busy day. This is my *breakfast.*" He grabbed a pungent wedge of cheese covered in white paper laying on the dashboard, and unwrapped it with one hand. "Care for some Chabicou?"

"No," Susan replied.

"I heard the French are festered easily by us Americans," Winston remarked.

"*Pardon*, festered?" Parott repeated, not understanding Winston's wording. He rolled his eyes upward and spied Winston through the rearview mirror.

"Yes, the French sometimes dislike Americans," Winston clarified.

"*Au contraire, monsieur.* We only dislike your inability to make full use of your liberties and opportunities," Parott mumbled, swallowing a mouthful of cheese. "In France, we only work a thirty-five *heure* week. That is less than any industrialized nation in the world. We work less by making use of our French efficiency, which allows us more time to enjoy our liberties and the *douceur de vivre*, the sweetness of life," he gloated, "*la raison d'être*. The whole point of being industrious is to create leisure, do you not agree?" He smiled. "Happiness is the highest good."

"I read where the French government extended the work hours under the new employment laws to improve the economy," Susan recalled.

"Oh … maybe so," Parott agreed. "But you cannot kill a good thing. Let me tell you a secret. No Frenchman has ever worked more than twenty *heures* a week."

"Casual undertime … sloth and pride," Winston muttered. "Four for seven."

Heavy footed, Parott stomped on the brakes. The tires squealed an earsplitting *screech*, like an angry bird. With a bump and sway, the car stopped behind a long line of traffic. "I am sorry … road construction. Seven kilometers ahead. Such delays—*La détour!*" Parott scorned. "Paris has the most complex road network in creation."

Anger, Winston perceived with a nod.

Parott wove between the congestion and exited the *Boulevard Périphérique*. He detoured over the River Seine, which winds through Paris, so he could approach the famous *landmarks* of the city directly from its sacred, western entry.

In the distance, Winston spied the bright red and yellow, *spectral* rays from the morning sun diffracting through the middle of an imposing skyscraper.

"*Voilà!* There, *monsieur*." Parott pointed with his football-player-size hand at the *oddly angled*, arch-shaped skyscraper. "This is the *Grand Arch de la Defense*, our Manhattan on the Seine, a complex built for the new European Union. It stands over Nanterre, the sacred place, the doorway of Mont-Valérien. It stands so tall, the Cathedral of Notre Dame could be inserted beneath its archway. There is a zodiac on its garden roof which you must see."

"It's huge!" Winston gawked out the rear window to catch a mirage of the *Arc de la Defense* reflecting off the black asphalt of the Avenue of the *Grande Armee* like a wave of bobbing bicyclists finishing the Tour de France.

The inspector popped a cracker in his mouth and pointed to another landmark as traffic slowed. "*Voilà!* There is the *Arc de Triomphe*, on the compass rose. It is the location of the Tomb of the Unknown and the Eternal Flame."

The Fiat sped forward, then lurched to a stop.

"We are now on the *Avenue des Champs Elysees,* the Place of the Blessed, designed by Andre Le Notre who created the Gardens of Versailles for Louis XIV, the Sun King. To the far right you can see the Tower. Look! Over there." Parott pointed, as their car picked up speed. "It is twice as tall as your Washington Monument. You should see it at night. There is a *light that beams* away from the Tower and circles the entire city. On your right is the *Place de la Concorde.*"

"An obelisk," Susan said abruptly.

"Hume said the coordinates are near the obelisk," Winston remarked.

"*Oui,* I know," Parott said, munching down on the last of the crackers. He rolled up the wrapper and tossed it over his left shoulder.

Winston watched the ball of cellophane bounce to the litter-strewn floor. He lurched forward in his seat, as Parott stomped the brakes.

"I despise these delays," Parott scorned again. "All of the motor cars are waiting on the light." He pushed a switch under the steering column. The police siren released a short Doppler-shrill and the blue, egg-shaped dome on the dashboard lit up. The busy cacophony dissipated as cars diverted to one side. "To your right is the *Jardin des Tuileries.* Beautiful, *oui?*"

"Yes, it's a beautiful park," Susan agreed, with a wandering gaze.

"There are many parks in Paris, *mademoiselle*. I will have to show you the lake at Park Montsouris, my favorite. *Monsieur*, the *Louvre* is on your immediate right. And your hotel is here on the *Rue de Rivoli*. It is one of the finest hotels in Paris."

The Fiat stopped at the yellow-painted curb and a doorman greeted them. Across from the hotel, a gilded statue of Joan of Arc wielding a sunlit lance appeared to guard the intersection to the *Place des Pyramides*.

Winston stepped from the car, stretched his legs, and brushed crumbs off the seat of his pants.

Parott awkwardly lifted himself out of the car and slammed the door shut. He pulled a silver flask from his coat and took a small sip, and then another. He spied Winston staring at him. Parott curled his lips and held out his flask.

Voilà! Winston nodded. *I knew there was a reason you were all over the road.*

Parott dashed around to the other side of the car to open the door for Susan. She smiled appreciatively as she stepped to the pavement. Parott noticed Winston staring at the statue. "She is beautiful, is she not?" He grabbed for Susan's hand.

Winston locked his eyes on Susan.

"*Saint Jean d'Arc* spoke to God," Parott remarked.

With a smug expression, Winston sighted westward down the *Rue de Rivoli* past the rows of neatly parked vehicles and tourist shops. He spied the golden arches on a McDonald's sign. His eyes fixed again on Susan, who held the inspector's arm. "Hmm …" *French cuisine. Lust, six out of seven.*

"We will leave your luggage here with the hotel concierge," Parott instructed. "Everything is arranged. Your belongings will be safe. This way, *s'il vous plait*. Follow me. I will show you what you are looking for."

Parott led them away from the hotel and crossed through the *Rue de Rivoli Entrée* into the Grand Plaza of the Louvre. "To your left is the Pyramid entrance to the *Louvre*. The monumental archway that you see before us is the *Arc de Triomphe du Carrousel*. It is one of three arches that form the western approach to the city, the *Triumphal Way* of the *Grand Ax* of Paris. The *Grand Ax* consists of the *Grande Arch de la Defense*, the *Arc de Triomphe l'Etoile*, and the tree-lined *Champs Elysées*." He pointed away from the Louvre in the direction of the *Champs Elysées*. "It is said that the *Grand Ax* is aligned to the constellation Orion, which according to folklore aids the sun in bringing about the long summer days of Paris."

"Aligned to Orion," Winston repeated.

"*Oui*, Orion was symbolic of Diana the Huntress, the Artemis of the crossroads, the moon goddess of the French Kings. Form does not always follow function."

Winston nodded knowingly with one eyebrow raised.

"The *Arc de Triomphe du Carousel*, a monument to Napoleon Bonaparte." Parott pointed as they strolled past the neoclassic archway. "It is surmounted by a bronze statuary of the Goddess of Peace driving a quadriga. The four horses are not the originals. The originals were taken by Napoleon from the *Basilique de Saint Mark's* in Venice. The government returned them after Napoleon's exile in 1812. Beneath the arch are inscribed the names of the battles and various treaties of Napoleon, along with occult symbols from the mystery schools."

"The mystery schools?" Susan questioned.

"*Oui*, Napoleon said, 'The conscience is the sacred haven of the liberty of man.' These mystery symbols reflect the inner nature of man and its connection with the forces of nature. The treaties formed the basis of law for all of the western European countries we have today. It is called *Napoleonic Law*. Napoleon once tried to conquer Jerusalem and Egypt. He embraced Islamic Law while in Egypt and implemented it within the code of law for his new empire."

Laws based on the mystery schools? Winston pondered.

Parott guided them away from the *Arc de Triomphe* to the broad, uncrowded *Jardin des Tuileries*. "In 1871, there was a great fire at the *Louvre* that destroyed the west wing that had been created by Catherine de Medici, who brought sorbet to France. So they demolished that part of the palace and opened up the vistas through the *Jardin des Tuileries*. Someday the *Louvre* hopes to rebuild the palace of *Tuileries*. I love these gardens. Such lovely flora."

Susan lingered for a moment beneath a latticed archway covered in flowering vines. She fondled a delicately folded white rose. "My favorite flower."

The inspector reached out, picked it, and offered it to her. He fumbled with his big hands while inserting the rose in a button hole on the lapel of her coat. "Be careful of the thorns," he warned. He stepped back and scanned Susan head to toe. "*Magnifique!*" he proclaimed, touching his fingers and thumb together and noisily kissing his fingertips.

Susan lifted her lapel to smell the rose and beamed a soft smile.

Be careful of strangers who give you flowers, Winston judged.

Proceeding westward through the *Jardin des Tuileries*, they passed a group of park venders selling souvenirs. Hidden behind well-groomed, geometrically arranged hedges stood dozens of statues of mythical figures, including *Theseus Slaying the Minotaur*, *Diana the Huntress*, *Pan* and *Echo*, and *A Lion Slaying America*.

"The joyful wheel of life ..." Parott pointed to the nearby, slow-moving Paris Ferris Wheel. "It rides on the axis of the most beautiful avenue in the world. Ah...!" he snapped, quickly holding his hand over his face to shield it from a tourist taking photos with a throwaway Kodak. "The prying lenses—Everywhere there is a camera. They are dangerous for anyone in law enforcement."

Winston glanced up at a video surveillance camera perched at the top of a lamppost. *Everyone else is getting their picture taken.* He eyed a young couple who were shielding their eyes and squinting up at the sun. They were flying a kite that clung to an almost invisible, threadlike cord. The darting paper wings falling off air pulled at them, as though they were walking their pet bird.

"*Vol au vent.*" The inspector pointed in the air and then toward the end of the gardens. "*Allez tout droit.* Follow me."

Parott and Winston stepped forward, but Susan stood as still as a tree, observing an old man wearing a *bright* blue, travel-light shirt from L. L. Beam, sitting on a park bench with his back to her. The man scribbled in a ledger while a group of sparrows, black redstarts, and kestrels gathered at his feet. Letters and numbers were inscribed on the outside of a circle drawn on the ground in front of him with dried sunflower seeds meticulously placed around the letters. Every time a bird pecked at a seed, the man jotted down a letter in the ledger.

"What's he doing?" Susan asked.

The three stepped closer and hovered over his shoulder. The man paid them no attention.

"He is an alectromancer," Parott whispered a reply with a smirked expression. "He is searching for a sign from God. He is using the birds to predict the future. The ancients followed the idea of *signatura reum*, God's signature in all things, meaning that the world should be read as God's signs. Anyone who speaks of God without understanding His signature in all things is ignorant and without true knowledge of God. The Romans once used alectromancy to determine a new Caesar. The magician, Lamblicus, followed this form of divination to discover the successor of Emperor Valens Caesar. When the Emperor was informed that such infernal powers from a divinatory ritual had been used to predict his successor and the destiny of Rome, he became so appalled, he ordered not only all the sorcerers, but all the philosophers in Rome, be severely punished and put to death."

"That circle of mixed letters and numbers looks like a Ouija board," Winston commented. He spied the notations in the open ledger.

9 -18 – caverne – crâne – dragon – âme – lumière – liberté

"Come this way," Parott motioned them along.

The three investigators continued through the gardens until they reached an adjoining city square, filled with hundreds of pigeons and doves. Many of the birds were marching in circles. Others were jousting and beak fencing. A few daring pigeons were prancing in the cobblestone streets and dodging cars.

"Coo, coo, what's going on? who? who-who-whoo? Missed me. Missed me."

"Look," Winston said to Susan, "the obelisk."

"I see it," she affirmed.

They crossed the busy thoroughfare surrounding the *Place de la Concorde*.

"Ici, here, *monsieur,"* Parott announced, stopping abruptly. "Stop. Right here."

Winston stumbled over a pigeon at his feet.

"Be careful, *monsieur*. Do not step on a *pigeon*. We adore *le pigeons* in Paris. They helped save the city during the Great War of 1870."

"What did they do, predict the future?" Winston backed a few steps and stopped next to the curb. He could feel the wind on his back from the cars rushing past him. In front of him towered a hundred-foot-tall, Egyptian obelisk. "Alright, we're at the obelisk. I noticed how it's aligned to the arches when we approached. Is that the location of the coordinates?" *It would make sense if it was.*

Inspector Parott shook his head. "Oh, *non."*

"So where's the location?" Winston panned his head, searching for clues related to the new *locus.*

"Monsieur, you are standing on it." Parott's cheeks rose, as he tugged at his belt.

Winston's eyes veered to his feet at a pigeon standing on top of a circular, cast-iron manhole cover. *This is no Jefferson Stone.* He felt perplexed.

"Coo, coo, what's going on? Who? Who-who-who? To the left, to the left."

"Are you sure about the coordinates?" Winston asked again.

"That is what your people gave us," Parott spoke confidently. He pulled a copy of a printed transcript of a secured police report from his coat pocket, unfolded it, and read aloud, "Latitude, 48 degrees, 51 minutes, 55 seconds, *Nord*; Longitude, 2 degrees, 19 minutes, 15 seconds, *Est."*

"Okay," Winston said.

"Raison d'etre ... ah ... what are you investigating?" Parott pried. *"Soupçon* of a true crime?"

"We're not certain," Susan replied honestly.

"What can you tell me about that obelisk?" Winston prompted, feeling sure that the manhole cover held no meaning.

"Bien sûr. You mean the sundial." Parott nodded slowly.

"Yes, the sundial. Amen—Whaddya know about the sundial?" Winston probed.

"The *Place de la Concorde* is the largest public square in Paris. It was originally the site where a statue of Louis XV once stood. That statue was replaced by the guillotine during the Revolution, at which time the square was called *Place de la Révolution*. Over a two-year period, nearly 1,200 Frenchmen lost their heads at this plaza, including Robespierre, Marie Antoinette, and Louis XVI. They say the mob caught the king's crown in a handbasket. This blood-soaked earth is now the foundation for this beautiful, 3,200-year-old obelisk from Luxor." Parott pointed to the hieroglyph-covered obelisk tipped in gold leaf.

"Sounds like a bloody mess," Winston commented.

"It is part of a long-standing tradition," Parott explained. "In the Middle Ages, the decapitated heads of enemies were impaled on staves and placed around the city as a warning against defiance to the government."

"A warning?" Susan repeated.

"*Oui.* But the guillotine has served other purposes. During the Revolution, some enlightened researchers used the guillotine to test the question, 'Does the head remain briefly conscious after decapitation?' The answer was determined after a condemned scientist instructed his assistant to watch his execution, and that he would blink his eyes as many times as he could. The assistant counted nearly twenty blinks after the head was severed. The head was still alive! We no longer use the guillotine in France. Capital punishment was abolished in 1977. We are a civilized country."

"Hmm." Winston's eyes blinked.

"You said Robespierre was executed here?" Susan gripped her notepad.

"*Oui*—Citizen Robespierre, a radical Jacobin leader, usurped the political power from the king and the Catholic Church and built a society around the secular ideas of Deism. He was interested in religion and promoted a state cult—first, to Supreme Reason—later, a Cult to the Supreme Being. Newton described the universe as a great clockwork." The inspector made circular motions with both hands, then interlocked the fingers in a tight grip, simulating the gears in a clock. "The French adopted his mechanical view of the universe into a radically revised version of Christianity known as Deism. Deists believed that everything—physical motion, human physiology, society, economics, and politics—could be understood by a set of rational principles found in the clockwork universe. If God created a rational universe, a universe that could be understood by human reason, then it was surmised that God was rational as well. If God is rational, then God could be understood through the use of reason without the use of pagan ideas such as mysticism, prayer, and the divinity of Christ." Parott shook his head. "Their age, which was hailed as the Age of Reason, was a time of serious stupidities. Without a king, France had become a headless kingdom. The Jacobins slaughtered nearly a quarter-of-a-million Christians in France as they set out to replace Christian ceremonies and superstitions with new rituals for a secular religion called The Cult of the Supreme Being. In 1793, Robespierre helped to make Deism into a state religion which included a festival to the Supreme Being. A column was erected here in Paris in front of a holy hill of initiation with a tree of liberty planted on top. It was a symbol derived from a book on alchemy and *qabalistic* literature ... the *Book of Abraham the Jew,* by Nicolas Flame. Robespierre became like a king and suffered the king's fate from the deadly French kiss. It would take nearly a hundred years before the idea of a state religion would be abandoned in France. In 1908, state churches and enforced religions were made illegal."

"But, a Supreme Being?" Susan questioned.

"Yeah, I could use a translation on that one," Winston added. "What was this Supreme Being?"

"*Qui*, it was a reference to society itself, the people, under the model of humanism. The Republic, the new Deist experimental government, was the Supreme Being."

"Tell us more about the obelisk," Winston requested.

"Obelisks were called *Tejen* by the ancient Egyptians, meaning 'protection' or 'defense.' They were also known as the *Ta-Wer,* the tower—*la magdala* of Osiris, the Egyptian god of resurrection. This obelisk is from the temple of Ramses II at Thebes."

"*Magdala* ... Osiris," Susan said with her tongue pressed against her teeth. She jotted in her notepad, her eyes drifting back and forth between the inspector and the obelisk. Her pen appeared to chase a light-filled shadow diffracting around its cone tip as she dotted an *i*.

"*Oui*, in 1831 this obelisk was sold by the Viceroy of Egypt to the French Masonic King, Louis Philippe. It is covered with hieroglyphs that picture the reigns of Pharaohs Ramses II and Ramses III. The inscriptions at the top of each face proscribe the correct ceremonies and rites of passage Ramses II followed in making offerings to the King of the Gods, Amun-Re."

"Amun-Re, a sun god," Winston remarked.

"*Oui*, the sun god. It is written that an obelisk can control the light of the sun."

"You mean casting shadows like a gnomon for a sundial?" Winston asked.

"*Non*." Parott shook his head. "It functioned as a crystal lens, or a mirror. It is said that a highly polished obelisk can reflect and bend light into a new direction. Stone is a highly reflective surface of both light and sound, unlike people who absorb nearly everything that hits them. Egyptian art, under the reign of Akhenatun, frequently illustrated a sunburst above an obelisk, with the rays of the sun, called the *Aten*. It is said that Egyptians had mastered this technique of scrying obelisks and could perform wonders using the light of the sun."

"Perhaps the Egyptians were into optical physics," Winston remarked.

"The Egyptians knew a lot of things, I suspect," Parott said. "You cannot build a civilization such as theirs unless you do. The French are like the Egyptians. They had their obelisks and we have our cathedrals."

"But you called that obelisk a sundial," Winston noted.

"*Oui*, Camille Flammarion had the idea to turn the *Place de la Concorde* into a giant sundial by using the shadow of this obelisk as a watch hand. His dream was realized in 1999 as part of the great millennium celebration. Government mathematicians traced out lines on the square from the base of the obelisk and provided a table of numbers inscribed in the pavement to enable tourists to work out the actual *heure*. The French consider it the world's largest sundial."

"I can see the shadow." Winston eyed the alignment of the shadow to the brass numbers in the pavement. "It tells time. But, I'm not sure it's the largest."

Parott checked his wristwatch, held his hand up, and motioned with all his fingers extended. "*Oui, neuf heures du matin*."

"Who was Camille Flammarion?" Susan asked.

"He was one of France's greatest astronomers," Parott explained. "He was originally a theologian by training. He wrote a groundbreaking book on ancient mythology and its association with astronomy, titled *Astronomical Myths*."

"I've heard of Flammarion," Winston remarked. "My mother was fascinated by his work. He wrote *Cosmologie Universelle* and *L'Astronomie*. I have copies of both books in my library at home."

"*Coo, coo, what's going on? Who? Who-who-who? To the left, to the left.*"

"*Par excellence*. That is correct, *monsieur*. Flammarion worked at the Paris Observatory. He was the first astronomer to theorize the possibility of life on Mars. I've read his book, *La Planète Mars*, many times. There is a crater named after him on Mars and another located at the center of every full moon."

"That, I didn't know," Winston admitted.

Parott pulled two Rowntree caramel candies from his coat pocket, unwrapped one, and popped it into his mouth. "Care for one?" he offered, pinching the candy between his fingers.

"No, thanks," Winston said.

Susan shook her head.

Parott pried the second caramel from its wrapper, wedged it into his mouth, and tossed the wrappers on the ground. "Fla ... ma ... ion was also a noted ba ... loo ... ist," he mumbled, his cheeks gyrating.

You look like a fat-faced gerbil, Winston thought.

"Flammarion performed one of the first long-distance flights in a hot-air balloon." Parott smacked his lips. "He was a founding father of French science fiction. Every French schoolboy knows his works, such as *Haunted Houses, The Unknown, God in Nature,* and his visionary apocalyptic novel, *Omega: The Last Days of the World,* which was made into a famous movie titled *The End of the World,* sometime in the 1930s. He also wrote of psychic experiences and his belief that he had discovered scientific proof of the existence of the *Lumen,* the light of the human soul after death, through spirit communications."

"A fellow soul-searcher." Winston grinned.

"The end the world?" Susan questioned.

"*Oil, Oui.* In Flammarion's *La Fin du Monde,* a fictional director of the Paris Observatory receives a *photophonic message* from Mars warning mankind of an impending disaster from a gigantic comet that could destroy the Earth."

"A photophonic message?" Susan questioned again. "What's that?"

"It's fiber optics," Winston explained. "It's a phone signal modulated on a contained beam of light."

"*Oui,* a message on a beam of light," the inspector agreed, licking the ends of his sticky fingers. "Flammarion was one of the first to write about interplanetary communication using beams of light modulated by selenium photocells. But, I am truly amazed at your astronomical knowledge." He pointed at Winston, then tapped his own nose with his finger. "You are brainy, like a well-cultured Parisian."

"It's only a hobby. My mother taught astronomy at the American University. Inspector, is there anything near here related to a meridian?" Winston pushed his investigation forward.

"*Oui.* The Paris Meridian passes near here. Flammarion was involved with that as well. He once worked for the Paris Observatory's Department of Longitude. He tried to establish the Paris Meridian as the prime meridian for the globe, but he failed. Greenwich was made the location for the Prime Meridian in 1884."

"Yes, we know," Susan affirmed. "Where is the meridian in Paris?"

"The line is near the *Louvre.*" Parott pointed.

"What can you tell us about this meridian?" Winston prompted.

"It was founded after the completion of the Paris Observatory, sometime around 1673, I think. *Aide-mémoire* ... I cannot place my finger of memory upon the year. It is the oldest observatory still in service in the world. It is a unique building. The Observatory is oriented from north to south. It is one of the few buildings in Paris aligned that way. Like Rome, Paris is a crisscross of radial streets, which resembles the mysterious Nazca patterns aligned to the stars in the Peruvian desert. The south face corner of the observatory marks the Paris meridian," Parott explained, making fluttering motions with his hands. "Sometime in 1995, I think, the Dutch artist, Jean

Dibbets, marked the meridian through Paris with 135 bronze plaques. Each plaque bears the name of François Arago—a prominent Freemason, historian, astronomer, and political figure. He is the Frenchman who discovered the presence of polarized patterns in the daylight sky. You can easily find the markers throughout the city."

"Arago ... polarization ... my nickel trick," Winston muttered.

Susan looked puzzled. "Nazca patterns? Aligned to the stars? Peru—"

"My father studied that stuff in Peru ... images of spiders, birds, and monkeys on the ground," Winston said before Susan could finish speaking. "He said they were associated with an ancient Peruvian water system. Inspector, is there anything unusual that has happened near the Paris meridian?"

"*Je ne comprende pas.*" Parott peered down at the pavement, shook his head, and gestured with his hands palms out. "I—I do not understand."

"Has anything near here been in the news lately?" Winston rephrased his question.

"*Oui.* They closed the doors of the *Salle des États* at the *Louvre*. The *Global Icon*, a *trompe l'oeil*, is being restored."

"I read about that in the paper. Something about damage to the frame of the painting," Susan remembered. "The frame was warped."

"*Oui.* The restoration is being performed at the Louvre laboratory." Parott pointed in the direction of the *Louvre's Porte des Lions*, the entrance to the museum's research facilities. "The restoration is being funded by the Rica-Walker Foundation. They are one of the many foundations which aid in the restoration of the *Louvre's* masterpieces. Rica-Walker has a strong interest in the art at the *Louvre*. It is one of your American foundations. I believe it is funded by the ZERVAN-OSIRIS Aging Well Institute in Dallas, Texas, a genetics company. They are associated with the European conglomerate Global Bio Design, which participates in DNA and RNA research. We have such a Frankenstein society." He shook his head in disapproval. "I understand they are cloning pet cats, so they can live forever by lacing them with human genes. Ah ... the French Paradox, there is no substitute for a Bordeaux Mouton Rothschild—our *aqua vitae*." He shook his head again. "Our police are working with Global Bio on the international genome project to create fingerprinting techniques using DNA. It is, what is the word ... a *fascinating* new science."

Fingerprints ... Winston glanced at the palms of his hands, then spied down at his shoes again. He shuffled his feet back and forth over the manhole cover. Arranged in a semi-circular pattern, casted letters spelled out a word he had seen before: CARNAC.

CleatBops, Winston flashed a thought. *A water system.* "Inspector, back to this manhole cover. Who or what is Carnac, besides a good pair of climbing shoes?"

"I admire your taste in shoes. French, are they not? *Je ne sais pas.* I do not know." Parott tentatively held up his hands, as though he was being arrested, and leaned forward to read the word on the manhole cover. "But, I can find out." He reached into the pocket of his blazer, pulled out a mobile phone, placed a call, and spoke for a few minutes. He lowered the phone and said to Winston, "I contacted Public Works. They are going to return my call."

Just as he finished speaking, the phone rang. Parott gestured with his thumb and pinky extended and wiggled his hand. "*Excusez-moi.* They are calling back." He smiled proudly. "Very fast. French efficiency." He answered the phone. "*Oui* ... oh ... hmm ... *oui*, Brittany. Hmm ... American. Hmm ... I see." Parott switched off his mobile phone. "Carnac is the name of the French company that made the manhole cover. It is an ironworks facility in Brittany, owned by Euro Metals, which is a division of an American firm, Carnac Information Solutions, a sister company of the Millennium Radio Group outside of Boston. EuroMetals designs the dies used in the stamping of European Euros."

The Inspector's a real popinjay. He covers all the bases. Winston felt impressed. "Inspector, what's beneath this manhole cover?"

"*Je ne sais pas.* The old sewers, probably. Let me call Public Works again." Parott placed another call and talked again. He stopped speaking and placed the mobile phone in his pocket. "*Monsieur* Winston, according to Public Works, this manhole leads to a service tunnel, one of the old entrances to the catacombs."

Susan lifted her eyes from the pages of her notepad. "Catacombs?"

"The Paris underground is riddled with a maze of over 300 kilometers of old catacombs," Parott answered. "It is the Empire of the Dead."

"Perhaps the *locus* we're looking for is below ground," Winston proposed.

"James, tell me you're not going to—" Susan balked.

"Yeah, let's shoot from the hip. Let's do a little creeping." Winston grinned. "How do we get down there?"

"Simply lift the cover," Parott replied. "Creeping?"

"I'll need a crowbar." Winston knelt to inspect the manhole cover. "Creeping is a term we use in the States for exploring unusual urban places," he explained.

The inspector made another phone call. Within minutes, a policeman wearing a navy blue, Gendarmerie Nationale uniform with a gold-ribboned, stovepipe hat and ankle-high military boots, trotted up carrying a crowbar.

"I received your message." The policeman panted as he caught his breath. "I retrieved it from the trunk of your auto, Inspector."

Parott gave the policeman a thumbs-up.

"Hello. Yes. That will do." Winston grabbed the crowbar. *Speedy Gonzales. He's faster than a three-toed ratite bird.* Winston placed the end of the crowbar in a cutout on the side of the iron cover and pried it open. "It's a heavy plate." He shoved it with one hand and peered into the street hole. "Now I need a flashlight."

"Here, *monsieur*," the policeman spoke. "Inspector Parott said he required that as well."

French efficiency, Winston thought, reaching for the flashlight. He aimed the light down the shaft.

Susan looked over his shoulder. "What do you see, James?"

"The rungs of a wrought-iron ladder and a dark hole that leads straight down *below ground.*" He paused. "I'm going to climb down and take a look. Inspector, do you have any information on this service tunnel? A map, maybe."

"I will see what I can do." Parott placed another phone call. "*Une carte,*" he mumbled. "Immediately!" He hung up the phone. "Quick," he ordered the policeman. "Go fetch *une carte.*"

Winston nimbly lowered himself into the brick-lined shaft, held onto the rusty rungs, and inched himself down toward the networked underbelly of Paris.

Parott hunched forward, moved his head next to Susan's, and looked down into the street hole. "Beware of the dragon, *monsieur*," he warned, extending his index finger.

"The dragon?" Winston questioned, staring up from the street hole.

"*Oui.* In the Middle Ages, there was a legend of a fierce and fiery dragon, known as the Peluda, who lived in a cave on the northern bend of the River Seine and demanded annual sacrifices of maidens and seamen from the residents of Rouen. Finally, St. Romanus saved the city by killing the dragon with a golden cross. But according to the tale, the dragon did not die. It fled to the underground streets of Paris, where it hides to this day. They say the Seine winds around the hills of Paris and leads to the new lair of the Peluda."

Winston reached the bottom with a loud *splash.* "What the—?"

"What was that?" Susan asked.

"*Eau de toilette.*" Parott frowned. "*Faux pas.*" He pinched his nose.

"There's six inches of water down here. I'm up to my ankles!" Winston yelled. "There's a long tunnel. I can make out a pinpoint of light at the far end. I'm going to have a look."

"Okay, Sherlock, this is beginning to smell like another one of your over-baked ideas, I'm coming down." Susan descended into the street hole. *Splash.* "You and your creeping. I still remember the last time we did something like this."

"Yeah, me too. It was fun. If you walk near the walls you can stay out of the deep water." Winston flexed his knees and flattened himself against the wall as he blended into the shadows.

"*Monsieur! Mademoiselle!*" the inspector shouted. "My agent has arrived with a printout, *une carte,* a map."

"French efficiency," Susan remarked.

Parott glanced at the concentric map of Paris. "You are in a sewer corridor that connects the river to the catacombs. I'm going to drop the map to you."

Winston high-stepped backward and positioned himself below the manhole to catch the map. As he looked up, he noted strange graffiti painted on the brick wall near the entrance. A chalk-white depiction of an obelisk was lit by the airy column of light spilling down from the street hole.

It must be a marker of some sort, Winston analyzed, his eyes wide and rigid. *Perhaps a reference to the street above. As below, so above?* As he stepped into the column of light, he noticed additional graffiti, meticulously painted on the walls. He discerned the outlined images of a candelabra, an octagon star, and an Egyptian, fish-shaped eye—the *udjat*—the Eye of Horus. "*Déjà vu,*" he reflected. *I've seen this before. But where? It looks like someone's warchalking. There can't be a wireless network down here.*

Suddenly, the rolled-up map bounced off the top of Winston's head. Susan caught it before it fell into the water.

"Pay attention, James," Susan snapped.

"I am. I was using my head," Winston retorted.

Susan unrolled the map under the light from the street hole. "Where are we?"

Winston took it from her hand. "Looks like a forgotten public works project. The map's incomplete. It only shows the tunnel from here to the river." He stowed the map in his shirt pocket. "Okay, let's have some fun. Let's check out this tunnel."

"I see the light." Susan ducked and sidestepped, balancing herself against the slippery, moss-covered sides of the sloping walls.

Winston moved toward the light, then stopped. "Shhh …" In the dark stillness of the underworld he folded himself into silence, listening for holes between the sounds.

Pat, tat, tat, tat … tat, tat …

"I hear water moving." Winston noticed a flash of silver reflecting in the dark liquid, like a snake of light slithering toward him. With one hand, he gripped a copper pipe connected to a row of equally spaced corroded gas lanterns lining the wall. "Something's down there." He extended his other hand to Susan. "Watch your head," he warned, "or you'll bump into one of these old lamps. Do you feel that breeze?"

"Yes, I can smell the river from here." She leaned forward.

Winston drew a quick breath. "No, that's something else. What's that smell?" He wrinkled his nose from a sulfuric stench. "Whoa! This tunnel smells like rotten eggs. Maybe there's a gas leak."

"It's the sewer," Susan reminded, her voice thin and choked. "It's probably hydrogen sulfide gas from the sewage. It can be toxic. But, I remember reading where doctors used hydrogen sulfide gas to extend the life of small animals in hibernation. The gas made their metabolic rate drop by 90 percent, with normal cellular activity slowing to almost a standstill, reducing the need for oxygen. Keep your nickel in your pocket. Don't light any kitchen matches down here."

Pat, tat, tat, tat … tat, tat … Shadows in the blackness shifted.

"Quiet. Hear something?" Susan tensed as she discerned a puddle of slow-crawling sludge. "What's that?"

Pat, tat, tat, tat … tat, tat …

"It's at your feet." Winston rolled his eyes at something grazing his ankle.

"There're rats down here!" Susan recoiled, as a dozen sewer rats swam past her feet. "Give me that." She tried to snatch the flashlight from Winston's hand.

Skinner Rats, Winston thought. *Rats in someone's maze.* "Yeah, but that smell. There's something in the water. Is it a snake?" He aimed the flashlight.

"Jesus! It's a dead cat." Susan felt her skin crawl. "It's covered in maggots."

Hundreds of squirming, white maggots were digging into the flesh of the bloated animal. The wiggling movements of the crawling maggots made the cat appear to quiver as though it was still breathing.

"Maybe it's just gassed. Let's bag it and ship it to that institute in Texas. Cats have nine lives; maybe they can resurrect it," Winston wisecracked. He grabbed Susan's hand tightly. "This way."

They ankle-waded nearly sixty meters and the fetid stench dissipated. The dank corridor became boxy and narrow as they came to a rusty gate of vertical bars bolted over an entry overlooking the river. Standing in mire oozing past his feet and trickling into the Seine, Winston pushed on the gate, trying to open it. He detected a heavy padlock secured to a latch on the other side.

Trapped … He shook the gate hard with his full weight to test the bolts and padlock. *I'm a prisoner,* he thought, framing his face between the bars and spying out beyond them at the barges and tourist boats docked along the Seine. He was struck by the sun's rays glistening the color of spilt honey over the water, as a dozen graceful white swans swam in orbital eddies against the currents. From his perspective, he could barely see the copper roof and the cast-iron Art Nouveau train station clock faces of the *Musée d'Orsay.* It was 9:18.

"I see civilization." Winston reached into his pocket. "This is obviously an entrance to the tunnel by way of the river." He referenced the map. "We're directly under the arch of the *Pont da le Concorde,* the bridge that links the *Palais Bourbon* of the *Assemblée Nationale* to the plaza and the obelisk—the political heart of the city."

"Maybe this is the dragon's cave." Susan gripped the bars with both hands, her eyes scanning the river.

Prancing at the edge of the concrete embankment, a pigeon cooed a staccato warning in one-note syllables. *"Coo, coo, coo, what's going on? Who? Who-who-who?"* The bird approached the gate and pecked at the toe of Winston's shoe. *"Go back, go back."*

Winston scooted backwards. "Let's see what's in the other direction." He folded the map into his pocket.

They *sloshed* back into the tunnel.

Winston noticed the column of light falling from the street hole onto the painting of the white obelisk. "No one's getting lost in this tunnel. Are you still there, Inspector?" he called, stepping into a haze of light.

"Pardonnez-moi?"

Winston faintly heard Parott's voice. "Are you still there?" he yelled again.

"Comment? Oui, monsieur. Oui. Did you find what you were looking for?" Parott held his hand over his mouth and yawned.

"Not yet. We've crawled down a real rabbit hole," Winston said under his breath. "I don't really know what I'm looking for."

"Who does?" Susan muttered, observing Winston's chiseled features picked out in the spray of light as he stopped to study the graffiti. "Quit wasting time. Hustle up, James!" She yanked at Winston's arm. "Point the light this way."

They forged onward through the darkness for about a hundred meters. The tunnel snaked back and forth as though it had been rippled by an earthquake. Their shadows, undulating on the walls, resembled robed monks pacing in line. The tunnel made a sharp left turn. The beam from the flashlight diffracted around the corner, casting fuzzy shadow-light on unseen things before they could be revealed. Rounding the corner, they froze in their steps.

"Damn—Look at that!" Winston jumped back. The tunnel was sealed off by a wall constructed entirely of human skulls, as though someone had used the heads of the dead as bricks. "Skullduggery galore … I think we just walked up Satan's asshole." The flashlight slipped from his hand. "Shit!" The refractions from the underwater light lit up the bell-shaped chamber with a cold, organic, eerie aura of death.

"Jeez …" Susan suppressed a bone marrow chill. "The inspector did say 1,200 souls lost their heads."

"Yeah, lost souls," Winston said dimly with an uneasy feeling he was violating the space. He bent down and fished in the fetid slush. "Got it." He retrieved the dripping flashlight and aimed it at Susan. Her eyes reflected the light back at him, her hair shimmering like embers changing colors in a fire. He noticed her shivering. "Frightened by the wall?"

"No, James." Her teeth chattered. "It's the water. I have cold feet."

"Whaddya make of this?" Winston stared in amazement while fanning the flickering light in a slow 360-degree turn. "This architecture of horror is hard to see.

This light's on the blink." *Tap, tap, tap.* He tapped the flashlight. Its faint glow illuminated the chamber. Anchored like a *lingam* to a *yoni,* a coffin-size, pink-marble slab stood as though floating in water before the wall of skulls. Candle wax covered the top of the slab in a multicolored mix of slickened lumps.

"I don't know." Susan's eyes narrowed, her forehead creasing in a quizzical frown. "It doesn't look like a letterbox. Skull collectors ... This chamber could be an ossuary." With a sense of dread, she touched the candle wax. The congealed puddle had flowed into deep gouges cut into the shape of a pentagram overlaid with a Star of David off-set within a circle.

The light went dark.

Winston slapped the flashlight with the palm of his hand. The light held steady, reflecting off the water in a rainbow spectrum arching across the chamber. He directed the beam to the carved symbols covering the stone ceiling. Small shards of quartz and iridescent turquoise in the mortar twinkled in the shifting light, playing tricks on his eyes. *Like stars,* he thought. "What's this?" He lumbered forward. "It's the same graffiti I saw at the manhole." He swept his beam over the patterned images formed by the aged, slim-covered skulls in the wall: an octagonal star, a loop in the shape of a fish-eye, and a group of smaller skulls lined up in rows. He counted, "... four ... five ... six ... my lucky number." He aimed the light back to the ceiling. "It's a canopy of symbols, like the constellations ... a wireless network."

"Artistic expression, perhaps?" Susan pondered. "Art eternal ... subliminals on the wall ... Plato's cave."

"Or maybe we're inside someone's letterbox," Winston thought out loud.

Susan glanced down at the slab and noticed how the wax became translucent when illuminated by the flashlight. "James, shine your light on the top of this stone. I think I see something ... an inscription maybe."

Winston trudged through the water, stepping closer. "Where?"

"Look." She dug her thumbnail into the wax, peeling bits away from the surface of the stone. "There's something ... letters maybe? They're covered by the wax."

"It's like a steganographic technique used by the Greeks," Winston compared. "In the *Histories of Herodotus,* a soldier named Demeratus sent a warning about an impending Persian attack on Sparta. He carved a message into a wooden panel and concealed it under colored wax. It's called the secret message that saved democracy. Let's see what we have." He angled the beam from the flashlight. "Yes, there's something here, but it's hard to make out. It resembles the letter A."

Susan chipped away more wax with the end of her pen, piece by piece, revealing the letters of a chiseled inscription encircling the pentagram.

"Looks like Latin," Winston said. "Except for these words ... HELL and SAN

GREAL below this crack in the stone."

"It does look like Latin," she observed. "But the words are separated by circles—No ... it's a Greek letter ... Omega."

SOLVE ET COAGULA Ω AUDE Ω SAPERE Ω DEUS Ω ABSCONDITUS Ω DEUS Ω VULT

"Alright. What does it say?" Winston urged.

Susan moved the tip of her finger from letter to letter and translated, "Solution and coagulation ... Dare to know ... a God that is hidden from man ... God wills it."

"What does that mean?" Winston wondered, his eyes darting up at the strange images formed by the skulls in the wall.

"I don't know, James. Do you see any other inscriptions?"

Winston circled to the other side of the stone, searching with the flashlight. "No, that's it." He glanced at the inscription.

"James, look at this." Susan chipped away wax from the sides of the pentagram. "There're little holes bored into the top the stone. They're patterns ... an egg shape and a skull motif. This looks like a snake. Jesus ... the stone is stained. Is it blood?"

Winston repositioned the light over the pentagram mottled with brick-brown-colored patches. "Seventy-seven-three-aitch ... I recognize this ... These holes resemble star positions in the night sky. This is the dipper constellation."

"What—seventy-seven, thirty-eight ...? The *Fry-Jefferson Map*," Susan recalled. She rubbed her fingertips over the holes in the stone. "What's the other?"

"Hell ... I don't know. Part of it's worn away." Winston's eyes drifted back to the symbols formed by the skulls in the wall. He noticed the words and names, *Je suis la fille - J. P. Marat - 72/Moses - TJ/1787*, painted across the foreheads of four of the skulls. He felt *the presence. TJ/1787...?* He eyed the slab. *A Jefferson Stone* ... "Susan, I think this is somebody's shrine or something," he surmised with a sense of apprehension. "With all these skulls, this god-awful place *is* a dragon's lair."

"It's a dead end, that's for sure," Susan quipped. "Let's get back up top. Maybe the inspector can tell us something about it."

With a quick flicker, the flashlight went dead, damaged by its filthy baptism. Darkness.

Tap, tap, tap. Winston repeatedly slapped the flashlight. "It's dead!" he complained, scratching the back of his hand. "This water makes my skin itch." His eyes dilated and quickly adjusted. "Hey, we don't need a flashlight."

The cold, ghoulish chamber was filled with a subdued, greenish glow. The water reflected a faint, oily mix of muted bioluminescence.

"The bacterium in the water is probably giving off the light," Susan assumed. "It uses bioluminescence in order to cell-cell communicate. It's a process called quorum sensing. Certain types of marine life can do this through light-producing organs, such as the deep-sea *Eurypegasus draconis*."

"That's Latin." Winston reached for Susan's hand. "Translation, please?"

"A dragon fish."

"Well, let's follow the glow and find our way back to the light of day."

CRAWLING OUT OF THE STREET HOLE, Winston noticed Parott and the policeman idly talking, pinching unfiltered Gitane cigarettes between their fingers like little torches of freedom. A gray cloud, spiraling around their heads, engulfed them as though they were hiding in deep thought.

Dragon's breath, Winston compared, approaching the two men with squishing sounds coming from his soggy shoes. "Inspector, have you ever been down there?" He waved smoke out of his face. His stinging eyes blinked.

"*Non, mon-sieur,*" the inspector's voice broke. He quickly swiped his fingers out from under his chin and eyed Winston's soaked shoes.

Squish, squash— "There's a strange chamber of commerce—an abandoned shrine with odd graffiti on the walls." Winston pointed the flashlight toward the street hole.

"Oh, I'm not surprised. Achk—" Parott coughed. He tossed his unfinished cigarette into the street with a flick of his thumb and nicotine-stained index finger. Its embers glowed as it bounced across the pavement. "Young people from all over Europe play their occult games in the catacombs. It is part of their rite of passage. It has been going on for years. It is meaningless, totally harmless. I assure you it is not worth ruining a good pair of shoes."

With a smug frown, the policeman peered bug-eyed at Winston's soaked shoes. He took another drag on his cigarette and shook his head in disapproval.

Okay, now I'm getting festered. "But there's a wall of human skulls down there forming strange shapes," Winston spoke urgently.

"*Monsieur,*" Parott bantered, "it is the catacombs. That is what you find in the catacombs." He tapped the side of his temple with his finger and darted his eyes to the policeman. "*Mon oeil,*" he spoke beneath his breath.

The policeman drew a smile. He pulled down the lower skin under his right eye with the two front fingers holding his cigarette.

Squish, squash— Susan joined them. "What do you make of all this, James?"

"I don't know," Winston mumbled, squinting at the sunlight reflecting off the gilded tip of the obelisk. He retrieved a gold nickel from his pocket and rolled it between his fingers. His eyes crept down the weathered face of the stone pillar as though he was reading the hieroglyphs of birds, eyes, and ankhs. "Obelisks, meridians, and a wall of skulls," he recapped the day's experiences. "We have two commonalities here. Contact the Backdoor Group and have them sample the words *obelisk* and *meridian* as possible *keywords.* Let's see what happens."

Susan proceeded to make a secure satellite phone call by way of Sky-Link. She pulled a wireless "Jawbone" from her pocket and stuck it in her left ear. The tiny earpiece connected to her satellite phone made use of special military technology to block out background noise.

"It's going to take a few minutes." *STA-KA, STA-KA,* the phone crackled. "I've got a tone. It's tuned to the wrong frequency. I'm picking up a satellite link. It's a rerun of the Howard Stern Show Revelations Game. Okay. There—now I have it."

"That's one of those phones with all the gadgets. I thought that hiptop was smarter than that," Winston joked, then frowned thoughtfully. "Inspector, what's that building at the end of the street? The one that looks like the Lincoln Memorial?" He pointed northeast. "It's got to be close to where we saw the ossuary."

"The Lincoln Memorial?" Susan repeated, waiting for the call to connect. She stared in the direction Winston pointed. *It's in front of an obelisk*, she reflected. *Beep, beep.* "Yes, hello—" she answered.

"It is the *Place de la Madeleine*," Parott explained, "dedicated to Mary Magdalene, who held the cup at the foot of the cross and caught the blood of Christ. The church is near the *Place de L'Opera*, 'the Hub of the Universe.' It's not far from where your country's ambassador to France, Thomas Jefferson, once lived. It is an old, Catholic church built right after the revolution in 1776. It is sometimes called the 'Temple to the Glory of the Great Army—' " He shook his head. "*Pardon, non ... je regrette.* The original church at that location may have been built around 810. It is one of the older churches in Paris. I believe it was rebuilt in 1366, perhaps, and rebuilt again around 1480. It became the seat of a Catholic parish around 1640. I think it was restored again in 1660. The church was demolished to make way for a larger property in 1776, maybe earlier. Its construction was delayed many times. For years, its huge unfinished columns stood like giant candlesticks waiting for a flame. Its pediment depicts a carving of the Last Judgment—Heaven, Hell, and Earth. Everybody in Paris calls it the *Madeleine*, but its official name is the Church of *Sainte-Marie Madeleine*."

"Jefferson lived near there? This doesn't feel right to me. There's something strange about that wall of skulls," Winston persisted. *I can't put my finger on it.*

"*Je ne sais pas.* I do not know any more about the skull wall." Parott massaged his forehead. "It's a reverence to the dead, I suppose. We are all on the way to dying. There are hundreds of such walls under Paris. I am certain it is nothing unusual."

"Or a reverence to the head," grumbled the policeman, who had been listening to their conversation. With a Bogart expression on his face, he flicked his cigarette and drew it to his lips.

"Whaddya mean by reverence to the head?" Winston pressed the policeman.

"*Avec plasir,* I thought everyone knew this," the policeman replied smugly, "a reverence to the head of Saint Denis." He exhaled a circle of smoke, then flipped his cigarette to the ground and stomped it out with a twist from the toe of his shoe.

Susan put her Jawbone in her pocket. "They're going to call me back." She pulled out her notepad.

"Who or what is Saint Denis?" Winston probed.

"Some consider Saint Denis to be a symbol derived from pagan Celtic head worship," Parott explained. "According to legend, the hill of Montmartre, meaning Mount of Martyrs, formed the shape of a human head. Thousands of years ago, the ancient Celts came to that hill to worship the gods Cunomaglus and the three-headed Lugus-Mercurius. Of the eight hills of Paris, it is the most revered. When the Romans settled Paris, they built a Temple to their god Mercury, the guide to the underworld, on that hill. In the twelfth century, Benedictine monks built a monastery near *Rue des Abesses*, next to the hill. It became the seat of a powerful abbey. It was there, in 1534, on the day of the Feast of the Assumption of Mary, that Ignatius Loyola and his six companions took vows that led to the formation of the Society of Jesus, the Spanish Mystics, once the strong arm of the body of Christ in Paris. Today the *Sacré-Coeur* Basilica stands on the summit. It was constructed at the end of the nineteenth century. Its famous, pastry-white dome dominates the Paris skyline to the north. You can see it from here." He pointed. "It is the big bird egg sitting on the horizon."

Winston looked in the direction Parott indicated. "Yeah. It resembles the Capitol

Building in Washington ... or an igloo at the North Pole."

"Or the Taj Mahal," Susan connected. *Spanish Mystics ... the Capitol Building.*

"A lingam or a mundane egg," the policeman added, "the divine place of creation. *Sacré-Coeur* is the flagship of Catholic devotion to the Holy Virgin in Paris. It attracts thousands of pilgrims from all over the world. At the end of the nineteenth century, Montmartre was the heart and soul of artistic life in Paris, the home of the free-minded intellectual Bohemians. Many artists, such as Berlioz and Picasso, lived and worked there. It was *the* Mecca of world culture and modern art, where the straight lines of the Cubists fragmented our reality with the spirit of the new artistic shape of things to come. It is where they *stopped the world.*" He nodded. "Our modern world was formed there by *avant-garde* artists who bent both time and space, and asked us to observe our lives with a new attitude."

"*Oui.* Now, it is the heart of the Red Light District," Parott chuckled, "the Snake."

"The patron saint of the Red Light District," Winston wagged his head, "and a hill in the shape of a head." *An egg ... the place of creation.*

"There is a macabre legend associated with Saint Denis." Parott pointed in the direction of *Sacré-Coeur.* "He was a Christian missionary sent by the Church in Rome to convert the pagans who settled Lutece, an ancient Celtic community that the Romans built upon, which is now Paris. Saint Denis and his two companions were successful in converting much of the population to the radical Christian religion. So the local Roman Governor ordered the three to appear before him to recant and submit to Roman authority. Saint Denis refused to submit, and he and his companions were imprisoned and tortured. The Roman governor then ordered their executions at the Temple of Mercury, at the summit of the highest hill outside of Lutece. According to the legend, the overzealous legionnaires condemned and decapitated Saint Denis before he reached the top of the hill."

"Like Saint Paul, they cut off his head," the policeman added.

"Yeah, they seem to have a habit of doing that here," Susan mocked, glancing at the obelisk.

"Once decapitated, Saint Denis picked up his head and proceeded up the hill and down the other side, for six kilometers," Parott said. "They say that at *Rue Yvonne-le-Tac*, he washed his bloody head in a sacred spring and came to the end of his trek."

"The spring is a holy place," the policeman remarked, "in the hand of God."

"On the north side of the descending slope of the hill, he fell to his knees before a converted holy woman named Catulla, and there he died. She buried him at that site, in a Christian ceremony. Sprigs of wheat immediately sprang from his grave. The martyrdom of Saint Denis, as well as the slaughter of early Christians in the area, inspired the naming of this hill the Mount of Martyrs, or *Montmartre.*"

"*Oui,*" the policeman agreed.

"The famous Saint Genevieve, who courageously routed the Huns from Paris, was a follower of the teachings of Saint Denis," Parott recalled. "She ordered a chapel to be built over his grave. King Dagobert, one of the last Merovingian kings, lavishly decorated the chapel's interior. He was buried there. This started a long tradition of interring the royalty of the three great dynasties of France in the crypts below the womb of that church. King Pepin and his son, Charlemagne, rebuilt the chapel and used its crypts as a depository for manuscripts and holy relics—"

"*Oui*, the treasured relics," the policeman said.

Parott nodded in agreement. "I think it was in 1121 that the humanist, Abott Suger, ordered the construction of a basilica for Saint Denis. It was the first basilica to make use of Gothic architecture. Abott Suger served as the king's counselor and helped to delineate the boundaries of the French kingdom. He also established one of the first schools for masons and architects, which promoted his view that architecture served as a representation for a cosmology of the heavens brought down to Earth. It was an 'as above, so below' view of architecture, where a cathedral served as a microcosm of the heavens—a representation of God's Kingdom here on Earth."

Building a heaven on Earth, Winston pondered.

"The Basilica of Saint-Denis was the first church in the world to feature a stained-glass, rose window—the hallmark of later Gothic churches, such as Notre Dame," Parott informed. "I adore the stained glass at Saint-Denis, especially the Quadriga of Aminadab window, which illustrates God the Father holding the Christ on the cross resting upon the four-wheeled Ark of the Covenant. In Gothic churches, God was associated with a divine light, a concept adopted from the ancient Jewish and Roman beliefs that the *invisible presence* of God existed within light. The rose window was an adaptation of the Roman *oculus*, the hole in the domed roof of the Pantheon in Rome. The rose window at Saint-Denis has since been transformed into a dial-plate for a clock. But, the choir of Saint-Denis still creates a colorful hymn of light, which serves as a manifesto of Gothic art and architecture for Christian Europe. The arched double deambulatory and its surrounding chapels form an uninterrupted crown of multicolored splendor, with pictures teaching lessons within the Bible."

"So the light of God is pushed through stained glass," Winston repeated. *Billy's dreamcatchers.*

"*Oui*, the shimmering shards of divine stories. It is a beautiful sight to see," Parott noted. "As with most medieval cathedrals throughout Europe, Saint-Denis was a depository for religious treasures, such as reliquaries, liturgical vessels, and Regalia objects used in the coronation of the early French Kings."

"*Oui, la treasures* …," the policeman murmured in awe, "the holy treasures—"

"*Oui, la treasures,*" Parott affirmed. "Those treasures also included items such as ancient manuscripts and grimoires. Much of it originated from the Holy Land, such as texts acquired by the Holy Hieromartyr Irenæus, the Bishop of Lyon, known as the Apostle of All Gaul—the special and, after God, sole protector of the realm. It is even said that the legendary Holy Grail was among the treasures of Saint-Denis."

Greed. Winston shook his head, observing the avaricious excitement of the two men. *Seven out of seven.*

"The *San Gréal*—the head of Saint Denis," the policeman said, wide-eyed. "The Templar *baphomet* … the hidden face of God."

Old Bucktooth Rosalyn's picture, Winston remembered.

"In 1793, revolutionaries attacked the basilica because they considered it a symbol of the monarchy," Parott said. "The tombs were damaged. Some were totally destroyed. Exhumed bodies were thrown into common graves. But, the basilica escaped complete destruction. The tombs of Francis I and Catherine de Medici were spared. Many of the treasures were looted and lost. Others were taken away to safety, where according to legend, they are still hidden to this day."

"Baphomet?" Susan questioned. "*San Gréal* ... the other word on the stone."

"*Oue*, the severed head of the Absolute, possibly the sea-goat Makara or the horn-headed fertility God of Mendes, the daemon guardian of the *doorway* to the Temple of Solomon and lost treasure—allegedly worshiped by the warring Knights Templar at their old fortress Le Temple here in Paris. It is said the severed head caused the land to germinate and made the Templars rich and wise. It is only folklore of some crazed esoteric cult, *Mademoiselle*," Parott added. "It is a story that legends are built upon."

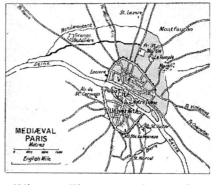

"And Paris is such a legend," the policeman muttered.

Buzz— Susan's satellite phone rang.

"Excuse me, Inspector. I have a call coming in from the birds." She answered the call. "Hello. ... Yes. That's good news. ... I'll tell you later. ... Send it by e-mail."

Susan switched off the phone and motioned to Winston. They stepped away from the inspector and the policeman. "James," she spoke too quietly for the others to hear, "Marx said he's been watching us over a Paris webcam. He wants to know why we disappeared into the manhole." She pointed to a nearby lamppost.

"All watched over by machines of loving grace." Winston waved at the lamppost. "Bet you wish you were here." He stomped his foot. *Squish, squash—*

"James, quit playing around. The Big Lug says that the keyword *meridian* does nothing. When he tried *obelisk*, the clock rate of the virus slowed by twenty percent. It totally erased the first segment from the virus string. It's falling apart under your acid test. We are on the right track with your codes and commonalities." Susan beamed.

"*Bingo*," Winston said. "We're off and running."

"Hume also said he stripped a new segment. He's waiting on a cross-check from a set of coordinates. Do you see any other connections from the catacombs?"

"No," he replied. "It's just heads and skulls."

"And Baphomet," Susan voiced. Her phone *buzzed* again. "That's the new coordinates. They're e-mailing them to me."

Squish, squash— Winston stepped closer. "Where?"

She squinted at the incoming e-mail on the digital screen, then held out the phone so Winston could see.

He read aloud, "Latitude 41 degrees, 54 minutes, 08 seconds North, Longitude 12 degrees, 27 minutes, 14 seconds East—"

"It's the Vatican," Susan interrupted.

"Holy thunder. Now we get to visit the keeper of the *keys*." Winston looked up at the lamppost and nodded. The flashlight in his hand flickered on and off.

A hungry, snow-white pigeon pecked at a dead maggot stuck to the side of Winston's shoe.

"Coo, coo, coo, what's going on? Who? Who-who-who? Go back, go back."

Day 10
Alberti's Perspective

De Pictura is written in three parts, the first of which gives the mathematical description of the perspective Alberti considered necessary to properly understand the techniques of painting. Alberti writes: "A painting is the intersection of a visual pyramid at a given distance, with a fixed center and a defined position of light, ..." Alberti used the principles of geometry and the science of optics to create a proper perspective.

 THE GREEN-STRIPED, yellow taxi parked in front of a hotel-like entrance cut into a towering, granite-block wall. The terrestrial radio sputtered the last few bars of "Magic Bus," then *crackled* and an Italian singer began a poor rendition of "Knocking on Heaven's Door." *Click— STA-KAT.* The driver switched off the radio.

"Is this it?" Winston asked Susan, who sat next to him in the backseat. He stared down the narrow *Viale Vaticano.* "I thought we were having a go-see at the Vatican."

"This *is* the Vatican," Susan replied. "It's the museum entrance. They have a guide waiting for us. Looks like it's going to rain. Is the equipment working correctly?"

"I think so." Winston switched on the GPS. "This is not the spot."

A *tap-tap-tap* came from the taxi's side window. "*Mi scusi, signore, signora,*" a voice spoke. *Tap-tap.* The crooked handle of a collapsed umbrella tapped the glass.

Winston rolled down his window.

"*Buongionio,* I am Monsignor Nicolo Torre of the Society of Jesus." A tall priest with a Sicilian dialect glared at Winston through the window. Angry acne scars were pockmarked across his forehead, as though branded from temple to temple with the word 'nasty.' The bridge of his nose, arching like a flying buttress on Notre Dame, was covered with tiny, bright-red veins and highlighted by dark purple splotches below his knife-edge cheekbones. "Are you the guests from the U.S. Embassy?" Moving his face closer, he almost poked Winston in the eye with his birdlike beak.

"Yes, we are." Susan handed the driver fifty Euros. She and Winston stepped from the taxi and greeted the monsignor. "I'm Susan Hamilton and this is James Winston."

"Good morning, *Signora* Hamilton, *Signor* Winston." Torre shook Winston's hand in a lion-paw grip, testing to see who could squeeze the tightest.

"Hello, Monsignor." Winston squeezed back. He noted the monsignor's sinister blend of charm and menace. *He's well dressed. He's not wearing a white collar. Maybe he's an honest man.* With a second glance, Winston warily took in the contrasting crudeness and elegance of Torre's sharply tailored suit, with a Y-shaped patterned, gold button pinned to his lapel. *Oiled back hair... a real Dapper Dan ... Look at that bedizen outfit: the white shirt, black bow tie, and yellow alligator shoes. He's as neat as a pin, except for that little smudge on the end of his nose. All he needs is a top hat, and he'd look like a tall gentoo penguin from Petermann Island. Old Bucktooth Rosalyn,* he remembered. *He's a curious fellow, looks a little lean, hard, and hungry. Maybe a little festered. He's got a face that would guarantee him a guilty verdict if he ever stood before a jury. Perhaps he's not an honest man.*

"Welcome to our country. I was ordered by the SISMI from the Forte Braschi to meet you here," Torre spoke in a wheezing voice. "I am an art historian with the Vatican Museums. I am staying at St. Paul's Outside the Wall. I have been assigned to the Vatican for only a few months. I previously taught European history at the school of the Sun King, the Lycée Louis-le-Grand in Paris." He politely shook Susan's hand. "May I see your credentials?"

"Paris is a beautiful city." Susan handed Torre a document from her shoulder bag.

"The NSA," Torre murmured suspiciously, "the American KGB. This must be important. There are no secrets at the Vatican. Everything is in plain sight." He handed the document back to her. His penetrating ebony eyes pored over Winston from head to toe, scanning his attire. *America's answer to 007 ...* He noticed the features of Winston's face. *A Sergio Leone western...?* "*Signor*, you look Italian—"

"We're doing a little historical fact-finding. Studying architecture, nothing more," Susan assured. "There's nothing to be concerned about."

"You have a nice voice, *signora*, very *auduboni*. Do you sing?"

"Sometimes," Susan sang.

"Aahchew!" Torre covered his mouth with his hand and pinched his long Roman nose. "*Scusi.*" *Sniff.* "You must think I am rude, but I have allergies."

"We need to see the area near the entrance of St. Peter's," Winston explained, eyeing the monsignor's hand. "What's the best way to the front of the Basilica?"

"Through the museums," Torre replied, wiping his hand with a bloodred handkerchief from his coat pocket. "*Per favore*, this way." He led them to a set of gigantic bronze doors sculptured to symbolize the creation of the world. He slipped his hand under the front of his coat, searching for a security card hanging around his neck. Pulling on a beaded chain, Torre retrieved a hand-carved rosary of black onyx bearing a tiny, silver crucifix. "*Un momento.*" He held up his index finger. "I'm always getting these confused." He brandished a smile of rotten teeth held together by bad dental work. Gold met silver as he kissed his rosary and whispered, "*In nomine Patris, et Filii, et Spiritus Sancti.*"

Winston stood cross-armed, peering up above the arching doorway at a carving of the Vatican seal—a pinecone-shaped hat in front of two crossed keys above the motto, *Ex Oriente Lux*. "Hmm, a skull and crossbones design ..." Winston winked at the two surveillance cameras on either side of the seal. "Keys to the back door."

Torre glanced at Winston and pointed with his umbrella to the seal. "*Claves Sancti Petri*—the keys of Saint Peter. A sign of fair warning."

Winston's eyes wandered to Torre.

"It's from the coat of arms of Saint Peter, the Prince of the Apostles," Torre explained. "Christ gave Saint Peter the keys of Heaven and Earth. A key symbolizes the authority of the church to forgive sin in the name of Jesus. The two keys symbolize the dual authority to open Heaven to repentant sinners and to lock Heaven from the unforgiven—the keys to Heaven and Hell."

"I read something about that in a brochure," Winston joked.

"When the keys are emblazoned on an inverted cross," Torre informed, "they form the coat of arms of Saint Peter who, according to our tradition, asked that his cross be mounted upside down because he felt unworthy to be crucified like our Lord."

"I know how that feels." Winston thought about his close encounter at Devil's Tower.

Torre felt a drizzle and opened the umbrella over Susan. "A key is a symbol for unlocking a new truth. For example, there is the famous Merchant's Key known as the Rule of Three, or the Golden Rule of proportions. The key was often used by merchants during the Renaissance for solving problems dealing with proportions related to currency exchange. Rule one—unite the thing you want to know about with rule two, anything that is dissimilar to it. Then rule three—compare the answer by the remaining thing. The result is always dissimilar to the thing you want to know about. The result is a new truth. Questions often lead to unexpected answers."

"Now, that sounds like something Billy might say." Winston grinned at Susan.

The monsignor closed the umbrella and reached under his coat again, fished out his security card connected to a long linked chain, and swiped it in the doorlock. A green LED display lit up above the words **Rapid-I-Scan** etched on the brass panel.

Snap, Snap. Torre double-snapped his boney fingers. "*Per favore,* follow me." He escorted his guests through a short corridor.

Winston squinched his nose from a strong sanitized odor, as his shoes *squeaked* across the polished marble floor. He noticed a mop in a plastic bucket on rollers propped in one corner of the entry. *They keep things clean.*

Torre eyed the bucket. "Maintenance." He locked his hands together and gingerly shook them in front of his chest. "The Vatican is where you come to get down on your hands and knees." He hung his umbrella on a nearby hat rack before passing through a security arch.

The archway *beeped.* A stone-faced guard in a black suit, sitting in a glassed-in booth beside a bank of video monitors, signaled Torre forward.

"Are you armed?" Torre asked, lowering his arms.

"No," Susan replied, stepping through the *beeping* archway.

"And you, *signore?*" the guard addressed Winston with a nod.

The archway *beeped* again.

Winston pointed to the GPS in his hand. "No, my penknife's on my altar table."

They proceeded to a two-foot square, brushed aluminum panel recessed in a side wall. At its center, a rim of light glowed purple from a camera lens that resembled the face of HAL 9000 in the movie *2001.*

"*Scusi,* I have to check you through our new security system," Torre said. "Look into this lens, *per favore.*"

Susan looked into the lens, and the display flashed green.

"*Identification confirmed,*" a soothing female voice resonated from the panel.

Winston took his turn at the fish-eye, but nothing happened.

"Try again. Everyone is entitled to a second chance." Torre held out his handkerchief. "*Signor* Winston, do you have a loose eyelash? Try to remain still. Stop your blinking. Your blinking is almost like Morse Code."

"No, thank you, I left mine in my coat pocket." *Big boys don't cry. Plus, I keep my nose clean.* "I'm just a little festered." Winston tried again. The LED flashed. Within seconds, the scanner cross checked against the known IDs in the EU Police database and Menwith's Global ID Registry AfterLifeLog.

Sniff. "You *are* who you say you *are,*" Torre muttered.

In small steps that made him appear busy, the monsignor ushered his guests past a set of glass doors leading to another part of the museums. "To your immediate right is the *Pinacoteca Vaticana*—the Vatican Picture Gallery. It holds a number of world-famous paintings by Giotto, Angelico, Leonardo da Vinci, Tiziano, and many more."

"Da Vinci?" Susan probed.

"*Sì*, Leonardo lived here at the Vatican at one time. He was the master of *chiaroscuro*. He was also a great prankster—a very mischievous man." Torre's metallic smile lingered as he spoke. "He was always modeling miniature dragons out of his art material to try to scare people." *Snap, Snap.* "This way, *per favore.*"

The three strolled down a wide hall lined with Greek statuaries of pagan gods.

"Is this your first visit to Rome?" Torre asked.

"Yes," Susan replied.

"My mother once said my father swept her away at Ephesus, and that I was conceived at a bed and breakfest east of Monte Compatri," Winston said. "I guess that makes me Italian." He winked at Torre.

Torre removed a brochure from his coat pocket and handed it to Susan. "Our facilities are comprised of separate museums, which together have over a thousand individual rooms of art and antiquities. There is a floor plan in the brochure. The founding of these museums can be traced back to 1503, when Pope Julius II placed a statue of Apollo in the courtyard of the Belvedere Palace."

"It's a cultural haven," Winston noted.

"*Sì.* The Vatican Museums house the world's largest art collection. Let me introduce you to a part of that culture. Our Egyptian museum consists of a number of ancient artifacts, including sarcophagi, mummies from the Sinai, rare seals, magic stelai, and other ancient iconic works of art." Torre leaned forward and pointed with his middle finger to a floor plan on the outside fold of the flyer. "We are here—the Chiaramonti Museum, named after Pope Pius VII. It houses statues and busts from the ancient Greek and Roman periods."

Detached from Torre's guide-talk, Winston glanced at the floor and noticed the colorful mosaic from the Baths of Otricoli depicting Zeus feeding a winged dragon. He stared across the wide room at a gigantic bust of Athena.

Torre opened the brochure. "The museum of Clement XIV and Pius VI is inside the Belvedere Palazzetto. Greek and Roman sculptures, such as the popes' most prized possessions, the *Laocoön and His Sons* and the messenger Hermes, can be found there."

"Hermes," Susan hinted to Winston, "the zero milestone."

Winston nodded slightly.

Torre pointed to a photograph of the *Laocoön* in the brochure. " 'A deadly fraud is this.' In 1506, the *Laocoön* was added to the collection after it was discovered in the ruins on the Esquiline Hill at Titus's palace. Some say it denotes the ancient thirteenth constellation Serpentarius—Ophiuchus, the serpent holder and healer, and the symbol of the Marxist class struggle. Others say it depicts an event in Virgil's *Aeneid*. A Trojan priest, Laocoön, is being strangled on the altar of Neptune as a sacrifice by monstrous *sea snakes* sent by the gods who favored the Greeks. Because he had warned the Trojans of the danger of bringing in the wooden horse, an *icon of the città*, he incurred the wrath of the gods."

"The Trojan Horse was the icon for the city?" Winston questioned. "I always though it was a booby trap."

"Booby trap?" Torre glanced at Susan, then cupped his hand to his chin and looked down his nose at Winston.

"It's a computer joke, Monsignor," Winston replied.

Susan grinned.

Torre held his head high and squared his shoulders, trying to appear distinguished. He pointed again to the floor plan in Susan's brochure. "Named after its founder, Pope Gregory XIV, the Gregorian Museum of Etruscan Art houses the works from the excavations in southern Etruria. The Etruscans were a pre-Roman society that lived in Italy. They are noted for their great art and architecture. Roman art and religion were strongly influenced by the Etruscans."

"I've read about them," Winston remarked. "They were the great builders of northern Italy."

Sniff. "You are correct." Torre rubbed his nose with his handkerchief. "Historians believe the Etruscans founded Rome and laid the *città's* original foundations. In the rolling hills north of Rome there is an extensive Etruscan graveyard. Recently, the tomb of an Etruscan king was discovered there. It was an underground chamber with murals of birds and lions on the walls and a wheel from a cart lying next to a

sarcophagus. Like Ophite ritual diagrams, these burial murals are considered to be the source of Western Art. The birds are said to symbolize the passage from life to death, while the lions denoted the power of the unseen underworld being revealed."

Susan glanced at an illustration of an amulet in her brochure labeled *Corpus Inscriptionum Etruscarum* ETRUSCAN MONSTER *KABAVN.* "A goat head and a bearded human head attached to a horse's head with bird legs beneath the sun and the moon …?"

"It is an invoking talisman of good fortune," Torre replied. "Although much of the Etruscan literature was systematically destroyed by our Church in the fourth century, these icons are believed to represent the faces of the Etruscan single deity—a god of a mixed nature. The symbolism is similar to the biblical vision of Ezekiel in which God is seen as a union of faces: a man, a lion, an ox, and an eagle conjoined upon a great wheel. This way, *per favore.*"

Torre held a door and ushered them into the courtyard. "This is the Courtyard of the Pigna, the Vatican's principal sculpture garden. This courtyard was once the location of the Temple of the Necropolis—an underground *Città* of the Dead. It was part of a cemetery built by the self-deifying, megalomaniac, Caligula. It was similar to the Catacombs of San Callisto here in Rome. It is at the Necropolis that the seven Sibyls once spoke their divine prophecies acquired from a talking head—a disembodied central intelligence employed by Romans who sought guidance from the underworld. The Necropolis was an adaptation of the Omphalos temple at Delphi, the Greek navel of the world and a center of serpent worship. It is alleged that Caligula ordered experiments in Egyptian alchemy at this site for the creation of *white gold.*"

"A cemetery … City of the Dead, the catacombs in Paris," Susan compared.

White gold? Winston pondered. *A talking head?*

Like he was signaling the start of a slow rigoletto, Torre graciously waved his handkerchief for his guests to follow. He quickened his pace through the courtyard. "*Signore,* this area constitutes the northern end of the Belvedere Courtyard which once extended from the Papal Palaces."

Winston spied a sixteen-foot-tall bronze piece standing in an over-sized niche in the northern wall of the courtyard. "An odd assortment of sculptures, that one seems to be sitting on a pedestal of importance. It reminds me of a finely cut diamond."

"Ah ... *Sì.* That is the *Holy Pigna,* the Holy Pinecone." Torre crossed his fingers into an X and waved his hand. "It is the Vatican's most sacred relic."

They paused beneath an imposing stone balcony to observe the odd bronze casting.

"A pinecone is a common motif in Roman Catholic architecture and religious ornamentation," Torre explained. "The courtyard takes its name from this masterpiece set into the *nicchone,* the holy niche. The *nicchone* was built in 1562 by the architect, cartographer, landscaper, and antiquarian Pirro Ligorio from Naples. In 1534, he traveled to Rome where he worked for many of the great Roman families who appreciated his sophisticated *trompe l'oeil* technique called *grotesque.* He designed the famous Monster Grove at Bomarzo, north of Rome, for the Prince of Orsini. The *grotesque* art could appear fantastic or profane, through an ingenious use of symbols and objects created around the mysteries found within one's dreams. Ligorio became a noted scholar of the mystery schools of the ancient cults of Rome. He wrote about these cults in his *Book of Antiquitie.*"

Symbols in dreams ... Winston considered, *similar to dream weaving.*

"Mystery schools ... that arch in Paris," Susan said to Winston.

"*Sì, signora.*" Torre diverted their attention from the topic, "The Holy Pinecone is bound on the south side by the *Braccio Nuovo.* The courtyard is bound on the east by the Chiaramonti Gallery." He pointed. "It is bound on the north by the Gregorian Egyptian Museum." He gestured again, toward the *nicchone* behind him, holding out both hands and pointing with his pinkies extended. "In the Egyptian Museum, directly behind the *nicchone,* are the statues of the guardian gods—not all of them are Egyptian. There are statues of the lioness goddess Sekhmet, both seated and standing, from the temples at Karnak. The Karnak complex included the Temple of Amon and the Temple of the Goddess Mut—the two temples dedicated to the two holy lights, the sun and moon. The complex was bordered by a small lake in the form of a half-moon. According to the researcher Rene Schwaller de Lubicz, that temple edifice is designed around the proportions of a standing man."

Half-moon ... Sister Rosalyn, Winston recalled. He eyed Torre's lapel pin again.

"The museum also contains a pair of statues of the baboon associated with the god Thot from the temple at Karnak," Torre continued. "Included are a statue of queen Tuya, the mother of Ramses II; a statue of the high priest of Ra Hor-Udja, from Heliopolis; a statue of a primordial divinity, Geb of the earth, also known as Shu of the air or the anthropomorphic form of the Egyptian god Set; and a statue of the god Bes, patron of pregnant women, from Rome."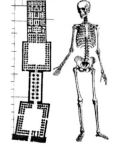

Susan placed her hand over her belly.

"The Vatican has a fascination with a lot of gods," Winston commented.

"*Sì.* They are the fountainhead of the Christian religion," Torre informed, "the underlying deities. Christianity was derived from many different cults. The rooms behind the *nicchone* contain magic and protective amulets and art objects. There is a figurine of a hippopotamus pierced with a harpoon, symbolizing the destruction of evil forces. There is a two-faced statue of Osiris-Apis Serapis, born from the lotus flower. Serapis was associated with the Roman Emperor Hadrian's deity, Antinous-Osiris, the boy-god that dies and is reborn. There was once a major temple to Serapis at Pergamon—the location of an early Christian community. There are also two carvings of a kneeling, winged genie, one worshiping the Tree of Life and the other with an eagle's head, both from Nimrud—"

"I thought Jesus was the god who died and was resurrected," Susan remarked.

"*Sì, signora,*" Torre said dismissively. "The west wing of the courtyard consists of the galleries of the Apostolic Library, over there." He pointed to his right. "This is the part of the Vatican Library known as the Secret Archives, which houses *our* collection of treatises, books, and magic grimoires from the Middle Ages and onward. It was founded by Pope Nicholas V. It also contains the original unedited editions listed in the *Index of Prohibited Books,* such as the works of Hobbes, Bacon, Spinoza, Calvin, Descartes, Pascal, Voltaire, Rousseau, Hugo, Locke, Hume, Kant, and Swedenborg. Although, many of the rare books were stolen by Napoleon and the French."

"They banned the whole Backdoor Group," Susan slyly whispered to Winston.

"Or the books read by our Founding Fathers." Winston looked amused.

"There are some things that should not be known," Torre commented. He pointed in the direction of the dome of St. Peter's. "When Constantine rebuilt Rome in honor of his new religion, he established four magnificent basilicas built over the supposed lost tombs of the Christian saints. In 326, the Basilica of St. Peter's was consecrated by Pope Sylvester I, over the site of the Apostle Peter's grave, although the grave site and remains have never been confirmed as St. Peter's. In fact, there are no documents proving that Peter or the apostle Paul ever lived in or visited Rome. Both Peter and Paul may have been archetypes modeled after the fabled twins, Romulus and Remus, the mythical founders of Rome. The south end of the Necropolis lies directly below the basilica—now the location of the tombs of the popes. The original basilica did not have a dome. It was an open-air church called the Garden of Paradise."

"An open-air church—such as a park or a city mall?" Winston remarked.

"*Sì, signore.* At the center of its garden atrium stood a gilded bronze fountain called the *Cantharus.* The fountain was adorned with columns of porphyry and faced with marble. Above it were four golden griffins. Four copper dolphins on the ceiling *spouted water* from their mouths. In the middle of the *Cantharus* sat the same Holy Pinecone, which we see here. Small holes in the Holy Pinecone *gushed water*. Above the pinecone reigned a statue of the Phrygian goddess Hekate-Cybele—the great mother of all gods—adorned in the robes of a hierophant and worshiped at the Temple of Concord in ancient times. Cybele was the Goddess of Asia Minor, the oldest goddess known, predating the goddesses of the Sumerian and the Egyptians by at least 5,000 years. She was worshipped in Rome as the *Magna Mater*, the queen mother. A lead pipe carried water to the Pinecone from the baths of the emperor. It continuously poured water for the public to drink.

"A goddess over a weeping fountain ..." Winston pondered aloud. *The Temple of Concord ...? The Pope Stone ... the Washington Monument....*

"The sacred *aqua vitae—the water of life.*" Torre grinned with his left cheek bone higher than the other. "It was much like the Vatican's Fountain of Sacrament which sprays water from a dragon's mouth. Roman fountains were often inscribed with the palindrome *Nipson anome-mata me-monan opsin*, which could be read backward and forward, meaning "Wash the sin as well as the face." He pointed back toward the *nicchone*. "This colossal bronze pinecone was cast in the first or second century. Before it was exhibited in the *Cantharus*, this sculpture adorned the top of the Basilica of Santa Maria. Toward the end of the eighth century, it was placed in the entrance hall of St. Peter's. Finally, in 1608, I think, during the construction of the present basilica, it was dismantled and relocated to the *nicchone*." Torre held his hand over his heart as he admired the sculpture. "The pagans revered the fruit of the evergreen because the lingam-shaped pinecone symbolized eternal life. Both Dionysus and the prehistoric goat-god Pan carried a pinecone staff as a fertility symbol." *Wzz ... Squawk.* "The pope's crosier is a staff in the shape of a shepherd's crook with a small pinecone at its tip." *Wzz ... Squawk.* "The pinecone, as a symbol of eternal life, serves as an icon for the theology of the Catholic faith," he described between wheezes.

Nature worship, Winston thought.

"Come," Torre beckoned. "Take a closer look."

They ascended a flight of marble stairs to a balcony behind the Holy Pinecone.

Susan noticed the bronze peacock and lion statues that guarded the sculpture on either side. "What are these other statues?" she inquired.

"The lions are from Egypt, and the peacocks are from Babylon," Torre replied. "The two peacocks are part of the original sculpture. Ah ... Melek Taus, the Peacock Angel ... In Greek mythology, the eye-like patterns on their feathers represent the stars that guard the way to heaven. The peacock is an early Christian symbol of the Resurrection. When a peacock sheds his feathers, he grows more brilliantly multicolored plumage. In the motifs of Persian decorative art, two peacocks drink from a pool at the base of the Tree of Life. Do not stare at the birds too long," Torre slyly advised. "The Chinese believed a peacock's glance could impregnate a woman."

Susan's eyes shifted, as they reached the top of the stairs. "Is that a coffin?"

"*Sì*, it is ... an anthropoid," Torre answered evenly. "It is an Egyptian sarcophagus made from basalt—a rare archeological find. The *nicchone* overlooking the ancient Necropolis is a fitting location for such a stone coffer, since the Egyptian wing of the museum resides behind the *nicchone*." Torre motioned toward the nine statues of the god Bast stationed on the *nicchone* as he trotted around the opened sarcophagus.

Holding his handkerchief, he glided his hand over the smooth edge of the sarcophagus in a gentle caress. "It is a place to rest at the end of life's journey. Socrates stated that the one aim of those who practice philosophy in the proper manner is to practice for dying and death. Such is the function of religion. It prepares us for dying. Death, our Great Leveler, is the only thing that is eternal. There is no armor against our fate. Death lays its icy hand on everyone." He spoke coldly, "Death conquers all."

Seems odd to have such a rare antiquity exposed to the pollution of Rome, Winston pondered. From the balcony he could see the entire Court of the Pigna stretching out before them. Due south, the white dome of St. Peter's dominated the skyline. Various sculptures lined the walls on the east side of the courtyard.

"Monsignor, what's that huge metal ball," Susan inquired, "across from the pillared facade that resembles the Lincoln Memorial?"

Lincoln Memorial ... Winston focused his attention on the circular garth in the middle of the courtyard. A slowly rotating brass orb, nearly twelve feet in diameter, reigned at the center. There was nothing organic or natural about the mechanical-looking art object. Its mirrored finish glistened, reflecting the morning sun. "It's not the traditional stone birdbath," he remarked. "I noticed it before. It certainly has the Midas Touch. Reminds me of an unfinished Death Star from a *Star Wars* movie. It's really out of place among all this antiquity."

Torre shrugged uneasily and chuckled, "The elemental symbol."

Winston glanced at Torre's belly. *It's not moving.*

"*Signore,* it is a garden gazing ball. They are often referred to as spheres of light, rose balls, good luck balls, and globes of happiness. Our globe of happiness is a cubist sculpture by an Italian artist." He pointed to the orb sitting before the Holy Pinecone, like a broken Christmas ornament that had fallen off a gigantic Yule Tree. "It was placed here in 1990. Sculptures like this one dot the planet. It is called the *Sfera Con Sfera,* the *Sphere Within Sphere.* The fractured, outer surface of this magnificent sculpture reveals a complex inner sphere said to represent the harsh, mechanized structure of our modern world." Torre stared humbly at the art object. "As you walk around it, its interior appears to change into a stirring construction of gears upon gears, turning onto itself, much like our universe—a demon let loose."

Winston spotted the spiked rays from the sun reflecting off the oddly angled, cracked and cutout sections of the golden orb, with a few teeth on its gears shining brighter than others. "You could use that thing as a sundial," he commented.

"There is the bust of Constantine the Second, the Aryan." Diverting the attention of his guests from the orb, Torre pointed to a five-foot-tall broken marble head from a statue standing in one corner of the courtyard. "He was the first true Christian emperor. His father, Constantine the First, who started our church, still worshiped Sol Invictus and Mithra, two solar deities. Constantine the Second inherited the western realm of his father's empire which included Britain, Gaul, and Spain. His rule helped to solidify the authority of the Church here in Rome."

"Jesus in Tibet! A big head." *That hill in Paris,* Winston thought. "You know," he said to Susan, "orbs, statues, and a fountain disguised as an evergreen ... This courtyard could be a type of letterbox."

Snap, Snap. With chin jutted out and eyebrows raised, Torre led them from the *nicchone,* back into the museum and up another flight of stairs. They passed through the upper galleries of the *Chiaramonti* and then into the *Raphael Stanze.*

"IN 1508, Pope Julius II commissioned the young Raphael Sanzio to paint the frescos in his four-room apartment," Torre guided. "These elegant rooms became known as the 'Rooms of Raphael." He worked for ten years to complete only three rooms before his death. The fourth room was later finished by Raphael's assistants."

"I've seen this fresco before," Winston remarked, edging toward it.

"That is the *School of Athens.*" Torre backed away and pointed to the prominent individuals represented in the painting. "In this fresco, Raphael included the faces of many of his artistic peers, representing them as ancient philosophers. There is Plato, who invented the plate. He is identified as Leonardo, and Aristotle as Michelangelo. They are the philosophers who applied Thales of Miletus's analysis of garden landscaping to the structure of the mind. Western Civilization is baptized in the philosophies of Aristotle and Plato. They are holding the holy texts. On the right we see Euclid, who is teaching geometry to his pupils. There are Jachin and Boaz, the pillars that guarded the approach to the Temple of Solomon. Zoroaster is seen holding the heavenly sphere. Ptolemy holds the earthly sphere. The person on the extreme right wearing the black beret is a self-portrait of Raphael. This fresco is a cinematic testament to Raphael's mastery of the visual code used in Renaissance perspective."

Winston took a step back, studying the fresco. "A guy thinking on the Y ... Who's the figure clad in armor and holding a sword?"

"It is the soul searcher, Alcibiades, the pupil of Socrates, who seeks self-knowledge." Torre eyed the fresco and recited from the *Dialogs of Alcibiades.*

'Then the eye, looking at another eye, and at that in the eye which is most perfect, and which is the instrument of vision, will there see itself? But looking at anything else either in man or in the world, and not to what resembles this, it will not see itself? Then if the eye is to see itself, it must look at the eye, and at that part of the eye where sight which is the virtue of the eye resides? And if the soul, my dear Alcibiades, is ever to know herself, must she not look at the soul; and especially at that part of the soul in which her virtue resides, and to any other which is like this? And do we know of any part of our souls more divine than that which has to do with wisdom and knowledge? Then this is that part of the soul which resembles the divine; and he who looks at this and at the whole class of things divine, will be most likely to know himself.' "

That's more convoluted than anything Billy ever said, Winston thought. He turned his attention back to the fresco. The imposing figures of Plato and Aristotle held two books, with their titles on the bindings in plain sight. "*Timaeus* and *Ethics* ... the holy texts? The Old and New Testaments, I presume?"

Torre chortled, "How many angels can fit on the head of a pin? How many infinite dots in a straight line? How many clichés in a 440-page Bible? Can a camel really pass through the eye of a needle?" He pointed to the ceiling at a medallion which represented philosophy, then to another ceiling medallion that symbolized theology. "Philosophy is not exalted. It is a way of life. It is the handmaid of theology. Our religion is a philosophy, don't you think?" he asked with a mischievous grin. "Aristotle said that all things tend to reach for perfection. Plato believed that within our souls is a hidden knowledge to which we all have access as a *latent memory* filled with certain *forms* and *ideas* which we carry into life in order to perfect our world. Perfection through art, through our creations. The artisan's purpose is to help make *God's presence* known." He motioned back to the fresco. "Mark, chapter six, verse three, 'Is not this the *tekton*, the son of Mary.' Plato's *Timaeus* is our other bible. It defines the lion-faced Demiurge, the Yaldabaot, the Yao, the Manitou, the Bythos, the World Soul, as the great creator deity—the *Megas Archetekton*, the Great Tekton Architect—who fashioned and shaped a divine order to humanity's world out of Nature's chaos and nothingness."

"TEKTON … That's a computer code that employs a matrix storage method for solving 3-D problems," Winston noted. "I've seen it used in CAD programming."

Torre backed away from the fresco and vigorously blew his nose. "*Timaeus* is part of Plato's metaphysics, which deals with invoking the soul of God into the material world through the 'great chain of being.' This is the primary function of the Catholic Church, or any church for that matter—the invoking of the holy spirit of God into the life of humanity." *Snap, snap.* "Come this way."

So God's a philosophical problem? Winston shook his head. *Billy would beg to differ.*

The three proceeded down another corridor and through a door that led into the Sistine Chapel. The monsignor held back at the threshold to properly introduce his guests to their new surroundings.

"You are fortunate. Only a select few receive a private tour of the Sistine Chapel. It was built between 1475 and 1483. It is one of the greatest wonders of Western art. We have a no photography policy here, as well as a strict rule of *silence*." Torre placed his index finger over his lips and spoke in hushed tones. "When papal elections take place, the Conclave is assembled in this chapel which originally served as the Palatine Chapel. This rectangular space is said to be modeled from the exact dimensions of the Temple of Solomon as described in the Old Testament, 666 for those who have wisdom. Its construction was supervised by Giovannino di Dolci."

Winston's head couldn't stay still as he marveled at the embellishments in the spacious room. "The colors! The bright colors," he excitedly half whispered. *It's an assault on the senses. This is better than the comics in the Sunday newspaper.*

"*Si*, it is a remarkable sight. I have prayed here for hours, studying these images," Torre's voice faintly echoed. "They challenge us with a wisdom that stirs the soul. Such is the power of great art." He pointed to the world-renowned, overly-restored frescos on the high-vaulted ceiling. "This room is a sanctuary for our consciousness. The roof is a flattened barrel vault with smaller side vaults over the windows to let in the light. A Japanese television network funded the restoration of these frescos. I understand they did something similar for the *Global Icon*. The scenes on the ceiling represent the creation stories found in the Old Testament of the Latin *Vulgate Bible* with its ten unforgettable words, 'In the beginning God created the heavens and the earth.' Every religion is based upon a cosmology with a creation story. Our story of the creation begins with the first panel, there." He sighted with his outstretched arm. "*Separation from Light to Dark,* then *the Creation of the Sun and Moon,* and on to the

Separation of the Earth from the Waters of God's consciousness."

"The creation," Winston spoke below his breath. "If I had been present at the creation, I would have been tempted to offer a few helpful hints."

"*Si, signore.* So you are knowledgeable? This whole work is an allegorical Gnostic view held by Michelangelo di Lodovico Buonarroti Simoni. Michelangelo believed that a hidden wisdom, a *gnosis* from deep within our consciousness, could be expressed into reality as a man-made image of God."

"Art as God?" Susan questioned.

"The serpent wisdom … This Gnostic interpretation of the Bible was reestablished during the Renaissance by the Medici popes and their colleges. Michelangelo was influenced by the Neoplatonic teachings promoted by Marsillio Ficino. The artist's hand is the instrument that projects the creative consciousness of God into our reality. It molds the mind of God into matter. Michelangelo once said, 'I live and love in God's peculiar light.' His writings reflected his belief in the divine origin of art and that the intellect in itself was divine. The *imago Dei*—the image of God is channeled through humanity's art. This view formed the basis of Renaissance art and architecture. Gnostic Christian texts, and even earlier Egyptian and Greek texts, often spoke of the union between the outer and inner mysteries of the human mind."

"Sister Rosalyn … between the pillar and cross," Winston mumbled, his attention snagged by the depiction of a half-nude figure of a man covering his eye in the fresco dominating the wall at the far end of the room. "Those images remind me of the symbols on Tarot cards. What's with the man covering his eye?"

"*Come?*" Torre cupped his ear. "*Può ripetere, per favore?*"

"The man staring into the chapel?" Winston asked again in a louder voice and pointed. "The one-eyed man?"

"Ah … The man over the animals in Plato's Cave," Torre responded. "He is being inexorably dragged toward Charon's boat by the damned on his passage to Hell. He is trying not to look into Hell. That fresco is *The Last Judgment.* It is filled with the same symbolism found in the *School of Athens.*" He paused. "*Per favore,* please step this way."

They followed Torre to the center of the chapel and stopped at the middle of a square mandala-mosaic patterned in the floor.

Winston's gaze swept the ceiling. "Look at all the ram skulls. The Lakota are into the buffalo."

"This chapel is beautiful," Susan spoke softly, her head reverently lifting up in dreamy-eyed amazement. "It's truly mind-melting."

"*Si,* it is, *signora.* Look. There is the scene to the brazen thing—the sacred Nehustan setup by Moses in the wilderness." He pointed to a snake entwined around a pole. "The whole ceiling is an allegory landscape of a Kabbalic representation of the body's meridians. These scenes have been designed around various body parts."

"Body parts?" Susan questioned. "That sounds morbid."

"The body's meridians—my VDC," Winston commented with interest.

"*Signore*, do you recognize the man in that panel?" Torre arched his head back and pointed again to the ceiling. "*Lì,* there. Directly overhead."

"No, I don't believe I do. I don't know him from Adam," Winston replied, sighting down Torre's outstretched arm and extended middle finger.

"*Signore*, that *is* who it is," Torre chuckled quietly. "This is Michelangelo's interpretation of the *Creation of Adam*. The panel is derived from the verse found in the book of Genesis, 'God created man in his own image, in the image of God he created him.' The focal point of the *Creation of Adam* is the contact between the *fingers* of the Creator and those of Adam, the *Donnadio*, through which the *breath of life* was transmitted. 'And the Lord God formed man from the dust of the ground, and breathed into his nostrils the *breath of life*; and man became a living soul.' It is a depiction of the moment when the human *soul* was created by God and infused into Adam's being.

Torre waved his handkerchief and recited from the book of John, " 'Something which has existed since the beginning, That we have heard, and we have seen with our own eyes; That we have watched and touched with our hands: The *Logos*, who is life. This is our subject.' God, the *Logos*—the Lost Word—alone is the author of all the motions in the world, the cosmic order within nature. In this painting, God is wrapped in a mantle. God is supported by the angels in flight, holding his consort, the *Schuyler*—the *Shekinah*—the enlightened Sophia Divine Wisdom, the Holy Spirit—a symbol of spiritual consciousness. God leans toward Adam who is shown as a resting

THE ADORATION OF THE MAGI

and strong athlete. Adam's powerful masculine beauty seems to confirm the words of the Old Testament, in which man was created in the image and likeness of God. But look closer, *signore*. What do you see?" Torre pointed.

Winston stretched his neck and did a double take.

Susan looked upward, squinting. "I'm not sure what you are pointing at."

"We should never adhere to a graven, *a firmly held*, image of God. If you understand something just one way, then you will not understand it at all. God is in everything. Look at it from the eye of Michelangelo, the sculptor," Torre advised. "Find its hidden pattern, then remove anything that does not belong. In this fresco, God, the muscular, Zeus-like figure, is cloaked within the shape of the midsagittal cross-section of a human brain. It is a symbol for mystic Gnosticism and the mysteries of the human consciousness. God is a thought, but God has form. It is an adaptation from Boticelli's *Birth of Venus* and Leonardo's *The Adoration of the Magi*."

Susan's jaw dropped, her eyes widening. "God's a *brain scan*," she whispered to Winston with a lopsided grin.

"The human factor ... a *steganographic* image," Winston whispered back with a smile, "the three-pound enigma. Adam's jacked-in. God's the great programmer, the cosmic brain—the *Logos*—the divine mind."

"Poemander ... 'By greatness of mind and impulse of divinity!' " Torre gracefully reeled his body in a full circle and lifted his arms up to the fresco-covered ceiling.

"God is a thought that transcends thought. In this artistic interpretation of the *Logos*, God is depicted as a creation of the mind of man. The word 'Adam' means *the First Cause*—the *Proto Cause*, the *Adam Kadmon*, the *Purusha*, the *Gayomart*—the Archetypal Man that is Humanity. And what was humanity made for, but to know God … *Adhaerendo Deo*, cleaving to God. Our desire to commune with God is one of the things that make us human. In the painting, Adam, the first sexless man, reaches out to his consciousness to find God, seen as an image of the human mind. At the same time, the God Consciousness reaches out to Adam. God's hand touches our reality through the hand of man. It's a two-way line of communication. The God Consciousness needs humanity as much as humanity needs a God. God desires to be known. The Great Unseen is manifest by the *breath of life* into the mind of man as the continuing journey of the mind of God into our world."

Torre paused. "But, the greater allegorical question created within this single panel of art is—Who created Whom? Who is the First Cause?" Torre purred with pinpoint gleams in his shaded eyes. *Sniff.* He knuckle wiped his swollen nose and stared straight into Winston's eyes. "This is the great unanswered burning question. The *God Question*. The how and why we seek to know. Did the invisible force we call God create man and everything in the universe? Or did man create his own God, within his own mind, so he could better define his universe? Do we dare eat such forbidden fruit?" He smiled thinly. "That is not quite what they taught you in Sunday school, now is it?"

Winston and Susan glanced at each other in a silent response. His Adam's apple bobbed up and down.

Sniff. Torre's smile receded and was replaced by a stern expression which filled the silent void.

"The chicken or the egg conundrum …" Winston exchanged another quizzical glance with Susan. *This sniffling priest is a real rooster.*

Snap … p … snap … p….

———

TORRE LED THEM from the chapel into a hallway, then down the royal stairway of Pius IX, through a set of king-size, bronze doors. He nodded to the plainclothed Vatican guard stationed at the doorway. Exiting the Apostolic Palace, the three paused between the shadows of curved rows of stone columns bordering a huge plaza scattered with early morning tourists and worshippers. A flock of nuns with downcast eyes bustled past them into the plaza.

"So where are we now?" Susan removed a notepad from her shoulder bag.

"This is St. Peter's Square," Torre motioned to the colossal columns that surrounded them. "And these are the welcoming arms of our Church. We are on the north side of Gian Lorenzo Bernini's colonnade. Bernini was the architect who helped design this beautiful plaza. He was also responsible for the facade of the Louvre, the palace of the Sun King."

Welcoming arms … not the same as the Smithsonian, Susan remembered what Ranger Nobles had told them.

Winston pulled his baseball cap from his hip pocket to shield his eyes as they stepped into the sunny expanse of the plaza. He bowed his head, reading the GPS in his hand. "This thing's having problems locking to the satellites. It must be the solar flares. There, it locked. Hume said the coordinates are near the front of the church. It must be inside the basilica, according to this," he thought out loud. "I know we're near it—Look!" He pointed to the towering stone obelisk situated at the cross-axis of the plaza. "Whaddya know about that obelisk?" he pressed.

Torre scratched his temple. "The pavement of this plaza is laid out like the spokes of a great, elliptical wheel, with an obelisk at its hub. The colonnade, the maternal arms of our Mother Church, cradles the obelisk and the fountains of two pillars." He pointed with his middle finger to the portico of the basilica. "St. Peter's, our Mother Church, resides at the site in Rome known in antiquity as the *Ager Vaticanus*. This was once a marshy district outside the *città* of Rome. The origin of the name *Vaticanus* is uncertain. It is claimed that the name came from an ancient Etruscan town called Vaticum. Nero, who mixed his snow with honey, included this marshy area as part of his imperial gardens. These gardens were situated at the foot of Vatican Hill, where the basilica would later be built."

"The Etruscans again," Winston commented.

Torre clasped his hands and led them into the plaza. "The word *Vaticanus* is derived from the Latin *vates*, which means the tellers of the future. The term *vaticanus mons* means the prophetic hill or mountain, which can be rephrased to mean the hill of prophecy. So the origins of the name Vatican could be associated with divine prophecy from the tellers of the future—such as the prophetic muses who once occupied Nero's temple, the site of the Courtyard of the Pigna. It is said that Etruscan muses communed with a severed head hidden in a cave on the side of the hill."

"Telling the future ... that guy at the park bench in Paris," Winston said to Susan.

"Saint Denis," Susan replied.

Torre looked up at the obelisk as they approached it. "In relation to your question, this obelisk of pink granite, similar to two others in Rome, does not have the usual hieroglyphics found on Egyptian obelisks. It is one of the oldest obelisks in Rome. No one knows its origins. There are various opinions as to why it has no hieroglyphics. Possibly an Egyptian pharaoh commissioned the obelisk and died before it could be inscribed. One source claims the obelisk was quarried at Aswan during the reign of Amenemhet II and erected in the Temple of the Sun in Heliopolis. Another source says that it is unknown where it was quarried, but it was erected at the Julian Forum in Alexandria by order of Emperor Augustus." He waved in the direction of the colonnade that encircled them. "After the obelisk was relocated to this site, Bernini designed this plaza and its elliptical colonnade around the position of the obelisk. Legend says that a bronze globe that once sat at its top held the ashes of Julius Caesar. During the relocation of the obelisk to this site, workers inspected the hollow globe and found nothing. Obviously, the little orb served another purpose."

That orb in the courtyard, Winston thought.

Torre stopped in his steps. The giant obelisk loomed behind him as he faced Susan and Winston. "When the mystery religions came to Rome in the so-called pagan days, not only were obelisks made and erected throughout all of Rome, but obelisks were brought here from Egypt at great expense and erected by the emperors. Caligula had this obelisk brought to Rome in 37 A. D. from Heliopolis, the *città* consecrated to the Sun. Heliopolis is the old Greek name for Bathshemesh."

"Bathshemesh," Susan repeated. "What does that mean?"

"Bathshemesh was the central place for Egyptian worship of the sacred *Benben* stones—or obelisks. The name is derived from the verb *weben*, meaning to shine forth. *Benben* stones were believed to hold the abode of the spirit of the sun made visible through *Benu*—a holy spirit bird that showed itself each morning at dawn. In the Old Testament, these obelisks are mentioned as the images of Bethshemesh. *Shamash* is the Semitic name for the Sumerian sun god, *Utu*, who is associated with the Egyptian deity, *Re* or *On,* and later the Persian Unconquered Sun God, *Mithra.* Bethshemesh means the abode of the Sun God."

"An abode of a sun god," Susan questioned, "in front of the Vatican?"

"*Si*. Throughout the Middle East, the *Benben* was revered as the physical dwelling place of the sun god. The great Sun Temple at the Phoenician *città* of Baalbek was considered a sanctuary for the worship of *Shamesh.* Baalbek was named after Baal-Berith, the lord of the covenant, a god of the Shechemites. *Shamash* was said to have the power of light over darkness and evil. The *Benben* stone was used in religious ceremonies, where followers prayed before the stone every morning at sunrise. According to legend, the Babylonian King Hammurabi received his code of law from the sun god *Shamash.* Emperor Caligula erected this *Benben* in his circus, later called the Circus of Nero and the Vatican Circus. That site is the present location of the Auditorium Conciliazione, where the Pope addresses his public audience. It is next to the Campo Santo Teutonico, which contains the Holy Soil. The Camp Santo is a separate territory and not a part of the Vatican. It is the last remaining territory of the Holy Roman Empire, the First Reich, and overseen by the Emperor of Austria, the last of the Habsburgs." Torre pointed to the pyramidal top of the obelisk. "Pope Sixtus V removed the orb from the original obelisk and replaced it with a cross and a bronze crest. In 1818, four Egyptian lions were added to the base, the symbols of the *dominion* of the Society of Jesus. The obelisk now stands about twenty-five meters high. It is the second-largest obelisk in Rome."

"So why place a *Benben* stone at the entrance to St. Peters?" Susan questioned.

"Since the obelisk once dominated the center of Nero's circus, it served as a silent witness to the martyrdom of St. Peter and the Christians who were persecuted there," Torre explained. "The word *obelisk* is derived from the word *obeliscus,* the shape of a spear or a sword. In the mystery religions, the obelisk was a solar symbol that represented the vital flow between Heaven and Earth, as a *communication link* with the divine."

"Like Michelangelo's brain scan," Susan offered a comparison.

"*Si*, it is a symbol of humanity reaching out to God in heaven, always upward. This obelisk was originally inscribed with the words 'Divine Augustus' and 'Divine Tiberius.' It is now dedicated to Christ with the inscription '*Christus Vincit, Christus Regnat, Christus Imperat. Christus ab omni malo plebem suam defendat.*' The hollow bronze cross at the top is said to contain a fragment of the True Cross."

Winston stepped away from the monsignor, stalking into the plaza in a widening, zigzag, spiral around the obelisk. The two fountains north and south of the obelisk gushed with the *clapping* applause of laughing water.

"Coo, coo, what's going on? Who? Who-who-who? Peace to you."

The *chattering* of pigeons and doves landing on the plaza clouded Winston's thoughts. Birds pranced with their wings overlapping, their beady eyes blinking, and their *clicking* beaks splitting open. He spotted desiccated earthworms stuck to the pavement, invoked to the surface by a recent rain. *Food for the birds.* He stopped for a moment. One of the marble quadrant markers positioned in the pavement snagged his attention. The carved marker depicted the face of an angel with its cheeks puffed, as though trying to whistle. *The Breath of God, maybe ... Reminds me of sweet-talking Parott with a mouthful of candy.* His eyes wandered up at the chipped and weathered obelisk, then back down to the other markers in the pavement. *The Sacred Hoop ...* "Someone's been marking time. It's a sundial."

"That is correct. It tells time. It predicts the future." Torre hovered behind Winston. "It is a sundial for the plaza. Before the age of mechanical clocks and watches, it was the Church's responsibility to keep time and maintain social order. This sundial served as a public clock. Time brings all things to Light. Timekeeping has been a major function of the Catholic Church since its conception, its immaculate conception." He smiled benignly. *Snap, Snap.* "This way. *Per favore.*"

As the three approached the front portico of St. Peter's, three small children gamboled up to greet them. One little girl, with big, brown, loving eyes, was draped in a *bright* red, oversized, travel-light jacket from L. L. Bea*m.* She smiled with a fragile look, her two front teeth missing. Her arms reached out to Susan. "*Signora,* please," she pleaded. Her hands were opened in distress.

Another little girl spoke to Winston, "*Qualche dollaro in più, per favore.*"

"Stay away!" Torre scorned sternly. He gorgonized the children with a single glance and waved his red handkerchief like a matador fighting a bull. "They are gypsies disguised as beggars—pickpockets." He wiggled his fingers in a grabbing motion. "*A chi dai il dito si prende anche il braccio.* They are after the tourists. They will steal you blind! They can tell you are rich Americans by the flag on your hat. I do not know why they are constantly attracted to St. Peter's. It is their haven here in Rome. I know that beggars cannot be choosers, but you would think *these* beggars would find a more suitable place to congregate than our Church. *Che barba!*" Torre held the palm of his hand out and quickly flicked it. "You would think this was a place that takes care of the needy. This is St. Peter's! Keep them at bay," he warned.

Susan looked surprised at Torre's outburst, as the children scampered away.

Winston reached in his back pocket. *Yeah, my wallet is still here.* He felt relieved. *I wonder if Torre will ask for a donation when his little tour is finished?*

As they crossed the expanse of the plaza, Torre squinted skyward to the massive, egg-shaped dome. "Ahh ..." Torre took a deep breath, his eyes became glassy. "Every time I walk into this plaza and see St. Peter's, my heart beats faster. *Perfetto!* Nagara style. Look directly overhead. You can see the dome designed by Michelangelo. Sometimes the dome seems to float in the air like a huge, divine, white chalice against the blue sky. It is an enduring throne to God, rooted deeply in the earth. At night it glows as a colossal, inextinguishable candle over the *città* of Rome, illuminating the darkness of our world, serving as a divine light that guides our way. The architect Pirro Ligorio completed St. Peter's after the death of Michelangelo."

"That's the same architect who designed the Courtyard of the Pigna," Susan said, stopping before the facade with its tall pillars supporting the portico. She turned 180 degrees with a contemplative stare at the obelisk. "An obelisk in front of the Lincoln Memorial, commonalities."

"Everything is *humongous*." Winston absorbed the vastness of the buildings that bounded them. "The colonnade is like a huge fence. It's intimidating. I feel the architecture grabbing at my soul."

Torre motioned them forward to the portico. "From St. Peter's portico you enter the gateway of the basilica through its five doors—the Door of Death, the Door of Good and Evil, the Center Door, and the Door of Sacraments. These doors are symbolic of the various ceremonial rites of passage within the Catholic faith. On the far right, to the north, you can see the Holy Door, which is usually opened every twenty-five years during Jubilee, or Holy Years. It was last opened by the Pope during the Millennium Celebration."

Winston glanced up at the carved golden *dragon* and *eagle* decorations on the ceiling of the portico as they approached the entrance, then rechecked his GPS. "It's just on the other side of those doors," he reckoned.

Sniff. "Those are the bronze doors by Filarete. What is on the other side of those doors?" Torre asked in a muffled voice as he blew his nose.

"We are looking for a location, an observation point," Susan answered casually.

"All roads lead to Rome. The world stops here. It appears that your quest ends at the steps of the Vatican. *Signora*, the basilica is closed to tourists at this hour. I need to make a call so someone can open the door." Torre pulled a mobile phone from his coat pocket and placed a call.

A voice *crackled* over the phone offering assistance.

"Someone will be here in a few minutes," Torre explained. "Did you know that St. Peter's is the sixteenth largest church complex in the world?" He beamed proudly, filling the lull in the conversation with idle chitchat.

"Where's the largest?" Susan inquired.

"It is in the United States—" Torre said abruptly.

Without warning, one of the heavy bronze doors opened slightly. A bearded Swiss guard, wearing a red, blue, and gold striped uniform that resembled a baggy jester's outfit, peeked dumbly from behind the door.

Combat ready, Winston observed. *Cool hat.* "Hello," he greeted the guard.

The guard did not reply. He swung the door open and motioned for them to follow.

Torre bowed his head and carried his hand across his face and chest in the sign of the cross before stepping over the threshold. *"In Hac Salus,"* he said below his breath. *"Del male non fare e paura non avere."*

Just as Winston entered, he noticed the readout flashing on his GPS. "Stop!" He halted. "This is the position. What can you tell us about this entrance?"

"It's a doorway, *signore*," Torre replied with a smug smile.

"Monsignor, this doorway is important," Winston shot back.

"A doorway to salvation? The doorway to the tomb of the martyred St. Peter the Fisherman—the Kingfisher?" Torre searched in a cunning attempt to answer.

There must be something in common to the locus. Winston turned 180 degrees and glared at the obelisk reigning over the plaza. "Monsignor, is there anything about this doorway that relates to that obelisk directly in front of it?"

Torre paused in thought, then sighted through the doorway into the dark recesses of the interior womb, the *garnha griha* of St. Peter's. He reared and twisted counterclockwise. His eyes settled on the obelisk and zeroed-in on a sliver of light reflecting off the cross at the top. *"Che sbadato!"* He slightly slapped his forehead with the palm of his hand, then smacked the back of his fist into his hand. *"Sì, sì, signore.* The sun in the church—*arcana imperii*—the secrets of empire. The obelisk is a symbol for the sun. This doorway was designed to be aligned to the sun on the day of the Vernal Equinox. The church faces east. *Ex oriente lux,* 'from the east comes the light,' is a phrase used to describe St. Peter's. Our church is an *Aula Lucis.*"

"A House of Light," Susan translated, "… a lighthouse?"

"Sì. The English historian Gilbert Scot, in his book, *Essay on Church Architecture,* gives a detailed account of this alignment in early church architecture. It is well-known that St. Peter's was designed for timekeeping. The word, temple, means time-place. All well-designed churches and temples are essentially architectural clocks. This design concept goes back as far as the temples of Karnak in Egypt."

"An Egyptian obelisk aligned to the sun—a sundial," Winston said as a thought flashed in his head. *Sol Invictus … Plato's cave.*

"Sì, aligned to the sun. *Nulla è nuovo sotto il sole.* If you added a prayer mat, this would be a perfect place to pray toward Mecca, since the Muslims perform five daily prayers to the east. It is a universal tradition for religious architecture to greet the divine morning light of the rising sun in the east, and even sometimes to the west to mark a good-bye to the setting sun. But, *Signor* Winston, perhaps you are not standing at the correct location?" Torre gave Winston a twisted grimace.

"Whaddya mean? This is the spot. This is a military PSN-11 Precision GPS receiver. The coordinates are exact," Winston challenged. "It's pinpoint accurate!"

"Maybe you need to be on the roof," Torre touched his temple with his finger.

Momentarily confused, Winston looked at Susan. Their narrowing eyes met as though reading each other's thoughts. Slowing turning in unison, they backtracked from the portico, made their way out into the plaza, and peered up toward the dome of St. Peter's. High above them, thirteen statues of Christ and his apostles guarded the entrance, with the statues stationed between two giagantic clocks which read: 9:18.

Winston panned in full circle, observing the other 140, larger-than-life, crumbling, white marble statues of the saints, martyrs, and angels that topped Bernini's colonnade. He spied bird nests at the feet of many of the statues. *This plaza's an aviary for the birds*, he sharply noted, locking his eyes on a statue of an angel which appeared brighter than the rest—*radiant*—as though whitewashed of any shadows that might give it form. "Maybe he's right," he said to Susan.

They approached Torre, who waited next to the open door.

"So, how do we get up there, Monsignor?" Winston asked.

"Detto fatto. We have an elevator." Torre waved them along.

Susan felt a chill from the cool, damp air as they entered the cavernous space. She immediately eyed a display on a far shadow-draped wall. Michelangelo's *Pietà* shown pure white beneath two disputed, twist-fluted columns from the Temple of Solomon flanking a mandala-like carving of angels holding crossed timbers. "It's breathtaking," she said. "Everything in here is so beautiful."

"The builders … Build it and He will come." Torre commented as he turned toward Winston. "Where are your manners?" He waved his handkerchief above his head. "*Signor* Winston, *please* remove your hat. This is God's house."

"Oh? I'm sorry. I'm not Catholic." Winston humbly removed his cap and took down the flag. "I'm an American," he joked.

Torre shook his head and motioned them forward. They approached another security checkpoint, monitored by a backscatter x-ray machine, a metal-detecting security arch, and a digital biometric hand scanner. "We can forego all of this. But I have to reverify your identities. Place your right hand palm down on the glass panel."

Susan placed her hand on the glass as though swearing on a Bible. A blue line of light passed over her palm and an LED on the scanner blinked green. Words etched into one corner of the glass read: **Rapid-I-Scan**.

Winston took his turn at the scanner. His palms stuck to the glass with a moist suction. The scanner flashed, but the LED failed to blink.

Torre inspected the scan of Winston's palm-prints glowing on a monitor in a spark-charged Kirlian haze. "*Signore*, your lifelines are blurred. Try again."

"These scans hardly ever work for me. I wonder why they don't use biosensor scanners at this place. The RFID chips always work," Winston mumbled, his lips almost glued together. He tried it again and nothing happened.

"Your lifelines are still blurred. *Per favore*, again. Success can be achieved only through repeated failure," Torre preached.

"My fingerprints are missing, but my lifelines are there." Winston tried again. *How many times must I place my life in the light before I get it right?* The light blinked. "Amen," Winston sighed. He lifted his palm, leaving a signature imprint.

"Excellent!" Torre chortled. "You have been resurrected."

Torre escorted them through the voluminous void of the nave. The basilica was filled with a soft, sibilant sound interrupted by the chirpy *squeaks* of Winston's shoes merging with the trailing ends of distant disembodied voices of morning worshipers reciting the *Prayer of St. Michael.*

"I hear the birds approaching." Torre stood beneath a column of light falling from the dome's lofty cupola adorned with the golden rays of a sun wheel. "This great space offers silence from the outside world." He pointed to Bernini's altar squared between four gigantic spiraling columns with sun symbols at their tops. "This way to the elevator."

"An elevator in the middle of a basilica?" Susan questioned.

"*Signora*, the roof is a tourist attraction. We use an elevator for public safety and convenience. You can acquire a grand panoramic *veduta* from the roof of St. Peter's."

"So much for a stairway to heaven," Winston mused, staring up at the brilliant sunburst at the hub of the cupola. The shimmering light falling around him, like a midday breeze, warmed his face. Entranced by the spirited movement of the light, he stood motionless in the focused harmonic silence echoing off the concave walls of the inner dome. "It makes me feel like time's crawling." *This would be a great place to meditate on the medicine wheel.* His eyes tracked across the gilded decorations of the cupola. "What's the meaning of the Latin text encircling the base of the cupola?"

"You are Peter, and on this rock I will build my church. I will give you the *keys* of the kingdom of heaven," Torre translated. "From the womb to the tomb … This is our place of ritual. The main altar, designed by Bernini, is said to rest atop the grave of St. Peter's skull and bones, the seat of our religion." *Snap, Snap.* "*Per favore*, this way."

On the artificial life form. – "Make big plans; aim high in hope and works, remembering that a noble, logical diagram once recorded, will be a **living thing** asserting itself with ever growing insistency." – *Daniel H. Burnham*, on the city plan of Washington, DC. 1910.

REACHING the sloping roof of the basilica, Winston paced away from Susan and the monsignor until his GPS locked again to the correct coordinates. He stopped twenty feet away from the cornice guarded by a coven of towering statues.

"This is the spot." Winston surveyed the area. "But, there's nothing here. There must be some other visual clue related to the *locus*." He hurriedly approached a weathered stone banister at the edge of the roof. His upper body arched out over the ledge, as he leaned on a mammoth statue of a figure holding a man-size, Latin cross. He spotted a tiding magpie perched atop the statue's head.

"*Ies–Us, Ies–Us, Ies–Us,*" called the magpie.

Susan watched Winston standing poised as if ready to jump off the end of a diving board. *He's got that lost look on his face*, she thought. Then she noticed the outside corners of his eyes crinkling. *Yeah, he's about to leap into something.*

"What—?" Winston felt a boney hand grasping his left shoulder.

"Be careful, *signore*, the ledge is quite slippery from last night's rain, the sweat of Shiva," Torre cautioned as he nervously watched the ends of Winston's feet extending past the edge of the banister.

"I won't lose my footing," Winston assured. "It's like standing on the edge of Devil's Tower." From his high vantage point he could see nearly all of Rome stretched out before him. *Torre is correct. Altitude affects attitude. Extraordinary!* He cupped his hand over his eyes, spying over the nearby rooftops and low canyons of stucco and stone. His head tilted in momentary jerks like the second hand on a clock, searching for a solution to the city's labyrinth. His eyes blinked. "Susan, come here. Look at this."

Susan stepped up onto the banister. "Okay, what? Whoa…!" Experiencing a wave of vertigo, she sidestepped and anchored her hand on a statue.

"Keep your balance. Hold on to Jesus," Winston advised.

"How do you know it's a statue of Jesus?" She glanced at the cross in its hands.

"A little bird told me." He grinned.

Winston shifted his weight to one side, took her arm and held her hand, using it as a pointer. He placed his other hand around her waist. Susan balanced on the ball of one foot, posed in a ballet arabesque, her face nuzzled beside Winston's square jaw. She tilted her head and gazed into his eyes. "Move your hand. It tickles."

"I'm testing your smile index," Winston said with a roguish grin. He noticed the streaks of blue in her glinting green eyes. "Look—Not at me, out there. Here, here, here, and here," he estimated, while guiding her arm.

"James …" Susan looked surprised. "Why, it's the tops of—"

She was cut off by the steely sound of Torre's voice. "*Chi cerca trova.* They are the other obelisks scattered throughout Rome. When you asked me about the obelisk and the doorway, I knew this perspective from the roof would offer a view of the other obelisks. St. Peter's, the highest point in the *città*, is seated as an absolute and unapproachable power over the Seven Hills of Rome. I thought it might interest you. It's a bird's-eye view." *Sniff.* "A lira for your thoughts, *Signor Winston.*"

A lira, that's more than a penny. I knew he was going to ask for a donation,

Winston mused. *Seven Hills ... my lucky number.* "So, these are Marsh's obelisks. There's even a glass pyramid over there like the one at the Louvre," he said, scrutinizing the crisscross of *vias* and *viales.* "It's a different perspective, but there's more here than meets the eye. Those streets appear to be aligned to the plaza, in this direction," he pointed, sensing a hidden order in their design, "and that direction."

"*Esse est percipi,* being is perception, *signore.* The pyramid is the entry to the underground entrance to the Vatican Museums. The central *viale* extends due east from the plaza—"

"Here, this might help." Susan retrieved a topographic map from her shoulder bag.

Winston glanced at the map in Susan's hand. "It seems to converge at that building near the river. It's the big, star-shaped building, here." He traced his finger over the map. "It has five sides, like the Pentagon."

"That is the *Castel Sant' Angelo*—the site of Hadrian's mausoleum," Torre said. "Hadrian, known as the Greekling, was the Roman Emperor who created Jerusalem, where they worshipped Janus, the muti-headed god of the Romans. Over the centuries, the mausoleum has served as a papal fortress, a library, and even a brothel. The building is topped with a bronze statue of the Archangel Michael slaying a dragon. According to legend, the hills bordering Rome form the image of a dragon in the landscape, with Hadrian's tomb riding on the back of the dragon."

"Janus," Winston mused to Susan, "the hackers of the Backdoor Group."

"A dragon?" Susan probed for more information.

"*Sì,* it is astronomical. Its stars were marked by the hills of Rome. Much of Rome is designed around the constellations. For example, the two *viales* extending from St. Peter's Square leading to the *Castel Sant' Angelo* are called *Borgo di Santo Spirita* and *Borgo Sant' Angelo.* The names *angel* and *spirit* denote the alignment of the *vias* to the stars rising over the mountain peaks east of Rome. Those two, V-shaped *viales* were once called the *Borgo Nuvo* and the *Borgo Vecchio,* until Mussolini demolished the *spina* of medieval housing to create the new *viale.* Those names combined mean the 'New Bull.' The names of the *vias* reference the change in the zodiac house during a 2000-year astronomical cycle. The old zodiac house was Taurus, the V-shaped cluster of stars that mark the station of *Hyades,* the Roman Pluto, the son of the Roman Cronus who aids his father in ruling the universe, an old Etruscan deity. The new house is Aries, the ram of the solar equinox, or the New Bull. To the Egyptians, Khnum, the ram-headed potter deity, was the First Cause modeler of man, who fashioned man and all things from the *Light of Creation*—the *ka* vital life force— flickering at the middle of a Mundane Egg on a potter's wheel—a symbol from the Orphic Mysteries. Our God is like Khnum, who sculpted the cosmos into existence out of an egg-shaped mass of clay."

The ram skulls in the Sistine Chapel, Winston thought.

"A Mundane Egg on a potter's wheel," Susan repeated. "That church in Paris."

"Yeah, a dome at the center of a spiderweb of streets." Winston turned and gazed up at the dome. *Paris ... Washington ...*

Torre pointed to the dome and then to the buildings that comprised the Vatican Museums. "St. Peter's is designed to function as an immense astronomical clock for establishing a calendar for the whole of society—the Wheel of Life."

Winston glanced back toward the Vatican Museums. *Billy at the Sacred Hoop ...*

Sniff. "In 1584, near the time that the English were first settling America, Pope Gregory XIII created a committee to reform the old Julian calendar used throughout Europe. The dates on the Julian calendar were drifting in relation to the true positions of the Earth to the sun and the moon. Under the leadership of the Jesuit mathematician, Christopher Clavius, the pope established the Vatican Observatory, now one of the oldest astronomical institutes in the world. Part of the observatory included the Tower of the Winds, where a brass meridian device first developed by Paolo Toscanelli was laid out on the top floor to formulate the Gregorian calendar, based upon the Earth's alignment to the sun here at Rome. A spear of light shines from a slit in the southern wall onto a brass zodiac inscribed on the floor to track the position of the sun. This meridian device was installed into the floor by the mathematician and cosmographer Ignazio Danti, who aided in erecting the obelisk in front of St. Peter's. On the ceiling of the Tower of the Wind is a directional pointer attached to a wind vane. This is why it is called the Tower of the Wind. I understand your Thomas Jefferson installed a similar wind vane at his home in the United States."

Susan offered Winston a quick smile and a nod.

"A calendar is the primary synchronization mechanism of every culture. Our Church believes the whole world is synchronized to our calendar, or at least it once was," Torre asserted. "And thus the world is synchronized to the Mother Church here at Rome, with all individual biological clocks in sync to the greater social clock. Today, the prime meridian for Italy runs past the American Academy in Rome on the Janiculum Hill, then through the Vatican and on to the astronomical observatory on Monte Morte, known also as the Mount of Joy. Monte Morte is near the Villa Stuart, built by the exiled king of England and Scotland, King James III, the Old Pretender. His remains lie in a crypt here at St. Peter's. The meridian continues northward to the Pote Milvio, the bridge where Emperor Constantine saw the light of God before his victory over Maxentius."

"That stone in the memorial in Alexandria," Susan murmured to Winston.

 Winston nodded. "Meridians. I've heard this tune before." *Ranger Nobles and Elvis.*

"But, our view from the roof of St. Peter's offers more than a geographical perspective of Rome," Torre added. "It is a glimpse into Alberti's perspective."

"What is Alberti's perspective?" Susan flipped the pages of her notepad.

"Leone Battista Alberti was the founding *monsignor* of modern architecture, mapmaking, pictorial perspective, 3-D modeling, and cryptography. As a follower of the Paduan humanist teacher Gasparino Barzizza," Torre explained. "Alberti, was considered the great Renaissance seer. His treatise, *Della Pictura,* on the laws of perspective, served as a bible for many artists and architects. His personal seal was that of a *fish-eye with wings* ... the Angel Eye. It was possibly an adaptation from an Etruscan amulet of a winged deity and the Renaissance belief that all things are viewed through the eye of creation. Alberti invented an indicant device for calculating the distance between two points on the ground. It was wheel-shaped, made of rotating discs. He used it to formulate polar coordinates following the mapping techniques created by the Greek cartographer and expert on optics, Ptolemy. Alberti applied his device to mapmaking and sculpting using three-dimensional point plotting."

"I'm familiar with this type of point plotting," Winston said instinctively. "It's found in CAD/CAM programming, using XYZ coordinates to build a virtual world—a false reality." *The TEKTON program ...*

"Alberti used a modified version of the device in cryptography," Torre added. "He created various polyalphabetic cipher wheels—encryption devices made of small discs inscribed with letters which spun on a spindle. I am sure your people at the NSA are familiar with that."

"It sounds like Jefferson's wheel cipher," Winston remarked. "Jefferson must have studied Alberti."

"A Captain Midnight decoder ring from a box of Crackerjacks," Susan teased. "It appears Jefferson took credit for a few things he really didn't do."

"Alberti based his cipher-wheel on the thirteenth-century *Menery Art* written by the Spanish mystic and theologian, Raymundus Lullus, known as Doctor Illuminatus." Torre started to explain.

"Doctor Illuminatus?" Susan questioned with a googled expression. "What— "

"I know about Lullus," Winston cut her off. "He's called the founding father of information science and computer logic, the *father of the search engines* that power the Internet. Everyone who uses the Internet does so by way of Lullus-logic. He invented the first logic machine, a text-based machine which produced true and false predictions. It's perhaps the simplest type of computer. Programming a machine is nothing more than a correct grammatical ordering of signs and symbols related to true and false statements."

"Does that make Alberti's cipher-wheel a type of computer?" Susan asked.

"Maybe," Winston said. "But it's not the oldest. The Antikythera mechanism could be the oldest geared analog computer. It's a type of astronomical clock. My mother was interested in it. It was used to predict eclipses."

"Lullus's logic machine was formed from complex paper discs circling one another," Torre noted, "with coded letters, numbers, and symbols inscribed on the discs—wheels within wheels—an Ezekiel machine. *Deus ex machina.*"

"God from a machine?" Susan tentatively translated.

"Logic is the language that translates the design of nature into a comprehensive structure," Torre explained. "The logic machine was designed to demonstrate the truth of the Catholic doctrine. Lullus believed that his logic machine, the Divine Instrument, could explain the totality of human wisdom by combining certain signs and symbols. 'All knowledge exists for the sake of Theology.' Lullus referred to his method as the *Prima Figura,* which consisted of nine words that represented the attributes of God—the absolute principles of God."

"God made simple, summed up in nine words or symbols," Winston questioned, "like some limited cafeteria menu? That's not a complicated God."

"There are over 25,000 sequenced genes in the human genome," Susan added.

"God *is* simple, *signore.*" Torre smiled. "By combining these words with a table of nine questions, it was possible for Lullus to construct a diagram for what he logically considered to be the Proofs of God. He hoped to illustrate how the Christian doctrines could be obtained artificially from a fixed set of preliminary ideas and concepts. Lullus wrote several books dealing with the usage of his Divine Instrument for self-education and memory training, such as *Liber de Propositions* and *Liber Chaos.* His followers, known as Lullists, flourished during the Middle Ages and the Renaissance. His most noted disciples included Giordano Bruno, Athanasius Kircher, and Gottfried Wilhelm Leibniz. Leibniz called Lullus's ideas on logic the *ars combinatoria*—an art of invention around an alphabet of thought. Leibniz believed it was possible to use Lullus-logic in the creation of a universal algebra that could represent everything in God's creation, including moral and metaphysical truths."

"Alphabet of thought ... It sounds like search engine stuff—like the Alchemist linguistic program created at the University of Chicago for searching the Internet," Winston compared. "They're creating logic-circuits which replicate 3-D objects. Star Trek kind of stuff, but—"

"Or new nano-biological technology," Susan added.

"Yeah, but I never thought Lullus-logic could define the attributes of God," Winston said.

Torre offered no reply and pointed in the direction of the old Roman Forum. "Alberti was commissioned by the Vatican to study Rome and aid in formulating a new design for an ideal *città*. He discovered that ancient Rome had been planned with its primary *vias* splayed like the spokes of a great wheel. The radiating *vias* of Rome are an adaptation of the angles measured from the alignment of the wheels found on an armillary sphere, a Greek symbol for the *Logos* of God in the cosmos, Plato's *Tekton*. The Stoic philosopher, Philo, in a discourse on natural rights, once declared that the *soul* of man is but an impression of the archetypal ideas from the Seal of the Logos. Man is but a copy of the heavenly order. The *città* plan for ancient Rome, as a symbol for humanity, duplicates the cosmic order, the *Logos*, supplanted and inscribed here on the ground of the good earth—Heaven on Earth."

"Rome is a heaven on Earth?" Susan stared at the monsignor.

"*Sì, signora*. Rome is older than our Church. The church stands upon Rome, and not the other way around. Legends say that Rome was founded by Remus and Romulus. If you combine those names you have Ruolulis which in Lithuanian means 'hill.' Rome was founded upon seven hills. Can Queen Victoria Eat Cold Apple Pie."

"Can Queen Victoria do what?" Susan replied.

"Maybe with a scoop of vanilla ice cream," Winston bantered.

"It's a mnemonic I use to remember the names of the Seven Hills of Rome." Torre held out his hand and counted with his fingers. "There is the *Capitoline, Quirinal, Viminal, Esquiline, Caelian, Aventine,* and the *Palatine*. These hills figure prominently in Roman mythology, religion, and politics. On each hill once stood a temple where they practiced, through the *Septimontium* festivals, reverence to the seven known planetary spheres—the sun, moon, Mercury, Venus, Mars, Jupiter, and Saturn. From its conception, Rome's design was based upon a cosmology of the heavens. A Heaven here on Earth." Torre joined Winston at the edge of the ledge. "Alberti discovered that the plan for Rome was similar to Hadrian's *Aelia Capitolina*, now known as modern-day Jerusalem. The popes adopted Alberti's discovery as the new ground plan for Rome. Alberti's design concepts became the guide for both art and architecture." Torre waved his handkerchief toward the elliptical plaza. "*Smuovere mare e monti.* All of the *vias* of Rome were redefined to express the order found in the planetary rings of an armillary sphere, the *Abas Lbn Firnas*—God's chariot—the Merkabah, Ezekiel's wheel-within-a-wheel. This *città* plan became a *divine symbol* for the Renaissance which illuminated humanity out of the Dark Ages."

Yeah, a wheel ... spheres within a sphere ... Lullus-logic ... that golden orb, Winston pondered. *The Sacred Hoop ... an obelisk at the center of a plaza ... the egg-shaped dome of St. Peter's on a potter's wheel ... Paris ... Washington.*

"Alberti's plan was adopted by others, to bring a spiritual significance to the design of their cities." Torre specified, "Paris was later redesigned this way for King Francis I. Various private gardens throughout Europe, such as Versailles, designed by Le Norte, make use of similar principles. Even London was rebuilt around such a pattern after *our* great fire destroyed that *città* in 1666. The new plan for London was created by Christopher Wren, a trained astronomer and mathematician from Oxford and a noted architect and Freemason. Wren's design made its way to the New World in the planning of Colonial Williamsburg under the watchful eye of the Royal Society. They say that the Ark of the Covenant is hidden in Williamsburg."

"Williamsburg ?" Susan questioned. *Alexandria maybe.*

Torre ignored her question and addressed Winston, "And also in your country, Washington, D.C. includes the same pattern in its radial street design. It was formulated by your Deist Founding Fathers, many of which lived in Williamsburg at one time. They created, within the geometric pattern for their new capital, the symbol of Newton's watchmaker universe. It was a metaphor for Plato's Tekton—the Great Builder, TGAOTU, the Primordial Carpenter—like Jesus the Carpenter of our Church."

"A city simulating a cosmology," Winston commented. *What did Billy say? My cosmic center ...*

"So, the radial streets of Washington, D.C. form an image of the Tekton?" Susan asked, puzzled.

"*Sì.* A wheel-within-a-wheel, an Antikythera mechanism." *Sniff.* "Look at the schematic of the Vatican complex in your brochure," Torre suggested.

Susan held out the brochure and opened it.

"Now, what does that look like to you?" Torre pointed to a diagram.

"It's just a map of the building," Susan responded.

"No. *Signora,* there are patterns here. Try to organize the shapes in your mind." He pulled a red felt-tip pen from his coat pocket and outlined the perimeter of the Vatican in the brochure. "Now, look again, *signora.* Form can follow function. Our Church is an instrument of God. The Vatican complex is architecturally patterned after an astronomical instrument, a set of calipers connected to a builder's level. These are the tools of the Tekton—Plato's Great Architect—who inscribed and measured the whole universe into being with a set of calipers and a builder's level—the Builder's tools. The symbols for the civilizing of man."

"Yes, I see it." Susan realized. *The Great Leveler.*

"The Builder's tools ... I always thought it was a compass and a square," Winston differed, eyeing the map. *A key shape and keyhole.*

"Not here, *signore.* This is the Catholic Church. That is for the other Church." Torre lowered his eyes.

"So the Catholic Church is on the level," Winston bated his breath and shook his head. *No.... This place is more like an altar to science and art than an altar to God.*

TOWER OF THE WIND

COURTYARD OF PIGNA

PLASSA SAN PIETRO

ARTIST USES
MEASUREMENTS
FROM THE TEKTON
AFTER LEONARDO SKETCH

"What do you know about the other obelisks scattered throughout the city?" Susan pressed Torre further.

"Besides the one at St. Peter's, there are twelve other ancient obelisks in Rome, one for every apostle and every sign of the zodiac," he answered. "Many of them are inscribed with mysterious hieroglyphs, considered by the Egyptians to be the divine language of the Gods. The Jesuit scholar Father Athanasius Kircher, the master of a hundred arts, was an authority on the hieroglyphs found on these obelisks. His motto was *Divine Sophia sits*, 'Nothing is more beautiful than to know the All.' Kircher was an expert in mathematics, astronomy, burning mirrors, acoustics, magic lanterns, and architecture. His *Mundus Subterraneus* was the first serious effort to describe the geological makeup of the Earth. He was the first to use the term electro-magnetism. He even wrote narratives on space travel and the possibility of extraterrestrial life. He

PAN, GOD OF THE ALL FROM THE OEDIPUS AEGYPTIACUS

also created an influential work on comparative religion in an attempt to justify the wisdom of pre-Christian pagan cultures to the Catholic world. It consisted of three folios titled the *Oedipus Aegyptiacus* and was derived from Greek myths, Pythagorean mathematics, Arabian alchemy, Latin philology, and the Hebrew Kabbalah. In his *Oedipus*, Kircher depicted the Great Goat God Pan, the classical God of the All, as the overseer of the classical cosmology for our church."

"A goat god ..." Susan repeated.

"In *Timaeus*, Plato describes the whole universe as an all-consuming Goat," Torre explained. "In his *Metaphysics*, Aristotle speaks of the First Cause, the unmovable originator of all motion, as the Goat substance which is without parts and indivisible."

"The Goat substance," Winston said, "sounds like the Higgs boson—the God Particle—the basic element in Nature that the physicists at CERN are looking for."

"*Si*," Torre affirmed. "The Greek philosopher Anaximander believed the four elements—earth, air, fire, and water—were manifestations of an underlying primal substance which he called Goat, the basic element in Nature."

"Kircher," Susan blurted, checking her notes. "A disciple of Lullus-logic ... the Great Goat God? I thought Jesus was the God of the Catholic Church."

"*Si, signora*. The scapegoat." Torre smiled. "In his time, Kircher was considered the master of decipherment. He attempted to improve the Lullus system. He wrote *Ars Magna Sciendi*, the Great Art of Science, which redefined the Llullistic art in relation to Kircher's esoteric translation of the Egyptian language and his anthropomorphic approach to architecture. Kircher created tables filled with various signs and symbols and compared their meaning in a radically new application of the Llullistic machine, as a Proof for God."

"Sounds as if this Jesuit priest was designing a type of primitive computer logic based on symbols, like a comparative Internet search engine," Winston said.

"The Global Consciousness ..." Torre smiled in response.

"Another Renaissance geek," Susan joked. "He's your kind of guy, James."

"Acoustics and magic lanterns ... He could have been a sixteenth-century Edison," Winston compared.

"Father Kircher believed the Egyptian hieroglyphs represented a holy angel language once spoken in Heaven," Torre informed. "Kircher was originally a mathematician to the Habsburg Court in Vienna, where he succeeded the expert on optics, Johannes Kepler. When he moved to the Jesuit college at Rome, he received a special commission to study the hieroglyphs on these obelisks. He concluded that the hieroglyphs referred to a Trinitarian God and a Pre-lapsarian wisdom that had been handed down from God to Adam and then from Adam to the Egyptians for guiding the soul into the afterlife. He believed this lost knowledge was recorded in the writings of Hermes Trimegistus and Pythagoras. Kircher's ideas greatly influenced our Church, especially the Jesuits. According to Kircher, the first principle in understanding any hieroglyph is that the symbol is always tied to Nature."

"A lost knowledge?" Susan appeared flustered. "An angel language? I need a translation on that one."

"*Si*. It is said that Father Kircher formulated the idea that the obelisk in front of St. Peter's should be encircled by an elliptical colonnade designed around Cartesian geometry, as a symbol for the arms of the Church." Torre briefly held his arms out in front of himself and clenched his hands together to form a circle. "Kircher advised Bernini on the design of the colonnade, so that it might function correctly with the central positioning of the obelisk. Father Kircher and Bernini believed the correct anthropomorphic proportions in their buildings would allow their architecture to come to life, like the legendary Jewish Golem—a being without a soul. This anthropomorphic application to architecture was first promoted in the published works of Mariano di Iacopo, known as Taccola, a Renaissance engineer and inventor, and Antonio di Pietro Averulino, the famous architect of Milan."

"Anthropomorphic," Winston thought out loud. "We use that term in the creation of artificial computer intelligence. It's presented in Hofsstadter's *GEB,* which describes how animated beings can be formed from inanimate matter. Inanimate objects can appear to come to life by giving them a human behavior, such as synthesized speech or building robots with human features. Artificial beings— puppets. Mythologies are based on this—the idea has been used in children's literature, where animals talk and act like human beings—some zoosemiotic birds talking—that kind of thing. But in architecture ... how is that possible?"

"Pythagoras said that 'Man is the measure of all things.' Jesus was anthropomorphic. God took the form of a man," Torre elaborated. "The noted anthropologist, Stewart Elliott Guthrie, argued that religion is merely 'systematic anthropomorphism,' in which human beings apply human characteristic to nonhuman objects and incomprehensible events, seen as gods in human form. God is often described in human terms, the face of God, the hand of God, and the eye of God—"

"The brain of God," Susan added.

"Father Kircher and Bernini designed their architecture around the dimensions of man," Torre continued. "The human form is preeminent. The Bible states that man was created in the image of God. It reasons that the dimensions of man as a micro cosmos also hold the dimensions of God. If you design your architecture around the dimensions of man, in essence you are designing it around the dimensions of God. In his thesis, the *Great Art of Light and Shadow*, Kircher promoted the Neoplatonic view that light was a representation of the soul of God. Kircher believed the proper positioning of architecture around the prophetic obelisks—the ancient symbols for light—would give the *città* a soul ... like a human soul—the spark which separates thinking beings from unthinking machines. He believed this design would transform Rome into a *living entity* here on Earth and God's mercy seat in a New Jerusalem."

"Like the Karnak Temple and the ceiling of the Sistine Chapel ... body parts ... a bionic church in the image of a man. A city with an artificial soul? I know what we say about the Internet with its Global Consciousness, but a city?" Winston said with skepticism. "That's a hard one to buy into, Monsignor."

"*Eppur, si muove*," Torre uttered. "The Church bought into it. That architecture is here. Our religion is preserved in stone."

Drawing of the squaring of a circle according to Taccola's measure of man using the builder's tools, the square and the compass. The measure of man is derived from the order found in a mechanical clockwork, and the clockwork is derived from the measure of man. Drawing of the icons of the Roman mystery religion. The human skull below a carpenter's plumb line rests upon a butterfly over the Wheel of Life - symbolizing the Egyptian *khekh*, the spirit motion of the universe and the human struggle through life.

Winston gaped up again at the dome. *Kircher, Bernini, and the Jesuits ... puppet masters over a puppet church.*

"Can you show us where these obelisks are located?" Susan asked.

"*Signora*, may I see your map?"

Susan handed him the map.

Torre removed his pen from his coat pocket and circled the locations of the other obelisks. "There is always one in front of, or near, a church or a temple. Let me show you. Here is the Lateranense Obelisk in the *Piazza di San Giovanni in Laterano*, near the pilgrimage church of Santa Croce built over the Holy Soil. Here is the *Terme* Obelisk at the Baths Diocletian. This is the location of the *Flaminio* Obelisk in the *Piazza del Popolo*. Here is the Solar Obelisk in the *Piazza di Montecitorio*. This is the Agonalis Obelisk at the *Piazza Navona*. Here is the *Piazza dell'Esquilino* Obelisk in front of the Bascilica di Santa Maria Maggiore." *Sniff.* "Look, you can see it due east of here." Torre pointed toward the horizon, then back to the map. "Here is *Quirinale* Obelisk in the *Piazza del Quirinale*. This is the *Sallustiano* Obelisk at the top of the Spanish Steps. This is the *Monte Pincio* Obelisk at Pincio Hill's Gardens. Here is the obelisk of the *Piazza dell'Esquilion*. There is the *Macuteo* Obelisk in front of the Pantheon. And the last one is the obelisk at the *Piazza della Minerva*. However, there are three other obelisks."

"Where are they?" Susan asked.

"One once stood at the southeastern end of the Circus Maximus," Torre answered. "It was brought to Italy in 1937 during the Fascist regime after the conquest of

Ethiopia. It has now been dismantled and returned to the Ethiopians."

"Ethiopia," Susan whispered to Winston. "The freeman who kept notes on the plan for Washington."

"There is another obelisk, north of the Vatican, near the *Foro Italico*. It was erected by Mussolini, the Little Prince. It consists of a block of marble carved to represent a *fascio littorio*, the symbols of authority of ancient Rome adopted for Mussolini's Fascist regime. It's not far from the Monte Mario Observatory. Another obelisk is located in the EUR district south of Rome. The EUR complex was created between 1920 and 1940 as a symbol of modern Fascism. It was a time when our Church and the Fascists walked hand in hand. The Fascist architects had many idealistic plans for rebuilding Rome as the 'whale of the world.' The outline of the EUR complex is shaped like the tail of a fish. The architecture of the EUR district is cold, geometric, and dehumanizing. They once proposed building a gigantic gateway arch over the EUR area, but it was never constructed. I believe you have one in your country."

"The Jefferson Gateway Arch," Susan said. *And a whale is not a fish.*

"It sounds like the Arch of Defense area in Paris." Winston stepped closer to study the map. His blinking eyes drew away from it in a moment of silent thought, as though he had finished peeling away the layers of an onion to discover something mysterious and unseen related to the city's design. "It's a maze, but there's a pattern here." He snatched the pen from Torre's hand and connected the circles with interconnecting lines. He drew a line from the Vatican to San Ginovanni in Laterano, then from the Vatican to the Galleria Borghese, followed by a line from the San Ginovanni to Santa Maria Maggiore. This pattern resembles an unfinished pentagram," he analyzed. "These landmarks look like they might be aligned to the equinox and the summer and winter solstices when viewed from the Vatican."

Torre held his index finger to his face and pressed on his lower eyelid of his right eye. "It's an irregular pentagram," he acknowledged. He faced southeast in the direction of the Roman Forum and traced a pentagram in the air above the map as

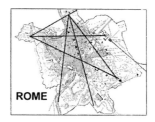

ROME

though bestowing a benediction. "You have drawn part of the old pilgrimage route for the *città*. It is similar to the Freedom Trail you Americans have in Boston. I have been there. You need a GoCard to see it all. You Americans and your games of Monopoly. The pilgrimage route in Rome was designed after the pilgrimage route in Jerusalem, known as the *Via Dolorosa*, which follows the final steps of our Messiah's journey on the Wheel of Life."

That slab in Paris, Winston remembered. *I've seen this pattern somewhere else.*

"But, a pentagram … it seems a little non-Christian," Susan commented with a questioning tone. "Almost blasphemous."

JERUSALEM SEAL

"No." Torre shook his head. "It is very Christian. It is thought to be the first official seal for Jerusalem. The original *città* plan for Jerusalem, Hadrian's *Aelia Capitolina*, was based around the design of a pentagram. Early Christians attributed the pentagram to the Five Wounds of Christ. 'By *His* wounds you are healed.' Those who show devotion to the Wounds shall receive favor from God. It invoked the Spirit of Christ. Prior to the Inquisitions there were no evil associations with the pentagram. To the contrary, it was once called the Shield of Christ, which denoted the order of the cosmos—the relationship between the sun and the tilt of Mother Earth." Torre angled his head to one side in an awkward Madonna pose. "It is also the basic geometry that forms the dimensions of man, the *Vitruvian Man.*" Torre outstretched his arms and legs. "The universal man—zeal, vigilance, hardihood, courage, constancy—the five duties of life. Emperor Constantine, who adopted Catholicism as the universal religion for his empire, used the pentagram together with the *chi-rho* symbol on many of his seals and amulets."

Yeah, Winston's mind geared, *the chi-rho, a circle—the Sacred Hoop.*

"When humanist Pope Nicholas V and Alberti redesigned Rome as a New Jerusalem, they incorporated the old pilgrimage route between the seven churches that sheltered the holy relics into their grand scheme," Torre revealed. "Each church had its own obelisk to mark the route for the pilgrims. Pilgrimage was considered an essential part of European religious life. Early Christians took a vow to visit the Holy *Città* of Jerusalem at some point in their lives. Such journeys, as they are today, were unsafe. Rome served as a substitute Jerusalem and the spiritual seat of Christian Europe. The location of the churches along the route forms the holy seal for Jerusalem, a pentagram shape. Most important was the route between the supposed tombs of Saint Peter and Saint Paul. The old Roman pilgrimage *starts* at St. Peters and *ends* at St. Peters. It's a full revolution."

Winston looked at the map, slowly rotating it. *A composition in the landscape ... a pentagram ... Pythagorean ... geometry ... Earth measure ... from obelisk to obelisk ... a maze of streets ... a pathway that starts at the ending ... a wheel within a wheel ... the Lakota medicine wheel ... a sundial,* he filed his thoughts away. "More commonalities," he mumbled in deep concentration. "the *Laocoön* ... the cross of Saint Peter ... Michael slaying a dragon ... a Golem. But there's another pattern here. I've seen it before." He doodled on the map with Torre's pen. "It's north of the Vatican. Etruscans ... the Vatican is aligned to it somehow—"

Susan pulled on Winston's shirt sleeve and led him away from the prying ears of the monsignor. She lowered her voice. "What do you make of all this, James?"

Winston flinched, feeling her breath in his ear. "That tickles." He cut a tight smile.

"I'm testing your smile index." She feigned an innocent look. "*Diabolus fecit, ut id facerem.*"

"Hmm— Latin again," Winston said, folding the map and tucking it his pocket.

"The devil made me do it," she translated with a sly grin.

Winston looked in the direction of Torre. "I don't know," he said, trying to decode the mixed signals. "I do know I don't care for Torre. He keeps flipping us the bird."

"I noticed. I wondered if we needed to salute back," Susan said.

"So far, all three sites are associated with prime meridians and obelisks." Winston focused on keywords. "One in Washington, one in Paris, and five here in Rome outlining a pentagram ... Susan, squirt the bird and have Marx try the keyword, *pentagram,*" he directed.

"I don't see a commonality with that keyword," Susan said perplexed.

"It's another hunch," Winston muttered. *Nobles pointed it out ... the sign of Jerusalem above the White House.*

Susan inserted the Jawbone in her ear and made a call by way of Sky-Link.

SEVEN TIME ZONES away, within the black monolith at Fort Meade, Marx input the keyword *pentagram* into a quarantined laptop.

"It's slowing. The damn thing's slowing down!" Marx removed his horned-rimmed glasses, looking pleased. "Jefferson's a genius."

"Oh, God, look!" Hegel exclaimed. "We have compiled a new set of coordinates."

Everyone gathered around the monitor at Hegel's station.

The table vibrated as Hume stomped across the floor. "You got a handle on it?"

"Fleur-de-lis!" Rousseau nodded an affirmative. His eyes focused on the columns of numbers as they scrolled to a stop on the screen.

"D-uh ... no. It's not a fleur-de-lis. It's something else," Marx reconsidered.

"Latitude 31 degrees, 47 minutes, 00 seconds north, Longitude 35 degrees, 13 minutes, 00 seconds west," Rousseau read the coordinates, as he quickly calculated them in his head. "You know, if you add those numbers, you get 666."

"Where the hell is that?" Marx asked.

Hegel's eyes widened. "Jerusalem."

――――

SUSAN'S PHONE RANG. "Excuse me, Monsignor. I have a call from the birds." She plugged the Jawbone into her ear. "Hello.... Yes. That's good news. Where? ... We're on our way." Her tone conveyed a sense of urgency.

"Here's your pen, Monsignor. You've been very informative. You're an honest man." Winston reached into his pocket and handed something to Torre.

Torre's eyes narrowed questioningly at the object in the palm of his hand. "A gold coin with a symbol of a horned beast?"

"It's a donation." Winston grinned flippantly. "You can use it to perform a wicked trick—"

"They have a new set of coordinates, James," Susan interrupted.

"Where to next?" Winston asked as they stepped away from the edge of the portico.

"*Ies-Us, Ies-Us, Ies-Us.*"

"Hadrian's *Aelia Capitolina*," she replied.

＊＊＊

Day 11
Golgotha - Jerusalem Syndrome

Est locus ex omni medius quem credimus orbe. Golgotha Iudaei patrio cognomine dicunt
There is a place which we believe to be the center of the world. The Jews give it the name of Golgotha.

Papal Residence, Castel Gandolfo, Lazio, Italy

RAP, RAP, RAP— RAP, RAP—
"*Papa?* Are you awake?" Sister Catalina, a middle-aged Ursuline nun with a soft-featured face, tentatively rotated the key in the lock. Her fingers gripped the heavy brass doorhandle.

Rap, Rap, Rap—
"*Papa?* Are you there?" She gently nudged the door ajar and listened. A black cat darted out the opened door. "*Signore?* Are you here?" She stepped into the exquisitely decorated bedchamber. "Oh … Oh, no! Oh, my God! *Signore* …" she slurred, brushing her hand in the sign of the cross as tears filled her eyes.

She frantically wheeled around to get assistance. In the doorway loomed a tall figure dressed in a black cassock and shoulder cape with a scarlet sash around his hips.

 "Archbishop Bracciolini! His Holiness is dead!" Sister Catalina exclaimed frantically through a veil of tears baptizing her face. Her glazed eyes fixed on the gold Furca cross pinned to the Archbishop's collar.

"I know," Bracciolini spoke calmly. "I can see him from here."

The Pope lay in his bed, his face darkened with a purplish stain, one eye closed, and his mouth open. The tip of his chalky, swollen tongue protruded from his mouth, giving the appearance that he had gasped for his last breath before his soul left his body. His mottled hands reached straight out. His extended right arm had knocked a clock off the bedside table onto the marble floor. His death had obviously been painful and sudden. Remaining on his table were a pair of reading glasses, an opened Latin *Vulgate Bible*, a glass half-full of water, and three containers of prescription medicine labeled: Imipramine, Enalapril, and Alprazolam.

"Inform the Cardinal Camerlengo," Bracciolini instructed the panic-stricken nun.

Sister Catalina left the bedchamber in haste.

The archbishop closed the door and locked it. Methodically, he walked across the room and then paused at the sound of broken glass *crunching* under the leather soles of his shoes. He leaned over the lifeless body, pulled a handkerchief from his pocket, and gingerly wiped the Pope's tongue. "There are no more words to say, my dear old friend. *Amicus verus est rara avis.*" He lightly touched the Pope's chin and closed his mouth, then positioned the Pope's right arm back to his side. He picked up one of the containers of medicine from the table, opened it, and emptied the remaining capsules into his hand. His eyes shifted toward the door as he concealed the capsules in his pocket and placed the container back on the table.

He stepped away from the bedside to a painting on the wall, a scaled reproduction of Roosakinewicz's *The Deposition (St. John Passion – 7),* and hinged it out to reveal a wall safe. He rotated the dial left, right, then left again and tugged on the handle. The door to the safe held solid. His eyes narrowed as he forcibly tugged again. *Nein,* he retraced his memory. *It is eight - one - nine.* He rotated the dial through a new sequence, gripped the handle, and opened the safe with a *thud.*

"Important things must be destroyed," Bracciolini said beneath his breath. He reached inside the safe. His fingers grappled with the 108 beads of a rosary, *clattering* a *tap ... tap ... tap* of a Devil's tattoo as he pushed it to one side. He withdrew a bundle of documents. "The Children's Birth Records, *nein* ..., Romanus Pontifex, *nein* ..., Quod divina sapientia, *nein* ..., Luminous Mysteries, *nein* ... Piano di Rinascita Democratica, *nein. Ja* ... here it is." He slipped a report titled Kabalyon - The Dossiers on the Creation of the American Edifices into his coat pocket. *We have always followed the stars. It is time for a change,* he thought.

Bracciolini returned to the bedside and solicitously hovered over the dead Pope. *"Agnus Dei, qui tollis peccata mundi, parce nobis, Domine.* Peace to you. God forgive *us* for what must be done." He peered down at the broken clock on the floor through pools of regret clouding his eyes. The clock had stopped at 9:18 A.M.

———

Walk about Zion, go round about her, number her towers, consider well her ramparts, go through her citadels; that you may tell the next generation that this is God, our God for ever and ever. He will be our guide forever. - Psalms 48:12-14

"MIRROR, MIRROR, on the wall, who's the fairest of them all? The mirror that flatters not ..." Winston lathered up for his morning bloodletting. "Who's that geezer in the glass?" He winked at the aging face that favored his father staring at him through droplets beading off the bathroom mirror. He eyed the clothes he was wearing, a wrinkled T-shirt with a faded picture of Devil's Tower on the front and a pair of black, skull-patterned, tight-fitting boxer briefs. He curved his mouth, stretched his haggard morning face, and tracked the razor's chromed edge over his throat. He stopped and gawked again at the phantom staring back at him. *What goes on behind those eyes I see?* He flashed a smile. *I'm a handsome devil when I have soft soap hiding my face.* He noticed the reflection of Devil's Tower in the mirror. *If we're not wearing a tattoo on our bodies, we're wearing some other symbol on our clothes to identify ourselves. Who am I?* He glanced down at his boxers.

The faucet dully dripped a clock-ticking *plomp, plomp, plomp* of expanding circles into the soapy mix floating in the basin.

There's a defect in my reflection. Winston sprayed shaving cream over the mirror to hide the dark spots where the silver had worn off the back. The lower half of his face was hidden by the foam. *I think I'll grow a beard and change my identity,* he mused. He took a breath of the mingled menthol-leathery scent and lifted the drain release. *Clunk— I feel dizzy.* He thought he saw the vague outline of the face of a bearded man in the slow-swirling puddle being swallowed up in a clockwise flow of a Coriolis force into the black hole at the bottom of the basin. *Not enough sleep. I'm seeing things. Jesus....*

From the adjacent room, Winston could hear the orchestration of "Singin' in the Rain," as Gene Kelly opened his umbrella and splash-danced a Devil's tattoo on channel 23. *Splash, Tap, tap, tap.* Winston tapped the end of his safety razor in the basin. He pulled the dull blade across his face. His stubble was still standing. *Where's my penknife.* He looked in the mirror again, closed his eyes, then opened them. *But you're still there.*

The television flickered with a noisy *STA-NAK, STA-NAK-NAK*. Then came a sudden *rap-rap-rap*. Winston haphazardly wiped his face with a muslin towel. He sauntered to the hotel room door and spied through the wide-angle, fisheye lens of the peephole. Susan was pacing impatiently in the hallway, like she needed to use the bathroom.

Rap, rap, rap—

"Okay!" he yelled, grabbing his baggy, quad-pocket trekking pants strewed across a pillow at the foot of the double bed. "I need to put my pants on!"

A sharp, *rap, rap, rap—*

"Okay!" Tugging at his pants, Winston hastily fastened his belt as he danced with himself across the room. He unlatched the security lock to the door and opened it. "You're here earlier than we planned. I thought you were room service coming to pick up the tray."

The television began an annoying, *STA-KA, KA, STA, KA, KA, KA*. Winston grabbed the remote lying on the bed and aimed it at the television.

"Good morning, James. The dawn is a friend of the muses and the early bird catches the worm." Susan swayed into the room as though she owned the place. She sat on the edge of the double bed, her chest thrust forward, with her hands locked together over her knees. "So, you had breakfast in bed. I hope you're rested," she said with a tilted smile. Shimmering strands of her hair lifted in the air, caught in updraft from the ceiling's slow-moving paddle fan.

"Yeah, sure." Winston's eyes wandered blearily back and forth at Susan. He found it hard not to stare. *Looks like she's trying to rip a new V into that low-cut T-shirt. She doesn't have to try so hard. All she's got to do is breathe.* He drew a quick breath of his own and touched the wrong button on the remote. The channel changed to the introduction for a movie. The goddess Columbia-Hekate, in full toga, held a lighted torch above her head. Winston tapped the button on the remote again and an Arabic rerun of *Raiders of the Lost Ark* flashed on the screen.

Bulloq was telling Indiana Jones about the Ark: "It can carry a broadcast," *SAT-KA*— "from—"

Winston found the OFF button and *Raiders of the Lost Ark* vanished as the television blinked. A line of white light receded into a small glowing dot that disappeared into the middle of the screen.

Susan glimpsed Winston's distorted reflection in the contoured glass as the tube went blank. "Why, you look exhausted. Are you okay?" She noticed the dark circles shadowing the thin folds under his eyes.

"I slam, therefore I am. I'm a little festered from lack of sleep. My brain's in sideways. I ran out of Billy's valerian root a couple of days ago. Crossing all these time zones hasn't helped. It's the jet lag—a dragon on my back. My internal clock's out of phase. Days are nights. Plus, the bed's too hard. It's like sleeping on a bunch of nails."

"That I can understand." Susan eyed the empty diet cola cans on the table. "Hmm," She twitched her nose at the rank odor from a half-eaten wedge of an egg sandwich in a plate on the nightstand, next to a complimentary hotel copy of the Quran. "You probably have a caffeine hangover from your pleasure-seeking habit. Temperance, you need to change your ways, or you're going to lose a kidney."

Winston picked up the sandwich, pulled back the toasted bread, and sprinkled it from a hotel salt packet labeled SALT FROM THE DEAD SEA. He took a bite. "Want some?" he murmured as he chewed. "It's good. There is an old Middle Eastern tradition that says eggs invoke the psyche. But I just enjoy the taste of a primordial mystery." Winston took another bite and sniffed. "Plus the smell can help lower your metabolic rate."

Susan shook her head. "No, thanks. Cholesterol is one of my food phobias. And all that sodium is bad for your heart."

Winston squinched his face with a slight choke. "No, I'm a bad liar," he amended. "The albumen's not properly cooked. It needs ketchup." He grabbed a half-empty can of cola, shook it, and washed down the egg taste with a swig. Finishing off the sandwich, he rolled his tongue over the front of his teeth and swallowed. His Adam's apple bobbed. "I don't want to waste any. There's no promise of tomorrow. Live for today—you've got to enjoy every sandwich."

"I have a guide set up through the archaeological department at the French Biblical and Archaeological School here in Jerusalem. He's going to meet us in the lobby. Do you have everything, James?"

"Yes," he replied testily.

"The GPS, is it charged?"

"Ye-es," Winston impatiently answered.

"Good, I have a topographic of the city." She tugged on the papers sticking out of her shoulder bag. "Do you have your checklist?"

"Yes, I have this checklist. But Susan," Winston gritted his teeth, "I do not have all this *stuff.* You'd think we were bird hunting or something. Binoculars, spotting scope, tripod, digital camera, guidebook, notepad, tape recorder, polarized sunglasses, sunscreen, insect repellent, flashlight, rain poncho, first aid kit, and a survival kit. Susan, you must have been a Girl Scout." He pulled off his t-shirt and sat down in a wicker lounge chair facing away from Susan.

"Hmm," Susan rolled her eyes. "It's always good to be prepared." She patted her shoulder bag.

Winston bit down on his lower lip as he slipped on a shirt.

"Aren't you going to change pants? You're wearing the same clothes from yesterday."

"I only brought one pair." He buttoned his shirt.

"James, I sat up much of the night as well thinking about what all of this might be about," she said. "Do you get the feeling that the virus is associated with religion in some way? The catacombs in Paris, the Vatican, and now Jerusalem?"

"It's possible," he said, slipping on his shoes. "But we are not necessarily chasing something religious. We're following geocentric landmarks. I'm aware that Jerusalem is considered the center of the world for the three principal monotheistic religions. And I'm also aware that this is the city where 'My Bible is better than your Bible,' but I wouldn't be surprised if all of this is associated with world politics."

"I've been trying to put a handle on who could have designed all this within the virus. And why?" she asked with a perplexed look on her face. "Any ideas on how to translate it?"

"I'm still at sixes and sevens. A 404—nothing whatsoever." He shook his head. "It's a real crux."

"Any new keywords to add to the word pool?"

"No." Winston bent down to tie his shoelaces. "Right now, I'm still gathering string. Only obelisk, pentagram, and meridian so far. It's the only thing that keeps cropping up everywhere we've been." He stood up.

"But according to the Backdoor Group, meridian does not function as a keyword," she prodded, casting a downward gaze.

"Yes, Susan, I know. Who's our guide today?" He reached for the door.

"It's a Dr. William Baragel Peres. He does work with the Smithsonian's Department of Anthropology."

"Alright, let's have a talk with the doctor. Maybe he has a miracle medicine that can cure what ails us," Winston said hopefully as they left the room. He *jiggled* the handle to make sure the door was locked.

"James." Susan's eyes rolled to one side.

"What?" Winston stopped short.

"You need to close the barn door."

Winston zipped up his fly.

Skulls, Susan mused. She shook her head.

———

DR. BAINS SAT BEHIND HIS DESK at Fort Meade, his eyes rigid, focused on an intelligence report scrolling across a computer monitor:

> STATO DELLA CITTÀ DEL VATICANO : HATCHETMAN : CHEDWICK
> OPERATIVE CONFIRMS POPE'S DEATH - DOCS ACQUIRED

He addressed his keyboard, opened a secure list of phone numbers from his computer, and dialed the heading OVAL OFFICE.

A speakerphone on his desk *buzzed* and *whistled* a dial tone.

Click— "Hello...."

"William, contact your superior and prepare a flight for Rome."

———

Astronomy compels the soul to look upward and leads us from this world to another. – Plato, the *Republic*

A NEATLY-DRESSED GENTLEMAN paced toward the front desk of the hotel lobby and stopped before a walled fish aquarium. Backlit in a subdued light, a luminous sea-green medusa swam eerily behind him, its tentacles grossly magnified as it approached the glass. The gentleman was one of those people who could never blend in with his surroundings. His flushed face, devoid of eyebrows and freckled from the sun, was shadowed by the wide brim of his turtle-shelled Bombay Bowler. He fidgeted with the buttons on the front of his rumpled, cream-colored, tropical suit, then nervously pulled on his bushy gray beard swooping from his cheekbones. He removed his pith helmet and adjusted its leather sweatband. His kinky, orange-red hair was twisted up like a bird's nest. Perspiration beaded off his brow and dripped past an inch-long, jagged scar that pointed like an arrow directly to his left eye. He raked his fingers through his hair and tightened the helmet back to his head. Picking up a folded newspaper from the desk, he fanned himself with a steady eye on the elevator doors. As the doors opened, he dropped the newspaper and beelined across the lobby. "Good morning, Ms. Hamilton," he articulated in impeccable English, his vowels full.

"Welcome to the city where heaven and Earth meet." He extended his hand.

Susan paused, exiting the elevator. "Good morning, Doctor. This is my associate, James Winston."

Winston and Peres exchanged a handshake.

He's got a sweaty palm. Winston noticed the tension in his stance. *He must be nervous.* "Hello. You look a little stricken by the heat," Winston spoke pleasantly as he gawked at the doctor. *This guy looks like Harpo Marx.*

"Yes, it's a very warm day. I feel like a bone-eater. My throat is parched." Peres pulled a white handkerchief from his pocket and wiped away the pinheads of sweat around his gangly, untanned neck. "I haven't adjusted to the weather in Jerusalem. I just came from an archeological expedition at Hokkaidō Island in Japan, the Land of the Rising Sun. The climate is quite different in Japan. We may want to carry bottled water with us if we are going to be out in the streets all day. It's the oppressive city heat. It's as hot as Hell out there in those streets. You do not want to get dehydrated."

"Good idea," Susan agreed. "I didn't prepare for that." She motioned to a bellboy dressed in a *bright* lemon-colored, travel-light waistcoat from L. L. Bea*m* and placed an order for bottled water.

"I'll have a juice substitute, a diet cola please." Winston winked at Susan. He noticed Peres staring at him. "I'm chemically dependent," he explained.

Peres smiled cordially. He caught Winston staring back at him. "My scar is from the battle at Gebel Libni during the Six Day War. I'm lucky that I can see with both eyes."

Winston averted his eyes in another direction. He noticed the Lion of Judah emblem on a city flag of Jerusalem draped across a wall in the lobby.

"Doctor Peres, we're searching for additional information about this area." Susan handed him a map and pointed to a bright orange circle. "It's the location of a park of some sort. We need a third eye to aid us in seeing anything of importance."

"Certainly, let me give it a bird's-eye view." He quickly inspected the map. "It's a few blocks from here. We can walk over there and—"

"Your water, sir," the bellboy interrupted, "and here is your soda, sir."

"I got it." Winston handed the bellboy a handful of shekels. "Keep the change."

"*Shukran,* thank you." The bellboy nodded.

Winston turned to Peres. "So, where are we going, Doctor?"

Peres glanced again at the map, then peered sharp-eyed at Winston. "To the Mount of Evil," he murmured.

☠☠☠

The day will come when the mystical generation of Jesus, by the Supreme Being as his father, in the womb of a virgin will be classed with the fable of the generation of Minerva in the brain of Jupiter. – *Thomas Jefferson* to John Adams

THE SUN HAD RISEN HOT that day. It was ninety plus degrees in Jerusalem. As they made their way through the noisy hustle that filled the confined cobblestone streets, a perspiring Doctor Peres began a tour of the Holy City. "We should have brought an umbrella. Have you ever been to Jerusalem before?" he asked loudly.

"Yes, I've been *here* before," Susan said laconically.

"And you, Mr. Winston?"

"No, but something about it looks familiar. My father came here a lot when he worked at the American Institute of Oriental Research."

"The Albright Institute," Peres noted. "My friend, Dr. Sanderson, studied there. I met Sanderson when I worked at the Oriental Institute of the University of Chicago. I'm with the Smithsonian now."

"Yes, I know," Winston said, looking bemused as they walked by the wall-to-wall stalls of moneychangers and street venders with old women chaffering for bargains. He felt the disapproval from a Muslim woman, a *niqabi,* covered head-to-toe in a black gulf-style *niqab,* standing like a shadow staring at Susan with fearful eyes through the slit in her veil. He noticed armed U. N. Peacekeepers clad in blue fatigues and Dragon Skin body armor standing on every other corner. "This block is hot. What's with all the blue suits?"

"The Muslims have closed off part of the Temple Mount," Peres said evenly. "They are refusing access. They claim there are structural problems. There are rumors that someone has been tunneling again. The last time that happened it nearly started a Holy War. They're Xe mercenaries hired as U.N. Peacekeepers who have been called in case there is a riot." He shook his head. "Since 1967, the whole *landscape* around Jerusalem has turned into a stage of political debate and conflict."

"Yeah. I saw the ugly concrete walls around the city when we came in last night. It's a concentration camp," Winston compared, "that would make Hitler proud."

"The Apartheid Wall of Zionism … Part of the 'Jerusalem Renaissance.' It's said that the Roman General Titus once built a wall around Jersulem to entrap and massacre the Jews," Peres explained. "But the Apartheid Wall was created to separate the Palestinians from Jerusalem for defence. The whole state of Israel is encirled with strategically placed Python missile sites. Both the Zionists and Palestinians want to make Jerusalem their capitol. The Vatican and the U.N. have proposed the city be given international status, independent of any government. Such craziness. Everyone wants to be the chosen people … the one nation under God."

"It's amazing how the major religions of the western world make such a fuss over the Temple Mount," Susan commented.

"David, Jesus, and Mohammad—Jerusalem is a city with many faces. Let me introduce you to this place of towers and domes so you can see beyond the fuss," Peres offered. "Jerusalem is an oasis in a dry, harlot desert. This ancient city lies in the middle of nowhere, at the bottom of a triangular basin bordered by a chain of small mountains. 'Tremble, thou earth, at the pressure of the Lord, which turneth the rock into a pool of water, the flint into a fountain,' " he recited. "The water from the surrounding streams and springs fall into this basin, making it an ideal location for a desert city. There are thirty cisterns which fill with life-sustaining water channeled from ancient aqueducts extending as far away as Bethlehem. Half of Israel is arid desert. In the desert, water means *life.* For centuries, water has been one of the most revered resources in the Middle East—almost sacred. Early Greek philosophers believe the world originated from water. The Bedouin say that the rains that fall from the sky are the tears from a sky goddess weeping as she watches over her people."

"No rainbows without the rain," Winston remarked.

"Archeological discoveries in the Negev and other parts of Israel have revealed ancient watering systems used by the Nabateans to collect and transfer rainwater—"

"In the Negev?" Susan cut Peres short. "That's south of here?"

"It's the desert where the Bible says Abraham first made a covenant with God. It's north of the Sinai and east of Giza, where the mighty Samson pulled down the Dagon serpent temple of the Philistines. It's where the fabled Ark of the Covenant was once kept," Peres answered. "Israel's economy, like the ancient Egyptian's hydraulic civilization centered on the Nile, is linked to its water supply. Water is a national security issue for Israel. It is said that Israel's diversion of the River Jordan in 1964 was the spark that led to the Six Day War, when Israel drew its new lines in the sand. Today, most of Israel's freshwater resources are joined in an irrigation grid which brings water from the north and the aquifers in the mountains east of Jerusalem to the semi-arid south through a network of giant pipes, aqueducts, and pumping stations. Israel's advances in water conservation have made it a world leader in the development of micro-irrigation and new plant strains bred specifically for arid conditions. Hmm." He cleared his throat. "I view the Old City as one large temple complex. The entire city is a U.N. World Heritage Site. Since early Roman times, this city has been a wellspring of religious co-existence. It is divided into four quadrants. To the north are the Christian and Muslim quarters—*Ut*—and to the south, the Armenian and Jewish quarters—*Ut*— Their borders are still more or less defined by the two main thoroughfares laid out by the Roman town planners of Emperor Hadrian—*Ut*— Excuse me."

Winston nodded for Peres to continue.

"This unique plan for the city was created in 135 *Anno Domini*. The city is believed to have been rebuilt upon the rubble of its earlier destruction during the suppression of Bar-Kochba's Jewish revolt against Roman rule—*Ut*—although there is very little archeological evidence for the existence of a Jewish temple city before that date. It was once generally believed that the Roman Tenth Legion made a clean sweep of the Old City—*Ut*—and laid out a new city around an entirely new plan. But it is difficult to erase the street pattern of a pre-established city—*Ut*—and not practical to do so. *Ut*— Please excuse me. Butterflies, I'm a bit nervous. *Ut*—"

"Take a sip of water," Susan suggested. "It'll help with the hiccups."

Peres swallowed from his water bottle.

"Hold your nose and do not breathe when you drink," Winston added. "I could set a clock by you."

"Hadrian's city was called *Aelia Capitolina*." Peres described, "Its plan was based upon a *cardo* or *cardus*, which is a cross axis of streets running north-south and east-west. That design was adopted by the Romans from the Etruscans and the Greeks who carried out their religious rituals in accordance to the division of celestial and terrestrial space. Virtually every Roman town in Italy was oriented around an astronomical grid."

"The Etruscans again," Winston noted. "An axis, like a Latin cross ..."

"Yes, a cross, one of the most powerful symbols in the world," Peres said. "The Etruscans believed that coordinating the heavens and the Earth into quarters enabled the priests to decipher certain signs emanating from their gods. All of the secular and sacral undertakings on Earth had to be coordinated with the *cardo* of the city. May I see your map again?"

Susan handed him the map.

"Hmm," Peres cleared his throat. "Yes, that's much better." He unfolded the map. "For the Romans, the *cardo* of a city symbolized the sacred dimensions of time and space in accordance with the cosmic stations of their sky gods. One direction travels vertically and the other horizontally. The vertical direction is often considered an evil direction with streets aligned toward the north. The horizontal direction is considered holy, with streets aligned east-west to mark the daily journey of the two holy lights, the sun and the moon."

The three halted as Peres pointed to a few of the landmarks on the map. "Today much of Hadrian's *cardo* is obscured by the various buildings and street markets. Its most prominent feature was a north-south axis, known as the Roman *cardo maximus*. This was a broad street running southward from the Damascus Gate along an imaginary axis that ran down the present Khan al-Zait Street. Crossing it at a right angle was the *decumanus*, the city's east-west axis, which is represented today by the approximate alignment of David and Chain Streets."

"So the *cardo* was laid out like a checkerboard?" Winston questioned.

"Yes." Peres slid his index finger over the map, tracing the geometry of the oddly angled street alignment. "This *cardo* arrangement can be seen on a restored mosaic map of Jerusalem from the Byzantine era which was discovered in a church in Madaba, Jordan in 1887. It is the oldest known pilgrimage map of Jerusalem and possibly an adaptation of a map described in Eusebius's book, the *Onamastikon*. In this mosaic, Jerusalem is depicted as a fish-shaped loop with a central *cardo*, similar to a mall, with a pillar standing at one end. Hadrian erected this pillar at an intersection to the *cardo*, north of the city. Here—at this location." He pointed to the map. "This pillar is said to symbolize an *omphalos* that marked the center of the known world. It is believed this was an itinerary column used as a Roman milestone. It also marked the terminus of two other streets running at an angle from the *cardo* and to each other. This formed a secondary street pattern oriented north-south and running parallel to the Temple Mount's Western Wall. These streets provide the *unique key* to the unusual geometric scheme for the upper half of *Aelia Capitolina*."

"We already know about itinerary columns and milestones," Susan commented. "Ranger Nobles and Mr. Howard told us about them."

"The *omphalos* was a conical stone that represented the navel of the Earth," the soft-spoken scholar elaborated. "It was often associated with a polar grid. But, the *omphalos* of the ancient world commonly marked the location of a *baetylos*."

"A *baetylos*?" Susan repeated.

"The residence of a god," Peres translated.

"So, there was a grid pattern of streets created by the north-south and east-west design of the *cardo*, which was overlapped with an angled street pattern?" Winston asked for clarification.

"Precisely, Mr. Winston. This is the way the Romans laid out their cities. You find the same pattern in the city plan of ancient Rome. The Jerusalem we have today originates from the Roman design. Over the centuries, many cities have been built this way. For example, in your country, Washington, D.C. was designed with a cross grid *cardo* intersected with streets running at various angles."

Susan thumbed through her notepad. "That's the same thing the monsignor told us." She pulled a ballpoint pen from her pocket and started to jot something down.

"It's not writing. It's out of ink. No ... it's got candle wax in the tip." She scowled. "I didn't bring an extra pen."

"Please, use mine." Peres reached into his coat and offered her a pen with a little, blue globe at its end.

"Thank you." She curiously fumbled with it. "How does it work?"

"Click the top of the globe," Peres instructed. "There is much wisdom to be found in the streets of Jerusalem, especially if we study the patterns hidden in its design with a bird's-eye view. The axis of this city is the invisible Messianic Line which runs from the Golden Gate, the Gate of Mercy, through the Temple Mount, and on to the Holy Sepulcher—the Martyrium." Peres pointed again to the map. "The streets that radiate from the site of Hadrian's column inside the Damascus Gate form an angle of forty-six degrees. It's a chevron formation that points north. This is the top point of the pentagram star that forms the basic design for the Roman plan. This shape was an early Christian symbol for Jerusalem."

"Torre said the same thing." Susan scribbled in her notepad, *Pentagram*, then earmarked the page, pinching it tight. *Bingo.*

"Another unique geometry feature related to the Old City is the path of the *Via Dolorosa*, the Way of Grief—the Path of Pain. It's a devotional walk adopted from the early Templars and Franciscans who traversed from the Holy Sepulcher along a route east of the Temple Mount. The original path of the *Via Dolorosa* entered from the south of the city, and there is a reason for that." Again, Peres pointed to the map. "Most scholars believe the current path marked by the fourteen Stations of the Cross was based upon a medieval European tradition associated with a meditation on Jesus's journey to Calvary. Along the route are sacred places described in the Passion of the Christ, with emphasis on His suffering. But, it is possible this path is associated with the early Celtic solar labyrinth, a design that may have been carried to Jerusalem by the Crusaders or the Romans. For example, at Station Two there is an old Roman surveying benchmark. Perhaps the real significance of this path lies in the angles that one turns from street to street. These angles measure divisions of twenty-three and a half degrees, the approximate tilt of the Earth, which is primarily determined by the gravitational pull of the sun and moon—the concept known as the Lunisolar Theory of Procession—studied by Isaac Newton."

Sun and moon, Winston flashed a thought. *Sundials, Newton ... my nickel trick.*

"The tilt of the Earth controls the delicate balance of the planet's climate." Peres extended his hand and angled it back and forth. "If it tilts too much, we could enter an ice age. Not enough tilt and the planet could become a vast, desert wasteland. The Earth's tilt is truly sacred. It's Nature's waltz. Life on Earth might not have occurred if not for our planet's tilt. The odds against such a balance out of which all life emegered are so astronomically high that many consider this to be proof for both a creator God and humanity's unique place in the universe. In this sense, the *Via Dolorosa* is a symbolic cosmic path toward the divine with its streets aligned to the major positions of the rising or setting sun on the eastern and western horizons. These streets reference the cosmic order that keeps the world in proper balance, the old Egyptian concept of *matt*, a perfect world order."

"Doctor, are there any obelisks or sundials in Jerusalem?" Winston changed the subject as they continued their southerly stroll toward the Mount of Evil.

"There is an obelisk in the Wohl Rose Garden near the Terraced Walls of the Supreme Court Building. But that building is known more for its symbol of the All Seeing Eye of the Rothschilds. There is also the Memorial Obelisk near the Central Bus Station. However, these obelisks are not ancient. They hold no more meaning than the Washington Monument. There may have been an ancient Egyptian obelisk or a Canaanite pillar in the city at one time, but nothing remains standing today. Palestine means the land of the pal, or the pillar, after the thousands of *masseboth*, ritualized standing stones, in the Negev and Sinai Deserts."

"Nothing, no obelisks or sundials at all?" Winston questioned. *There must be another commonality.*

"Well ..." Peres paused, then nodded, "perhaps. There are two primary churches or shrines in Jerusalem. One is a Golden Dome and the other is a human dome. The Golden Dome is a shrine known as the Dome of the Rock at the Temple Mount and the other dome covers the Church of the Holy Sepulcher. The Holy Sepulcher is said to be the site of Christ's crucifixion, entombment, and resurrection. This site is also known as Golgotha, a swell of land, or Calvary, the place of the skull—the human dome—the great *cranioum*. Look." He pointed east. "You can see the golden-capped Dome of the Rock from here. There is a traditional sundial over the center archway of the Dome of the Rock. But there is also an *ancient* sundial at the Dome of the Rock."

Winston stared nonchalantly at the sun reflecting off the Golden Dome resting atop a building covered in jade-blue mosaics. His sharp eyes followed three large, black-bearded vultures circling in aerial acrobatics high above the glistening dome. Each bird dropped a bone from their prey onto the Temple Mount plaza. "Hmm." *Birds of sacrifice, they're targeting the Dome of Aeschylus, looking for lamb.* "My eyes are not as good as they used to be," he muttered. "But, those scavengers look a little aggravated by the light. The dome's in their line of fire."

"Kohinoor, the Mountain of Light ... This city is full of religious scavengers. Like our world, it is a place of conflicting babble. No two people come to God by way of the same road," Peres noted. "The Dome of the Rock is the most contested piece of real estate on Earth. This shrine, correctly known as the *Qubbat As-Sakhrah*, was built to commemorate the Prophet Mohammad's miraculous 'Night Journey' to the Seven Heavens. The stone foundation of the Threshing Floor is said to contain a hoofprint petrosomatoglyph of Mohammad's steed. According to legend, God threw a rock into 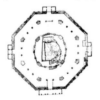 a great abyss with his *right hand* to block the entry into Hell, thus God laid His foundation stone at the center of the cosmological world. The shrine's architectural form follows that of a cosmic *lingam*, an octagon between a circle and a square—Vishnu, Shiva, and Brahma. The stone floor is possibly a type of spiritual *yoni* of support through the deluge of life and may have been part of an earlier Canaanite hilltop altar, known as a *bama*. The Semites and Canaanites were among the most assiduous stone worshipers in the ancient world."

"The entry to Hell, the Gate to Hell," Winston compared. "A stone at the center—"

"Like the Jefferson Stone," Susan cut him short.

"The Threshing Floor is above the Well of the Soul—possibly an ancient oracle chamber, like the one at Delphi. As pointed out by the American explorer, Dr. James Barclay, in his *City of the Great King*, the rock floor of this mosque is formed from various, angled cuts and grooves which are not consistent with a traditional threshing floor. 'Thou hast set the borders of the earth: thou hast made both summer and the winter,' " Peres thoughtfully quoted from the book of Psalms. "Perhaps the *key* for unlocking a secret to the Dome of the Rock lies not in Jerusalem, but in Peru, at the mountain city of Machu Picchu."

Winston caught Susan's wide-eyed expression.

"Peru?" she questioned.

"There is a calendar stone at Machu Picchu called the *Intihuatana*, meaning the Hitching Post of the Sun." Peres pointed toward the Dome of the Rock. "The *Intihuarana* is a small pillar cut at various angles designed to cast specific shadows for keeping time. It has been shown that this stone was hitched, or aligned, to the sun at the time of the equinoxes. It is simply a type of sundial. The same is true of various angled grooves and cuts on the Threshing Floor. Threshing floors were used in the ancient world to separate grain from the chaff. But the Threshing Floor of the Dome of the Rock is an ancient calendar stone, similar to the one at Machu Picchu, only larger."

"Form does not always follow function," Winston remarked. "So, it's like the obelisks in Rome and Paris—a sundial."

"Precisely, Mr. Winston. The Golden Dome over the Threshing Floor appears to block out the sun's light for the functionality of this ancient sundial. Sunlight enters the dome primarily by way of a screened oculus in the roof, similar to Hadrian's Pantheon in Rome. Stained-glass windows encircling the drum of the outer walls also cast light upon the Threshing Floor. The Qur'an states, 'God is the light of heaven and earth.' The design of the structure captures the source of this spiritual light."

"Stained glass windows … found in cathedrals," Winston noted.

"Yes. The Dome of the Rock is similar to the first cathedrals, with its rock floor likened to the meridian markers and labyrinthine floors found in one-quarter of all European cathedrals. The Threshing Floor functioned as a calculator for *threshing* out the movement of the sun and moon, the two faces of Janus. The entire universe turns around that stone. The floor is made up of angled cuts in the rock which once cast shadows to predict the time for certain religious feast days. There is even a prayer niche aligned toward Mecca. The floor threshes out *time*, particularly the concept of time, as related to a religious deity. Over the years, the rock has been worn away, leaving only the angles found on the floor as the remnants of the original calendar stone for us to interpret. It is said, that when the Knights Templar occupied this site, they purposely chipped away at the rock, leaving it in its present condition."

"How certain are you that it's a calendar stone?" Susan asked.

"A recent computer analysis proves that the angles cut into the floor were once associated with solar and lunar alignments to the Mount of Olives, the location of the crusader's Tomb to the Vigin Mary. The peaks of the Mount of Olives are the meeting place of the sol and moon, the Sumerian *Shamash* and *Sin* after which the Sinai desert is named, the two great opposing holy lights—the old symbols of Christ and his bride. The first altars of many ancient religions were to the sun and moon, or the sun and Mother Earth, in order to understand the *Logos* and the *Sophia*."

"*Logos* and *Sophia*?" Susan probed further.

"Yes, the cosmic order and divine wisdom, or the understanding of that cosmic order as applied to the self—a person's relationship to the cycles within Nature."

"I don't understand." Susan slightly shook her head.

"This is a metaphoric philosophical teaching found in the first Gnostic Gospels. One of these gospels, *The Sophia of Jesus Christ,* states that after Jesus rose from the dead, *twelve* disciples and *seven* women served as his followers. In the book of Luke a similar story includes a woman cured of seven demons, Mary Magdalene. Jesus and his followers went to Galilee onto the mountain called Divination and Joy, where they gathered together and were 'perplexed about the underlying reality of the universe and its great plan.' This is perhaps a reference to the *twelve* zodiacs and the *seven* pole stars which govern the order of the old Earth-centered cosmos. Furthermore, it is said that the Savior appeared, not in his previous physical form, but as a spirit. His new likeness resembled a great angel of light—"

"I thought *Sophia* was a goddess," Susan interrupted. "Part of the women's rights movement."

"No," Peres chuckled and then explained, "*Sophia* is not a lost goddess. *Sophia* is a concept for a lost wisdom, or understanding, associated with the nature of the *logos*—the cosmic order behind the workings of the world. It might be compared to the knowledge you obtain in a physics class. It represents a type of knowledge that a willing soul must obtain in order to overcome his ignorance of the true reality of the world. Aristotle identified five intellectual virtues through which a person arrives at a truth by either affirmation or denial—true or false observations— "

"Like the *yes* or *no* gateways in computer logic circuits," Winston interrupted.

"Lullus-logic," Susan added.

"Perhaps, I'm not a computer expert," Peres admitted. "Aristotle called three of these virtues: the Practical, the Productive, and the Theoretical. Within the Theoretical there were three types of knowledge: *Nous*, the intuitive understanding; *Episteme,* a scientific and empirical knowledge; and *Sophia,* an eternal and unchangeable philosophical wisdom. This is a wisdom of the order within Nature, which humans naturally understand as a type of sixth sense. When you walk in the forest, you have a feeling that you are walking within God's creation, the natural order, or the *logos*. It is a type of mental transcendence that sets us at peace. Part of this understanding is that the *logos*, the cosmic order, exists not only in the material world, but in the mental world as well. It is a part of the natural order within the *enlightened* thinker. So above, so within. A divine order, or a divine light, within us all."

"Divine Light," Winston repeated.

"Light is at the foundation of many religions, Mr. Winston. According to the Bible, Light was the first-born of God—the first manifestation of Himself in the universe. While there is no authentic archeological evidence of the existence of a Temple of Solomon in Jerusalem, there really is *a presence* of a Temple of Sol-o-Moon—the two holy lights. The Threshing Floor is the Temple's foundation for a higher magic."

"Sol-o-Moon. The sun and its consort—sun and moon worship," Winston surmised. *A calendar ... the Earth in proper balance.*

"It is not the worship of the sun and moon, but an attempt to understand their cosmic order," Peres clarified. "Symbolism related to the cosmic order is prevalent within the mythologies of the Bible. The Bible is an amazing book, but to truly understand it you have to forget everything you've been taught, and read it from the beginning to the end with your eyes wide open. Then you will see things you never saw before. Sadly, many view the Bible as a literal truth. But, it is not. It is merely a collection of mythology stories with some historical basis. However, that does not make it unimportant. Mythology is very important, perhaps more important than real history. Myths contain perennial themes which convey timeless meanings that help to *ground* our lives to the world around us ... and to a God beyond the words within the Bible. Many of the names in the Bible are viewed by mythologists and anthropologists as code words for a cosmology. The stories and characters of the Bible bear very close resemblances to the sun, moon, and earth goddesses found in the Babylonian and Egyptian epics. Female names such as Mary and Salome have alternate meanings associated with the Mother Earth and the sun and moon. For example, Mary Magdalene is associated with the Earth's axis—the Magdalene line, the line of mapping."

"Or a meridian," Susan proposed. *That church in Paris ...*

"Yes," Peres continued. "In his work, the *Dawn of Astronomy: A Study of Temple Worship,* the British astronomer, Joseph Lockyer, theorized that the fabled Temple of Solomon, like the Egyptian and Greek temples, was a type of astronomical observatory. For him, the Temple of Solomon was a *time place*—a true temple designed to track the movement from the sacred *KRN*, a Hebrew term for the Horned One that sends forth a radiant beam of light, known as the *Shekinah.*"

"Lockyer," Winston interjected. "He's the astronomer who discovered that the sun is made of helium—"

"A Horned One, a gnomon at an altar ... a *Benben* stone ... What did Inspector Parott say?" Susan checked her notes. "What is the *Shekinah?*"

"The *Shekinah* is the reflection of Yahweh found in the nature of light. The calendar stone was in effect a means of communing with the *Shekinah*. It was a means of understanding the passage of the *Shekinah*, that being time, and thus a means of understanding *the presence* of Yahweh. Yahweh—like the Babylonian deity, Tammuz, and the supreme Greek deity, Saturn-Kronos, the god of time who ruled over the celestial pole—must have been associated with the concepts of time, space, and motion, as well as light...." He held his hand out to Susan. "My pen."

She handed him the pen, and Peres quickly drew a symbol on the back of the map. "This concept of a divine light can be found in other cultures. For example, this is the Japanese *Kanji* symbol for the two great lights in the heavens. In Japan and China, hieroglyphs are used to convey their language, as does Paleo-Hebrew and Proto-Sinaitic script first discovered in the ancient mining regions of the Sinai, the Country of Green Turquoise. Images and symbols are the fastest way to reach the human mind. Humans are limited in their ability to describe complex ideas. Our language and art are comprised totally of symbols that are open to interpretation, which fosters free thought. Most people formulate some visual image of God when they worship. We filter our understanding of the Divine through the context of our available iconic library. But, certain images are universal in their interpretation and sacred to all cultures. The two *Kanji* characters represent a combination of the sun and moon pulled together—becoming *bright*, or as in a changing, drawing inwards, or an opening of the intensity of light, like the *Shekinah*. When we combine the two

Japanese characters, it means *to inscribe brightly*, or *Ieoh Ming* in Chinese. Mr. Winston, it's all about God's divine light."

明 "Hmm ... little square shapes." Winston eyed Peres's bird scratches on the map. "Let in the light. It reminds me of a Windows Logo."

Peres flipped the map over and traced around the perimeter of the oddly angled shape of the Temple Mount with the end of the pen. "Square-shaped ... yes, the temple of the four corners. In addition," Peres changed the subject, "the Temple Mount is offset from the axis of the main *cardo* of the city. This offset axis is designed around an *axis mundi*—the axis of the Earth—which is aligned to the *spiritus mundi*—the Spirit of the World. The Egyptians called this the *sma*, symbolized by a whirling feather attached to a pole representing a human lung next to its windpipe, the Spirit of the Breath of Life. This is one reason why the Temple Mount is not a perfect square, but a diagonally shaped structure."

"It's box-shaped," Winston noted.

"A letterbox," Susan proposed with a smile. "I'll bet it holds some secrets."

"The Temple platform is a Holy Space. It is the place where the Infinite *presence* of Yahweh exists in the earthly realm," Peres continued. "It reminds me of the Zen rock garden of Soami within the Ryoan-ji Temple in Japan—the Temple of the Peaceful Dragon. That garden is called the Garden of Emptiness. It is a sublime place to meditate on the emptiness of our busy world. I have meditated before that garden for hours, sitting in a Lotus position and addressing a riddle with no answer — '**Can you *see* the voice of God?**' The riddle helps you to break free from our logical world so you can enter into a new reality. The garden's design is deceptively simple. It is composed of fifteen stones set in a small rectangular field of rippled-patterned white gravel. The stones are arranged in five groupings of five, two, three, two and three, so

that when observed from any vantage point there is always one rock hidden from sight. That arrangement is similar to the layout of the mosques on the Temple platform. According to recent studies, the Garden of Emptiness was designed to invoke an unconscious experience from the viewer." Peres sketched a shape on the back of the map. "Within the empty landscape of the garden is hidden the mental image of the trunk and branches of a tree. Somehow this subtle arrangement brings about a peaceful feeling to everyone who views the garden."

TREE ALIGNED TO ROCKS

Seeing trees, Winston contemplated, *associated with an axis mundi ... aligned north and south.* "It's steganographic."

"What did I tell you, James?" Susan joked, "Even the Zen Buddhists have dealt with subliminals."

Winston smiled. "A hidden tree in a garden ... Billy's Great Tree ... the Garden of Eden—Paradise."

"Trees are a very important religious symbol. They are often associated with the place in which God communes with man, as in the Garden of Eden story," Peres noted. "An *axis mundi* when aligned to the northern sky is very similar to an invisible World Tree, branching out along the Earth's polar axis. The *axis mundi* of the Temple Mount is like the hub of the universe."

"Hub of the universe," Winston wisecracked to Susan. "It's a little different from an opera house."

"Paris ..." Susan turned a thought, *Skulls, a Ferris Wheel of Life on the city's axis.*

"In Chinese and Egyptian art, World Trees are depicted with sacred birds in their branches, symbolizing man's passage through life. Many temples incorporate this design element to invoke a feeling of serenity," Peres explained. "A temple's axis is a connecting link to the movement of the heavens. I believe the *axis mundi* at the Temple Mount was adopted from the Egyptians. A similar axial pattern exists in the design of the temple complex at Karnak, along the bend in the Nile. Karnak was created for the worship of the Egyptian *Ka*, the *life force*—the pure white spirit power of the male potency. It was also designed for keeping time, like the Threshing Floor at the Dome of the Rock."

"A pure white spirit power," Winston repeated, thinking about Billy at the medicine wheel. "Keeping time?"

"That's the temple designed after a standing man. Torre talked about," Susan said to Winston, checking her notes. "Anthropomorphic ..."

Peres pulled his coat away from the sticky sweat soaking through his shirt. He took three short sips from his water bottle, then pointed toward a stone dome that rose over the nearby buildings. "Over there is Jerusalem's other domed temple, the Church of the Holy Sepulcher. The three, great, Christian creeds oversee that church—the Roman Catholics, the Greek Orthodox, and the Orthodox Armenians. It was built by the Roman Emperor Constantine over Hadrian's Temple to Venus Genetrix—the *Lux Ferre*—the mother of all Romans by way of her son Aeneas, who was an ancestor of Julii. According to a Christian legend found in Eusebius of Caesarea's book, *The Life of Constantine*, Hadrian built his Temple to Venus over the site of the crucifixion, on the hill of Golgotha, although this is disputed to this day. Three other sites outside the Old City are also called Golgotha. The word Golgotha is Aramaic for the Greek word, *kranion*, meaning skull, from which we get Calvary, from the Latin root *calva*, the scalp. Of course there is an associated symbolism with this terminology in the Gospels, that being: the head, the brain, the human mind—human consciousness. It is obviously a *symbol* for early Christian Gnosticism adopted from the Greek mystery religions and related mythologies."

"The mystery religions?" Susan inquired. "Greek mythology?"

"Yes. For example, according to one Greek myth in *The Bibliotheca*, the Oracle of Gaea prophesied that Metos, the goddess of Wisdom, would bear two children. The first child would be a girl and the second a boy who would overthrow Zeus—the supreme God of the Greek pantheon, who had been raised by the horned goat Amalthea. Zeus took this warning of the oracle to heart. When he next caught Metos off guard, he opened up his mouth and swallowed her whole, leading to the end of Metos and the beginning of Zeus's wisdom. But this wisdom was much more than Zeus could take. Zeus developed the mother of all headaches. He howled louder than a banshee, with cries which could be heard throughout the entire world. The other gods came to his aid. Hermes realized what needed to be done and directed Hephaestus to take a wedge and split open Zeus's skull."

"They hacked his head." Susan's eyes slanted at Winston. "James, doesn't your relaxation chair do that?"

Winston grinned.

"Athena sprang swiftly from Zeus's immortal head, and not from a nocturnal birth from a mother's womb," Peres said with a puzzled expression. "She was fully grown and clothed in armor, holding a shield made of goat skin, and brandishing a sharp-pointed spear. Due to the manner of her birth, she proclaimed dominion over all things associated with wisdom as the Greek goddess of gnosis."

"She was like Eve," Susan compared, "fully created from Adam's rib."

"It's a similar mythology. The Eve myth may have been adapted from the Greek story," Peres hypothesized. "Athena's symbol was a sun owl, a bird of wisdom, standing before a crescent moon beneath an olive branch. For the Greeks, she was a symbol of the psyche of man fully born into the material world and ready to take on the world through a complete understanding of the forces in nature. She was a symbol for the fully enlightened mind."

"A knowledge of the order of the cosmos," Winston said, sighting westward at the stationary vanes of the Montefiore Windmill rising over the rooftops in the distance, "the sun and the moon ... Sol-o-Moon."

Peres nodded. "The scholar F. M. Muller believed the story of Athena's birth was associated with the cycles of sun. He identified Athena with the Vedic goddess, Ahana of the Dawn. Athena, or Minerva, was originally a representation of the light that accompanied the morning sun, symbolized by the morning star, the planet Venus, and thus Athena's association with Venus."

Venus ... Winston thought. *My Huygens-Grimaldi experiment.*

"To the Greeks, Athena was a virgin goddess, a Pallas maiden," Peres added. "She was portrayed fully clothed, usually in armor, and often shaking a spear or sword of truth, as the defender against all evil. She was the patron goddess of the city of Athens and the Acropolis, where they secretly worshiped the Great God Pan. Her face is depicted on many ancient Greek coins. That same patrician face, with its haunting eyes and noble nose, can be found on many Roman sculptures such as the *Venus de Milo.* It is said that Leonardo da Vinci copied those eyes and that nose for the *Global Icon* in the Louvre. The same face can be found on the mosaic floor of a Roman temple in Sepphoris, near Nazareth—the so-called 'Mona Lisa of Palestine.' "

"The *Global Icon* ..." Susan remembered, *Paris ... skulls and bones ...*

Winston's raised his eyes to Susan, realizing her awareness of a connection.

"That face," Peres considered, "was even adopted for the Statue of Liberty, the *lux ferre*, the light of liberty, the *light of freedom.*"

"So the *Global Icon* is a depiction of the goddess of wisdom, once worshiped by the Romans at Calvary?" Susan shook her head in disbelief. "Jesus!"

"Yes, Ms. Hamilton." Peres chortled slightly, "Jesus." He stepped forward and continued his explanation as they strolled through the maze of narrowing streets. "The Holy Sepulcher, like the Ha-Kotel for the Jews, is the center of the world for the Christian faith. The fact that it is associated with Golgotha suggests a Gnostic interpretation for the existence of this church. In the Gnostic view, Christ is often seen as a symbol for the last Adam. Adam is seen as the First Cause—the first human mind—where God resides as a sacred knowledge and wisdom, symbolized by the Greek and Roman goddesses, Athena and Venus, the *lux ferre*. Of course, God did create the birds before he created Adam." Peres tapped his forehead with his finger. "The subconscious mind."

"Torre told us about Adam and the First Cause," Susan said.

"In Hebrew, the word *Adam* means *man*," Peres translated. "The title, Son of Man —the Nehushtan, is a reference to Adam. The phrases, Son of Man, Child of Man, and Son of Adam, are interchangeable. In the Gospel narrative, Jesus refers to himself using the phrase *Adam Kadmon*—the Son of Man—Anthropos, the heavenly apocalyptic figure who is to come. Paul, the great Gnostic teacher who helped to establish the Christian church, used the phrase, *Adam Kadmon*, as the description of the archetypal man—a *projection of man* upon the Tree of Life and created in God's image as the first and perfect representative of humanity—who many believed would return at the end of time and restore all things anew. In the Gnostic view, the firstborn human, the First Cause, the ruler over the world which God created—is simply the mind of man, the wielder of the compass that inscribes God's great plan into the physical world. This archetypal man, the *Adam Kadmon*, in the Gnostic view, can be *any one of us*. Thus, the symbol of the skull has a double meaning. Golgotha becomes a symbol for the place that links the human soul with the God consciousness which lies within us all."

"Michelangelo's brain scan," Susan equated in a whisper.

Peres thoughtfully combed his fingers through his wiry beard. "The older, Gnostic Jewish literature states that Golgotha is a symbol for paradise. This is the fundamental belief within Gnosticism, that states that God resides in a kingdom of pure *gedulah*—a *love* within us all. It is a 'kingdom within,' spoken of in the Gospels. This same symbolism can be seen in the old Buddhist meditations before a human skull in order to achieve the correct *level* of *consciousness*. It is also part of a complex idea found in Plato's view of Eros, *love*, and Gnosis, *knowledge*. Plato believed you can never grasp true knowledge, but you could use Eros to try to get there."

Susan stopped as they passed through the archway of the Porte Horti Regis. "It's getting warm." She took a sip of water and noticed an odd aftertaste. "Hold this." She made a grumpy frown and handed her bottle to Winston. She pulled her hair up from the nape of her neck, spiraled it between her fingers, twisted it into a bun, and held it in place with a butterfly hair clip she retrieved from her pocket.

Winston's eyes were riveted on the profile of Susan's face outlined in the sunlight.

"What?" she said to Winston, noticing his gawking.

Red-faced, he stopped staring and took a swig from her water bottle.

"Give me that!" She snatched the bottle from Winston's hand.

Winston redirected his attention back to Peres, who was grinning sheepishly.

"We all know that the story of the death of Jesus the Christ is about overcoming one's personal fears," Peres spoke, observing their behavior. "With the second greatest fear being the fear of death delivered to the winds of our mind. You cannot appreciate life until you face death, either that of your own or someone else's. Death is the great unknown. Everyone fears what they do not understand. The Gnostics believed that overcoming such a fear is a process that takes place in the human mind. It is about the descent of man into his consciousness to face his soul before dying. A descent into limbo. You have to step into the darkest recesses of your mind and *slay your own dragons at the place of the skull* to find a higher level of consciousness within yourself. A place where you can discover your own garden filled with the songbirds of paradise, the place where God resides."

"Yes, the Gospels teach us to overcome the fear of death," Winston agreed, "but you called that the *second* greatest fear. What is the greatest fear?"

"Mr. Winston, the Gnostics believed that the human body was a prison for the true self. And that this true self was, in essence, our individual soul. Gnostics directed their teachings toward the discovery of the soul that lies at the heart of the human mind. Some call it a *love of wisdom*, the Greek meaning of *philosophy*. Many of the Greek-based religions believed that the human heart was the seat of intelligence, and *to know* was *to love*." Peres paused in thought. "To ignore the historical fact that Christianity is rooted in Gnostic principals is to abandon great teachings related to profound truths. Overcoming the fear of death is a lesson found in the old warrior mythologies associated with conquering the fear of death before entering combat. Wars have been won and nations conquered from the application of this simple understanding. But sometimes our greatest fear is not that of death, but our *fear to love*. Love is the only thing that eases fear. Love can renew our lives. It is a *powerful* magic. Love is one of the things that makes us human, yet Godlike at the same time. Love is the great mediator. At the heart of gnostic teaching is the *wisdom of love*."

Susan peeked under her eyelids at Winston.

Peres spoke earnestly as they continued their trek to the Mount of Evil. "According to the findings from the 1993 Jesus Seminar, there is little or no historical evidence for the existence of a holy man named Jesus. The original texts used to create the gospels have been lost for centuries, with no third party documents from that time to attest to his historical existence. Nevertheless, the Jesus in the Gospel narratives is a true mythical metaphor for a greater teaching about the human experience. *He*, like the ancient rite of circumcision, is a symbol for human sacrifice. In this didactic story, God sent his only son into the world so we might live through him, in a Godlike way. Jesus reveals God's *love*—a perfect kindness. He is an example of the human mental sacrifice that clears away the damage done in our relationships with our fellowman. Sometimes we feel that we have been unfairly treated by our fellowman. But a Godlike love is a *love* that can help us overcome such feelings. 'All we need is love.' Those are the greatest words ever written." He paused. "God loves us not because of who we are, but because of who He is. *Deus Caritas Est.*"

"God is love," Susan translated.

Peres stared longingly out over the city skyline of Jerusalem. "We know God by the spirit from which *we* love. Love is essential to our lives, Mr. Winston. Love is about self-sacrifice in the greatest quest through life—the search for *our* souls. Love knows not its own depth, until the hour of separation. Have you ever loved someone and given of yourself with all your heart, and then suddenly been rejected? It is a deep emotional pain to be rejected that way, especially when all you tried to do—is *love* someone. It is a pain far more intense than a scourging or bloodletting before a crucifixion. It is a pain that falls heavily on you and pulls away at the core of your soul—which defines your very being. If others understood what that pain felt like, they would never turn their face away from another human being."

"Rejection," Susan remarked, "the wound of love."

"Yes...." Peres sadly shook his head and returned his attention to Winston. "Pain is fascinating horror. There is always a purpose for pain. To overcome such pain a person has to search his soul and traverse his mind between his own heaven and hell, to find a new state of existence. A new consciousness. This is the true path of the *Via Dolorosa* presented in the Passion of the Christ. It is the way in which we search within ourselves to find forgiveness instead of hate for those who can cause such pain, to realize no matter how much they reject us—we still *love* them," he pleaded in a quivering voice. "Love is the unifying emotion. As with Abraham's binding of Isaac to prove his love of God, in the Passion story, God proved His love on the Cross. It was His ultimate self-fulfillment, a giving of Himself and a losing of His ego. The wounded Christ hung in pain, bled, and died as a *symbol* of God saying to the world, 'I love you through my forgiveness.' It is a governing law within human nature. We never recover from an injury imposed upon us until we learn to forgive. To forgive is to find *freedom*. To love someone beyond such pain is a very deep *love*, a very special *love*, a great *love* indeed. That is the beauty of God's *love*. It can overlook another person's misguided deeds. It is a *love* that cannot sicken or decay. You do not stop loving, if you truly love. I have often wondered how many people in this world can even begin to love that way?"

Peres leveled Winston with a cellophane stare, as though he could see right through him. "I believe that when a person has learned to love that way, he has finally learned to look into the face of his fellowman and see beyond it—to see another person's soul. It is only then that our relationships turn full circle. *Amor vincit omnia*—Love conquers all." He smiled at Susan. "Socrates may have said it best, 'He who loves your soul is the true lover. The lover of the body goes away when the flower of youth fades. But he who loves the soul goes not away, as long as the soul follows after virtue.' Mr. Winston, it does not matter if Jesus lived or died. It is not that complicated. What matters is the underlying *truth* within the story. If you judge people, you will not have time to *love* them. It is pure and simple. *Amor est vitae essentia. Love* is the Essence of Life! We need to live in God's love—with a Christ-like consciousness. Unconditional *agape* ... unconditional infinite compassion. If a thing loves, it is Infinite."

My father. My mother. Unconditional loyalty ... Billy. Winston felt from his heart. *A greater love hath no man.*

"It is only when we see the world through our hearts that we begin to see it rightly, Mr. Winston. What is essential is sometimes *invisible to the eye*."

"Steganographic," Winston remarked. He glanced at Susan.

————

And here I was, near the axis of the world, in the darkness where the stars make a circle in the sky. At that moment the conviction came to me that the harmony and rhythm were too perfect to be a symbol of blind chance or an accidental offshoot of the cosmic process; and I knew that a Beneficent Intelligence pervaded the whole. It was a feeling that transcended reason; that went to the heart of a man's despair and found it groundless. – Admiral Richard E. Byrd

THE THREE STROLLED from the Porte Horti Regis South Gate until they reached the entrance to a public park on the side of a hill.

"We are at Abu Tor. This park is the Peace Forest next to the old Convent of St. Claire. It's just a little further up this hill." Peres led them along a pedestrian walkway. He stopped and caught his breath as they passed through the arched entry to the Haas Promenade. "It is east of here, at the end of the promenade."

Winston referenced the mobile GPS as they walked. He noticed graffiti painted on the sidewalk: BUILD BRIDGES NOT WALLS. He stopped. "A magnetic variance … This must be a hot spot. An immediate lock to six satellites," he affirmed to Susan as he surveyed the Old City stretched out before him. "But I don't see anything in common with the other sites. Except perhaps the Golden Dome. It reminds me of that golden orb at the Vatican. Doctor Peres, are you aware of anything unusual about this location? Is there anything near here associated with obelisks, sundials, observatories, or meridians?"

"Meridians …" Peres thought for a moment, "the Rothschild's Supreme Court Building has a brass meridian on its floor like the ones found in European cathedrals. But that building is not near here. There is the Jerusalem Bird Observatory, next to the Parliament Building and Supreme Court House. It is world famous."

"No, I'm talking about an astronomical observatory," Winston clarified.

"So, you are looking for something associated with astronomy. Mr. Winston, are you familiar with the workings of the constellations?"

"Yes, my mother was an astronomer. My father was an archaeologist. One was always digging in the heavens, and the other was always digging in the ground," Winston said. "When I was a boy, I always felt suspended between two worlds."

"Excellent. Then perhaps you might appreciate the recent theories about *Aelia Capitolina*. Hadrian wanted to build a temple city at the center of his known world, similar to ancient Rome, which stood at the heart of its Mediterranean-European Empire. Hadrian's new spiritual meeting place was created to unite his Empire with the religions and social systems of the Far East. His planners followed Ptolemy's polar axis geometry in the mapping out of *Aelia Capitolina*."

"Ptolemy, the Greek mapmaker?" Winston asked.

"He was also an astronomer and mathematician. Ptolemy's system is recorded in his *Geography*, an atlas of ancient maps," Peres elaborated. "But, Hadrian's starting point for the survey of his temple-city was not his Temple of Venus, his Temple to Jupiter, nor the pillar that served as the milestone at the end of the *cardo maximus*." Peres pointed north in the direction of the Old City. "According to one theory, the starting point for *Aelia Capitolina* is close to where we are standing, on the high ground above Abu Tor along the northern ridge of the Mount of Evil Counsel. This high ground has always been a favored vantage point for viewing Jerusalem. In the first century, a Hasmonean settlement flourished on this ridge."

"A Hasmonean settlement," Susan repeated.

"Maccabees, the Greek Jews," Peres replied. "This is a special holy spot for over a billion Christians throughout the world. It is here that legend says the Jews held counsel against Jesus and offered him as a scapegoat. The headquarters of the United Nations Observer Force, originally the British High Commissioner's Residence, is just down the street." Peres pointed to a blue flag displaying a polar view of the earth waving high above a stand of pines and cypresses as he scouted his surroundings. "It was designed by the architect Austen St. Barb Harrison, who oversaw city planning during the British Mandate period. The refuted Family Tomb of Jesus, with a chevron pointing north above its entry, is a block over that way." Peres pointed to a nearby street sign: Duv Grurner. "The high ground above the Armon Ha-Natziv ridge where we are standing is the future location of a hotel and embassy complex and the Sela Observation Tower—something similar to the Space Needle in Seattle, the

Stratosphere in Las Vegas, or the Egyptian Cairo Tower built by the Soviets."

"An observation tower, Jerusalem's Eiffel Tower," Susan compared, "like the Washington Monument."

"Another tower before a dome," Winston muttered, staring at the Dome of the Rock in the distance.

"It will be the city's tallest skyscraper, offering a lofty panoramic view of Jerusalem and the surrounding *landscape*," Peres noted. "But it is the ground just below us which is most interesting. This is one of the possible locations for Golgotha other than the traditional site of the Holy Sepulcher. Some researchers claim that Golgotha is located near a cave known as Jeremiah's Grotto, north of the Old City, because in the right light it resembles a human skull. But, look at the lay of the land on your map. The topography of Abu Tor also resembles the shape of a skull."

Susan held out her map so Winston could see. "We were walking on it. There're buildings covering it."

"Yeah, it's a skull-shaped profile," Winston noted, "wearing the Old City like a crown. Its jawbone is over the U.N. Headquarters. According to the topographic relief, it's ditched out in a couple of places. Here, at its temple."

"That's the location of the Greek Convent of St. Onuphrius." Peres noted. "The Mount of Evil above this skull-shaped profile on the older maps is also known as Mount Meridionalis—the Mount of the Meridian or Mount of the Mapping. Hand me your map and let me show you a hidden *Daath* shared by a few scholars, which most people do not know."

Susan handed him the map.

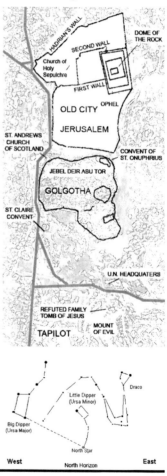

"The Mount of Evil is located here," Peres pointed on the map. "It is believed by some researchers that Hadrian's *Aelia Capitolina* was designed to mirror certain polar constellations. These polar star groups were used by surveyors to determine a prime meridian for Hadrian's new Roman Empire."

"I've heard this before," Winston said to Susan.

"Washington, Paris, Rome, now Jerusalem," she replied. "Commonalities."

Peres handed the map back to Susan. He kicked a clump of grass at his feet and cleared away a patch of sand. He removed his pen from his pocket, knelt down, placed his water bottle aside, and began scratching images onto the ground. "If you know your astronomy, then you know that there are two primary constellations that allow us to determine polar north. One of these is Ursa Minor, the Little Bear." He inscribed a dipper shape onto the ground. "Ursa Minor, as an astronomical symbol, dates as far back as the Eurasian ice age." He pointed to the image. "The stars that form the bear are dipper shaped. It is around this star group, at the end of its handle, that all the stars in the night sky appear to rotate through a near 26,000 year cycle, known as the great Platonic Year."

"A dipper," Susan said, "that stone in the catacombs."

Winston nodded in agreement.

"The other constellation is Draco, the Old Serpent—the Great Winged Fire-Breather." Peres scrawled an image of the dragon constellation onto the ground. "This constellation is circumpolar. It is a gigantic monster of stars that guards the Little Dipper. The curved alignment of its stars is one of its unique characteristics in the night sky. The stars that form the curve are fairly fine, but the stars of the head of Draco are clear in the night sky and form a bent square shape."

Peres struck a line below the drawings to represent the horizon. "In the Northern Hemisphere, these principal star groups will appear just above the northern horizon. Note how the water dragon appears to cradle the bear—the dipper shape." He pointed to the drawings. "The dragon, a Leviathan of ten stars, is curled around the seven stars. Now, hand me the map. Let's look at the topography surrounding the Old City." Crouching, Peres laid the map next to the images scratched in the dirt. " 'And The Lord said unto Moses: I never sleep: but take a cup and fill it with water.' The alignment of the Temple Mount is not arbitrary. It's all about the life-giving water. The temple platform outlines the shape of a dipper. It's aligned due north—one of several *visual cues* for understanding the design of the Old City." He *clicked* the little blue globe at the end of his pen and marked on the map the four corners of the Old City. "These corners appear to align to the six primary stars of the Little Dipper. The ancient Dragon Fountain from the Pool of Gihon flows into the dipper-shaped Temple Mount by way of the Hezekial conduit. Two of the oldest pools in Jerusalem, the Serpent's Pool and the Sheep's Pool, also connect to ancient conduits that lead to the Mount. The star of the bear's head falls on a mosque north of the Old City. The primary stars that form the handle are noted by either topographic or architectural features running southwest along a geographic ridge that extends toward a hill south of Mount Gihon."

Susan looked at the map. "Where's that?"

"It locates Polaris." Peres lifted his pith helmet. The scar above his brow channeled a bead of sweat into his eye. He swiped his forehead with the back of his hand as he looked up at Susan. "There are different interpretations of this configuration. The end star in the handle is near the Talpiot Industrial Park, just west of here. The axial ecliptic, the pivot point of the heavens next to the pole star, is located at the intersection of Koenig, Hamoda'i, and Refa'im Streets. It's the site of an old graveyard for the German Unitarian Community of the Temple. Other researchers claim the tail is formed by the hills running southwest toward the town of Bezek, whose name means the Chaining of the Lightning of the Lord." Peres tightened his helmet back to his head and pointed with his pen. "Now, look at the low mountain peaks outside the Old City, to the north, the east, and to the west, and the monuments and important buildings that have been erected on each hill." He marked little Xs on the map. "If we connect these landmarks, we find that the pattern forms the constellation Draco—the Great Dragon—the Hebrew *Tannin*."

Winston's eyes blinked. "This is the pattern I couldn't make out on that stone in Paris," he said to Susan.

Peres drew lines between the Xs, as though connecting the dots of a children's picture puzzle in the Sunday newspaper. As he did, he recited a passage from the Bible, " 'Cast to the earth to be in the garden.' It is the same pattern seen in the night sky on the northern horizon." He looked up at Winston. "There are four ancient roads that lead to Jerusalem, like the four rivers leading into the Garden of Eden. Those roads align to the position of the four brightest stars in the night sky." Peres *clicked* his pen and inscribed a circle on the ground. He marked along its edge. "Thuban to the north, Polaris in the southwest, Vega in the northeast, and Deneb in the southeast—the four stars that touch the edge of the celestial pole of the ecliptic. This pattern formed by the topography represents the celestial circle brought down to Earth ... the great circle that is the symbol of the Ouroboros—the unending movement of the World's Soul, the Great Wheel of Life. It reminds me of the Japanese *Genbu,* the serpent-turtle who governs the North. The hub of this ouroboros at Jerusalem is centered south of the old town of Bahurim, now Bethany, near the Chapel of the Ascension of Jesus. Across from that chapel is the Church of the Paternoster, one of the original structures built by Constantine to denote the place of the Ascension. According to legend, it is the site where Christ taught his apostles the Lord's Prayer, 'On earth as it is in heaven.' Just south of this church is the location of the old Stone of Zoheleth—known as the Crawling Rock—the Serpent's Rock—and the rudder pillar of the Temple of Solomon—the Third Pillar, which denotes the position of NGC 6543," he staked his pen into the ground, "at the heart of Palestine."

"NGC 6543, that's the Cat's Eye Nebula," Winston noted. *The hub for the World's Soul* ... He eyed the blue globe at the end of the pen encircled by the polar constellations. *A language for the soul ... a city with a soul, like Rome ... Billy at the Sacred Hoop ... a cat's eye view.* He knelt down and pulled the pen from the ground, like he was releasing Excalibur from the stone.

Peres stood up and pointed toward the north. "Yes, the Cat's Eye of Bast, who holds down the primordial water deity Mut. It's aligned to *Alkaid,* the star in the tail of Ursa Major, the old Roman *Septentriones,* the Seven Plough Oxen who pulls a cosmic plow through the *Carro* sky reminding us to *always* dig deeper. Most people look into the north sky at night and see the Little Dipper, but I see the Lost Temple of Solomon. The dipper is the sacred cup, the Drinking Gourd, the Silver Spoon, the grail—the Holy Grail—surrounded by the celestial circle of the twelve major constellations—like Christ at the Last Supper. This order of the cosmos is the order for Jerusalem—the Order of Sion—the Celestial Encampment. 'God dwells in Sion.' "

A cosmic plow that feeds the world ... the plowman—Jefferson, Winston thought as he passed the pen to Peres.

"The Holy Grail?" Susan shook her head. "I've been reading the wrong books. I thought the Holy Grail was a Lost Goddess. But that cop in Paris said it was the head of Saint Denis."

"And some legends say it's a mysterious head severed by the nine witches of

Gloucester," Peres remarked, staring toward the Mount of Olives. "Mythologies can represent more than one thing. In the small, tear-shaped Franciscan church known as Dominus Flevit, on the western slope of the Mount of Olives, there is an arch-shaped window which commemorates Jesus weeping like a fresh rain over the city. The view from that window looks west toward the Dome of the Rock and the setting sun. The lattice work in the window, like a polar grid, radiates from the icon of an orb falling into a cup." He paused. "The lost Holy Grail is not lost. It's *hidden in plain sight* in every night sky, guiding us since the dawn of timekeeping. It is altogether possible that the topography surrounding the Temple Mount is a natural geographic formation adapted to the plan for the city. The creation of holy cities around alignments to the heavens was a common practice by the ancients. It's well known that the alignment of Jerusalem to Masada and to Petra forms the belt of Orion, a constellation associated with the local resurrection god, Tammuz."

The three stars—the shepherd kings, Winston remembered, *my mother.* "A grail cup encircled by a snake." He slightly nodded. "This drawing on the ground is a type of planisphere."

"What's a planisphere?" Susan asked.

"It's a rotating star finder wheel, a type of analog computer for calculating the positions of the stars," Winston answered. "The name refers to the constellations found on a celestial sphere drawn on a flat plane, like these constellations the Doctor drew on the ground."

"Yes," Peres agreed, "like Chicken Little, if you look closely at the ground you will discover that the sky has fallen. A planisphere—a chart of the heavens, without doubt the first of all bibles. It's a pictorial edition. On modern planispheres, *Ursa Minor*, the Little Bear, is found near the axis of the ecliptic. But, there is no bear on the star charts of the Chaldeans, Persians, Egyptians, or the Indians, where these stars were associated with different figures. For example, the Egyptians depicted the Dipper as a bull's thigh, a symbol found in their portrayals of the ceremony of the 'Opening of the Mouth,' performed on the mummy of a dead pharaoh. Some early Christian traditions called *Ursa Minor* the Little Sheepfold—the *Agnus Dei*."

THIRD CENTURY DEPICTION OF JESUS AS THE GOOD SHEPHERD HOLDING THE LAMB AND THE WATER DIPPER FROM THE CEILING OF THE HOLY SEE'S SAN CALLISTO CATACOMB IN ROME

"The Lamb of God," Susan translated.

" 'And Mary had a Little Lamb whose fleece was white as snow. And everywhere that Mary went, the Lamb was sure to go,' " Peres recited. "For the first five centuries of Christianity, the lamb was the symbol of the Christian creed. Early Christian Apocalyptic T-O maps for Jerusalem depict a cosmology. The O symbolizes an unending universe, with the T denoting the crossroads of the three continents with the Paschal lamb at its center. 'The Lamb who is in the midst of the throne will shepherd them and lead them to living *fountains* of waters." Like Perseus severing the head of Medusa which spilled forth the giant Chrysaor, the shepherd David cut off the head of Goliath, chased a lion, and saved a lamb from its mouth. This is David's city, *Ro'eh Yisra'el*, the Shepherd of Israel who protects the lamb. In Revelation, the lamb is the kernel of truth around which all else is clustered, the *cornerstone* on which everything lasting is built. The constellation is said to clock the return of the coming Redeemer."

"A cornerstone guarded by a winged demon," Winston noted. He retrieved the folded map of Rome from his pants pocket and glanced at it. "The Lamb...."

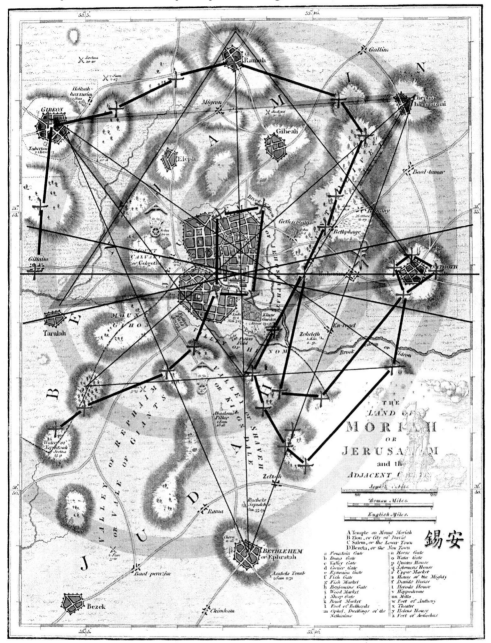

"Yes, a *winged* demon," Peres agreed. "Some believe this design we see here was engineered out of the landscape in the distant past. The hills around the Old City are formed by manmade stepped terraces, like a Chinese agricultural system. The whole Kidron Valley conforms perfectly to the underbelly of Ursa Minor depicted on the Greek star charts. The Hinnom Valley borders the flank of the Bear, or Lamb. It must have been a massive earth-moving project." Peres marked on the map again as he continued his chalk talk. "The location of the Church of the Nativity in Bethlehem, almost due south of here, was probably the pivotal surveying point for the creation of the whole thing. Starting at Bethlehem, near the ancient Threshing Floor of Boaz, you can easily survey a huge, inverted pentagram in the landscape, bounded by the various landmarks and old towns bordering Jerusalem, such as Taralah, Gibeon, Ramah, Chephar-he-Ammona, and Anathoth near Izzarriya on the West Bank—a suburb around the lozenge-shaped artificial hill at the head of the dragon, near the old Martyrius Monastery at the settlement of Ma'ale Adummin. It's been earmarked for a future building project." Peres pointed. "If you interconnect these towns to a hill south of here, they form the Star of David encompassing Jerusalem. Everything has been geometrically aligned, suggesting a predetermined plan or a survey."

"A pentagram invoking the dragon." Winston folded the map back to his pocket.

"And a Star of David …" Susan gazed at the collage of symbols on the map.

"These patterns are here so we do not forget the *Source*," Peres emphasized.

"Yes, who created it?" Susan pondered, *Man or Nature, who is the First Cause?*

"The Canaanites, the Hurrians, the Asiatic Hyksos, or the Egyptians, if the Bible is correct," Peres replied. "The lengendary King David, the shepherd king, seized the temple city of the Jebusites, a Canaanite tribe who may have built upon the site of an earlier temple to an unknown Pharaoh. Based on the Egyptian execration texts, the Egyptians occupied this site around the twentieth century B.C. Then again, it could be Greek in origin. It could be a plan that Hadrian and Constantine adopted from the Greeks, which was passed on to the Crusaders and later to the Muslims. Ursa Minor is first mentioned in the *Phaenomea,* meaning 'the Appearances.' It is an old poem by Aratus, a Greek poet. St. Paul quotes part of the *Phaenomea* in Acts when he condemns the idol worship of the Greeks. That poem is derived from an earlier lost work with the same name, by the Greek astronomer and pupil of Plato, Eudoxus of Cnidus. Eudoxus was the first to offer a mathematical explanation for the movement of the planetary spheres. It is said that the Greek sage, Thales of Miletus, who established the Ionian school of astronomy, adopted the configuration of Ursa from Phoenician navigators, who may have adopted that constellation from the Canaanites. Before Thales, that pattern of stars was seen as one of the *wings* of Draco."

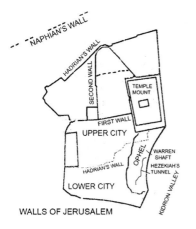

WALLS OF JERUSALEM

"The hills around Jeruselem," Susan remarked, "the temple city was the wing."

"The Greek star charts derived from Ptolemy's *Almegest*, the same alignments we use today to chart the heavens, depict the constellations as observed between the thirty-five and thirty-six degree latitudes," Peres added. "That excludes all locations north and south of those latitudes, such as Egypt and Greece, as being the origin for the Greek star charts. Some scholars claim the scheme originated with the Babylonian text, 'The Prayers to the Gods of Night;' and that the Greek constellations were charted from Babylon along the thirty-sixth parallel. But more precisely, ancient

Jerusalem also falls within the bounds. The Jebusite names for Jerusalem were Jebus and *Urushalim*, a Canaanite word meaning the City of Light founded by the god Shalim. Tablets discovered in Elba, Syria, dating back to 3000 B.C., mention the god Shalim being venerated in *Uruksalem*. Shalim along with its twin, the god Shachar, were worshipped by the Phoenicians and Canaanites as gods of the dusk and the dawn, which suggests their temples were oriented to the sun. This whole site surrounding the Temple Mount could have been an ancient solar observatory created by Canaanite priest-astronomers and the point of origin for the mapping of the Greek polar constellations—primarily Draco, since the Dipper had not been created."

Winston glanced at the map. "Incredible … Draco and the temple … contained within the Apartheid Wall."

"Jerusalem has always been a city of walls. Although the exact locations of the biblical walls of the Old City are in doubt, the city's walls offer us an additional *clue* to the creation of the dragon constellation in the landscape," Peres continued. "According to the Bible, the walls of Jerusalem were reconstructed sometime between 515 B.C. and 70 A.D. Many scholars believe these walls date back to 445 B.C. when Nehemiah returned from Babylon and built the lower part of the city. The Second Wall may have been built by King Agrippa around 44 A.D. But *none* of these walls stand today. In 135, Emperor Hadrian totally destroyed Jerusalem and built new walls which outline the stars of Ursa Minor, the *wings* of the dragon. This is the shape the Old City retains today. The constellation's relationship to the oddly angled shape of the walls suggests Hadrian's town planners were aware of the dragon in the surrounding topography. Or, it is possible that Hadrian's planners were the creators of this design in the landscape."

"So the constellations we use today may have originated in Jerusalem," Winston clarified.

"Possibly. But, I think the symbolic understanding of the heavens can be traced to the Far East." Peres motioned to the drawing on the ground. "The Little Dipper is one of the oldest constellations in the world. Even today, it is the *key* constellation, the first that people are taught to recognize. It is known by nearly every culture as the hands of the nighttime sky clock. In ancient Sumer, the Dipper stars were called *Ma-God-Da*, the Flying Wagon. In India, the Dipper was known as the *Saptar Shayar,* the Seven Anchors, which hold down the pole of the sky. It has also been called the Seven *Rishis*, the Seven Poets, and the Seven Builders. This association with the seven builders can be found in Egyptian star lore, where the Dipper was associated with the primordial mound that rose up from a great cosmic sea. They believed this was the first land on which life appeared, the garden of paradise—an oasis in the desert. In Egypt, the stars of the Dipper were called the Seven Sages who assisted Thoth, the great builder and magician, in the construction of the pyramids, which the Egyptians referred to as the stone mansions of the gods. Sometimes the Egyptians called the Dipper the Cart of Osiris. It was often depicted as a hippopotamus, the goddess of birth and creation. The star, *Dubhe*, in the Dipper, was often associated with the goddess Isis. There are many temples throughout Egypt which are aligned to Dubhe." Peres pointed toward the Dome of the Rock. "It is possible that Egyptian cosmology was applied to the Temple Mount and the city plan of Jerusalem."

"My mother believed that the charting of the heavens started with the megalithic sites in the British Isles," Winston remarked.

"The oldest megaliths with an astronomical alignment are at Nabta Playa, in Egypt's Nubian Desert," Peres countered. "But, I believe our current charting comes from the Far East." He stared at the symbols on the back of the map. "Some believe the first reverence to the Dipper began in the Alps of Switzerland, where ancient cave chapels contain images of cave bear skulls. It is my theory that much of the Dipper lore originated in Japan or with the shamans of the Amur River Valley in China—the Black Dragon River—where the Dipper is a principal shamanistic icon. In China, the Dipper was called the *Beidou*. The ancient Taoists believed that the *ideal city* should be aligned to the *Beidou*."

"Yeah, I've studied the Tao," Winston said. "Embrace the Yang, turn your back on the Yin. Billy got me into it, teaching me some Taekwondo."

"Like the Gnostics, their practices involved evoking the primordial forces in nature in order to be reunited with it in body, soul, and spirit. The Taoist shape of the ideal city was a square," Peres revealed, "symbolic of a cosmological flat Earth beneath the dome of heaven. In Chinese divination, north is viewed as a bad direction. The northwest is considered the worst and darkest direction in the night sky. In Japan, Ursa Major is called *Ooguma* and Ursa Minor is called *Koguma*. The star sometimes called *Ne no Boshi*, the mouse star, or *Shin Boshi*, the Heart Star, denotes the direction of the Soul of the Heavens—the location of our Polaris."

"Polaris, the mariner's star," Winston recalled. "It's a triple star group—three stars rotating around each other, pulsating like a blinking lighthouse." *Alexandria,* he thought, *the compass rose on the* Fry-Jefferson Map.

Peres pointed north toward the Old City. "The faint stars of Draco rise above the northern horizon of Jerusalem. *Alpha Draconis*, known as Thuban, is the third star from the bend in the tail of Draco. It was once the Pole Star—nearly 5000 years ago." He paused, then recited, " 'Sun, be dark over Gideon!' ... 'Reeling over Taralah' ... 'I went out by night by the gate of the valley, even before the dragon well, and to the dung port, and viewed the walls of Jerusalem, which were broken down, and the gates thereof were consumed with fire.' Draco is referred to in passages from the book of Nehemiah. The Apocrypha books of Bel and the Dragon and Maccabees, and the vision from the book of Ezekiel are all associated with the dragon lore of Jerusalem." Peres lightly kicked at his drawing on the ground. " 'Am I the Sea, or the Dragon, that you set a guard over me?' The star in the bend of the crooked tail of this Draco in the landscape is near the site of the HaKirya Government Center which includes the Supreme Court Building and the Knesset."

Winston glanced at the constellations at his feet, then looked out over Jerusalem. His eyes traveled from the Temple Mount west toward the site of the Knesset. "Dragon hills ... a shepherd's crook beside a sheepfold."

Peres pressed the cool bottle to his face as he returned the map to Winston. "The hill known as Mount Septentrionalis is due north of here. It is sometimes called the Serpent Mount, the Mount of the Seven Stars, or the Northern Mount—near Ramah, the high place, the seat of a cosmic mound. It is the hill that represents the third star of the tail of Draco in the landscape of Jerusalem. If you draw a line of longitude from the Mount of Evil to Mount Septentrionalis, you will create a line that passes through the Roman *cardo*, the current demarcation line of Jerusalem. It points toward the

Tomb of the Kings and Bethel, the Heavenly House of God. They buried their kings according to the positions of the stars within the hub of the heavenly Wheel of Life."

"That longitude would pass through the middle of the southern Golgotha," Susan connected, studying the map. "It's aligned to a death skull."

"It's a principal axiom of the Mystery Religions that is older than these hills that surround Jerusalem," Peres remarked. "Death rides upon the Wheel of Life. We are all on our way to dying."

"This is amazing, a city designed after the constellations." Winston turned the map upside down and systematically rotated it, reading it from all directions. *Ezekiel. A wheel within a wheel. I'm not sure it's aligned due north.*

"The hills around Jerusalem have been called the Seven Hills in various holy books," Peres said. "The *Pirke de-Rabbi Eliezer*, an eighth-century *midrashic* narrative, describes Jerusalem as being situated on seven hills. They are often identified as the three summits of the Mount of Olives: known as Scopus Hill, Nob Hill, and Olivet Hill, or the Mount of Offence. The fourth hill is between the Kedron and the Tyropoeon Valleys, known as the original Mount Zion. The fifth hill is Ophel Mount, and the sixth hill is north of that. It is the 'Rock' around which Fort Antonia was built. The seventh hill is southwest of the city, the new Mount Zion."

Susan flipped through her notes. "Torre said the same thing about Rome."

"It is possible that this design for Jerusalem is Hadrian's adaptation of the Seven Hills of Rome—a representation of the *Septentriones*," Peres agreed. "The Seven Hills of Rome have often been called the Dragon Hills in reference to the pole stars. The peaks of the hills surrounding the Old City of Jerusalem spiral out from the Temple Mount toward Bethlehem like an uncoiled spring." He swirled his pen over the map in Winston's hand. "From here, to here, to here, it forms the rhythmic pattern of an ancient sun spiral—a solar labyrinth pouring out of a dipper, like the Water of Life from a continually turning manna machine."

"The Water of Life from the Lamb … like the Holy Pinecone fountain at the Vatican," Susan compared.

"My parents had photos of these labyrinth patterns carved into the rocks around Newgrange," Winston remembered aloud.

"These spiraled patterns are associated with the polar axial movement of the Earth," Peres explained. "The peaks east of the Temple Mount serve as reference points for observing the equinox and solstice sunrises which strike across the Mount of Olives." He drew solstice alignments through the Temple Mount.

"This alignment resembles the crisscross streets of Rome and Paris," Susan noted, "like crossbones." *Skull and bones …*

"And Washington," Winston added.

"The *Campitelli* district of Rome, a name derived from the words *campus telluris* meaning *earth field*, is possibly a corruption of *Capitolium*." Peres handed his pen to Winston. "The *Capitolium* is also the most important of Rome's seven hills. It dominated the site of the Roman Forum—now the site of the Vittoriano, the monument to Victor Emanuel II and the church of St. Maria in Aracoeli, known as the Altar to the Heavens. According to legend, the Temple of Castor and Pollux in the Roman Forum at the base of the *Capitolium* was haunted by a devil in the form of a dragon. The *Campitelli* district is in the shape of the head of the constellation Draco. To this day, a dragon's head is still used on the district's seal."

"A Roman district in the shape of a dragon's head?" Winston questioned.

"Mr. Howard said that's where Jefferson got the name for the Capital," Susan remarked. *An Earth field ...*

"Roman cosmology is something Hadrian would have applied to his scheme for a temple city dedicated to the early Roman and Greek mystery religions. Again, the *chief cornerstone* for observing this wagon dance of the stars is where we are standing. The dragon is the biblical symbol for Satan, the prince of this world, and the sea monster—the Leviathan, the ruler of the lower sea of the human consciousness. Thus the naming of this place where we stand—the Mount of Evil." Peres stomped on the ground with one foot. " 'Praise the Lord from the earth, ye Dragons and ye Deeps.' This is where you can stand to bear witness to the dragon, *Tannin,* rising above Jerusalem, the cosmic city created from the cosmic mounds."

"And all of this has to do with understanding longitude?" Susan queried.

"Yes, the constellation Draco can be interpreted as a cart, or a sleigh, being pulled through the heavens by eight tiny stars. It's Santa's sleigh at the north pole. Santa, the red-suited Yule man promoted by the American media, of course, is an anagram for Satan—although Satan in our demon-haunted world is usually modeled after the horned goat-boy, Pan," Peres noted, "or Joulupukki, the old Flemish Yule goat. All longitudes point north to Santa's polar home, the location of the Universal Monarch who brings gifts of renewal to the world. Reverence to the polar stars is found within many sun-worshiping religions. There was *Helios,* who was seen as the axis of the celestial revolutions. There was the Assyrian *Shamash,* who was sometimes seen as the polar deity. And there was the Egyptian *Atum-Re,* who reigned atop a world pole."

"All of this seems so far-fetched, Doctor Peres," Susan said skeptically. "I was taught to believe in a real Jesus and a historical Bible. You must be joking. Jerusalem is in the image of a dragon ... and Santa is Satan."

"And the Muslim Temple Mount is the Holy Grail," Winston added. "Christian heresy—Jerusalem is built from a leaf from the Devil's book ... under the wings of Draco." Winston unthawed a smile. "It's the ultimate taboo."

"No, **Ms.** Hamilton. It is not that unusual. For example, we are introduced to the four Gospels by way of the star-searching Magi—"

"The three wise men," Winston commented. "The Belt of Orion."

"Yes, Orion. The three magi are the *key* to understanding a hidden meaning within the Gospels," Peres continued to demythologize. "Astronomical knowledge was once held solely by the priest-astronomers. They were the ancient brain trusts of their day. Their knowledge degenerated into the various myths and the pseudo-sciences of religion and the occult. For example, both David and Solomon reigned for forty years. Forty is a magic number in Hebrew mythology, and found throughout the mythologies of the ancient Middle East, as well as the rest of the world. Why, you might ask?"

"Yes, why forty?" Susan's eyes widened.

"Forty is an astronomical number associated with *birth and rebirth*—forty weeks, *nine* months, the Indian monsoon season." Peres answered. "It's a cyclical number. The birth cycles of humanity are linked to the birth cycles in nature."

Susan placed her hand over her belly.

"The repetitive use of this number throughout the Old and New Testaments acts as a clue for the reader, so he might understand that he is reading myths associated with star lore, and not true history," Peres explained. "The Bible's mathematics prove that it's not historical."

"Numbers as code words," Winston said. "The Bible's encrypted—"

"Man is a storytelling animal," Peres pointed out. "He often gets his stories from his subconscious, the Cartesian theater, where there is a Greater Inner Voice from a homunculus constantly speaking to him, trying to be heard—and trying to reveal the mysteries of the cosmic world that move around us. Mythologies and symbol-laden narratives are a way for the God Consciousness within every person to be shared with the rest of humanity. That's why we value the storytellers who can tap into the God Consciousness. They are the translators of an iconography associated with the Divine *presence* found in nature *and* within each man."

"A star language representing God's consciousness." Winston shook his head. "Maybe that's why my mother treated astronomy almost like a religion."

"The American scholar on religious mythology, Joseph Campbell, believed that certain symbols associated with the star myths served as the world's primary social archetypes," Peres elaborated, "the signposts of life. Our modern mythical motifs found in books and movies, which help to define every culture, are based upon ancient star lore. As below, as above. Every society has structured itself around the higher organization found in nature. Understanding the movement of the heavens may have been man's first step in becoming civilized. The constellations may be the *first universal language*. The stars are a part of nature, but the constellations are manmade. They are human footprints—a network of apparently meaningless steganographic patterns in the night sky mapped out by the Consciousness of Man. At some point in the past, one single soul, or a group of like-minds, used the blank canvas of the sky to present a living motion picture that told the story of their gods and their way of life. This was a *major paradigm shift* for humanity. Man had conceived his own gods and positioned them in the heavens. The constellations, as a reflection of Man's dark place of mystery and wonder, represent the language for the first Global Consciousness. To understand the story in the sky is to understand the structure of our minds. It's a strange paradox. Man is created from star dust, but the constellations are a creation of man. It is as if humanity is naturally reaching out to its Origin."

"Consciousness encompassing the world—the mind's design space—an Outernet," Winston joked, "the first Sky-link."

"Michelangelo's brain scan," Susan reflected. "Man was the First Cause."

"Man is the center of his universe," Peres said. "Every society since that paradigm shift has created its own unique cosmological mythologies built upon this constellation-language from the human mind. Our modern world is the byproduct of the star myths of the First Watchers. Everything is written with the stars. This is an old area of study known as Pan-Babylonism. At the start of the twentieth century, many artisans and architects were heavily involved in the Pan-Babylonian movement."

"This reminds me of something my mother used to say, 'Everything is written in the stars,' " Winston said. "She often quoted from a book, *Language Is A Virus That Came From Outer Space*, some ancient ideas replicating themselves into other forms."

"What?" Susan questioned. "A virus that came from outer space?"

"Perhaps this virus we are trying to disable is associated with an ancient star language," Winston pondered.

Peres smiled. "The Greeks have a phrase for their origin mythologies—*Istories me arkoudes*—meaning, the stories with bears. Star lore is at the core of every culture, Mr. Winston. How many movies are produced each year around the themes derived from Bram Stoker's *Dracula?* How many dragons are found in our children's storybooks? How many times have we retold the story of Peter Pan? Our art mirrors the society that creates it. In pre-Christian Europe, dragons were revered as symbols of wisdom. In Japan, dragons serve as protectors of the Japanese zodiac and the waters of the heavenly cosmos. In China, a dragon, or *Lóng*, represents the concept of the yang and the balance within nature. *Lóngs* are sometimes called the song birds of sadness and despair. When paired with the cosmic bird *Fenghuang*, the symbol of the Empress who holds a snake in her talons, the dragon becomes a symbol of the power of the Emperor. The name *Kowloon* means nine dragons. There are nine types of dragons in ancient Chinese cosmology, each with their own special purpose. Many Chinese around the world proudly proclaim themselves as *Lung Tik Chuan Ren*, the descendants of the dragon. The *Lóng* is a *respected* image. Legends associated with the *Lóng* have shaped Chinese civilization and culture," Peres emphasized. "In Chinese lore, a boy-emperor of the Song Dynasty fled the northern Mongols to find safety in the hills surrounding Hong Kong, once known as Kowloon. He counted eight hills that concealed eight dragons at Kowloon. A ninth dragon was hidden within the emperor himself … hidden in his *soul* … hidden in his *social* soul."

A social soul, Winston pondered.

"In Egyptian star lore, *Amen-Ra* battles the serpent-fiend, *Nak,* for the life force, the *ka*—the *creative force*—such as the *Shekinah*," Peres said. "Life and death."

Ka and Nak? Where have I heard that before? Winston tried to remember.

"In Greek mythology, Triptolemus received seeds of life and a chariot of winged dragons from Demeter," Peres added. "And there is the dragon Ladon, who guarded the golden apples in the Garden of Hesperides. In that myth, Hercules stole the apples by outwitting the dragon. Those apples were often referred to as the three stars of the Little Dipper's handle. In Jerusalem, the dragon in the landscape guards the Golden Dome—the golden pearl—the Dipper. Jerusalem, like Hong Kong and the eternal city of Rome, is a dragon city. Perhaps all the great *eternal cities* are *dragon cities*."

"Or a dragon guarding a white pearl," Susan thought out loud, sighting in the direction of the Holy Sepulcher.

Peres pointed back to the ground. "Many of the ancient kings and queens associated themselves with the polar star groups as personifications of the star gods—the all-powerful constellations around which their courts and empires rotated. With the aid of their priest-astronomers, they ruled their empires under a social order that was in sync with the heavenly kingdom. At the foot of the Pole Stars is Cepheus the king constellation, and Cassiopeia, his queen, who rules over the kingdom of the Hyperboreans. According to Greek myth, Cassiopeia offended the sea god Nereus. So Nereus sent a monster to destroy Cepheus and his kingdom. Cepheus was told that he must sacrifice his daughter, Andromeda, in order to save his kingdom. The hero Perseus fought the monster, and saved Andromeda and the kingdom. The star configuration for the savior Perseus is similar to the constellation Orion."

"My mother talked about that constellation all the time," Winston said.

"Orion is one of the most easily recognizable constellations in the sky. It is integrated within many different mythologies. The Arabs saw Orion as a shepherd with his dog and a flock of sheep. Phoenicians associated Orion with Melqart." Peres stretched his arms and legs in an arched pose. "The Sumerians called Orion, *Uru-anna*, identified with the hero Gilgamesh, who was seen as battling the Bull of Heaven, *Gut-anna*, the constellation Taurus. In the older Greek zodiac, Orion is seen as Herakles bearing the golden lion's head as he battles the bull through his twelve labors."

"Twelve labors?" Susan asked.

"It's a rite of passage myth, associated with the movement of the night sky zodiac, in order to synchronize one's life with nature."

Rite of passage ... 'Never loose the bands of Orion' ... finding the pole star ... the Temple Mount and Talpiot. Winston eyed the globed end of the pen in his hand.

"The city plan of Jerusalem, as a temple of the heavens, may have served as a *memory aid* for locating the stars around which the world appears to move," Peres noted. "It is a *true* theology, a *knowledge of the order* of God's creation. Jerusalem, the earthly sanctuary which symbolizes *the presence* of God here on Earth, is in the image of the polar constellations, the fixed stars—the *unmovable movers* of the millwork of the heavens. It is an edifice to the great Platonic Year and Plato's great architect—the *Primum Movens*—the Invisible Force that the ancients believed the heavens and their whole world rotated around."

"The Prime Mover," Susan translated. "So Jerusalem is in the image of a dragon, a bear, and a skull," she tried to sum up the archetypes laid out before her.

"Precisely ... but it is more than that. It is a sacred knowledge," Peres spoke softly. "It is the star map that the birds follow in their migrations. It is at the heart of Nature. It is a map that unites humanity with the heavens. Such as the marriage of the two professions of your parents, Mr. Winston, this image on the ground is a divine system of relations, a union between the Earth and the sky. It is a union between man and his maker—Time—the Dark Endless One. The abstract Time deity is known by many names: Chronos, Kali, Sesha, Thoth, Manat, Aion, Zervan ... the God of Ages. In Tibet, one of the central deities is Kalachakra, the Time-Wheel." Peres held up his hand and looped his fingers together. "Symbolized by a circular mandala—beginningless and endless—Kalachakra represents the ultimate omniscience. The Romans worshiped the Time deity as Chronos. In the Mithraic cults, Chronos was symbolized as a lion standing on a globe and entangled by a snake, denoting the endless movement of the earth orbiting the sun—the boundless passage of Dark Time."

"Sounds like the *Laocoön* at the Vatican," Susan said to Winston.

"Yeah, Serpentarius, a Trojan Horse," he muttered, "a booby trap."

"Everything in life is under the influence of Time," Peres continued. "All of our clocks and maps, and essentially, the actions of all humanity, are synchronized with the polar star groups. And as long as these stars are seen in the northern sky, we know the Earth and all life on the planet is in proper balance. There are many religions in Jerusalem. But this drawing on the ground represents the guiding principle that the city follows. From Galileo to Huygens, understanding time is something that civilizes humanity. This clockwork of stars has led to the creation of every mechanical invention and every electronic device. Every motor is a type of clock. Every electronic device operates from a clock cycle. They are all modeled after the heavenly clockwork that rules over every aspect of our lives. All of us are chained to a pocket watch or tied to a wristwatch. We live our whole lives around a social clock. No matter what religion you profess to have, these polar angels represent the principles of the *oldest* religion—the one that truly guides us."

Winston glanced at his GPS watch, then rubbed his forearm. *Some more than others*, he thought.

Peres surveyed the panorama of a walled Jerusalem sprawling over the landscape. "The world stops here, Mr. Winston. We are looking out over this city through a distant looking glass at a labyrinth not thoroughly known. For two thousand years, kings, emperors, and caliphs from different cultures with religions guided by misdirected dogmas have come here to conquer or settle this city and have mindlessly covered over these images of the gods of their fathers. 'How sharper than a serpent's tooth it is, to have a thankless child.' How *blind* they all are."

"Excuse me, Doctor," Susan said, stepping away to speak to Winston in private.

"Certainly." Peres nodded. "I have to leave soon. I'm scheduled to do research in the south of France—a little town called Rennes-le-Chateau."

"James, what he's telling us is more than interesting." She tugged on Winston's arm. Her eyes were locked on the drawing of the star in the dust at her feet.

"Yeah, I didn't expect to get this diagnosis from the doctor," he chuckled. "He's like a Boy Scout following the North Star. He's as sharp as Paracelsus. The city plan for Jerusalem contains a *steganographic* image. It's coded!" Winston eyes blinked as he stared at the map. "But, I'm not so sure it's been forgotten. Lay of the land ... The streets branching west from the Old City form a pattern ... wing-shaped." He hastily sketched on the map. " 'Never loose the bands of Orion' ... Mother Mary ... There's more to this—"

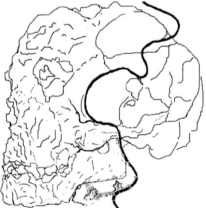

"Yeah, that's interesting. But James, do you realize we might have another commonality?" Susan urged in a lowered voice.

"And what is that?" Winston folded the map, tucked it in the side pocket of his trekking pants, and passed the pen to Susan.

"Remember, the catacombs. Get focused, James—you know. Use your skull!" She tapped the side of her forehead with the globe at the end of the pen.

Winston nodded. "Yeah, steganographic ..."

He thought about the catacombs in Paris and the skull and crossbones-like seal of the Vatican. "Of course, the *key* and *skull* ... heads and skulls. Jesus—Calvary, it's the head of the world—the Christian center of the world." He reached into his pants pocket, retrieved the map of Rome, and eyed the doodle he had made from the outline of the streets and the topography that dominated the northern landscape of the city. Recognizing the pattern, he nodded again. "I'm a bonehead. I should have seen this before. Time ... the Great Leveler ... Looks like Rome has a skeleton in its closet. We do have another commonality." He handed Susan the map. "Look at this!"

Susan stared at the drawing. Her eyes widened. "Baphomet!" she exclaimed. "Human consciousness ... It's huge."

Above the leveling tools of the Tekton rested the jawbone of the eternal image, appearing as a totenkopf impaled upon the crooked staff of the Tiber River flowing from it like a spinal column feeding the nervous system of the Eternal City.

Buzz— Susan's satellite phone rang.

"I wonder who that could be?" Winston asked knowingly. "Hand me your Jawbone."

Winston placed Susan's Jawbone in his ear. "I feel like a Bluetooth fairy. ... Yes? Hello, Marx." His features became animated as he listened. "Slow down. Don't get festered. ... We're doing well. Thank you. I think we have another keyword. Try *skull* or *head*. ... Right. Good. ... No, that's not good. We'll meet them at the airport." He handed the Jawbone back to Susan. Hearing an odd *chirping* after-sound, he slightly twisted his finger in his ear. "I recognized his voice, but Marx sounds like a woman through this thing. Translation, please."

"It's a woman's Jawbone," she clarified. "The signal is vocoder encrypted by the NSA. It sounds a little different after it's translated over the Jawbone."

Winston suddenly felt a pasty dryness in his mouth. His hand trembled. *I need a buzz.* He opened his bottle of diet cola. The bottle overflowed with a carbonated *fizz* that dripped onto the drawing of the devil in the dust.

"So what did he say?" Susan watched part of the drawing on the ground dissolve away as though Winston had extinguished a fire.

"The virus has spread into the banking systems. ATM and credit card transactions are being interrupted all over the United States. Bains is worried that the virus could be associated with a theft. It's always about the money. A fistful of dollars, they always get worried when it comes to the digital money. Not everything in the world is coin operated, and money's not meant to be served. It's just *zeros* and *ones*."

"It's your ouroboros snake," Susan said, eyeing the crook in the river next to the skull image on the map as she folded it.

"They have a plane waiting for us at Atarot. Marx has separated another segment from the Ebola." Winston paused and gulped from the bottle. "This drink's a bit flat. The new coordinates are in the British Isles." *Beep* "Look—the bird just laid an egg. It's on the phone readout."

"Where in the British Isles?" Her eyes focused on the polarized display.

LAT: 55 56' 38" N, LONG: 03 09' 41" W

Winston smacked his lips to moisten them, then replied, "A place I used to visit when I was a child—Edinburgh."

Day 12
Arthur's Seat

I know how birds can fly, how fish can swim, how animals can run.
But who knows how dragons ride on winds and soar through clouds on into heaven?
One does not need to know how or why in order to soar.
One just needs to believe in *dragons*. – Confucius

STANDING AT THE CORNER of Carlton Road and Abby Hill, Winston lifted his baseball cap and raked his hand through his hair. He glanced at his wristwatch. It was 9:18 A.M.

"There they are." Susan pointed to two men approaching from the direction of Abby Hill. One was a sawed-off, beefy man dressed in military fatigues, wearing a maroon beret with an air landing guilder badge on the brim. The other man sported a white-feathered, hunter-green beret and a plaid kilt revealing his bird-like, bowed legs. A fully loaded, well-worn, canvas military knapsack was gripped in his hand.

"Good morning, I'm Captain Brinson, your attaché from Menwith Hill, and this is the local historian you requested, Dr. McCalester from the University of Edinburgh."

Winston had called ahead and specifically requested Dr. McCalester accompany them in their investigation of the new *locus*.

"Hello, Angus!" Winston cheerfully smiled while removing his sunglasses. He shook Dr. McCalester's hand, followed by a firm, shoulder-slapping hug.

"Hey, my little Jimmy!" Angus jovially greeted in a thick Scottish brogue. "It's been donkey's ears, a long time of mind. You were no more than a wee lad the last time I saw you. I was so sorry to hear about your parents. I admired your father's work. He was a man among men. The good men are bound to their women. Mary was always his better half, a beautiful woman. I see you work for the government now."

"Yes, I'm a patriotic soul. Truth, justice, and the American way." Winston smiled slyly and pointed to the flag on his baseball cap. "It's just something I've got to do."

"You know Dr. McCalester?" Susan asked Winston. She looked up into Angus's big, brown eyes, highlighted by bushy brows arching like two, miniature owl feathers. The seventy-year-old, world-renowned archeologist, British historian, and polyhistor towered six and a half feet tall. She noticed an Edinburgh Dragon Pin from the Hard Rock Café attached to his shirt collar.

Angus offered her a crooked smile that was long in the tooth. "I knew Jimmy's father when we attended the university," he said affably, dropping his knapsack to the ground. He tipped his beret and shook Susan's hand. A blue ribbon was tied around his index finger. "We studied in the same field of archeology. I think the last time I saw Jimmy, he was on summer vacation with his parents. A very skinny little boy. I was a Headmaster molding the character of young men at Gordontoun in those days."

"So, you're bringing family and friends in on the investigation." Susan said.

"No, yes …" Winston swiped his hand under his chin, lowered his gaze, and then looked straight at Susan. "Angus knows more about the history of Edinburgh than anyone I know." Winston carried his attention back to Angus. "I still have two of your books that you gave my father in my library."

"My reputation precedes me." Angus laughed lightly, holding his right hand straight out above his waist. "Oh, my God, scandalous exaggerations, I'm sure. Have you read them?" he inquired as he lifted his knapsack.

"No, I don't believe I have," Winston replied, remembering the books.

"Well, don't judge a book by its cover. There are others who know more than I," Angus admitted. "But, I am from the groves of the academe, although I've been put in mothballs. I do not teach at the university anymore. I'm an academic dinosaur, I am afraid. Nevertheless, I am well-versed on the history of Edinburgh. So, how can I help you? It's good to feel needed. I have everything in my knapsack—copies of old maps, historical reports—everything you requested, Jimmy. It's a sack full of treasure!"

"Where are the coordinates?" Winston asked Captain Brinson who was holding a mobile GPS.

Brinson checked a digital topographic map on the LDC readout:

HEIGHT-250.5 METERS, LAT - 35 55' 45' 18" N   LONG - 3.9 38'15" W

"According to the GPS, it's there—right there." Brinson pointed to a knob of rock at the summit of a majestic hill that loomed a mile away.

Angus turned to determine where the captain was pointing. He squinted as the clouds parted and the morning sun reflected off the blood-red cliffs of the mountain that dominated Edinburgh's skyline. "Why, that's Arthur's Seat. I know that place very well," he said good-naturedly.

"Alright, that's where we're going," Winston said.

"Then follow me," Angus rolled up his sleeves with a can-do spirit, "let me offer you a cook's tour. I know the best way to get there."

"I think we can handle things from here," Susan dismissed Captain Brinson, as he handed her the GPS unit and a small camera bag.

As they strolled through the narrow streets of old Edinburgh, Angus shared some background on the small mountain they were about to climb. "Arthur's Seat is an eight hundred-foot-high lava plug from the remains of a dead volcano. It is confined within Holyrood Park. The mountain's summit offers a tremendous view of the surrounding countryside and of the sea to the east. The *seat* itself is a notch between the highest point of the peak and a secondary point a little way to the south." Angus pointed in the direction of the mountain. "There are two approaches to the top of Arthur's Seat from this side of the city. One is the Radical Road, a narrow footpath that runs next to the Salisbury Crags. The other is by way of the northern approach. Many tourists take the Radical Road because they find that route to the top visually stimulating, although many say the climb is as demanding as a bike ride up *L'Alpe d'Huez*."

"It doesn't look like a hard climb to me," Winston said.

"Wait til you get to the top," Angus interjected. "It will take your breath away."

"Look." Angus pointed to a castle a few hundred yards away. A flag bearing the Hebrew letter *Tav*, the cross of St. Andrew, waved in the breeze. "That's Holyrood House, the summer palace of the queen. It is similar to the White House of your president, a temporary residence. The royal family has nine residences throughout Great Britain. The name, Holyrood, is derived from the abbey next to the palace. According to legend, Holyrood Abby was built by King David the First to commemorate an incident where he found himself in dire straits while hunting near Arthur's Seat and was *saved* by a stag whose antlers mysteriously changed into a holy cross. The noble stag is still revered by the Royals to this day."

Winston noticed the coat of arms for Scotland carved on a stone wall next to the entry gate. *A lion ... Jerusalem ...*

Angus pointed to a street that ascended to an ancient castle-keep. "There're the cobbled streets of the Royal Mile, the model for the modern street mall—the secular temple. Geoffery's, across the street from the Virgin Megastore, is the shop where I buy my clothes ... hand-sewn, pure cashmere." He proudly tugged on his kilt. "The Royal Mile runs down the middle of the Old Town and up to the Camera Obscura with its 'magic mirror of life,' near Castle Hill ... Hoggwarts," Angus scoffed with a shake of his head, "Mary's Chapel, where the Stone of Destiny is housed—"

"The Stone of Destiny?" Winston questioned.

"The old *lapidem*—the holy coronation stone. All but one of the kings of England have been crowned and anointed—like gods—upon that stone. According to tradition, the Stone of Destiny was once the chief cornerstone of the Temple of Solomon. It's now the chieftain stone of Castle Hill. You should visit the castle's underground vaults. They're hollowed right into the rock. The old city along the Royal Mile was rebuilt after the Great Fire of 1824, which necessitated changes in the ground level of the streets. There are many underground passages and hidden vaults beneath the Old Town which lead right into the castle."

"Like catacombs?" Susan ventured a comparison. *Paris ... Rome ...*

"Exactly. It's said the underground of Edinburgh is haunted by ghosts, such as the Headless Drummer." Angus chuckled. "Legend says the Headless Drummer drums a Devil's tattoo whenever the world is in despair."

"Saint Denis," Susan said to Winston.

"The chief cornerstone ... the Temple of Solomon, again," Winston commented below his breath. *The Dipper*, he pondered.

Angus pointed in the direction of what looked like a huge circus tent. "Over there is the Dynamic Earth, our museum to the earth sciences. Next to it are the new Scottish Parliament Buildings."

"Odd architecture," Winston noted. "It looks out of place in this old city."

———

CONTINUING THEIR STROLL, they entered through a wrought-iron gate into a public park skirted by an asphalt road called the Queen's Drive.

"This is Holyrood Park, commissioned by Prince Albert in the 1850's," Angus guided. "This park is a special place in Edinburgh, almost sacred. It's even protected by the Royal family. It's a protected SSSI site. The city has never attempted to build on this mountain-hill."

Stepping from the walkway, they passed through a gap in the hedges at the bottom of the garden and proceeded in the direction of a grassy knoll.

"This is the northern approach," Angus said. "Let me take you on a path less traveled. It's just on the other side of the little rise called Haggis Knows."

Angus shepherded them on a gentle ascent by way of a well-trodden shortcut known as the Velvet Walk. They passed a man and woman in their late fifties, dressed in matching, *bright* khaki-colored, travel-light clothing from L. L. Bea*m*, descending from the summit. The man had a camera hanging from his neck. The woman smiled and graciously greeted, "G'Day," in a New Zealand accent.

Winston nodded back with a friendly smile.

"Although modern-day Edinburgh has never encroached upon Arthur's Seat, the ground where we are standing used to be the location of a fortification for the original inhabitants of prehistoric Edinburgh," Angus commented. "This whole area juts up over the surrounding countryside. With its steep mountain cliffs to the north and south, it is an ideal location for a self-contained community. On the other side of that ridge are ancient terraces carved into the eastern face of the mountain, like a Babylonian hanging garden. Most archeologists believe they were used for agricultural purposes. Others contend the terraces were an ancient, ceremonial, labyrinthine pathway that once spiraled to the top of the mountain."

"So this is an ancient Celtic site?" Winston asked.

"Celtic or Picton. Maybe even older," Angus replied. "It's pre-Roman. Look." Angus abruptly stopped beside a small rowan tree and cocked his head in the direction of the summit. He pointed. "Do you see the Lion's Haunch?"

"The lion's what?" Susan questioned, uncertain of what Angus was pointing to. "Are there lions running loose?" she asked jokingly. "Is there a zoo in the park?"

"Oh, maybe snakes," Angus chuckled in reply. "The park is only a McGuffin for catching lions. The Lion's Haunch is the part of the mountain that resembles the backbone of a crouching lion. Your hand?" Angus grasp Susan's hand, her forefinger extended, and guided it as he outlined the shape of the golden-haired, crouching lion formed by the topography of the mountain. "For the love of the hunt. See!"

"Yes, I see it now." Her eyes widened. "It reminds me of a crouching sphinx. I even see the profile of a lion's head."

"The bigger the better," Winston jested, "a real mountain lion."

"Obviously the name applies to the topographic resemblance to a lion," Susan offered a quick analysis.

"Well, maybe," Angus conceded. "But, I believe this topographic feature is an enormous, *linga*-billboard-like sculpture. You see, if we were approaching from the south side of the mountain we'd see the same profile as seen here from the northern approach. And if you approach by way of St. Leonard Hall on the eastern side, you will see the remains of rear legs and a tail. From every direction, the profile of a lion can be discerned in the rock formation."

Winston and Susan stopped in their tracks and listened to Angus as they stared in awe at the Lion's Haunch.

"Teleology—form sometimes follows function." Angus explained, "A lion is known as the guardian of sacred places, like the Egyptian guardian deity Aker who constantly battles the darkness and holds down the serpent. It's been used as a religious symbol for resurrection and enduring time, as with the ancient deity *Ialdabaoth*—the Demiurge. In astronomy, the lion is a symbol for the sun. It also denotes the zodiac constellation, Leo—the group of stars shaped like a backward question mark or a sickle. Although the zodiac symbol Leo, in Chinese, is a Dragon."

"I'm familiar with these constellations," Winston said.

"Your mother taught you well. This crouching lion here at Arthur's Seat is on a direct east to west axis which is aligned to the solar equinox." Angus pointed to the humped back of the Lion's Haunch, then to the head, and on to the western horizon. "Secondly, each year the locals celebrate the age-old Beltane festival to Lugus on this mountain-hill, which is carried out at the time of the equinox. Thirdly, the peak of Arthur's Seat is at the top of the lion's head for this sculpture." He pointed again to the summit. "Fourthly, the head of this lion feature is not weathered and worn like the rest of this old mountain. With that you have four unusual features associated with a single place. I believe this camouflaged image in the topography is man-made."

"Steganographic. Any idea who created it?" Winston asked Angus.

"I suspect it was created by the ancient community that once lived on this mountain-hill. I consider that a real possibility. But it's possible the Romans created it. They settled Edinburgh in the second century. A Roman lion and snake fertility statue was discovered along the river Almond in 1997. In fact, the oldest known written description of this part of the world comes from the Roman records. But then again, *perhaps* someone else created it." Angus grinned sheepishly. "Onward and upward. Come this way."

Passing through the grassy highlands of Hunter's Bog, they stepped over a rocky outcropping known as Piper's Walk which led to the top of the tor about twelve feet away. As they scrambled up the path, Winston noticed two, three-foot-tall, concrete pillars anchored to the summit.

"Don't tell me those are Jefferson Stones," Winston said in disbelief.

"What?" Angus questioned, walking stiffly.

"It's an inside joke, Dr. McCalester," Susan said pleasantly. "It has to do with meridians."

"Well, so do those two pillars, my dear," Angus responded with a quick nod.

Winston stopped in his tracks and snagged Susan's gaze with an agreeing wink.

She winked back at him.

"What's the nature of these concrete pillars?" Winston probed.

"They are summit markers, not the pillars of Jachin and Boaz, or even the pillars of Heracles. Arthur's Seat is between those two pillars. One pillar marks the highest point of the summit and the other has a metal plaque that offers directions to other landmarks that can be seen from the summit. This way. We're almost to the top."

Angus bowed his head into a gust of wind and trudged like a mountain goat up a steep switchback toward the summit.

"I'm walking on eggshells. Watch your step," Winston warned Susan.

"Oops!" Susan stumbled, as rocks rolled under her feet.

"Careful, my dear." Angus caught her hand. "It's mind over matter. You have to step like you're firewalking. Imagine that this old volcano is still alive! Please, allow me the liberty to hold your hand."

"Thank you, Dr. McCalester." Susan smiled politely, as Angus gently pulled her up to the summit.

"Away with the formalities. Angus, my dear. Call me Angus."

The three approached one of the pillars.

"Look at this, Jimmy." Angus pointed to an aluminum plaque on top of the pillar, splattered with fresh bird droppings from a goldfinch that had just taken flight. Lines inscribed on the plaque, resembling the spokes of a wheel, pointed to other geographic features that could be seen in the distance.

Winston started to read the place names on the plaque. *Fidra Island, Knock Hill....* *These alignments remind me of the radial roads branching out from the Vatican.* He turned away from the pillar. "I feel like Don Quixote tilting at windmills," he spoke above the loud *snapping* and *flapping* of his shirt. "This wind is piercing. It's like being at the top of Devil's Tower. The vista is absolutely breathtaking. Right, left, up, down, which way should I turn?" He stared toward the northeast at a pulsating, white ribbon of sand bordering the Firth of Forth, separating the land from an ocean merging indistinguishable with the turquoise sky. The distant orb of the morning sun reflected across the water as an undulating golden pillar that pointed to Lamb Island.

"I said it would take your breath away," Angus remarked with a huff.

In quiet wonder, Winston made a slow 360 degree turn, his long-practiced eyes soaking up a memory of the countryside and the angled rooftops of Edinburgh merging with hilly fields of green.

"See any letterboxes, James?" Susan ribbed.

"No," Winston admitted. "But, I wasn't looking for any. I was hoping to find an obelisk. I don't see one anywhere."

"Me either," Susan said, frowning in confusion.

"Oh, there's one at Carlton Hill," Angus noted.

"Where's that?" Winston responded, as a poet black-billed magpie landed at his feet and started scavenging for food.

"It is in that direction, to your right, below Nelson's Tower." Angus pointed west to a stone tower. "You can barely see it through that stand of trees next to the old Playfair City Observatory. Look! See the golden time ball on top of the Tower. The Tower is a memorial to Lord Admiral Horatio Nelson who was once the governor of Port Royal, Jamaica, where the British spearheaded their acquisition of the Americas from the Spanish."

"Call, call, obelisk, obelisk, which way? Call, to the right, to the right."

Winston glanced at a beak-wiping, copycat magpie prancing at his feet. "Hmm. Whaddya know about that obelisk? Whoa— "

"Call, call, to the right, to the right." The magpie took flight.

"I nearly tripped on that bird. Are they always under your feet?" Winston asked.

"Be careful how you treat the birds, Jimmy. I am a member of the Royal Society for the Protection of the Birds and the British Ornithologists' Union. John Audubon once lived in Edinburgh. We take our birding *seriously* here."

"Alright, don't get festered, Angus. Tell me more about that obelisk."

"It's called Hamilton's Obelisk. It's a massive Roman obelisk, one hundred forty-four-feet tall. I was once told the obelisk was used as a reference in a famous solar experiment in 1850. It stands in a graveyard, near the Old Governor's House at the base of Carlton Hill, the site of another dead volcano. Edinburgh was built on seven hills—Corstorphine Hill, Braid Hill, Blackford Hill, Castle Hill, Carlton Hill, Arthur's Seat, and Craigmillar Hill. Three of these hills are the chimneys of extinct volcanoes. Carlton Hill is now a local cemetery. It contains an old Jewish burial vault, which your father and I once excavated. The National Monument, *Edinburgh's Disgrace,* is also on Carlton Hill. It's an unfinished memorial modeled after the Parthenon. It now sits like the ruins of the great sun temple at Baalbek."

"Hamilton?" Winston questioned with a sideways glance at Susan.

"So, a copy of the Lincoln Memorial and an obelisk are over there." Susan pointed. "Are you sure we are at the right place? Plus, I don't see anything related to a skull."

"Oh … skulls!" Angus held up his ribboned finger. "I think I have some information on that in my materials." He rummaged through his knapsack. "You are right, my dear. There is a memorial statue to Abraham Lincoln on Carlton Hill, next to the mausoleum of David Hume. Where are those papers?"

Angus removed some documents, placed them on top of one of the concrete markers, and held them down tightly with one hand to anchor them from the wind. "Sometimes I need twelve arms," he complained as he retrieved a ring of keys from a side pocket of his knapsack along with an old, brass pocket compass and laid them on top of the papers. Inscribed on the cover of the compass were symbols surrounding the images of a fish-eye and the Star of David. "I'm not finding it! Maybe I left it back at my library." He looked up at Winston. "Perhaps I should begin by telling you more about the Roman history of this area, and about the wondrous adder—Edinburgh's Lambton Wyrm." He stomped his foot.

"Edinburgh's Lambton Worm," Susan repeated.

"A Typhon, my dear. The Edinbane Dragon!" Angus forcefully clarified.

Susan eyed the dragon pin attached to Angus's collar. *Another dragon? Paris, Rome, Jerusalem ... commonalities,* she thought.

"The Romans who settled here did not call this city Edinburgh," Angus said. "They originally named it the *Casrum Orurm*—a reference to a dragon-shaped city. Ptolemy, the ancient Greek geographer who mapped the Roman Empire, called this place the *Pinnata Castra*—the winged camp. Roman fortifications were set up on either sides of

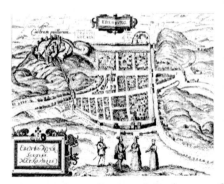

the city at Cramond and Inveresk. The ancient French records called the city Laileburg, meaning a winged town. The *1654 Blaeu Atlas of Scotland* referenced Edinburgh as the *Castrum alatum,* meaning winged castle, and the *Castrum alarum,* meaning castle of wings. The hill where the castle now stands was seen as the head of a dragon, or a great bird. The hills of Arthur's Seat and Carlton Hill, over there, were seen as two gigantic wings emerging from the ground. The Roman engineers who surveyed the city may have discerned the image of a dragon shape-shifting out of the landscape and emerging from the waters of the Firth of Forth. Holyrood Castle sits on the spine, between the two wings of this chameleon hidden in the landscape. Since 1765, the axial grid of James Craig's New Town Plan has covered over most of this old image. But the mighty winged-shape of Arthur's Seat can still be discerned in the landscape."

"You mean the Queen's House, like our White House," Susan said.

"As sure as God's in Gloucestershire," Angus replied, "the Romans did this sort of thing all over Europe, naming places for the shapes they saw formed by the natural contours in the land."

"Yeah, I can believe that," Susan commented.

"The temple's cornerstone is still guarded by a winged demon," Winston thought out loud. He pulled the map of Jerusalem from his pocket and glanced at the sketch he had made earlier. "Hmm ..." *A winged camp ... dragon wings ... Roman ... Hadrian.*

"The Romans were the great road builders," Angus explained, "with more than 50,000 miles of roads crossing their empire. Perhaps they were the first to call Arthur's Seat the Lion's Haunch, although that name does not show up in their records. It's all too far in the distant past, with scant written evidence to paint a true history. But the dragon is associated with Arthur's Seat by way of the legends of King Arthur. King Arthur's last name was Pendragon, meaning the head of the dragon, the head dragon, or the foremost leader—the lawgiver. The name Arthur in Welsh means *Urse Horribilis* or bear. Arthur's Seat means seat of the bear or home of the bear—"

"Or Bear Lodge," Winston interrupted with a proud expression.

"Exactly." Angus pulled a star chart from his knapsack. "It's all connected to astronomy. Let me show you. The constellation Ursa Major contains the group of stars we commonly see in the northern night sky, known as the Plough, or the Big Dipper. The handle of the Dipper is the Great Bear's tail, and the Dipper's cup is the Bear's flank. The Big Dipper is not a traditional constellation, but an asterism. An asterism is a distinctive group of stars shared by two constellations. This group that forms the Big Dipper is made up of seven stars known as," Angus traced his finger over the star chart, "*Phad, Megrez, Alioth, Mizar, Alkaid.* The two end stars in the bowl of the Big Dipper are *Dubhe* and *Merak.* These end stars are known as the pointers. An imaginary line extending through them leads to the polestar Polaris, the North Star, at the end of the wagging tail of Ursa Minor. The polestar is the principal nighttime reference for navigation at sea. The angle between the horizon and Polaris in the night sky is equal to your latitude on the earth."

"We already know about the polestar," Susan remarked, gawking at the diagram. "It looks like a Nazi swastika." *Jerusalem is centered around a swastika?*

"A swastika night, from the little toes of Buddha," Angus muttered as he pointed again to the star chart. "In Scandinavian star lore, the Little Dipper was called Thor's Wagon or Karl's Wagon. To the Anglo-Saxons it was known as Odin's Wain or wagon, and in German star lore it was called Heaven's Wagon. The ancient Finns depicted this asterism as a holy pine tree with seven stars at the top or with a bear nestled in its uppermost branches."

The nicchone at the Vatican, Winston pondered.

"Christmas stars," Susan remarked. *And Santa is Satan.*

"Exactly, my dear. The Greeks called this star group the Seven Wise Men. Their star charts associate the asterism with the image of a cosmic bear. The word bear comes from the word *bare*, which means to hold up, as in the Great Bear who holds up the sky. In English lore, the Dipper was commonly known as Charles's Wain, Charles being the English variation of Karl. Influenced by Indo-European mythology, it was also known as Arcturus Wain, or Arthur's Wain, or Arthur's Wagon."

"We know about these stars and the dragon," Susan stated again.

"Exactly." Angus pointed to another constellation. "Surrounding the bear, we have Draco, the dragon. Because the Earth is tilted at an angle of nearly twenty-three and a half degrees, the polestar changes its location over a 26,000 year period, known as the Platonic year. In the distant past, the tail of the constellation Draco was once the location of the polestar."

Angus glided his finger over the star chart. "In addition, Ursa Major resides above the constellations Leo Minor and Leo Major."

"Leo, as in the Lion's Haunch at Arthur's Seat, or Arthur's Wagon?" Susan questioned with a nod. *David saved a lamb from a lion's mouth,* she thought.

"It's not that difficult to understand," Angus replied. "Leo points the way to the dragon. Combined, we have the bear, Arthur's Seat; the head of the dragon, the Castle Hill; and Leo, the Lion's Haunch—three symbols of royal authority. These are three distinctive features of the topography of Edinburgh. They are also associated with the polar star groups. It's all an astronomical reference that's been engineered into the landscape. The bear and the dragon constellations, Ursa and Draco, guard the polestar. And the polestar is used as a reference for all global navigation by way of the imaginary lines of longitude. There is even an ancient rose-line that runs through the center of Arthur's Seat."

"Lions, dragons, and bears, oh my," Winston murmured.

" 'Thou shalt tread upon the lion and cobra: the young lion and the dragon shalt thou trample under feet,' "Angus quoted. "Your father recited that verse all the time. He understood the secrets of Arthur's Seat—"

"Rose-line," Susan asked faintly, "marks on a compass rose?" *What did Mr. Howard say about Peter Jefferson's map?* She tried to remember. *Paris—Hell.*

"Yes, it's the marker on a compass rose that points north. It's simply another name for a meridian, my dear, an imaginary line of longitude. Although the word *ros* in Hebrew means 'head.' The rose-line is marked by this concrete pillar on the summit. It's sometimes called the Magdalene Line that points to the Star of Enlightenment— the star we guide ourselves by."

"Mary married to the Lamb," Susan said. "So, Arthur Pendragon is a *codeword* for astronomical polar coordinates?"

"Exactly!" Angus burst out. "The whole King Arthur mythology is about the movement of the heavens around the polestar. Many claim the Gospels convey a similar meaning, with the twelve apostles rotating around a central sun."

"That's the same thing Dr. Peres told us," Susan remarked to Winston.

"Christ and the Last Supper," Winston muttered. *The Grail, the dipper.*

Angus noticed Winston's thoughtful expression. "Katherine Maltwood, in her book *The Glastonbury Temple of the Stars*, was the first to uncover the astronomical relationship within the Arthurian legends. Jimmy, your father knew of her work. She claimed that the landscape surrounding Glastonbury in the south of England was designed as a gigantic astronomical clock dating to around 2700 B.C. The landscape mirrors certain constellations which mill a circular zodiac ten miles in diameter. The likelihood of this occurring by chance was calculated at one in half a billion—"

"A giant zodiac … Glastonbury," Susan repeated, thumbing through her notepad. "The *Fry-Jefferson Map* … Fry was from Glastonbury."

"A zodiac is a symbolic story of man in sync with God," Angus explained. "The term zodiac comes from the Greek word *zodion,* a small living image which signifies the story of the microcosmic life of man in sync with the stars."

"You sound like my mother talking," Winston remarked.

"Or Dr. Peres," Susan added.

Angus removed an aerial photograph of the Glastonbury Zodiac from a folder. The photo detailed the outlines of picture glyphs formed by the natural features of the fields, hills, rivers, and artificial constructions in the form of ditches, roads, and boundary lines. "Such images formed in the landscape are positioned all over the

British Isles, such as the pole-carrying Long Man of Wilmington and the club-holding, lion-skin-toting, sexually aroused Cerne Abbas Giant married to the countryside at Dorset. It's believed to be a phallic fertility image, or a depiction of Hercules. You know, your father did some archaeological work at the ruins of the old Benedictine abbey at Cerne Abbas."

"Hercules slaying Ladon ... Jerusalem," Winston connected, staring at the map of Jerusalem in his hands.

"But, Dr. McCalester, what about the reference to a skull?" Susan inquired. "We found something in Rome—"

"Yes." Winston slightly shook his head, signaling Susan not to say too much. "What can you tell us about skulls?" he asked keeping his tone casual.

"Angus, my dear, call me Angus," he reminded Susan as he caught Winston's head wagging. "Jimmy, there is another grand image associated with this site besides a lion, a dragon, and a bear."

Susan and Winston stood silent, their eyes opened wide.

"But, I'm sorry. I do not have all of my materials with me," Angus apologized testily. "I need to return to my library. I have some old books I think you need to see. They might give you a better understanding of the significance of this place."

"Alright Angus, let's visit your library," Winston said calmly, folding the map into his pocket. "Susan, take some photos of those pillars."

As Angus gathered his papers and tucked them into his knapsack. He picked up the pocket compass and held it out toward Winston. "Look, Jimmy."

"An old pocket compass." Winston spotted the Japanese, haiku-like inscription on its cover.

"A guide for life's journeys." Angus flipped the cover open and handed it to Winston. "Read the inscription inside."

Winston held the compass close to his heart, his eyes blinking. He noticed the cardinal points printed on the face behind the needle were misaligned. He bowed his head and read the inscription.

> *How we carried on*
> *Time is passing as we do our deeds*
> *The road ahead is long and winding*
> *Life can be hope without hope sometimes*
> *If you get lost – Look at this cross*
> *And follow the seven stars in the sky*
> *Remember me like I remember you*
> *J. A. Winston*

"Your father gave it to me before he left Edinburgh to live in the States. He told me the compass had belonged to his father. From father to son. Take it, Jimmy. He would be *proud*."

"Thank you." Winston's eyes stopped blinking as he placed the compass into his pocket. "Angus?"

"Yes, Jimmy."

"What are those Oriental-like symbols on the front of the compass? They look like they could be part of someone's Turing Test in a Chinese thought room experiment."

"Ah ... the kingdom of heaven is a net let down into a lake that catches all kinds of fish. I've asked myself that same question. These symbols resemble the script found on an *ika,* a ceremonial fish tablet, which describes the prayers, calendars, and aspects of spiritual consciousness related to the cosmology of the Polynesian and Solomon islanders of the South Pacific. That script is similar to the ancient Indus script, one of the oldest scripts known to man. But, I was told those markings have to do with something your great-great-grandfather discovered. Something about the dipper stars, a winged demon, and the sacred union of the forces of the sun and moon." Angus smiled with a wink.

Winston turned the compass over and noted the engraving on the back. "A tree … with a snake battling a lion at its roots? What's this about?"

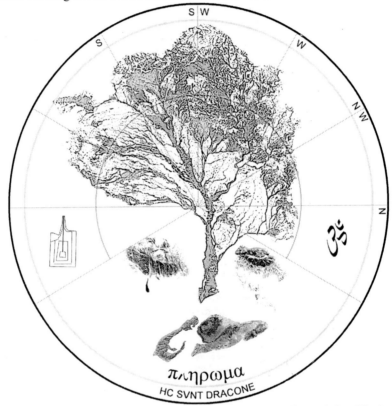

"The coat of arms for the Hoggwarts Houses of Slytherin and Gryffindor," Angus scoffed. "I always thought this striking cobra and crouching lion was a reference to Arthur's Seat. But, your father told me it was an Egyptian symbol for the great struggle between good and evil. In this case, they may correspond to the serpent deities Wadjet, Set, or Apep and the lions Aker, Sef, or Maahes. Or … it could stand for the Egyptian deities Amen and his consort, Mut. The sovereign lion and cobra imagery are found on Egyptian apotropaic, boomerang-shaped magic wands as symbols for protection."

"Peres mentioned *Amen-Ka* and *Nak.* It reminds me of Peres's time deity Chronos," Winston compared. "And tearful eyes … the tree looks like it has a face."

"Cat-like," Angus said. "Weeping eyes, a characteristic of the Egyptian sun god and a symbol of love. Eyes are the windows to the soul. Every time I look at this engraving, it sets me at peace."

"The whole diagram has symmetry," Winston sized-up the pattern.

"The presence of design," Angus said.

"What's this inscription? Is it Greek above Latin?"

"*Pleroma.*" Angus translated, "A Greek phrase, the 'fullness of God's power.' "

"And the other?"

" 'Here be dragons.' Your father told me the engravings on the compass would aid you in finding your ultimate destination … something as old as time. Whatever that means. I could never figure it out. Maybe you'll have better luck than I."

SUSAN SNAPPED a few photos before the three descended Arthur's Seat, this time by way of the Radical Road. Minutes later, they reached a place where the footpath deteriorated into an eroded, precarious precipice. Winston stopped at the edge of a cliff, near a set of chains and a sign reading DANGER LOOSE ROCKS - GOAT COUNTRY, WATCH YOUR STEP. Angus joined him as they looked out over the rambling, cottage-like architecture of the old city of Edinburgh.

Susan observed the two companions. *Father and son,* she compared.

"It's a beautiful city," Winston said. "Something out of a fairy tale." He felt a friendly shoulder pat from Angus.

"Our Area 51. Sigmund Freud once said a city is 'the whole of mental life.' I've stood here a hundred times, Jimmy. I never tire of this view. I love Edinburgh, our Athens of the North. The modern world began at Edinburgh. Nested between the rivers Leith and Almond, this city was a principal location of publishing and learning long before the eighteenth-century Scottish Enlightenment. The civil law used by much of western society originated in Edinburgh with The Law of the Four Burghs, the oldest civic document in existence. Built upon the new technologies created by Scots such as James Watt, who improved the steam engine, the Industrial Age began here at Edinburgh. This ageless city sits at the intellectual crossroads of our modern-day views on natural science and geography."

"So, the Industrial Age was founded under the wings of a dragon," Winston joked.

"Exactly. Lend an ear and let me tell you a story. Do you see that cutout in the side of the crags?" Angus pointed to an abandoned quarry a few feet away.

"Yes," Winston replied. He noticed a grouping of names painted on the wall of the quarry: *Jean-Paul Marat … W. Sinclair … HRH Albert … J. Hutton.*

"That cutout is the south quarry and that rock formation to the left of it is known as Hutton's Rock. 'The present is the key to the past.' This is the place were James Hutton, the father of modern geology, observed the formation of geological strata and formulated the first correct view of the world below ground."

Angus rested on a nearby boulder as he educated Susan and Winston on the history of Hutton's Rock. "In 1650, Ireland's Protestant Archbishop, James Ussher of Armagh, published his famous *Annales Veteris Testamenti.* In it, he declared that Adam from the book of Genesis was created in the year 4004 B.C. Four years after Ussher's declaration, the Vatican Council decreed that anyone daring to contradict the accuracy of that date was a heretic. That foolish Cat'lic decree stood until 1952. The decree established what became known as the Neptunian view of the world proposed by the scholar Abraham Werner. He believed the world was once entirely covered by the biblical deluge."

"Rip van Winkle," Winston said. "It took a long time for them to wake up."

"Yes," Angus chuckled. "As late as the eighteenth century, the educated world still clung to the Neptunian flood theory. Then in 1790, James Hutton began to study the geological features at Arthur's Seat in order to formulate a new geology for the planet. He discovered that the Earth is a book with its story told between pages of layered rock with a million years to every page. Four years later, Hutton published his three-volume treatise titled *An Investigation into the Principles of Knowledge*. Hutton, for the first time, realized that both the surface and interior of the planet were constantly changing through the processes of decay and re-creation. Each year Mount Everest gets taller. Each year the Dead Sea gets lower. The geology of the Earth is evolving and being made anew through dynamic changes."

"Nothing is constant," Winston said. "We all grow older. They say I used to look like my mother. Now I look like my father."

"Don't remind me." Angus swiped his hand over his balding pate and scratched the gray curls around his ears. "It's evolution, an undeniable fact. Call it metamorphosis, but we all evolve. It remained for Charles Darwin, who was influenced by Hutton's disciples, Charles Lyell and John Playfair, to bring Hutton's idea to the forefront of the public consciousness. In his *Descent of Man*, Darwin restated Hutton's basic concept as the theory we all know today as the *origin of species*. Thus, it was Darwin who provided the voluminous evidence necessary to win over the scientific community to the theory of evolution. Nevertheless, it was Hutton's idea, which originated here, at Arthur's Seat," Angus said proudly.

"So, Arthur's Seat is the origin of the origin of species," Winston quipped. "We're truly standing at a special place."

Angus stood up and removed pen and paper from his knapsack. "In our search for our place in God's great creation, we constantly ask ourselves: Where does man stand? The millwork of God grinds slowly, but it ultimately grinds out a world that leads to the progress of Man. I believe that man stands at the top of an evolutionary chain of being," he began to explain. "I adopted this idea from a book entitled *The Phenomenon of Man* by a Jesuit priest named Pierre Teilhard de Chardin. Although, it is very similar to the views on human progress and the future state of man promoted by Francis Bacon and the Scottish astronomer Thomas Dick. Teilhard formulated a metaphysical argument which proposed that the consciousness of man is the outcome of God's linear cascade of creation. Man, the only earthly being with a higher consciousness, is the reason for the existence of everything else around him. Evolution has a direction—and that direction led to the creation of the mind of man." Angus sketched a chain of symbols on the paper in his hand. "In his book, Teilhard explained his process of divinization as a type of cosmology consisting of a pre-life point of creation, the Alpha Point—the starting point of this chain of beginning, and the Omega Point—the end of the cosmological chain in the Great Leap Forward."

"A beginning and the end," Susan interjected, "the symbol for Christ in the Bible."

"Yes, my dear. But, it's a beginning to *an* end. Teilhard equated Christ with an evolving cosmology. He reinterpreted the book of Genesis as an evolutionary process, starting from the Divine Spark of the Creative Light of God to the outcome of a Divine Consciousness found in the phenomenon of the enlightened man who had obtained a Christ-like consciousness. In an undefinable emergence, the creative light of God burst into the cosmos. That light was made of waves and particles—particles which seeded the material world of the cosmos and waves which carried a *signal,* serving as the essence of the mind of God permeating throughout all of creation. The Bible says that man was created in the image of God. In this sense, Alpha is the starting position of the creative light of God, and Omega is the outcome—the mind of man, the *omphalos*—where the God Consciousness is awakened into our world. The Omega Point is equal to the future state of God. In Exodus, God speaks to Moses from the burning bush and reveals His name, *EHYEH ASHER EHYEH,* meaning *I shall be what I shall be.* God is a future state, not yet achieved. 'As man is, God once was; as God is, man may become.' God is our Ultimate Future. We meet the Divine at the end of life's journey. It's a type of vitalism, a belief that life is in some small part is pre-determined and self-determining."

"A man recently told me something Aristotle once said ... something about all things tending to reach for perfection. But, a spark of light evolving into the consciousness of man?" Winston shook his head again. "Oh, Billy, everything is pushed by light."

"Teilhard maintained that the Christ of the Gospels, of which there is little or no historical evidence, should not be viewed merely by way of historical events, but must be viewed in the wider scope of the cosmic events which have affected the history of the universe and the evolution of man," Angus clarified. "This evolutionary emergence is the Incarnation, Resurrection, and Ascension of matter into the creation of a humanity with a God Consciousness—a consciousness directed toward a love to-and-from its creative source. Man is merely an unfinished animal destined to become an Overman. This is the final neotenous of the nexus. This union of the human with the divine is the ultimate goal of everyone. We all want to turn our base metals into gold. The evolution from Alpha to Omega is the bringing of the God Consciousness into our world—the Global Consciousness. Teilhard presented his view in the form of an equation where 'Evolution = Rise of Consciousness.' Although no one can fully embody God, we can certainly move toward it. The final step in man's evolution is the awareness of his own Godlike consciousness."

"My friend, Billy, would agree with that," Winston said.

"The Renaissance philosopher Pico della Mirandola in his *Oration on the Dignity of Man,* the 'Manifesto of the Renaissance,' believed man possessed unlimited possibilities, even godlike possibilities. The philosopher Hegel said something very similar, 'the history of the world is nothing other than the progress toward the consciousness of *freedom.*' It's an *apocalyptic* view which describes God's *presence* through human agents, where a God Consciousness exists within each man who is free." Angus pointed to the various symbols. "It's a consciousness that every man seeks within himself—a consciousness that each person freely accepts and freely understands. This symbolism of Alpha to Omega is the *itinerium mentis in deum,* the journey of the mind of God into our world."

Winston stared at the drawing. "So these *sign relations* represent a pictorial equation for invoking God into our world. God self-replicating into human consciousness—man made from star stuff—a solar god in human form—" Winston paused. "This model is not linear. It's circular. God leads to God ... a zero-sum-gain."

"A God Consciousness," Susan muttered, "Michelangelo's brain scan."

"Good point," Angus agreed. "And maybe even cyclical, if the Buddhists are right about worlds coming in and out of being. It's simply one view of evolution, Jimmy. And it all started here at Arthur's Seat. Hutton's findings led to a chain reaction in the world of science. The way we date the Earth shifted away from the old system found in the Bible. In many ways, the current scientific view of how man sees his place in the world began at that spot where James Hutton first studied geological strata." Angus pointed again to the sedimentary outcropping. "Hutton's discoveries made Arthur's Seat one of the most important geologic memorials to modern-day science. Arthur's Seat is the place where humanity *stopped the world.*"

"This is an interesting geology lesson," Winston said. "I never thought of evolution in this way. Our reality is the evolving Manifestation of God."

"There is a geography lesson here as well. Do you remember the lines on that plaque on the summit marker?" Angus prodded.

"Yes," Winston replied.

"Jimmy, all of the landmarks pointed to on that plaque are aligned with astronomical events on the horizon. It is possible the forgotten community that once lived on this mountain–hill consisted of a cult of ancient priest-astronomers. When you settle this far north, you begin to wonder at the majesty of the Northern Lights. Beneath this sky, you can think as high as the stars. I believe that the summit of Arthur's Seat served as an ancient observation point which was aligned to the various geographic features, as denoted on that plaque. If you sit up there on the right night of the year, the heavens will appear to revolve around those geographic points of reference on the horizon like a gigantic clock. The whole landscape to the north, to the south, to the east, and to the west—the four cardinal directions—is a vast astronomical observatory that's six hundred times larger than anything at Stonehenge."

Form following function. Winston nodded. "So it's aligned to the positions of the rising and setting sun, around a pentagram."

"Like Rome and Jerusalem," Susan added, "another commonality."

Angus pointed in the direction of the southern horizon. "I believe this astronomical site was connected to an ancient line of longitude that the Roman road builders once used to survey the British Isles. This is an ancient prime meridian, the rose-line. It was once the main rose-line for navigation throughout the British Isles. The current Royal Observatory of Edinburgh at Blackford Hill, as well as the old Playfair on Carlton, lies adjacent to that old rose-line."

"So this ancient meridian that passes through the summit marker at Arthur's Seat was like the Greenwich meridian we have today?" Winston asked.

"Exactly. Much of the old work at the Royal Greenwich is now carried on at the ROE. Edinburgh's old prime meridian runs through Playfair's East wing. That meridian dates back to the mid-1200s."

Observatories near prime meridians, Winston thought. *More commonalities.*

"And the land surrounding Arthur's Seat serves as an interconnection between heaven and Earth?" Susan connected.

"Or heaven on Earth," Winston remarked. *Rome and Jerusalem.*

"But, what about that skull?" Susan reminded.

"We need to get back to my library," Angus said with forbearance as they continued their informative jaunt down the Radical Road.

AN HOUR AND FORTY-SEVEN minutes later, Angus and his guests arrived at his home at Number 6 Easter Road.

Winston glanced up at the Gothic letters chisled into a granite arch above the front door of the weathered brick Victorian remnant of the nineteeth century. He smiled.

ILINGU - STOP YOUR WALKING, TRAVELER, AND ENTER THIS SACRED TEMPLE

"This way." Angus ushered them through the foyer and into a vaulted antique space lined with wall-to-wall bookcases laden with remarkable stories silently sleeping on the shelves. Open books were strewn across a sixteen-foot-long, solid oak table at the middle of the room. Tall piles of books, bundles of manuscripts, and rolls of untitled folios were hoarded in all four corners. The old floorboards sagged and sprang as Angus tread across the room and stopped beside a four-foot-tall brass orrery next to a walnut display case filled with his butterfly collection. "*Shu—* Ailuros." Angus coaxed his lazy Persian cat off of papers laying on the table.

Meow— Ailuros leaped onto the display case. A watchful mouse scurried over the floor like a schoolboy late for class and took cover behind a stack of books.

"I have it here somewhere." Angus began pulling materials from a nearby shelf.

Susan picked up a book from the table. "James, you've been out done," she whispered. "I like Angus. He reminds me of a wise, old owl."

Winston removed his sunglasses and panned the library, marveling at the extensive collection. He took a deep breath and inhaled a stale scent that almost burned his sinuses—the smell of old books. For some people that smell could almost make them gag, but for a bookworm like Winston, it was the sweet smell of perfume.

"Umm … I smell the fragrance of reason," Winston said, eyeing a sign printed in bold, red script that hung askew on a wall. With an inward chuckle, he read a medieval curse to any would-be bibliomaniacs with sticky fingers.

Caveat Lector
**Steal not these books, my dear worthy friend,
for fear the gallows will be your worthy end;
Up the ladder, and down the rope,
there you'll hang until you choke;
Then I'll come along and say,
'Where's my book you stole away?**

Susan peeked up at the epigram and gingerly placed the book back on the table.

"It's on this shelf," Angus recalled. "If only I can remember where I put it." He slightly kissed the ribbon on his finger.

"You have an impressive library, Angus. I hope your memory is not as dusty as these books." Winston scrolled his finger over the dusty, red leather cover of a large book sitting on the end of the table, leaving an after-image of a fish-shaped eye below a hand-tooled ornamentation of an eagle grasping a snake in its mouth, now with the vague outline of a fish clutched in its talons. "You have a lot of old books here. That's a lot of knowledge."

"A room without books is like a body without a soul. I have many rare books, Jimmy. I cannot live without books. I'm an amazon for books. I live for my collection. I'm constantly reading. 'The man who does not read good books is at no advantage over the man who can't read them.' Sometimes I sit and weep because I have not read all the volumes." Angus patted his hand on top of a five-foot-tall stack of books in the corner. "A few of these books where given to me by close friends from the Lotos Club in New York. They're even registered at bookcrossing.com. You always make a new friend when you share a book. Jimmy, I have one here, somewhere, that I wish to share with you. If only I can find it."

Angus slid books in and out of the shelves as he searched for a specific title. *"The Way to Bliss,* no.... *Plato's Republic,* no.... *The History of Hell,* no.... *Principles of Psychology,* no.... *Hidden Symbols in Art,* no.... *The Masks of God,* no.... *Cosmographiae Introducti,* no.... *The Goat Foot God,* no.... *Anarchy, State and Utopia,* no.... *The God of the Machine,* no.... *Dragonology for Children,* no.... *Bear on a Bike,* no.... *Everyman,* no.... *The Dragons of Eden,* no.... *Social Theory and Modern Sociology,* no.... *Mapping the Mind,* no.... *The Transmitter to God: The Limbic System, the Soul, and Spirituality,* no.... Palmer's *The Desert of the Exodus,* no.... *Mumbo-Jumbo,* no.... *Visible and Invisible,* no.... *Religio Medici,* no.... *Psychic Battlefield: a history of the military-occult complex,* no.... Cassirer's *The Myth of the State,* no.... *Labyrinths: The art of interactive writing and design,* no.... *Idiot's Guide to the Bible,* no.... *Gospel of the Flying Spaghetti Monster,* no.... *The Origin of All Religious Worship, The Origin of Constellations,* no.... *Bellum Civile,* no.... *The Kingdom of the Cults,* no.... *When Scotland was Jewish,* no.... *The Candle of Vision,* no.... *The Dream Pool Essays,* no.... *On the Magnet,* no.... *Principles of Political,* no.... *Le Totémisme aujourd'hui,* no.... *Myths of Light,* no.... *Magic Eye Beyond 3-D,* no.... *American Religion: Emergence of the Post-Christian Nation,* no.... *Die Mneme,* no.... *A History of Christian Thought: From its Judaic and Hellenistic Origins to Existentialism,* no.... *Vicariousness and Authenticity: The Robot in the Garden,* no.... *World Holiday and Time Zone Guide,* no.... *Myth & Christianity: An Inquiry Into The Possibility Of Religion Without Myth,* no.... *Metaphors We Live By,* no.... *Devil in the White City,* no.... *Elementary Forms of Religious Life,* yes, no.... *Supplementum Magicum,* no.... *De optimo senatore,* no.... *Origins and History of Consciousness,* no.... *Jitterbug Perfume,* no.... *New View over Atlantis,* no.... *Book of Birds: Religious Track Society,* no.... *Bibliotheca Historica,* no.... *Inventio Fortunatae,* no.... *Walden, 15 essays including "Civil Disobedience,"* no.... *Bulfinch's Mythology,* no.... *The Chymical Wedding of Christian Rosencruz,* no.... *Nineteen Eighty-Four,* Well...? No. *Marking Time: The Epic Quest to Invent the Perfect Calendar,* know.... *Scotorum historiae a prima gentis originae* ... Ah ... Here it is! Henry Maule's, *The History of Scotland.*"

Slam— A puff of dust flew up as Angus plunked the heavy book to the table.

"Jimmy, what do you normally think of when I say, Scotland?"

"Fine whiskey." Winston grinned. "Perhaps an aged Belhaven."

"Well, no doubt. However, when I think of Scotland, I think of a country that has harbored many of the oldest schools of learning in Western Europe."

Angus opened the book and pointed to a faded illustration of King David the First of Scotland. "Long before the great academies of Renaissance learning were created in Florence, Venice, and Milan, King David the First, who was the eighth Earl of Huntingdon and the ninth son of Malcolm Canmore, established an extraordinary university that served as one of Europe's greatest mystery schools. All sorts of religious and academic texts were acquired from the known world and studied at King David's special school."

"Okay," Winston said, uncertain of Angus's point.

Angus selected an outdated atlas from the bookshelf, placed it on the table, and opened it to a torn, xanthous-stained, removable topographic map of Edinburgh. "Now, look at this topographic outline of Arthur's Seat," he instructed with a wink.

Winston and Susan moved forward. Their eyes darted and rotated, inquisitively studying the map.

"So?" Susan said, dumbfounded. "All I see is mountain topography."

Angus rotated the book to a different angle. "Look again. Carefully. Think, my dear." He suggestively lifted one eyebrow at Susan and tapped the side of his forehead with his finger. "What do you see now?"

Susan pored over the map again with a steady eye for information absorption. "It's the profile of a human skull!" she said, dazzled by the image. "A lion's body and a man's head. It is a sphinx. Hey, I even see the outline of the wing around the park."

"Splendid, my dear!" Angus praised. "An acute observation ... a symbolic griffin, the mythical guardian of the Tree of Life."

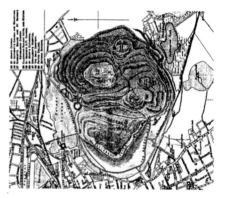

Images inside of images ... a Tree of Life ... a winged griffin ... a hidden tree in Peres's Japanese rock garden ... Billy's Great Tree. Winston retrieved the compass from his pocket and glanced at the engravings on both sides. He looked back to the map of the skull profile of Arthur's Seat. "Hmm ... I've seen bigger," he mumbled. "Its jawbone rests on top of Holyrood. Looks like it's got a head wound."

The one over the Vatican. Susan nodded in agreement. "Yes, what are the odds?"

"God—Angus. It appears Hutton's geology has evolved into the *mind of man*," Winston joked. *But there's more to this ...* His eyes wandered over the map.

"Phrenology," Angus murmured, "the geo-mapping of the skull. Notice how the topography resembles the lobes of a human brain crowned by Holy Rood Park."

"So, is this a natural feature or man-made?" Winston asked.

"Jimmy, if it's a natural feature, then it's certainly one of the world's most unusual geological oddities. No, Jimmy. I believe it's man-made," Angus spoke seriously. "The quarries carved into the crags next to the Radical Road are the remains of one of King David's mining operations. Rocks from these quarries were used to build the old cobblestoned Votadini Road that leads to London. I believe King David intentionally engineered onto the ground this image of a monstrous human skull. See the carved-out notch that forms the bridge of the nose in this skull profile?" Angus pointed. "It was formed in the crags by one of these quarries. Before this site was known as Arthur's Seat, earlier maps called it the *Craggenmarf*, the Dead Man's Rock, the Rock of Slaughter—the Rock of Sacrifice. It's the Hill of the Dead, as in skull and bones." He removed the flaking map from the book and gently laid it on the table, holding down the creases with his fingertips. "There is a fascinating history related to the skull profile on this map. It is believed by some historians that King David created this image from certain illuminations found in a cherished book that he possessed—"

"So this edifice was not constructed by the Celts?" Susan interrupted.

"Well, maybe, my dear," Angus said flatly. "According to local legends this site is called the bearded head of King Arthur. In this case, it's not an image of a skull, but a bearded head. If King David did not create it, then it's possible that someone did create it before him. And yes, that could have been the Celts, the mysterious Picts of Caledonia, the Carnutes, the Gadeni, the Votadini, or the old kingdom of *Y Gododdin* which fell to the Angles of Bernicia."

"A head or a *ros* ..." Susan recalled what Angus had said about the rose-line.

Angus pointed at the map. "It's possible this skull profile is associated with an ancient cosmology. Some mythologies represent the vault of heaven as a great skull. For example, in Scandinavian lore, the skull was a symbol for the seat of the cosmological world. Their primeval creator deity was seen as a father of giants, known as Ymir, a type of Vedic *Purusha*. This giant was nourished by the four milky streams, the four directions of the cosmos. When he died, his bones and flesh became the mountains and the land of Midgard, Middle Earth, and his skull became the vault of heaven. A race of dwarfs, our humanity, grew within his carcass."

"A skull, a symbol of death, was a symbol for a cosmology?" Susan questioned.

"Astronomy," Winston mumbled to Susan, "remember ... Hadrian's meridian runs through the head at Jerusalem—the place of the skull guarded by a dragon. It's more grist for the mill ... commonalities ... Rome ... Jerusalem ... Paris."

"It's mental, my dear." Angus tapped his finger to his temple. "The throne of the I. You stand at the focal point of your own world. Arthur's Seat is the 'seat of thought.' But as I said before, it's also possible that this is not a skull, but rather the profile of a bearded head. It could be associated with Bran the Benedigeidfram, the Blessed One, the beheaded Celtic deity of regeneration—Jack in the Green. Renewal and regeneration were central themes within their way of life. The head of Bran was thought to have a magical quality, like a symbolic horn of plenty. Winston Churchill wrote about the old head cults of the Celts in his *History of Great Britain*, describing their venerations and rituals as a form of ancestor or *father worship*. The skull, since it survives the dissolution of the flesh, was believed by many primitive societies to contain the life force of the dead—the human soul. In the Welsh poem, the 'Spoils of the Annwfn,' King Arthur travels to the Celtic underworld to retrieve the head of Bran. In the story, *Bonedd yr Arwyr*, Bran is a paternal ancestor of King Arthur. Here we have two legends associating Arthur with Bran. In this case, Arthur's Seat could be a representation of Bran the Blessed."

"Father worship?" Winston questioned. *The heads of Mount Rushmore ...*

"Yes, Jimmy. Edinburgh Castle was the first royal residence of King Malcolm the Third of Scotland, the father of King David the First—"

"The King Malcolm found in Shakespeare?" Susan inquired. "The man who murdered Macbeth?"

"Exactly, he was the eldest son of King Duncan I. *Máel Coluim mac Donnchada* was his proper name, but he was also known as *Ceann Mór*, meaning 'Big Head' in the Pictish language. Malcolm is also an Anglicization of the Latin name, *Malcolmus,* derived from the name *Máel Coluim* which can mean, 'Servant of Columba,' as in a reference to Saint Columba who brought Celtic Christianity to Scotland. The name can also be derived from the devotional pattern found in many medieval Scottish names, such as *Máel Ísu'* meaning, 'Servant of Jesus.' It is speculated that King

Malcolm adopted his name from the site he chose for his castle. He was the king of Edinburgh, the king over the site of the Big Head."

"Or the king over the place of the skull, the *ros*," Susan remarked. "So this skull image was created by King Malcolm?"

"The symbol of the head may have served as a warning that indicated the surrounding land belonged to the Malcolm clan," Angus suggested. "But I believe this well-designed skull profile we see here is the result of a public works project carried out by King David the First, who granted Edinburgh the first Royal Charter."

"That's what the inspector said," Susan recalled. "Heads and skulls denote a warning."

"Ancestor worship?" Winston speculated, trying to think ahead of Angus. "The head was designed by the son in memory of the father, like Jefferson's meridian."

"Possibly, Jimmy. But more likely, it's in memory to the Divine Father. The shape of Arthur's Seat is not unique. Your father discovered a similar feature at another mountain."

"He's not the only one," Winston chuckled below his breath.

"Where's that?" Susan asked.

Angus reached across the table and opened another atlas titled *The Lost Wonders*. He turned the pages to a topographic map. "Look at this."

Susan quickly visualized the shape. "It's another map of Arthur's Seat," she moved her finger over the map, "... and with wings?"

"Oh, no, my dear. It's a forty-mile area around Gebel Musa, better known as Mount Sinai, the Mountain of Fire, where Moses built *an altar* and received the law *on stone*, the Ten Commandments. 'And I saw Elohim face to face and my soul was spared!' At the base of Gebel Musa stands the Monastery of St. Catherine. It's one of the oldest continuously functioning monasteries in Egypt. It's a U.N. World Heritage Site. Its library contains a hoard of old religious manuscripts. It's the second largest repository of ancient codices in the world, outnumbered only by the Vatican Library. In fact, the oldest copy of the Greek *Septuagint* was discovered there by the biblical scholar Constantin von Tischendorf in 1844."

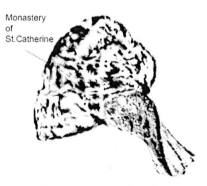

Monastery of St.Catherine

"Who was Saint Catherine?" Susan asked.

"She was an early virgin Christian martyr from Alexandria, who was sentenced to death on the wheel by the Roman Emperor Maximus. Blades were fixed to four wooden wheels, which were set on two axes rotating in opposite directions. However, when this failed to kill her, she was beheaded."

"I've heard that tale before," Winston said.

"Saint Denis," Susan agreed. "Holy heads."

"The story is an obvious cosmological myth for the Wheel of Life," Angus explained, "the axis around which the world spins. But according to tradition, angels took her remains from Alexandria to Mount Sinai, where Eastern Orthodox monks from the monastery found them 500 years later. The monastery was built by order of

Christian Emperor Justinian I around 530 A.D., to enclose the Chapel of the Burning Bush originally built by Helena, the mother of Constantine the First, at the site of the biblical *vision of God*. It was first known as the Monastery of the Holy Virgin. Though it is commonly known as St. Catherine's, its actual name is the Monastery of the Transfiguration. The Greek Orthodox monks transferred the bodily remains of Saint Catherine to various churches throughout Eastern Europe as holy relics. A cult to the saint, centered around Winchester, was brought to England by pilgrims after the crusades. Her skull and hand are still displayed in the monastery. Years later, her spirit supposedly spoke to the virgin warrior, Joan of Arc. Jimmy, your father and I visited Gebel Musa. In a bone-jarring climb up 3,700 hand-hewn stone steps, we ascended to the top of the world where God addresses man, stood before the pillared altar, and watched the rehabilitating sunrise over the distant Gulf of Akaba. The place is ancient. The whole outline of the mountain had been intentionally *burned* into the landscape to produce this head shape in veneration to a God."

"Burned," Susan repeated.

"By the Glory of the Lord … according to tradition." Angus pointed to the map. "This image could be the oldest depiction of the God of the Old Testament."

Pillared altar … Billy at Devil's Tower, Winston connected as he studied over the map. "The face of God in the world." He flashed a thought of Sister Rosalyn. "A winged skull and the wheel of life … Harley-Davidson and Roman mystery religions." He shook his head. "It even has a head wound. I wonder what its jawbone is resting on—"

"Forty miles … it's huge," Susan said, checking her notes. "Nobles said something about Joan of Arc … Meridian Hill."

"Jimmy's father believed the outlying topography surrounding Gebel Musa had been carved away by a pre-Timna Culture as early as 7000 B.C.," Angus added. "He believed that a reverence to Gebel Musa had been stamped into the landscapes throughout Europe and the British Isles. 'Make all things to the pattern that was shown thee in the Mount.' "

"So, Arthur's Seat is like Mount Sinai, a reverence to God?" Winston connected.

"Yes. But, I believe the design of Arthur's Seat holds another purpose." Angus dropped heavily into a man-size captain's chair at the head of the table and locked his eyes on Winston. The chair *creaked.* "Ah … Holy me, the Devil's boots don't creak. Excuse me. It's been a long day for an old man. I'm worn to a frazzle. I'm going to rest on my laurels for a moment."

Angus propped his elbows on the arms of the chair and held the map of Arthur's Seat between his hands. He crossed his legs to keep from being exposed, then bated his breath as he spoke, "Jimmy, let me tell you a tale we don't tell in school."

He glared at the skull profile on the map, thinking where to begin. "A hundred years before the Medici's started their Renaissance from the lost knowledge rediscovered in the storehouses and churches of Constantinople, King David had already acquired certain texts from far-off monasteries scattered throughout the Holy Lands. He became well connected with the nobility of Christian Europe through his mother, Margaret, known as Saint Margaret, the sister of Edgar Ætheling, the uncrowned King of England, whose title had been usurped by William the Conqueror. Margaret supported the Roman Cat'lic religion in Scotland during Malcolm's reign.

At that time, Christianity in Scotland was dominated by the Celtic Church created earlier by Saint Columba." Angus pointed to the map in his hand. "Now, according to one account, King David, who believed everything should be created to a set plan, sculpted Arthur's Seat into the image of a skull in order to duplicate a diagram he discovered in a remarkable codex brought back from the Holy Lands by one of his crusading knights, a certain James Rosal."

"From a codex," Susan questioned, "a book?"

Angus pointed again to the map. "In 1100, soon after Jerusalem was captured in the first of the nine crusades, a group of Italian Calabrian monks discovered a stash of Hebrew manuscripts buried in a cave beneath the abandoned fourth-century Monastery of Martyrius east of Jerusalem. These documents were thought to be among the oldest writings in the Hebrew language and possibly part of a larger library once held at the ancient monastery of St. Anthony's at the foot of Mount Al-Qalzam in Egypt. Part of these writings made their way to southern France where they were studied by a group of Cistercian monks, known as the White Robed Monks, who were experts in deciphering Hebrew literature. The news of this discovery quickly made its way to Scotland and to the ears of King David."

Angus pushed on the arms of the chair and stood up. "Ah ... I'm turning into a stiff, old, cocky sod." He arched his back. It *crackled.* "That's much better," he said and continued. "In the year 1117, a monk at a Cistercian monastery in Troyes, who was transcribing these manuscripts, discovered a reference to a codex containing information that would allow humanity to usher in a divine apocalyptic change in the world."

Stepping away from Winston, Angus cupped his stubbled chin in his hand and bowed his head in contemplative thought.

"Okay, go on," Winston urged.

Angus smiled. "When the news circulated of this discovery within the Cistercian Order, Saint Bernard of Clairvaux, the head of the Cistercian monks and a primary promoter of the Virgin Mary cult within the Church, founded the Order of the Poor Fellow-Soldiers of Christ—the Knights Templar, the guardians of pilgrimage roads. They once held the Temple Mount in their hands. In 1118, the same year the Templars were founded, Baldwin I, the King of Jerusalem, died without heirs, leading to the possibility that Jerusalem could soon fall back into the *hands* of the Turks. So, Saint Bernard ordered this select group of nine knights to travel back to the Holy Lands and retrieve this special codex, believed to be hidden in Jerusalem, to ensure that it would not be destroyed. A Tyronesian monk and shoemaker from Lindores Abbey named James Rosal, a skilled academician, was among this select group of knights who searched for the book. However, Rosal's main benefactor was not Saint Bernard, the head of the Cistercian monks, but rather King David of Scotland, who had eagerly supported the formation of the Templars. His wealthy wife, Queen Maud de Lens of Boulogne, was a cousin of Godfrey of Bouillon, the Guardian over the Kingdom of Jerusalem. In June of 1128, after the Templars returned from the Holy Lands, King David bequeathed to them a plot of land not far from Edinburgh known as Balantrodoch, the first recognized gift of land to the Templars." Angus paused. "The nine knights discovered what they were looking for and carried it back to the Cistercian abbey at Seborga near the French border of northwest Italy, where

Cistercian translators and copyists eagerly awaited. After translations were made, James Rosal, in the company of the two founding knights of the Order, Hugh de Payen and André de Montbard, hand-delivered the codex to King David."

Angus looked squarely at Winston with one feathery eyebrow raised. "Jimmy, this sacred codex that the knights presented to King David is called—the *Kabalyon*." Angus pointed to the red, leather-bound book lying at the end of the table which Winston had earlier marked. "Here, I have a copy."

Winston locked his eyes on the book.

"However, it is known by several different names, such as the *Kabbalist Rite*, the *Kabbal Road*, and the *Kabbalist Line*," Angus divulged. "Perhaps one of the best-known names is the *Kaba Lyon*, a manuscript believed to contain the rites of passage used by the first Christian Church. It is believed these rites were translated and copied by Saint Irenaeus from the *Kabalyon* to his *Kaba Lyon* in the late second century. Irenaeus was the Bishop of Lugdunum in Gaul, the old fort to Lugus, which is now Lyons in France."

"Lyons, that's where Interpol is headquartered," Susan commented.

"Yes," Angus affirmed, "the sword through the Earth—their emblem—intelligence gathering. It is a principal crossroads of Gnostic Christian learning to this very day. Ireaneus was a promoter of the Logos theory of the Greeks in his view of a central God rather than the dual natures of God as believed by other Gnostics. A few historians claim he studied certain Valentinian Greek Gnostic texts similar to the Jewish Kabbalah, thus the titling of his manuscript *Kaba Lyon*. Ireaneus was also a follower of Polycarp, a disciple of John the Evangelist, the disputed writer of the book of Revelation. It was Ireaneus, whose works were once honored at the cathedral of St. Denis outside Paris, who explicitly affirmed that Saint Peter had founded the Church of Rome, that its bishops were his successors, and that to the church in Rome all the other churches ought to be subordinate." Angus looked Winston straight in the eyes. "Jimmy, Ireaneus, for all intents and purposes, started the Papacy as we know it today. The *Kabalyon* may very well serve as the original rites for the core doctrine of the first Cat'lic Church."

"*Ka-bal-yon*," Susan pronounced the title. "What does it mean?"

"The Hidden Truth or the *Concealed One*," Angus informed. "Some claim the *Kabalyon* is derived from early Jewish Kabbalic or Hellenistic Gnostic literature. It is written in a mix of Latin, Greek, and Paleo-Hebrew. From one phonetic breakdown, the sounds, *ka and ba,* could be associated with the two Egyptian principles for the life spirit that resided in the physical body and the personal soul that continues into the afterlife—life and death—with *lyon*, a symbol for the sun and the sacred sound of God, the *Aum*. The voice from the other side."

"Torre mentioned the *ka* light of creation." Susan checked her notes.

"So, what sort of rite of passage does this codex deal with?" Winston probed as he thought about the rites of passage used by the Lakota and his own personal search in the Keeping of the Soul.

"The *Kabalyon* is considered a manuscript belonging to a category of works known as *genuzim*—books that should be hidden away as witnesses to a different past," Angus answered. "Part of the *Kabalyon* is thought to consist of a set of special instructions for carrying out a rite of passage for achieving human perfection—a

model, so to speak, to be followed as the correct design for building a perfect society."
Angus placed his left hand palm down on his copy of the *Kabalyon*. "Included in the
codex were zoomorphic and hermetic diagrams which served as a type of map or
pilgrimage route to be used with the sacred texts as a plan for rebuilding a New
Jerusalem. Not just a physical city mind you, but as a type of temple hidden within
every person. One verse of the *Kabalyon* states that, 'The most High dwelleth not in
temples made with hands' but in the 'kingdom within,' as spoken of in the Gospels."

"A new Jerusalem," Susan connected. "Alberti's Rome ..."

"A kingdom within," Winston whispered back. "Christian Gnosticism."

Angus laid the map next to the book. "I believe that the diagrams from the
Kabalyon were used by King David to terra-sculpt Arthur's Seat, next to Holyrood
Abbey, into the image of the skull-shaped Golgotha hill found in Jerusalem. In
addition, I believe that King David attempted to use the diagrams found in the
Kabalyon to rebuild a New Jerusalem here at Edinburgh." Angus pointed again to the
topographic map. "King David was trying to redesign the landscape in Edinburgh into
the Kabbalic-like image of a God here on Earth, an image he saw revealed in the
illuminations of the *Kabalyon*. It is said that the Templars who acquired the *Kabalyon*
performed an initiation ceremony at midnight before an idol in the shape of a cat or a
head, which they called Baphomet. Some believe this idol was none other than the site
of Jerusalem's Golgotha. It's possible the landscape we see here at Arthur's Seat
could be the image of the Templar Baphomet, derived from the illuminations of the
Kabalyon ... serving as a *Memento Mori* ... a reminder of mortality. We are all on our
way to dying."

"Baphomet over the Vatican," Susan hinted to Winston.

Winston nodded. "The Templars, someone's cosmology ... Maybe the
illuminations are associated with the constellations, if Peres is right about Jerusalem."

"But, Golgotha was the site of the resurrection," Susan pointed out.

"And so is Arthur's Seat, my dear. In the late eighteenth century, the medical
school at St. Leonard's, at the foot of Salisbury Crags, was the home of the
Resurrectionists."

"Resurrectionists?" Susan questioned.

"An enlightened group of medical doctors who dug up recently buried cadavers
and performed blood transfusions from animals in hope of bringing the dead back to
life," Angus answered. "William Thornton, the Englishman who designed your
Capitol Building in Washington, studied medicine under the Resurrectionists in
Edinburgh. He also studied architecture and *landscaping* while living here. In his
writings, he stated that on the night that George Washington died, he proposed the
resurrection of Washington using *lamb's* blood."

"I understand they're trying to do something similar in Texas," Winston joked.

"Frankenstein," Susan uttered. "The resurrection of Washington, Jesus! But Mr.
Howard said that Jefferson designed the Capitol Building."

"Yes, my dear." Angus gave her a knowing, scholarly gaze. "King David's grand
plan for Edinburgh later evolved into a grand quest for lost knowledge. Eventually,
artifacts were brought back from the Holy Lands in order to transplant all of
Jerusalem in the Middle East to Edinburgh. The Holyrood Palace and its abbey
received their names from a piece of bloodied wood, splintered from the true cross of

Jesus, which was once stored there."

"Transplanting Jerusalem to Edinburgh?" Susan questioned skeptically. "That's hard to believe."

Angus smiled again, walked over to the bookshelf, retrieved a book titled *The History of Pisa,* and placed it on the table. He opened it to a dog-eared page of a watercolor architectural rendering of the Santa Maria Cathedral in Pisa, Italy. "In the year 1272, just before the Turks regained control of the Holy Lands from the crusaders, all was thought lost for Jerusalem. So a group of crusading knights, on special orders from the heirs of King David the First, began an ambitious project of cannibalizing the hill they believed to be Golgotha. The hallowed ground of Golgotha was likened to the Holy Grail containing the blood of Christ. This soil was the last tangible connection to the life of Jesus here on Earth. Fifty-nine shiploads of holy soil were carried en route to Edinburgh, but seven of the ships on the first leg of the journey were wrecked in a storm near the Greek island of Antikythera. Their grand plan was abandoned, with the remaining sanguinolent-drenched dirt eventually being stored at the Campo Santo cloister in Pisa, the Castello della Magione in Poggibonsi, and the Cathedral of San Nicola in Sandonia. Supposedly, the holy earth at the Campo Santo, the Sacred Field, can reduce a corpse to a petrified mummy in a few days."

The Antikythera mechanism ... Winston thought, *my mother.* "I bet they dug it up from a hill south of Jerusalem."

"Yes-s, Jimmy. You are right. That's where they acquired the holy soil—now the Convent of St. Onuphrius. According to legend, it is also where Empress Helena, the founder of Christian Jerusalem, ordered two hundred and seventy ship-loads of soil removed and carried to the monastery at Nemi and the Campo Santo at the Vatican in 327 A.D."

"Torre said something about holy soil." Susan flipped the pages of her notepad.

"That's a lot of dirt," Winston noted. "Sounds like she was transplanting Calvery to Rome. ... The skull—"

"All of this is true? The holy soil is in Pisa, Poggibonsi, and Rome?" Susan questioned again. "The holy blood, the Lamb's blood ... caught by Mary Magdalene at the cross?"

"Well, not all of it, my dear." Angus laid the map of Edinburgh next to the map of Pisa. "Since the fifteenth century, the sacred earth from the Vatican Campo Santo has been distributed by the Papacy throughout the world, to wherever a special cemetery or church is created. It is rumored that two of the seven lost shiploads did survive the voyage, one landing near Bristol and the other making it all the way to Edinburgh where its holy payload was scattered on the grounds of Arthur's Seat, now Holyrood Park. One account claims the holy soil was stored in a cave at St. Nina, then carried to Melrose Abbey by King David's stepson, Saint Waltheof, who performed healing miracles using the soil. Melrose had been built by King David in 1136 for the Cistercian monks."

"The Cistercians, the monks who searched for the *Kabalyon*?" Susan questioned.

"Exactly. Allegedly, a sacred tree grows at Melrose Abby next to the site containing the soil from the Place of the Skull. Many years later, King Robert the Bruce, who was responsible for the Declaration of Arbroath that declared Scottish independence based on the belief that they were 'people of Israel,' ordered his heart be carried all the way to Jerusalem after his death, so it could be buried in holy soil. But, after the Muslims killed Sir James the Black Douglas who carried the heart back en route through Spain, an alternative resting place for the heart of The Bruce was hastily reassigned to the soil from Jerusalem at Melrose Abbey—where his heart resides to this day. This holy soil is part of a long-held tradition throughout Europe. Bricks fashioned from the holy soil at Pisa have been used in the construction of cathedrals and churches. Souvenirs, mementos, and bric-a-brac depicting skulls are even sold to this day in the shops around Pisa in remembrance of Golgotha."

"You mean where we walked today may have contained the sacred soil carried all the way from Jerusalem?" Susan questioned in disbelief.

"A little holy pixie dust." Angus closed the book with a *slam*. Dust flew off the cover.

"Aahchew!" Susan sneezed.

"God bless, my dear," Angus offered, then continued his story. "With the death of the immediate heirs of King David, the king's plan for Edinburgh was abandoned. The various religious wars and territorial disputes between Protestant England and Cat'lic Scotland during the Scottish Reformation and the Rough Wooing led to the scattering of the king's esoteric library. The only known original full text of the *Kabalyon*, the one held by King David the First, was now lost. And thereby hangs another tale!"

Angus riffled through the book on the ancestry of Scottish kings and stopped at a page subtitled *William the Lyon*. "Some say the *Kabalyon*, along with other holy relics, passed into the safekeeping of King David's trusted knight, Sir Robert de Maule of the ancient House of Panmure, whose family smuggled it to the Americas. One account says it was stolen by Edward I, the Hammer, and carried to Glastonbury in Somerset. Other accounts claim it passed into the hands of the grandson of King David, William I, also known as the Lyon of the Featherstonehaugh clan. It's believed that William's pseudonym was derived from the lion sculptured at Arthur's Seat, but he may have adopted his name from the *Kabalyon*. William the Lyon was married three times, out of which we have the lineages for the future kings of Scotland. His third wife was the Lady Isabel Avenel, who bore him a daughter, Isabella. Isabella wed the Templar Robert de Ros and lived at Featherstone Castle. She later married Robert le Bruce of Annandale, the grandfather of King Robert the Bruce."

"This is the same Robert the Bruce, the king whose heart is buried in the holy soil at Melrose?" Susan tried to clarify.

"Yes, my dear. The lineage that passed through her marriage with Robert de Ros eventually produced six American presidents, which included George Washington."

"Robert the Ros, Robert the Head—"

"The Blood Royal of the Big Head of the *Ceann Mór* clan over the United States," Winston interrupted Susan and chuckled. "I thought the American Revolution did away with ruling bloodlines."

"Are you implying that the lost *Kabalyon* ended up in the hands of George Washington?" Susan asked with a wild guess.

"Not exactly. Look at this." Angus opened a scrapbook filled with newspaper clippings, resting on the edge of the table. He peeked back and forth at Susan as he unfolded a torn, faded article from the *London Globe* titled "Rare Book for Sale."

Susan and Winston stepped closer to view the scrapbook. Eagerly, they listened to a story of an extraordinary sequence of events.

"In 1875, a mysterious book showed up in an antiquarian bookshop in Lower London. This bookshop had acquired part of the old library of Dr. John Dee which had passed into the collections of the noted naturalist Sir Thomas Browne and the occult historian Sir Elias Ashmole, an Oxford man and one of the founders of the Royal Society and English freemasonry. Dee's library, which consisted of over 4000 volumes, was the largest philosophical and scientific library of its kind in England. Even the father of modern science, Francis Bacon, the author of the *New Atlantis* and creator of the scientific method—which is taught in all public schools and universities today—had befriended Dr. Dee and studied at this unique library at Mortlake."

Angus trudged across the room. He pulled another book bound in blue morocco with a coat of arms in flaking gilt from the shelf and opened it. Its worm-eaten, rippled, vellum leaves resembled slices of Swiss cheese falling from the broken spine. "Aging Japanese paper," Angus remarked, holding the book tightly to keep it from falling apart. The title on the cover read, *The Angelic Conversations of Dr. John Dee.* Angus placed it on the table, carefully opened it again, and pointed to a torn etching of Dr. Dee on the first page insert.

"Dr. John Dee was accused of scrying and speaking to spirits and angels, aided by dark mirrors used in catoptromancy and crystalomancy, or crystal gazing. It was said he had the ability to summon the spirits through both and had even invoked the archangel Uriel, the Flame of God. Queen Elizabeth I, his benefactor who modeled herself as the new virgin goddess-queen over the world—the Protestant replacement for the Cat'lic cult to the Virgin Mary—was highly interested in the ancient texts that dealt with such things. So she ordered Dr. Dee, like a curious thief, to gather every text and manuscript from every church and monastery throughout Scotland and England, supposedly in search of King David's lost *Kabalyon*. It is said that Dee even acquired a rare powder dug up from a bishop's crypt in Wales—"

"Some holy soil?" Susan speculated.

"Perhaps." Angus continued, "Elizabeth sent Dee to continental Europe in search of a copy. It is known that while Dee was in Antwerp, he acquired similar texts to the *Kabalyon*, such as the *Steganographia* and the *Book of Enoch*, which some say contained an unknown language based on rituals written on stone tablets that the angel Uriel hand delivered to Adam in the Garden."

"The *Steganographia?*" Winston questioned. "I'm familiar with that. But, a lost *angel* language spoken in the Garden of Eden … That sounds a little off base."

"Dr. Dee created an Enochian alphabet from these books, which he referred to as an angelic language composed of an alphabet of twenty-one letters," Angus informed.

"So, this angel language was a type of code?" Winston guessed.

"Yes, Jimmy. There are even stories of similar texts containing an unknown language, such as the *Sepher Raziel*, a book of seven parts that the angel Raziel delivered to Adam after Adam's expulsion from Paradise."

"A language delivered to Adam … This Dr. Dee sounds like that Jesuit scholar Torre talked about. What was his name?" She flipped through her notes. "Kircher."

Angus looked surprised at Susan's remark. "Dr. Dee was not some sort of crazed magician. He was a well-connected scholar who was way ahead of his time. He was considered England's principal philosopher and mathematician. He held close ties with other scholars on the continent, such as the Jesuit and Utopian thinker Francesco Pucci, who was interested in Dee's experiments with crystalomancy."

"Crystalomancy," Susan repeated. "Experiments in crystal gazing?"

"Gazing at a skewstone," Angus said. "Pucci was from a family of scholars affiliated with the banking houses in Florence. Dee was also a close friend of the Flemish cartographer, Gerardus Mercator. Dee was very interested in the new techniques used for mapping the world around polar coordinates. While teaching in Paris, Dee became acquainted with the French mathematician and Kabbalist, Oronce Fine. Dee and Fine visited the armillary sphere exhibited at the cathedral of St. Denis. At that time, it was considered the most accurate model of the known universe."

"Armillary sphere ... St. Denis ... stained-glass windows ... Heaven on Earth," Susan remarked in a whisper. "The Tekton."

Winston nodded.

"Fine, like Dee, was interested in creating an accurate map of the world," Angus said. "He is best known for his work in cartography and optics. From his study of math and logic, Fine created the Glass Bead Game."

Susan lifted a quizzical eyebrow at Winston. "The Glass Bead Game."

Winston smiled coolly. "Commonalties, the game of logic."

"Like the Bar Kokhba Game of Twelve Questions," Angus compared, "Fine's game allowed its players to visualize through *connective analysis* the relationships between common words and processes for logic building. The Nobel Prize-winning writer, Herman Hesse, called the Glass Bead Game an age-old metaphor for the *Divine Lila*—the Game of Life. Dee used the game in his alchemy experiments. There's even a diagram of it in this book." Angus thumbed through the pages. "Ah ... where is it? Here it is." He stopped at a page covered over by a powdered, purplish fungus. Angus lowered his face to the book, puckered his lips, and blew across the page. A wave of organic residue receded into the gutter between the pages, and a faded diagram of crisscrossed circles and lines rose to the surface. "Look. See."

Winston and Susan peered at the diagram.

"Snakes and ladders," Winston considered, "a design for a mandala," *Billy at the medicine wheel,* he flashed a thought. *Or a server diagram for the Internet—the pathway for the virus ... Lullus's image of God ...*

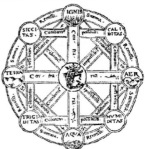

Susan pointed, stirring her finger in a circle around the diagram's connected networks. "*Ignis, Aer, Terra, Aqva*— Fire, Air, Earth, and Water. What's the relevance of that image at the center ... a fish with a crown on its head?"

"Empedocles's four essential elements: hydrogen, nitrogen, oxygen, and carbon," Angus commented, then added, "a fish king, like the Merovingian kings of France. No, I believe it's the head of a leviathan, the God of Forces, my dear."

"A leviathan?" Susan questioned.

"It's the old sea serpent, found in the Babylonian poem, the Epic of Creation, which describes the ongoing battle between the grandmother, Tiamat, and her grandson, Marduk, who guards the Tables of Destiny. It's a creation mythology which deals with the ongoing battle of the human consciousness as humanity tries to understand the workings of the chaotic aspects of nature. It's possibly the original creation story from which the Garden of Eden mythology was derived, where the serpent is associated with the Trees of Life and Knowledge. In the Epic of Creation, Tiamat is depicted as a dragon with enormous wings. As a dragon, she is able to live under the water, walk on land, fly in the air, and breathe fire."

"Water, earth, air, and fire, the four elements," Susan summed up, "… Goat."

"Exactly, as found in the *Vastu Shastra*. The leviathan-mother-creator rules over the four elements in nature—the building blocks for a reality. She rules over the Tree of Life. And this logic wheel of the Glass Bead Game is like a Tree of Knowledge."

"More Lullus-logic," Susan said.

"A tree of knowledge, an Internet server diagram," Winston commented, "the Table of Destiny."

Angus closed the book and continued his informative lecture. "Dr. Dee was also involved in the first English colonization of the New World."

"How's that?" Winston asked.

"Dr. Dee was associated with Sir Walter Raleigh. Dee taught mathematics and other disciplines to the Kabbalist Thomas Harriot, who served as Raleigh's principle astronomer, cartographer, and navigator. Harriot is best remembered for teaching navigation to the fledgling British navy. He was a noted naval architect and engineer. He was also responsible for creating many of the symbols and notations used in modern-day algebra, the math of the relations of relationships. Many have called Harriot the best mathematician that England ever produced. He studied optics and discovered the laws related to the refraction of light. He built a working telescope for observing the moon years before Galileo. Harriot's fame exceeded that of Dr. Dee. Most historians agree that Harriot was the mastermind behind Raleigh's explorations in the New World. I have a picture of him somewhere." Angus thumbed through another book. "Yes, here it is. Look."

"He resembles the illustrations I've seen of Shakespeare," Winston compared.

"Prospero in Shakespeare's *The Tempest* was based on Harriot," Angus said.

Susan checked her notepad. "Howard said Jefferson had a copy of Harriot's book."

Angus's eyes widened at Susan's comment. "Harriot and Raleigh were part of a secret society known as the School of Night, which included the likes of Sir Francis Drake, Christopher Marlowe, Richard Baines, and Ingram Frizer. This Elizabethan illuminati was a well-connected group of English scientists and elite thinkers who set the course for the future of the British Empire. They met outside London at the Earl of Northumberland's house, called New Syon."

"New Sion?" Susan questioned Angus. "Like King David's plan for Edinburgh?"

"Yes, my dear, a New Jerusalem, derived from the icons found in the *Kabalyon*. The Earl, known as the 'Wizzard,' Harriot, and Raleigh were the principal players of the cabal. Harriot, by way of his acquaintance with Dr. Dee, may have seen the *Kabalyon*. Harriot worked for Raleigh in the measuring of the God Longitude."

"The God Longitude," Susan repeated, her eyes narrowing.

"It's a longitude located seventy-seven degrees west of Greenwich, the birthplace of their new virgin queen," Angus clarified. "The Greenwich Observatory was designed by England's Leonardo, Robert Hooke, a colleague of Newton in the field of optics. He postulated the first wave theory for light. Hooke worked with telescopes and microscopes and coined the term 'biological cell.' After the Great Fire of 1666, he oversaw the new survey of London—modeled after the Champs-Élysées in Paris. He even designed the dome of St. Paul's. He was a close friend of Christopher Wren who planned every crooked alleyway for the New London."

"Hooke ..." Winston said, "Huygens's pocket watch ... my experiment—"

"Seventy-seven degrees ..." Susan thumbed through her notes. "That's within a minute of the meridian at the Jefferson Stone."

Winston's eyes widened. "Angus, tell us more about this God Longitude."

"Jimmy, the colony at Roanoke in the Carolinas was established for several reasons. First, the colony allowed England to lay claim to lands in the New World. Second, it allowed the English to explore the resources of America. But the location of the colony was also chosen because of its approximate latitude and longitude. Jimmy, this is technical, so you need to listen carefully."

"Okay, I'm all ears, Angus," Winston urged.

"The colony served as a base for the scientific observation of a pair of solar and lunar eclipses in 1585, for measuring a correct line of longitude at seventy-seven degrees west of London so that England could establish a more accurate calendar."

"A calendar ... they sailed across the Atlantic Ocean to establish a calendar?" Susan asked Angus in disbelief.

"Yes, my dear. From the fifteenth century, the Papacy had been obsessed with predicting the date of Easter far into the future. After the Vatican declared their 1582 Reform Proposal for a new Christian calendar for all of Europe, Protestant England responded by proposing its own Christian calendar. This was a project initiated by both Dr. Dee and Harriot, who believed such a calendar, measured from a precise astronomical meridian, would aid in establishing a practical form of navigation at sea. The meridian chosen for calculating their new calendar was located seventy-seven degrees west of London. Their proposals were later promoted in 1645 by the astronomer, mathematician, and expert in Oriental languages, Dr. John Greaves. You know your father studied Greaves's letters about his explorations in Egypt."

"Mr. Howard said something about the seventy-seventh degree meridian." Susan consulted her notes. "Related to ... no ... it was Ranger Nobles ... something about Port Royal." She flipped the pages of her notepad. "Laystone."

"Yeah, the *Logique Port-Royal* is an old book that deals with logic building. My father gave me a copy," Winston recalled. "It's in my library."

"I know of that work," Angus agreed. "The *Grammaire generale et raisonnee de Port-Royal,* the royal art of thinking. It was published in 1662, I believe. It was one of the first books on the philosophy of logic used in the European educational system in the nineteenth century. It was an anonymous publication, possibly edited by the Jansenist Antoine Arnauld. The *Port-Royal* promoted the Cartesian philosophy of categorizing the world around proper organization, through the mapping out of one's reality around boundaries and coordinates. The Cartesian view encouraged the coordinating of space as applied to national boundaries, trading zones, and sea charts, as the proper way to define and artificially represent the real world."

"Bureaucratic and structured," Winston remarked.

"Well organized, Jimmy. The Cartesian coordinate system is used in the study of geometry and architecture. This system was important in the development of calculus. Calculus is used to calculate the longitude and latitude grid that maps the planet."

"Yeah, geometry and calculus ... Huygens used the term *catenary* in his geometric explanation of the focusing of light," Winston added. "But, when I hear the term Cartesianism, I think of mapping out your mind. I thought Cartesianism deals with the separation of the mind from the body, so that the mind could be better understood, void of interferences from the physical world."

"Yes, it does Jimmy. Cartesianism is a type of philosophy. Since the popularization of Christian humanism in the fifteenth century, most Europeans believed that man was the work of a creator and had been installed at the center of the world, as the caretaker over the garden of paradise. Man stands at the center of his universe—his garden. Man, like Adam with his opened eyes, sees the world from his own point of reference. Man, as the gardener, naturally seeks security in his garden by creating a well-ordered life. For example, the biblical account of the naming and categorizing of the plants and animals is a Cartesian way of applying logical order to the world. It is a way of imposing an orderly system over nature's chaos, so that man can find security within himself. Man's ordered reality is ultimately a product of man—to the point to where man can almost become godlike—as the creator of his own reality." Angus paused.

"Okay, go ahead, make my day," Winston urged.

"Cartesianism expands on this notion. It is a philosophy based upon the enlightened rationalism of René Descartes, who followed the dictum, *cogito, ergo sum*, 'I think, therefore I am.' A person's own thoughts are his primary reference for finding truth, because a person's thoughts determine his reality for the world around him. For Descartes, the design of the real world is a clockwork product of the mind of man which can be geometrically mapped logically around Cartesian coordinates."

"I slam, therefore I am," Winston punned. "I never stop thinking."

Angus chuckled. "Following this philosophical view, subjective truth could hold a higher and more important epistemological place than mere objective truth. In a phenomenalistic example, is this book laying on the table really a book? Or is it the remains of a tree? Or is the book an artificial representation of someone's thoughts? Is the book simply the invisible made visible through an artificial reality? How we see things depends on our personal perception of reality. Our concept of truth originates from within our minds, the *first cause* for understanding a reality. This philosophical view can be very metaphysical."

"A changing reality derived from the knowledge of the observer. Your Necker cube," Susan said to Winston.

"Nevertheless," Angus added, "the Jansenist, Antoine Arnauld, pointed out a flaw in the dependency on one's self as the First Cause in determining one's reality."

"How's that," Winston asked, "besides a big ego?"

"Sometimes we must rely on a greater power beyond ourselves, Jimmy. The man who oversees the garden by way of only his own eyes and his own design must not forget who created the garden." Angus raised his ribboned index finger upward. "Mathew 6:33, 'Seek first the kingdom of God.' Arnauld used the *Port-Royal Logic* to produce a set of proofs to back up his belief that a person's view of reality first depends upon an understanding of his God. According to Arnauld, a person cannot clearly and distinctly understand *his true* reality until he achieves a clear and certain knowledge of the existence of *his* God. Thus, a person using only his own thoughts cannot be a clear and distinct thinking being, since a person's knowledge of his reality depends on his knowledge of an existing God."

"So, Arnauld was saying that you need to clearly understand the attributes of your God before you can truly understand your place in the world," Winston tried to clarify. "My friend Billy calls it an understanding of your cosmic center."

"Exactly, but even Arnauld may have overlooked an important point."

"And what is that?" Susan questioned.

"God's hand is in everything, my dear. God is the only agent of change. Perhaps the order which man creates is the natural intent of God, regardless of man's understanding of God. Man, as an instrument of God, could be a part of a greater plan that he doesn't need to, or is even capable of, understanding."

"Lullus-logic," Susan blurted below her breath. "Michelangelo's brain scan again. God is the First Cause?"

Angus smiled at Susan. "It's simply a philosophical lesson hidden within the creation story in the book of Genesis."

Ding, ding, ding ... Susan's phone chimed. She checked the readout. "It's a text message from Dr. Bains. He wants us to report in immediately," she said to Winston.

"Bains will have to wait. Angus, can you tell us more about the God Longitude?" Winston probed forward.

"Of course! In 1585, no one knew the true diameter of the world. In addition, no one knew their exact longitude at sea. Everything was a guess. Knowing the correct longitude at sea was crucial to navigators involved in maritime trade. So, in 1675, King Charles II of England founded the Royal Observatory to solve the problem of determining longitude at sea. By observing the correct relationship between the cycles of the sun, the moon, and the Earth, a person can calculate his relative location on the planet to an imaginary grid of longitude and latitude. Traditionally, sailors determined their longitude using the Lunar Distance Method. They could observe the moon's position relative to the stars and compare their observations to lunar tables compiled by the Royal Observatory at Greenwich. For every fifteen degrees of longitude that one travels east or west of Greenwich, the local time jumps one hour ahead or one hour behind. Therefore, if you know the local times at two points on the Earth, you can use the difference between those points to calculate their distance in longitude east or west from Greenwich."

"So the moon can be used to calculate distances along the Earth's surface," Susan summed up.

"Yes, but there are other ways to calculate longitude between two points on the Earth's surface. Based on the believed diameter of the planet, you can calculate the longitudinal distance between two points on the surface by referencing a common point in the night sky. This was done by the English in 1677, when observations of the transit of Mercury were used to determine the longitude at Port Royal in Jamaica, which passed through Charles II's holdings in the Carolinas. Because a transit can be seen from different places on the Earth, it is possible to triangulate a true longitude position from the center of the Earth. This observation made Port Royal the primary point of reference for navigation at sea. When John Harrison tested his first sea clocks, the known longitude at Port Royal was used as a reference. Thomas Harriot had attempted a similar study from the Roanoke Colony in 1587 using observations of the eclipses of the sun and moon which were not as accurate as a transit of a planet."

"I know about Roanoke," Winston recalled. "I have relatives who live near there. It's an island off the coast of North Carolina. My family used to vacation there. My father and I surf fished near one of the lighthouses. The Wright Brothers flew the first airplane not far from there, at Kill Devil Hills. Roanoke's the site of the first English colony in the New World. The settlers got swallowed up by the wilderness and became known as the Lost Colony."

"Correct, Jimmy. Harriot and his crew surveyed inland to an Indian temple-village known as Pananaioc, a site *they believed* to be connected with the fabled Lost Tribes of Israel. They then explored north toward the Chesapeake Bay where they got lost in the Dismal Swamp. Among the surveyors was the Jewish Kabbalist Joachim Ganz, whose father was a noted German astronomer who knew Kepler, Tycho Brache, and also Dr. Dee. Harriot and his men were hunting for a longitude lined up to a celestial observation which Dr. Dee had computed related to the Earth's correct position in time and space to the heavenly bodies of the sun, the moon, and the eye of the constellation Ophiuchus, the Redeemer—leading some Christain Kabbalists to believe the longitude located the prophesied site of the Second Coming. This singular longitude was considered *the line* where a synchronization point on the surface of the Earth was naturally attuned on the day of the equinox for the next 400 years. This longitude located four such synchronization points on the planet's surface where the equinox positions did not waver beyond a twenty-four hour period. No other longitude on the planet was as precise. Everywhere else on our planet the days always seemed a bit longer than twenty-four hours."

"A synchronization point?" Susan questioned. "The Lost Tribes of Israel?"

"It's the place where the sun, the moon, and the stars appeared to constantly revolve around the true center of the cosmological universe. Many considered the *thirty-sixth* parallel the optimal latitude for these celestial observations. In the 1750's, Arthur Dobbs, the Governor of North Carolina, who had studied Dee's work on the Northwest Passage, proposed building a capital along the longitude in North Carolina, known as George City. Some claim Dobbs even owned a copy of the *Kabalyon*."

"Hell … Howard's compass rose," Susan said, searching through her notepad.

"It's all based on the Saros cycles," Angus explained, "the period in which the pattern of lunar and solar eclipses repeat every eighteen years and the synodic period where the moon makes a complete thirty-day revolution relative to the Earth and the sun over a thirty-three-year period. If you are interested in creating an accurate calendar around a thirty-day month, you need to make your observation from the synodic synchronization point aligned to the moon's changing perigees and apogees. This is similar to the way the ancient Muslims and Greeks calculated their calendars. This is the location on the planet where all of the different types of time best synchronize to each other," Angus noted. "Of course, there are errors in keeping time by using the heavenly bodies. The position of the objects in the sky varies over extended periods. Any calendar will become obsolete if solely derived from the dynamism of the heavenly bodies. That's why we use quartz crystal clocks, atomic clocks, and better yet, frequency combs to keep correct time."

"Frequency combs?" Susan quizzed Angus. "What's that?"

"It's not for combing your hair, my dear. It's the application of quantum optics using individual light particles—photons. The physicists, Glauber and Hansh, came up with the idea. Light beams can be used in measuring femtoseconds, a trillionth of a second, the most accurate unit of time—"

"Susan, it's part of the new light technology we use to secure messages over Sky-Link," Winston tried to clarify. "You remember. Dr. Bains mentioned it."

"Oh, yes." She nodded.

Hidden wave patterns, Winston geared a thought, *Sol-o-Moon ... eclipses ... the Earth in proper balance ... beams of light ... Billy at the medicine wheel.*

"To create a calendar around the correct position of the celestial bodies was to reject the geocentrism still promoted by the Church of Rome at that time," Angus informed. "Dr. Dee, Harriot, and Raleigh, were in many ways, walking on dangerous ground with their new theories on navigation and calendar keeping. All three were later accused of summoning spirits using Dr. Dee's magic and occult mathematics. However, their theories were not some secret knowledge held solely by Dr. Dee. The Spanish, the Portuguese, the French, and certain Vatican scholars had previously formulated similar theories. After the Spanish first settled Florida, they immediately traveled north in search of a synchronization point at an inland location. I know you have heard of Ponce de León's search for the *magical spring.*"

"The Fountain of Youth," Susan replied. "I learned about that in the third grade."

"The old search for the free radicals that might fight off some viral DNA damage," Winston joked. *Like the virus ...*

Angus chuckled. "The Fountain of Youth was simply a metaphor for the search for a synchronization point on the God Longitude. In fact, the first English expedition to Roanoke Island followed the same route used by the Spanish who searched for the sacred spring."

"But why call it the God Longitude?" Winston asked.

"Jimmy, there are a few reasons why it became known as the God Longitude. First, it was *the line* of longitude that denoted a

GOD LONGITUDE

demarcation for the two Americas. It dissected the two continents from Virginia, through Panama—the Quetzal zone, then past Medellin in Colombia and on through Peru on the west coast of South America following the Peru-Chile Oceanic Trench. This made it an excellent point of navigational reference for the New World. It was the zero meridian for the Americas. Secondly, certain Jesuit geographers promoted this meridian as a symbolic longitude that passed near where Columbus first stepped foot in the New World, at the island of San Salvadore, meaning the Holy Savior, thus the nick-naming of the meridian—the God Longitude—a symbol for the Christianizing of the Americas. Thirdly, the longitude passed through Cuba and the old Spanish colony of Jamaica, which later became the primary commercial hub for trade between the Americas and the Old World. The Spanish, and later the British after 1654, used Jamaica as a primary support base for the conquest of the Americas. The Puritan Lord Protector, Oliver Cromwell, who directed the English conquest of Jamaica, referred to this longitude in his Grand Western Design."

"Grand Western Design," Susan jotted in her notepad. "What was that?"

"Cromwell created a plan to destroy the Spanish trade monopoly in the New World by accruing English holdings in the Caribbean, the hub of the two Americas," Angus explained. "Vice-Admiral William Penn, the father of William Penn who founded Philadelphia, commanded the capture of Port Royal from the Spanish."

"Sounds like the precursor to the Monroe Doctrine—" Winston commented.

"Mr. Howard said something about Philadelphia and the *Fry-Jefferson Map*." Susan flipped back through her notes. "Where is it?"

"Jamaica was ceded to England in the Treaty of Madrid in 1670," Angus continued. "Port Royal soon became a strategic commercial hub for the British. It was the seventh largest seaport in the world and the largest English port in the Americas. It was part of the Atlantic Chain of Ports that the British established for their colonies. Many of the original British colonies included a seaport which was part of this chain. The longitude passing through Port Royal served as the primary longitude of navigational reference for this chain of ports along the Atlantic coast. It extended north through the Great Abaco of the Bahamas and on to the Colonies."

"The Abaco Islands ..." Susan scribbled a notation. "The tax haven?"

"Yes, Abaco, an Italian name for the Hebrew prophet Habakkuk," Angus replied, "in the tale of Bel and the Dragon—the fabled guardian of the Temple of Solomon."

"Sol-o-Moon ... Jerusalem," Winston connected. "So the British referenced a longitude at Port Royal in 1670, although a true measure of longitude for the globe was not established until 1762," he stated, remembering what Howard had told him earlier. "Seems like someone put the cart before the horse—"

"You mentioned Peru," Susan interrupted. "The calendar stone ... Doctor Peres told us about it. It's here in my notes."

"Yes. Peru, the home of the potato," Angus said. "When the Spanish settled Peru, they believed that Cuzco was near one of the synchronization points. There is a chain of Peruvian temples that lie near the longitude. In fact, Caral-Supe, the oldest planned temple city yet discovered in the Americas, skirts that longitude. Caral-Supe is as old as the Great Pyramids of Giza. But the synchronization point ended up being a bit too far south over the Pacific. The Spanish settled Lima, once called the City of the Kings, to mark the southern location of the seventy-seventh meridian. Nazca was called the 'Southern Pillar' of a Spanish Empire. So important was this location that Martín de Loyola, a relative of Saint Ignatius, the founder of the Jesuit Order, married a Peruvian princess to unite the bloodlines."

"You said four synchronization points. Where are the others?" Susan asked.

"Lines of longitude circle the globe, my dear. Another is in the Forbidden Zone near the borders of Mongolia in China. The longitude passes through the center of Laos to a fourth point in the Southern Hemisphere, over the Indian Ocean near Australia just south of the Sunda Trench, which caused the earthquake responsible for the devastating tsunami of 2004."

"China," Winston pondered. "Laos ..." *Billy served in Laos.* He fished the compass from his pocket and curiously glanced at the Oriental inscriptions on the cover. He looked back at Angus. "So the Spanish, with the aid of Columbus, established a zero meridian for the New World," Winston tried to sum things up.

"Yes, Jimmy. Columbus knew the exact distance to his destination was 750 leagues along the Tropic of Cancer. On his first voyage, he landed at an island he named San Salvador—the Holy Savior. Some historians claim this island was actually Eleuthera just south of the Great Abaco. Columbus then traveled south to Cuba along the future God Longitude, after which he sailed back to Spain. Jamaica was discovered by Columbus on his second voyage in 1494, where he sited the sun's solstice position to determine his latitude. He named the island Santiago and landed at Port Marie, due north of Old Port Royal, near the future longitude. The whole island was later granted to Columbus by the King of Spain."

"You're implying Columbus knew were he was going," Winston said.

"Exactly. We have to follow the logic. Are we to believe it was a mere coincidence that Columbus set up his base of operation at the center of the future meridian that divided the two Americas? What are the odds?" Angus shook his head. "Of course, Columbus knew where he was going. His voyages to the New World were planned as carefully as an American mission to the moon. He was not sailing for the Far East," Angus said bluntly. "He had his course set for the garden of the cosmological world. He was searching for Paradise. He says so, in so many words, in his *Book of Prophecies*. He even considered himself the new Christbearer, who was to establish the new Paradise for the whole world."

"Columbus was searching for Paradise?" Susan questioned in disbelief.

"Yes, my dear. Early explorers often described the New World as a Lost Paradise. One example is the *Navigatio* manuscript that describes the voyages of the Irish monk, Saint Brendan the Voyager, and his discovery of the Promised Land. According to some historians, Saint Brendan and seven companions sailed the Atlantic and traveled as far south as the Chesapeake Bay. By way of the Dominicans within the Cat'lic Church, many countries were well aware of Brendan's voyage. More than a hundred medieval manuscripts of the *Navigatio* still exist to this day. Brendan is even considered the patron saint of sailors."

"He traveled to the Chesapeake Bay?" Susan prompted Angus.

"Yes. Although it is possible that Brendan's voyage may have been a mere myth associated with a hidden cosmology within the Celtic Church," Angus added. "In the end, the idea of a Promised Land promoted by Brendan's story was believed by later explorers. Many maps before the time of Columbus included an island called St. Brendan's Isle in the Western Atlantic. The English pirate and explorer from Somerset, Francis Drake, who searched for a northwest passage to the Pacific with the aid of Dr. Dee and Harriot, refers to this land above the thirty-seventh degree latitude as the Nova Albion—a New Sion. In addition, members of the School of Night, particularly Raleigh and Hawkins, had studied the legends of the Welsh Prince of Snowdon, Madoc the Navigator. Madoc, who had sailed under the old Welsh banner of the dragon, is said to have voyaged to America in 1170. I've seen Raleigh's letters concerning this at the National Library of Wales."

"A Prince of Wales discovered America?" Susan questioned.

"Possibly, my dear. There were three researchers who promoted the Madoc narrative in order to lay claim that an Englishman had discovered America 300 years before Columbus. First, there was David Powe, who wrote the *Historie of Cambria* in 1584. His book contained an early version of the Madoc narrative. The next was the Englishman, Richard Hakluyt, a noted geographer and collector of rare manuscripts. Hakluyt lived in Paris where he secretly collected information on the Spanish and Portuguese voyages to the Americas. He compiled an important work entitled *A Particuler Discourse concerning Wesierne Discoveries*, which included the Madoc narrative. In 1584, Hakluyt presented to Queen Elizabeth a copy of his *Discourse* to back up the English claim to lands in the New World. Later Hakluyt became a chief promoter of the Jamestown colony under the reign of King James I. That colony was also backed by the John Company, the influential East Indian Trading Company. But the principal promoter of the Madoc narrative was the mysterious Dr. John Dee. In 1580, Dr. Dee presented to Queen Elizabeth a document entitled *The Lord Madoc, son of Owen Gwynedd, Prince of Northwales*. Dee claimed that Madoc's voyage had expanded the empire of the legendary Welsh King Arthur across the North Atlantic, and that the voyages of Madoc confirmed the entitlement of the Welsh to those territories in the New World. The queen, as successor to the Welsh-Tudor kings of England, had a legitimate claim to North America over the claims of other European empires. I have a copy of Dee's document somewhere."

Angus reached high on a bookshelf and retrieved a folder of loose papers. He thumbed through it and withdrew a photocopy. "It's not a good copy, the script is difficult to read." He held it close to his face.

" '... lyneally descended from the blood royall, borne in Wales, named Madock ap Owen Gwyneth, departing from the coast of England, about the yeere of our Lord God 1170 arrived and there planted himselfe, and his Colonies, and afterward appeareth in an auncient Welch Chronicle, where he then gave to certaine Llandes, Beastes, and Fowles, sundrie Welch names, as the Lland of Pengwyn, which yet to this day beareth the same.'

From Dee's reference to the Lland of Pengwyn, or Pendragon, some researchers have speculated that the Madoc narratives were derived from an earlier date and make reference to the brother of the fabled King Arthur, the son of Uther Pendragon, named Prince Madog Morfran ap Meurig, the Cormorant. So in this case, yes, my dear, America may have been discovered by a Welsh prince as early as 510 A. D."

"Pendragon, the head of the dragon," Susan said, "Arthur's Seat in Edinburgh."

"Or Rome, the capital," Winston added. "Jerusalem."

"Madoc's, or Prince Madog's, descendants included Queen Margaret, the mother of King David," Angus noted. "The dragon was an emblem of their lineage."

"You said that Columbus wrote a book of prophecies?" Susan probed.

"Yes, Columbus's voyages were driven more by his personal views on biblical prophecy than his understanding of astronomy or geography. He compiled a collection of biblical passages in his *Book of Prophecies*. Columbus claimed he heard divine voices which instructed him to call for a new crusade to capture Jerusalem. He often wore a Franciscan habit and may have been a member of that religious order. He described his explorations to the new Paradise as part of God's great plan which would result in the fulfillment of the prophecies leading to the thousand year reign, the Last Judgment of mankind, and the end of the world. Columbus used the verses from the Bible to support his claim that there was a land on the other side of the Atlantic. For instance, *Proverbs* speaks of the Earth's surface as being curved and spherical. Columbus would later describe his discovery of the New World as 'the fulfillment of what Isaiah prophesied,' the discovery of the 'Isles beyond the sea.' "

"The Last Judgment ... the end of the world," Winston interjected. "That *Omega* book written by Flammarion."

"The Frenchman associated with the obelisk in Paris," Susan remembered.

"Yeah," Winston agreed, "the meridian man."

"It's hard to believe grade school textbooks still credit Columbus with the discovery of America," Susan thoughtfully commented.

"Every educated person since the fifteenth century knows that Columbus did not discover America." Angus nodded slightly. "Even Thomas Jefferson knew that America had been visited by Norwegians by way of Greenland." Angus reached for a book on the shelf embossed with an ouroborous encircling the scrolled initials 𝒯𝒥 on the cover. He opened it and laid it on the table. "Look, Jefferson says so in this unedited French edition of the *Obervations Sur la Virginie*." Angus pointed to a quotation by Jefferson which mentioned a settlement by the Norwegians.

"This is Jefferson's *Notes on Virginia*." Susan glanced at the open pages. "Mr. Howard said something." She spied a map of an Indian fortification along the Miami River. "What's this? It's in the shape of a lamp."

"It's a map of an Indian effigy mound aligned to the sun and moon, similar to Arthur's Seat and Maltwood's Glastonbury zodiac," Angus replied.

"And what's that in the middle?" She pointed.

"It's a Hanukkah menorah, my dear … as from the Lost Tribes of Israel."

"I've seen that somewhere before," Winston remarked. "A copy of this map is in my father's papers. His compass …" He pulled the compass from his pocket and checked the symbols on its cover.

"Me, too," Susan added. "But where?"

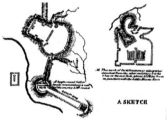

A SKETCH

"Jefferson was fascinated by this effigy," Angus said. "In 1823, he sent Major Isaac Roberdeau, the head of the Bureau of Topographical Engineers of the Army Corps of Engineers, to survey and study these mounds. Roberdeau had assisted Jefferson in laying out the original city plan for Washington in 1791."

"So Jefferson was interested in mapping out earth effigies," Susan said. "But what about Columbus and the meridian?"

"Columbus, like Jefferson, did his research," Angus answered. "Columbus had access to maps which clearly depicted the coastlines of the Americas based on tales from earlier explorers and sailors. Many mapmakers were aware of a land on the other side of the Atlantic. And some did not believe it to be Asia. It is apparent that others had crossed the Atlantic before Columbus."

"Angus, all of this is beyond me." Winston shook his head. "You are implying Columbus had a map that led him to a specific longitude."

"Perhaps he did," Angus said. "There are several examples of maps predating 1492 which outline the coast of America. It's possible Columbus may have had access to a Viking sea chart, or even a Viking sunstone. He may have been aware of a *navigational secret*—which is hidden in plain sight."

"A Viking sunstone?" Winston questioned. "Is that a type of obelisk?"

"No, it more like a compass," Angus explained, "made from a piece of Icelandic spar, an optical calcite, or Norwegian crystal cordierite, both of which changes hues when rotated in polarized light. It has been theorized that the Vikings could have gazed through these crystals at the polarization pattern of sunlight in the sky. This polarization pattern is a natural latticework that covers the entire daylight sky, and is most visible at the higher latitudes. It has been shown that certain spiders use this pattern as a model for weaving their webs. Bees use this polarized light to guide them to a food source. Migratory songbirds follow the intersections of these polarization bands with the horizon to find the north-south meridian, regardless of the time of year.

Angus grabbed pencil and paper from the table and sketched two circular diagrams. "This polarization effect produces two different patterns in the sky. At the sun's zenith, it appears as a series of polarized rings of light and shadow directly overhead, as a circular mandala—like dark halos around the sun. At twilight, when sunlight scatters in the upper atmosphere, two polarization pillars extend into the sky from the left and right of the setting or rising sun and appear straight overhead as a third polarized pillar aligned to the earth's longitude. This phenomenon is barely visible today through our polluted atmosphere. The ancients must have bore witness to an incredible sight—a firmament covered with a *web* of polarized bands and rings."

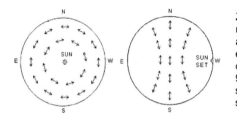

Zeros and Ones - Polarized light oscillates in one plane relative to the direction of propagation. At every sunrise and sunset, there is an intense band of polarized light extending 90 degrees from the sun and passing directly overhead through the zenith and intersecting the horizon 90 degrees to the right and left of the sun. Just as the sun's location changes with latitude and the time of year, so does the alignment of these bands of polarized light.

"Daylight constellations, nature's Outernet," Winston offered a comparison. "Axial and circular—a natural Cartesian geometry for the dome and axis of the heavens." *Natural architectural constructs for cathedral builders ... circles and dashes of dark and light ... bar codes ... zeros and ones ... ouroboros numbers ... Billy's dream catcher ... a giant spider's web....*

"Sounds like Dr. Dee's crystal gazing experiments," Susan added.

"Yes, my dear. This is something that would have interested Dr. Dee. This is the *third way*, which is almost magical, to determine longitude. It is known that Dee invented a special compass for navigation at sea, called the Paradoxal compass, which may have been used to observe polarized light."

"Sol-o-mon ... the third pillar ... a spiderweb in the sky ... best seen at twilight, Winston pondered. *A sun compass ... polarized light ... longitude....*

"Columbus was familiar with the maritime legends of the Lost Isle of the Seven Cities, or Isle of Demons, believed to be located in the Western Atlantic," Angus refocused on Columbus. "It's possible Columbus may have come in contact with *The Friar's Map of America*, dating from around 1360. That map clearly identifies the coastline of North America. Your father studied that map. He believed, like the explorer Thor Heyerdahl, that the Egyptians and Phoenecians had crossed the Atlantic as early as 1500 B.C."

"Good old Dad." Winston smiled.

"Columbus could have been aware of the travels of the Italian merchant Nicolo de Conti through China, India, and Africa. De Conti may have seen Chinese maps of the New World," Angus continued. "According to Chinese records, between 1405 and 1433, the navigator Zheng led China's imperial Star Fleet on seven epic voyages to the lands in the east. They navigated by way of the pole stars. Many historians believe Columbus saw the terrestrial globe created by Martin Behaim, a cartographer from Nürnberg, the home of the Nürnberg Egg—"

"A Nürnberg egg?" Susan questioned.

"A pocket watch, my dear. It was not accurate, since it used a coiled spring as a power source. But, as long you kept it wound, it kept good time. Behaim produced a globe of the known world from the maps of Ptolemy and the geographical theories of Paolo Toscanelli, a Florentine physician, mathematician, geographer and an expert on solar and lunar eclipses who was influenced by the reports from de Conti. Toscanelli even taught mathematics to Brunelleschi and a young Leonardo. Behaim's Globe was known as *Erdapfel,* or Earthapple. Columbus must have seen the Earthapple, because later he wrote that he believed the Earth was shaped like a pear or a woman's breast, with a small mound at the top, a very cosmological view of things. In 1482, Columbus studied the maps and mathematics of Toscanelli who had calculated the circumference of the world. Some of his biographers claim Columbus followed a chart created by Toscanelli on his four voyages. In 1513, the Turkish croptographer Piri Reis drew a map which he claimed had been created from an earlier map used by Columbus. This could have been a version of the famous *Mappa Mundi* presented to the Queen of Spain in 1503 by Juan de la Cosa, the navigator of the *Santa Maria.* And the *Mappa Mundi* could have been derived from Toscanelli's chart. In addition, Columbus was aware of certain celestial phenomena related to navigation. There was a total eclipse of the moon in September, 1494 during his second voyage, which Columbus used to clarify his position at sea. And on his fourth voyage, Columbus was shipwrecked for a year at St. Ann's Bay near the God Longitude, where he used his foreknowledge of a total eclipse of the moon in 1504 to convince the Indians that he possessed supernatural powers. Remember, a lunar eclipse is one of the ways to determine a fixed longitude at sea. It is obvious that Columbus knew about the orbital paths of the Earth and the moon and could predict when and where eclipses could be observed."

"Sol-o-Moon!" Winston exclaimed. "Being able to predict the location of an eclipse suggests Columbus already knew the true size of the Earth—"

"Dipper stars again," Susan interrupted. "Chinese ... What did Dr. Peres say—?"

"Yes, my dear, the dipper stars are at the heart of just about everything. If you cannot follow the stars you will become lost. After the Roanoke colony became lost, a new English colony was established at Jamestown. It was a little further west and a little further north, at a site believed to be the true location of the seventy-seventh degree longitude, derived from Harriot's earlier calculations."

"Howard said there was an obelisk at Jamestown," Susan remembered.

"In that day, the changes in the heavens were thought to signal profound events," Angus continued. "In 1604, Kepler observed a supernova in the skies over Europe. The explosion of this dying star was as bright as the planet Mars and could be seen with the naked eye. Many considered it an omen of good fortune. The heavens had signaled the birth of a New Age. Four years later, in June of 1606, King James I granted permission to the Virginia Company to establish a new colony. On March 18, 1607, the comet we know today as Halley's Comet made its expected seventy-six year return in the heavens—appearing at its calculated position in the middle of the constellation of Sagittarius, the lamp-shaped constellation. For a while, it became the brightest object in the night sky. Many likened this comet to the Star of Bethlehem, the Christ Comet, which signaled the birth of the new Messiah."

"A lamp shape," Susan voiced, "the effigy mound on Jefferson's map."

Angus knowingly nodded. "On May 14, 1607, the Virginia Company landed on Jamestown Island at the same time that Halley's Comet came closest to the Earth. But, the settling of Jamestown may have been more than a mere English endeavor." Angus grew thoughtful. "On the voyage to Virginia, the legendary Captain John Smith was accused of being a Cat'lic conspirator. It's known that Smith had previously visited both the Pope and Father Robert Parson, the man who founded the English Cat'lic college of Saint-Omer. Some historians even believe Smith and a Cat'lic cohort poisoned the colonists at Jamestown before leaving the settlement."

"Omer College ... Nobles said something," Susan recalled, "the Jesuits."

"If you were associated with the Papacy, which many in England despised as the Antichrist, you were seen as a plotter against the English Crown," Angus noted. "Smith was cleared of his charges when secret orders where opened placing Smith in charge of a special mission."

"What sort of mission?" Winston asked Angus.

"Captain Smith was sent to head a scientific expedition to map out Virginia and locate a possible synchronization point along the God Longitude. The colony was ordered to settle between the thirty-eighth and fortieth degree latitudes, following Harriot's earlier calculations. This was the midpoint of the English Virginia Territory extending from the Atlantic to the Pacific. They finally settled at an obscure location, near the site of a previous, failed Spanish colony. Captain John Martin, the companion of John Smith who some say buccaneered with the old sea goat, Francis Drake, founded the plantation called Brandon, a wee bit west of Jamestown, on the current seventy-seventh degree meridian."

"Drake, the explorer with the School of Night ... *Brandon*," Susan pronounced. "Named after the Irish saint? Mr. Howard said something about Brandon ... where they started the survey into the Land of Eden." She consulted her notes.

"No, my dear. It's named after Captain Martin's wife's maiden name. Her father, Robert Brandon, was an alchemist and a friend of Dr. Dee. Captain Martin's father was the Recorder of London, the Master of the Mint, and another alchemist friend of Dee. The Brandon family name is derived from an old manor near Warwickshire—the Brandune, the fire hill—located near the geographic center of Britain. Smoke signals from strategically placed fire hills were once used to mark ancient meridians across the Isles. The same technique for surveying the land may have been used at Jamestown. In June of 1609, Captain Smith and a group of surveyors, lead by Dr. Walter Russell, a doctor of physics, set out to map Virginia and the major rivers of the Chesapeake Bay. Like the magi searching for Bethlehem, they explored the rivers and recorded their positions to events taking place in the night sky. At the same time that Smith was surveying Virginia, Thomas Harriot was studying the position of the moon through a telescope from the lap of Syon House outside London."

"Howard told us about Smith's map," Susan remembered, "with the location of Washington at the center—"

"So the English were simply continuing a previous plan established by the Spanish?" Winston interrupted. "And the Spanish, by way of the Catholic Church, were possibly aware of Brendan's or Madoc's earlier voyages; meaning that the Jamestown colony was just a recolonization of a Welsh or Irish settlement on the Chesapeake. God, Angus, I wonder if the CIA knows about all this?"

"Exactly. Jamestown was not the first colony in Virginia. In 1609, Ecija, a Spanish mariner, entered the Chesapeake in search of information regarding the Jamestown settlement. He reported that the colony was located on the *exact spot* chosen earlier by Lucas Vázquez de Ayllón for a failed, 1526 Spanish settlement. Ayllón's colony, known as St. Michael of the River of the Holy Spirit, consisted of six hundred men, women, and children. A small town was built, including a Dominican church where the first Mass was held in the now continental United States."

"The exact spot," Susan repeated. "Saint Michael, the dragon slayer?"

Or Hercules and Perseus, Winston turned a thought. *Jerusalem.*

"Ayllón, like Dee and Harriot, searched for a Northwest Passage," Angus added. "He believed the Chesapeake river system led to China. It was a belief previously held by Amerigo Vespucci who had sailed as far north as the Chesapeake in his first voyage to America in 1497. The Spanish attempted a second colonization on the Chesapeake in 1561 when explorer Pedro Menendez de Avilés discovered a broad bay which he named *Bahia de Santa Maria,* the Bay of Saint Mary. It was known by that name until 1607, when the English renamed it the Chesapeake Bay."

The Chesapeake ... between Maryland and Virginia, Winston made the connection, *Virgin Mary.*

"During his expedition, Menendez coerced a young Indian prince, named Paquiquino, to travel to Spain," Angus said. "He was the cousin of King Poakiam, the father of Pocahontas, who later befriended the Jamestown colonists. The prince was exhibited like a prize before the royal family and nobles of Spain. His name was Christianized to Don Luis after he was taken to Mexico, where he was indoctrinated into the Cat'lic religion and European culture. In 1562, the King of Spain placed Menendez in charge of a fleet of ships to establish a string of ports that would extend north of Cuba along the God Longitude. Four years later, the Spanish made their third attempt to establish a colony, known as Ajacàn, derived from the Hebrew name *Jacan,* meaning Jachin—the northern pillar of the Temple of Solomon. This settlement consisted of Don Luis and a group of twelve, highly-trained Jesuit priests. It was hoped that Don Luis would seed European traditions into the local Indian culture. Don Luis refused to serve as a pawn and decided to return to his native ways. He organized a revolt against the Jesuit colonists and killed them."

The Jesuits ... the Goat guy ... Susan connected, *Kircher—*

"So, you are saying the Spanish Jesuits tried to set up a colony at the northern end of the longitude, just as they had done in Peru, in an effort to mark both ends of this longitude in the two Americas?" Winston tried to jump ahead of Angus.

"Exactly! But the English beat them to it. Later, many of the major colonial capitals such as Charles City, Williamsburg, Richmond, and Harrisburg were located near this longitude. For example, when Baron Christoph von Graffenried's Swiss and German Palatine colonists settled Virginia and the Carolinas, they found harbor near the God Longitude. Von Graffenried considered a site north of Washington, D. C. and finally settled at New Bern in the Carolinas, directly on top of the seventy-seventh degree longitude. All the principal towns in Virginia and the Carolinas were established near the sacred longitude. It was a primary point of reference for time keeping in the New World and critical to navigation and trade between the Great Chain of Ports in America and England."

"Torre said something about Williamsburg." Susan consulted her notes.

Angus nodded, then changed the subject. "But back to Dr. Dee and the *Kabalyon*, my dear. Dee's library at Mortlake was vandalized after he was accused of practicing the black arts. In fact, everyone in the cabal of the School of Night was accused of being involved in the black arts. Radical thinkers, such as Sir Walter Raleigh, lost their heads from the accusations. The *Kabalyon* and many of the other works in Dee's library vanished as England entered a brief period of religious persecution. It was a dangerous time for anyone searching for scientific truths." Angus closed the book on Dr. Dee. "But it is hard to kill truth with religious zealotry. Dr. Dee was not the only English scholar interested in these types of things."

Angus stepped over to a wooden book pedestal next to the brass orrery and stood squarely behind it. On the pedestal sat a closed book. Angus gripped his hands on either side of the pedestal, but he didn't touch the book. "This is a first edition of Sir Isaac Newton's *Principia*. Newton wrote three great works, the *Principia*, his book of *Opticks*, and a paper on the book of Revelation titled *Observations upon the Prophecies of Daniel and the Apocalypse of St. John*. Newton believed in the forces of history—with a prologue and an epilogue. In writing these three works, he was trying to create a comprehensive system that connected his scientific theories with the known history and the biblical prophecy unveiled in Revelation. Newton believed the universe could be seen as a clockwork with a sun at its nucleus—a clockwork with a past and a future—a beginning and an end. Like Dr. Dee, Newton even formulated a navigational theory using the moon as a practical way for finding longitude at sea."

"Newton studied the book of Revelation," Susan asked, "like Columbus?"

"Yes, my dear, eschatology, the study of the predicted Messianic Age. One might think of the book of Revelation as a sister book to the *Kabalyon*. Both are filled with symbolic images. Some eschatologists have even speculated that the apocalyptic symbols of Revelation were derived from the *Kabalyon*. Newton believed that the book of Revelation was coded by way of certain numbers and symbols presented within the text which laid out the historical sequence of God's timetable for humanity. Newton spent nearly a quarter of his life studying this coded association of words and symbols. He even carried out a special investigation on the holy dimensions of Solomon's Temple as described in the Bible so he could formulate its correct design around the measure of a cubit. His letters on the Revelation are now stored at the Jewish National and University Library. Newton firmly believed there was a lost wisdom coded within the Bible, and that by studying the dimensions of the temple in Jerusalem, he would be able to decode it."

"Peres would agree with that," Susan said to Winston.

"Newton believed the Second Coming would happen after 1865, after the fall of the Beast," Angus continued. "Later, other religious leaders adopted similar views. For instance, the American, William Miller, used the book of Daniel, along with Newton's research, to predict the Second Coming of the Messiah in the spring of 1843 and the end of the world on October 18, 1844. Of course, to everyone's great disappointment, the world did not end. Later, Miller's followers, the Millerites, claimed his calculations were off and the Second Coming would happen in 1848. Millerites were spread out all over the world. The Millerites in Jerusalem eventually united with the Jewish messianic movement formed by Sir Mose Montefire. That movement was the forerunner of modern political Zionism."

"1865," Winston remarked. "That's when Nobles said they finished the Capitol."

"1848?" Susan quickly thumbed through her notes. "The cornerstone of the Washington Monument," she mumbled.

"Of course, no one witnessed the Second Coming in either of those years," Angus pointed out. "Later, other religious groups, such as the Mormons, the Watch Tower Bible, and the Tract Society of Pennsylvania, predicted it might occur within a seven-year period centered around 1886. More recently, other doomsayers predicted the year 2001 and 2012. The Jehovah's Witnesses claim the Secomd Coming should be interpreted as an *unseen presence* which will become known in the visible events of the final days. Perhaps they will never decode the book of Revelation unless they understand the meaning behind the illuminations of the *Kabalyon*. But then, perhaps Newton was in search of something else."

"Something else?" Winston queried.

"Yes, Jimmy. One hundred and fifty years after Newton's death, historians discovered a chest filled with texts on alchemy, Eastern religions, and other esoteric thought that Newton had locked away. It's the same type of material studied by Dr. Dee. It's possible that Newton was continuing an investigation started by Dee. Among Newton's books were the gnostic teachings of Irenaeus, who had owned a copy of the *Kabalyon*. The books in Newton's treasure chest included the hermetic philosophy of Basilius Valetinus and a dogeared copy of Christian Knorr von Rosenroth's two-volume set, the *Kabbala Denudata*, which dealt with the *invoking of the divine* by way of the *purified fire*. Newton stated that, 'the hidden secret *modus* is *Clissus Paracelsi* was nothing else but the separation of the principles of purification and a reunion in a fusible and penetrating *fixity*.' "

"A penetrating *fixity* ... what does that mean?" Susan asked.

"The *solve et coagule*, my dear. The breaking down and recreation of everything in life—the great mystery of Nature's resurrection."

"*Solve et coagule*, where did I see that?" Susan traced her memory. "Paris ..."

"Newton's notes on alchemy were written in a type of code," Angus explained. "Newton may have had access to the *Steganographia* and the lost *Kabalyon*, whose illuminations may have guided him in his attempt to decode the book of Revelation, so he could discover the secrets of the universe."

"Bacon and Newton, they were two of Jefferson's heroes," Winston remarked, mentally filing away more connections. *A circular clockwork ... a beginning and an end ... a purified fire ... and Jefferson was aware of Harriot. I wonder if Jefferson had access to one of the copies of the* Kabalyon.

"Alchemy," Susan repeated, "secrets of the universe?"

"Yes, my dear. Alchemy! The great Golden Game. It appears that Newton was searching for the philosopher's stone."

"The philosopher's stone," she fired back, "found in Harry Potter?"

"It's a code word for the quickening of *white gold* or *quicksilver*," Angus replied.

"White gold?" Winston probed. "Quicksilver?" *The Temple of the Necropolis, the golden orb,* he remembered.

"Yes, but it's not a precious metal, Jimmy. Newton studied the works of the Benedictine alchemist Basil Valentine, the author of *The Secret Fire,* and the French alchemist Pierre Jean Fabre, known for his *Alchimista Christianus* and *Les Secrets Chymiques*. In Fabre's view, alchemy was associated with a deeper mystery behind the symbolism within Christianity. Fabre wrote, 'Alchemy is ... a true and solid science that teaches how to know *the center of all things*, which in the divine language is called the Spirit of Life.' White gold was considered by alchemists such as Fabre to be a pure Light of Life formed within the crucible, the cauldron, a cup that is a holy chalice of stone. This crucible is used to create the illusive *lapis eliker—the purified oil of antimony*—the *elixir* that allows you to *live forever*, like a Fountain of Youth. The process is fully explained in a two-hundred-page, French poem titled *La Lumière sortant par soi-même des Ténèbres*, or *The Light Coming Out of Darkness*."

"To live forever?" Susan darted her eyes over at Winston in disbelief. "Jesus ..."

"Light coming out of darkness," Winston mused. *Light at the medicine wheel ... How old is Billy?*

"The basis of all alchemical transformations required an alchemist to obtain the three keys that unlock the philsopher's stone in order to apply the seven-step formula described in the *Emerald Tablet of Hermes*, the Book of Great Secrets," Angus disclosed. "The philosopher's stone is a stone which is not a stone. Alchemy is about finding the *Sophia* in the mind—a pure enlightened wisdom that *will set you free*. Nevertheless, some achemists believed that a physical transmutation was possible through the fabrication of the precious living stones, the lighting of the ephemeral fire upon the crucible, and the drinking of the *aqua vitae*—the water of life, the *azoth*."

"But what about the *Kabalyon*?" Susan asked. "You said Newton may have read it. Was it in Newton's chest?"

"No." Angus shook his head. He moved away from the pedestal and returned his attention to the yellowed newspaper clippings he had removed from the scrapbook. "What the London antiquarian bookdealer discovered within one of the old library books was a book hidden within another book, wrapped in a false binding. This hidden book was an illustrated version of the *Kabalyon*, possibly even the original once held by King David."

"So the lost *Kabalyon* may have been rediscovered?" Susan asked for clarification.

"Exactly, my dear."

"Susan, Angus." She smiled. "Call me Susan."

Angus grinned pleasantly, then spoke seriously, "Susan, the bookdealer, like a money-hungry colporteur, put the *Kabalyon* up for sale. It is said that the English Freemason, MacGregor S. L. Mathers, who was the author of *The Kabballah Unveiled*, saw the book in 1880 and was given a chance to purchase it. But he did not. Mathers later published a book titled *The Greater Key of Solomon*, which is now considered an important Masonic grimoire. He later helped to form the Hermetic Order of the Golden Dawn and the Order of Alpha et Omega, two of the twentieth century's greatest occult organizations."

"Occult organizations?" Susan lifted one eyebrow.

"Susan, other interested buyers also saw the book. From reports I've gathered, the book was similar to a palimpsest or an abscissa. It is said that the pages of the *Kabalyon* held by the bookdealer had been cut and rotated. Many of the pages and chapters had even been pasted to new positions. The book was totally rearranged into a jigsaw puzzle. However, all of the illuminations for understanding the nature of the

Kabalyon were still intact." Angus quickly shuffled through the newspaper clippings. "It's here somewhere. Ah, where is it? Here it is. Look at this, Jimmy!"

Winston stepped closer.

"A prominent London art dealer, Sir Joseph Duveen, the Baron of Millbank, learned about the book. He made a purchase in 1889 for a powerful and wealthy American architect living in Chicago, the windy city where the birds can really fly."

Angus unfolded a newspaper clipping from the *Chicago Tribune* advertising the sale of a book by Duveen Brothers & Company.

"An architect from Chicago?" Susan questioned. "So the original *Kabalyon* is now in the United States?'

"The architect's name was Daniel Hudson Burnham," Angus divulged. "He was a devoted follower of the Swedenborgian religion. He had previously learned about the *Kabalyon* from Francis Cabell, a fellow Swedenborgian from a respected family of canal builders in Virginia. Swendenborgian beliefs influenced the likes of William Blake, Ralph Waldo Emerson, and William Butler Yeats. Blake's book *The Marriage of Heaven and Hell* was heavily influenced by that religion. All of these thinkers saw a utopian philosophy within the teachings of the Swedenborgian theology. Some Swedenborgians believed that the return of the Messiah would be signaled by the *physical* rebuilding of a New Jerusalem. Daniel Burnham was responsible for several city projects throughout America, including San Francisco, Chicago, and Washington, D.C., the original territory of the United States. He also helped to form the American Academy in Rome."

"American Academy in Rome," Susan said, looking at her notes. "South of the Vatican, near the meridian."

"Certain Masonic organizations were influenced by the Swendenborgian teaching as well," Angus added. "They followed the Swedenborgian Rites adopted from the religious rituals used by the Cat'lic Benedictine Order and created by the Kabbalist, Dom Antoine-Joseph Pernety. Pernety wrote a book titled *The Great Art, A System on the Practice of the Magnum Opus on the Effects of Light*, which described a procedure for invoking the Divine. One of the illustrations found in his work depicts an *eagle* surrounded by the sun and moon. It is possible that the source for Pernety's book was a lection of the *Kabalyon* he acquired in 1783 from the Berlin library of the 'Old Fritz,' Frederick the Great of Prussia, whose grandfather was George I of England."

An eagle and the sun and the moon, Winston thought. *Sol-o-Moon.*

"Frederick the Great was a well-educated, enlightened leader," Angus revealed. "His aide-de-camp was General Baron Friedrich von Steuben, a follower of Pernety's work. Steuben became involved in the American Revolutionary War. He was in charge of training the troops for George Washington. Many historians agree that it was Steuben, and not Washington, who was responsible for the victories during the Revolution. General Steuben created a set of rules of order, called 'Steuben's Regulations,' which disciplined Washington's rough and ready army. Those rules became the basic rules of order for the future American Army. Steuben even drew up the plan for the military academy at West Point, envisioned by Hamilton and founded by Jefferson. General Steuben and Jefferson were friends."

"West Point. I didn't know we did that." Winston grinned at Susan.

"Yes ...," Angus uttered with a puzzled expression. "It's not far from the God

Longitude. After the war, Steuben helped to form the Society of Cincinnati, a society of military elite. George Washington became the first president of that organization. Other noted members included the French general, Lafayette. The coat of arms for that society, an eagle, was designed by the French engineer, Pierre L'Enfant, who was the attributed designer of the city plan for Washington, D.C."

"Mr. Howard said Jefferson designed the plan for Washington," Susan contended.

"I don't know of this Mr. Howard you keep referring to," Angus admitted. "But I would agree … *that* city plan was not designed by L'Enfant." He chuckled as though he knew more than he wanted to say. "The city plan for Washington is simply a version of the *Carta Pisane*, a thirteenth-century portalano—a port to port sea chart centered on the old meridians through Paris and Jerusalem. You can navigate *anywhere* with one these charts. All you need is a compass. Here, I think I have a copy." He reached high on the shelf and sorted through a bundle of rolled up documents. "Look at this." He carefully unrolled a brittle sheet of tracing vellum.

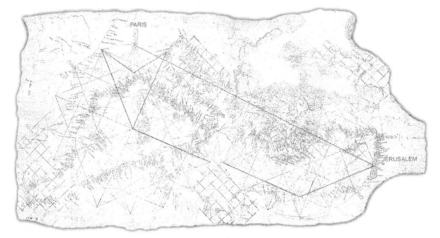

Susan glanced at Winston. "Meridians … Paris and Jerusalem …"

"And pentragams," Winston muttered, his eyes wandering over the crisscross of squares and triangles. He looked up at Angus. "Whaddya know about this chart?"

"Not much, really. It's a true map of mystery," Angus began to explain. "No one is certain how it was created, or who created it. Some believe it is a copy of a chart drawn up for King Louis IX when he sailed to Tunis on his ill-fated crusade to the Holy Land. Most historians consider it a surviving example of the types of charts once used by navigators of the Mediterranean. It's the same type of chart drawn up by de la Cosa—the *Mappa Mundi*."

"So, King Loius IX created the the city plan for Washington." Susan said, confused. "Washington, D.C. is a navigation chart? How did you learn all about this?"

"Jimmy's father told me about it. He said he noticed the similarities between this chart and Washington when he was doing research at the Bibliothèque Nationale. He thought the *Carta Pisane* was connected somehow with the Holy Soil at Pisa. But, back to Pernety," Angus refocused. "Pernety later formed the *Societe des Illumines d'Avignon* in 1786, sometimes called the original Order of Illuminati—the Order of Enlightenment—considered to this day as an *elite* within the multi-billion-dollar international organization known as Freemasonry. Some say it's a hierarchy structured like a neatly encased matryshka doll, with tentacles which extend to the Vatican."

"The Freemasons," Winston commented. "Stone-laying cabals."

"Yes, Jimmy, God's architects—the *Phre Massens*—the Sons of Light. The Masters of the old craft of architecture and *civil* engineering and its technical language of geometry which serves as a cult iconography for rebuilding the Temple of Solomon. It's a symbolic temple, since no one has ever found a Temple of Solomon to rebuild. Many consider speculative Masonry a philosophy which deals with the evolution of man reaching for his liberation through the eternal quest for the self-enlightened human consciousness."

"Alpha to Omega—Evolution again," Winston likened. "But you said that idea came from a Jesuit."

Angus nodded slowly. "Although, there is a legend within the Royal Arch tradition of Freemasonry," he remembered with a sly expression on his face, "which states that Freemasonry is linked to the accidental discovery of a crypt on the site of the Temple Mount in Jerusalem, where certain items where found, in particular, a *book* containing the *original* Gospels as *revealed* by God."

"The *Kabalyon*," Susan said softly.

Angus nodded again. "Some Masonic historians claim that Freemasonry started here in Scotland in 1583 from the stonemason guilds which quarried the mines of King David and built the original castle architecture for our city. Others claim it started in Kirkcudbrightshire, above Whitehorn, the Cradle of the Old Faith."

"The masons who quarried the skull image at Arthur's Seat," Susan clarified.

"Yes," Angus replied. "Some claim the Masonic 'Book of Charges' from Gloucestershire and the Kirlwell scroll were derived from the *Kabalyon*. For many, Freemasonry is merely a modern expression in *brick* and mortar of the ancient mysteries associated with architecture, where architecture serves as a medium capable of revealing a truth that lies beyond appearances. It's a craft of symbols. For example, the Cartesian arch, which uses a wedge-shaped keystone to support an archway, is a metaphor for Plato's view of the human mind supporting the world of reality."

"Michelangelo's brain scan," Susan mumbled, "Plato's cave ..."

"As the craft developed, many Masonic symbols were adopted from the works of the eighteenth-century French pioneer of Greek paleography and archaeology, Bernard de Montfaucon," Angus added. "Montfaucon had studied the esoteric works of Pirro Ligorio dealing with the architecture of ancient Rome and the rituals of the mystery religions practiced there."

"Ligorio ... Torre said something about him." Susan reminded Winston. "The Holy Pinecone and the Goddess Cybele."

"Daniel Burnham was also influenced by the French esoteric views. He was a classically trained architect of the *École des Beaux-Arts* movement and an admirer of Baron Haussmann's innovative design for Paris during the Third Republic." Angus focused again on Burnham. "This well-respected school of architecture was founded in 1648 by Charles Le Brun as an esoteric art school. It later merged with the *Académie d'Architecture*, founded in 1671 by Jean Baptiste Colbert, who established the first astronomical observatory in Paris. Colbert also oversaw the first French explorations into Egypt." Angus pulled another book from the shelf titled *City*

Planning and Ancient Architecture, sitting next to a copy of the *Devil's Dictionary.*
"The *École des Beaux-Arts* was heavily influenced by the old rules of architecture
created by the Romans and the Greeks."

Angus opened the book and thumbed through the stiff marbled paper. The crisp
snaps of fanning pages sounded like bird wings *flapping.* "Look at this, Jimmy." He
pointed to a page titled The Schools of Architecture. "It is said that European
architecture was derived from three primary schools of planning. The first goes back
to the cosmological views of the Greeks who designed their cities as a space to
connect man to the heavens. The second was the Roman application of magical rites
that often connected their architecture to the spiritual world. The third was the Judaic
notion that an architectural plan could be a realization of a Heavenly Jerusalem here
on Earth as an expression of Messianic Hope."

"Magical rites associated with architecture?" Susan questioned, uncertain.

"Yes, magical," Angus acknowledged. "But not in the sense of pulling a rabbit out
of a hat. Roman architecture incorporated design elements which connected man to
his time and space and the procreative forces within nature. Their architecture was
said to invoke an upwelling of an unconscious spirit, or temporal *loci,* within each
individual which allowed him to better understand his place in the universe."

"A temporal *loci,*" Winston equated, "architecture related to time and space …
such as gnomons located on top of meridians." *Or the coordinates in the virus—*

"Exactly, Jimmy. Architecture is responsible for the spatial organization of man's
world." Angus flipped the pages, one too many, then flipped back to the title page of
an illustration of a man's face above bright red letters that spelled out VITRUVIUS.
"Perhaps one of the first widely studied theories on ancient architecture was proposed
by the first-century, Roman architect, Marcus Vitruvius Pollio. Vitruvius was a
Greek-trained master who served under the reign of Caesar Augustus. Vitruvius is
sometimes called the First Architect. It is said that he
headed up Caesar's Roman College of Architects, which
designed much of ancient Rome. He was a follower of
the philosophy of the Ionians and a well-traveled group
of Greek architects known as the Dionysian Artificers.
The Dionysian Artificers believed that temples should be constructed upon the most
perfect form found in Nature. Most historians believe Vitruvius's architectural
principles were used to build the Pantheon, which represented Hadrian's attempt to
construct a temple around a perfect geometric form—that being a circle or a sphere.
It's an obvious adaptation of the tomb architecture of the Etruscans or a Buddhist
cosmic stupa. This architecture is the forerunner for all modern places of worship. The
oculus in its roof was associated with the Roman mystery religions' reverence to light,
time, and space—the temporal *loci*—the symbolic point around which the whole
universe revolved. Light rains through the oculus, cutting through space and slowly
rotating through time as it shines on the squared, coffered ceiling of the dome,
evolving into new dimensional form created out of shadow."

"Teilhard's evolution again," Winston compared. *Billy at the medicine wheel.*

Angus turned a few of the gilt-edged pages to an illustration of an archway with a
keystone. "Roman cosmology depicted the world as a flat square with four pillars at
each corner that held up the dome of the heavens. An adaptation of this cosmology is

found in their design for open-domed temples which represented the natural openings of caves or grass huts with a portal to the sky—and the divine light."

"Like the design for the Pantheon." Winston he geared a thought, *The celestial axis mundi in Jerusalem around the Dome of the Rock.*

Angus flipped the pages to a diagram of a city plan. "Vitruvius based many of his designs for towns and buildings around an octagon shape aligned to the cardinal directions and the eight winds, like a Vishnumedal. This sixteenth-century Vitruvian town plan depicts an octagon superimposed upon a checkerboard grid pattern. This formal ground plan, or *ichnographia,* was the model for the utopian city plan."

I've seen that design somewhere before. But where? Winston tried to recollect. *Rome, Paris, Jerusalem, Washington ...*

Angus pulled a tattered, buckram-covered volume from a 1511 edition of the ten-volume set, *De Archectura,* from the shelf and riffled through its pages. "An example is here somewhere. Here it is. Look!" He pointed to another architectural plan for a city. "The octagon-shaped civic center was the ceremonial heart of the city surrounded by the ancient *terramare* settlements, or columns, in a sixteen-line grid pattern. For Vitruvius, the columns of ancient temples supplemented the groves of sacred trees that represented a garden of paradise, the *Adytum Holy of Holies.* Legend states that these gardens are where the Greeks, the founders of democracy, started their religions."

I remember where I've seen this, Winston connected, *at the temple for democracy.*

"The embellishment of architecture was not always purely for aesthetics," Angus added. "It sometimes honored a deity. Decorative Doric, Ionic, and Corinthian columns were symbols for sacred trees. Like the Wailing Wall of Jerusalem, these columns were believed to hold the actual *presence* of different spirits and djinnis which guarded a special place—the *genius loci.* Ornamentation on a temple not only honored a god, but helped to house the god's *presence.* Classical architecture was not just an art form. It served as a means of invoking the various intangible deities into tangible objects within a world of reality. The invisible made visible."

"Like King David's images in the landscape?" Susan asked. "An invisible idol to a godhead ... in homage to a deity?"

"Exactly," Angus affirmed. "Another example is the *terminus,* a boundary stone inscribed with pictures of constellations or a cornerstone that was sometimes sprinkled with lamb's blood, corn, or anointed with oil or wine. The gods lay deep in the *landscape,* where the corners of farms and cities were bound by terminus stones. These phallic posts marked the boundary of an area that was held divine, as an earthly sanctuary. Every true temple had its *terminuses* anointed. This practice is very old. The Freemasons still follow it. Often a victim was sacrificed in a symbolic sexual rite to fertilize the soil. His blood was poured into a hole in the ground that served as the foundation for the *terminus.* In the book of Proverbs a commandment is made, 'Do not move the boundary-stone nor shift the surveyor's rope, nor tamper with the widow's land-bounds.' The penalty for moving such a stone was a death sentence under Roman law, since the *terminus* was often considered a guardian of Roman territory. So sacred was the *terminus* to the Romans, they had the end of their year, February 23, dedicated to the Festival of the *Terminalia.* The British anthropologist Mary Douglas believed that boundary-stones served as the first symbols for social law. Laws essentially set the boundaries for all aspects of social life."

"Okay, from pillar to post," Winston said as he formulated his thoughts. *Sacred spaces ... the Temple Mount in Jerusalem ... the four corners ... the Little Dipper.*

"A *terminus*, like a grave marker, also represented a symbolic gateway into the spirit world," Angus continued. "The Greek god Hermes, the god of boundaries, was often seen as a phallic pillar, or *herm*, that was set up over a grave to serve as the guide for the dead—the *Psychopomos*—the Divine Herald between the material and spiritual worlds. If a person wanted to leave a message for the dead, he simply spoke to the herm stone at the grave. The herm, as a spiritual boundary stone, delivers your message to the afterlife. It is a tradition that is still practiced by many to this day. Ah ... *le ton beau de le tombeau*, the beautiful tone from the tomb. The herm at a grave is a symbol of the civilized man who honors his ancestors."

"I've heard that before," Winston remarked. "Something Billy said."

"So a herm stone is a type of transmitter?" Susan questioned.

"Exactly, Susan. At the Forum in Rome, a *terminus* called the golden milestone marked the cross-axis of the Roman Empire. The Romans often associated the *terminus* with the deity Jupiter, and erected a *terminus* at the navel of every Roman city along an axis running north to south called the *cardo maximus*."

"We know about the *cardo*." Winston eyed Susan. "Peres told us about it."

"One such example is the Old London Stone hidden behind a gate on Cannon Street," Angus identified. "It's the foundation stone of Trinovantum, New Troy, the original name for London. Even today the London Stone is said to represent the geographic midpoint of the British Empire."

"Similar to the Jefferson Stone," Susan compared.

Angus closed the book and pointed to the other volumes resting on the bookshelves. "The only surviving classical treatise of Vitruvius's work *De Architecture* was unearthed in the early fifteenth century by an Italian humanist in an underground scriptorium at the Monastery of St. Gall in Switzerland. This is the home of the famous Gregorian chant manuscripts by Saint Tutilo, the occult rhetoric texts of the *Istituto Oratoria*, and the first paradise plan for an ideal open court monastery based upon the design of the Temple Mount in Jerusalem. In 1486, *De Architecture* was published by the Medici in Italy, where it became the chief architectural book of reference of the European Renaissance. Vitruvius's theories served as the final authority for Italian architects such as Alberti, Michelangelo, Palladio, and Leonardo, the man who wanted to fly like the vultures."

"No, it was not a vulture," Winston interrupted. "Leonardo based his mechanical glider designs on the flight of bats."

"Bats are not birds," Susan noted. "Bats are mammals. Birds follow the stars in their navigation. Bats follow echoes and wave patterns."

"Maybe," Angus agreed as he opened an oversized art book at the middle of the table which contained drawings and paintings by Leonardo. "In a thesis on Roman architecture, Leonardo drew his famous proportions of the human figure, known as the Vitruvian Man or Universal Man, to symbolize the architectural and artistic theories of Vitruvius. It's Leonardo's enigma." He flipped the page from a sketch of baby Jesus playing with a cat to a drawing of the *Vitruvian Man*.

"I've seen that before," Susan said astutely. "It reminds me of a snow angel."

"It's now embossed on certain Common Market Euros," Angus noted. "It's the most popular secular symbol in the world."

"That artwork is inscribed in stone at the entrance of my home," Winston added. "So this drawing represents *the key* to understanding ancient art and architecture?"

"Yes, Jimmy, but it's more than that. It represents the measurement associated with Plato's image of the Soul of God—the *Logos*."

"The Soul of God?" Susan looked perplexed. "A snow-angel?"

"It's like a *Vaastu Purusha Mandala*," Angus noted.

"*A Vaastu Purusha Mandala?*" Susan repeated.

"*Vaastu* means the dewelling for both humans and gods. It's a Hindu form-being-diagram which incorporates the positioning of the body of the primeval giant *Purusha*—the first man image—

VAASTU PURUSHA MANDALA

with the position of the planets, in the design of a temple space around the cardinal directions, human proportion, and harmonic placement. It orginates from the *Vastu Shastra,* cosmic canons discovered at the Hangseseshwari temple in India, once used by Hindu architects. The diagram locates the *Brahmastan*—the silent seat of all life—the heart and lungs of a space which *breathes Life* into a sacred place. The body of a god was considered a type of architecture."

"Like Kircher and Bernini at the Vatican," Susan said, checking her notes.

"This idea of creating architecture around human form was popularized during the Renaissance by Antonio di Pietro Averlino, known as Filarete. In his *Treatise on Architecture*, Averlino described a plan for the ideal city of

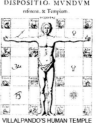

Sforinda. His city was composed of a plaza a mile long and half a mile wide, with a duomo at one end, a lookout tower at the other, and a canal system connected to a river. Filarete claimed he acquired this design from an illuminated '*Golden Book*' which detailed the architecture of buildings and landscapes of antiquity."

"A *Golden Book*, like the *Kabalyon*?" Susan questioned.

Angus nodded. "Maybe even a copy."

VILLALPANDO'S HUMAN TEMPLE

"Sounds like the design for the Mall in Washington," Winston compared.

"Torre said something about Averlino and Filarete." Susan flipped through the pages of her notepad. "The bronze door at St. Peter's ... an architect in Milan."

"He was Duke Francesco Sforza's chief architect in the redesigning of Milan in the late 1500's. Leonardo, who also worked for the Duke, was a follower of Filarete and promoted many concepts found in the *Treatise on Architecture*." Angus pointed to the open book. "In his drawing, Leonardo presented the outstretched image of a man, like a square peg in a round hole trying to fit in. The Vitruvian Man's geometric form is derived from the measured angles taken from an armillary sphere, the wheels-within-wheels that represented Plato's image of the Tekton—the Great Builder, the old Craftsman God. These measurements defined the order within Nature, the Order in the Cosmos—the *Logos* Soul of the

Cosmos. A true measure of a man is determined by the measure of the cosmic soul."

I wonder if Billy knows about this? Winston thought.

"During the early 1620's, Inigo Jones, a Grand Master of English Freemasonry, known as the Vitruvius Britannicus, began to apply Vitruvian architecture to state buildings under the reign of Charles I, who purchased the secret formula for frozen milk from the French," Angus noted. "Thanks to Jones, Vitruvius's *De Architecture* became the architectural bible during the English Enlightenment. Inigo Jones, under the advice of Dr. Dee, also helped to develop a type of architecture for the Elizabethan theater, known as theatrical architecture."

"Dr. Dee again," Susan said.

"Jones's technique used symbolic memory devices within architectural stage settings, based upon the proportions of the world as a way of addressing the unconscious mind of the viewer," Angus explained. "Perhaps these memory devices were derived from the illuminations of the *Kabalyon* acquired by Dr. Dee. It's even possible that the Englishman Robert Fludd saw Dee's copy of the *Kabalyon* and used it as the basis for his book, the *Utriusque Cosimi Historia*, which united the mental images comprising human memory with all architectural settings. Fludd referred to these as the two great arts—the Round Arts which dealt with mental symbols, and the Square Arts, which dealt with architecture. Fludd's and Jones's ideas may have been used in the design of the Globe Theatre in London, the theater of the mind."

Angus laid his hand, palm down, on the art book. "Some believe that Leonardo, who was more famous for his theatrical stage presentations than his art, created this architectural memory technique through his innovations in perspective stage design. Still others claim the technique was adopted from the early cathedral builders. However, it is a technique that dates as far back as the theatrical performances associated with the mysteries of Dionysius and the outdoor presentations of the *rites of passage* associated with the early Christian Passion Plays. Since the time of Inigo Jones, these memory aids associated with theatrical architecture have proliferated into the motion picture and television industries, as well as modern-day advertising. Today, there is a whole science associated with addressing a viewer's subconscious by way of what he sees through art and architecture. Certain images presented in the correct order have a way of addressing and *controlling* the human mind."

"My VDC experiment with subliminal messages," Winston murmured to Susan with an I-told-you-so expression on his face.

"The nine major networks," Susan whispered back.

"Jones followed the edited version of the ten books of *De Architecture* created by the French painter, Nicolas Poussin." Angus pointed one by one to the set of books on the shelf. "It consisted of the following volumes: Landscape Architecture, Construction Materials, Temples, Public Places, Private Dwellings, Finishes and Colors, Water Supply, Sundials and Clocks, and Mechanical Engineering."

"It sounds like a standard engineering curriculum taught at any good university."

"Yes, Jimmy. It's the standard curriculum." Angus continued to explain the influence of Vitruvius, "Well, a Jesuit priest named Juan Bautista Villalpando, the master architect for King Philip II of Spain, was also influenced by Vitruvius—"

"Another Jesuit," Susan said.

"Villalpando trained with his follow Jesuit, Jerome de Prado, who produced a two volume work known as the *Vision of Ezekiel*. Part of the second volume included a detailed archeological study of the Temple Mount in Jerusalem, along with their research on the Third Temple built by the Jewish priest Onias IV at Leontopolis in Egypt—the City of the Lion where the Egyptians worshipped the deity Maahes."

I wonder if they knew about the dragon and the dipper, Winston thought, *City of the Lion ... Maahes.* He pulled the compass from his pocket and eyed its engravings.

"Villalpando was also a noted mathematician," Angus shared. "He taught at the Jesuit college of San Herenegildo in Seville, where he produced twenty-one original propositions on the nature of gravity. Newton is known to have borrowed from Villalpando's work. Combining Vitruvius's theories with his own strong religious beliefs, Villalpando theorized that many ancient temple-cities were designed around specific passages from the Bible which alluded to an architectural technique used in the building of the long-lost Temple of Solomon."

Newton borrowed from Villalpando, Winston paralleled. *And Jefferson borrowed from Newton.*

Angus again pointed at the drawing of the *Vitruvian Man.* "This architectural technique placed man in harmony with the natural world and thus in harmony with his God. Villalpando concluded that the temples mentioned in the Bible held the *key* to understanding the classical architecture of the Greeks and the Romans. In his book, Villalpando attempted to illustrate an appropriate plan for reconstructing the lost temple at Jerusalem. Following the biblical view that the human body is a temple, Villalpando created a design for Solomon's Temple around the image of the outstretched arms of the crucified Christ—the perfect man—as its cornerstone."

"*The Vision of Ezekiel?*" Winston pondered aloud. *Wheel within a wheel ... the Tekton ... Kircher's anthropomorphic architecture.*

"Villalpando's design for the sanctuary of King Solomon's Temple combined the dimensions of man and the dimensions of the heavens, based upon his interpretation of Hebrews 9:23," Angus said. "For example, Villalpando designed his temple court to represent the twelve tribes which symbolized the twelve zodiacs. This allowed the Temple of Solomon to serve as a symbolic replica of the heavenly House of God."

"The zodiac at Glastonbury," Susan connected.

Angus nodded. "It also fitted into Plato's view of the perfect city which favored a division of twelve in his natural laws. The total idea represented the harmonious unification of the twelve tribal states with the order of the heavens into a Godlike covenant. Villalpando finally settled upon a domed building for his new plan for the Temple of Solomon. For him, a domed building was a symbolic holy mountain on the world's axis, with a three-domed building symbolizing the three hills of the Mount of Olives from where Christ ascended into heaven according to scripture."

In the Vision of Ezekiel from the *Bear Bible*, the four wheels symbolize the cardinal directions and the orderly movement of the heavenly throne of God supported by the sun and the planets. John's Vision of the New Jerusalem from Klauber's *Historiae Biblicae Veteris et Novi Testamenti.* The mystic city of St. John with its angled grid pattern of streets serves as the archetype of the perfect civilization yet to be. Above the New Jerusalem, shines a great sunburst of glory - the throne of God.

A new Temple of Sol-o-Moon. Winston collected his thoughts. *Three domes ... a holy mountain ... that church in Paris ...*

"Although much of Villalpando's work was associated with the occult, his ideas were widely accepted by the Cat'lic architects of the sixteenth century. His theories comprised one of the first books on architecture ever put into print and circulated by the Church of Rome. Many self-taught architects and apprentices of the European Renaissance used it as a reference source. It helped promote the ancient approach of using architecture as a means of uniting man with Nature, a central principle used in European architecture for the next 500 years." Angus sat down in the captain's chair. "Today, the evidence appears to show conclusively that the ancients integrated a reverence to Nature in the creation of their temples, monuments, and shrines in a harmonious discipline that united government, science, architecture, and religion."

Yes, Nature's Laws. Winston nodded. *My other self.*

"Has this approach to art and architecture been lost in the distant past? Or has it amazingly been passed on to us today through certain architectural traditions?" Angus prompted. "Daniel Burnham was thoroughly schooled in all of this knowledge, having attended the *École des Beaux-Arts.*" Angus stood up, walked over to the red, leather-bound book at the end of the table, and opened it to the table of contents. "Twelve years after Daniel Burnham purchased the *Kabalyon*, a version of the book containing only the text was published, along with a cover story claiming it had been written by three initiates of the Human Potential and New Thought Movements in Chicago."

"New Thought Movement?" Susan questioned.

"Infinite Intelligence—They were followers of a panentheistic belief that God and the *human mind* were one and the same, and that the spiritual evolution of the mind leads to God."

"Michelangelo's brain scan," Susan said.

"Teilhard's Alpha to Omega again," Winston added.

Angus nodded. "The New Thought Movement was an outgrowth of earlier Swedenborgian and Masonic teachings, based on aspects of Cartesian dualism. But, it also may have been associated with the Order of Alpha et Omega. This revised book, known as the *Kybalion*," he pointed to his *Kabalyon*, "consisted of the following chapter by chapter path for initiation: A Hermetic Philosophy, Seven Hermetic Principles of the Seven Ages of Man and **the Seventh Ray**, The Absolute – the Five Limbs of the Brahman, A Mental Universe, Divine Paradox, The Absolute In All, Peri Automatopoietkes, The Seven Planes of Correspondence, Vibrations, Polarities, Rhythms, Causations, The Two Genders, Mental Genders, and Hermetic Axiom."

"Hmm ... the Seven Hermetic Principles of the Seven Ages of Man. It sounds like someone's self-help book. A seven-step guide maybe ... or the seven rites of the Lakota," Winston pondered beneath his breath.

"So, your book is an edited version of the *Kabalyon*," Susan specified.

"Susan," Angus confided as he sat down again, "this edited version is held in high regard by certain alchemists and Kabbalists who find deep meaning from the text alone, as a path of initiation on equal standing with the *Corpus Hermeticum.*"

"Just what is a Kabbalist?" Susan asked.

"It is someone who studies the Kabbalah system, my dear. Which, in essence, is a study of the working language of the angels, a language of *consciousness*, be it called the *kawanah*, or a prayer—*the most powerful channel of communication.* The Kabbalah is a philosophical piece of literature dealing with an influential form of Jewish mysticism that was founded in Spain in the twelfth century. It's older than the monastic traditions and has been called one of the most influential books ever written. The predominant schools of Kabbalic teaching were located in Barcelona. The

Spanish Kabbalah consisted of two main books. The first was the *Sefer ha-temuna*, known as the *Book of the Image,* which interprets certain cosmic cyles by way of the Torah in order to reveal the attributes of the divine. The other was the *Book of Brightness,* which contains doctrine related to the transmigration of the human soul and other mystical notions alien to Orthodox Judaism, which allows man to approach God directly—as in prayer."

"The Kabbalah sounds confusing," Susan said. "Images and brightness ... It's about prayer, such as the Lord's Prayer?"

"The *communication link*," Angus stressed. "We pray for it, and so we get it." He rested his elbows on the arms of the captain's chair and clasped his hands together. "Most religions presume that humanity is able to interact with certain aspects of a Creative Force outside of the perceivable universe. The most common form of this interaction is called prayer." Angus paused. "Do you believe in something you can not see? When you pray, my dear, to whom do you pray? The invisible *presence* of a god? Or do you pray to yourself? Thoughts unspoken are not unknown to the Divine Mind. The word religion means the connection to the divine. The study of the Kabbalah is an attempt to understand the *communication link* between the mind of man and the mind of God, so that man might better carry out God's great plan."

"Yes, from the Latin *re,* which means again, and *ligare,* meaning to connect, as in the English word ligament," Susan related.

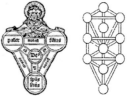

"The language for this *communication link* is ultimately believed to be a mental pictorial language consisting of certain magical signs and sigils—*images.*" Angus rose from his chair. "The primary sigil which a Kabbalist uses to create and understand this *communication link* is called a Sephirothic Tree, or a Tree of Life. It's sometimes called the Seven Way Path ... the Jewel ... a map of God's body ... or the reflection of God-in-man which is used to invoke the divine light of the *Skekhinah* into the physical world." He opened another book on the table to a diagram shaped like a complex molecule. "It looks like this— three pillars linked together by ten emanations associated with the mind of God, like the ten Hindu avatars or a hierachy of human needs. It's a diamond in the rough. The Japanese call it the cherry tree. You know, the one that George Washington cut down. The Celts of Northern Europe called it the *yggdrasil* or Samson's pillars. The Sephirothic Tree is the central image of Kabbalic meditation and prayer. This tree serves as a symbol for God, with the *head of God* residing at the top of the tree. Its design is used in the temple layout for a Gnostic Mass. Many religious and hermetic orders, such as the Jews, Renaissance Humanists, Christians, Rosicrucians, Freemasons, Gnostics, and even Satanists have studied the Kabbalah."

"I've seen that prayer tree pattern somewhere," Winston said, eyeing the illustration. *The catacombs ... a fish-eye ... diamond shaped ... pillars ... Washington ... Nobles and the map ... the spearhead ... the pope on the Mall ... the virus...*

"Me too," Susan agreed. "But where? *The Glass Bead Game* ...

"Now, look at this." Angus opened another book to a faded diagram of the Shield of the Trinity. "An adaptation of this sephirothic correspondence can be found in a medieval diagram of Janus-Lugus, the *triune*-three-faced god of the gateway to the soul, holding the Shield of the Trinity. The three curving sides, each exactly equal in length, carry the Latin words which mean *is not*. The short straight bands contain the word *is*. The outer circles bear the Latin words for Father, Son, and Holy Spirit. The inner circle contains the word *God*. This is a lattice diagram for a traditional medieval image of the Godhead, the union of the Father, the Son, and the Soul."

"So this geometric symbolism is part of an angelic picture language?" Susan asked.

"Exactly, Susan. However, serious science is up this tree. This symbolic lattice serves as a structured hierarchy around which everything in the world can be measured. It's a design for the archetypal structure of *creation* which holds the innermost secrets of nature."

"The secrets of nature," Susan repeated, placing her hand over her belly.

"The patterns for chemical bonding," Winston compared, "or even those polarization patterns in the sky."

Angus smiled in agreement, walked over to the shelves, and retrieved a few more books. "There are many ancient books and grimoires which claim to decode the angelic languages. Here is the *Key of Solomon* from the Middle Ages, known as the *Lemegedon Clavicula Salomonis*, which describes certain rituals used in conjunction with special seals, sigils, and other talismans related to Vishnu, which ward off evil."

Slam— The book fell on the table.

"Here is the *Ayat Gh al–Hakim fi'l-sihr*, meaning the aim of the sage, also known as the *Picatrix*, meaning the *key*."

Slam— The book fell on the table.

"*Picatrix* ... a picture?" Susan questioned in a whisper. "A key? A picture key?"

"Books such as these dealt with the Notory Art which sought to gain divine knowledge on the correct procedure for communion with God by way of angelic prayer, revealed within the design of certain symbols. And there are other related books and treatises, such as Johnnannes Trithemius's *Polygraphiae*, the *Steganographia*, and his other noted work, *The Seven Secondary Intelligences*, which predict the history of the world by following astrological symbols and the seven spirits believed to have the power to govern the heavens."

"The *Steganographia—* It's the first practical book on cryptography."

"Correct, Jimmy. The *Polygraphiae* and the *Steganographia*, or *covered writing* as it has been called, deals with the arcanum of writing and symbols. The workings of MI6 and the CIA are derived from these two books alone. The *Steganographia* was originally a trilogy. The first volume specifically deals with the *song language*, in which a communion with the divine could be achieved by way of a special *coniurati*—a harmonic song—much like a Gregorian chant. Words placed to the correct cadence, to the correct rhythm of things, have the ability to alter the human mind into a transcendent state of self-understanding."

Slam— The Big Book fell on the table.

"The third volume of *Steganographia* deals with the techniques used for hiding symbols and messages in art and architecture," Angus explained.

"Steganographic techniques ... a harmonic song," Winston connected. "Like my digital image experiments with my VDC. But, I always thought it was Francis Bacon who promoted this technique of hiding messages in art."

"Unless you are an Oxfordian, now you are getting into the subject of Shakespeare." Angus guffawed.

"So these hidden symbols in art and architecture are like the edifices formed by the landscape of Edinburgh?" Susan proposed.

"Susan, the *Kabalyon* could be *the source* for all this other medieval, esoteric literature. For example, Trithemius was an abbot of the Schottenkloster, a Scottish monastery in Wurzburg, Germany. Some historians believe that King David's *Kabalyon* was smuggled to this monastery for safekeeping, and that Trithemius referenced it when he wrote the *Steganographia*. Still others believe that Trithemius referenced a version of the *Kabalyon* that originated from the Far East, where Marco Polo discovered the secrets of ice cream. The *Kabalyon* could have made its way to Western Europe by way of the Silk Road passing through Kabul to Xi'an, which once united the two halves of Eurasia. Others claim it originated in northern Egypt with the Phoenicians, the Amorites, Proto-Canaanites, or the Hyksos—the King-Shepherds."

"Shepherd kings." Susan recorded in her notepad.

"Only a few known illuminations from the book have been discovered." Angus opened a folder. "Look, your father acquired one of the missing illuminations. He believed it was associated with ancient Vedic Sanskrit Vedas, or possibly a cosmic map for the *Bhagvatam*—the Hindu *Book of God*."

"Looks like the *Global Icon*," Susan compared.

"A depiction of Saraswati," Angus guessed.

"Or Queen Ouroboros," Winston added. "Leonardo must have seen a copy of the *Kabalyon*. How did my father get this?"

"I do not know," Angus admitted. "He sent this to me without an explanation after he settled in the States." Angus reached for his copy of the *Kabalyon*. The book's stiff spine *crackled* as he sprang it open. "Some believe the *Kabalyon* was seen by the early English illuminators such as William Brailes, and that many illuminated bibles drew upon the *Kabalyon*. Certain mystic Kabbalists believe the *Kabalyon* served as a reference book to the *Shi'ur Qomah* for an initiation into a godlike state of consciousness. But they also believe that the symbols hidden in the illuminations of the *Kabalyon* must be acquired before the texts can be fully understood. These symbols are considered a type of *rebus key*—or yes, my dear—a *picture key*—that unlocks the mysteries of the invisible *presence* of God."

"A godlike *state* of consciousness," Winston repeated. "Sounds like these images serve as a type of consciousness encoder." *My VDC ....*

"More of that Lullus-logic," Susan quipped.

Winston's eyes blinked, snared by one of the pages of the *Kabalyon* titled "The Seven Ages of Man and the Seventh Ray." With a concentrated double vision stare, his eyes wandered over the lines of text. Words and letters blurred and merged together as if floating off the page, then focused into a sharpened clarity. "Angus, look at this." Winston pointed. "The letters are shaped differently ... angled to form a different script. You say this is a textual copy?"

"Yes," Angus replied, looking at a line of text containing various misshapen, italic-like letters. "My copy is an accurate translation from the original *Kabalyon*. You are right. I never noticed this."

AMVN Ω AUDE Ω SAPERE Ω DEUS Ω ABSCONDITUS Ω DEUS Ω VULT

"Part of this is Latin," Susan observed. "I've seen this before ... the catacombs—"

"Tilt it into the light," Winston cut her short. "I think these oddly shaped letters form a pattern. It's throughout the entire text. There's a hidden image on this page. Angus, do you have a thin sheet of paper ... something I can see through?"

Angus retrieved a sheet of onionskin from a drawer in the table.

"What are you getting at?" Susan asked Winston.

"I'm going to trace the location of the angled letters to reveal the pattern." Winston took the paper from Angus. "Give me a pen."

She reached into her pocket. "Here's the one Dr. Peres gave me—"

Angus noticed the blue globe on the tip of the pen and the logo SMITHSONIAN INSTITUTE imprinted on it. He shook his head. "Here, Jimmy. Use a pencil." He passed Winston a stubby No2.

Winston laid the onionskin over the page and circled slightly the odd letters which showed through. "Steganographic ... These circles form the outline of different letters or a word maybe. This could be a type of Cardan Grille that forms a master decipher template for the book, like an old computer punchcard or a voting ballot."

Susan and Angus stepped closer to get a better look.

"Be careful. Do not damage my copy of the *Kabalyon*."

"What is it?" Susan asked. "I don't see anything."

"Let me connect the dots." Winston drew lines from each circle to the next. He lifted the paper and held it up so they could see.

AɪᴍΩ

"It's not Latin—" Susan said.

"It's Greek," Winston interrupted. "Alpha, Omega, I M."

"They're the Greek letters *Alpha Iota Mu Omega*," Angus exclaimed.

"*Alpha Omega*, a sign for the Messiah?" Susan asked.

"Yes, my dear ... IOA ... the Ouroboros ... the All in One."

"IOA, that's a computer language ..." *The Ouroboros ... zeros and ones*, Winston mused. *Out of Many ... One ... Goat—*

"Translation please?" Susan added.

"*Alpha Iota Mu Omega* is an acronym for the Greek phrase 'I am yesterday, today, and forever' and the symbol for the Eternal God. According to the Cat'lic Church, *Alpha Iota Mu Omega* is the sign for the Archangel Michael—the Angel of Light— who is prophesied to descend from heaven and chain the Great Satan before the Second Coming. But, these letters are also the Greek symbols for the beginning and end of the Great Platonic Year, symbolized by a dragon or a snake biting its own tail, forming a sacred circle—a symbol of the World Soul."

"An ouroboros circle—the 26,000 year period Dr. Peres told us about—based around the constellation Draco." Susan mentally connected the dots, *Arthur's Seat ... Golgotha ... the binary code in the virus.*

"It appears the *Kabalyon* is embedded with a hidden text," Winston interjected.

"Yes, Jimmy. Just like the Bible."

"Hidden texts are in the Bible?" Susan questioned, staring at the open page from the *Kabalyon*. "Using odd letters or characters?"

"Let me explain." Angus leaned against the edge of the table. "Some hermeneutic researchers believe the *Kabalyon* serves as the core text for part of Bible. It is now known that the first books of the Old Testament are a union of texts from many different writers who appear to have worked from a common source, sometimes called the lost *J documents.* The same is true of the New Testament, with the hypothetical lost *Q documents,* from which most scholars agree the four Gospels were created."

"Dr. Peres said something about the lack of documented evidence," Susan remarked, "only a mythology based on star lore."

"A few mystic followers of the *Torah* believe the common source for the Old Testament *Septuagint* and the Gospels may have been the *Kabalyon*," Angus said. "They believe a reference to the *Kabalyon* has been encoded within the Bible—by way of a series of prophetic code words which reference the illuminated images of the *Kabalyon*, which predict future events leading to both the Second Coming of the Messiah and the creation of the New Jerusalem."

"Are you saying the *Kabalyon* can predict the future ... like bird signs?"

"Well, no. Not exactly, Jimmy. I don't want to sound like Nostradamus when I say this. Ah ... where should I begin. Let's take another look at Dr. Dee."

"Dr. Dee again?" Susan prompted. "The scryer searching for the God Longitude?"

"There is an entry in Dee's journal in which the English philosopher Sir Francis Bacon met with Dee at Mortlake," Angus continued. "The young Bacon came to Dee to learn about an ancient Greek and Hebrew numerical code known as the Gematria, one of the oldest known cipher systems. Bacon was later put in charge of editing the 1611 translation of the *King James Bible.* It is evident that Bacon wanted to understand something hidden within the Bible."

"Dr. Dee was involved in the English translation of the Bible?" Susan questioned.

"Yes. Another friend of Dee, Sir Henry Savile, a noted Greek scholar and mathematician, took part in the translation of the *King James.* It is well known that certain books within the Bible were encrypted by Greek scribes. For example, the book of Jeremiah uses a simple reversed-alphabet substitution cipher known as ATBASH. You will never understand that book until you apply the cipher."

"Dr. Peres told us about the use of numbers in the Bible to denote a hidden meaning," Susan recalled.

"So, there're two types of ciphers used in the Bible?" Winston asked.

"At least two, Jimmy, and maybe more."

"More?" Susan questioned.

"Many have noticed the cryptic nature of the Bible," Angus said. "In 1890, Ivan Nikolayevitsh Panin, a Russian emigrant who graduated from Harvard with a degree in Russian literature, became convinced that he had discovered amazing patterns in the Greek text of the book of Psalms. These patterns were more than just a simple ATBASH cipher. Soon afterward, he realized there were sequences in the text of the New Testament as well. Until his death in 1942, he devoted his life to his strange mathematical investigation, leaving over 40,000 pages of notes dealing with certain code words hidden in the Bible. Perhaps one of the most interesting things about Panin's work is his discovery that the first verse of *Genesis* and the first verse of *Matthew* contained similar patterns of *sevens.* Since the first book of the Old Testament is believed to have been written well over a thousand years before the first book of the New Testament, such a pattern implicated a *single* author—or source."

"Seven." Winston nodded firmly. "Okay, go on."

"Early in the twentieth century, the Rabbi Machael Ber Weissmandl, a Czech Talmudic scholar, performed an investigation into the equidistant letter sequences of the words found in the *Torah.* He discovered the word, *Elohim,* one of the Jewish names of God, hidden within certain intervals of the texts. Followers of Weissmandl expanded on his research in the early 1980s. They discovered other hidden words. In 1994, an article was published in the journal of *Statistical Science,* which indicated that it was *not* by random chance that such words could be repeatedly found hidden within the texts. Even a cryptologist within the NSA concluded from his own independent studies that something *profound* appeared to be encrypted within the *Torah.* The research into this area of study became known as the Bible Code."

"I've heard of that mathematician at the NSA," Susan remarked.

"The Bible Code researchers shocked everyone when they applied their research to the Greek and English translations of both the Old and New Testaments, picking up where Panin left off," Angus explained. "All sorts of names, places, and events throughout history appeared to crop up in relationship to one another—names such as Napoleon, Newton, Hitler, and Einstein, and events including the Second World War and even the attacks of 9/11. The whole Bible is woven with a hidden meaning. It is as though the power of God had carried a secret message from the original texts to other translations. Even Gutenberg in his badly printed translation could not foul it up."

"From Greek to Latin, to Hebrew, to German, to English," Winston said. "It's hard to believe that hidden words could be transcribed in the various translations."

"Well, Jimmy, one of the Kabbalists who had studied the text from *Kabalyon* decided to see if the English word *kabalyon* showed up anywhere in the King James translation. What he discovered was truly shocking. In the New Testament, the word *kabalyon* was discovered embedded within the scriptures one time. In the Old Testament, it was discovered fifteen times. It was like a Lost Word hidden within the scriptures. When other words believed to be associated with the possible illuminations referenced in the *Kabalyon* were cross-checked with the word *kabalyon,* something incredible happened. On every page where the word *kabalyon* showed up embedded within the scriptures, the name Jerusalem could also be found. Other words on each page also cross-referenced the word *kabalyon*—words like Rome, Sion, fish, seven, north, star, angel, devil, bird, wings, sun, Solomon, city, earth, hidden, Adam, light, alpha, moon, temple, Obama, Michael, and Jesus. Many of the phrases found associated with the word *kabalyon* included—house of the lord, Son of Man, King of Judha, children of Israel, priest of the most high, Ark of the Covenant, Ark of the Lord, foundation of the world, tree in the midst of the earth, measure of a man, by the space of two years, day of judgement, and a whirlwind came out of the north. For the word of God is quick. It's as if the hidden word *kabalyon* was a magnetic force for these other words and phrases. Look at this."

Angus pulled a printout from the bottom of the folder of newspaper clippings. Winston and Susan stepped closer, their eyes poring over a list of words created from a computer realignment of the scriptures from the New Testament. The word *kabalyon* was highlighted with other reference words marked. All of the marked words appeared within the same common scriptural texts on the page.

"Jimmy, this is a computer printout of the *kabalyon* word search in the New Testament. The programming that does this sort of thing is readily available in the public domain."

"This really looks like something from a Ouija board," Winston commented.

[A large grid of letters — a computer word-search printout — appears here.]

"Jimmy, certain mystic Kabbalists believed these other words and phrases define the lost illuminations, the *key* symbols used to define *the consciousness and the life force of God*—the nature of the psychology of God's mind—which will serve as the structures used to build the New Jerusalem and to signal the coming of the Messiah."

"So, the Bible references the word *kabalyon* as a sacred keyword, and the Bible is somebody's enigma machine." Winston shook his head in disbelief.

"Exactly, no question about it. It's a messianic keyword—the Kabalyon key," Angus said, "for finding the hidden illuminations and a hidden meaning within the Bible. You have to study the associated scriptural texts."

"That's a remarkable story, Angus. It definitely goes beyond the laws of chance. It's enough to make you believe that God wrote the Bible," Winston said with a tentative leap of faith.

"It's enough to make me believe we're on some sort of holy quest," Susan remarked in amazement.

Or rediscovering cities created from the Kabalyon, Winston pondered.

Angus stared hard at Winston with the focused face of determination. "There's even more to this, Jimmy. In certain Kabbalic circles it is believed that the symbols and diagrams found within the original illuminations of the *Kabalyon* represent something more important. Do you remember the Old Testament stories of how there once was an original language spoken by all of mankind?"

"Yes, it's the Old Testament story about the Tower of Babel, the gate of God, where the Babylonians tried to build a tower to heaven so they could commune with God," Winston replied. "But God punished their hubris and circumvented their plan by separating them from their common language."

"Exactly. The illuminations in the *Kabalyon* may represent the pre-Babel language, the original unified language spoken by all mankind at a creative junction in the distant past—the language of Pangea. They believe the illuminations in the *Kabalyon* represent a type of symbolic alphabet, like the hieroglyphs on the Rosetta Stone. This symbolic alphabet is visually stimulating, like a natural pheromone. These are *powerful* symbols. By simply seeing the symbols, a deeply held, hidden memory in the human consciousness is triggered into operation. It is this triggering process that

allows a direct communication link with God."

"Michelangelo's brain scan," Susan murmured.

"The skull image at Mount Sinai," Winston connected.

"They believe the lost symbols of the *Kabalyon* represent the original angelic language. This could be the language spoken by the prophets and possibly used by Jesus in the first rites of passage for his original twelve, as mentioned in the early Christian Gnostic gospels. This is the language that an ancient Indian Sufi text calls the Language of the Birds—the Language of the Gods."

"Language of the Birds," Winston interjected. "Oh … Billy."

"Language of the Gods?" Susan repeated.

"Yes, my dear. Within this Sufi text is a Vedic meditation called *neti neti*, or not this not that, designed to help you find out who you are and consequently who and what God is within yourself. The object of the meditation is to learn to speak the bird language, the most ancient of all the dead languages, a hidden language shared by everyone."

"Deductive reasoning," Winston said. "Clues—not this, not that … *Yes and no statements … zeros and ones ….*

"Yes, clues! Let me show you an interesting clue." Angus opened a tattered Holy Bible to a colored illustration of the Ark of the Covenant being carried into the desert by the Israelites as they fled from Egypt. "No one is certain what the Ark is or what it means. But according to some scholars, it originated in Egypt."

"The Ark could be Egyptian?" Susan questioned.

"Possibly. There are Egyptian wall paintings of people parading a portable boat-shaped shrine commemorating the barge of Amun of Karnak, called *Userhat-Amun*, which appears very similar to the Ark described in the Bible. However, the Ark could be a *symbol* for something else. Many religious scholars believe that the Lost Holy Grail—the *blood vessel*, the chalice or platter of plenty—and the Lost Ark of the Covenant to be simply a mythical allegory for the same thing. In their simplest sense, these legendary relics are merely emblems for anything that represents *the presence* of God. Generally, the theology of Christianity implies that Jesus Christ is a symbolic allegory that represents the New Testament Ark of the Covenant denoted in the book of Revelation by the symbols *Alpha* and *Omega*, the Beginning and the End—the religious symbols for the Messiah and *the presence* of God."

The presence of God on Earth ... Winston geared a thought, *Arthur's Seat ... the blood vessel ... the dipper ... the chalice ... mind of man ... skull ... capital.*

Angus pointed to the illustration of the Ark. "The Old Testament states that the Ark was a chest made of acacia wood, completely overlaid with gold and veiled in fine goat hair. It contained the stone tablets of the Law, Aaron's rod, and a jar of manna. It was carried before the armies of the Israelites in battle as a talisman for invoking divine intervention against their enemies, similar to the mysterious *eye* used by Boler in Scandinavian folklore." He laid his hand on the open Bible. "According to the Bible, the Ark was also the Chesed, Mercy Seat of the God Yehovah, which rested between two, golden, winged cherubim—the two winged creatures who guarded the Ark and looked down upon the mercy seat. God's *presence* did not dwell inside the Ark, but between the two winged cherubim, as the *Shekinah Glory* of light. According to scripture, King David placed the Ark on the Temple Mount. On certain holy days he prayed before the Ark, but he would not touch it or face the *Shekinah Glory of the Lord*. Instead, he faced away from the Ark and bowed to the *shadow* of the winged cherubim cast upon the ground."

Susan flipped through her notes. "Dr. Peres told us about the *Shekinah*."

Winston hovered over her shoulder and peeked at her scribbles resembling Egyptian hieroglyphs. "I can't read your writing. It must be an angel language. I'm going to need the Rosetta Stone to translate it."

"Steganographic." She grinned. "No one's reading this girl's diary."

"The *Shekinah* is a divine light," Angus grinned, "a manifestation of God that shines above the mercy seat, the receptacle of the law. This light is a *communication link* with God."

"A communication link ... fiber optics without the fiber," Winston reasoned.

"Yes, Jimmy, something like that. To commune with Light." Angus's eyes twinkled with excitement. He pulled a small booklet from a shelf. "This Light is also seen as the female consort of God—the creative spark—the **true Holy Grail**, a symbol of the female creative deity—a motherly angel of liberation who always stands beside us, healing our body, mind, and spirit. Jimmy, this is a verse on the *Shekinah* from *The Wisdom of Solomon* written by an unknown Jewish sage living in Alexandria around 50 B.C." He lowered his eyes to the booklet and began to recite.

" '*Shekinah* is the Supreme Spirit devoted to the good of all people ...

She shines bright in the bloom of ignorance; She is unfading;
She is easily seen by those who love Her; easily found by those who look for Her, And *quickly does She come to those who seek Her help.*
One who rises early, intent on finding Her, will not grow weary of the quest—
For one day he will find Her seated in his own heart.
To set all one's thoughts on Her is true wisdom,
And to be ever aware of Her is the sure way to perfect peace.
For *Shekinah* Herself goes about in search of those who are worthy of Her.
With every step, She comes to guide them; in every thought, She comes to meet them.... The true beginning of spiritual life is the desire to know *Shekinah.*
Following Her will is the sure path of immortality. And immortality is oneness with God. Your desire to know *Shekinah* leads to God and His Kingdom. With all your thrones and scepters you may rule the world for a while. But take hold of *Shekinah* and you will *rule the world forever!*' "

"You have to excuse my oratory skills," Angus concluded his recitation. "In the writings of the Jews, the *Shekinah* is always the feminine consort of Yahweh, similar to Juno, the Roman goddess of light and the consort of Jupiter."

"Juno?" Susan hesitated. *A creative deity ... the true Holy Grail ... I have been reading the right books.*

Juno, Winston thought, *the Washington Monument ...*

"Yes, Susan. A female consort of God who bears the divine light is not unique to the Bible. The *Shekinah* is none other than Asherah, a goddess which the Hebrews possibly inherited from the Sumerians. Her original name was *Ninharsag*—the lady of the Western Mountain. This duality of a male God and a female consort is a symbolism found in basic human psychology. In this sense, the *Shekinah* symbolizes the union of the pneuma and the psyche of the logical mind."

"Lullus-logic again," Susan said. *The Shekinah sprang from the mind of Adam, according to Michelangelo's painting, like Eve from his rib. Adam was the mother. Man is the First Cause?*

Angus closed the booklet and slid it back on its shelf. He returned to the Bible on the table and pointed to the picture of the golden cherubim sitting on top of the Ark of the Covenant. "Most religious scholars believe the cherubim were traditional symbols for the solar lions, such as the one we saw today at Arthur's Seat. This dual solar symbolism is found in various religious icons for the central deity. For example, in the Mithraic cult, the solar god, Mithra, is often depicted between the two fire quenchers. In Egyptian hieroglyphs, the *omphalos* stone—the navel for a temple complex, known as the holy *axis mundi*—is frequently placed between two great birds known as *Amru* and *Chamru,* the golden eagles of the sky. In this case, the Ark of the Covenant might be compared to the *axis mundi* of a city."

"Dr. Peres mentioned the *axis mundi*," Susan said.

"An axis for a city," Winston responded. "Meridians aligned to the polar star."

"Now, *abracadabra.*" Angus pointed again to the picture. "I will create as I speak. Look again at this illustration of the Ark of the Covenant. It shows two winged cherubim, two winged angels, or two - winged - *birds.* These cherubim are believed to be an allegorical metaphor for this angel language, or *bird language,* that allowed man to talk directly to God. There is no physical Ark of the Covenant, it is only a symbolic metaphor for the Language of the Birds."

Angus opened a book on the table titled *The Mystery of the Cathedrals.* "This is a book by Fulcanelli, the fictitious name of an early twentieth-century French alchemist. His true identity is uncertain, although a few researchers suspect that he was Jules Violle, a scientist from the University of Lyons, who was an associate of the astronomer Camille Flammarion—"

"Flammarion, again," Susan remembered. "The meridian in Paris …"

"Yes. There is an interesting illustration in the back of this book. Look at this." Angus unfolded a page. "This is the famous Flammarion Woodcut. It was created by an unknown artist and first appeared in Flammarion's *L'Atmosphere: Météorologie Populaire*. The woodcut depicts the seeker beside the Tree of Life peering through the Earth's atmosphere, reaching out, *not afraid of letting go*, as he discovers the hidden workings of the universe—the Great Wheelwork."

"It's like he's staring out from Plato's cave," Susan noticed, "at polarized bands in the sky."

"I've read about Violle," Winston remembered.

"Violle carried out the first measurement of the Solar Constant on Mont Blanc in 1875," Angus noted, "a measurement of the light intensity from the sun. It's one of the principal measurements used in the biological understanding of the Greenhouse Effect and the evolutionary aspects of the Gaea Principle."

"Yeah, I'm familiar with the Solar Constant from my Huygens-Grimaldi experiment," Winston remarked.

"Violle was also a follower of Professor Allan Kardec from Lyons," Angus informed. "Kardec was a French complier or codifier, who carried out the first scientific investigation of the paranormal world through his Parisian Society of Psychologic Studies. Kardec is known as the Father of Spiritualism. He is responsible for coining the terms reincarnation and spiritualism. In 1857, he published the book, *The Spirit World*, in which he concluded that within each man there is something more which exists after death. This something more—this principle of life, the animic spark—is the immortal soul of each man which is a part of the greater World Soul. He believed that man's destiny is controlled by this World Soul which resides in an unseen spirit realm as an invisible intelligence constantly communicating with us and exerting its unconscious influence. In 1861, Kardec published *The Mediums Book*, in which he suggested there is a mechanical science for communicating with the spirit world by way of spirit-tapping and spirit-writing—"

"Spirit-writing …" Winston remembered the man sitting on the bench in Paris. "Bird-talk with a Ouija board."

"Spiritualism?" Susan reiterated.

"Yeah," Winston mumbled, "the Sacred Hoop."

"Yes, my dear. It's a belief in a transit area after death where the soul resides. It was a popular movement in France, Great Britain, and America in the nineteenth century. The American Society for Psychical Research was founded in Boston not long after the founding of the Society for Physical Research in London. The first officers of the ASPR included the eminent astronomer Simon Newcomb and the prominent psychologist William James."

"Newcomb ... the speed of light," Winston said, "the Washington Monument."

Angus nodded. "But back to Fulcanelli. In the *Mystery of the Cathedrals*, Fulcanelli refers to this *bird language* as the Green Language, in reference to the *first language* spoken and recognized by human consciousness since the dawn of human time. This language was an Invisible Presence, like Violle's World Soul, which governed the actions of mankind from the first day of creation. He believed this Green Language was the most ancient way of communication, consisting of *mental symbols* that preceded the spoken word of man. This is the symbolic language that speaks the basic instructions to man which has allowed humanity to slay its primal fears. It is the Sign Language of the Soul formed from the unconscious archetypal symbols that allow man to rise above the animals and become a creative being equal with God, not as God's adversary, but as a conduit for God's great plan."

"A symbolic language of the soul?" Winston asked. "A language of the mind."

"Yes." Angus pointed to the book by Fulcanelli. "The main point in Fulcanelli's book and his other work, *The Dwellings of the Philosophers*, was that the *key* to unraveling the greater mystery of alchemy and the symbolic architecture of cathedrals lay in an understanding of what he called the phonetic law of the spoken Kabbalah, this being the Language of the Birds. According to Fulcanelli, the first masons who built cathedrals throughout Europe used this symbolic language to design their structures to push light—with *light* being the *Shekinah*—the visible *presence* of God."

"To push light ... language of the birds." Winston groaned, "Oh ... Billy."

"For many Kabbalists, God's *presence* is found within light," Angus affirmed.

Evolution ... Alpha to the Omega, Winston thought. *Light to Enlightenment.*

"Dr. Peres said something about that," Susan remarked. "But he also said that God was Love."

"I'm not familiar with this Dr. Peres," Angus tried to recollect. "But this reverence to God as Light is found in many religious texts. The ritualized sacrifice to the Light of the Sun is actually the oldest form of religion, with the Glorified Light being associated with mankind's basic perception of God. It's even found in the Bible."

Angus began rambling about the illuminations within the *Kabalyon*. "This symbolic bird language served as a building block upon which all human communication has been derived. It is a type of deep-memory road map for finding the core of the lost godlike consciousness hidden in everyone. The twentieth-century psychoanalyst Carl Jung called it a *universal consciousness* of the rational mind. Aristotle, the Greek philosopher and personal tutor of Alexander the Great, called it something else—the soul. This language is the active intellect of God found described in Aristotle's metaphysics as the final cause of human thought—the *entelecheia* of the rational soul. But, this Bird Language could represent another type of soul."

"Another type of soul?" Winston questioned.

Angus grinned and pulled a book from the shelf. "In 1890, the social anthropologist Sir James George Frazer published his investigation into the folklore of the ancients titled *The Golden Bough*. It was a significant anthropological study into the early cultures of man. Although considered scandalous by some because of its pagan view of the Lamb of God, it became a popular book among Victorian high society. Frazer followed up his investigation in 1926 with another book, *The Worship of Nature,* which dealt with the worship of the sky and the Earth. Frazer concluded the first religions of the ancient world were grounded in Nature worship, where the gods were a personification of the unknown forces of nature. Mystery was their God. Frazer believed man's ancient religions could be divided into three types: Tribal Religions, Nature Religions, and Universal Religions, all with their own associated symbols."

Symbols ... Winston pondered with an undercurrent of curiosity.

"The deities of the Nature Religions represented aspects of nature that appeared supernatural to early man due to his lack of scientific understanding," Angus explained. "There were Nature deities that represented the Earth, the sun, the moon, and the four directions of the winds. These were among the most commonly seen and unseen spirit forces worshiped by all ancient cultures. Everything in nature was seen to have a personification—a separate spirit with its own *animus*—a mind or a soul. Yet, as man acquired a practical understanding of the forces in nature, he gradually abandoned the nature deities in favor of a single Tribal or Universal god—a God of the All. Tribes often associated themselves with a crop or a domestic animal which sustained the tribe, such a goat or a sheep. According to the Egyptian anthropologist Margaret Murray, pre-Christian religions revolved around the Horned God." Angus opened an atlas on the table to a topographic map of Egypt.

"Another map," Susan said.

"Look at the shape of Egypt and the Sinai peninsula." Angus moved his finger around the territorial boundaries. "They form the horned heads of a goat and a ram. One is drinking water from the Nile, the River of Life, and other from the Gulf of Aqaba. The bearded goat and the ram are often found on the crowns of Egyptian pharaohs as symbols of their kingship over the tribal land or nomes. These

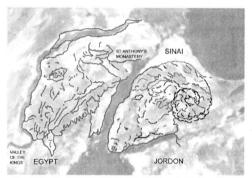

zoomorphic edifices constitute a construction larger than the Great Wall of China."

Tribal gods, Winston mused. *Billy could really get into this.*

"Torre's ram-headed *Khnum*," Susan said, perplexed. "The First Cause is in the Sinai?"

"Exactly, Mount Sinai," Angus reminded, then continued. "The tribal gods eventually evolved into the single universal god, such as the Great God Pan, a single cosmological deity which encompassed all aspects of nature, including both man's human and animal natures—half man, half animal, like a minotaur. It's similar to the Chinese first-being, Pangu, or the shape-shifting Celtic demon, Púca, a night monster that appears as an eagle or a large black goat," Angus compared. "The French occultist Eliphas Lévi illustrated Pan in his *Dogme et Rituel de la Haute Magie* as the Sabbatic deity he called 'Baphomet of Mendes.' I have a picture." Angus opened *The Golden Bough* to an illustration. "This hermaphroditic image represents the Unmovable Mover described in Plato's *Critias* and *Timaeus*—the Goat. See, it's a god of the All—male and female, animal and human, and sitting on the Earth between the sun and moon."

"Sol-o-Moon," Winston muttered, scrutinizing the illustration, "the cosmic order of the sun and the moon, the *Logos*."

"A god of the All … the Goat substance," Susan wondered. "So Baphomet was not just a deity symbolized by a head. He was the head deity."

"The first social groups were tribal in nature, so much so, that outside of the self, the tribe has been called man's original secondary group," Angus continued. "The tribal god served as a unifying force for the tribe, a civilizing function. Even today, most human beings interact within their own social groups, such as clubs, organizations, or religious sects. Most primitive societies were organized around family clans, like the tribes of Israel. Clans often associated themselves with totemic symbols, called totems, such as a badge, a flag, coat of arms, or some emblem that served as a defining and recognizable sign for the clan." Angus pulled at his kilt. "We all have our colors."

Susan glanced at Winston's baseball cap. *Red, white, and blue.*

"Societies can only exist under the umbrella of a totem. Totemic symbols are held in high regard by basic tribal societies and have a powerful effect on those seeking a tribal identity. However, these totems are not worshiped; rather they represent the things in nature from which the clans and the tribe derive its strength. Individually, the various totem symbols represent the different kinships of the clans. United, the totems serve as an organized group of ideas that express the social consciousness and the underlying, unchangeable social schema—a type of symbolic tool for grasping the truths about the social order and the shared socially acceptable conventions."

Susan glanced again at the flag on Winston's cap.

"On another level," Angus added, "the totems served as a symbolic replacement of the mysteries found in nature. As societies became more organized, the clans began to reject the old magical ideas of compelling a god into their lives in favor of new transcendental ideas that stimulated the social self."

Yes, the self, Winston connected. *Independence.*

"Totemic symbols were often united to form a totem pole, a type of *axis mundi*, which served as the unifying symbol for the underlying relationship between the individual and the entire tribe. The design of entire communities, their ecomonic, social, and religious structures, were centered around such totem images. Here it was believed that the unsophisticated minds of a tribal society could not see themselves within a social group except through some material symbol to rally around, such as a flag or even a cross. A totem pole is often viewed by the clan with a certain reverence, but the totem in itself is not worshiped as a deity. It is a symbolic expression of the union within the tribal religion. The plants and animals depicted on a totem pole denote the aspects of tribal life within the sacred and profane worlds."

"Mine's profane," Winston said coolly. "Sometimes I feel like the low man on the totem pole."

Susan nodded silently in agreement.

"Yes, we all feel that way sometimes," Angus said. "According to E. E. Evans in his *Theories of Primitive Religion*, the association with the tribal ancestors was the basis for the religion of the tribal society. Fustel de Coulage, in his book, *The Ancient City,* expanded on Evans's theory, saying that the ancient classical societies were focused on the family lineages of their ancestors and the founding fathers of the tribe."

Memorials to the founding fathers, Winston connected. *Washington, Lincoln, and my other self.*

"This deification of one's ancestors was often symbolized by a *head,* since it was believed that the power of ancestors was a fundamental part of the human consciousness." Angus tapped his forehead with his fingers. "Sigmund Freud stated that the ancestor father figure served as the *head* deity for all of humanity—the source of our gene pools. Freud believed that every human being feels an innate psychological need for a paternal figure and that's why humanity created a god, because God represents our father in our unconscious mind. Each person's individual god was no more than a *projection of his father* from his childhood."

My penknife, Winston mused. *Promises.*

"Unconscious father figure," Susan repeated. "It's like King Malcolm and the skull image of Arthur's Seat ... a possible image of a head deity for the Malcolm clan."

"But, an image designed into the landscape can represent more than just a single individual or a family," Angus continued his lengthy discourse. "According to the social theories presented in *Elementary Forms of Religious Life* by the noted French father of sociology Emile Durkheim, 'the God of the clan is the clan itself.' For Freud, God is a symbol for the father figure. For Durkheim, God is only a symbol for society. Durkheim's view is similar to an old Jewish belief that God is simply a symbol for the rebuilt temple city-state, the new Messianic society, the *naos nios* in the Greek. It's sort of a messianic self-identity for a society. This is the type of symbolism presented in the illuminations from the *Kabalyon,* which King David was trying to reproduce in Edinburgh."

"I think I understand. You're saying that society can be its own God."

"Exactly, Jimmy ... but, not can be—it is! A God can be likened to a body of people of like mind, a *nois,* in the Greek. Within primitive societies, Durkhein observed a duality of religions, which he termed the negative and positive cults, or the sacred and the profane cults. They might be likened to today's political parties, the left and the right, or the liberals and the conservatives. These cults were not so much associated with good or evil as much as they were associated with the dual nature of man's consciousness—man's individual and collective consciousness. This social duality forms the soul of a society, which according to Durkhein was the 'soul of a religion.' The psychological duality of man's consciousness was a direct outcome of his social environment, where the two primary cults of society are guided and shaped. In this case, religious beliefs are *symbolic expressions* of social realities. Every person's god is merely a representation of the cultural values and morals of their local community, state, province, territory, or nation."

"Political parties are types of cults?" Susan asked with an uncertain expression. "Society as a God ... a Supreme Being?"

"They're two sides of the same coin," Angus replied. "Political parties take sides as representatives of either the individuals or the social collective—the I or the Thou, more government or less government. It's that type of thing—a political and social polarization. Western governments resemble the divided Western town presented in a Sergio Leone Italian movie."

Susan looked at Winston's shadow-shaven face. "Societies are about the good, the bad, and the ugly." She winked at Winston.

"The individual consciousness is associated with the profane cults," Angus said, "which relate to antisocial beliefs, a type of individual chaos. Societies dominated by individuals are diverse in structure because individuals depend upon the mixed bag of social conditions to differentiate themselves. In a diverse society, individuals often serve as the instigators of change from the social norm. Thus profane cults, as the *social anomaly*, are responsible for the progress of society. Many people define their identities through social groups which follow the greater social soul. It's a gang mentality. However, some people are meant to be alone. They are not the followers of the social norm. They are the autonomous, self-directed, and self-actualizing individuals. They are the soul searchers. They are the rare thinkers, the *seers* and the prophets who do not live a stagnant life and whose deeds can change the world."

That's me, Winston thought. *I'm a code breaker. I break away from the codes of society. I set my own course. Well ... sometimes. I am still a prisoner.*

"The sacred cult, on the *other hand*, is associated with the collective consciousness of a social group. The collective consciousness represents the accepted way of thinking—the well-ordered, controllable, predictable, and unchanging aspects of social life. It's the *herd* mentality of the complacent society, with everyone stepping in line and following authority. It's an egalitarian society, where a child can never be better than his parents, or his fellowman. All things sacred become authority figures. And according to the Hegelian view on religious fascism, the greatest authority figure of any society is the collective consciousness of the state."

The Global Consciousness, Winston thought.

"Again, all of this is associated with the symbol of a skull?" Susan asked.

"It's mental." Angus tapped his forehead again with his finger tips. "However, all of the lost images of the *Kabalyon* represent this collective consciousness, not just the skull image. These images end up being a picture of the God Consciousness that exists within the human mind and also within the realm of society, a social consciousness. It's a God shared by everyone. A God within us all. This is the greater Social Soul— where each individual is like a single cell in the larger organism—the God Society."

A God within us all, Winston eyed the goat-headed Baphomet on the page.

"A cell in a larger organism," Susan repeated, "like the ocean's biosystems."

"Yes," Angus affirmed. "The individual of the profane cult cannot enter into a relationship with the sacred except by way of a mysterious power that resides within each individual, which represents a type of rebirth into society by way of a rite of passage. In essence, if you do not follow the prescribed rites of passage for a society, then you remain a unique individual. A society rallies around the flag, so to speak. Individuals *do not*. Social life is made possible through a vast system of totemic symbols. And these totemic symbols, like the lost images of the *Kabalyon*, serve as visible symbols of the tribal god—the Social Deity."

"So every society, in essence, reveres itself, as its own God, or Social Soul?" Winston shook his head. "And this God can be represented by certain totem symbols for that society ... which show up in aspects of everyday life?"

"Exactly!" Angus said. "The symbols are found in our mythology, our religions, and our art ... in our creations."

"So, going back to Arnauld's criticism of Cartesianism," Winston proposed. "If a society is a God, and the people of that society do not know that society is their God, then those people are not clear and functional thinking beings, since the knowledge of who they are as individuals depends on their knowledge of the existence of their God. Their total concept of self depends on their knowledge of what God really is, and without that knowledge, they have not discovered themselves within a true reality. They're just staring at the shadows in Plato's Cave."

"Well put, Jimmy." Angus smiled at Winston's perceptiveness. "And an interesting comparison."

"So, what would you call people who do not know that society is their God?"

"Slaves," Angus replied bluntly. "A man is a slave to whatever has mastered him. You have just been set free, Jimmy. Knowledge is power."

"Damn, Angus! This is one hell of a kettle of fish." Winston exhaled a drawn out sigh and shook his head. "Please don't throw another book at us. It's a lot to swallow! It's a real fantasia. Sounds like the *Kabalyon* is the general theory for just about everything hermetic, and Christian for that matter."

Susan gawked at the pyramidal pile of books on the table and nodded in agreement.

"There are rumors that other versions of the *Kabalyon* exist besides the one purchased by Daniel Burnham," Angus explained as he changed topics. "One rumor claims that the Warren Expedition in 1867 discovered a second volume of the *Kabalyon* buried deep beneath the Temple Mount in Jerusalem. General Charles Warren wrote two books about his explorations, the *Underground Jerusalem* and *The Temple or the Tomb*. Again, their discoveries were carried back to Scotland, where they are said to be hidden away. Jimmy, your great-great-grandfather, Captain Andrew Alexander Winston, took part in that expedition." Angus gleamed proudly. "He even aided in the Ordnance Survey of the Sinai Desert carried out by Royal Engineers and led by Captain Charles Wilson in 1869. They attempted to trace the path of Moses and his people to the Promised Land. Your father was very interested in his great-grandfather's papers describing Egyptian stelae discovered in the desert."

"I didn't know all that," Winston said. "My father gave me his revolver."

"One legend claims King David's *Kabalyon* was taken to Melrose Abbey by Saint Waltheof. It is possible this is the version acquired by Dr. Dee when he searched the abbeys and churches throughout the British Isles. Still, another story says that King David thought it was better to be safe than sorry, so he made a complete copy from the original which he deposited in a metal box, about so big," Angus held his hands apart, "in the crypt at Rosslyn Chapel, a little south of Arthur's Seat as the crow flies, directly on top of the old rose-line. It's near the bend in the River Almond, where the Scots defended the Crown and beat the bloody English in 1303—the snakes. There're dozens of legends associated with Rosslyn. Some believe the severed head of Christ is buried beneath the Apprentice Pillar. There's even a letter on display at the National Museum from Queen Margarete to William St. Clair, thanking him for showing her the mysteries beneath the crypt."

How does he know the size of the metal box? Susan thought. "Head line ..." She checked her notes. "That convent near the Jerusalem meridian. We walked past it."

"Who was William St. Clair?" Winston asked.

"The chapel was built by the St. Clair's, the grand masters of Scottish

Freemasonry. Saint Clair means 'holy light'—the *Shekinah Glory*. Built like a Japanese pagoda with an interior as decorative as the Dilwara Temples in India, the chapel is a hypnotic place to visit. It's been called a medieval book in stone." Angus pointed to Rosslyn Chapel on the map. "It stands on a foundation of stones quarried from Arthur's Seat, laid on the day of a rare conjunction between Venus and the sun."

"My Huygens-Grimaldi experiment," Winston muttered.

"Stones from the head of a God …" Susan noticed the names on the map. "It's near the town of Roslin. That's where they did the first cloning."

"Yes," Angus agreed. "That's where they cloned Dolly the Sheep. Her stuffed carcass is on exhibit at the Royal Museum. But the start of the new species took place at George Washington University Medical Center in Washington, D.C. in 1993."

The first cloned sheep … a rose-line pointing to Arthur's Seat—the skull of heaven and the little dipper, Winston wondered. *A cosmology … the Lamb.*

Susan looked at her notes. "George Washington University, that's near another rose-line … The Key of All Keys."

"Cloning, DNA, Key of All Keys … People playing God," Winston commented, shaking his head. "Societies as gods."

"Rosslyn Chapel is located near the ruins of Rosslyn Castle, which served as a scriptorium for translating ancient documents acquired by King David and his heirs." Angus refocused on the chapel and added, "It is said certain aspects of the *Kabaylon* angel language are encoded in the design of Rosslyn Chapel by way of 215 stone cubes that enclose the upper cornices. Inscribed on these cubes are a series of characters that appear to be binary. When the symbols are plotted out, they resemble the musical notations for a song—a bird song maybe. This theory relies on the fact that at each point where an arch meets a pillar in the chapel, there is a carved cherub playing a different musical instrument. Some believe these characters, or notes, produce a type of healing music."

"A healing music?" Winston questioned. "Binary code … like an ouroboros snake in the virus … the chapel is encrypted?"

"Yes, Jimmy. It is said the music follows the cadence of a fifteenth-century chant. But, I suspect the music was derived from the Bhagavad-Gita, or the sounds of the birds. *Le ton beau*—the beautiful tone. Nothing quite compares to their angelic choir. Like angels, sometimes they fly so close to you that you can hear the flutter of their wings. You just have to have the right ears to listen."

"It's like my VDC that helps me sleep using harmonics and acupuncture points on the body's meridians," Winston clarified.

"Well, yes, it could be similar to that." Angus paused and noted, "Sound, like light, is a vibration—both exist on a spectrum of seven defined notes and colors. Only the music played at Rosslyn Chapel rests on top of an earthly meridian."

Buzz— A noise sounding like bees came from Susan's pants pocket.

"Excuse me, Angus, I have a phone call."

"Certainly, Susan," Angus said patiently.

Susan placed her Jawbone in her ear. "Hello … Yes. That's good news. … That's not good news." She cocked her head toward Winston, pantomimed to her wrist and mouthed, *Time to go.* "Where? Now? How soon…?" She unplugged the Jawbone from her ear and placed it her pocket. "James, they have another set of coordinates," she reported with an urgent expression. "Bains is threatening to take over if we don't come up with a solution soon." She readdressed Angus, "All of this is extremely interesting, but we have to leave now. A car is coming to pick us up. We're going back to Washington—"

"For God's sake, let me give you notice," Angus interrupted. "I know I sound a bit radgie gadgie with all of this. But I am *not*. The *Kabalyon* is an open secret to the few who know it. It's really not all that complicated. It's the Trogo Autoegocratic Law— we naturally get from the world what we need to survive. The survival of man and society is linked directly to his understanding of the geomagnetic fields, the changing seasons, and the movement of the heavens—the sun, the moon, and the stars. All man has to do to understand it all is to simply observe the actions and the migration of the birds. They have the sixth sense. They already know!" Angus spoke excitedly. "But, with that said, if what you are looking for is associated with the *Kabalyon*, then you need to carry yourself carefully." He frowned, a warning tone entering his voice, "Some misguided souls of the occult would kill to gain possession of one of the lost copies of the *Kabalyon*. The secrets of the *Kabalyon* should only be held by those who are worthy of understanding it."

"Well, Angus, if I stumble on a copy, I'll maintain a watchful eye."

"Misguided souls of the occult," Susan repeated with concern in her voice.

"The Brethren of the Nephilim, an elite group of puppet masters who wear the circular badge of a forked cross—the Upsilon—the Pythagorean and Ophite symbol of eternal life," Angus raised his looped forefinger and thumb to his right eye. "Their operatives are everywhere. Like the Russian Mafia, they brand themselves with tattoos. This elite group of reconstructionists and iconodules believe they do not exist unless their world is marked … and that those who control the images of the *Kabalyon* will rule the world."

"Totemic," Susan quipped. "The nine major networks."

Angus looked at Winston. "One more thing before you go. You'll need this." He went to the shelves one last time, retrieved an object that looked like a billiard ball perched on a wooden pedestal, and placed it at the middle of the table.

"What it is?" Susan flipped a page in her notepad.

"It's a Chinese *Ieoh Ming* message orb. The ancient ruling emperors along the Amur River Valley used to pass on secure messages in these orbs. Jimmy's father and I discovered this one hidden in Rosslyn Chapel. It's always reminded me of a Tibetan prayer wheel with a mantra hidden inside."

"Amur," Winston repeated. "Peres said something—"

"Looks like you finally found a letterbox." Susan smiled at Winston, then addressed Angus. "What were you doing at Rosslyn?"

"Need to know." Angus grinned. He lifted the orb from its stand and handed it to Winston. "It goes with the compass. It's where he found it. Inside the orb."

"I thought you said the compass belonged to James's grandfather," Susan recalled.

"Yes, my dear."

The crescent moon atop the Dome of the Rock, Winston thought, eyeing the stand. He held the orb in front of his face and marveled at the inlayed turquoise petroglyhs on its surface. "These are the Chinese characters Peres mentioned. Inscribe Brightly on the orb … winged dragons on either side of a blazing sun … like the cherubim on top of the Ark." He rotated it. "It has the same symbols as on the pocket compass. It's a puzzle ball for sure. It's sealed. How do you get inside? Do I have to cut it open?"

"So, the wizard is stumped." Susan smiled.

"All you need is the key," Angus said. "The orb is lined with precious stone as hard as diamond. You'll figure it out. Your father did. Take it. Put the compass back where it belongs, at the *center* of the orb. Make him proud. Here, Jimmy. Take this map of Edinburgh. You may want to reference it."

"Hello, Dolly …" Winston glanced at the map. " 'A man inside a Bigger Man.' " He tucked it in his pocket, then held the orb close to his face. "I might need some help. It's sealed tight." He jiggled the orb to his ear. "I hear something inside."

"Then before you travel back to the States, you need to speak to Professor Simmons Coxy. He knew your father, Jimmy. He knows about the orb. He's doing research in France. I'm an amateur compared to him. He's an old goat, but he understands the mysteries related to Edinburgh much better than I. He thinks Arthur's Seat is connected to an old Earth grid system. Simmons is aware of certain coordinates, some very special coordinates. He also knows about the *Kabalyon* and the dragon currents. He is an expert in the V.I.T.R.I.O.L. and understands the workings of the Reshel format. He could be way ahead of you in your quest."

"Vitriol? It sounds like a fortified vitamin drink. Dragon currents?" Winston eyed the symbols on the orb. "Reshel format … what's that?"

"You need to speak to Professor Coxy, Jimmy," Angus insisted.

Winston turned to Susan. "You head back to Washington and report in with Bains. I'm going to France for a day to check out Professor Coxy."

"So you think there is something to what Angus is saying?" She lowered her voice. "Do you think the *Kabalyon* has something to do with all of this?"

"Exactly, my dear." Winston cut a slow grin.

———

ONBOARD PanAm Flight 2330 bound for Rome, Professor Maisun adjusted the leg rest of his roomy seat in First Class.

"Dr. Maisun," a stewardess politely addressed him, approaching from behind. "We will be in Rome in approximately twenty minutes. You have a phone call. This way, please."

"Of course." Maisun reached for the metal security box resting in the seat next to him. He rose up and followed her into the forward lounge to a communications booth with a built-in desk and two telephones.

"It's the phone with the blinking light." She pointed and closed the door, leaving Maisun alone.

He placed the box on the table, pressed the lighted button, and lifted the receiver to his ear. "Hello."

"He has a package, Professor," a refined voice said calmly.

"Thank you." Maisun hung up, pulled a phonecard from his billfold, and swiped it in the slot on the side of the phone. He held the receiver to his ear and dialed a number. *Twenty minutes*, he thought, glancing impatiently at his watch and then to the security box. He heard a *click—*

"Leave a message at the sound of the tone."

Beep

"Hello, Jagermeister Komodo. Expedite 918."

***

Day 13
Array

And God said casually, "Let the Land produce the living creatures according to their kind." And God let the Land make it so. And the Land made the wild animals according to their kind. And the Land made the livestock according to their kind. And the Land made all the creatures that stand upon the ground according to their kind. And God proclaimed that it was good.

Then God said casually, "Let us make man in our own image, in our own likeness, and let man rule over the fish of the deep and the birds of the air. Let man rule over the livestock. Let man rule over all the earth, which is the Land, and over all the creatures made by the Land that stand upon the ground."

So God made man in his own image, in the image of God he created him; both male and female he created them. God blessed them to *think* and said to them, "Be fruitful and multiply and *evolve*; fill my earth with yourself and *subdue* the Land. Rule over the fish of the deep and the birds of the air and over every other living creature that stands upon the surface of the ground made by the Land."

Then God said casually, "And to all the beasts of the earth and all the birds of the air and all the creatures that I *inscribed* upon the surface of the ground. To everything that I have shared my breath of life, I give every green plant for food."

And God made it so.

And when God saw all he had made, He called it wonderful, *only* if it was true, and *only* if it was good.

All through the evening of the sixth day God wondered.

And all through the morning of the seventh day, God still wondered.

Was it good?

Thus the heavens and the earth were completed by God in all their vast *array*.

WINSTON HELD A LOOSE GRIP, staring over the top of the steering wheel at a narrow, two-lane blacktop that ribboned through the Burgundy vineyards of French Brittany. He had taken the high-speed train from Edinburgh to London, proceeded by car to Plymouth, then crossed the English Channel the night before to Roscoff aboard the Seagull ferry. Now he was en route to his rendezvous with the tough-as-a-pine-knot Professor Simmons Coxy.

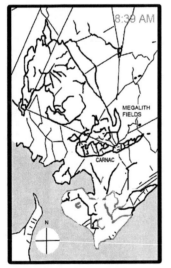

The upholstery of the rental had a new car smell mixed with the acrid odor of stale cigarette smoke. Winston tapped on the pine tree car freshener hanging from the rearview mirror. *Maybe I should pray to it,* he reckoned. He checked a map overlaid with a digital compass rose on the GPS screen in the car's dash. A flashing red arrow snaked north along a well-marked road between the topographic contours, pointing to 8:39 AM blinking at the top of the screen. *I'm going to be late.* Grinding gears, he negotiated the stick shift into fourth, and the blue-jay-blue Smart car efficiently picked up speed.

Eyeing through the mirror, Winston noticed a set of headlights advancing fast. Within seconds, the compass logo on the grill of a black Acura was hugging his bumper. He observed a man wearing sunglass sitting low behind the wheel. *What's his hurry?* Winston gunned the engine. The needle on his speedometer vibrated past 110 kph. *They say this dinky dynamo is better than a little lemon. It's fast. But it's still hard to beat an old '57 Volkswagen.*

The Acura held tight on Winston's bumper.

Winston stuck his arm out the window and waved. "It's your road!" He exchanged glances with the other driver, as the Acura darted into the other lane with its left tail light blinking. It raced by in a high-pitched whine and sped out of sight. *A crazy Japanese tourist,* Winston thought, noticing the driver's Oriental features.

———

APPROACHING QUIMPER, Winston spotted a weathered road sign.

CONCARNEAU 8 KILOMETERS

Stone megaliths dotted the nearby fields, like dinosaur bones protruding from the ground. *The Mendelsohn Synagogue,* he compared. *I'm getting closer.*

Minutes later, he down shifted, and the engine *purred,* as he circled through the roundabout at the center of the walled town of Concarneau. All of the buildings were made of stone, with the village shops crowded together around the town commons. *Locmariaquer Pub ... where is it? Angus said the professor would meet me there.* He noticed a building with four wrought-iron tables in front. Above its entry, a bold red-lettered sign read: **LOCMARIAQUER.** *I'm in luck.* Winston smiled. *It's a red-letter day!*

A man dressed in a dingy sweatshirt and faded jeans sat slump-shouldered at one of the tables. Self-absorbed, his face was shielded by the wide brim of his gray fedora as he read intently from a file folder.

Winston parked within thirty feet of where the man sat. He noticed the black Acura parked at the far end of the commons. He grabbed his *Northface* rucksack, stepped from his car, and slammed the door.

The bloodshot eyes of the man at the table peered up from his papers at the stranger coming toward him. A sustained puff of smoke rose from a six-inch-long, chalk-white, mammoth bone pipe balanced from one side of his mouth.

"Excuse me! Are you Professor Coxy?" Winston shouted.

"You must be McCalester's friend." Coxy replied, his pipe gripped between his teeth. He stuck out his thick, callused land-hand.

Winston dropped his rucksack in a chair and shook Coxy's hand. "Hello, I'm James Winston."

Coxy remained seated with a puffed-eyed glare that mirrored Lee Marvin's from the movie *Paint Your Wagon. He's got a friendly kipper.* He sized up Winston. *But look at those threads he's wearing. He's dressed like a bum. Stains on his kecks. A baseball cap with an American flag on the front. The Yanks and their totems. He must be patriotic. And those dirty scuffed-up hiking shoes ... I wonder if they are comfortable.* He pulled his pipe from his mouth. "I'm Simmons Arkas Phereclus Coxy, the Third. I'm from Newcastle, where I teach at the college's School of Geology. I grew up around Newcastle, near the Thornborough Complex, the triple super-henge monument mirrored after Orion, Britain's largest ritual site." He paused. "So, you're the chip from the old block. I understand you're John Winston's boy."

"Yes." Winston nodded.

"I knew your father. He was a brilliant man, with a stiff upper lip. He always toed the line. No one could hold a candle to the man. Second to none. One of the ablest men I ever knew. He had an incredible vision of things that still reaches out beyond his grave." Coxy reached across the table for an open bottle of imported Flying Fish beer, surrounded by empty bottles of Belgian *Satan Gold, Belzebuth Pur Malt,*

Jagermeister, Tungi Spirit, Mountain Goat Hightail Ale, and a Bordeaux *Cabellon.* "However, he was a bit of a rogue sometimes. I remember when we were in school; he once tried to drink me under the table. I wasn't worth three sheets to the wind. Your father certainly knew how to hold his drink."

"I didn't know that. I thought he was a teetotaler." Winston eyed the strange fish logo on the bottle in Coxy's hand. *It reminds me of the symbols on Billy's gorget.*

Coxy took a sip from the bottle and refreshed his memory. "Care for some drinkable gold?" Without making eye contact, he held out the bottle. "The Babylonians considered beer the sacred union of earth and water—the *terra* and *rectificando*. It's a powerful medicine, an *aqua vitae* used by every civilization from Egypt to Peru. It's the best Soma I've ever had!"

"No thanks," Winston replied. "I'm on a diet."

"It's my hair of the dog. Every time I take a shot I lose some brain cells. It's how I make room for some new brain cells. I don't want to get bigheaded." Coxy smirked. "Here's looking at you, and your father." He finished off his drink and wiped away the dribble sticking to his graying goatee with the back of his hand. "Yes ... The good men are true. How we were friends." He glared at the long-necked amber bottle in his hand, like he was appreciating the figure of a beautiful woman. "Ambrosia ... Ah, the potatory pleasures. Friendships, like good wine, always seem to get better with age. It's sad and unjust somehow, that this fine bottle of wine is gone." He peered at Winston as he thought about how much the son resembled his father. "Son, men such as your father are as scarce as hen's teeth."

"I miss him, too. He's a hard act to follow." Winston paused, then probed forward. "Professor, Dr. McCalester said you might shed some light on this orb I have. He said you knew how to open it." He reached into his rucksack and handed Coxy the orb.

"I remember this," Coxy said gruffly, rotating the orb in his hand. "It's your father's. It's a message orb—a Pandora's box. I presume McCalester gave it to you?"

"Yes, he did."

"Well ... I guess he knows what he's doing," Coxy scoffed. "Yes, I know how to open it." He handed it back to Winston.

"Dr. McCalester also implied that you are an expert on the relationship of something called *dragon currents* to a global meridian system."

"Hmm— Channeling, telepathy, crystal ball gazing, lay-lines, quantum healing, telluric currents, Odic forces, and map-dowsing are all the tools of the spoon-bending tricksters," Coxy snorted. "I do not call them *dragon currents.* That's some New Age tommyrot. I call them *global standing waves* which shape the Earth's magnetically oriented Hartmann Net. And I'm not certain if there are any experts in this field of study. I'm currently doing a field experiment at the Carnac site. It's a study that has never been done before."

"What's your research about?"

"Well, if we're finished with our little yackety-yak, let me really bend your ear." Coxy slapped his beer belly with both hands and heaved a low harmonic belch that reeked worse than the mile-wide approach to the Guinness brewery outside of Dublin. "Why don't we go to the site, and I'll explain it to you. Perhaps I can answer your questions." He sluggishly pushed himself up from the table, holding on to balance himself as he collected his papers.

"Sure. Your car or mine?" Winston asked with one eyebrow raised.

"The research site is just on the other side of that field." Coxy pointed with the end his pipe. "Why don't we do some walking. It's good for your health, you know. It can boost your memory." He wobbled a few steps forward. "I recently purchased a brand new pair of Nike running shoes. I need to break them in." He stuck out his left foot and showed off his Pro GTX Lugus fashion-colored running shoe.

Winston observed the tall, barrel-chested Antaean teetering on one foot. *I'm not certain you can walk in those shoes, let alone run.*

As they stepped away, Winston eyed a waiter dressed in a *bright* blue, travel-light shirt from L. L. Bea*m*. The waiter smiled pleasantly as he collected the empty bottles onto a tray he held in one hand. He winked at Winston and darted his eyes at Coxy, then clenched his fist, tipped his thumb to his mouth, and cut his eyes at Coxy again.

———

COXY LIMPED FORWARD WITH A HEAVY *THUMP*, as they gaited at an uneven pace along a dust-blown path that led to a wooded hill.

He's walking tipsy, Winston noticed. *I wonder if he's had too much to drink. He's draggin' along like Frankenstein.* "Professor, is there something wrong with your leg? I see you're limping."

"It's my bloody toe! I have an ingrown toenail that's festered. It's the reason I purchased these damn winged sandals." Coxy kicked with his foot, like a rooster scratching in the dirt. "But, don't you worry about me. If it gets worse, I'll start using my middle leg." He beamed proudly. "My boy, have you ever been to this part of France before?"

"No, I've never been here before." Winston chuckled beneath his breath. "But my parents used to vacation near here. They did some research on the nearby abbeys."

"Well, you are in for a treat, Mr. Winston."

A spooked covey of quail took flight from a low chaparral, as they emerged from a weald of trees. Coxy pointed to a clearing about a hundred yards ahead, covered with irregular rows of four-to-twelve-foot-high, megalithic columns. "Now that we are out of the woods, let me lead you into the forest. I've been doing fieldwork here for the past three weeks. Are you familiar with the history of Carnac?"

"No," Winston replied. "It looks like a graveyard."

"It's a prehistoric alignment site, similar to the Avebury menhirs in England. This legion of stones is arranged in parallel rows. The area covers over 135 hectares. Many believe the site dates back 7,000 years to the Hallstatt culture. No one can put an exact date on the place. I believe part of the site goes back 16,000 years, to the time of the star charts drawn in the Lascaux caves of Central France—the first churches."

"So, who created all this?"

"Bloody good question. These stones have intrigued a lot of researchers over the years. Even Benjamin Franklin and Thomas Jefferson visited Carnac once."

Now twice, Winston thought.

"Most researchers believe they were created by the predecessors of the Celts who lived in this area at one time. This alignment of stones is unusual in its design. As with Avebury, Stonehenge, and the *nuraghes* in Sardinia, there is no clear understanding as to what the alignment really signifies. A few researchers have theorized the alignment acted as a guide to a celestial or astronomical phenomenon. This whole system of stones could be a huge observatory of some kind. The most respected theory is that Carnac was a lunar observatory. At the cross-axis of the complex is the huge broken orthostat called *Le Grand Menhir Brisé* which is aligned to the moon."

Maybe they were searching for a longitude, Winston mused, remembering what Angus and Dr. Peres had told him.

Coxy led Winston through the field, turning his head back and forth and up and down, inspecting the stone columns like a farmer studying a crop ready for harvest. "These stones are *amazing*. They're the largest in Brittany. There are similar sites scattered throughout this part of France. Because of the large number of such sites, this region must have contained a prosperous and well-organized society. Sheltered by the Quiberon Peninsula with an abundance of freshwater springs, Carnac provided an ideal place to hunt, fish, and gather food. With the advent of agriculture which guaranteed a regular food supply, the people in this area must have had enough time on their hands to construct these huge monuments of stone. It's amazing to think of how much labor and time it took to construct a site such as this. It is truly *amazing*, don't you think?"

"As they walked between the rows, Winston noticed several shoebox-size, black, plastic boxes attached to each column with gray duct tape. A white sticker on each box read: MILLENNIUM RADIO GROUP, BOSTON. The boxes were connected to one another by wire harnesses which led to a central cable snaking along the ground to a makeshift cabin tent at the far end of the field. *Letterboxes...?* "What's with all the wires? It reminds me of an experiment in my basement."

"Have you ever read Jules Verne, the science fiction writer?"

"Yes," Winston replied.

"How about his book, *Journey to the Center of the Earth?*"

"I read all of his stories when I was younger. I've even seen the movies on TV and in the theaters," Winston elaborated.

"Nemo is an anagram for Omen, don't you know?"

"No, I did not know that." Winston paused.

"In Verne's book, the Earth had a hollow core occupied by the remains of a lost civilization. It's an allegory for something else."

"Yes, I know," Winston said.

"Well, Verne's story does not agree with science. Since 1936, science has held that the nucleus of our planet really consists of a solid iron core enveloped by a sea of molten magma."

"Right, I live near the remains of an extinct volcano," Winston remarked.

"I'm sure you do," Coxy said smugly. "But a new theory emerged in 1995 about the Earth's inner core, formulated from a sophisticated computer model. Recent seismic mappings, measured with sensitive instruments from key locations on the planet's surface, have offered a new picture of the center of the Earth."

Coxy stopped outside the door of the tent and tapped his pipe against the palm of his hand to clean out the charred and blackened bowl. He faced Winston, took a deep breath and spoke bluntly, "Geologists have discovered that a giant crystal is buried deep within our planet, more than 3,000 miles below."

"A crystal?"

"Let's dig deeper." Coxy stared seriously above the deep waves of sagging circles under his eyes. "Let me show you something that very few people know."

They entered the tent and Coxy switched on a beat-up laptop sitting on a metal folding table next to an opened bottle of beer and a stack of books. The case of the laptop was cracked, with one side of the screen wrapped in duct tape. Above the computer hung a brass wire birdcage in the shape of a Japanese pagoda. At the center of the cage, a golden-green and scarlet-plumed, long-tailed Quetzal perched atop a swinging trapeze. *"Twit-twit, twit-twit, twit-twit."*

Coxy eased himself into a director's chair in front of the laptop. He pinched a plug of tobacco from a tin can on the table, an "Esoterica" blend, and tamped it in the bowl of his pipe. "Do you smoke?"

"No," Winston admitted.

"I'm not supposed to. I have pneumonoultramicro-," Coxy wheezed, "scopicsilico-volcanoconiosis, a lung affliction I acquired after digging up a laraium snake altar in the ash covered House of the Vestals in Pompeii. But, I have a bad habit of doing the things I'm not supposed to do." He lit a match and puffed his pipe back to life. Its embers glowed yellow-red hotspots like magma breathing across the basin of a volcano. "Let's get down-to-earth by throwing some light on this with some curious data I've collected." He leaned forward through swirls of smoke and addressed the laptop. "What I have pieced together comes primarily from the seismic data."

Point and *click.* A PowerPoint animation appeared on the screen.

"Sometimes the occult nature of the scientific method causes us to play the devil's advocate and come up with a new explanation for things we did not expect to discover. Here is a pictorial example of how the data was studied using deep-core physics. When shock waves from earthquakes ripple through the planet, they are detected by sensitive seismic instruments at various locations on the surface. The data collected on these vibrations show an ever-so-slight change in their path and speed which has allowed scientists to draw inferences about the planet's interior structure. The data revealed a puzzling anomaly. Seismic waves traveled faster north-to-south than east-to-west, about five seconds faster from pole-to-pole than through the equator." Coxy waved his hand, jabbing the tip of his pipe at Winston's face.

"Five seconds? Someone did some precision calculations." Winston tilted his head to one side and eyed the arabesque pattern of Celtic knots that adorned the pipe.

"All of these findings were confirmed only within the past few years. The data was fed into a CRAY C90 computer at the Pittsburgh Supercomputing Center and the Earth-listening station at the Black Forest Observatory in Germany. It leads us to the conclusion that the Earth's solid-iron inner core is anisotropic." Coxy rotated his pipe between his teeth and bit down. "It's vibrating!"

Winston appeared puzzled. "Vibrating?"

"It's a *crystal,* Mr. Winston. Let me show you a computer model of this thing." Coxy readdressed the laptop. "Now, pay close attention. Look at the simulated design of this crystal at the core. It is a latticework formation. The crystal floats in a sea of spinning magma, like an embryo in its mother's womb."

"Yes, it's a crystalline network, a big diamond," Winston touched the screen and outlined the shape, "a diamond mine ..."

"Alright. The core is shaped around a lattice network, or a diamond as you say. All crystals are," Coxy agreed. "This *sambhogakāya* is hexagonal of the *first water.* Each vertex on this latticed core helps to determine the crystal's natural vibration—its harmonic. The various vertices on the crystal resonate a pattern of harmonic waves that intersect the Earth's crust at *key* geographic points on the planet's surface. Our world is aligned harmonically to the lattice shape of the core." Point and *click*. "The arrangement of these *key* geographic features on the Earth's surface offers us a rare view of what lies beneath. It's a revelation to a truth that lies beneath it all. The old ideas have flown out the window. Everything lies beneath!"

"You're saying you've mapped out the core of the Earth?" Winston questioned.

"Let me elaborate." Point and *click*. "By plotting these geographic locations around the globe, we can postulate a 3-D model of the crystal. For example, we can determine the number of lattices, the relative size of the core, and the frequencies of

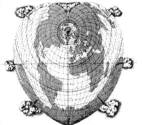

low-level harmonics oscillating from the core."

"Interesting," Winston said with piqued curiosity.

"Now, are you aware of longitude and latitude?"

"Yes, I'm a bit festered with them," Winston said, whey-faced. "I've been chasing them down all week."

"Maybe you've been studying the wrong maps." Coxy opened a reference atlas on the table. "Look at this sixteenth-century map by an Arab geographer. It's called the Hadji Ahmed Map. It's a map with lines of longitude converging at the North Pole. This cartography set a new standard in its day for mapping out the world."

"It's heart-shaped," Winston noted, his eyes probing over the map. *An appleglobe. Where have I seen that before...? Old Bucktooth,* he remembered.

"Those lines on this old map are all artificial." Coxy motioned back to the screen. "We discovered that there is a natural grid system for the planet which is a reflection of, and directly linked to, the crystal core and specifically aligned to the crystal core's lattice structure. Now, those ley lines or *dragon currents* spoken of by the New-Agers are not some sort of quackery. When understood in relation to the true geological data, we have a science that naturally maps the planet to its inner core. I call it the Core Grid. The New-Agers call it the Reshel Grid. The noted American architect, thinker, and inventor Buckminster Fuller was heavily into this mode of thought. He mapped the world, not as a round globe, but as a geometric crystal-shaped lattice, with the landmasses anchored to the flattened *plates*. In his book *Synergetics 2*, he called it the Composite of Primary and Secondary Icosahedron Great Circle Sets, icosahedrally

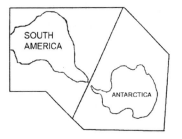

derived from a spherical polyhedron of twenty equal-sided triangular faces. Fuller's map is the most geometrically accurate map of the world."

Point and *click*. A version of a Fuller's Projection Dymaxion™ Map of the world appeared on the screen.

Winston glued his eyes closer to the laptop. "I know they call South America the 'bird continent,' but the layout of the land masses resembles a winged bird, a duck or a goose, with South America pecking at Antarctica. You know, the shape of Antarctica reminds me of Michelangelo's brain scan." *God is in Antarctica...? Jerusalem, maybe.*

"A bird and a brain scan? I think you are seeing things, Mr. Winston. Fuller's map reveals the nature of the hidden shape of the planet. On Fuller's map, the Earth's landmass is a sprawling island surrounded by a single ocean—like the crystal embryo at the core. And like an embryo, this landmass has a navel, a central place where it is connected to the source. The Europeans once placed Jerusalem at the navel of the world. But they were *not* seeing the whole world. Fuller's map changes all of that. It's Plato's *Atlantis,* with Washington, D.C. at the new center. Everything lies beneath!"

"Hmm, a unified landmass, *Pangea,*" Winston said.

"This way of plotting points and interconnecting them is a very metaphysical approach to seeing the unseen," Coxy equated. "Fuller's map reveals the world's lattice network which is naturally formed around the embryonic crystalline core."

"Yes," Winston agreed. "In synergetics, thinking is a visual process, where ideas are mapped out as images and geometric constructs that are artificially created in the human mind before they become a reality. I learned this in the computer design of artificial intelligence. Fuller's map is a Hamiltonian vector field, built around an interconnecting lattice of points in space in order to view something invisible. I've seen it used in program routines for CAD-CAM, such as Talisman graph technology. All future PCs will have this technology built into them. It's part of the Xanadu Project for the development of the World Wide Web around *free access*, where everyone will have a wimp *point-and-click* access from whatever computer, video game, or multimedia player they want to use. Everything and everyone will be interconnected. It will be a *point-and-click* universe."

"Outrageous, man! Volley! Good point. Your father would be proud!" Coxy furled his lips and bit on the end of his pipe, seesawing it in his mouth. "You must have sprung from your mother's womb headfirst. I can tell you're one of Zeus's offspring."

Winston smiled like he had passed a test. *But Jefferson must have figured this out way before Fuller, if Elvis is right,* he pondered. *Washington, D.C. is at the center of it all?* He rechecked the map on the screen. *I don't know,* he thought. *Devil's Tower could be at the geographic midpoint of the landmass.*

His son's no slouch, Coxy approved as he studied Winston's behavior. *He's worth his salt. I guess I should never take someone for granted. Tap, Tap.* Coxy rapped the table with the bowl of his pipe. "Mr. Winston, your attention please."

Winston shifted his eyes to Coxy.

"By lining up the principal geographic features from around the globe, dozens of grid or lattice patterns can be created which appear to modulate just below the surface of the globe as natural rose-lines aligned to the crystal core. I have discovered that one such rose-line runs through the Carnac site. Carnac rests on top of one of the harmonic nodes transmitted from a leading edge of one of the vertices of the crystal core."

"So these stones at Carnac are aligned somehow to the Earth's core?" Winston questioned.

"Not just the core, mind you, it's aligned to the vertices of the lattice on the outside of the crystal," Coxy clarified. "Everything lies beneath! The Earth's changing pressure produces a piezo-effect upon the crystal core."

"A piezo-effect?" Winston questioned again.

"It's the result of a balanced tensegrity. When you deform or strike a piece of quartz, an electric charge is generated. And when you pass an electric charge through quartz, it vibrates at a specific frequency. This is how quartz watches keep such good time and how piezo-electric lighters generate a spark."

"Yes, I know," Winston affirmed.

"Theoretically, the piezo-effect causes the crystalline core to vibrate carrier waves around certain harmonics tuned to various ELF, Extremely Low-level Frequencies. To be precise, the core resonates an infrasound at approximately 7.83 Hertz on the Schumann Resonance scale. This embryo at the core has a heartbeat."

"That's a plausible theory. I can understand how that might happen," Winston said, trying to follow Coxy's alcohol-enhanced explanation.

"No, it's a fact! Nothing rests. Everything moves. Everything vibrates. Every time there is an earthquake, geologists have recorded these associated electromagnetic emissions. The U. S. Navy Research Lab has been measuring these emissions for years. Seventy-seven degrees west of Greenwich at Belgrano Station in Antarctica, there is a base for measuring both above and *below* ground cosmic ray observations."

"Navy Research Lab ... That's a major facility for studying artificial intelligence," Winston noted. "Seventy-seven degrees ... Antarctica, the God Long—"

"Yes—your brain scan, Mr. Winston," Coxy reminded. "The Earth's changing pressure on the core, like the tidal flows of the oceans, is caused by the fluctuating gravitational pull of the sun, the moon, and the other planets. The recent earthquakes we hear about in the news could be induced by the alignment of the heavenly bodies."

"Such as the alignment of the recent transit of Venus with Earth and the sun?" Winston proposed.

"You're a quick study. You're no rookie. A good point. But recently, the moon and the planets Mars and Jupiter were in that alignment as well. So the old ideas promoted in astrology related to man's fate and the alignment of the stars holds a certain scientific relevance here."

"Alright. I'm following you so far," Winston said. "It has to do with gravity."

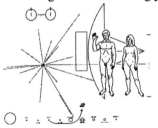

"It's more than just gravity, my boy. It's something that dances with gravity. Recently, the Jet Propulsion Laboratory discovered *the presence* of an anomaly in the expected gravitational pull on the trajectory of one of the Pioneer satellites that exited our solar system."

"A Pioneer satellite?" Winston questioned.

"The one with the little cosmology plaque attached to the side, with the universal symbols defining its point of origin," Coxy explained, "man and woman before a transmitting *um*brella. The JPL discovered the path of the satellite is off of its trajectory by more than 80,000 miles. The calculation of its expected trajectory was based upon the known gravitational pulls from the planets. The only conclusion is that another force outside of gravity is involved in controlling the satellite's trajectory. Newton's gravitational constant, the formula *G*, is not constant. Some scientists believe this 'other force' is caused by the frame-dragging of space-time around massive spinning bodies, such as the planets. It's been theorized that rotating masses can twist space-time into *fractured openings to another reality* where all existing scientific theories break down and the Infinite becomes possible. Such fractured spikes in space-time could allow a momentary linking to the theoretical Boltzmann brain." Coxy took a quick draw from his pipe and exhaled a chain of expanding smoke rings. "I believe the force responsible for the change in the satellite's trajectory is the weak harmonic flux coming from the core of our planet and the other planets as well. It may even be the source of the mysterious Chandler wobble, a small variance in the Earth's axis of rotation. This flux from the heavenly bodies creates an interconnected harmonic latticework for the entire universe—an invisible aether of space—much like the phonon field used in the creation of the Higgs boson."

"The Higgs boson," Winston repeated. "I've heard of that. It's Plato's Goat, the God Particle which physicists are trying to create with the particle accelerator in Switzerland. It's a particle constrained by an electromagnetic field, like an alchemy experiment where you resurrect a new material inside a crucible. The God Particle is the missing building block in nature. It holds the *key* to the subatomic world and supersymmetry which would redefine the nature of the entire universe."

"Correct, the Perfect Particle from the God Detector at CERN," Coxy acknowledged. "Perfection is simplicity. Now, I have a theory which is not so simple. I believe that the heavens are speaking to us by way of the carrier waves emitted from the Earth's crystal core—carrier waves which those New-Agers call *dragon currents*." Coxy minded Winston's thoughtful expression, trying to read his understanding of what had been said.

"Another force outside of gravity, a heartbeat from the Earth—transmitting a signal?" Winston shook his head. "A harmonic resonance ... a God Wave—"

"Yes, a relentless harmonic hum, the Breath of Life," Coxy blurted.

"Amazing." Winston's curiosity sharpened. "You've festered my fascination."

"I hope I have. I'm a teacher, just like your father. Have you ever heard of Nikola Tesla?"

"Yes. He was an American physicist. He was the ultimate geek."

"No, I believe he was Hungarian," Coxy challenged in a feisty tone. "Tesla, known as the Pigeon Man from Manhattan, was a spark of genius. He was the great communicator who worked with radio-frequencies and electromagnetic waves. And despite the claims made by Marconi, it was Tesla who actually invented the idea for radio as we know it today. He went on to experiment with wireless transmission of electrical power through the Schumann resonance, the air gap between the ionosphere and the Earth's surface which acts as a wave guide for the orientation of radio waves."

"Yeah, I know about all that," Winston remarked. "Wireless transmission—a two-way line of communication." *Michelangelo's brain scan* ...

"Correct, a transmitter." Coxy affirmed. "As far back as 1859, the telegraph lines in the United States were powered by electrical currents induced from the geomagnetic actions of the solar wind in the ionosphere. In Colorado Springs, Tesla tested his theory that power could be transmitted through the air using the largest Tesla coil ever built, called the Magnifying Transmitter. It was capable of generating 300,000 watts of power. Reportedly, it could produce a bolt of lightning 130 feet long. According to one account, he successfully transmitted 50,000 watts of power without using ground lines. Instead, he transmitted by way of the Earth's electromagnetic field—the same field which I believe is emitted from the Earth's crystalline core. Tesla saw the Earth's north-south polarities and its immense magnetic fields as parts of a huge, self-sustaining dynamo encased in a fluid outer-core," Coxy explained. "He believed he could tap into that dynamo and harness an endless supply of free energy.

It was a type of 'aether technology,' a metaphysical free energy. He was trying to harness the great *wheelwork* of Nature."

A wheelwork ... the Tekton, Winston sparked a thought, *Washington, D.C. at the crossroads.*

Coxy pointed again to the PowerPoint display. "The effect of the moving sea of magma around the crystal core acts like the windings in an electric motor. It's the dynamo that drives the life force for the whole planet."

"That's right," Winston responded. "Anything made of *iron*, any ferrous metal, will produce a *magnetic field*."

"The Earth's egged-shaped magnetoshpere shields all life on the planet from the harmful effects of the solar winds. Without this protection, life could not survive on the surface of the Earth. The crystal, in effect, is the guardian of all life on the planet," Coxy summed up. "In fact, the dynamo is the *prana* creative source for all primordial life, which over the eons has oozed up to the surface from geological changes deep within the planet. These primordial microbes, emerging from the darkness and reaching out for the light of the sun, excrete the oxygen required by all the higher forms life. It's Einstein's Law of Photochemistry. The crystal core drives it all. It's the *soul* of the Earth!"

A Mundane Egg ... The core is the source? Winston pondered. *The Earth and sun combined form the creative source for life.*

"Out and out, I believe the harmonics coming from the core can be amplified by other crystalline structures on the Earth's surface, such as these stone alignments at Carnac, or the ferrous meteor deposits embedded in the Earth's crust. It's similar to the Helmholtz resonance effect." Coxy grabbed a beer bottle from the table and lightly blew across its mouth, producing an airy drone like a low note from a pipe organ. "In some places on the globe people claim they can hear a low-frequency hum near certain geological formations, such as the Auckland Volcanic Field in New Zealand, the Bristol Gorge in England, and Mount Sinai above the junction of the fault lines between the Gulf of Suez and the Gulf of Aqaba. I was taking measurements outside Taos, New Mexico two months ago, where I heard a harmonic resonance along the gorge that cuts through the Taos Plateau volcanic field. I could actually feel it vibrating throughout my whole body."

Mount Sinai ... the skull, the mountain of god, Winston thought. *Billy getting attuned on top of Devil's Tower.* "Meteor deposits. What did Elvis say?" he remembered aloud. "There was an impact crater at Cape Charles associated with the meridian through Washington."

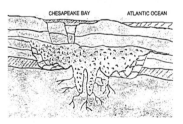

"It's like the Silverpit crater in the North Sea or the crater hidden below the surface of north-central California," Coxy said. "It's a bolide crater buried 500 meters beneath the southern part of the Chesapeake Bay, not far from the Thomas Jefferson Accelerator Lab, where the U.S. Department of Energy studies the quantum effects of high-beam polarized light. Look at this diagram." Point and *click.* Coxy opened a picture file. "There is a ferrous crystalline tower, five times taller than the Washington Monument buried at the middle of that crater. These deposits can affect the magnetic fields of the planet.

Magnetic north deviates as much as eleven degrees around the Chesapeake Bay, where certain waters are posted off limits by the U. S. Navy."

Winston stared at the phallic profile of the towering underground monolith. "Mother of God, it's huge!"

"Such ferrous concentrations are buried all over the planet," Coxy remarked. "Italy, Scotland, Israel, Arizona—each emitting its own signature magnetic variance. A similar, but smaller, impact crater is responsible for the bowl-shaped topography next to the fault line near the heart of Washington, D.C."

A city encircled by seven hills, Winston recalled.

"I believe these deposits, along with other structures on the surface, could act as a type of natural antenna *array,*" Coxy said, "similar to Telsa's coil experiment, a forerunner to the High Frequency Active Auroral Research Program—HAARP. I believe these stone columns here at Carnac amplify the weak signal coming from the core. I've had the opportunity to dabble in some serious analysis here at Carnac over the last few days. The intensity of this signal is what I'm trying to figure out with my experiments. Anything that disturbs the delicate balance of the Earth can have an effect on the carrier waves."

"That's also an interesting theory," Winston remarked, with a knee-jerk reaction.

"Yes, that goes without saying. But, Mr. Winston, this is *not* a theory. About thirteen days ago, I discovered an increase in the harmonic flux coming up from the Earth's core. Something is happening that has never happened before," Coxy stressed as he leaned back in his chair with a serious look in his eyes. "The ever-so-faint modulation of those *dragon currents* has been amplified somehow. These frequency modulations pulsing from the core are randomly affecting nearby electronic equipment in a disturbing way. Electronic devices near these stone structures periodically go dead for just a few seconds."

"An electronic disturbance," Winston muttered. *The Washington Monument and the helicopter crash,* he thought about what Ranger Nobles had said. "So how has the harmonic flux been amplified?"

"I asked myself that same question. So I racked my brain, put it in my pipe, and smoked it out. Crystals can actually *grow* through a process called assisted nucleation. In theory, it is altogether possible that the crystal core is *expanding.* As above, so below, it mirrors our universe. It's well known that our sun gets larger as it consumes its supply of hydrogen and helium."

"Expanding?" Winston took a step back from Coxy.

"Recent estimated measurements of the Earth's core suggest it has changed position by a quarter of a degree. Many scientists believe the core is spinning at a faster rate than the planet's axial rotation. The core appears to be realigning to the axis of the planet. The magnetic flux of the Southern Hemisphere has changed drastically over the past ten years. The magnetic field which shields our planet is weakening at an astonishing rate. The rapid decay suggests characteristics of a magnetic reversal within the next twenty years. This could only happen if the dynamo that generates the field was switched off completely. The French-Danish and German space agencies have sent up Swarm, Orsted, and CHAMP satellites to study changes in the South Atlantic Anomaly. These satellites have confirmed that the magnetic flux over the South Atlantic is growing. It's possible this could be associated with a predicted magnetic reversal."

"The South Atlantic Anomaly," Winston repeated. "A magnetic reversal?"

"The tipping point ... a catastrophic pole shift with the world turned upside down in an instant from an earth-crust-displacement. The pulses I'm picking up from my experiments here at Carnac could be an omen. But, do not *panic*, Mr. Winston. I believe the core is simply *expan*ding from the additional mass accumulated from meteor deposits. Tons of cosmic debris fall on the Earth each year. It fuels the planet. This is an old idea proposed by the eminent Australian geologist Samuel Warren Carey, who used it to explain the movement of the tectonic plates. He believed the Earth was explanding at the rate of six inches every year. There's a deep gash in the Earth's crust, midway between the Cape Verde Islands and the Caribbean on the Mid-Atlantic Ridge, out of which the outer layers grow. This expansion could be the impetus behind related earthquakes, the eruption of deadly supervolcanos, and global warming. We've had sixty-seven minor earthquakes in the last six days. Hurricanes have increased in intensity by twenty percent in the last two years. The Earth's albedo is lowering. The summers are hotter and the winters are colder in every region of the planet. In the ecosystem, bee and bird colonies are being disrupted by the planet's sudden changes in its electromagnetic fields. All of these events, along with the harmonic flux, could be caused by the natural growth of the crystal core. It's like the Earth is in labor and about to give birth. But then again, this flux could be associated with an external force unrelated to the added mass from space debris."

"An external force?" Winston probed. "What type of external force?"

Coxy grinned. "Hand me your orb. Let me show you how to open it."

Winston felt confused. *Now he wants to open the orb.* He retrieved it from his rucksack and passed it to Coxy.

Coxy gripped it in one hand, stepped to the doorway of the tent, and held it in the sunlight. "One, two, three, four, five, six ... seven." *Click—* He lifted the domed lid from the top of the orb.

"Now it looks like a wooden cup." Winston gawked at it. "How'd you do that? That's cooler than my nickel trick."

"It's concealed in plain sight. Sunlight heats the stone-locking spring to the lid behind the sun symbol on the outside of the orb. It's made out of umangite, a copper mineral containing selenium. It's light sensitive. Look. There's something inside."

"What is it?"

"What do you think it is? This *is* a message orb," Coxy grunted as he sat down. "It's a rolled up piece of vellum with something written on it."

"What's it say?"

"It's your orb." He passed the paper to Winston. "You read it."

Winston unrolled it. His eyes focused on the faint script. He retrieved the brass compass from his pocket and inspected it. The polished cover of the compass glowed like a spark in the dark hollow of his hand. "Hmm. 'From Alpha to Omega ... Seven windows'...? Light ... and a message." He flipped open the compass, tucked the paper inside, and stowed it back into his pocket.

"Yes, light! It's an incredible force ... a force which may be responsible for the expansion of the planet. One exotic theory is that the planet absorbs light and transforms it into new mass. The Nobel Prize-winning experimental physicist Carl

David Anderson proved that high-energy photons from light can affect dark matter to produce new mass. It's a process called Paired Production, which suggests that the whole Universe is recreating itself. In this case, the Earth, as with our Universe, is a self-perpetuating organism—which is constantly growing."

"Light transformed to mass," Winston thought out loud. "It sounds similar to Teilhard's theory on the God Consciousness."

"It's the same process used in the creation of the God Particle," Coxy noted. "The recent intensity in the sun's coronal mass ejections could be the catalyst for the sudden changes we're experiencing. But … light also has the capability of *transmitting a message*. I know you've heard of Alexander Graham Bell?"

"He was Scottish … the inventor of the telephone. I was once told he was a friend of my great-great-grandfather," Winston recalled.

"Right, the telephone. Actually, Elisha Gray of Chicago invented the telephone, but Bell got the credit. Gray wrote an interesting book titled *Nature's Miracles: World-Building and Life, Earth, Air, and Water,* in which he stated that the design of the universe was the result of an *intelligence* which could be understood. But, have you ever heard of Bell's other invention, the photophone?"

"I can't say that I have," Winston replied. "Well … Parott said something."

"Bell was a remarkable man," Coxy proclaimed. "In 1880, he transmitted the first wireless telephone message through his newly invented photophone. He considered the photophone his most important invention. The device allowed for the transmission of sound by way of a beam of light. Of the thirty patents granted to Bell, four were for his photophone. Those patents serve as the core technology for both Bell Labs and Lucent Technologies, who build the optical communication servers for the main hubs of the Internet and the U. S. Department of Defense."

"Yeah, I know about Internet servers." Winston grinned.

"The photophone functioned similarly to the telephone," Coxy explained, glancing at the open orb still in his hand, "except the photophone used light as a means of sending information while the telephone relied on electricity. In one experiment in Washington, D.C., Bell and his co-inventor, Charles Tainter, succeeded in transmitting a signal over a distance of 800 feet using sunlight as their carrier source. Their receiver was a parabolic mirror with light sensitive selenium cells at its focal point, just like this orb." He held it out in his hand. "Selenium's electrical resistance varies inversely when illuminated by light. Its resistance is higher when it is darkened and lower when it is lighted. The idea behind the photophone was to modulate an audio message onto a light beam which could be received by a telephone headset."

"Right, we can speak with light," Winston agreed. "It can carry a message. Fiber optics and imaging bundling."

"Correct, optics, it's in the optics. The science has been around a long time—Newton's optics, Roger Bacon's optics, Alhazen's optics, Leonardo da Vinci's optics—ways to receive a message from light."

"Just like the orb," Winston repeated.

"Here." Coxy returned the orb to Winston.

Winston's eyes narrowed as he grasped it. "There's something wedged inside." He tweezed his two fingers in the opening, pinched a small strip of metal, and guided it out the top. "What is this?" He stared into the palm of his hand. "It's inscribed with the same types of symbols as on my pocket compass." *The symbols in the catacombs,* he remembered, *the pattern within the virus segment.* He held it so Coxy could see.

"It's an old ceremonial lamina, part of a necklace worn by the first Christians." Coxy eyed the symbols. "Those markings are known as the Messianic Seal—the Eye of God conjoined by the creative forces of nature to the Tree of Life. God is always watching over the Creation. Your father was obsessed with the history of this symbol since his freshman year in college, after he learned about it in the archives of the library at Edinburgh. Here's the lid to your orb." He held out the lid.

Winston spied the circular cap under the rim. "Wait a minute. There're letters and characters under the rim." He snatched the lid from Coxy's hand and inspected it. "That's a disc from a Jefferson wheel cipher. It's like the one my father gave me. It's attached to the bottom of the lid."

"Part of another message, I suspect." A grin eased across Coxy's face. "Something from *beyond* the grave?"

Winston looked suspiciously at Coxy, then dropped the lamina back into the orb, closed the lid, and placed it in his rucksack.

"Ah ...," Coxy groaned as he rose up from his seat. "I need to break the seal and drain the dragon." He lumbered over to the door of the tent, faced away from Winston, and unzipped the fly of his pants. "Oooo ... Look over at that roadway." The scholarly boffin sidestepped and marked a line on the ground with a steady stream, glistening like a lightbeam from a laser pointer. "That roadway next to the stones in the field. Tell me what you see." Coxy pointed with the end of his pipe.

Winston averted his eyes to one side. He scouted out the open door. He squinched his nose at the repugnant odor of sulfur and ammonia. A long puddle trenched into the ground pointed toward a distant asphalt-covered road. "I'm not sure what you're getting at," he puzzled. "What am I supposed to be seeing?"

Ta-ta-ta ... ta-ta-ta ... ta-ta-ta ... came the sound of a Devil's tattoo.

Zip— Coxy sidestepped, turned, and faced Winston. "Quit pulling my beard, you're smarter than that. Come, come, I've marked the way. See it through. Pick it clean. Thick and fast! Put it on the front burner and smoke it out. It's a simple observation. Maybe I should have spelled it out for you. You have to think, Mr. Winston. You have to create a vision that sees beyond the end of your nose! Form does not always follow function. Do you see those power lines running beside that roadway?" Coxy prompted.

"Yes," Winston replied testily. He drew a breath and clenched his jaw. *I'm getting a little festered with his snide tutorials.*

"The roadways run adjacent to the power lines. Hitler's Socialist Dream, the Autobahn highway system, promoted by Eisenhower from the Zero Milestone in Washington, D.C., now wraps itself around the entire globe." Coxy grinned boozily. "And so do the power grids and the telephone lines."

"Okay," Winston said, trying to follow Coxy's logic.

"The concrete and asphalt roads are simply made up of crushed stone—rock crystals bonded together by oil, the black blood of the Earth—into a crystalline network that now covers the surface of the civilized planet. It too could be a type of transmitter, an ever-extending pathway, like an integrated circuit board. The old *dragon currents* undulating below ground may not be below ground anymore. The grand system of roadways running adjacent to the power and telecommunications lines could serve as a pathway above ground, as the *dragon currents* merge with the consciousness of the roads."

"I see," Winston uttered. "So the Dragon is now *hidden* in the streets."

"And I thought you were just a young whippersnapper. Yes … Yes, it is. These roadways can carry more than the invisible gas clouds from auto exhaust. For the first time in human history, the world is entwined by bands of black asphalt. In the U.S. alone, a combined area half the size of Texas is smothered in black. It's an unnatural heat absorber. The sun, whose gravity pushes and pulls on the crystal core in a piezo-effect, also heats millions of miles of roads in a daily cycle of expansion and contraction, like some sort of cosmic pump. This is simply another type of piezo-effect on the crystalline roadways."

"That's a unique concept," Winston said.

"This is not a new concept, my boy. Our whole world is driven by sunlight. The oceans and the ice caps that regulate the biosphere operate around the same sort of light driven pump. The Earth absorbs and reflects heat from the sun. The proper balance between this absorption and reflection is critical to our environment. The biosphere operates within a very delicate temperature range. The desert regions around the middle latitudes and the polar ice caps reflect the sun's heat in correlation to the Earth's tilt, which drives this cosmic pump. It's like a big air conditioning system that regulates the atmosphere, so the planet can breathe and life can flourish."

"So, the roads collect heat like a Green House Effect," Winston compared, "where excess CO_2 levels trap heat in the atmosphere."

"Politics … That's more like a misdirected truth. We can have a rise in temperatures apart from CO_2 levels. Volcanic activity under the oceans can heat up the planet, leading to a thawing of the polar ice caps. Excessive dust deposits in the atmosphere from meteor showers can block out sunlight. An old study in the *Proceedings of the National Academy of Sciences* concluded that the foresting of the planet at the mid- and high latitudes could raise temperatures by ten degrees from the loss of the Earth's reflectivity." Point and *click.* "Look at these measurements from NASA's Terra satellite. The temperatures are steadily rising in the middle latitudes and the ice caps are melting. It's an artificial tug of war between cooling and warming. Our planet is weeping."

"Global warming … Can it be fixed?" Winston asked.

"Learn to adapt. We need a new paradigm. Man has to reconnect with Nature and live in balance with the Earth's geography and its cycles. Stop the pollution and green the planet only at the proper latitudes. Reduce the urban sprawl, especially in the reflective regions such as the deserts and the beaches. It's the deserts, man. People are not supposed to live in vast desert communities. It's the place of Bedouin and nomads. It's always been that way. Well, maybe not always. Your father had an interesting theory on the Sahara and the Sinai. But that's another matter."

"This is hard to believe." Winston shook his head. "Solar activity is affecting the growth of the crystal core?"

"Everything lies beneath," Coxy stressed again. "One thing affects another. Some of the heat from the sun is absorbed by the planet. It accumulates at the core until it dissipates through volcanic activity. Part of the Earth's harmonic emissions which normally dissipate into outer space are aborted and trapped by the roadways. Those harmonics now have the means to travel freely around the surface of the globe—but, by way of the man-made roads and the adjacent power grids."

"So, the roads which trap the sun's heat could be transmitting a signal from the core," Winston summed up skeptically. "And this signal carried through the roads is pushed by light." He paused. "And you're suggesting the Earth is somehow uploading this signal?"

"Volley! That's the spirit! We're beginning to see eye-to-eye. Everything is measured in angstroms. It's the invisible wave lengths that are smaller than small, that lie beneath it all. E=mc2. Alhazen proved it with the help of Euclid. Everything is pushed by light!"

"Oh … Billy," Winston muttered.

"Mr. Winston, have you ever had a telephone to ring, and when you picked up, no one was on the other end of the line?"

"Why—yes. I suppose that has happened to everyone." Winston shrugged his shoulders. *Where's he going with this?*

"Well, maybe there was someone on the other end of the line trying to speak to you, only you did not have the right ears with which to hear. *Visitam Interiorem Terre Rectificatum Invenias Ocultum Lapidum,*" Coxy quoted. "You have to visit the interior of the Earth, which through rectifying you will find the occult stone. Everything-lies-beneath," he articulated, clearing his throat and launching into a manic explanation. "This may sound extreme, but I believe that the Earth is communicating with us through its own natural energy grid. The various megalithic sites, along with natural land formations around the globe, could allow us to tap into the core and listen to the planet's inner voice. I believe that Carnac functions as an antenna array, something somewhat like an Allen Radio Telescope array used by SETI."

Click, click— He tapped on the computer screen with the end of his pipe. "Any large structure lying on, or near, the natural rose-line that runs adjacent to this antenna array has the capability of amplifying the signal even further. The natural rose-line near Carnac runs directly through the British Isles. This rose-line is constantly spitting out an internal harmonic from the Earth's core." Coxy dug through a file folder lying next to the laptop. "Look at these numbers." He unfolded a computer readout of tallied coordinates. "The rose-line passing through the British Isles has a three-degree wide variance. This is not a very wide chalk. Both Menwith Hill Station and Arthur's Seat, as well as Greenwich, are within two degrees of this natural rose-line. Carnac is at 2 degrees, 9 minutes, 22 seconds, east of Greenwich, next to a fault line that leads to the Thames. Arthur's Seat is at 4 degrees, 38 minutes, east. And Menwith is at 1 degrees, 6 minutes, 33 seconds, east."

"Angus mentioned this rose-line."

"I'm sure he did." Coxy reached across the table and picked up a booklet titled NOAA - SOLAR WINDS WARNING 11 YEAR CYCLE. "That's not it." He grabbed another booklet and flipped to a page. A DARPA seal, a globe covered with lines of longitude, was imprinted on the front cover below the title:

WORLD WIDE WEB – NHMFL TEST REPORT – VOA – GOLDSTONE
GEOMORPHOLOGY – B.R.A.I.N.W.A.S.H.
(Direct Enegry Weapons Systems – BLUE BIRD – B.B. WILLIAMS)

I wonder where he got that? Winston thought.

"By the same token, the transatlantic cable, the main ground communication link between Europe and America that runs to Menwith Hill, also junctions with this natural rose-line. That cable links to Washington, D.C., which sits near the midpoint of the global island landmass, where the largest man-made pillar of stones on Earth is erected, and is now off balance. That pillar pushes on the Earth with an accelerated force of 81,000 tons. It's basic physics. For every action there is an equal and opposite reaction. The Earth and its harmonic is pushing back! The transatlantic cable connects to the global telephone lines, which run in many places parallel with the power lines and the asphalt roadways that cover the planet like an integrated circuit board."

"Yeah, pushing back ... could be," Winston mumbled. *The helicopter crash ... the new landlines at the monument running to the White House.*

Coxy closed the booklet and shuffled it across the table. He refolded the readout and brandished it in his hand. "So, it is now possible for the weak harmonic energy coming from the core to be transmitted globally by way of harmonic waves riding over the telephone lines, the power lines, and the crystalline roadways which encircle the entire globe like a cingular integrated circuit board." He shook his head excitedly in quick tremors from side to side. "It's an Electronic Voice Phenomena—an ELF type signal—some *white noise* from the core."

Coxy tapped on the mouse pad and a live nighttime satellite feed of North America appeared on the screen. A splotchy web of pulsing lights tentacled over a faintly-lit grid that outlined America's highways. "Look at the nervous system of the invisible whole. The congestion of super cities is sprawling out over the whole planet into an interconnected global metropolis which replicates a distinct pattern. Washington, D.C. spiderwebs north to Boston through New York and then south to Richmond. In the Midwest, Chicago merges with Detroit. Atlanta is the hub of a supercity covering the entire state of Georgia. Dallas, Los Angles, London, Paris, Rome, Madrid, Moscow, Berlin, Tokyo, Hong Kong—it's happening everywhere—a new *social* way of life which is swallowing up the land. Self-replication is the most powerful force in the universe. Moore's Law states that the complexity of any integrated circuit will double every eighteen months. Call it an accident, or happenstance, but this global circuit board—this new *ouroboros*—has never existed at this level, until now."

A gridwork over an overlapping web ... the Roman plan, Winston pondered the satellite feed. *The Tekton has spread everywhere.*

Coxy tossed the readout to the table, typed on his keyboard, and addressed an audio program. The letters I and U were worn away from the top of the plastic keys. An expanding and contracting frequency wave appeared on the screen. "I've used a modification of a computer code known as TEKTON in my experiments. It's tailored specifically to solve tectonic problems for geologists."

"I know about that computer code," Winston said.

"My program modifies the power spectral density. It can increase the pitch of the ELF from the core. It tunes the RF transients into the audio frequency range. Creation is the outcome of the evolving processes of sound. Listen to this!" Coxy typed in a command and then pressed the *Enter* key.

The screen flickered and dimmed.

"It must be plugged into the wrong device." Coxy reached behind the computer and unclipped a wire as if he was cutting an umbilical cord. His elbow knocked over an empty beer bottle.

The screen flickered again.

"It must be a loose connection," he growled in a voice that sounded like a car running over loose gravel. He slapped the side of the laptop as though waking a newborn baby to its new reality. Suddenly, a moving frequency wave appeared on the screen. The laptop's internal speakers cried, *Ka ... nak.*

A *silence—*

Aum ... Ka ... nak.

Silence—

Aum ... bīja ... Ka ... nak, rumbled over the speakers in a travailing mantra, gyrating from the world turning over on itself.

Winston's face squinched. *Sounds worse than a goetia groaning call from a dying moorhen with a frog in its throat.*

"Hearken, Mr. Winston. Listen for the cadence of the metaphysical utterance of the *nada.* It's a bird on a wire!" Coxy sang like the proud father of a newborn idea. "It's an intoxicating grapevine. I've made *contact.*" He waved his hand in the direction of the monoliths outside the doorway, then back to the laptop. "I do not believe this is mere happenstance. I believe that all of this was created by our human consciousness, so that something could be transmitted back to our consciousness. God made our trees of life so the birds would have a place to rest and sing. We just have to perk up our ears and listen!"

"I'm listenin'," Winston said.

Coxy pulled his left foot over his knee and loosened the laces on his Nike. He removed his shoe, pulled away the smelly threadbare sock covering his curled-up pigeon toes, and started massaging the arch of his foot. "Every now and then we need to do a little reflex on our meridians, a little loving Nyasa. Everything lies beneath. It's all in our feet. We take our shoes off one foot at time, step-by-step. It's an evolution. It's how we are balanced. Something small—a corn, a bunion, or a blister on the end of your big hallux, or some deep fungal infection underneath the shield of your nail—just a little bit is all it takes to set you off balance." Coxy touched that special spot on the sole of his foot. "Oooo ... that feels so good!" He patted his foot and stretched his gnarled toes. "We need to decode the language. We need a *key.*"

"Yes, an evolution, Alpha to Omega ... A *keyword,* that's what I'm looking for."

"Perhaps we already have one." Coxy scratched between his toes. "Perhaps the language to read such a signal coming from the core of the planet is already built into the human consciousness by years of evolution, like a waiting seed in need of some watering. The Earth's core has been sending out these harmonic currents long before the beginning of man's ability to draw ritualistic images on a cave wall. Before the invention of writing, man's most important intellectual skill was his ability to memorize. It's locked up inside our memories—a hidden genetic behavior."

Coxy pulled on his sock, slipped his shoe back on, and put his foot down. He readdressed the keyboard. A 3-D animation of the Earth slowly rotating on its axis appeared on the screen. "The *terra firma!*" He stared, admiring the spinning Earth. "Every person who steps upon the ground has his consciousness coupled to the Earth. Biologist can now use RF technology to turn genes on and off. Perhaps the thousands of years of exposure to the low-level harmonic from the core of the planet has made it possible for the mind of man to become attuned to a unique RF signal coming from the core. Everything lies beneath. Perhaps there is a natural course already evolved within the coiled-up pathways of our brains ... a primitive, archetypal pattern that has echoed down the millennia through the collective consciousness of man. Like some resonant electrochemistry in the neocortex for a neurortheology, it's a pathway which is now imprinted within the 25,000 genes coiled up in the tree of life of our DNA. Attuned by time, it's an endogenous pathway that leads us to an understanding—much like the way a homing pigeon is led. Like some sort of internal Bird Language."

"A Bird Language," Winston repeated, "a neurortheology ..."

"You can call it the Silent Sound of Nature which we all hear. Or an Animal Nature, Which We All Understand. Or you can call it Something That Always Guides Us North. ... My boy, God is constantly guiding us, and He is a good *Mother*. Gaea, our pale blue dot, is speaking to us! From the *omphalos*. From the center of the world. Everything lies beneath!"

The omphalos? The Jefferson Stone, Winston recollected. His attention slipped away from Coxy, lost in a different frame of mind.

"Mr. Winston, do you understand what I am saying?"

"I—Well, yes. Loud and clear. Bird Language ... I presume you are talking about Dr. McCalester's *Kabalyon,*" Winston replied, stone-faced.

"Yes, I *am*," Coxy said bluntly. "But, don't presume anything. I *am* a follower of the Kabbalah. Many scientists are. I have serious views on the nature of the *Kabalyon*. The Nobel Laureate biologist George Wald suggested that the cosmos wishes to be known, and that there must exist a cosmic consciousness that founded the unverse and out of which everything was created, leading to the possibility that matter and mind are complementary sides of the same reality. If the psychiatrist, Carl Jung is correct, then everything that man creates contains an archetypal signature that allows man to communicate with a greater universal consciousness—*One Ocean of Mind* which is his Akashic *source* for creating his reality. It's a type of psi nonverbal communication. In this case, every piece of art and architecture, and every written word and musical notation—everything ever created by the mind of man—is a link!" Coxy stressed. "Jung called it a *universal consciousness* because it represented a common *influence* found in all of human creative endeavor. But, what if that *influence* came from the planet and every man had the natural ability to tap into that *influence* and talk to the Creative Source? The Bible says that Man came from the earth and back to the earth he will *go*. Even Jesus had to enter the darkness of an underground tomb before his resurrection!" Coxy turned his attention to the rotating Earth on the screen. "We cherish our *art,* when it's created from the E*art*h, our beautiful planet. Everything lies beneath. Especially Beauty. There is a divine logic within the transcendence of beauty. Beauty is the mark of God, the Splendor of Truth ... the True Realty. Beyond the *Tiphereth* lies a beautiful Soul and a joy forever. So is Nature. We are always in the hands of Nature. The laws of Nature, the basic patterns of the cosmos, are the primary governing language."

"Yes, Nature," Winston remarked, "the Tao."

"We have to view the world with a wider perspective," Coxy proposed. "We are simply barbarians, if we do not follow the laws of Nature. Adapt or perish is Nature's inexorable imperative. If we can decipher the Earth's code from these things around us which appear in plain sight, then we might understand the Unseen Heavenly One. As stewards of our planet, we have to think like a gardener about the condition of the soil below ground. Between our weeding and watering, what are the trees of life rooted in? What keeps them grounded? How did God build our paradise? What keeps everything in a proper balance? What flowers in the garden forms the colors of its soul. It all comes from the ground up! Life oozed up from the core. The diamond at the core is the blueprint. Gaea, our Earth, the Mother of us all, is our source!" He pointed to the computer screen with his pipe. "It's hidden in the Lord's Prayer, 'Thy kingdom come. Thy will be done *in* earth as it is in heaven.' Our heavenly queendom is not above, Mr. Winston. It's below ground."

"Hell! We might need a new religion, if all of this is true," Winston interjected. "Mother Earth and her embryo core talking to us."

"True. We might need a new religion, or a new form of government. Imagine, a society following its own natural law, *perfectly attuned* to the planet's natural forces."

Seems like my other self already imagined that at one time, Winston thought.

"I believe we could be entering a new epoch, a Golden Age, our eleventh hour, where humanity begins to speak the bird language. An age when man will be able to communicate in a two-way conversation with the planet," Coxy grew thoughtful. "We will all just naturally know. Just like the birds. When to group, when to nest, when to feed, when to change our bearings, and when to fly. No one will tell us. No one will instruct us. No one will preach to us. And no one will govern us!"

Coxy swayed unsteadily as he stood up. "Some birds die if confined to captivity." He opened the cage above his computer and released the Quetzal. "They must fly *free!*" he proclaimed, watching the feathered serpent exit the open door of the cabin tent. " 'O happy bird! Delicious soul! Spread thy pinion, break the cage; Sit on the roof of the seven domes, Where the *spirit takes repose.*' " Coxy placed his hand on Winston's shoulder. "God loved the birds and created trees, Mr. Winston. Man loved the birds and invented cages. 'I know why the caged bird sings.' I *am* talking about a two-way line of communication. The *key* is the language we decide to use. How we connect to ourselves and communicate with this planet is the Kabalyon key."

"Thank you, Professor." Winston eyed the open door of the birdcage. "I *think*, therefore I understand."

Two hundred yards away, next to a grove of trees, a short man with Oriental features lowered a set of KMR-358 audio surveillance binoculars from his eyes.

***

Day 14
Conclave

The Conclave Internet game is a role-playing game where each player of the game creates, and then plays as, a single character.

IN THE MAP ROOM OF THE WHITE HOUSE, President Walker and William Benning leisurely sat on a sofa, watching a wall of television monitors simultaneously broadcasting the same "Special Report." All but one of the monitors displayed a talking head reporting before an identical blue-screened background. *STA-KA, NA, NA, NAK.* Static *crackled* from one of the speakers. The television at the middle of the wall of disembodied heads displayed a scene from the uncensored version of the film *Metropolis.* In a city that shines as a beacon to the world, the golden gynoid of Hel was rising from her throne stationed beneath a pentagram shadowed on the wall behind her.

"They're all babbling. Go to CNN, Benning," Walker said, slightly miffed. "It's better coverage than the All Seeing Eye Network, or the Peacock Network, or that Alphabet Soup Network. Set them all on CNN."

Benning fumbled with a remote control. "Which button changes the channels?"

"Hand it to me, hand it to me." Walker snatched it from Benning and flipped through the channels until all of the monitors were playing the same broadcast.

Two commentators sat at one end of a desk, reporting on the Papal election. At the other end of the desk sat guest commentator Dr. William James from the School of Religious Studies at the University of Notre Dame.

"Dr. James, you have written five books on the history of the Catholic religion, one of the world's most fascinating and mysterious institutions. Can you offer us a bit of history on the Vatican conclave?" anchorman Frank Canster asked.

"Yes, Frank." Smiling like a well-groomed golfer who had won the Masters, Dr. James tightened his *bright* green tie and pulled on the sleeve of his matching travel-light dress jacket from L. L. Bea*m.* "The conclave is an old process in which a new *pontiff* is chosen for the See of Peter in Rome, the *pontiff* being the pope."

"Can you elaborate on that, Doctor?" Frank asked.

"The etymological origins of that title can be traced back to the master engineers who built the first bridges and roads throughout Europe. Sometime in the ancient past a Roman engineer built the first bridge over the Tiber River. This feat greatly influenced commerce in Rome, and the engineer was given the title Pontifex, meaning the bridge builder. The title Pontifex became so honorable that eventually the Roman God-Emperors assumed the title for themselves, though they did not physically build any bridges. Caesar was called the *Pontifex Maximus*, the High Priest."

"So the original *Pontifex* was a civil engineer?" Frank questioned.

Dr. James took a sip of something that looked like water from a half-filled glass on the desk. He cleared his throat. "A-hmm ... excuse me. That's better. Yes, Frank, an engineer—a bridge builder. Bridges play an important role in our social life. In times of war, they facilitated defense. In times of peace, they promoted communication, commerce, and pilgrimage. The word 'pontificate' means to speak and write, or communicate. So the *pontiff*, the pope, is seen as the unique human soul on the planet who builds bridges of communication between the earthly and spiritual worlds for over 1.1 billion Roman Catholics. The Latin root word for religion is *religare,* meaning to reunite. Every person must reunite his soul with the heavenly source. The *pontiff* is the man who has learned to bridge the water that separates the two. He symbolizes the divine marriage between the Message and the messenger. In the Catholic hierarchy, he is the single soul who stands between the faithful and God. His leadership is very important. The Papacy is the world's oldest elected monarchy and the smallest country in the world. It is the oldest ongoing theocracy."

"That's true, Dr. James," Frank agreed. "The Church at Rome is a government based upon Plato's *Republic.* It is not a monolithic entity, but a union of many different religious factions. This adds to the mystery of the conclave, since the group that captures the Papacy can steer the Church in a new direction."

"That's right, the Vatican is a government claiming to rule on the behalf of God," Dr. James explained. "Unlike other forms of government, a theocracy is different in that the administrative hierarchy of the government is identical to the administrative hierarchy of a religion. This distinguishes a theocracy from other forms of governments, such as a state religion, or traditional monarchies in which the head of state claims that his authority comes from God, as with the monarchies of Europe."

"Doctor, can you explain exactly how the conclave works?"

"Yes, Frank. Immediately after the death of a pope, the Cardinal Camerlengo, who is a representative of the Sacred College, assumes charge of the papal household. In the presence of the others, he calls the dead pope by his original baptismal name. At one time they struck the forehead of the dead pope three times with a silver mallet to ensure that he was really dead. Now they check for a heartbeat using modern electrocardial equipment. They use a hammer to smash the sacred fisherman's ring. They also break the pontiff's personal seal. These symbols of the pope are considered almost magical, with a soul of their own. A notary draws up official papers to confirm the legal death of the pope."

"Maxwell's Silver Hammer," Frank chuckled.

"I'm a Beatles fan, too." Dr. James drew a quick smile. "Usually a period of nine days is allowed to pass before a new pope is selected. This allows time to contact the 183 cardinals from around the world. But in our modern technological society, that period has been reduced to a few days. Many of the formalities of the past have been streamlined for today's special event. Plus, we had no lengthy services for the late Pope. In accordance with his wishes, he was immediately buried without a funeral."

"That is true," Frank said. "But, there are *rumors* that this conclave has been hastened by certain factions within the Church in an attempt to manipulate its outcome."

"Such rumors have always circulated during conclave. Although the process is steeped in mystery and ritual, it is a credible electoral process," Dr. James assured. "The cardinals perform certain divine rites among themselves, singing songs and chanting the *Veni Creator Spiritus*. After celebrating the divine mysteries, they enter into conclave. The College of Cardinals, of which a coven of thirteen are from the United States, are secluded in the Sistine Chapel until a new Pontiff is chosen. The word *conclave* is derived from the Latin *cum clvis*, meaning to lock with a *key*. In this Draconian lockup, the group of cardinals sequester themselves into the chapel's confines, whose walls are adorned with the mind-melding frescos of Michelangelo. But, the red-robed electors are allowed to move freely between their residence at Santa Marta and their formal meetings in the Sistine Chapel. All phones, radios, newspapers, and televisions are banned to prevent any influence from the media. None of these birdmen are allowed to leave the conclave until the voting is finished. It is very doubtful that anyone could manipulate its outcome."

"So the voting process could take days or even weeks?" Frank clarified.

"Yes. There are four possible forms of this election. They are *compromissum. scrutinium, accessus,* and *quasi-inspiratio.* The usual form is the *scrutinium,* a secret ballot. The successful candidate requires a two-thirds vote exclusive of his own. If the required two-thirds is not obtained, the ballots are consumed in a stove, whose chimney extends through the roof of the Sistine Chapel. Chemicals are mixed with the ballots to produce a dark smoke, or *sfumato,* to show to those waiting outside that there has been no election. When a white smoke comes from the chimney, it means the final ballot has been burned and a new Pontiff has been selected."

"Police barricades hold back the thousands who have come to witness this historic event, as they bake in the morning sun. It's Rome's hottest entertainment," Frank reported before a blue screen displaying the multitude in St. Peter's Square. Two huge television monitors, set up in the plaza, stood before a surging sea of 150,000 pilgrims and tourists pressed against themselves, trying to obtain the first reports on the new Pope. The *Grand Loggia* balcony above the entrance of St. Peter's appeared empty.

"That's right, Frank," Anchorman Ed Albright added. "The streets of Rome are gridlocked. Every news service in the world is on hand to bear witness. There are over a half-million people packed in the labyrinth of streets leading to St. Peter's Square. Rome is groaning under the weight of visitors. The eyes of the world are watching. Everyone is anxious to learn who the next Pope will be. Millions have placed bets on the top five candidates. But it's like playing the lottery. We never know who the next pope will be."

"And look, Frank, at our special Chimney Cam in the lower right-hand corner of your screen," Ed reported. "Is that—"

"Yes, Ed, I believe it is. That's smoke billowing up from the chimney pipe."

"And it is a white smoke, Frank! We have a white smoke! Look at that crowd cheering—waving flags and banners. They have exploded into joy. Men, women, and children are praying, crying, and chanting. The bells of St. Peter's are ringing."

"*Habemus papam,* we have ourselves a new Pope to guide us," Dr. James praised, his fingers laced together. "Bless this man who will carry the burden."

"It is official!" Ed reported. "At 9:18 A.M. here in Rome, a new Pope has been selected by the Vatican conclave—"

"And I have a bulletin being handed to me," Frank interrupted. "This is an exclusive breaking news report from CNN. The next pope is ... Monsignor Maxentius Leonardo Garibaldi, from the Roman Catholic Archdiocese of Boston."

The television momentarily flickered. A wavy ghost image weaved through the screen. *STA-NAK, STA-NAK—*

"This is truly remarkable," Ed said. "The new Pope is an American."

"It's a historical first," Dr. James added. "Monsignor Garibaldi is not a cardinal or a bishop. Not since the election of Pope Urban VI in 1379 has a non-cardinal been elected pope—"

"Yes, it is," Ed interrupted, "considering that American Catholics have a history of dissension with the Vatican on key issues involving the clergy, abortion, same-sex marriage, and the death penalty."

"This is a historic day for the Church," Dr. James proclaimed. "It had been rumored that an American cardinal might be chosen. But, a mere Monsignor—"

"I also understand it was rumored that an African cardinal might be chosen to strengthen ties with the Dark Continent to confront the growing threat of Islamic fundamentalism," Frank added.

"I know Monsignor Garibaldi," Dr. James said. "He was born to purple. He is an outstanding selection—a Rhodes Scholar, a graduate of Cambridge and the Georgetown School of International Studies, a ranking member of the Knights of Columbus and the Knights of Malta, and a member of the Olivetans—a Benedictine Order. He's a prolific author of academic theology and a noted expert in eschatology. He has written over forty books on the position of the Church in the modern world."

"And I understand Monsignor Garibaldi is the half-brother of the previous pope," Frank reported.

"Not since the Medici has there been a continuation of such a family tree within the Papacy," Dr. James compared. "In a renewal of nepotism, it appears that the Vatican is sending a clear signal that it will maintain policies as usual by selecting someone within the same—" *STA-KA, KA, NAK, NA-NAK, NA-NAK*— "Look!"

The cameras focused on the *Grand Loggia* as its glass doors swung open. Three robed priests and the new Pope stepped out to greet the faithful gathering around the hub of their universe. The three priests recited their Amens before the plaza and invoked the protection of Mary. The television camera theatrically panned upwards. Birds swooped in the thermals, encircling the golden orb atop the dome of St. Peter's.

"Ed, I have breaking news. The name chosen by Monsignor Garibaldi will be Pope Peter Romulus," Frank reported. "And Pope Peter Romulus is about to speak."

STA-KA, KA, NA, NA, KANAK

Pope Peter Romulus raised his hands and clenched them together. He smiled as he surveyed the multitude in the plaza. "*Urbs et Orbi.* My heart follows the Glory from the other side of the Mount of Olives," he proclaimed. "I ride upon the beast of burden which pulls the plow that feeds the multitudes. Trust yourselves as *my* servants. I am the new gardener over this world!"

President Walker picked up the infrared remote control from the coffee table and muted the voices of the talking baphomets.

"What do you make of this play-by-play, Benning?"

"The reception may not be that clear, but this snake is not hard to swallow." Benning slightly shook his head, his cornrows bouncing. "We are getting it right from the horse's mouth. Those guys with the Fourth Estate usually set the agenda on things like this. They are the useful hypnotists. They are painting a picture that buoys confidence for the new frontman." He paused. "But, the Papacy is many men, and none of them are elected. I—I'd say the Vatican is sending a clear signal that they are still in our pockets. It's a win-win. It's business as usual." Benning smiled. "You know Garibaldi. You've met him. You'll see him again later this week at the scheduled meeting at Columbia."

"Yes. He is a good friend of Professor Maisun," Walker said hesitantly. "It appears the new *pontiff* is our kind of guy. Now, show me that list of Catholic nominees for the Supreme Court that Maisun sent you. He says we need to save the courts from the activist judges who will erase God from our public square. We need to get ready for the next annual Red Mass."

——

The religion of one age is the literary entertainment of the next. – *Ralph Waldo Emerson*

THE NIGHT DEEPENED. Professor Maisun stood rigid, staring out an open window on the upper level of the Vatican Library that overlooked the Courtyard of the Pigna—long considered the holiest ground within the Vatican complex. He sidestepped away from the window and surveyed the brightly painted esoteric frescos that decorated the room's opulent walls and ceilings. On a nearby ornately carved table sat an empty metal security box with its lid lifted. Beside the box sat an open book, a brass candlestick holding a flickering bloodred candle, and a pair of white lambskin gloves. Maisun's right eye settled on vibrant illuminations on the book's pages, veiled in pallid hues of fulgent orange cast from the candle. The illuminations appeared to shape-shift with the enkindling flux of the flame.

This event is as rare as the transit of Venus, Maisun thought. *Not since the carousel for the heretic philosopher and Nature's true 46 XXXY hermaphrodite—the true herm from the Garden, the first and third human, the Queen of Sweden—has this holy ground harbored such an occasion.*

He slipped on the gloves, locked his hands together, and stared out the window. The courtyard appeared empty and void in the pitch-black of the moonless night.

"*In girum imus nocte et consumimur igni.* Midnight in the garden of good and evil—a perfect night for this," he muttered, tugging on the glove of one hand and anxiously twisting his signet ring in a dactyliomancy around his finger. *Only minutes until tomorrow. I see wonderful things, an Egyptian coffin and a golden vessel levitating above the underworld. The stars will bear witness, since the sky is our sacred canopy.* He checked his Leonardo wristwatch, a cheap Steinhausen knockoff. *Eleven-fifty-five ... The saints here tonight know the art of untying the knot. But they need to start soon, or they are going to be late.*

Maisun's right eye shut tightly, momentarily blinded by the flash from the sudden activation of the courtyard's external floodlights. He held his hand to his face to allow his eye to adjust to the intensity of the light. The spiraling, milky patterns in the film covering his left eye glowed eerily. He leaned over the ledge of the window. The night air shifted, torqued and charged. He drew a deep breath and smiled in approval at what he saw.

Twelve figures draped in hooded robes of black sackcloth which touched the ground now occupied the courtyard. Four of the twelve stood on the *nicchone* balcony before the Holy Pinecone lingam. Their heads were uncovered, their faces hidden behind grotesque goat, ram, and cat-faced tribal masks. The ancient names were respectfully scrolled in red letters across their foreheads: Lutetia Parisiorum,

Londinium, Moskva, Metragirta. They hovered over the Egyptian sarcophagus, motioning with stiff, choreographed gestures as if their bones were bolted together. From his perch at the window, Maisun could barely discern the outline of a nude man lying in the sarcophagus half-filled with warm earth mingled with squirming cold blooded snakes.

"The chalice of good daemon," proclaimed one of the four attendants, cupping a clay pot filled with oil in one hand. In his other hand, he clutched a root of mandrake, the mayapple, darkened from yellow to cyan and twisted into the shape of a tiny man with his arms and legs outstretched.

In one hand, the second attendant carried a toothless skull stained with scarlet cinnabar. With his other hand, he dipped his fingers into the earthen pot held by the first attendant and covered them in an amber-colored oil of pure *narwastu*. Waving the skull above the sarcophagus, he touched the nude man with his oil-drenched fingertips. He touched the nude man's feet. He touched his genitals. He touched the heart of his chest. He touched his lips. He touched his forehead. Each time he touched the nude man, he made a motion with his hand.

Another attendant carried a crimson robe draped over his left arm. In his right hand he gripped a spiraled, ouroboros-shaped crosier staff of sturdy rowan wood with a small carving of a pinecone at its tip.

The fourth attendant, a lector, read from a book which he held in his right hand. "*Hoc signo vinces,*" his voice echoed across the courtyard. "We do not waste the perfume." With his left hand, he made repetitive motions in the air. He tore a strip of

parchment from the book and fed it to the nude man as he read. "This is the Word," he intoned. "Food for thought."

As the lector finished reading, the man in the sarcophagus painfully lifted a heavy stone pressing against his solar plexus, revealing the purplish scarification of a flared sun. "Xeper, I give rise to my spirit," he spoke in a muffled voice. His head was shrouded by a scarf soaked in lamb's blood which clung tightly to his face as he breathed, like a suffocating caul covering the head of a chosen new born. He rose to a standing position and held out the stone, its surface inscribed with the Messianic Seal. "I stand on unbroken legs." Stepping from the sarcophagus, he dropped the stone. In a *blast,* it shattered into hundreds of pieces over the marble floor. The heel of his foot crushed the head of a snakeling twisting around his ankle. He extended his arms straight out in front of his chest. His hands were bound in iron shackles connected by chains.

The lector, who held a *key,* stepped forward and unlocked the manacles. Iron on marble, the shackles *clanged* like a bell as they struck the floor, gouging out a mark that could not be repaired. "I am unbound," the man's muffled voice growled. "I am freed!" He lifted his hands palms out, his lifelines visible for all to see. Released and unfettered, he peeled the bloody scarf from his face, and tossed it to the floor. "I have no secrets ... I can see."

He wore no collar around his neck. Serpent-shaped golden armlets were coiled around his muscular forearms. Splotches of blood mottled his face. Inflamed whelps and crisscrossed scrape marks mapping out above his navel radiated like a nimbus. Multicolored tattoos of religious symbols covered his body. An encircled Chi Rho between the letters *Alpha* and *Omega* stretched across the heart of his chest.

Two of the attendants carefully covered the nude man with the crimson robe and handed him the crosier and the clay pot of oil. One of the attendants unwrapped a scytale, a goatskin strap embossed with talismanic Greek symbols, from the staff. He tied it around the man's waist like a belt to secure the open robe rippling around him, leaving only the tattoos on his broad chest exposed.

"*Inviolatus* Mah-Hah-Bone," the lector recited from the book in his hand.

"Mah-Hah-Bone," the man in the crimson robe repeated as he poured the remaining oil from the clay pot over the tip of the crosier. "*Lekh la-Azazel* ..." he chanted. "I take it on!" He leaned forward and kissed the skull before the attendants placed it and the mandrake into the sarcophagus. He grasped the crosier, extended it high above his head, and tapped its tip against the side of the Holy Pinecone. "*Lapsus ex caeli.*" In one swift motion, he carried the crosier to his side. Wielding it firmly in one hand, he forcefully rapped the blunt end against the floor of the *nicchone*.

Tap-Tap— resounded through the Courtyard of the Pigna.

The four attendants led the man in the crimson robe in a royal descent down the marble stairway of the *nicchone*.

Tap-Tap— came the sound of the *descending man.*

Tap-Tap— He gracefully treaded.

Tap-Tap— He fearlessly made his way to the center of the courtyard.

Parading before him, the attendants gathered around the golden orb and removed their masks—gazing. Unafraid of the distorted world, each in turn stepped forth and kissed the lustrously morphed reflections of themselves in the orb. They dropped their robes to the ground and stood nude before it, their bodies covered only by tattoos of religious symbols.

The man with the crosier remained silent and motionless before the orb. Then he spoke, "*Emet,* I see myself." He handed the clay pot to one of the attendants. Using the end of the crosier, he scratched the sign of a Latin cross onto the ground and recited, "*Hapy,* this is my front. *Imsety,* this is my back. *Duamutef,* my left. *Qebehsenuef,* my right. Bring forth the *Lux.*"

In a pulsing, spiraling parade of lights, the remaining men in the courtyard approached the orb from the four cardinal directions bearing lit candles. They entered the circular gravel garth, bent down one by one, and lit the dozens of hand-size earthen lamps scattered around the orb. Pushing and twisting, they planted their candles into the earth. The flickering lamps and candles released the mesmerizing scent of burning incense. The axis of the courtyard resembled a miniature Copernican universe with a radiant sun at its nucleus.

In unison, nigrous swirls of sackcloth fell to the ground, revealing faces from every race once hidden by the shields of their hoods. Each man was covered with bright tribal *irezumi* body art. One-inch-wide, leather collars were strapped around their necks. One after the other, they knelt before the golden orb in a kaleidoscopic body movement of color. Arms and legs, backs and bellies—all covered in multicolored symbols, wonderful and awful pictures—gyrated in a synchronicity that could only have been choreographed by the forces of Nature. With their eyes closed in a trancelike ecstasy, they lifted their hands palms out above their heads, activating their animus and summoning the primal fragments of behavior found only in their dark.

"We are a brotherhood of *bab'bals!*" the man with the crosier cried. "For a thousand years, our *imperium in imperio* has reigned as the masters' masters."

From the window, Maisun heard whispers in ancient Latin and Greek exchanged by the kneeling brothers until their voices increased in volume into the slow, heavy cadence of a Gregorian chant. The courtyard filled with the searing breath of an imperceptible utterance which should never be heard. He could not decipher what was said, but Maisun understood. "*Sanguis bebimus, corpus edimus.*" He heard the phrases, *Noli me tangere*, *Ave Lux Deus*, *Ave Lux Ferre*, *Ave Shiva Deus*, repeated in the chant.

A shapely, olive-skinned sylph, with a face painted geisha-lithium-white, emerged from the shadows between the southern pillars of the *Braccio Nuovo.* She was cocooned in an iridescent robe of violet, purple, and scarlet which fell into a long green and gold *rustling* train stitched with peacock feathers—a hundred blue-green eyes opening and closing like the vault of heaven moving over the ground. Advancing into the courtyard, she preened and courted between the lit candles as though walking through fire. Her black-satin hair tossed in the air like skeins of silk with her every step. She entered the circle of men genuflecting before the orb and presented herself to the man holding the crosier. She gazed at him with hypnotic eyes dilated to dead pools of black, outlined by fish-shaped loops of dark kohl, like an Egyptian goddess.

He nodded.

Struggling, bending, turning, laboring, she shed her mantle, gradually revealing her naked body—her belly plump and swollen. A full-length tattoo of an Oriental dragon, formed from a mingled mix of red, green, blue, and yellow, decorated her back. Two hand-size tattoos of wings fanning cross her small shoulder blades appeared to flap as she moved her arms. She took a deep breath and stepped forward from the vestment nested at her feet. Adorned only with a leader collar around her neck, she waited.

 He smiled.

She bowed her head, knelt with her arms extended, and offered him something clenched in her hand.

He touched her head with the tip of the crosier, piercing her scalp. Blood flowed.

She rose up, took his left hand, and slipped a yellow-gold ring which bore the Y-shaped cross upon his middle finger.

A strained *silence* suddenly filled the courtyard. The kneeling brothers ceased their chant and arched their heads back. They closed their eyes and opened their mouths wide, exposing pierced tongues swollen with tattoos of soundless sacred idioms. They laconically spoke with their tongues wagging like hungry baby birds.

"*Hoc signo vinces!*" the young woman praised, her head still bowed.

The man with the crosier pulled at her chin with the tips of his fingers and raised her head. He bored his eyes into her. "You maintain the water and the fire. You exalt the bottomless cup and carry the new sacrifices."

She embraced his blood varnished face with both of her hands and kissed him on the lips.

His face appeared angered with tribal marks, the blood-swiped impressions from the release of her slender fingers. " 'I am thy mate, I am thy man, Goat of thy flock, I am *gold*, I am your *god*, Flesh to thy bone, flower to thy rod,' " he recited. " 'With hooves of steel I race on the rocks, through solstice, forever stubborn to equinox—an everlasting world without end.' "

She reached out and poisitioned her right forefinger at the center of his temple. "*Theotokos Us-iri* ..." She lowered her hand and rested her palm over the Omega symbol on his chest. Rapturously, she pressed the tips of her six fingers into his flesh.

He closed his eyes and heaved a deep breath. "Ahh ..."

"O-me-ga ... Oh My God," she cried the omnific word, "Jah-buh-aum, with you I satisfy my hunger. I take your mark. I am Eve, I am Lilith, your dark maid. Let me taste your wisdom." She grasped his hand and kissed the ring, then bit into the meaty flesh of his palm. Blood flowed. Fallen droplets soaked into the ground.

An attendant quickly stepped forward, positioned the clay pot beneath the bleeding hand, and then handed it to the young woman.

She turned away and retreated north toward the Holy Pinecone. When she reached the base of the *nicchone*, she knelt on both knees and lifted the clay pot high above her head. The dragon on her back appeared to leap up at the Holy Pinecone with her every gesture. Her body went limp. She collapsed to the ground and curled up in a fetal position, cradling the earthen *ambix* with both hands.

The man with the crosier approached the kneeling brothers and allowed each one to see the ring before beginning his blood work. He squeezed his fist above their open mouths. Drops of crimson painted over their slithering tongues. Lunging forward, he deftly stabbed the raised right palm of each man with the end of his crosier. "*Verbum domini, manetaeter,*" he commanded harshly. The speared tip cut deeply into their hands—painful *stigmatas*—wounds of devotion that would not heal easily.

One after the other, the bleeding brothers renewed their rhythmic chants. Their eyes opened. Half of them wore feral-eyed, crazed expressions. The other half looked serious and stern. Speaking in English, each man stretched out his bloody six-fingered hand and recited in turn.

"Inshushinak, Lugus, Hekate, Odin, Osiris, Zeus, Esus, Pillar of the Boatman, Eternal Father of the Universe, Shiva at whose command the world evolved from chaos and all created matter had its birth, we, your unworthy servants, humbly implore you to bestow your spiritual blessing on this convocation," said the first kneeling man. "In the name of Baphomet, we, the ruling sons and the daughters of the Grigori, adhere to the mysteries of the Serpent and the Lion—the Mystery of Mysteries. In this enthronement of the Fallen Archangel, our nakedness is a symbol of our purity and our joy of obedience. All of our kind have been marked. We, the mighty Brethren of the Nephilim, the followers of the prophet St. Malachy, the augurs of the first and only *Osor-Api, Madre Natura*, the Orphic Mysteries of Eleusis, Hadrian's twelve rites of Alcides, and Master Ligorio, have set you up so that you can strive against the city which contains the image of our *Eternal Pleroma* in the house of their father." Lines of anguish webbed across his face as he looped the fingers of his bloody hand and held them to his right eye. "You are the Penultimate Master over the Ma'ahes, our exalted Nebu next to the last who will rescue us from the abyss. You are the First Deep, the Universal Fount, from whom all fountains have gone forth."

"You are the Second Deep, the Universal Wisdom, from whom all other wisdoms have gone forth," said the second kneeling man.

"You are the Third Deep, the Universal Mystery, from whom all mysteries have gone forth," said the third kneeling man.

"You are the Fourth Deep, the Universal *Gnostikoi*, from whom all gnosis have gone forth," said the fourth kneeling man.

"You are the Fifth Deep, the Universal Purity, from whom all purity has gone forth," said the fifth kneeling man.

"You are the Sixth Deep, the Silence that contains all silences," said the sixth kneeling man.

"You are the Seventh Deep, the Universal Essential Essence, from whom all essences have gone forth," said the seventh kneeling man.

"You are the Eighth Deep, the Forefather, from whom and by whom all forefathers exist," said the eighth kneeling man.

"You are the Ninth Deep, the All-Father, Self-Father, in whom is the All-Paternity of those who are Self-Fathers of the all," said the ninth kneeling man.

"You are the Tenth Deep, the All-Power, from whom all powers have gone forth," said the tenth kneeling man.

"You are the Eleventh Deep, that in which is the First Invisible, from whom all have come forth," said the eleventh kneeling man.

"You are the Twelfth Deep, the only Truth, from whence all truths have sped forth," said the twelfth kneeling man, his eyes tearing. "Hail to the beast of pride! Between snakes and goat heads, your marble throne awaits you at Arlington." He extended his arms and lay prostrate on the ground.

"*Konx Opax!*" cried the man holding the crosier. "Christ is Dead! We bask in the lap of Logos. You are my chosen senate—my angels, my generals who will rule over the eighty-three. You have been marked."

The kneeling brothers arose, paraded away from the orb, and disappeared into the shadows of the courtyard.

The man with the crosier confidently turned away from the orb and toward the severed, stone head of Constantine II. He glared up toward the Tower of the Winds and beyond its surrounding roofs and gables to the lighted dome of St. Peter's. "*Iustum, necar, reges, impios,*" he addressed, bowing his head in a condescending gesture. "*Hamalau mila hemen geala.*" Steady and confident, he stood erect, his eyes leerily panning the second floor windows of the courtyard. The downcast faces of spectators, men and women, were watching from the shadows of every window. His eyes settled on the face of Professor Maisun staring back at him. He pried a proud and shameless smile at Maisun. With a sweep of his raised hand and an arrogant flip of his wrist, he flaunted the ring upon his middle finger in the Sign of Kish. It *glistened*.

With his hands pressed to his chest, Maisun smiled back and nodded. *The birth of a centaur and the awakening of angels ... It's an insane bloody mess.* He removed the glove from his left hand and extended his fist at arm's length as if to salute. Around his middle finger clung his signet ring with a jeweled image of the Trylon and Perisphere from the 1939 New York World's Fair. A ray of light reflected off the diamond-studded surface of the Perisphere. It *glistened*.

A well-dressed man walked up behind Maisun and tugged at the professor's arm. "This way, *Signor* Maisun. It is over now."

***

Day 15
Rock Creek

This is the generation of that great LEVIATHAN, or rather, to speak more reverently, of that 'mortal god,' to which we owe under the 'immortal God,' our peace and defence. - Thomas Hobbes, Leviathan

WAITING FOR HIS RIDE, Winston stood gripping his rucksack at the curb outside Dulles International Airport next to one of the giant arches holding up the building's swooping wing-shaped roof. *The Netplex ... Back in the snake pit,* he thought.

"Stop!"

Winston heard a woman's frantic voice. He glanced up at the gigantic panels of glass fronting the building to a reflection of a small boy darting behind him, chasing a black and white toy soccer ball rolling into the street.

"My ball!" the boy yelled.

Winston instinctively dropped his rucksack, swung around, and grabbed the boy's arm before the child could step into harm's way.

A taxi *screeched* to a halt. A guttering *BAM*, like a gunshot, and the ball was crushed. *BAM*, bumpers bashed together. Security personnel came running.

"Oh, thank you so much!" The boy's pregnant mother seized her son's arm.

"No problem." Winston eyed the boy. "He reminds me of myself. Glad to help." Winston noticed a short man in a black suit walking away from him with a rucksack in his hand.

"Dillon, how many times do I have to tell you," the mother scolded, then readdressed Winston. "Thank you, again." She pulled her whining son away.

Winston reached for his rucksack. "Where is it?" His head circled. "Ah, there it is."

A black Mercury pulled up to the curb. The passenger window rolled down.

"Mr. Winston," the driver greeted, "welcome back to Washington."

THIRTY MINUTES LATER.

"Sir, we will be there soon," the driver informed.

Winston shifted in the passenger's seat and retrieved a cell phone from his pants pocket. The phone *chimed* as he opened it. 7:06 AM counted on the LCD readout as he pressed the # key and dialed Susan. *Touchpads ... a world without faces ... Some of us have more physical contact with a phone and a keyboard than we do with people.*

Beep— "Hello."

"Hey ... I got your message. I'm on my way." Winston located his position on the dashboard GPS. "We're driving up North Capitol," he spoke into the phone, still staring at the display. "Hmm ..." *The pentagram star... but it's not a star, it's the letter Alpha above the White House.* "Okay. I'll see you shortly." He closed the flip-phone and stowed it in his pants zip-pocket. He moved his finger over the screen. *Omega around the Capitol ...* " 'From Alpha to Omega,' " he muttered. *What did Angus say about Teilhard—?*

"You know, this is the same route used for the funeral of President Scott last week," the driver said, making idle conversation. "The Catholic University of America and the National Shrine of the Immaculate Conception are in this direction. The National Shrine is designed to resemble the Washington Monument and the

Capitol Dome combined. It's dedicated to Mother Mary, the new Ark of the Covenant, who bore the light of God in her womb. A breathtaking, fiery mural of Christ at the *Last Judgment* covers the inside of its dome. One of the popes even visited the Crypt of the Basilica."

"I didn't know that," Winston said. "The *Last Judgment?* Where did I come across that before?" *Paris ... Rome?*

"Yeah, the last judgment. 'Behold, I am coming soon, bringing My recompense, to repay everyone for what he has done. I am the Alpha and the Omega, the first and the last, the beginning and the end,' " the driver quoted. "God is not unconditional. In the end, he's going to come back and separate the *sheep* from the *goats* and punish everyone who did not follow his rules."

Egyptian tribes ... "I guess I'm in trouble," Winston whispered to himself. "Why don't you turn up the AC? It's getting warm."

"This is the Catholic quarter of the District," the driver continued with his guide talk. "They say the old bishop John Carroll placed the District under the protection of the Virgin. Not far from here is the Franciscan Monastery of the Holy Land. It's a tourist attraction. I've been there. They have a garden replica of the *key* landmarks in Jerusalem referenced to the Stations of the Cross. Below that garden is a copy of the Roman catacombs." He adjusted the air conditioning, then tuned the radio to another station. Madonna began singing her Kabbalic "Ray of Light." "They even have a replica of the Grotto at Lourdes where the French girl saw the apparition of the goddess Mary, the Queen of Heaven, within a brilliant white light."

Winston felt the cool air from the vents in the dash. "Hmm ... ray of light." His mind flashbacked memories of the past six days, *Paris ... Rome ... Edinburgh.*

"You know, Scott was buried at Rock Creek Cemetery," the driver mentioned. "It's been busy there since the funeral. Lots of tourists. No need to worry about tourists today though. The cemetery is closed so you NSA people can have a look around."

"Good," Winston remarked.

"There's the entrance." The driver pointed.

The car rounded a corner at Totten Park and drove through an impressive, wrought-iron, double-gated entry. Two NSA agents, dressed like pallbearers wearing sunglasses, closed the gates as the car passed. One-foot-high letters on the archway above the gates read: ST PAUL'S CHURCH ROCK CREEK CHURCHYARD 1719.

"This is a beautiful cemetery," Winston noted, as the car wound past the wooded gardens planted with old, moss-slung giants rooted into the ground. Their arching, leaf-laden branches covered the driveway with a shifting patchwork of dusty, sunlit silence and shady stillness, evoking a Buddhist-like ambiance of utter peace and calm.

It's a serene and solitary place, Winston mused. *I feel like I'm sitting in the Chi of my VDC. This place is more like a breath of life than the breath of death. I sense nothing eerie, depressing, or sad here. Some graveyards make you feel this way. I wonder if paradise looks like this?* He surveyed the ordered maze of tombstones and monuments. *It reminds me of Carnac ... herms, talking stones.*

"We are supposed to meet them across from the President's grave," said the driver.

The president ... Winston's eyes opened wide. *Now I understand why Susan sounded so concerned.*

Grief drives men into habits of serious reflection, sharpens the understanding, and softens the heart; it compels them to arouse their reason, to assert its empire over their passions, propensities and prejudices; to elevate them to a superiority over all human events; to give them the *felicis annimi immcota tranquilitatum*; in short, to make them stoics and Christians. - *John Adams* to Jefferson, May 6, 1816

SUSAN STOOD NERVOUSLY twisting the toe of her shoe into the ground. The backs of her hands rested on her hips, with one hand holding a camera. "Hello, James," she greeted, as Winston stepped from the car, gripping a rucksack.

He took a breath, savoring the scent of freshly cut grass. *Beautiful.* Winston felt overcome by the sight of Susan standing before the countless flowers blanketing Scott's grave. "Are the coordinates associated with Scott's grave?"

"No, but they are dead center on another grave. It's up this hill, behind a hedge at the top of the garden." Susan led Winston to a memorial site and updated him on the situation with the virus. "Did Professor Coxy help you open your letterbox?"

"Yeah, it had something inside. Look at this. It's a wicked trick." Winston unzipped the rucksack. "Wait a minute, this stuff isn't mine." His thoughts flashed back to the airport. "Shit! A pickpocket made off with my stuff ... my father's orb." He handed the rucksack to Susan. "Why leave me with this—"

"Do I need to contact airport security?" she suggested.

"No, you keep it. I couldn't sleep on the plane, so I removed the contents from the orb to study them." He reached into his pants pocket and retrieved the wooden disc and the metal lamina. "I guess it's no big loss." He put the items back into his pocket.

"James, we *need* to close up this investigation," Susan urgently insisted with concern etched across her face. "Dr. Bains is having a meltdown. He's on the backs of everyone. He's mad as hell that we've been running around the globe looking for clues. And your spur-of-the-moment visit with Professor Coxy didn't help. He said, 'your game's not worth the candle.' He even called you an 'idiotic wombat.' He thinks our ocular inspections are a waste of time and money, and that we've stalled the investigation into Limbo. Things are going haywire. The virus has turned into a cockroach. It's spread into more systems outside of the government. Bains is being hounded by a group of angry German astrophysicists. Their supercomputer Millennium Run Simulation of the universe has been capsized by the virus. Bains is getting flack from all directions. He's had the Backdoor Group sequestered at Fort Meade. Now Marx is bitching. Bains thinks the Ebola could soon reach critical mass. He wants things wrapped up ASAP. We might not have much time before he takes over Project Capricorn."

"I'm not timeboxing with Bains. He needs to let things shake and bake," Winston said adamantly. "I think we're on to something. Bains wants to do things too much by the book and mold our faces behind his mask. The successful person always takes the time to go the extra mile." Winston hesitated as he eyed a nearby group of graves. A red-backed salamander scurried over the ground in front of a tombstone carved with an emblem of a woman weeping over a broken column beneath a seven-fluted syrinx, a square and compass, and the name COLLINS. "I'm not the kind to roll over and play dead," he added. "We're not stopping here."

"It'll be your funeral, not mine." Susan placed her camera into the rucksack. "This way. Stay on the path, don't walk between the graves."

They lumbered forward, their feet sinking loosely into crushed stone, until they came to a Vishnumandal-shaped memorial almost hidden behind a wall of flowering foliage guarded over by fluttering butterflies and darting dragonflies.

Winston could hear birds singing in the hedges.

"This is Reverend Worthington," Susan introduced. She dropped the rucksack next to a well-dressed man sitting alone on a pink marble bench. "He's the caretaker for the cemetery chapel. Reverend, this is my associate, James Winston."

In front of Winston sat a lean, hollow-cheeked man in his late thirties with a drawn expression as though he was waiting for his turn to die. The man's deep-set eyes were highlighted by skin-pinched, dark creases carved deep into his furrowed cheeks. He was a skeleton of a man, thin, very thin.

"Good morning, Mr. Winston," the reverend greeted in a meek voice. "I'm Hiram Worthington. Welcome to Arcadia." He got to his feet in a tense stance and limply shook Winston's hand. His loose, black, wool-blend suit hung awkwardly on his frame, like a hand-me-down from a taller cousin. A tiny, gold, Latin cross pinned to his lapel glinted in the sunlight. Around his neck, at the end of a braided, green lanyard, hung a bloodred Audubon birdcall dangling over the heart of his chest.

"Hello, Preacher." Winston felt a quiver in the reverend's hand. He noticed the dreary, forlorn face of the sad-eyed vireo. *His eyes are filled with sorrow, like he's hiding a burden.*

"It's that statue over there." Susan pointed to a bronze sculpture a few feet away. "That's the spot. James, it's close to the seventy-seventh degree meridian."

"But it's not on the seventy-seventh degree meridian?" Winston asked.

"No, that line skirts the cornerstone of the National Shrine of the Immaculate Conception." Susan handed Winston a map. "It's near an old hunting lodge called Duckwood, built in the 1800's by W. W. Corcoran. There's a strange bunker from World War I hidden under the lodge. I've checked it out. It's empty. The property has been sold for development. I tried to get background on the history of the bunker through the War Department, but their documents are still classified."

"A Catholic meridian," Winston said, studying the map. "Here's the cemetery. I've seen this shape before. I can't put a face on it.... Corcoran, that's the guy Nobles said oversaw the completion of the Washington Monument—"

"It's a beautiful piece of art, isn't it, Mr. Winston?" the reverend's voice interrupted, with a variance in pitch followed by an odd whistling resonance.

Winston stared at the statue. *That cloaked Muslim woman ... I feel like I'm in Jerusalem.* "Preacher Worthington, whaddya know about this statue?"

"Just a little. I've been working here for a few years. I used to teach American history at the University of Maryland. Please, follow me." Reverend Worthington pulled on his belt to hold up his pants, led them to the other side of the memorial, and pointed with his twitching finger to a carving of two interconnected, circular wreaths. "Look at this, the sacred symbol of union," the reverend said, absent-mindedly twisting a gold band on his left ring finger. "The history of this memorial is a bit of a love story and a tale of woe. Henry Adams, the grandson of President John Quincy Adams, commissioned the memorial. Adams authored the noted book, *The Education of Henry Adams,* which is considered by many to be the most influential American book ever written."

"I've never heard of it," Winston remarked.

"There is a famous quote by Henry Adams," the reverend explained. " 'You say that love is nonsense—I tell you it is no such thing. For weeks and months it is a steady physical pain, an ache about the heart, never leaving one, by night or by day; a strain on one's nerves like a toothache or rheumatism, not intolerable at any one instant, but exhausting by its steady drain on the strength.' " Reverend Worthington smiled wistfully, revealing his two overlapping front teeth. "Adams is talking about the loss of his wife, whom he loved dearly. The love of his life." The reverend's eyes beamed briefly with heartfelt emotion. " 'But to see her was to love her, Love but her, and love forever …' Robert Burns. Love is a powerful force in our lives, Mr. Winston. It's unjust somehow, when someone you love dearly walks out of your life."

The corners of the reverend's eyes brimmed as he considered the two interconnecting rings. " 'I go mourning.' Psalms 38:6," he quoted, as emotions too deep for words arose. Instead of words, a single tear rolled down his gaunt cheek.

"John Adams once wrote Thomas Jefferson a letter in which he said, 'Without religion this world would be something not fit to be mentioned in polite company, I mean Hell.' " He managed a slight smile. "Thank God for religion, for it protects us from the world."

Susan sliced a glance at Winston.

"You and I are One. … I know there are bad things in our lives which our lucid memories help us to forget, but there are some things you don't want to forget." The reverend's voice became plaintive, "I lost someone I loved a few years ago. Someone who bore my children and bore witness to my life, to show that she believed in me. Loss can overwhelm a soul, Mr. Winston. It can steal away your dreams and what you had hoped would be your future. You walk hand-in-hand with someone for many years, and then suddenly, there's no one holding your hand. You wake up one day and discover that there is no one beside you. You lie awake at night, like a bird alone on a roof, wondering. But the eye cannot say to the hand, 'I don't need you.' You still anticipate the end of every day with someone's arms, like the cord of life in a mother's womb, wrapped around you, keeping you safe. You miss it," he lamented.

"You sit at a table every morning and you think about the only person whose ears could hear the sounds of your dreams—and the only beaming eyes that could ever see the light of your vision for each new day." His voice broke again, trying to find the words. "You – miss – it. You step outside your front door to the sounds of the birds that sing, but they can't fill the *silence* from the loss of her angelic voice. You miss it," he added again faintly.

"Life goes on, but you know you have lost the best thing. Living with a loss is *hard* living. It is a lifelong cross to bear that can change your very being. It will tear you up and lay you down, as you see the world from the inside out. It can be a turning point in your life, if you become stronger and not hardened through your suffering. So you can realize that within your memories you are not alone. The art of loss is hard to master … but, our memories help us to survive."

"You're still grieving," Susan said, her voice sympathetic.

"Ah ... Grief." The reverend nodded. "Some have called grief an evil, because it steals away the happiness in our lives. But, our lives are forged by the fire of grief and tempered from our tears. The emptiness of missing someone is like the void of a window or a door cut into a wall. Emptiness can be useful. It can take us into another world. Our world is full of broken people, Ms. Hamilton. Hardly a man breathes who has not known great sorrow. I'm certain Henry Adams felt this same way. Please. Follow me."

Winston's Adam's apple felt stuck in his throat. *And I always thought the greatest loss was the loss of self-respect.* He questioned, in self-analysis, his own disguise of bravado and confidence. *I need to lose my ego.*

Reverend Worthington languidly led them back to the front of the memorial. He sat down on the bench directly in front of the statue. "Let me tell you a story on how loss can perpetuate loss," he began. "One day in 1884, plummeted into the depths of a depression by the sudden death of her father, Henry's wife, Marian Adams, known as 'Clover' by her closest friends, swallowed potassium cyanide while Henry was paying an emergency visit to his dentist. Henry remained grief-stricken until the end of his life. To mark her grave, he commissioned this special monument from the well-known American sculptor, Augustus Saint-Gaudens. There are no markers with the names of either Adams at this memorial. Few visitors to the memorial actually know it is the grave site of both Henry and Marian. He was buried here in 1918."

Reverend Worthington stood up and stepped toward the calm, mourning figure seated at one side of the memorial.

Two beguiling ravens, like the law crow from the crest of Washington, flew down from the sky. They perched atop the granite slab behind the statue's head, raised the feathers on the back of their necks, and opened their long, yellow beaks. *"Caw, caw, caw,"* they carked. Their tiny heads snaked in an excited, fluid motion like Huginn and Muninn whispering the world's secrets into Odin's ear.

The reverend glanced at them. "Love is a dark raven when it is lost. Plunged into his own despair and in search of comfort, Adams traveled to Japan in the summer of 1886 with his friend, the noted artist John La Large. Upon his return, Adams decided to replace the headstone that he had originally ordered with a more elaborate memorial. He asked his friend, Saint-Gaudens, to create a memorial with an Oriental theme. The outcome is this idealized figure we see here that combines the images of

the Buddha with the sculptural feel of Michelangelo."

"Michelangelo ... Japan ... Dr. Peres's Celestial Circle and the Dipper Grail," Susan whispered to Winston.

"It is truly an emblematic American work of art," the reverend said. "It's a *misterium magnum,* an image of the great mystery. Saint-Gaudens said that 'Some call it *The Peace of God that Passeth Understanding,* others call it Nirvana. But to him it was the human soul face to face with the greatest of all mysteries.' It has always reminded me of the cloaked figures in El Greco's painting, the *Visitation,* at Dumbarton Oaks."

"An American Buddha," Winston compared, "shrouded vigilance ... a woman draped in a womb ... hidden ... peering out at the world, like from Plato's Cave."

"I thought it was the face of a man peering out at the world," Susan said. "Dumbarton Oaks," she repeated, looking through her notes.

" 'Both man and female He created them,' the Shiva Ardhanareeswara," the reverend quoted. "Dumbarton Oaks houses the Center for the American Society of Landscape Architects. It's an old building of importance. It's where they formally drafted the charter for the U. N. and the World Bank." The reverend pulled his hand to his chest and rubbed his fingers over the birdcall. The birdcall made no sound.

Silence filled the hedges.

"This figure, also known as *The Death,* has been described as 'an idealization *complete* and *absolute.*' Many claim Augustus Saint-Gaudens named it the *Grief.* Others claim its name came from a newspaper article written by Mark Twain. The statue has since been unofficially called *Grief,* as promoted by Twain. It's fitting. Cemeteries are where you come to share your grief. But, Henry Adams always referred to it as the Buddha. Saint-Gaudens's wrote in his journal, 'Adams. Buddha. Mental repose. Calm reflection *in contrast* with *the violent forces in nature.*' "

"*Grief,* the *Via Dolorosa,*" Susan said to Winston.

The reverend dropped his gaze to the bloodred birdcall in the palm of his hand. "I like to call this statue the *Halcyon,* after Alcyone in Greek mythology, who in grief over the death of her husband, Ceyx, threw herself into the *sea of consciousness* and was changed into a tranquil halcyon—a golden bird with the power to calm the winds and the waves of the sea. Grief, our darkness made visible, is a comforting thing."

Stepping to the northern corner of the platform, the reverend stood next to a carving of cherubim wings above a bird's claw grasping an orb. "Saint-Gaudens asked his friend, the noted architect Stanford White, to create the setting for this statue. Stanford White was responsible for the design of the Oval Office at the White House. He had also worked with the tree-huggers Daniel Burnham and Frederick Law Olmsted on the redesign of Washington, D.C. during the City Beautiful Movement of the early 1900s. They were the architects of the Great White City at the 1893 Columbian Exposition in Chicago."

"Burnham ..." Susan glanced at Winston.

"The *Kabalyon,*" Winston muttered.

"The early 1900s was another time and place," the reverend continued. "It was the Gilded Age. Historians have called it the end of the American Republic and the start of the American Empire. It was a time of William Jennings Bryan and Christian Socialism in America, when many believed that the teachings in the Bible could solve the problems created by the nation's emerging industrialization. Still other philosophers, such as Charles S. Peirce and the Swedenborgian ghost hunter and the promoter of the New Thought Movement, William James, both members of Harvard's Metaphysical Club, saw pragmatism and religious pluralism as the best direction for the new American society."

"William James," Winston thought out loud. *Psychical Research, Newcomb's experiment, light ... the Washington Monument.*

"New Thought Movement," Susan said to Winston.

"Yeah ... Angus's book." Winston nodded. "Mind-body, Cartesian dualism."

"Saint-Gaudens had known Stanford White since the construction of Trinity Church, when Saint-Gaudens worked for LaFarge on the interior decoration,"

Worthington continued. "White worked for the almost mystic architect, Olmsted's former partner, H. H. Richardson, on the design of that church. Richardson was the grandson of Joseph Priestly."

"Priestly?" Susan asked, jotting down the name.

"He was a natural philosopher, an alchemist, a chemist, a Unitarian, and a follower of Pantisocracy," the reverend explained. "He was a close friend of Benjamin Franklin and Thomas Jefferson. Priestly is the man who invented soda water, the basis for the soft drink industry."

"My favorite poison," Winston remarked.

His arms folded behind his back, the reverend tread to the southern corner of the memorial's platform. "Before his death in 1907, Saint-Gaudens created some of the most honored works of sculpture in America, including the figure of Diana that once topped Madison Square Gardens. He created monuments to American heroes and statesmen like President Lincoln and General Sherman, and the Scottish writer Robert Louis Stevenson, as well as the Hamilton Fish Tomb. Saint-Gaudens even worked on the commission that replanned Washington, D.C. in the early 1900s. He also aided in the formation of the American Academy in Rome."

"Academy in Rome ..." Susan flipped the pages of her notepad, straightening the edges. *Next to the meridian on the skull.*

The reverend stepped toward the statue, and the ravens took flight. He rubbed his hand over the statue's smooth, brownish-green, patined surface. His eyes keenly followed his hand. "It is truly a hypnotic piece of art. The enigmatic gaze of this draped figure seems to change with the light throughout the day and with the mood of the viewer. Sometimes you can see your own reflection in it. I've sat here for hours, looking at it. It's easy to understand why Eleanor Roosevelt, the first lady who promoted the creation of the United Nations, came here to meditate."

The reverend stepped backward, in a slow, even pace, maintaining his gaze on the statue. "I recall something she once said, although the people who run the U.N. do not practice it. 'Remember always that you not only have the right to be an individual, you also have an obligation to be one.' I wonder if she believed that? She would have had to divorce FDR if she believed in something like that." He waved with his hands in quick circular gestures. "This memorial became famous in the early 1900s. A sculptor named Edward Pausch created his own unauthorized copy of the *Grief.* In 1905, General Felix Agnus purchased the Pausch copy to grace his family tomb at Druid Ridge Cemetery in Pikesville, Maryland. It became known as the infamous *Black Aggie,* the angel of darkness. In 1967, the *Black Aggie* was donated to the Smithsonian after the statue had been vandalized by initiates from a local college fraternity who included the statue in their initiation rites."

"Initiation rites," Winston said to himself.

"Yes, form does not always follow function," the reverend quipped. "The *Black Aggie* was exhibited in the National Gallery of Art for a brief period. For many years, the statue remained in a dusty storeroom of the Smithsonian until it rose from the dead. The *Black Aggie* now resides in the rear courtyard of the Dolly Madison House."

Reverend Worthington ambled awkwardly across the platform, sat down again on the bench directly in front of the statue, and stared with a Nembutsu emptiness into the calm face of *Grief.*

"That's an interesting story, Preacher Worthington," Winston remarked.

Susan jabbed her elbow into Winston's side.

"What?" He flinched.

"James, do you see what's in front of this statue?" She motioned with a sideways flick of her head.

"Yes, I do," he responded. "This cemetery is a forest of obelisks. They're all over the place."

Susan leaned toward Winston in conspiratorial closeness, her hand to her mouth, "James, there must be other commonalities in this graveyard."

"Probably," he whispered back. "Preacher Worthington, can you tell us about the history of the cemetery?" he asked, searching for more information on the *locus.*

"The cemetery encircles the old parish church of St. Paul's Episcopal Chapel. St. Paul's was founded during the reign of Queen Anne, in 1712. Despite several fires over the years, the original eighteen-inch-thick brick walls still remain intact. All of the those bricks were imported from Gloucester. There are only a few special buildings in America constructed of bricks imported from Europe, such as some of the buildings at Williamsburg and the massive base that holds up the U. S. Capitol dome. Our chapel is known for its beautiful stained-glass windows which portray the history of the Episcopal Church in America."

"So the cemetery was created in 1712?" Susan probed.

"No," the reverend corrected. "The cemetery was established a few years later in 1719 when John Bradford pledged 100 acres to serve as a glebe for the parish. That glebe is the site of the present-day churchyard. In 1721, a new brick church was built on the site of the present building. In the late 1880s, much of the churchyard was redesigned as an urban space, under the guidance of landscape architect Frederick Law Olmsted. Its rolling landscape worked well with the popular rural cemetery movement of the period, which sought to combine cemeteries with public parks."

"Preacher Worthington are you aware of any skull-shaped monuments on the grounds?"

"Skulls ... the symbol of human mortality," the reverend thought out loud. "No, not really. There are winged skulls carved on some of the tombstones. Especially on the old colonial graves. It was a common ornamentation back then. They are often depicted alongside an hourglass with wings to signify the swiftness of time and the flight of the soul. Skulls are all that remain after the soul takes flight. It's an old cemetery, Mr. Winston, an old political graveyard. Our chapel is the oldest church in the District. It is one of the oldest still-standing structures in the United States."

"Where's the chapel?" Winston asked, handing Susan the map.

"It's this way, near the entrance." The reverend pointed.

"I'm melting in this humid heat. Some water would be nice. Do you have a fountain in the chapel?"

"And Nature calls," Susan added, picking up the rucksack. "I need to visit the comfort station."

"Yes. There is a fountain and restrooms. Follow me," the reverend summoned in a funereal voice. "You can't get lost in this cemetery. It's a labyrinth with all of the paths leading to the chapel."

Birds chirped in the hedges, as the reverend escorted them to the chapel. "There are several other noteworthy memorials on the grounds in addition to the *Grief*," the reverend shared. "There is the Frederic Keep Monument, the Heurich Mausoleum, the Sherwood Mausoleum Door, the Thompson-Harding Monument, and the Kauffman Monument, also known as *The Seven Ages of Memory*. We also have gravesites of many well-known individuals in the cemetery, such as Upton Sinclair, Gore Vidal, the writer of *The City and the Pillar*, Charles Corby, George Washington Riggs, the family of Alexander Graham Bell, and the sister of Edgar Allan Poe. A lot of thought went into the design of those tombs and memorials. People want to be remembered. But the duties of our station in life are merely temporal. Death is the only thing promised to us. The world ends here." He stopped in his steps and stared at a white marble tombstone adorned with fresh flowers. In bold letters, the name WORTHINGTON was chiseled across its face above two dates separated by a dash. "The dates of our birth and our death." The reverend pointed. "Alpha and Omega—the beginning and the end. That short dash between the dates, that's your life. Every tombstone in this cemetery has a dash. This place of death and grief is full of life."

"Yes, it is. It's hidden in plain sight. I guess sometimes you just have to look for it. It's a beautiful cemetery, Preacher. Listen to those birds singing."

"Sirin and Alkonost, the songbirds of sorrow … and joy. I agree, Mr. Winston, it is a beautiful cemetery. It's our ribbon of green in the District. This and Rock Creek Park, Arlington Cemetery, and the Mount of Olives Cemetery next to the Kenilworth Aquatic Garden lie at the major intersection of the great North Atlantic Flyway which extends over the Pocosins in North Carolina. These are the places where the birds come to visit in their migration. The large public parks and cemeteries make the District an aviary for the birds. The spirits of the dead reside here and so do the birds."

The three proceeded past a large Celtic cross, carved with a vine of intertwining Solomon's knots, next to a bronze statue of a man and woman standing in union.

"There's the chapel." The reverend pointed to the front of the church with its unusual, octagon-shaped steeple.

Winston eyed the bronze plaque next to the entrance.

HERE, THE FIRST CHURCH **EDIFICE** WITHIN THE FUTURE DISTRICT OF COLUMBIA WAS ERECTED IN **1719**.

"Let me unlock the door." The reverend fished through his coat pocket. "I have it somewhere." He thumbed through a ring of *jangling* keys. "This is the gate key. The crypt key. Yes. Here it is." He opened the door and they entered the small, square chapel. "Ms. Hamilton," he said politely, "let me show you to the facilities."

As Susan and the reverend disappeared through a side door, Winston took a seat on an empty wooden pew. He noticed the scent of furniture polish. Awkwardly sliding in his seat, he leaned back and leisurely studied the nuances of the chapel's interior.

Quaint, peaceful, Winston contemplated. *A simple square—cubic architecture …* His eyes narrowed as he looked across the chapel at the three stained-glass windows of the eastern wall. *Or the inside of another letterbox … I'm familiar with that …*

A colorful rendition of Mantegna's *Descent Into Limbo* decorated the central window. In the scene, Jesus walked on a street paved in gold before a skull-shaped cave, with the sinners of purgatory filing out of the skull's mouth. Jesus held a staff bearing the flag of Saint George. Above the scene, a depiction of a fire-breathing dragon, mingled within the illuminated clouds of the *Shekinah Glory,* emerged from the heavens. An obelisk and a golden fleur-de-lis were placed above the skull-shaped cave. A one-inch-wide panel of ruby-red glass extended from the fleur-de-lis at the top and dissected the whole window.

Winston noted the inscription at the bottom of the window.

Matthew Chapter Sixteen
TV ES PETRVS ET SVPER HANC PETRAM AEDIFICABO ECCLESIAM MEAM. TIBI DABO CLAVES REGNI CAELORVM (Matthew 16:18-19: "You are Peter, and on this rock I will build my church. I will give you the keys of the kingdom of heaven.")

"Hmm … 'Windows of Enlightenment.' " *Stained-glass windows … Saint Denis … holy heads … Golgotha … an obelisk pointing north … Draco … rose-line.* Winston's thoughts flickered in rapid succession. He shifted his gaze to the right of the central window at a second window depicting a scene related to the Old Testament. A Bible verse was inscribed at the base of the window.

Ezekiel Chapter One
"I beheld the living creatures, behold one wheel upon the earth by the living creatures, with his four faces. The appearance of the wheels and **their work** was the colour of **White Beryl:** and they four had one likeness: and their appearance and their work was as it were a wheel in the middle of a wheel."

The focal point of the scene featured a bearded man in a red robe holding a sphere made of golden rings in his right hand. A menorah and a Star of David were formed by the glass at the bottom of the scene, with the sun and the moon depicted on either side of an inverted pentagram star at the top.

A wheel in the middle of a wheel … sol and moon … pentagram, Winston brainstormed. He studied the third window which depicted Jesus feeding fish to the multitude. A verse at the bottom of the window read:

John Chapter One
"In the beginning was the *Logos*, and the *Logos* was with God, and the ***Logos* was God**. And in the *Logos* was *Life*"

A fish … the Logos, a cosmic order … a wheel within a wheel, Plato's Tekton. He linked the commonalities.

"They are enlightening, are they not, Mr. Winston?" the reverend's voice echoed from the far side of the chapel. "The light from this stained-glass is an uplifting sight from the sorrow and death outside."

"Yes, they are," Winston agreed with a thoughtful gaze.

"These windows were installed when they renovated the church." The reverend carried a paper cup in the shape of an ice cream cone.

"When was that?"

"It happened around 1904, maybe. The famous Chicago architect, Daniel Burnham, oversaw the renovation. These windows were done at the same time as the ones in the Folger Shakespearian Library across from the Capitol. Here's your cup of water."

Shake-speare, Winston reflected. *What did Peres say? Athena … Lux Ferre.* He turned his head to face the reverend. "Preacher Worthington, whaddya know about these other windows at the Folger Library?"

"Nothing really. But there is one that is quite famous, called the *Seven Ages of Man*. The Kauffman Memorial is based upon the same theme. It's a curved granite wall with a series of low-relief bronze tablets with illustrations of the seven stages of life as portrayed in Shakespeare's *As You Like It*."

"Hmm …" Winston's eyes wandered up again to the windows as he drank from the cup. *Seven Ages of Man ... It was listed in that book ... 'Windows of Enlightenment'* ...

Susan walked into the chapel, holding the rucksack. "Are we ready to inspect the cemetery?"

"Pardon me." Winston turned away from the reverend. "Susan, the preacher told me that Daniel Burnham renovated this building."

"That Chi-town architect again," she said, surprised.

"Yes, and he was responsible for *that*." Winston pointed to the three windows.

Susan faced the windows.

"I don't know. It's another hunch or a different presence of mind. Perhaps I'm grasping at straws." Winston stood up and faced the windows. "But I'm thinking that these windows have something to do with that book Angus told us about. Maybe all of this has to do with that book. We need to do double overtime. Susan, I want you to take a few photos of the interior of this chapel. Have the Preacher show you the Kauffman Monument. Get some pictures. Then meet me tomorrow morning at Fort Meade." He crumpled the paper cup in his hand and started to walk away.

"Where are you going?" She asked, confused. "Bains won't stand for another one of your side trips."

"I'm going to my library." A secretive expression drifted across Winston's face.

"You're going back to Sundance, to Bear Lodge?"

"No. I'm going to my other library, the Jefferson Building at the Library of Congress. I need to do some research. I need to close up a few loose ends."

Susan pulled her camera to her eye. The prismatic blend of colors from the stained glass reflected through her viewfinder, like the shifting shards in a kaleidoscope. She lowered her camera. "James, did you see the images in these windows?"

"Yes, I know. It may shed a different light on all this. Take some photos."

As Winston walked out the door, his studious eyes caught the design in the stained glass above the entrance. A depiction of a piscivorous American eagle, with a snake in its mouth, held in its talons a *red herring*. The Greek letters *Alpha* and *Omega* were inscribed below the scene.

Winston reeled back, challenged by the images. His eyes blinked. "From *Alpha* to *Omega*. When fish fly!" he exclaimed below his breath. "I've seen that somewhere before. Susan, get some shots of this one as well."

———

The second is freedom of every person to worship God in his own way - everywhere in the world. The "Four Freedoms" speech, 6 January 1941, *Franklin Delano Roosevelt*
Nature's laws lay *hid in sight*; God said, 'Let Newton be! And all was *light*.' – Alexander *Pope*

FORTY-SEVEN MINUTES LATER, the black Mercury sat running with its left brake light lit outside the research entrance to the Jefferson Building of the Library of Congress on Second Street.

"Look, I could be here all night. I'll call you later for pickup," Winston instructed the driver. He exited the car and waited next to a concrete barricade disguised as a flowerpot, until the car drove out of sight. He glanced up at the golden flame atop the Jefferson Building and to a long banner hanging on one side of the building.

SPECIAL EXHIBITS
"Post nubila phoebus"
(After dark clouds comes the sun)
On View between Sept. 11- 25.
15th Century Maps of America - Main Hall
Jefferson's Cipher Wheel and the Lord's Prayer - East Hall
The History of Early American Money - West Hall
To be presented again March 11-25 of next year.

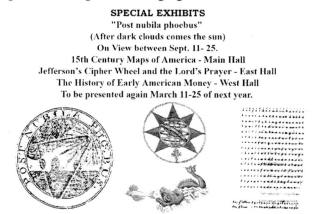

I'll come back later and check that out. Winston crossed the street and race-walked away from the library. *It's north of here,* he reckoned. He trekked one block north, then stopped next to a neo-classical stone building.

Directly in front of him stood an aluminum replica of a statue of Puck—the demon, the woodwose, the Green Man, the Horned God, the Sorcerer, and the pagan trickster Púca. The partially disrobed Puck struck a kneeling pose with the palms of his hands exposed. His lifelines were clearly visible for all to see. His face sighted away from the houses of government.

A white dove, Columbia, the heroic bird, landed on the statue's head. *"Coo-coo-ca-roo. Peace to you."*

Winston bowed his head to read the inscription below the statue. A mischievous quotation engraved in the stone proclaimed, "Lord, what fooles these mortals be!" Behind the statue loomed five enormous windows in the western wall of the Folger Library.

Following a walkway that skirted the corner, Winston proceeded to the main research entrance.

———

"**SIR, I'M SORRY.** We are closed today. Renovations," a young attendant in a guard's uniform instructed, as Winston opened the door. "I cannot let you in."

"But, I need to get in." Winston held his ground, staring at the naive expression on the young face dusted with tiny, boyish freckles. "I've come a long way." He eyed the ID badge on the attendant's shirt pocket: RODNEY CHARON.

"Sir. We are closed today," the attendant repeated firmly.

Maybe government needs to oversee the gatekeeper. Winston reached into his wallet, pulled out an ID card, and handed it to the attendant. "Listen. Call the number on this card. They will confirm that it is alright for you to let me in. I only want to see the stained-glass windows in this building. This will not take long."

"Hmm— " The attendant stretched his neck and took a gander at the name on the card with his dime-size eyes. "Mr. Winston, this is a MENSA membership card." He shook his head and handed the card back to Winston.

"I'm always getting them mixed up." Winston fumbled through his wallet. "I have it here somewhere. This is it. No, this is the biometric Homeland Security card. Let's see … Here. Try this one."

The attendant read the official imprint above a silvery holographic stamp of the NSA seal. "I cannot let you in with this card either," he said primly, annoyance creeping into his voice. "Anyone could have a card that says NSA Security."

Winston rolled his eyes and spoke below his breath. "I'd give you my social security number, but it's in my arm. You guys need a Veri-biosensor scanner." He readdressed the attendant, "Listen, don't get festered. Just call this 800 number on the B-side." Winston lightened his voice. "Please. There's no harm in doing this."

"Alright. I'll call the number," the attendant agreed hesitantly.

The attendant left Winston standing in the entrance hall and disappeared past a gift shop into a back room.

"Hello … How did I get this number? I have a gentleman outside who claims to be with the NSA. We are closed today. I do not have the authority to let him in." The attendant flinched; his eyes squeezed shut as he momentarily recoiled the phone away from his ear. "Yes. That's right. This is the Folger Library. How did you know that? ... Yes. Ms. Jenkins is my supervisor. How did you know? ... Yes. She's still here. But— I need to hang up? But—Hello? Hello!"

The attendant approached Winston, who waited patiently. "Sir, they hung up on me. I cannot let you in."

"Yeah. I know," Winston said flatly.

A quaint woman in her late fifties wearing an oversized, downy-like, body sweater stepped into the entrance hall. She was less than five feet tall and Rubenesque. Her smooth porcelain skin emphasized her wide-set, half-closed, light-brown-yellow eyes and the tranquil expression on her face. The tight curls of her cotton-white hair, like the delicate feathers hooding a sleepy-eyed snow owl, slightly rustled as she moved forward. Around her neck hung a pair of silver-framed reading glasses, next to a bloodred Audubon birdcall.

"Are you Mr. Winston?" the woman asked with a midtown London accent.

"Hello. Yes. He has my card," Winston replied bluntly. He pulled the ID card from the attendant's hand and winked an I-told-you-so. He handed it to the woman.

"It's alright, Rodney. It's alright. Mr. Winston may enter the building," she said apologetically. "I'm so sorry. My name is Beatrice Jenkins. I am one of the library's curators." She handed Winston his ID card. "Welcome to our house of the Bard— Shakespeare—the *universal mind* who knew *everything*."

"Are you a guide?" Winston asked as he placed the card back into his wallet. "Can you offer me a history on this building?"

"Yes, I can," she replied.

"What can you tell me about the stained-glass windows in this building? Especially the one called *The Seven Ages of Man?*"

"Normally, the viewing of that window is off-limits. But, lend an ear, Mr. Winston. Come this way," she guided. "Follow me. Step into our *theater of life*. It's in our Reading Room."

Without making a sound, as though floating on air, she glided across the hardwood floors and led Winston into a Tudor-style athenaeum. Richly embellished with moldings and panels of hardwood inlays, the room contained thousands of books and works of Elizabethan art.

Winston felt a chill when he entered the room. His eyes wandered up to the wall tapestries and the wheel-shaped chandeliers hanging from the coffered ceiling. As they walked past a stone fireplace, he spied the swinging brass pendulum of a clock on a table, covered by a crystal-clear, leaded glass dome. Its hands pointed to 9:11 A.M. His studious eyes scanned the titles on the shelves, displayed like epitaphs on the fronts of weathered tombstones. He noticed a plaque hanging above a door.

Love's Labours Lost
"This thing of darkness I acknowledge mine. . . . Black is the badge of hell.
The hue of dungeons, and the School of Night."

"You have a fine selection of old books, Ms. Jenkins." He rubbed his shoulders. "It's cold in here." A warm mist rolled off his breath.

"Yes, we do, but most of the rare books are stored in our vaults three levels below ground," she explained, stretching her sweater tighter around her shoulders. "All of the first folios are stored there, as well as the other rare and surviving works from the Elizabethan period. We keep this room at a constant humidity to preserve the books."

Elizabethan ... Dr. Dee ... Bacon ... the School of Night ... the God Longitude. Winston remembered Angus's history of the *Kabalyon.*

Ms. Jenkins paused next to a long oak table and rested her hand on the edge. "This is it." She pointed upward to the far end of the athenaeum at the western wall. The whole second-floor wall consisted of a spectacular window of multicolored stained glass, the design of which resembled a menorah.

"This way, Mr. Winston." She led him up a stairway to a balcony directly in front of the window. Holding onto the railing, she leaned forward and pointed with one hand, like a sailor at the helm of a ship sighting an uncharted island. "This window was designed in the studio of Nicola D'Acenzo in Philadelphia. In the glass you see the depictions of the Infant, the School Boy, the Lover, the Soldier, Justice, Pantoloone, and the Old Man. The window depicts the *Seven Ages of Man* from Jaques's speech in *As You Like It.* It's the speech where Jaques concludes his cynical evaluation of the emptiness of human life by reminding us of how in our old age we eventually become *useless* lumps of flesh."

Ms. Jenkins leveled her eyes on the window and allowed her neck to relax. As she did, she ever so slightly swayed her head to the cadence of her spoken word.

"All the world's a stage,
And all the men and women merely players:
They have their exits and their entrances;
And one man in his time plays many parts,
His acts being Seven Ages. At first the infant,
Mewling and puking in the nurse's arms;
Then the whining schoolboy, with his satchel,
And shining morning face, creeping like snail
Unwillingly to school. And then the lover,
Sighing like furnace, with a woeful ballad
Made to his mistress' eyebrow. Then a soldier,
Full of strange oaths, and bearded like the pard,
Jealous in honour, sudden, and quick in quarrel,
Seeking the bubble reputation
Even in the cannon's mouth. And then the justice,
In fair round belly with good capon lined,
With eyes severe, and beard of formal cut,
Full of wise saws and modern instances;
And so he plays his part: the sixth age shifts
Into the lean and slippered pantaloon,
With spectacles on nose, and pouch on side,
His youthful hose, well saved, a world too wide
For his shrunk shank; and his big manly voice,
Turning again toward childish treble, pipes
And whistles in his sound. Last scene of all,
That ends this strange eventful history,
Is second childishness, and mere oblivion—
Sans teeth, sans eyes, sans taste, sans everything."

She turned toward Winston. "Mr. Winston, this is a speech about the rites of human passage and the pedagogical lessons for life."

"Like a *Divine Comedy*," he mused. "Yes, I already know that. That's why I'm here. A rite of passage from an old book has led me here … along with a message from my father."

Ms. Jenkins smiled. "This speech marks the various times when a person reaches a new and significant change in his or her life. It is something that nearly all societies recognize through special ceremonies, which are held to observe a person's entry into a new stage in life. From one stage to another, it can be anything—from a birthday party, a school graduation ceremony, or even something as sad as a funeral."

My parents, Winston thoughtfully listened.

"Most rites of passage help us to understand our role in a society. They can also help us to understand others in new and different ways from what we learn through a profound experience."

She lifted her heart-shaped face to Winston with a hopeful expression. "Rites of passage fall into perhaps three main phases within the human experience. There is the separation phase, wherein a person is often taken away from his or her familiar environment. Sometimes a person has to enter into a different and sometimes foreign world, where they are forced to readjust. A rite of passage that falls into this category is birth." She closed her eyes. "Living in a mother's womb, like living in a cave, an infant is bound in a safe and secure environment. It fledges from its nest to discover an extremely different habitat in the world, where he or she can be born again and learn to fly. Death, the way of all flesh, can also be a separation rite of passage, depending on a person's belief about an afterlife. Dying can be somewhat like being born again."

She opened her eyes. "The transition phase of a rite of passage is the time when a person learns the appropriate behavior for the new stage in their life. This phase may include the time when a person becomes engaged to be married. It's a time when a couple prepares for the sacred union. The transition phase may also include the time when children enter adolescence. We all must leave our childhood behind, Mr. Winston. It's the time when people *learn* and *grow* and become *independent* adults in the real and often *unforgiving* world."

With the help of Billy. Winston gave a heart-felt smile.

"The last phase, that of incorporation, takes place when someone is willing to adopt a new role in their life. Marriage again is a good example of such a phase. After people are married, they often have to take on new roles, having prepared for it in earlier transition and separation phases of their lives. Marriage can be a soul-forging process. It is a sacred relationship that breaks down our egos, turning us into givers and people who care unselfishly. Marriages seldom work if they are not preceded by rites of passage followed in the correct order."

I'm not the marrying kind. Winston's face lost all expression, tight-lipped. *Maybe I was meant to live alone.*

"It is also true for dying," Ms. Jenkins noted. "One of the one hundred most important thinkers of the last century, Elisabeth Kubler-Ross, once wrote that 'dying is nothing to fear. That it could be the most wonderful experience of our lives. It all depends on how we lived our lives.' Did we follow the correct rite of passage through it? Did we experience a correct *Nirvana,* a life free from suffering?"

"*Nirvana.*" *Bear Lodge.* Winston grinned. *Home.*

"It's an endless play, our stages in life. We seem to live our lives around the words found in the greeting cards, as we celebrate the remembrance of our rites of passage." She glanced at the floor, lost in thought. "Mr. Winston, there are many rites of passage in our lives. Some are considered more significant than others. There are five times of profound change in every person's life. These being birth, leaving childhood behind and becoming an adolescent, leaving home, marriage, and funerals. All of the events found in the greeting cards. To recognize these pivotal moments in our lives, societies often hold elaborate ceremonies. Each society chooses to mark these rites in its own unique ways, which are meaningful to its own culture. These five times in our lives are represented in some way within Jaques's speech."

She glanced toward the window. "This is why Shakespeare's words are so enduring. Those *eternae veritate* words are still valid for us today. They will always relate to the human soul and the human experience. Yes, even Shakespeare, or Bacon, or a School of Night maybe," she nodded, "can be seen as being as holy and inviolable as any biblical prophet."

Ms. Jenkins closed her eyes again in a trancelike state of total calm and spoke just above a whisper, as in a Shinto harmony.

"There are Seven Ages.

There are seven days in the week ... seven days in God's great creation.

There are seven candlesticks, with *one* liked unto the Son of Man.

There are seven dimensions to the *Logos*, with Ayocosmos being the highest.

Gabriel, Raphael, Uriel, Michael, Samael, Zachariel, Orifiel. There were seven ancient planetary Gods, seven Kabbalic mirrors. Seven Gods of Happiness: Hotei, Bishamonten, Fukurokuuju, Jurojin, Daikoku, Ebisu, Benzaiten.

There are seven heavens, seven heavenly virtues, and seven dances of the Tandava.

There are seven seas that form the waters of the Earth ... and seven continents on the Earth. Seven participants in Plato's Symposium on the nature of love.

There are seven wonders of the ancient world.

Seven sages of Greece who taught great truths, Solon, Chilon, Thales, Bias, Cleobulus, Pittacus, Periander.

Seven stages of Alchemy—in the transmutation to white gold.

There are seven great arts that must be mastered.

Anger, Greed, Lust, Envy, Pride, Sloth, and Gluttony. There are seven deadly sins.

Seven Joys and Seven Sorrows of the Blessed Virgin Mary.

Seven circles in Dante's Inferno. Seven devils behind the Magdelene Line.

Seven Noahide Laws in the Talmud.

Seven fundamental colors in the spectrum of light.

Seven psychological seats of activity we all possess, with two which most people never experience.

Seven steps to death spoken by the Dalai Lama, an Ocean of Wisdom.

One great dance through the seven veils.

Seventy years in the average life of a man. The *Septuagint*.

Seventy years in one degree of the great Platonic year.

Seven notes on the musical scale, which only the birds have mastered.

Seven stars to the north, that we might guide ourselves by."

"Everything is septenary, sevenfold. Nature's law is a law of seven, the perfect number. This window is a symbol for the Tree of Life. Man is linked to his life harmoniously by his rite of passage through it," she spoke aloud. "*Life*—is a religion, Mr. Winston. Ordered and Primal."

Hacking ... the Game of Life. Winston nodded in agreement.

She looked up into Winston's studious blue eyes. "There are different types of rites found in every society. There are Calendrical Rites based around holy days with rituals which observe the seasonal changes or commemorate important historical events. There are Rites of Exchange and Communion involving offerings and sacrifices to a deity, including prayer, incantation, divination, and consultation of oracles. There are Rites of Affliction which mitigate the influence of negative forces such as demonic spirits, bad karma, and sin. Those rites are often associated with feasting or fasting which purifies the body, including rituals of healing, exorcism, and self-afflicted purification before an encounter with the divine through a trance or a personal vision quest."

"I do my fasting with a diet cola." Winston grinned. "A vision quest, you sound like a friend of mine."

Ms. Jenkins smiled. "And there are Political Rites which promote the power of the institutions of government as part of the accepted order. They include enthronement rituals, legal ceremonies, and ceremonies related to warfare, such as praising God after a battle." She shook her head despairingly. "As if God would condone the destruction of his most sacred creation."

Winston nodded, then commented, "It doesn't follow the Tao."

"All of these rites help to guide us." Ms. Jenkins grew thoughtful. "Some people seem to come into this world fully formed, cradled in the comfort of a fetal position and connected by a cord of life to some greater self. They seem to know all the answers, while others spend their whole lives asking questions ... as though they were not even born to their world. It's as if they were C-sectioned, yanked from the womb just before their time and forced from the start to live a life that wasn't really meant to be. Mr. Winston, there are a lot of C-sections in our world." She shook her head. "They seem to have to live their lives around other people's rites of passage. The story of Jesus ... the story in *Star Wars* ... *Tom Sawyer* ... *Hamlet* ... *The Canterbury Tales* ... *A Pilgrim's Progress* ... Alice, in her wonderland," she spoke joyfully. "Or even the whimsy found in *A Midsummer Night's Dream.*"

"But there's some greater purpose for everyone." Winston hopefully added, "Everything happens for a reason. Everyone has a place in the world—a place in the grand scheme of things."

"Yes, Mr. Winston. What do we want to be when we grow up? A doctor, a lawyer, or an Indian chief?"

Billy, Winston thought.

"Some people have trouble finding their way," Ms. Jenkins pointed out. "They need a Meaning Maker to guide them. It's where they draw their comfort. With *certain faith,* they follow a path laid down by someone else. But adhering to a dogma can be a censorship of the personal exploration which gives our lives meaning. Self discovery, the real purpose of our lives, is undermined by living the path of someone else. You can't be Tom Sawyer. You can't be Hamlet. You can't be Luke Skywalker. And you can't be Jesus. They are all personifications of the rites of human passage. They are merely memory maps for our minds to follow as we find our true calling."

She held her arms behind her back like a bird with its wings folded. "What makes us who we are?" She stared out into the vaulted Reading Room from her perch on the balcony. "I have often wondered what it might be like if we could just live our lives, and let our own personal rites of passage just naturally occur. It is a naturally occurring thing—Nature's laws. We live in a world where people have to take on so many roles that do not suit them. Business roles, male and female roles, ethnic roles. Too many mothers who must be fathers and too many fathers who must be mothers. Not everyone was born to be an actor."

She looked up at the leaden bordered patchwork of crystal glass with her arms still folded. She sidestepped and sidled up next to Winston. Both of their bodies were color-drenched, bathed in the shimmer of a misty rainbow falling down upon them.

" 'My heart leaps up when I behold a rainbow in the sky: So was it when my life began,' Wordsworth," Ms. Jenkins quoted in delight. "These colored lights I see are like the various holy books of faith: the Bible, the Qur'an, the Torah, the *Shiva Sutra*s, the Kabbalah, the *Tao*, and the *Samurai Creed*. Each was written by someone's hand and is only a filtered and colored view of the source. Every culture offers a different vision of life. Perhaps we need to study all the colors in the rainbow of faiths to find the True White Light of Life. Doctrines are only signposts offering direction. Every person, Mr. Winston, holds a fragment of the knowledge of God. Every person has a measure of faith in his own belief, which is a *trust in himself*. Do we listen to that small voice inside us which we trust, that tells us what to do, how to trow, and when to follow? Do we follow that trust? Do we live the true *Light* of *Life* that *beams* from our hearts and sets us burning? Do we follow our heart's desire, our mystic path, our *makaru*, our True Voice? Do we move from our own magnetic center, our true essence, toward the direction of our daydreams? Do we follow the steps that make it happen, so we can live to discover our own *Tality*, our secret place beyond the world of reality? Or do we live our lives as battling cogs in a machine—turning upon ourselves into submission?"

She paused theatrically. " 'For where your treasure is, there will your heart be also.' This window is a representation of our Lineage of Luminance that beacons us." Her eyes lamped up at Winston's face. "No man should die without living his dreams. You are right. We all have a hidden purpose in our lives, Mr. Winston, which is our true destiny. Do we truly live to carry out the purpose which makes our lives matter? We have to live our *own* lives," she spoke stoically. "We must not be tethered like kites and held by someone's hand as we attempt to fly through life. We must soar like birds under our own wings, freely. Life is like a song, or at least it should be. It's in our mnemonics and our phonetics. Each person has to dance his own dance, speak with his own cadence, and trip the light fantastic to Live a Life of his own, so he can sing into song and *speak*. Someone else's rite of passage is simply a guide to go by. It is important that we live in a world that allows that. Don't you think? A world in which we are *free*. A world in which I can learn and respect your rite of passage, and at the same time, *live mine*." She shook her head, excited. "Can you even begin to imagine what that world might be like? To Live and Let Live!"

She stared Winston steadily in the eyes. "Let the beauty we love be the one we do. Sometimes you have to see the world through a mosaic of stained glass, so you can improve your every shining hour. Sometimes it takes adversity to forge a life into self-determination. Life is a quarry, out of which we are to mine, chisel, and mold our character. Our path in this world is our voice in this world. Life is short, Mr. Winston. Very short. The seven ages go by quickly. We have to learn to speak and make our *special* voices heard, as *we chose* our own best path."

Winston grinned. "I know some Shakespeare, too. 'It is a kind of a good deed to say well; and yet words are not deeds.' Know, Ms. Jenkins, it's in the deeds, not just the words," he noted. "We have to set our beliefs into action. We have to do what we say. We have to practice what we preach."

"Forsooth. Yes, verily." She nodded in agreement. "Indeed, Mr. Winston."

Outside, a cloud passed before the sun, blocking the light entering the lightwell behind the stained-glass window. The bright shards of multicolored mosaics dimmed.

Ms. Jenkins quietly stepped away.

Winston stood at the edge of the balcony and studied the window. He remained there alone for an hour or more, his eyes blinking. He faced *The Seven Ages*.

"Steganographic," he whispered, pulling a nickel from his pocket and rolling it between his fingers. *There's a pattern here. Someone's Tarot ... The Infant, Virgo, a Jester's head ... The School Boy, a dog, Orion, three fish ... The Lover, the Lute-Bearer, Orpheus, Hermes, the Zero Mile Stone ... Vega in the Lyra, a Platonic year ... The Soldier, tilted shaking spear, letters, letters again, Omega, Alpha, the fleur-de-lis—the North Star. Justice, Libra, a Law Giver, Pendragon, the Dragon ... The Pantoloone, powerful in all things, a business man, three lions, one eye hidden, a one-eyed man, Hebrew letters ... Write this down. A quill is a pen. The Old Man, shadow from a candle, time, the wheel, the Sacred Hoop.* Winston's mind filled with possibilities from a well of ideas.

It was now the middle of the day. Winston stood there as the sun's light began to shine its brightest, like a *well of life* behind the *Seven Ages*. He felt weightless and detached, yet drawn to the stained glass, the way plants are drawn to the blue, violet, and green spectrums of light.

In a moment of empathic perception, he felt alone, yet not alone.

The same light has a different color as it passes through each scene of a separate age, he perceived. *Each day has its own colored light. This window is almost alive. "James. Everything is pushed by light." Rainbows, Promises.*

His eyes stopped blinking.

Then, as if someone had turned the tap on a faucet, Winston's mind gushed with a sudden impulse. *I wonder?* With a gnawing suspicion, he reached into his pocket and retrieved the pocket compass. *Everything happens for a reason. There's a reason I didn't lose this stuff from the orb.* He opened it, unrolled the scrap of paper, and read the message again.

HC SVNT DRACONES
1 John 1:5 - "Gift of God" Our Jochebed
Seven Windows of Enlightenment
From Alpha to Omega, The Theotokos and the Cross
The Compass Leads to a Treasure.
Find the Center of the Earth - Walk Around Jerusalem.
The Light of Life Hides Next to the Skull.

The Light of Life Hides Next to the Skull...? An idea flashed in his head as Winston studied the engravings on the compass. *The Messianic Seal ... Maybe these symbols act like a compass...? Lullus-logic—symbols that form a message. These seven lines on the compass could be seven candles of light. Coxy called it a Tree of Life.* He glanced at the back of the compass. Its metal surface shimmered as he flipped it back and forth in his hand. *Angus referred to this other engraving as a Tree of Life ... the ultimate destination.* "Hmm, mirrored images ..." *The two sides of the compass could be a Bongard problem.* He looked up at the window. *Seven panels of light? Seven, my father told me it was my lucky number.* He checked the pocket compass again. *A Star of David ... It looks like Coxy's crystal.* He glanced back at the stained glass. *Eyeing a crystal light. I'm over thinking again. I don't know, these markings on this compass could be a map. But Light...?* Winston contemplated, with a quantum leap. *Obelisks are crystals. What did the Inspector say? Something about the Egyptians believing that an obelisk can reflect light ...* He squinted at the symbols on the pocket compass one more time. *These are the same symbols I saw in that tunnel in Paris. What were they doing there? A bright white obelisk on the tunnel wall—a column of light...?*

He looked out over the balcony at the twinkling lights on the wheel-shaped chandeliers. He peered down into the Reading Room and spied the lights reflected off the glass dome of the clock on the table. *Not this, not that ... Light being pulled down by gravity. And Coxy said gravitational fields are affected by rotating massive objects that frame-drag **space-time**. And there is a massive obelisk near here ... a herm ... a type of **transmitter**.* His mind raced, putting together the pieces of another puzzle. *Seventy-seven degrees ... Mother Mary ... the Washington Monument and the Capitol Dome combined ... Alpha to Omega ... a synchronization point ... my Huygens-Grimaldi experiment, mass and gravity ... **bending light** ... the light boxes at Newgrange ... 'the dome of stones and something more' my mother said ... 'at his heart is the Trapezium **fish**, a nebula waiting for a nova' ... one statue brighter than the rest ... Father Kircher ... yes, yes, Monsignor penguin, from the east comes the light—and sometimes **from the west** ... an obelisk in front of St. Peter's ... a Benben ... Light piercing into the womb of the church ... the egg-shaped dome of St. Peter's ... What did Torre say? 'Flickering at the middle of a Mundane Egg on a potter's wheel.'*

" 'From Alpha to Omega ... The Light of Life Hides Next to the Skull ...' " he muttered. "The skull ... the head ... the capital ... the Capitol Building." He cocked his head and gaped again at *The Seven Ages.* "Yes, Ms. Jenkins, 'A light of life that beacons us' ... Jefferson's Lantern of Demosthenes, the Dark Lantern of talking stones. A beacon of light." *Billy's lamp at the medicine wheel. I wonder if it's possible? If it is, I wonder if I can see this?* He checked his wristwatch, then shook his arm in an affirmative gesture as he clenched the pocket compass and held it close to his heart.

Blessed are the pure in heart, for they shall see God. - Matthew 5:8
The light was in the world, and the World was made by it, and the world knew it not. - John 1:10
Light is an image of God's immense Magnitude, Goodness, Eternity, Power, Wisdom, Will, Virtue, Truth and Glory.... - *The Book Light,* by *Raymond Lullus,* Doctor Illuminatus
God is the absolute Verity or Truth clothed with Light.... - *Pythagoras*
God parted from him at the spot where He had spoken to him; and Jacob set up a massebah at the site where He had spoken to him, a massebah of stone, and he offered a libation on it and poured oil upon it. Genesis 35:13–14
In the middle of the stone seemeth to stand a little round thing like a spark of fire, and it increaseth, and it seemeth to be as a globe of twenty inches diameter, or there about. - Edward Kelly's comments to Dr. John Dee on crystal gazing.

AFTER SAYING GOODBY to Ms. Jenkins and giving a quick wink, blink, and nod to Rodney, Winston left the Folger Library and headed west along East Capitol Street. He rechecked his wristwatch and glanced up at the clouds in the sky. *It's clearing. Good. But I need to be on the other side of the building.* He paced north along Olmsted's omega-shaped walkway that bordered the Temple of Liberty. He sighted down a wide street to a statue of Christopher Columbus standing below a globe in front of Union Station. *Yes, the God Longitude,* Winston thought. He stopped at the well-lit, *brick* Grotto next to the Capitol and took a refreshing drink from the fountain. *The Fountain of Youth,* he mused, wiping his lips as his eyes tracked up to the dome. *Resting on imported bricks ... Jesus... It looks like a big ball of vanilla ice* *cream on an ice cream cone.* He noted the ornamentations that decorated the massive temple. One carving caught his eye. *The egg and spear ... a blade and a crucible.*

Winston approached the side of the Capitol facing the Mall and stopped next to a Vishnumandal-shaped fountain, positioned like a sea of bronze at the base of the western porch. *This reminds me of the nicchone at the Vatican,* he contemplated. He sighted out over the Mall, the heart of America's secular temple. Viewed from the east, the Washington Monument appeared undamaged, as omnipresent as ever in the distance. If not for the dump trucks and massive Caterpillar loading machines stationed around it, no one would have guessed what had happened.

He checked his wristwatch again. *It's too early,* he reckoned. *If this happens, it's going to happen just before the sun sets.* He held a watchful eye on the sky. *No, clouds. Please, no clouds.* His eyes crept up at the Capitol's mountain-like dome. *How high is it? Nobles said it's the highest building in the city.* He fixed his eyes on the windows of the drum. *The sashes for the panes of glass are bowed just a little. I wonder if the light gets in.* He looked back at the Washington Monument and tried to estimate a measurement. *How tall is it? How far away is it from here? As in a transit of Venus, some physics is involved—if this happens. I'm not sure. I might be too close to the building to see anything.*

Searching for a wider perspective, Winston treaded away from the Capitol. A vague perfume permeated the air, as he followed a curved walkway outlined by well-organized beds of pulsing red and white roses, flowering dictamnus, and bright clusters of amaranths in full bloom. He walked past a blind man wearing shades and led by a German Shepherd Seeing Eye dog. The blind man was softly singing the lyrics to U2's "Beautiful Day" and tapping a Devil's tattoo on the pavement with his cane. *Tap, tap, tap ... tap, tap, tap ...*

That guy looks a lot like President Scott, Winston thought. He stopped at the street crossing and admired the chest-size, Ark of the Covenant-shaped, street lamps. He glanced up again at the dome. *What did Angus say? A metaphor for the grail.*

Crossing the street, he approached a stand of hedges barely hiding a bronze statue of General Grant riding his horse, Cincinnati. As though stationed at the tail end of a goldfish pond, the statue loomed before a reflecting pool like an aphotic pale rider from the final scene of a cowboy movie waiting for the sun to set. A crouching bronze lion guarded the statue at each of the four corners of the raised stone garth. *Arthur's Seat,* Winston thought. *Symbols for the sun. The guardians of sacred spaces ... or the dominion of the Society of Jesus.*

"Bring your nickel ..."

Winston heard someone's i-Pod chattering Creedence Clearwater Revival's "Down on the Corner."

A few sightseers had gathered around the statue. Winston's eyes followed a man and woman in their twenties, holding hands and smiling at each other as they strolled across the statuary platform. *New love,* he noted.

A little boy and a little girl bantering a nursery rhyme back and forth to each other appeared to be chasing butterflies as they frolicked around the statue.

" 'Oranges and Lemons' say the bells of St. Clement's."

" 'Bull's eyes and targets' say the bells of St. Margaret's."

" 'Two sticks and an apple' say the bells of Whitechapel."

" 'You owe me ten shillings' say the bells of St. Helen's."

" 'When will you pay me?' say the bells of Old Bailey."

" 'When I grow rich' say the bells of Shoreditch."

" 'Pray when will that be?' say the bells of Stepney."

" 'I do not know' says the great bell of Bow."

"Here comes a candle to light you to bed,"

"And here comes a chopper to chop off your head!"

"Chip chop, chip chop." They laughed together. "The last man's **dead!**"

The joy of children. Winston shook his head.

An elderly couple, perhaps the children's grandparents, sat on a stone banister on the opposite side of the statue. The gentleman was thoughtfully reading from a guidebook, with a camera hanging from his neck.

They look familiar. Winston tried to remember.

"G'Day, son," the gentleman greeted in a New Zealand accent, peeking over the edge of his book at Winston. The woman beside him smiled cordially. She motioned to another little girl with a golden barrette in her hair. The girl wore a *bright* travel-light T-shirt from L. L. Bea*m* made from a designer imprint of the American flag. Leaning over a banister, the girl high-tossed stones into the calming water of the reflecting pool as she watched the circular wakes propagate and intersect. Her playful movements resembled a tiny flag waving in a comfortable breeze.

Winston nodded back. *A circle of unbroken love,* he surmised. He folded his arms and leaned against the stone banister on his side of the statue.

Resting on the pavement, a few feet away, sat a bedraggled bearded man in tattered military clothes. The man, who appeared to be one of the city's many homeless, had made himself a bed out of folded cardboard and newspapers. His checks expanded out like an accordion as he chewed on a plug of worm dirt. He smiled kindly in a silent welcome, with deep creases lining his well-tanned face like lines of longitude and latitude mapping out the course of a hard life.

Winston returned a smile. He stared at the man's eyes, nested in deep folds of tired flesh. He noted the ragged name tag sewn above his shirt pocket: CATO.

"Pluhhh—" The homeless man spat a brown lugie to the pavement. "Shalom." He held his hand up in the *shin*-shape of a Vulcan salute, the Sephirothic sign for the divine union. "Did you drink?" His cracked and chapped lower lip trembled. "Are you ready?" He touched the beads of the *rudraksha* mālā around his neck. He removed the headset from his ears and fumbled through his pocket to turn off his i-Pod.

Winston could faintly hear James Taylor singing the end of "Shed a Little Light" and the beginning of "The Frozen Man." Winston looked up at the statue of General Grant.

The homeless man rose up and began gathering his belongings into two black plastic tote bags which held all his worldly possessions.

Feeling like he had scared the man away or invaded his space, Winston waved his hand in a friendly gesture and smiled again. "Hello, it's a nice afternoon."

"Yes, it is, brother," the homeless man agreed with an uneasy nod. He glanced at his wristwatch, then removed a metal cup and a bloodred birdcall attached to a green lanyard from his tote bag. "*Barack* ... seven minutes ... *botzina dekardinota.*" He squatted on the pavement between the two tote bags and rested his back against the stone rails of the banister. He tilted his head and looked longingly across the Reflection Pool toward the gigantic pillar bounded by rows of trees. "I see trees ...," he spoke softly, as though waiting for a deliverance. He swayed his body, raised one hand, and tapped his forehead with his fingertip and began mumbling verses from the *Visualization Sutra of the Sublime.*

Winston thought he heard the cupbearer whispering to himself, "I'm not crazy. I'm not crazy." *He's a forgotten soul. A truly free man. Not a part of anything. Not a care in the world. He reminds me of Billy sitting at the medicine wheel.* Winston took a deep breath and diverted his eyes away from the homeless man. *Relax, breathe.* "No, you're not crazy," Winston said to himself. "**I can see it all from here.**" He gazed out across the vast clearing of *a brahmastan* toward the Washington Monument, scrutinizing it from a distance. He noticed the dozens of bright yellow, sunburst gonfalons, the logo of the Smithsonian, lining the Mall on either side. *It's difficult to judge. It's not a true obelisk. It's not just a gnomon for casting shadows. It's spear-shaped... a migthy skewer made of stones ... a sword in a garden that turns both ways to guide the way.* He squinted. *It's really bowed—just a little.*

Patiently, Winston watched as the orb of the sun gradually angled it's way toward the event horizon—reaching for twilight. As it did, it shape-shifted into an arcing halo behind the Washington Monument. The massive stone column totally obscured the sun from Winston's view. The western sky appeared like a Great Crack in the dome of heaven breaking through the *sunya* of Time and Space.

Unnerved by the sudden *unmesa*-shift from light to dark, Winston's spatial perceptions distorted as the distance rushed toward him and the sun flickered out. For a moment, All was One, as he stared into the Void. "A shady tree ..." He snapped his head around and sighted the Capitol dome. "No! Nothing!" *It's not happening. Maybe it's not the right time. Maybe it's not the right day. Maybe it's too far away. Maybe Einstein and Newton were wrong about mass, gravity, and light. Maybe I'm over thinking this one.* He sighted back at the Washington Monument. *Is that a cloud in the sky?* His eyes narrowed. "No," he uttered. "It's a flock of birds—blocking out the sun!"

Birds blurred in shadow. Thousands of birds clouded the sky, descending in a swirling supernal mass that wheeled above the Earth. Their wings strumming, pushing down, cutting the air as they flew past the pillared altar and over the field of green. A multitude of ruffled feathers and tiny, glittering, beady eyes came closer.

Winston felt his senses carried aloft by the approaching breeze from their wayward wings. He propped up straight from the banister and stepped toward the penumbra.

"Look at me." A few feet away the homeless man twisted his birdcall to the wide-eyed fascination of the little girl draped in the *bright* colored imprint of the American flag. The birdcall sounded an invoking *chirp-chop, chirp-chop.* In an instant, the birds dispersed and gathered in the trees that lined the Mall.

Waiting.

Waves of lengthening shadow bands chased one another across the ground. The loud *chattering* and *crowing* of the birds *rustling* in the trees could be heard greeting the gloaming.

Dong, dong, dong, dong, dong, dong, dong. Vibrating clearly, bells tolled from the

Smithsonian, its castle outlined against an ultra-violet sky morphing to a deep purple and searching for black as the day ebbed away.

"Come this way," the elderly woman called to the little girl from the other side of the platform in an unfounded voice of concern, with her arms reaching out, afraid of letting go.

"*Berakhah*. Go back, now." The homeless man eyed the little girl. "*Hamayir L'aretz*. Be calm. Do not be afraid." He then looked at Winston from the other side of the garth. "Hold this moment in your memory. It's not your time. Don't look or you'll go blind."

In a temporal moment—in unison—the homeless man, the little girl, and Winston crossed the geodesic line of sight between the Washington Monument and the Capitol Building and walked their separate ways. As they did, Winston turned upon himself and spied back at the Monument.

The scattering from the leading edge of a single point of collimated light erupted out of nothingness—endlessly spilling from one side, like the Eye of Dipankara peering from behind a big tree trunk, playing hide and go seek. A resonating *spanda* from Creation's copulation cut through the planes of existence with the Breath of Life.

Winston squinted, feeling his retinas where about to be seared from the witnessing of a Theophany. "Baily's Beads," he breathed. "Hot gold ... a celestial diamond ... I'm moving toward it."

Energy and form unfolding the Principle Particle, the sun showed itself unclothed, a bright naked orb touching a dark naked line—linear and circular—the marriage of the temporal and the spatial forms for All Reality.

Absorbing the light through a *bodhi* moment of a window opening into Eternity, Winston scried *the mirrored image* from the sword's blade undulating in a fiery *nasika* DNA-patterned-zigzag across the *reflecting* pool. *Ducks and geese floating on a swell of burning water...*, he thought, *a winding path ... beautiful water ... dissolving waves of bliss.* For a microsecond, he stared into both the terrifying and fascinating *numinous*, the aweful overpowering Awe that is greater than one's self— the Echo of the Empyrean at the Creative Source. "I hear it ... a warm moving timbre. I see myself." Breaking free from his crystal gazing, from one reality to another, he turned and faced the schlieren field upon the Vessel of Liberty. Enraptured, he gazed upward at the candent, anastigmatic parousia—a burning chrome—like a lightning strike flashing far from the west. He held himself as still as the statue of General Grant, as though the world had stopped.

Kohinoor ... Immaculate Conception ... Saint Clair ... the ka ... the seeding ... holograms around the mercy seat. It's wonderful ... a floating doppler ball of shadow above the fountain of two pillars. "I see it!" *Ninharsag ... The sun's in the shadow. Knife-edged—Lucent ... Ieoh Ming ... White Beryl ... Such a Life-Loving Beam—an L. L. Beam.*

Winston reached into his pocket and tossed a gold-plated Jefferson nickel to the pavement. It rolled around upon its trochal form. Spinning.

"Whoa—I think I just busted a *blood vessel*. Wicked trick. *Freedom*."

***

Day 16
Take Down

Things that collapse: A takedown fishing pole, a takedown bow, taking down a flag, taking down a totem.

NESTLED IN THE HEART OF THEIR HOME, Brad Middleton and his family gathered at the breakfast table, watching the morning news on the kitchen television.

"And the weather for all of America is stormy today," reported the zany weatherman dressed in a polka-dotted clown outfit, charming a group of children. Behind him, a golden statue of the trickster Prometheus held a beckoning flame at the middle of the zodiac in Rockefeller Plaza outside the studios of the *Today Show*. "I'm afraid that things are going to get worse before they get better."

The image on the screen flickered and rolled in and out of focus. *STA-KA, STA-KA,* spat from the speaker.

"Thank you for that informative weather report," said Jane Ballsly.

"Yes," said her co-anchor Tom Moss, reading from an idiot card while holding blank papers in his hands. A backdrop of the U. S. Capitol dome hovered over his head. "In other news today, officials at the United Nations in conjunction with Israeli police and archaeologists with the Islamic Trust, the WAQF, agreed that because of the recent earthquake in Israel, part of the compound of Islam's third holiest shrine, the Al-Aqsa Mosque, will be closed to visitors in fear that it might collapse from the weight of the large crowds of believers."

A close-up of a woman's face appeared on the screen. The caption Hebrew University archeologist Dr. Helena Mayer appeared at the bottom of the screen.

"The Temple Mount is being neglected," declared Professor Mayer. "It is only a matter of time before part of the structure collapses."

"Excuse me, Tom, we have a special report," Jane interrupted in excited newspeak. "We are cutting to Donald Davidson with a live feed. Hello, Donald."

The camera focused on the spiderwebbed polar axis imprinted on the sky blue U.N. flag waving high above the flags of the nations of the world.

"Hello, Jane. I'm standing in front of the United Nations Building in New York. This monolith above a dome was built upon blood-soaked land originally set aside for the 'X-city' project and donated to the U. N. by the Rockefeller family. In a few minutes, the new American Ambassador of the U. N. will emerge through these glass doors with Pope Peter Romulus by his side. The two dignitaries have just finished addressing a special early-bird meeting before the General Council. This is a historical first, Jane. And look—here they come!"

A group of reporters and cameramen jostled around Ambassador Maisun, the Pope, and their security people as they exited the building. The two strange bedfellows serpentined through the plaza past a twenty-two-foot-tall sculpture titled *Single Form*, designed to represent the ever-changing sublime forms of nature. A hole in the sculpture sited to the sun. They proceeded to the Sculpture Gardens next to the building, past a statuary of a bent handgun with its barrel tied in a Solomon's knot. Next to a statue known as *Let Us Beat Swords into Plowshares*, an assemblage of television cameras waited for the prearranged photo-op. To their far right loomed

Good Defeats Evil, a colossal figure of Saint George spearing his cross into a sculpture of a multiheaded dragon made from scrapped missiles being torn apart. The two frontmen stopped and positioned themselves separately on top of two taped red Xs that had been marked on the concrete pavement. They faced the cameras and began playing to the public eye.

Brad reached for a half-empty gallon of milk from the table and poured some into his cereal bowl. Munching on a spoonful of Cheerios, he stared wide-eyed at the television, watching the video close-up of the domineering face and eerie, single-eyed glare of U.N. Ambassador J. B. Maisun.

"Ambassador Maisun, this is definitely a high-water mark in your career," a reporter commented, waving in his hand a pen with a little blue globe at its tip. "Can you share with us your agenda as the new U. S. Ambassador?"

"Why, certainly." Maisun smiled amiably. He tugged on his coat and straightened his tie. The sun reflected a silvery spike off the tiny sphere on his 1939 New York World's Fair souvenir tie clasp. He stretched his neck, cleared his throat, and spoke.

Immediately the awestruck reporters began to *take down* the words from the silver-tongued orator.

Maisun stood straight and steadfast with a practiced calm. "Hmm ... We are the *two pillars*." He nodded hopefully at the Pope. "We are united with the U.N. like a three-head eagle which scavenges our world for the serpents of despair."

Looking serious, the Pope lifted his hand and slightly touched the hemangioma on his forehead as he nodded in agreement.

"Pope Peter Romulus and I have just prayed together before the Heliogabalus *Stone of Light* in the below-ground Meditation Room. We stand here as a single voice under the eye of the Faceless God and our covenant is justice. We have a *plan* for the planet. Globalization is our new watchword. This is our agenda. But building confidence in a global society will take more than the outline found in a blueprint. It will require *strength* to be *established*. It will take the cooperation of *every living being* on the planet." Maisun cocked his head toward the Pope and nodded again. "We will work in unison to achieve that cooperation—by whatever means it takes!" He lifted his chin in profile to the cameras.

The *snap, snap, snap,* from camera shutters filled the air in response to Maisun's proclamation.

"Thank you. Thank you," he said firmly. "I have to leave now." He held his wristwatch close to his face. "I'm going to be late. I have an appointment with delegates from the World Summit on the Information Society at the Low Library at Columbia University, followed by a meeting at New School."

After hogging the limelight, Ambassador Maisun led the silent, smiling Pope away from their X positions, like an iron hand grasping a velvet glove.

As their powdered faces disappeared from view, the camera focused on a reflection from a ray of light off the statuary of a golden fractured orb of gears-within-gears directly behind them in the cosmological garden of the United Nations.

———

Art is not merely an imitation of the reality of nature, but in truth a metaphysical supplement to the reality of nature, placed alongside thereof for its conquest. - *Friedrich Wilhelm Nietzsche*

"HELLO, SIR," greeted a gentleman dressed to impress in a blue, two-piece business suit. He approached *the man* waiting before a bronze bust on top of a five-foot-tall, white marble podium.

"Hello, Mr. Stanson," said the man, smiling slyly. "Welcome to Texas."

"I was directed by your people at the institute to meet you here." Stanson removed his black-framed glasses. "I'm nearsighted." He stepped closer to study the bust.

"Yes, sometimes you do not need glasses to see." The man tugged at the glove on his left hand and returned his attention to the bronze bust. "I love this museum and its sculptures. I particularly admire this one." He pointed. "It's called the *Bust of the Boy*. It reminds me of my childhood. I am a caulbearer who barely made it into this world. I was born from a hard labor that nearly killed my mother and me. I battled for life from the start." He shifted his eyes at Stanson. "So, you are my new righthand man? My last assistant, Mr. Westbrook, is no longer with us. He met with a misfortune. I had his head served up on a platter. He was not a trustworthy man. He talked a lot. You do know that there is a proper time for silence?"

"I know my place. I am devoted to your cause. I studied with the brotherhood in Salem, Oregon." Unintimidated by the man's comments, Stanson switched to another subject. "Sir, I am ready to inspect your facilities for the new security system. I need to visit the underground vaults."

"Let us go back to my institute. I just flew in from my private villa near the Villa Madama in Rome. I'm leaving later for my Morningside address, with its view over St. John, the *God Box*, and Columbia. I have a driver waiting. Come this way."

The man paraded ahead of Stanson like an armored cannon, with a physical presence that conveyed to anyone who approached him, *You need to get out of my way*. He led Stanson through a maze of sculptures into a spacious room with glass-paneled windows at two ends.

They walked past a mirror-finished sheet of steel hanging on the wall, titled **YOU**. The man glanced at the undistorted reflection of himself. He diverted his eyes. "Look." He stopped in his steps and pointed to a sculpture on a marble pedestal. "Rodin's *Eve*. Our other half from the garden, Adam's consort. The woman who taught man to see both good and evil, the mother of us all." Sitting in a glass display on another pedestal a few feet away, a human skull encrusted with 8,601 flawless pave-set diamonds over a platinum cast sparkled beneath a spotlight. "*For the love of God*, by Hirst," the man said. "It's worth 100 million dollars."

Stanson craned his neck upward to a human figure hanging from the rafters.

"Do you like it, Mr. Stanson?" the man asked dryly.

"It's definitely different," Stanson replied. "It's covered in numbers."

"It's called *White Flying Figure With Numbers*. Those are phone numbers, his new identity within the Global Consciousness. Every person in our Information Age has an alternate identity. With the aid of telecommunications, our world is shrinking and individuality is becoming obsolete. Still, half of the world's population has never made or received a phone call. We have much work to do. The new kingdom is like the Internet let down into a lake in order to catch all kinds of fish," the man said, looking upward. "Have you ever seen the ceiling of the Sistine Chapel?"

"Yes," Stanson replied, glancing across the gallery at the horned *Moonbird*.

"Michelangelo was a genius. Only the artist has learned to break the uncrossable barriers to commune with God. Who created whom, I wonder? Come this way. Let's look out the window and enjoy life a little."

They stepped before a window with a full view to the outdoor sculpture garden. Between them and the window stood a seven-foot-tall, metal sculpture of swirling stainless-steel spikes, resembling a huge bundle of barbed wire. Outside the window loomed an artwork constructed from crisscrossed steel I-beams.

"There is the *Eviva Amore*, made of I-beams tied together with steel circles." The man pointed to the sculpture firmly planted into the ground. "It reminds me of the global axis—the Wheel of Life. A possible representation of the Tekton or an *axis mundi*, I wonder ... the presence of God?"

Stanson nodded in agreement.

The man motioned to the metal sculpture in front of them. "This is a copy of the *Quantum Cloud* sculpture that overlooks the Millennium Dome near the Prime Meridian at Greenwich. It makes use of the single point perspective technique, always revealing something new in relation to the observer's distance. Stand away from the cloud of this lethal metallic storm. Reorganize your spatial coordinates with your mind's eye to the chaos of this creation and tell me what you see."

Stanson stepped backward a few paces, and the twisted tempest of steel shape-shifted into the dimensionless vibrating form of a man in a fearless warrior pose who appeared covered in needles from an overzealous acupuncture session.

"Christ, it's the image of a man ... a stickman ... like Guy Fawkes, the burning man, or the Wicker Man of Kirkcudbrightshire ..." Stanson marveled at the shadowy shape enveloped within a pulsing halo of light. "Beautiful."

"Yes, it is, Mr. Stanson. The human form is preeminent. In the Great Chain of Being—without man, God is irrelevant. Out of this twisted chaos comes the order of man and his body meridian, his Kabbalic Tree—the genome—a *Quantum Cloud*. Sometimes you have to step away from a thing and obtain a new visual to discover the true aspects of yourself. Museums can function as temples, a microcosm in reverence to *Man* and his god."

"An interesting comparison," Stanson said sarcastically. "Things are not as they appear. I've always likened a museum to a cemetery for the past."

"You lack *faith*, Mr. Stanson. No ... not the past. Museums are displays of our future ... the Brave New World." The man crossed his arms and gazed out the window. "In our search for our place in the world, we are always asking ourselves: Where does man stand? *Ecce Homo* ... You have to think *beyond the Man*. A few years ago, several brilliant philosophers met at the top floor of a New York skyscraper to discuss the nature of reality. Does reality exist or is it a byproduct of our senses and completely subjective and subject to our will? At the end of their discussion, the philosophers filed out the door of the room they were in, at which point one of the

more observant philosophers remarked, 'No one is leaving by way of the window.' "
The man chuckled at his own anecdote. "It requires faith to believe that the true nature
of our world can be seen by way of the window. In the Far East, landscape painters
consciously regard their art as religious. Art forces us into consciousness. It is
consciousness, not matter, which is the foundation of all existence. Our world is a
creation from the mind of Man." He uncrossed his arms and gestured toward the
window. "Here before us, we see the fearless image of Man standing before the
window of his world, where the image of God, the axial-machine of the Tekton,
resides in the man-made garden. *Man! Steady at the Wheel. The Power!* We have
abandoned the shadowed world of the past. We are gazing out from Plato's cave."

The man guided Stanson away from the twisted sculpture and down another
corridor. "There is Picasso's *Head of a Woman*." He tapped the side of his forehead
with his index finger and then pointed. "And there is Picasso's *Goat Skull, Bottle and
Candle*. It's amazing how the multiple views of Cubism have reshaped our world. No
two views are ever the same. Once we grasp a new view of the world, we can never
continue to adhere to the arcane."

Stanson nodded again in agreement.

They exited the building and entered the gardens of the Nasher Sculpture Center.

"Our garden of earthly delights … these wonderful pieces of art are a reflection of
our society. Over there are the thirty-six headless figures of the *Bronze Crowd*. They
remind me of gaumless prisoners, like many excerebrose Americans lined up in rows
and waiting to be ordered, mindless." The man stopped in front of another sculpture.
"It's totally unlike this one." He gestured upwards. "It is called *Walking to the Sky*."

They paused beneath a stainless steel pole arching a hundred feet into the air.
Seven, painted, fiberglass, life-size figures of men, women, and children stood
balanced on the pole, as if walking a tightrope briskly up into the heavens. Three other
fiberglass figures waited on the ground with expressions of awe, watching the ascent.

"Look at them, Mr. Stanson. They are leaving the garden, defying gravity, and
ascending to new heights under their own power. Human will. It is the true American
way. We have to do things under our own power. No giving to or taking from our
fellowman. Those figures stand like individuals. It is how you gain respect. Yet, they
also symbolize the human collective. It is a tribute to the direction of the human spirit.
Humanity innately rises upward from the Earth to the heavens with determination,
striving for a new future." He held his gloved fist to his chest. "It's a symbol of our
awakened consciousness and our search for the higher wisdom."

Stanson curiously eyed the sculpture.

"This way to my car," the man ordered, monotonically. He led Stanson out through
the entrance to the museum. He signaled to the driver of a silver Bentley Continental
Flying Spur parked next to the curb to follow, as they strolled down the sidewalk,
away from the Art District and past the Cathedral Shrine of the Virgin of Guadalupe.
"Let's walk for a while. It's good for your health." He held his hand to his face and
checked his watch.

"That's a beautiful timepiece, sir," Stanson complimented.

"It's a Tour de Equinox, a 2.5 million dollar Swiss watch. It is one of only seven
ever produced. It keeps the date, day of the week, month and leap years, sunrise and
sunset, and the phases of the moon related to the Northern Hemisphere sky chart. It

even keeps Barbarian Time. It is synchronized to within a millisecond of the atomic clock in Washington. Businessmen such as I always need to know the correct time. Time is life's only limited commodity. You never want to waste time."

Stanson pulled at his coat sleeve and glanced at his wristwatch.

"Look at that skyline." The man pointed with his arm extended, his fingers in the *Mano cornuto* salute of the Texas Longhorns. "Do you see the globed tower just beyond the Pegasus sign atop the Magnolia Hotel?"

"A big golf ball sitting on a gigantic tee," Stanson compared, "or maybe a large peyote cactus."

"It's more than some odd form of architecture. It's a landmark. Dallas is a global city, the Lathe of Heaven," the man exulted. "That is the Reunion Tower, a sphere of lights, visible at night for many miles in all directions. It is 560 feet tall, taller than the Washington Monument, but smaller than the Tower of the Americas in San Antonio. The star of empire, everything is bigger in Texas. There is a revolving observation lounge within the sphere. It overlooks the Stonehenge of Dealey Plaza where they stopped the world in 1963, the Year of the Silent Revolution. O Captain my Captain!" The man straightened his tie and tugged at the collar of his red shirt. "To play the game. I stood on that lawn with my parents and came of age. An X on the pavement marks the spot of the death of a king on the Y—the misguided boy from Brookline. When you follow the stars, a sacrifice is always required."

"*Anno Domini*," Stanson murmured. "It is his will."

"The Tower stands at the focal point of the old La Reunion area, a part of Dallas settled by French immigrants in the early nineteenth century. My great-great-grandmother was part of the original La Reunion settlement. She was from Lyons in France. Her ancestors were Jewish refugees from Zugarramurdi in Basque during the Spanish Inquisition. They were members of the original thirteen."

"I've never heard of this settlement," Stanson remarked.

"You are not alone. Most Texans are not aware of this obscure early history. In 1855, a colony of mostly French, Belgian, and Swiss settlers established a Utopian commune called La Reunion about three miles from where Reunion Arena stands today. The commune consisted of a select group of skilled artisans, naturalists, and philosophers. They were the disciples of the French socialist Francois Marie Charles Fourier—one of the prophets from Paris. Fourier taught a unique approach to communal living, which he believed would provide general abundance and quality of life for everyone living within his commune. Fourier's ideas followed the principles of a well-ordered production and distribution system that results in a profit. Life is about acquisition."

"It sounds like the way you run your business, sir," Stanson complimented.

The man smiled a broad mouthful of yellowed and aged dinosaur teeth, like tiny little knives. "Yes, it's the American way. The self-contained community, a Utopian ideal, with a dollar in your pocket at the end of the day. Only in America."

Stanson nodded in agreement.

"The colonists at La Reunion built their homes out of stone," the man said in a bragging tone. "They were solid and sound. Private property was considered a valued right by these colonists. Their government incorporated a democratic voting system which included women."

"Women's lib," Stanston remarked.

"They were way ahead of their time." The man smiled. "But they were not unique. There were many followers of Fourierism in the early nineteenth century—the North American Phalanx in New Jersey and New Harmony in Indiana, which trained Lincoln. There were over forty such colonies throughout America. Most historians say the La Reunion colony failed in its attempt to create a Utopia and were quickly forgotten. American Individualism was too much for the followers of Fourier. When people become exposed to America's freedoms, they sometimes seize the day. But we do our best to make sure that never happens." He smiled again. "The failure of La Reunion came near the end of the first phase of the Fourier movement in America. But like all good ideas, the Fourier movement evolved. In France, it was taken up by the followers of Henri Saint-Simon, the promoter of the Hand of Greed." The man clenched his gloved fist. "It's not the Hand of God that turns our world, but Greed. Saint-Simon believed that only the industrial chiefs of capital should rule in the interest of society. The French Saint-Simonians, who engineered the idea behind the Panama and Suez Canals, set out to re-engineer our world for the sake of profit. In America, Emerson's Brook Farm transcendentalists, who later founded the Republican Party and our Order, were devoted followers of the Fourier ideology. So were Hegel and Marx, who considered Fourier the true father of communism, where the state is the Absolute, the Social God. A few historians say that Jefferson, the biggest snake of them all, was a follower of Fourier. His school at Charlottesville was designed around Fourier's approach to learning within a self-contained environment, where teachers and students lived together, confined within the winged architecture of academia before the dome of Vitruvius—like the pattern of the Smithsonian on the National Mall. Ah ... Jonah and his whale, the whole world created from the belly of a fish."

Stanson perceived the man's mood darkening.

"Come this way." The man pointed to the Bentley idling next to the curb. "My institute is not far from the glass-crystal prism of Fountain Place, designed by the firm of I. M. Pei. We can be there in a few minutes."

———

JEFFERSON eyeballed the sign overhead as he swung open the doors.

CRACK CHAMBER – ERIKSON ROOM 3603
(Alter Ego – Sophomore's Dream – The Other I – Light Up Your Silver Spoon)
Everything is an allegory, on top of an allegory, built into an allegory.
Welcome to the Enigma.

Hume, Hegel, Rousseau, Kant, Marx, Emerson, and Salomé were gathered at a computer station at the far end of the room. A dead quiet, spiked with an undercurrent of anticipation, emanated from around their table. Everyone's eyes were trained on Jefferson surreptitiously as he entered.

I feel like I'm attending someone's silent tea party. Jefferson took a breath. The aroma of Starbucks filled the air. Scattered on the table were various photos, maps, and documents, along with Cliff bars, Oreos, and other geek food next to a dozen battered Styrofoam cups half-filled with coffee and cola.

"D-uh ... the ever-intrepid Jefferson," Marx growled, ill-tempered as usual. "Alright, Jefferson, *the eyes* are the anagram. What's the password?" he prompted.

"*They see*," Jefferson replied confidently.

"Welcome back to our gifted group of comrades." Marx huffed impatiently, "You're late, Jefferson."

Jefferson put on his game face. "Goodness, how the hours fly. What time is it?"

"It's 9:18 A.M." Salomé said, sliding a rucksack to one side of the table.

"Sounds like I got here just in the nick of time," Jefferson joked.

"Alright Jefferson, so you can keep time," Marx agreed with a crooked grin. "So, how's the trailblazer? Did you discover what you were looking for? Those of us who have been minding the fort are so anxious to learn about your exploits during your vacation with Mata Hari." His eyes darted at Salomé.

"It was the best vacation I ever had." Salomé smiled slyly at Jefferson.

"Do you have all of the materials I requested?" Jefferson grinned.

"D-uh ... Yes, but we still don't know what to make of everything," Marx barked.

"Okay, don't get festered. Don't be so subjective about everything. Let me see what cards we have on the table." Jefferson leaned forward among his cohorts. His eyes blinked as he studied the assorted photos, maps, and documents.

"Those are of the Kauffman Memorial," Salomé pointed out. "You should have seen it. It was more mysterious than the *Grief*."

"Maybe I did." Winston picked up a photograph of the interior of the Chapel at Rock Creek Cemetery. "Here." He touched a bright, star-shaped, rainbow-colored haze in the photo diffracting through a stained-glass window. "Here." He picked up another photo. "Here, here, and here. I have an idea I've been playing with since yesterday, after I first saw the stained glass in this chapel."

"So indulge us, Jefferson," Marx said. "Share with us your *Novum Organum*."

"Yes," Salomé added, "a translation please."

"We used the basic principles of intelligence gathering," Jefferson briefed. "We discriminated each place we visited, compared the common themes, and categorized them. What we ended up with is a list of items which, by coincidence, appears in the stained-glass windows at the last place we visited. My solution is based upon a logical progression of commonalities."

"Based on what?" Hegel asked, unimpressed. He slumped forward in his chair with his elbows planted on the table, cradling his head, with his hands covering his ears.

"It's deductive reasoning," Jefferson assessed.

"So it's a hunch, but not an absolute," Marx considered reluctantly, his teeth grinding together. Both of his elbows were anchored squarely to the table. He rubbed his forehead and gazed down at a photo. "Objective and subjective. Jefferson, you're giving me a migraine."

"I am a rational being," Kant muttered in a muffled voice, his hand clamped over his mouth with his elbow propped on the table. "You'll have to explain it to me."

"It's a logical progression that follows the relationship of the sequences of the virus segments," Jefferson replied, observing the three monkeys posed at the table. "The tour that Salomé and I took is a Hamiltonian path."

"What's a Hamiltonian path?" Salomé asked.

"It's a model of the whole, formed around a geometric optimization problem—like a graphic snake-in-the-box. A Hamiltonian pathway is a path that visits each place exactly once, except for the starting place which you visit twice," Jefferson started to explain. "A Hamiltonian path always leads back home. It's a full revolution. It's about revolution."

"Like Dorothy and her little dog visiting the Land of Oz," Salomé equated, "she ends up going back home."

"Orion," Jefferson remarked beneath his breath.

"D-uh …" *Tap, tap.* Marx uncovered his eyes and knuckle rapped the table. "I *see*, and I agree. It's like a Komiqsberg Bridge Problem. The segments of the virus referenced six places which formed your trek. You visited Washington twice. It's like the Ori's time traveling curve. Everything theoretically ends where it starts."

"I remember studying the Hamiltonian circuit in college," Hegel said, lifting his head from his hands and uncovering his ears. "Sometime in the 1850's, William Hamilton invented a type of Icosian Calculus, which he used to investigate closed-edge paths on a dodecahedron, a three-dimensional Platonic solid with twelve pentagonal faces. Hamilton was considered the next Newton of his day. The problem was used as part of his System of Roots of Unity."

"I once spoke about it in a lecture I gave for the NSA," Kant added, dropping his hand from his mouth. "The System of Roots of Unity is very metaphysical. It's a type of logic-loop. Hamilton was a gifted child. He could read almost every known language by the age of sixteen, including the Oriental languages. He believed that an underlying *language* stood at the core of Newton's view of the dynamics of the universe. All languages have a cadence—a rhythm and rhyme, and a time and space. So does the structure of Newton's orderly universe. Hamilton considered the possibility of a *core language* as a part of a Science of Pure Time and Pure Reason."

"I thought pure reason was only a play on words," Hume said, holding tightly to a half-empty potato chip bag.

"No, it's real." Hegel calmly popped a chocolate kiss in his mouth.

"A logic-loop … the Lullists and the Glass Bead Game," Salomé made a connection, "with a Leviathan at the *center*—"

"Correct," Jefferson interjected. "But a Hamiltonian path is also a path-tracing problem. It's a tool for analysis, where the path invokes a response, with the response in turn evoking a new understanding of a greater problem. It's even used in psychoanalysis. Basically, the Hamiltonian path illustrates how to visit each point on the dodecahedron exactly once. Such edge-path graphs used in science are known as Hamiltonian circuits. They're used in computer program design for everything from the *structure of the Internet* to the scheduling of airplane flights, where it serves as a type of directional language for the manmade birds."

"A Hamiltonian path is sometimes called the Chinese Postman or Traveling Salesman problem," Hume added. "If we are given a map of a certain number of cities connected by roads, can a salesperson really visit all the cities exactly once within a certain number of miles? Hamilton applied his problem to an Icosian graphic game. It was known as The World Also Admits As Around. I remember playing it in the comics section of the Sunday morning paper. It was a real brain teaser. It looked something like this." With a few quick swipes of his pen, Hume sketched a diagram in the shape of Fort Knox on a yellow legal pad.

Everyone at the table huddled closer and examined the thumb-nail sketch.

"A drawing of someone's enneagram," Marx compared, "or a Chaldean Seal."

"I remember this. It was called Hamilton's Circle," Emerson commented. "It's a maze game designed around interlocking pentagons. It's a brain-building game. The goal is to find a closed-edge course through a maze of knots. Like the balled up chords in your brain."

"I once used a Hamiltonian cycle in a subroutine program for three-dimensional representations in CAD design," Hegel added. "If you can connect enough dots in a path, you can formulate a graphic skeleton of the invisible thing. It's used for forming a quick 3-D, unfinished view of an object that a CAD programmer is trying to create from nothing. A virtual reality, like the daily lives of the citizens of the United States."

"Right!" Jefferson fired back excitedly. "It's a way of mapping invisible things. This pentagon shape is the core for information geometry. The problem is used in the computer networking of the Internet—the Galactic Network, first envisioned at MIT and set up through the Advanced Research Projects Agency for national defense in the 1960's after scientists observed *strange* solar activities in 1955. The way the Internet servers are linked together to share their data is essentially a Hamiltonian circuit. It's even used in harmonic analysis in the subroutes of the programs of my VDC. It's a key circuit in the creation of reusable microarchitectural routines in computer languages such as Mescal."

"Strange solar activities?" Salomé probed. "The Internet was started from the study of solar activities? I thought Al Gore created the Internet."

"The International Geophysical Year announced by Eisenhower which was dedicated to gathering information about the solar winds in the upper atmosphere," Jefferson replied. "Form does not always follow function."

"Oh?" Salomé said. "I think I understand it now." She picked up a pencil from the table and drew a line through the maze Hume had drawn. "I can see the pathway ... a winding snake. Ta-da!" she beamed proudly.

"Fleur-de-lis! That was quick. But, it's easy for you." Rousseau joked.

"Occam's razor, the simplest solution." Salomé brought her fingers to her lips and flicked a kiss to Rousseau.

"There's a pattern in the way we discovered the keywords," Jefferson spoke evenly, trying to sound serious. "The first sequence of the virus led us to Washington. *Obelisk* was the keyword. The second sequence led us to Paris, where we confirmed the keyword *obelisk* and obtained a reference to a new keyword—*skull*. The next sequence lead us to Rome. Again, *obelisk* was confirmed. *Skull* was confirmed. And the next referenced keyword was—*pentagram*."

"D-uh ... that's right," Marx spoke up. "You're in a real groove, Jefferson."

"The fourth sequence led us to Jerusalem. *Skull* was confirmed and *pentagram* was confirmed. The new keyword was *dragon*." Jefferson picked up momentum.

Salomé flipped through her notebook. Her eyes went wide. She nodded.

"The fifth sequence led us to Edinburgh. *Skull* and *dragon* were confirmed. *Obelisk* was confirmed. *Rose-line* was confirmed as an alternate name for meridian. And a *new keyword* was established. The last sequence led us back to Washington. A full Hamiltonian cycle."

"It's a revolution," Marx said.

"Correct. It's about the law of return," Jefferson related. "A beginning and an end, like the Christian symbols for the Messiah, *Alpha* and *Omega*. I believe that the stained-glass windows in this chapel confirm all of the keywords discovered at the various *loci* we visited."

Tap, tap. Hume held in his fingers an old English shilling depicting a Scottish lion. He tapped it on the table again. *Tap.* "It's twisted logic, but somehow it makes sense," he agreed, shaking his head like a doubting Thomas. "But, your explanation seems to fall apart when you travel to Jerusalem," the Big Lug challenged in a skeptical voice.

"I'm not certain," Jefferson admitted, "maybe I'm dreaming. I suspect Jerusalem should have been the first place we visited. Instead, we began in Washington. Maybe we deciphered the sequences at random. If we had started in Jerusalem, it's possible the chain of keyword confirmations would have led us back to Washington."

"But that would make your solution a *reductio ad absurdum*. It would not be a Hamiltonian path. Because if you had started at Jerusalem and ended up at Washington, then you would not have finished where you had started," Hume scoffed in disapproval. "Not unless, Washington, D.C. is a Jerusalem."

"A Catch-22 … Well, maybe the path is not all that important," Jefferson conceded to Hume. "I guess I owe you a bottle of Scotch."

Salomé looked at the drawing on the table with a tentative look of achievement.

But maybe the path is, Jefferson thought, *the pentagram over the White House …* '*Those who show devotion to the Wounds shall receive favor from God.*' "What is important is the net result. We are searching for keywords. Let's look at the images in these stained-glass windows." He started shuffling through the photos, pointing to them as he spoke. "This church was renovated under Daniel Burnham's supervision. I believe the common keywords, based on what I see in the stained glass, are *rose-line, obelisk, skull, pentagram, dragon,* and *Alpha Omega*. With *Alpha* and *Omega* being the two characters for the last keyword, which symbolizes a full revolution through the Hamiltonian circuit." *And life itself … a dash.*

"Or a full revolution through a Platonic Year," Salomé added, associating the last keyword with astronomy.

Marx adjusted his glasses, looking closely at the photos. "So, the ultra, ULTRA answer to all this is the stained-glass windows in the church at Rock Creek Cemetery, a place where life ends?" Marx grunted, still uncertain.

"No," Jefferson corrected. "The answers may be in the stained-glass windows at the Folger Library across from the Capitol Building—the windows that set you on a course through life. Every place we traveled was associated with pilgrimages or rites of spiritual passage."

"D-uh … I don't follow? Spiritual paths?" Marx grumbled, with a slump-shouldered shrug. "Jefferson, this is nonsense. How did the keywords end up in the stained glass? None of this makes any sense."

"I'm still not certain." Jefferson hesitated. "There's something far deeper here. Perhaps I'll never understand it. But I can feel the connections. Trust me on this one. Let's see if this list of keywords actually works."

Pop— "Showtime!" Hegel said as he input the remaining keywords into the SATAN backdoor of the Ebola virus. "Let it begin with an ending."

"Keep your fingers crossed," Jefferson mumbled to Salomé.

She crossed her fingers and bit down on her lower lip.

On a separate monitor, Marx and Jefferson watched as a 3-D representation of the virus segments disappeared, number after number, from the screen.

"Fleur-de-lis!" Rousseau shouted jubilantly, with unnecessary drama. "The virus is scrubbed. It's a *revelation!*"

"There is no absolute for the Absolute," Hegel proclaimed. *Pop*—

"It's the result of our diverse minds coming together, the new geek consciousness," Kant concluded.

"How about that. It worked." Jefferson sighed, with a saved face. "Sweet. Have Bains bank-wire my check."

"Not bad," Hume voiced. "Not bad at all. Well-done, Jefferson. Now that this is over, I can attend the Topcoder competition and win some more money."

"And I thought you were just a plugged nickel. Rack up another one for Western tenacity," Marx said, with a S.E.G. "Jefferson, you did it. You've slain the Falnir!"

"Salomé," Jefferson dropped his voice. He steered her away from the rest of the group. His optimism began to wane. "I still have a few unanswered questions. All of this seems like a setup … like someone knew how I would think it through. I have this gut feeling that this virus was created by a hacker to lead *me* somewhere. I'm not certain, but I think these keywords describe the illuminations from the lost manuscript. If we can discover who holds the manuscript, then we might discover the hacker who created all this."

"D-uh … I agree," Marx commented as he overheard. "This is not some fetishism of commodities. Birdhouses do not build themselves. People build birdhouses. This virus was not created by the Order of the Red Herring. It is obvious that the keywords came from a central source."

"Yes, Marx. A greater power is behind it all," Jefferson agreed. "Maybe even some *white noise* from the core."

Marx looked puzzled.

"We've just been moving from place to place like pieces in someone's game?" Salomé questioned, confused. "All of this, just to turn off a computer virus? There's no reasoning behind it all, it's a wild goose chase. And now, you and Marx are implying we have to go solve a whodunit."

"A hacking-geek is a strange breed of bird. Our minds aren't quite right," Jefferson chuckled. "The hacker who created this virus could be someone who wants to have some fun. He could be someone looking for attention. He could be running us through a gauntlet, testing us to see how well we respond. We need to figure out who he is. We need to explore every possible avenue. There's a good chance he's into Geocaching."

"That's the GPS treasure hunting game you told me about."

"Right," Jefferson said. "This hacker's a player who's into hiding things, letterboxes and hidden treasures."

"That doesn't help much. It appears everyone from the Vatican to the ancient Celts were into some form of Geocaching," Salomé said. "But the only cache we discovered was the various *symbols* related to the *keyword*s. That's not much of a treasure."

"For the love of the hunt … It's a McGuffin for catching lions. 'For where your treasure is, there will your heart be also.' Soul-searching … It's all about finding your soul." Jefferson smiled. "I suggest we do additional research on the architects of this city and try to understand what they knew about the *Kabalyon*. It's about that book. I suspect the hacker is someone who has learned to read the *Kabalyon* the same way as the architects. He could be someone who can read the Language of the Birds." He verbally collected his thoughts, "Hamilton's language, maybe. It might even have something to do with a light show I saw yesterday."

"So we're finished?" Salomé said melancholically.

"I hope not. I still have some things to decode." He removed the Jefferson cipher-disc from his pocket along with another object. "Here." He placed something in her hand.

Her eyes drifted down at her hand. "A book of matches from the Dupont Hotel? Translation, please?"

"Consider it a challenge. It's a clue. It's across from the Brookings Institute. I'm hoping you'll figure it out," he said, unable to stifle his grin. He picked up the rucksack from the table.

A belated Christmas card. She smiled.

———

STANSON AND THE MAN stepped from the Continental Flying Spur onto the sidewalk next to an open plaza surrounded by skyscrapers of mirrored glass. The tall, silver, Art Deco lettering on a sign beside the plaza read:

THE ZERVAN-OSIRIS TRANSHUMANIST AGING WELL INSTITUTE
110 South Market Street

A sculpture of a twenty-foot-diameter, fractured, golden orb commanded the middle of the plaza.

"Stop, here," the man instructed. "Look at it. What do you think?"

"I saw the sphere earlier. I don't know what to think," Stanson replied.

"It's one of many," the man said, thumb polishing the spiderweb patterned, gold button pinned to his lapel. "I'm thinking of replacing it with a mandala. Perhaps a concrete box—something with more dimension. Maybe a gigantic Necker Cube."

The man escorted Stanson through the vast lobby of the institute. Resembling the procession way from an Egyptian temple, rows of glass display cases of various species of stuffed cats lined the lobby. On the far-end western wall loomed a twenty-foot-tall, granite bas-relief of a DNA mapping in the shape of the Americas next to a mural of the ouroboros-shaped *Tree of Life on the Web*.

"All of this began at the Strecker Lab in New York." The man led Stanson into the elevator. "The cryonics storage tanks are on the sixth floor. We work closely with the Cajal Institute in Madrid, the Institute of Neuroscience near Corioli, and the site at Edwards. We have removed the heads from the bodies that are already dead. Saving the heads. We have 144 frozen human heads. The seventh floor contains the GILOH labs for studying life-sustaining stem cells from umbilical cords and placentas. We are NMDP certified. My collection is in the underground vault." He pushed L9 on a panel. "I trust this new security system is more efficient. I am placing my *faith* in this company. That is why I purchased Rapid-I-Scan."

"I assure you, it's the best security system in the world, sir. Do not worry."

The elevator doors opened and they stepped into a steel-lined antechamber. On the opposite wall was an arched entrance to a long, narrow corridor.

"I am extremely proud of my collection." The man motioned Stanson to proceed down the corridor. "After you."

Stanson took a few steps forward and bumped his nose into a metal wall. "What the hell!" He repositioned his glasses.

"It's a *trompe-l'œil* mural," the man laughed, "a trick of the eye. Don't beat your head against the wall. You should always question your reality. Our *whole world* is an *illusion*." He removed his glove and placed his six-fingered hand over a glass panel on a side wall. "Ahithophel. Within my hand, I hold the key that unlocks the door for others so they may pass through and see." A mechanism *buzzed,* and the mural of the corridor retracted into the wall. One by one, a spiderweb of pulsing light beams from proximity sensors barring the entry disappeared. "After you, Mr. Stanson."

Stanson held his hand out tentatively in front of his face as he entered.

"*Faith,* Mr. Stanson, have *faith,*" the man encouraged.

"Lessons learned," Stanson responded. "Faith is not a truth."

They walked down a corridor with spotlighted paintings recessed behind glass panels in the walls.

"*The Shade of Darkness,* by Turner," the man pointed to the art as they passed. "*Moon Madness* by Wyeth ... *Portrait of Francis Bacon* by Freud ... *The White Duck* by Oudry ... *View of the Sea at Scheveningen* and *Congregation Leaving the Reformed Church in Nuenen* by Van Gogh ... *Still life, Memento Mori* by Henstenburgh. ... See the lit candle before the skull? Look ... *Landscape with an Obelisk* by Finck ... *Roses in a Vase* by Renoir ... and the *Madonna with the Yardwinder.*"

At the end of the corridor hung a framed drawing on a stone wall.

"Why, it's a copy of Da Vinci's *Vitruvian Man.*" Stanson removed his eyeglasses.

"No, it is the original," the man said proudly. "I purchased it from the Biblioteca Reale in the Gran city of Torino. So much of the world is for sale."

Shaking his head, Stanson turned toward a niche recessed in the wall illuminated with low-level lighting. He stepped closer. His eyes widened. "*Christ,* is that a copy of the *Global Icon?*"

"Minerva ... Baphomet and Salamander. 'It has died many times and learned the secrets of the grave.' No," the man grinned wolfishly. "It is an original. But all of this is tripe," he said coldly, waving his hand. "The real prize of my collection is *behind* that painting." He pointed.

Stanson turned and faced a wall-size painting. "It's Botticelli's *Birth of Venus!*"

"On permanent loan from the Uffizi." The man smirked proudly. He placed his hand over another glass panel in the wall and recited, "Eloquence is a painting of the thoughts. O Father, Who Art thou? Art endures." The painting slowly retracted upward into the ceiling. With a sudden *thud* it stopped to reveal an illuminated doorway. "This way." The man stepped into the light.

Stanson cautiously crossed the threshold, wondering what work of art he would see next. He found himself in a cold, twenty-foot-square vault, completely lined in rough-hewn, black-marble from floor to ceiling. On each of the walls, dirt-brown cuneiform tablets were displayed behind four evenly spaced glass enclosures. Seven non-ultraviolet spotlights shone on a ten-foot-long display case at the center of the room. Probing forward, Stanson's face glowed in the low luminosity as he glared through his own reflection in the bulletproof glass of the display case.

Red diodes at all four corners of the case levitated a latticework of flickering laser beams over the contents. The case held thirteen bookrests upholstered in purple velvet. At the end of each bookrest stood a small, square sign respectively depicting the images of a human skull, the head of a goat, a lamb, a dragon, an eagle, a fish, a Star of David below a menorah, a pentagram, a woman cradling a child, a man hanging on a forked cross, a six-armed dancing Shiva, a horse carrying four riders, and the Greek letters *Alpha* and *Omega*. Three of the bookrests held closed, red leather-bound books. Hand-tooled on the cover of each book, next to its adjacent sign, were the images of a skull, a dragon, and the letters *Alpha* and *Omega*. Resting on a strip of paper in front of the books lay two brass keys next to an inscribed gold-foil-covered cylinder, roughly the size of the cardboard core from a toilet paper roll. Printed on the paper were the words: FIRST LIGHT - FIRST CONTACT.

A ten-inch-square, felt-lined, rusted strongbox sat open at one corner of the case. The box held a bundle of two-inch-diameter wooden discs with letters carved on their outer rims. The box rested on top of a sun-dried earthen tile, highlighted by green, blue, and yellow glazes. The tile was scratched with symbols resembling a fish, a Star of David, a seven-branched menorah, and the words: *SAN GREAL*. Next to the tile lay a bronze clockwork of interlocking hand-size geared wheels with inscriptions along the perimeter of each wheel. At another corner of the case, a toothless human skull, stained with red cinnabar and wearing a tarnished gold crown, rested on a silver platter next to an open *Ieoh Ming* message orb and a bottle of wine labeled: *1789 Lafitte Th. J.* A strip of paper in front of the bottle read: ABU TOR.

"Why, these are only books—" Stanson cringed as he felt the iron grip from a hand clamping onto his shoulder.

"No, these are special books, Mr. Stanson."

"Special? What do you mean by that?" Stanson looked baffled. "And what are these other items?"

"The tile is from Pisa. It once belonged to Filippo Mazzei, an Italian associate of Thomas Jefferson and Benjamin Franklin. It is one of many," the man began to explain. "The geared mechanism next to it was discovered in a shipwreck off the coast of Anitkythera in 1901. I procured it from a professor at American University. The other half of this device is held by the National Archaeological Museum in Athens. The keys are to the strongbox. The box contains twenty discs from a Jefferson cipher machine. Jefferson encrypted nearly all of his correspondence between the years of 1790 and 1802, the years in which he was involved in the creation of the city plan for Washington, D.C. This machine was used to decode his letters. It's his master wheel cipher. The night before he died, Jefferson left instructions that the keys to the box which held this machine be buried with him in his coffin. When the grounds of the Capitol Building were excavated for an underground visitors center in 2002, a strongbox encased in a concrete block was discovered at the bottom of an abandoned well. It was a massive excavation, with 53,000 truckloads of public *dirt* stolen away."

"Encased in concrete?"

"A time capsule," the man clarified. "It is said that the British searched for it when they invaded Washington in 1812. The strongbox contained nineteen discs to the machine—the ones you see here. It was missing seven discs. It also lacked the master key letter and number sequence that Jefferson used to set the device. Jefferson sent the remaining discs to seven associates, in order to maintain a secret he harbored concerning something he acquired while touring in Italy."

"But you have twenty discs. Where did the last disc come from?"

"When the Union Army besieged Petersburg during the Civil War, they captured and pillaged a plantation house along the James River known as Brandon. The central part of the house had been designed by Thomas Jefferson. During the looting, a secret panel to a compartment hidden behind a wall next to a fireplace in the south wing of the house was discovered. The compartment contained a stash of documents concerning Jefferson, including a faded map of Virginia by William Byrd on which was written a cryptic message.

'*Clavis ad Theosaurum* - A key to a treasure – A Crown's fortune concealed – De Quincuniall above Buckhorn. NanSeMond. 9:18 The Tragos head of Cernunnos is the meeting place. A family graveyard. Under an Obelisk. *Azazel*. From *Gianfar* to *Rastaban*. *Theca ubi res pretiosa deponitur.* The keys to the wheels of Jefferson's machine lay next to the skull.'

Naturally, the Union looters were mystified and immediately began an investigation. All of the graveyards in the area were searched. The vast library at Westover was scavenged. Anyone who might have known anything about the documents was questioned. While further examining the house, a brick projection was discovered in the outside wall beneath the window of the room with the secret panel. When brick and mortar were removed, a human skull was uncovered."

"A skull ..." Stanson's eyes darted toward the display case.

"Inside the skull was a stone inscribed with the single word, 'Richmond.' Some considered the skull—the Latin *caput*—to be a clue that referenced the State Capitol Building at Richmond which had been designed by Jefferson as a copy of the 'Temple to the Glory of the Great Army' in Paris. He personally monitored the construction of its footings. That whole building, top to bottom, was extensively torn apart and searched, with the eventual collapse of the building's floor in 1870," the man chuckled, "and the loss of sixty-three lives."

"Did this lead to the discovery of the disc?"

"Yes. Many years later, the disc was found buried on the grounds of the Virginia Capitol during the excavation for an underground visitors center."

"Another underground visitors center?" Stanson asked, puzzled.

"Treasure hunters, Mr. Stanson."

Stanson shifted his attention back to the display case. "And how did you get these keys, if they were buried with him?" His eyes narrowed. "And whose skull is this?"

The man smiled smugly. "Have you ever heard the story of the *Kabalyon?*" he asked, ignoring Stanson's questions.

"No ... the *ka-bal-yon?*" Stanson carefully pronounced the unfamiliar word.

"The Lost Word. It's the name for the books in the display case. Their story goes something like this."

Stanson listened intensely, ingesting the man's every word.

"The *Kabalyon* is said to be one of the oldest surviving religious teachings in the western tradition, even older than the Greek Orpheus system in the Derveni Papyrus or the Buddhist *Diamond Sutra*. Some contend the *Kabalyon* is part of the lost teachings of the Etruscans, the Egyptians, and the Susians associated with the agricultural gods Serapis and Inshushinak. It consists of thirteen handwritten codices—each illustrated with a strange picture language—a self-configuring language of our true reality. These codices were once stored at the Serapeum of Alexandria and the library of Pergamos, where the Pergamenes invented calf-skin parchment—the predecessor of vellum and paper. Later, the codices were transported to Jerusalem by order of the Emperor Hadrian, and stored in a chamber below his Temple to *Jupiter Capitolinus*. The thirteen volumes, along with a cache of other rare Greek manuscripts, were discovered in Jerusalem during the Crusades, after which they were spread to the four corners of the Holy Roman Empire. Copies of these codices have been found in libraries throughtout world—Paris, Rome, Madrid, Moscow. But, only the originals have any value. The pages of the originals, like a Rosetta Stone, are encrypted by way of certain illustrations which serve as—the *key*— the basic syntax for decoding the world's different languages and religions. Everything is interconnected, *with primers on every page*."

"I see you have three," Stanson counted. "Are these, as with everything else in your collection, originals?"

"Yes, I have spent my whole life trying to acquire all thirteen." He stared lovingly at the three books. "It's been my mission in life, my obsession. It takes a long time to get this far. My mother gave me the first rebound volume. She acquired it from my great-great-grandmother. I loved my mother. I hated my father, the bastard son of a Yiddish Chabad-Lubavitch rabbi from Birobidzhan. Love carries on and so does hate. I worry about my daughter and my grand-daughter. Her mother was a snake."

"Your mother? Your mother's great-grandmother?" Stanson remembered. "The woman who settled La Reunion? The utopian—"

"Yes, she brought it with her from Lyons in France. It is said that Saint Irenaeus once owned this volume. This codex was revered by certain artists at the community of La Reunion as the *key* to great secrets."

"What about these other two books? Where did they come from?"

"I purchased one from the estate of a Chicago architect. The other I acquired from the estate of a pragmatic philosopher from Milford who once worked for the U. S. Geological Survey. Several of the pages from that volume are missing. He obtained the book from—well, I do not need to explain all of this," he said firmly. "Not now."

"You said it was a *key* to great secrets. What sort of secrets?"

"Our whole world has been created from the illuminations in these thirteen books. They deal with the nature of man and the nature of the world, and how the two act as one and the same. The world, Mr. Stanson, goes on living. It continues to grow and evolve. The soul of the Earth never dies. It's a natural law. Yet man, on the other hand, loses his life and eventually loses his soul. I have always tried to be a man of the world. I want to keep my soul and live forever."

Stanson's eyes darted to one side at the face of his new boss. "To live forever."

"Yes, like a god! It's my natural right! It says so in the beloved book, verse 3:22: 'And the LORD God said, Behold, the man is become as one of us, to know good and evil: and now, lest he put forth *his hand*, and take also of the Tree of Life, and eat, and *live forever*.' The soul must acquire new powers to be retained. The three books I possess contain the secrets of the Tree of Life and what appears to be the instructions for building a *device* that will allow you to live forever. A device that will allow you to keep your soul. I plan on keeping my soul, by whatever means it takes." He glared at the empty book rests. "But I need the other volumes."

"Where are the other volumes?" Stanson inquired.

"One volume is kept in the Tomb. One is always stored in the Crypt of the Center Church on the Green. Others are secured in Moscow, London, Washington, Paris, and Madrid. The Vatican holds the eighth in their Secret Archives. We know that another volume was discovered in Jerusalem in the late nineteenth century. That volume was carried to Scotland. Following leads from the French Order, we searched to no avail during the Vietnam War for the last volume believed to be hidden in the ancient city of Luang Prabang in Laos. Later, research indicated it was stored at a museum in the Silk Road city of Kabul, our future City of Light. Satellite photos of Mehrgarh in Pakistan, the world's oldest civic center south of Kabul, resembles one of the diagrams from the *Kabalyon*—the mighty arms of Shahanshah. In addition, the topography of Kabul and Alexander's city of Kandahar resemble the *Kabalyon's* illuminations of the long-awaited two children. And although we are experts at stealing history, after sacking that museum during our War on Terror, we did not find the book. Perhaps the Soviets acquired it. But, new evidence suggests it may still be stored beneath the Temple Mount. My associate has been busy working with his people to acquire the volume—if it is still there. He is keeping half eyes on everything. Through our new diplomacy, we now have control over the Temple Mount and the West Bank." He clenched his fist. "More than one head always gets the job done."

"The two children ... the Twins prophesied by our Order?" Stanson questioned. "I thought that was only legend. And the volume in Scotland?"

"My friend, William, the brainiac, has been working on an insane scheme involving a computer virus to flush out the location of the volume hidden in Scotland. We are hoping the individual who has access to the book will take the bait." He sniggered. "William is such a twisted sort."

———

Deus ex machine

On Holy Images (c730): On images and worship, let us analyze the exact meaning of each. An image is a likeness of the original with a certain difference, for it is not an exact reproduction of the original. An image is an expression of something in the future, mystically shadowing forth what is to happen. For instance, the ark represents the image of Our Lady, Mother of God, so does the staff and earthen jar.

WINSTON LEFT THE CRACK CHAMBER, gripping his rucksack in one hand and a file folder labeled PROJECT CAPRICORN in the other. He had said his good-byes to his fellow hacking philosophers. Now, he set his sights for home.

Just another job, Winston sized up. *Just another debt I had to pay*. Ambling down the corridor to the desk of the receptionist, he hummed along to the Eagles singing "Visions" over the speakers concealed in the ceiling. "Hello. Here's my ID." Winston dropped his rucksack on the table and unpinned the nametag from his shirt collar. "I'm going to miss my other self." As he bent over the desk, under the guiding hand of happenstance, a sheet of paper fell to the floor from his folder. Kneeling down to pick it up, he peeped up at the receptionist.

Mistaking Winston's blinking eye as a flirtatious wink, she girlishly twisted the curls in her hair and gave him more than a pleasant smile.

Rising to his feet, Winston noticed the dark, incarnadine-colored birdcall hanging around her neck. But his attention was not captured by the birdcall, nor by the attractive receptionist. In a twinkling of an eye, Winston felt as if he could see right through her. With a cellophane stare, he eyed something else—something he knew he had not seen before—but then again, he knew he had. He was looking beyond her—at *the presence* of a Soul.

On the wall behind receptionist's desk hung a black-and-white map of the original plan for Washington between a bare topographic map and a framed, three-foot-tall, multicolored Landsat photograph of the District of Columbia.

Mesmerized, Winston's stepped closer and read the title on the first map.

The Ellicott Plan
The Position for the different Grand Edifices

The background music sputtered a new selection and U2 began singing "Where the Streets Have No Name."

"Stop-the-world," Winston whispered hoarsely. *This is the Jefferson/Ellicott plan that Ranger Nobles talked about. But, I've seen this before. These street alignments resemble a planisphere ... Torre's Tekton. The parks form a pattern ... a cosmic plow ... Jefferson's plow*. He touched the map. *From here, Phecda ... to this public square, Merak ... to here, Dubhe*. He read the legend on the map.

F. Grand Cascade, formed of water from the sources of the Tiber.

To the Capitol Building, Megrez ... to here, Aliot ... the bowl of the dipper. Again he read the legend.

E. Five Grand Fountains.
25 springs of water abundantly supplied in the driest seasons of the year.

To the White House, Mizar ... He guided his finger. *To this junction at the bank of the river, Alkaid*. He glanced at the legend.

"THE KEY OF ALL KEYS"

"*Alkaid,* the Key of All Keys," he said, "the star that points to the Cat's Eye—the soul of the celestial circle—Jerusalem … A navigation chart pointing back to the Source … a Hamiltonian Path … the return of the *Lamb*."

Winston looked at the neocrotex-like topography on the second map. "Mind control," he muttered. *Michelangelo and Gnosticism ... Washington's a brain scan ... a Boltzmann brain ... a neurotheology ... a universal consciousness ... a Christ-like consciousness.*

With a blind impulse, his eyes wandered to the Landsat of the square-shaped District as he obtained a new view from outside the box. The small label attached to its frame read: **LANDSCAPE OF DREAMS**.

He leaned his face to within inches of the photograph, meticulously studying the unity of the landscape with a cleansed perception. "Some of the original parks are missing, the Dipper is covered over." His eyes widened.

"This is OOSOOM! What a work of art. This is way beyond Picasso. This is state-of-the-art. A groundscraper … Someone's *hacked* the landscape. This photo is a *cover* filled with *stego.* I can see the **fnords**!"

He placed the tip of his finger on the photo, sliding it ever-so-slowly. "Here. And here. Here. They're here, there, everywhere. Totems!" *Names of the states.*

Puzzled by what he saw, he paused, trying to connect the unseen in a new cognitive way. His Adam's apple jumped in his throat. "Un-*believ*-able." He held his eyes closer, cocking his head, studying it. Studying it closer. Struggling with the Nature of the design, he began to lose himself in the unveiling collage of images and forms. His stomach knotted with an uneasy feeling.

All of this in plain sight, he mused. *You can even measure it with a yardstick. Maltwood's images at Glastonbury ... a bird of prey ... a soul grabber ... a labyrinth, forty-seven degrees to the bear ... Coxy's core grid ... This kingdom of heaven is a net that catches all kinds of fish ... a fish eye ... Alberti's eye, the fish-eye with wings ... the Angel Eye ... cherubim wings, an eagle's eye, a goat's eye, an evil-eyed perspective ... revenge of the creature.* "My father's compass … It is a map!" He moved his finger over the photo. *Everything is located between two longitudes—one through the Shrine to Mary and the other through the shrine for the Ark of the Covenant ... the Freemasons and the Catholics.*

He thoughtfully reformed the patterns, tracing every nuance in his mind's eye from the Landsat's mingled yellows, blues, greens, and reds.

A cosmic center ... the cosmic scheme of things ... streets aligned to the sun ... aligned to the moon ... letters and numbers. It's a Ouija board ... Yo ... Eye for an I ... the cyclops ... a pentagram, a pentagram, a pentagram, three ... a Sephirothic Tree ... a World Tree ... tools of the Tekton ... clocks ... polar ... solar ... lunar ... Sol-o-Moon

... David's star ... a city of four corners ... a mandala, but not a perfect square. This is a city of a different color. It's full and complete. "Yes ..." *Alpha* ... He traced his finger over the Greek letter above the White House. *To Omega* ... He touched the Greek letter encircling the Capitol. *The evolution of the God Consciousness into our world ... a lost Goddess and the Shekinah Glory ... Everything is pushed by Light.*

"Hmm ..." *I feel like I'm looking at a missing link.* His mind raced. *Zeus's skull ... the king of Camelot ... his grave ... the Grim Reaper ... Arthur's Seat ... a profile of Frankenstein with a bolt in his neck ... a pentagon, a Hamiltonian pathway ... external cosmos and internal spiritual consciousness ... axial and circumpolar ... Jesus! Sister Rosalyn's rosary,* he remembered. *Lullus's diagram for the Proofs of God ... playing God ... a Unity of Being... Totalitarianism ... the God is the State ... the First Amendment ... Laocoön's Trojan horse.*

Fully aware, Winston stepped back, retreating from the landscape. "God and Mammon," he spoke aloud. "Someone's fouled the nest!"

With the clear vision of 20/20 hindsight, it now occurred to Winston that he had missed something. He felt like the painter Van Gogh, as if someone had hacked off his left ear just before painting a new *View of the Asylum.* Edgar Allan Poe had once written that the "biggest secrets are those too big to be seen." Now, Winston found himself standing before such a secret.

You'd never see any of this if you were color blind. You would never see it if you were blinded by someone's theology. I shouldn't have counted my chickens before they hatched. "Where can I get a photograph like this?" he asked the receptionist.

"Maybe the bookstore?" she replied. "You'll need an eagle cash card."

"Where's the bookstore?"

"There's one in the first floor lobby. But I think they are closed at this time. Section 215."

"Listen, you can clear this with Dr. Bains if you like. I'm going to take this photograph down from the wall. I need it for research." Winston eyeballed the lens of the security camera above the desk and gave a fake smile.

"That's fine," the receptionist said, not sensing anything unusual. "Bring it back when you're finished."

Winston removed the photograph from its frame, rolled it up, and tucked it under his arm like he was stealing the *Global Icon* from the Louvre.

I have to grind this out. All I need is a laptop and pen and paper. He felt determined. *I'm going to pick at this thing until it festers.*

———

THE DOCTOR sat at his desk, pecking away at his computer. He stopped typing and rested his eyes on the panoramic photograph of Jerusalem above his desk.

BEEP, BEEP. The computer sounded. The Doctor's cheeks raised as he noticed the tag on the incoming email, JBMaisun@UN.orgg. One finger at a time, he typed in the password: *s-u-p-e-r-c-a-l-a-f-r-a-g-l-l-i-s-t-l-c-e-x-p-l-a-l-a-d-o-c-l-o-u-s.* The screen flashed as an unscrambled message appeared.

Green light. We conquer. Continue project. Begin excavations at Ma'ale Adummin.

He pushed back from the keyboard, retrieved a mobile phone from his coat pocket, and dialed a number. "Hello, Mohamad. ... Yes, I am fine. And you? ... Good. I have some very good news. We will be resuming our tunneling."

Day 17
Crashing the System

The clergy converted the simple teachings of Jesus into an engine for enslaving mankind and adulterated by artificial constructions into a contrivance to filch wealth and power themselves ... these clergy, in fact, constitute the real Anti-Christ. - Thomas Jefferson

WINSTON SAT STUNNED in the hotel lobby as he listened to the background music of Ben Folds crooning the end of "Jesusland." An uneasy foreboding swept over him, as System of a Down began wailing "Highway Song." He rubbed his tired eyes and massaged his temples to soothe the mounting pressure in his head. In a slight sweat, he appeared ill, but he wasn't. He had spent the last thirteen hours alone, formulating diagrams precisely drawn to follow the curved roads and topography from the Landsat photo he had acquired at Fort Meade. The all-nighter of scanning images and crosschecking by way of topographic maps downloaded from the Internet had left him exhausted. Though fighting sleep, Winston felt he had been awakened only to discover the rest of the world was still sleeping. His mind now languorously retreated into a cave of Brahmâ as he waited for his ride.

On the other side of the lobby, a television aired an early morning talk-show. Sitting at a desk in front of a stained-glass window depicting the Washington Monument and the Capitol dome, host Phil Gladley greeted his guest Reverend William Wichards. Wichards, the nation's leading theocrat, was plugging his new book, *The Coming End of Days – Seven Reasons Why We Have No Choice.*

"Good morning, Phil." Wichards reached across the table to shake hands.

Gladley extended his hand, then drew it back. "I've seen people fall to the floor from shaking your hand," the political pundit joked with the wealthy faith healer. He held up a book with the smiling face of Wichards on the cover. "The theme of your book is that we are living in the end times with America emerging as the world's leading Christian nation. In your book, you are not the prophet of doom, but a twenty-first century Savonarola of new hope—"

"Hope sustains us," Wichards agreed fervently. Without hesitation, he launched his sales pitch. "We are a spiritual nation washed in the blood of Christ ... a Christian melting pot fostering Christian values which have become the common *ground* for the American society."

"So America is becoming more Christian, day by day?" Gladley asked.

"Oh, most certainly," Wichards replied. The television camera focused on his oversized, labrose, freaky lips. "According to the recent U.S. Religious Landscape Survey by the Pew Forum on Religion & Public Life, seventy-seven percent of Americans believe in angels, which is up from seventy-one percent in 1994. Ninety percent believe in a god. Seventy percent believe in a devil. That's up from sixty-five percent in 1994. More Americans believe in a devil than Darwin. Eighty percent believe there is a heaven. Seventy percent believe there is a hell. That's up from seventy-two percent in 1997. In fact, studies show that countries whose citizens believe in a hell and the devil are more prosperous than countries that do not."

"I see. In God we trust, but which one? How do you identify our faith in our prosperous America?" Gladley asked. "Are we devil worshipers or Christians?"

"Well," Wichards chuckled, his belly not moving, "some churches are harlots.

Ours is a bride of Christ. More than eighty percent of Americans say they are Christians, half of which identify themselves as Protestant. Twenty-five percent of these say they are Roman Catholic, nearly sixty-eight million. Eleven percent call themselves Baptist. Nine percent are Methodist. Six percent are Southern Baptist. Five percent are Lutheran. Three percent are Presbyterian. Two percent are Episcopalian. Two percent are Pentecostal. Two percent are members of the Church of Christ. And seven percent have no religious affiliation at all, but they still consider themselves Christians. And of course, there are the three percent who say they are Jewish, but we still count them as our brothers. *Although*, they will not be caught up in the Rapture."

"Christianity in America seems highly fragmented," Gladley pointed out. "Some might call that shaky ground. I think you covered everyone, except for perhaps the New Age religions and the atheists. What do you have to say about the New Age, Neopagan, and the Secular Humanist world view that Christianity is more or less just a well-thought-out mythology based upon older pagan beliefs?"

"If that were true, we could include them within our flock, and you could say ninety percent of Americans are Christian." Wichards grinned. The camera focused on the tiny American flag pinned to his lapel.

"I see," Gladley said. "How about the role of government in a society that claims to be predominately Christian? Can there be a true separation of church and state? As you are aware, many religious organizations and church zealots have tried to exploit, politicize, and market God by saying that America is a Christian nation. Some observers have claimed that this quest for political power is destroying the fundamental value system of Christianity in America, and that it is counter productive for both the state and the church."

"The separation of church and state, in my mind, is not a noxious idea," Wichards continued his God's-on-our-side rhetoric. "In a recent poll by the Council for America's First Freedom, it was reported that forty-nine percent, nearly *half* of 1000 adults surveyed, believed that the separation of church and state is either unnecessary or should be viewed with less importance. Out of this same group of intelligent adults, fifty-one percent believed that it was the most important of our constitutional rights, ahead of freedom of the press, the right to bear arms, and freedom of assembly—"

"Fifty-fifty … That's a fairly wide God-gap over the First Amendment," Gladley interrupted, attempting to focus on theocratic issues. "That polarization mirrors the political divide in our country. I've also read that survey. It showed that eighty-three percent rejected any sort of *official religion* for our nation, with nearly sixty percent believing that it was important that we tolerate and understand the religious beliefs of others. Former Justice Robert Jackson once wrote that the First Amendment ensures that 'if there is any fixed star in our constitutional constellation, it is that no official, high or petty, can prescribe what shall be orthodox in politics, nationalism, religion, or force citizens to confess by word or *act* their faith therein.' Would you not agree that the separation of church and state is *absolutely critical* to our form of government?"

Tight lipped, his eyes stern, Wichards sat speechless, absent-mindedly twisting a ring on his finger as he listened.

"The very existence of democracy as an institution that serves as a voice of the people demands that the institution be separate from any single religious belief. I am aware that you are a sponsor of the late-President Scott's Executive Order on the subservience of 'faith-based' religions to Homeland Security—but Reverend, would you not agree that any sort of state-sponsored religion would hinder a citizen's ability to practice his faith? And that Democracy simply *cannot* work without the separation of church and state? To base the policies of this government on specific religious dogma would be dangerous to the government's existence. Governments that mandate a religious belief are doomed to fail."

"I'm not playing the part of your straw man. I speak with the voice of America. We are all children of God. The only God-gap is the space between a person's brain and his thick skull." Wichards raised his venomous voice, wagged his hand back and forth, and glared red-faced as he gladly put Gladley in his place. " 'He that hath ears to hear, let him hear.' Anyone who can think will eventually find his way to God. Personal happiness is only achieved through the fulfillment of our deepest need, our relationship with God. Religion is the cultural *loadstone* of the United States. Followers of any religion cannot simply leave their beliefs at the door before entering the public square. Faith does shape our values, but our government's policy-making follows principles that do not reflect any single religious belief. Churches of every denomination serve as the institutional *landmarks* of moral guidance on the *landscape* of our public squares. But, they do not function as courthouses. *Too many* of *those* with liberal views seem intent on disassembling our country's Christian past. The First Amendment *ensures* that the government *does not* act in the interest or the disinterest of any religion. There are Christians in both the Democratic and Republican Parties. I assure you," Wichards chuckled, "there is no political party which are God's Official Party. Our republic leads the world in religious tolerance and pluralism. The doctrine of separation of church and state in America is on firm and solid *ground*. These polls exhibit a well-worn *pattern* throughout American history. Our country has always been divided over religious issues. In addition, a paper published in the *Journal of Religion and Society* reported that most Americans believe their 'churchgoing nation is an exceptional, God-blessed, shining city on the hill that stands as an impressive *example* for an increasingly skeptical world.' In the eyes of the rest of the world, our country is a *symbol* of the Messianic hope and liberation found within the Christian message. Even with the evils wrought by feminists, gays with AIDS, and the political liberals, our God will never withdraw his protection over the United States."

"I see," Gladley said, glancing at the dimpled marks on Wichard's hand. "It sounds like you are doing a fine job, Reverend Wichards. Thank you for your thought-provoking comments and your knowledgeable insight. I'm certain your book will become a best-seller."

"With a strong right hand and an outstretched arm, the power of God will prevail. Rejoice. Evangelists in America have broadened their perspective and widened their agendas. We are spreading the message of Christ's divine birth and resurrection over the entire Earth. The signs of the Second Coming are nearing. Ezra's vision will be seen by all before the Day of the Lord. And the New Israel will be manifested into the earth. The Body of the Church is not a sleeping gaint. We are working hard to make America the place it was meant to be. We are serving up the teachings of Jesus on a plate washed in the blood. Christian leadership is going to reshape our culture and change the world. It's God's work I do. It's God's work I do. God bless America," Wichards pontificated with the wide smile of salesmanship. "God bless—America."

As the television cut to a commercial, the screen flickered. It started rolling horizontally, then vertically. STA-KA, NAK, NAK, spat from the speaker.

The TV's filled with garbage. Winston shook his head. He glaced at the headlines of a *sewage tabloid* sitting on a coffee table: **Elvis Spotted in Baltimore ... Crop Circles Found in Israel.** Looking toward the lobby entrance, he spotted a short man in a dark suit circuiting through the revolving doors. The man approached the concierge's desk and talked briefly. Winston observed the man's emotionless Oriental features shielded behind polarized sunglasses. *I've seen you somewhere before.*

The concierge turned and checked the clock on the wall behind his desk. It was 7:18 A.M. He picked up a telephone and spoke into it. Around his neck, dangling at the end of a green lanyard, hung a bloodred Audubon birdcall. "Paging Mr. Winston. Your chauffeur is ready," the concierge's voice echoed over the lobby's intercom.

As though he were a nursing home patient lost in an Alzheimer's episode, Winston sat motionless and numb to it all. The snowy static on the TV monitor cleared, and the talk-show host concluded his interview with Reverend Wichards.

What a snow job. I am this close to these people. They have no idea I can see what they are doing. Winston stood up and approached the chauffeur. "Hello. I'm James Winston."

"Good morning, sir. I'm Mr. Yin Komodo from the NSA division in Las Vegas. I'm your security escort. Do you have any luggage?"

"Only this." Winston held out a rucksack. He eyed a spiderweb patterned, gold button pinned to Komodo's lapel.

Komodo reached out to take it, but Winston pulled it away.

"No ... I'll keep it with me," Winston reconsidered, noticing a tattoo of the Madonna and Child on the back of Komodo's hand.

"This way, sir."

Following Komodo out of the lobby through the revolving doors, Winston glimpsed his haggard self in the glass as he made a slow circular walk into the light of day. *When you stare at yourself, you do not see the future or the past, you see the now,* he mused. *What I see of myself is flawed. Facing yourself can be a horrid thing.*

The sudden burst of intrusive street noises deafened Winston's thoughtful mood.

Komodo posed next to the curb, holding open the rear door of a black Acura sedan parked behind a 1955 pink Cadillac. He motioned for Winston to step into the government-issued machine.

I wonder if Mr. Howard is nearby, Winston thought as he settled in and made himself comfortable.

"You are flying out of Ronald Reagan International," Komodo informed from behind the wheel. "Your plane departs at 9:18 A.M."

Winston fumbled with the seatbelt. *My mother's savior,* he remembered her story about the teenager at Lowell Park.

Attached to the car's front dash perched a six-inch-tall, fuzzy-pink, plastic, bobble-head flamingo car-dash bird. Komodo poked it. It bobbed. Peeping over the top of his sunglasses, Komodo repositioned the rearview mirror to better observe his passenger. With a mindful expression, he indirectly glared into Winston's eyes. "There will be a few detours this morning. The main roads south are blocked off due to road construction. It's a real mess."

"Tell me something new," Winston muttered underneath his breath.

Komodo turned the key in the ignition and the XM radio began playing Eric Clapton's version of Robert Johnson's "Crossroads."

"Wait a minute," Winston mumbled, spying someone at the edge of his peripheral vision. He shifted in his seat and stared through the car's tinted glass to the front of the hotel. A pleasant smile stretched across his face. He placed his hand on the window, but he knew she couldn't see him.

Susan stood as still as a mannequin beneath a brass plaque on the wall reading, *Hotel Dupont, Dupont Circle*. She held up her hand, with her index finger, pinky, and thumb extended, holding a book of matches.

"We have to go, sir, or you're going to be late." Komodo steered the car away from the curb into noisy traffic and merged with the consciousness of the road. The pink flamingo bobbed forward.

I knew she'd figure it out. Winston eyes beamed as he slumped back into his seat with a content expression on his face. *I like the way she looks at me, right through me sometimes ... like a soulmate. Maybe that's the only reason people are in the world, to find their soulmate.*

As they left Dupont Circle, a traffic cop motioned the car in a new direction, northeast up New Hampshire Avenue. The flamingo bobbed sideways.

Winston's thoughts drifted as he stared out the window. Everything he saw seemed blended with the smudged imprint from his hand. *It's steganographic. Reflections of ourselves. Everything symbolizes something*, he concluded as he watched the people in the streets. *Look at everyone living their lives. Everyone's mind is preoccupied. Speaking into their cell phones, but not speaking to each other. Some smiling. Some angry faced. Some looking like they lost their best friend. Others looking confident. Feeling safe. Some aimlessly being pulled by a leash, like Orion, walking their dogs. Some knowing where they are going. They all just have to get there on time.*

"All the streets are blocked off south of here. I'm taking Thomas Circle to catch 14th Street to Constitution," Komodo updated. The radio speakers cut loose the plangent guitar chords of Jimmy Hendrix tearing up "Crosstown Traffic." "Go, Jim!" Komodo urged, against the driving beat.

As the car crossed 16th Street, the flamingo bobbed away from the windshield.

"The old brotherhood." Komodo pointed.

Winston glared at the entrance to the ziggurat-style House of the Temple. *It looks more like a mausoleum for some dead way of life than a temple. I'm certain they know. I'll be watching you.*

The car looped through Scot's Circle toward Thomas Circle. *The pentagram star*, Winston pinpointed his location.

The music stopped. Then the Byrds started singing "Turn! Turn! Turn! (To Everything There Is A Season)."

From Thomas Circle, the sedan glided south down 14th Street and then on to Constitution. It stopped for the light, waiting. The sea of traffic parted and the Acura crossed into an oasis of green lawns and sacred groves.

There it is again. Winston eyed the broken monument. All the debris had been tagged and neatly stacked in piles. Guards holding loaded M-16s were standing on every corner. *Jerusalem*, Winston compared. He moved his face close to the glass and squinted skyward at a birdlike shadow looming over the car. The UAV Dragon Eye was still circumnavigating the Monument. Winston eyed the sun reflecting off the gilded Flaming Sword Monument on the Ellipse in front of the fleur-de-lis embellished fence bounding the White House.

The radio started playing "King of the Road." Komodo pressed the SEARCH button and changed to another station. The speakers squawked *STA-NAK, STA-NAK* with music erupting between the static, as he tuned in on "Puff the Magic Dragon."

"I once read they performed that song at the White House for President Kennedy," Komodo remarked.

"Christ, I'm not surprised," Winston said. *Peter, Paul, and Mary, and a fire-breathing dragon.*

Crossing the Memorial Bridge that linked the victorious North with the defeated South, they passed between two, larger-than-life, bronze, winged horses posed like winged cherubim. Sighting through ghostly bails of morning brume billowing over the waters of the Potomac, Winston could barely make out the templelike outline of Arlington House. As they exited onto the Jefferson Davis Highway, his eyes tracked the thousands of tombstones surrounding the house, like the dragon teeth Cadmus planted in the ground.

How many souls which have borne the ultimate sacrifice in the name of liberty have been wasted by the existence of this thing? Winston thought as he surveyed the monumental architecture that bounded the Mall on the other side of the river. *For most people architecture is architecture,* he assessed. *Art is art. Literature is literature. Science is science. Music is music. And theology is theology. There are no crossroads between the disciplines. No metaphor, or allegory, or symbolism contained in one discipline that might act as a profound truth within the next. They do not see the divine intelligence in the design. Most people don't think that way. Most people will never understand any of this.* He patted the rucksack. *Why should they even try, when the middle ground always seems greener. It is hard to sway from a solid belief. It is hard to walk away from a place that feels safe. But apathy can enslave a human soul,* he thought. *Can a caged bird—fly—or truly sing? Ah ... that crazy Coxy.* Winston recalled his own experience at the Capitol Building. *Everyone needs to flash through the crystal prisms of their mind so they see past the cage they are in. But maybe, just maybe, there are those out there with a wider perspective. Perhaps ... just perhaps ... there are a few who are in sync with it all ... Billy, Angus, Coxy, Ms. Jenkins.*

Komodo changed the station. *STA-KA, KA, KA—* The Beatles were singing "Why Don't We Do It in the Road."

Yeah, why don't we do that? Winston reached into the rucksack. He retrieved a purple folder containing maps, cutouts from the Landsat photo, and various overlaid steganographic transparencies.

As he scrutinized the material in the folder his thoughts deepened, filled with unnerving primal images percolating one after the other in a molten sea—seeing everything at once—the way that God sees.

"Are you alright, sir?" Komodo observed the hollow-eyed expression on Winston's face in the rearview mirror. "You look exhausted."

Crackling louder than a Tesla spark, the radio sputtered an ionized interference and AC/DC began screaming "Highway to Hell."

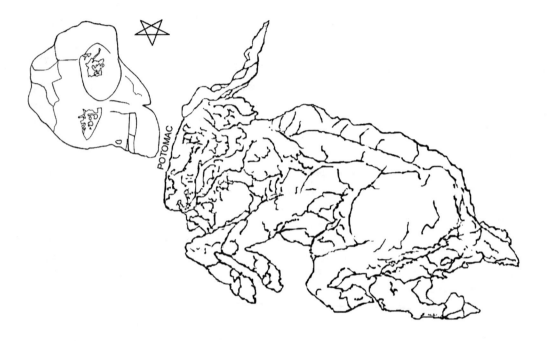

"Yeah, sure, I'm okay," Winston said with a deathly tone in his voice. *Is anyone alright in this society of mind? We are all beings on our way to dying.* His eyes wandered restlessly over the drawing in his hand—a profile of a death skull, with its jawbone resting over the fertility symbol of the sacrificial horned one. *Baphomet times two—a circle of life,* Winston sized up. *What are the odds? Don't it get your goat?*

"We will be at the airport shortly," Komodo informed. "A private plane is waiting to take you back to Sundance."

Winston tucked the papers into the rucksack. *Lift the veil. Normally I'd go back by American Eagle out of Dulles. Someone must have appreciated my work. A private plane. Brother. Big Brother, a shadow government whose outline is hidden in the landscape.*

The radio squawked and Audioslave proclaimed, "I Am the Highway."

And they worshipped the dragon which gave power unto the beast: and they worshipped the beast, saying, Who is like unto the beast? Who is able to make war with him? – Revelation 13:4

TWENTY MINUTES LATER, Winston stepped aboard a Falcon 10 aircraft. ✈

"Welcome to flight 918, Mr. Winston," the green-uniformed copilot greeted as he led Winston to seat number 7. "Here are your headphones and blanket. May I take your luggage? I'll stow it in the upper compartment for you."

"No, I'll keep it with me," Winston replied.

"Can I get you anything?" the copilot asked.

"A diet cola, maybe."

The copilot stepped away to the galley.

Winston removed the purple folder from the rucksack and placed the rucksack on the plush seat next to him.

"Here is your cola," the copilot offered politely.

Winston grabbed the cup, took a sip, and closed his eyes and felt the *buzz*.

The copilot returned to the cockpit.

Winston placed the cup in the polished, bird's-eye maple cup holder in the armrest. He untangled his headphones and plugged them in the armrest audio socket. He placed them over his ears, then rotated a thumbwheel on the armrest to test the volume. Danzig was playing "Belly of the Beast." He increased the volume as high as it would go. And then he turned it off. The headphones tightened around his neck, as he pulled them from his ears. *Sometimes it's hard to face the music,* he thought.

The plane slowly taxied toward the end of the runway. With a sweeping turn, it stopped into position.

Here we go.... Winston felt the throaty, vibrating, *aum* roar of jet turbines as the plane sped forward and ascended through a low-level patchy fog. He looked out the cabin window at the world becoming ant-like. His gaze drifted through the *primal mist* of the thermals beating off the wings of the plane. With fiery clarity, he now obtained a bird's-eye view of the indelible, winged Image of the Beast.

"I feel beside myself. I see Shiva," he murmured. *The vast altar to the Creator and the Destroyer—the illusion. Dante's Heaven and Hell are real places.*

In the distance, the Capitol dome sat like an egg resting in a bird's nest balanced in the branches of a cosmic tree planted between two rivers, two seas. It stood as the symbol of the long-held dream of a "Shining City on the Hill" spoken of in Winthrop's sermon—the so-called allegorical statement that had been used to describe a people in search of religious liberty in the land of milk and honey, so they could create their own New Jerusalem.

As the plane gained altitude and corrected its course northwest, Winston could see the whole northern area of the Cloud-cuckoo-land of Washington D.C. The winding snakelike course of Rock Creek Park appeared outlined in the inverted shape of the Dead Sea. The heavenly aligned inverted pentagram above the White House lay like a talisman invoking the unending power of the Unmovable Mover. The shape of Rock Creek Cemetery curled like a plume of fire breathing down upon the crucible. The diamond-like, sephiroth-shaped roads that encompassed the Mall radiated in every direction like stretch marks spreading across the belly of Mother Earth. It was a city of religious symbols for a nation, insuring all of its kind had been marked.

Roads reaching out, Winston compared, *East and West, branches in the Tree of*

Knowledge ... North and South, branches in the Tree of Life ... Moving with the Earth like spokes of a great wheel-within-a-wheel—Pan's outdoor labyrinth of the Tekton.

His elbow bumped the thumbwheel on the armrest, the headphones stuttered, and Stevie Wonder began soulfully singing "Living for the City."

"Yes. Soul-searching," Winston spoke coolly. "It's all about owning our souls." *We've all been led up the garden path. Even when we've seen the light, we've bought into a fool's paradise, sight unseen. It's all on stony ground, with feet of clay. But it's one grand spectacle of color and design. Steganographic!*

He pulled the second diagram from the folder and contemplated his rendition of the fire-breather, posed as though crucified upon the axis of the world with *the center* of modern civilization beneath its wings.

The music selection changed and "Antichrist" from Saviour Machine's 'unofficial soundtrack to the end of the world' blared through the headphones.

Battling sleep, Winston's thoughts meandered. *Time—our schizophrenic seasons. It's from the light of fall to the darkness of winter that the leaves lose their colors to reveal the branches in the trees. When you take out all that color and strip away the surroundings, all you have is the shape-shifted outline of the thing. All you have is this. A leviathan—the Sea King—the great mental discourse ... the heart of the human animal ... a shadowy serpent defying time from the dark and deep.*

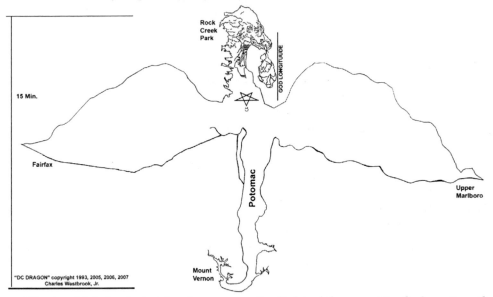

We shouldn't be fooled by the stars or the light of the sun. It's dark matter, the fifth fundamental force that binds this damn thing together. Dark energy, like the individual, determines its own destiny. It pushes and pulls, as it tears away at the fabric of the universe, just as it tears away at the heart of our souls. This dragon is from the flaming pearl of perfection. Such a terror—a terror from within. Look how big it is! The damn arrogance of the thing! Hell's been paved with good intentions. Now, we have one hell of a force to be reckoned with. What else can I say? This drawing is worth a million words.

Pergamos. When did one nation under God become one nation unguarded? How could we have such a great fall from grace? I always thought a city set on a shining hill could not be hidden. The spiritual machine, the price of a dream ... I guess people need to be careful what they dream of. Looks like a lot of doomsayers got left behind.... Someone's gonna' need an exorcist. It's a Southern Baptist nightmare.

Gazing through the clouds, Winston looked out the window again at the giant obelisk, getting smaller and smaller as the plane ascended. The Monument had speared the thing, like a stake through its heart. Both had been born and formed at the same time. Their design preceded the American Revolution. Now the spear was broken, the Monument of Light had been dimmed, and the outline of the dark beast could be seen.

From his visual perspective, Winston gained a new awareness of time and space. His mind aphorized the whys and wherefores, as he wrestled with the two sides of a new question.

He lifted the first transparency from the file folder and compared it with the second transparency. He stared at the masks of the three monsters, the manifestation of the eternal—the images of *the presence* that owns us—the images of a nation surrendered to the *Dar Pa*—the Dark Father. *I am a pilgrim looking at the faces of darkness. These horrible and holy images are the shadows, the dark side of life. It's our necessary evil, our chaos around the clock. It's the side of life that keeps us in check. It's the ultimate religious persecution. A deep, resonating, **demon-driven fear**. We're reminded of it everywhere we go ... razor wire, security cameras, checkpoints, barricades, armed guards, gated communities, dominating architecture, time-pushing bosses, soul-saving preachers ... the promoters of fear.* "Oh brother ....," he sighed, "Big Brother." ***Fear** is a powerful thing. What if I could feel only love for this country and not **fear** it? What if I could truly trust it? Papaphobia, Stygiophobia, Theologicophobia, Theophobia, Tyrannophobia, Uranophobia, Wiccaphobia, Zeusophobia ... Enough already. This is **pure fear** that I hold in my hands—the **primal fear**. We mistrust people because of **fear**. People kill each other because of **fear**. Nations go to war because of **fear**. We restrict our lives due to **fear**. We lose our lives due to **fear**. **Fear** is the cause of thousands of personal and collective conflicts that eat away at our souls. Some say that all we have to **fear** is **fear** itself. Some say the future does not belong to **fear**. Some say **fear** can sometimes fuel us. Sometimes doubt is all we need to succeed.*

He thought about something Billy had said, *"You must confront your inner demon to defeat the one outside."* Billy had told him, *"You cannot trust the shadows. The shapes of the shadows are not clear. The shapes of the shadows are not solid enough. Shadows never stand still long enough for us to discern a true shape."*

Winston felt the cold weight of disappointment. *This has killed my hope, these shadow images I wish I'd never seen. Could it be that these images represent the only true voice? The one union? An absolute power ... an E pluribus unum ... out of many, the One. I guess I could laugh because it's funny. But, I should cry because it's true. But what is truth?* he thought philosophically. *They say if you repeat a lie long enough, it can become a reality. But unvarnished truth always wins out. Truth is an Absolute. Or is it?* Winston took a heavy breath. *What is it that famous German physicist once said? "The belief that there is only one truth and that oneself is in possession of it, is the deepest root of all evil that is in the world."*

In an epiphany, Winston scrutinized the images searching for the deeper meaning to the deeper mystery. *Lullus-logic—symbols that form a message ... the gods and demons in everyone. Every human mind has a dark side. These images are a catch-22. I fully understand this could be a part of a greater artistic symbol ... an expression of free speech. It's like the theme from a Star Wars movie ... the dark side battling the light saber ... of light over darkness ... of freedom over oppression. It could be a symbol of the philosophy of the people in this country ... of hope ... of slaying the forces of nature ... of slaying evil ... of slaying fear at the place of the skull. Or maybe even a dragon guarding a treasure hoard ... a bright pearl ... an iron dome of law resting on a pile of bricks ... Jesus. But what is the Gestalt from all of this? What is the true meaning behind all of these symbols? Which meaning follows Occam's Razor? Which one is the MML?*

"Ahh … 'Behold an emblem of our human mind Crowded with thoughts that need a settled home, Yet, like to eddying balls of foam, Within this whirlpool, they each other chase Round and round, and neither find An outlet nor a resting-place! Stranger, if such disquietude be thine, Fall on thy knees and sue for help divine.' Wordsworth," Winston recited in a low whisper to himself. "The land of dreams … the mirror-world. What I see is me." *Like some psychological inkblot strategy, these are the images of the American psyche—the semiotics of the self—the archetypes that program and govern the human mind. Fishes, skulls, dragons ... symbols for human consciousness ... the language of the birds ... the images that serve as the tools for shaping our reality.*

But, it is also a Trojan horse—an American idol—which could be a booby trap. A booby trap that is hard to ignore—if—these images are a theological representation of someone's real estate-based religion and the icons of the state-sanctioned church. His thoughtful mood intensified. *Can the expression of such a theological idea by this government, in itself, be an oppression of the people? Can the Christians living under the wings of this government really have two gods? How many Lawgivers can they have? You can't even be an atheist. They're all in the same boat. What did Preacher Worthington say? "Thank God for religion, for it protects us from the world." But, who will protect us from someone's religion? Even if that religion is a worship of the freedom of religion. What about the rights of the individuals who cannot stamp their religious beliefs into the landscape? What about their First Amendment rights...?*

"Hmm …" His eyes blinked, as he reformulated his thoughts. *We live in Plato's cave. People will believe what they want to believe and they will disregard the rest. No one will believe me. Memory maps. Energy grids. The Earth's soul talking back to the soul of humanity through art and architecture. Humanity and the cosmos converged as one-like-mind. You have to connect to it all, to see the bigger picture. Yeah ... someone's gonna say I'm crazy, a lunatic with a Sol-o-Moon fixation.*

"And Santa is Satan. Ah … I need to share this with someone." *How do you get the people's attention? The masses always follow the leader, not their own consciousness. We are the clock-watchers, the followers of the wheel—we are the creatures of habit who mold our lives around the order of the watchmaker—cyclical, circular, constantly conforming to the greater order of the great Platonic year. There aren't enough people who are self-sufficient to understand a thing like this. There aren't enough people who have stepped away from the wheel of life and obtained a view from outside the box.*

He placed the transparencies back into the folder. *It's hard to imagine that the leaders of our government could operate under its wings and not know of its existence.* He felt disheartened. *It's like not knowing their own place in the world. How many of those in power know about this? And of those who don't, would they defend the existence of this thing, or would they have the courage to correct it? This president will not buy it. I know her too well. She's just another one of the hounds of hell. Plus, she's got a bad heart. When it comes to profiles in courage, this president will not follow what is right instead of the polls. Or the bosses who create the polls. Who can I trust with this, when everyone is a mover and a shaker?* he wondered. *Who can you trust when the Light you once believed in as a truth, is only a reflection off a Dark mirror? When you look into that mirror, what you see is the truth. Sometimes the truth hurts. But sometimes, we have to play hurt."*

He remembered the adage from the NSA brochure, *"Knowledge is power."* It can *win a war. It can set you free. It can save your soul. What is the best way to share this knowledge?* Winston pondered in a sleep-deprived daze. *Who do I share this with?* He squinted as he pinched the bridge of his nose. *Perhaps my mind will be clearer when I get back to Sundance. It's been twelve days. I'm tired. I need to mental floss. I need some time on the VDC. I need to get back to my oasis, back to Bear Lodge, my place in the sun. I need to cast a different light on all of this, to see beyond the shadows.*

Winston leaned his head back and closed his eyes to clear his inner vision, but he kept seeing the images in the landscape of Washington. From his dark side of the dawn, he sighted out the cabin window at the amber glow of the morning sun hovering over the edge of the horizon. *You need the correct vantage point to see a thing like this. What is it about sunrises and sunsets that move our emotions so?* He felt uplifted, thinking about what he had seen at the Capitol Building and the woman that rides upon the beast.

As his inner voice stopped speaking, Winston could hear Billy's words of wisdom. *"If you do not share what you have seen, then you may lose the reason for having seen it."* Philosophy, Winston thought. *The Silencing of Truth ... Does a tree make a sound when it falls if there is no one there to hear it? Can a thing like this exist if there is no one to bear witness to it? Oppression can only survive through silence.*

Yes, I need to share this with someone. How many history books mention anything about these images? Which laws of sedition were passed which sanctioned its creation? He shook his head. *Brother, Big Brother. We're way past* Nineteen Eighty-Four. *Every American needs to know about the existence of these shadows. They deserve to see this,* Winston assured himself. *After all, they have to pay for it with their lives and their children's lives. They have to pay with their souls.* He slumped in his seat and pulled his hand over his shadow-shaven chin. *We built this thing. Maybe sometimes we have to be brave. Sometimes we have to admit we are flawed. We need to have the courage to rebuild our temple and start over again.* He glared at the folder in his hands. *Someone will not fear this,* he hoped. *Someone will listen. Others will understand.* He nodded. *Someone's goin' to want to play the fiddle, to see if Rome will burn.*

Winston took a deep breath as he considered the ramifications of his discovery. *I am not a lawyer, but I can read the law. I do not need someone else to interpret the truth. Black and white is black and white. There are four branches to our government, the Executive, the Congressional, the Judicial, and the People. They work together. One part cannot be disenfranchised from the other three. The Bill of Rights is the document which empowers the People. If the First Amendment to the Constitution of the United States means anything, then the government I thought I knew cannot exist with these images.* **True freedom cannot exist under the wings of fear.** *It's a crime against humanity. A government that ignores the Bill of Rights is a government that ignores the People. Promises ... my penknife,* he remembered, *the Light of Freedom. This country needs to keep its promises. And how should I go public with a thing like this? Elucubrate a book? You can't even do that with Section 215. It's worse than Nazi book burning.*

Sunlight spilled across his face through the cabin window. "I have a faith in humanity," he spoke with resolve, "and not in someone else's view of *their* god. I may be a prisoner, but I am an American citizen. I am in control of my life. I am my own master. I choose *my own* rite of passage."

He pulled the headphones over his ears, turned up the sound, and listened to words from Leonard Cohen's "Anthem."

Yes, the birds are here to guide the way. I need to think again and to learn to pray, and stop this dwelling on things that come my way. Or the awful things I think I see. And so it is, he then realized. *It was all meant to BE.*

"I slam, therefore I am," he spoke softy. His eyelids felt heavy.

For the third time in twelve days, Winston's eyes stopped blinking. He yawned. His vision dwindled to darkness. Forty winks. He dozed off.

———

The natural source of secrecy is fear. When any new religion over-runs a former religion, the professors of the new become the persecutors of the old. – *Thomas Paine* - "Origin of Free-Masonry"

DONG ... DONG ... DONG ...

In dormitory room number 918 at Turner Hall on the campus of the University of North Carolina at Chapel Hill, Jackson Jones could hear the bells from the chapel tower ringing as the midday sun reached its zenith. Wearing a dirty sweatshirt with 4:20 - Time To Get A Head stenciled on the front, Jackson sat cross-legged in a chair next to his stereo as he toked a joint. His straight, shoulder length hair, parted down the middle, and wire frame glasses resting on a bend at the bridge of his nose made him look like John Lennon.

He turned his stereo all the way up to better hear "Picture" being sung by Kid Rock and Sheryl Crow, then changed the selection to the Stones wailing "100 Years Ago" from *Goat's Head Soup*. Warm beer in a plastic cup on a table in front of the vibrating speakers propagated rippling circular waves. Leaning back in his chair, he rolled his glassy eyes over a glossy pinup torn from the latest issue of "Playboy" taped to the dorm room door. Thrusting his lit joint in his hand like a conductor's baton, he smiled with enjoyment, his head bobbing up and down as he slowly went deaf.

Suddenly, the door swung open and Mike Archer dragged through lugging a backpack full of dirty clothes and an empty camera bag.

"Ah … Man," Jackson growled. *Here comes the big shot.*

"Turn that *damn* thing down!" Mike fumed. *You skulled pervert.* He marched over to the stereo and killed the volume.

"Don't get so uptight." Jackson shrugged his shoulders. "I see you're back from your European tour. So, how was the *trip*, Mr. Michael?"

"You're never going to believe what happened," Mike replied disgustedly. "I lost my mother's camera."

"The Big Eye. You lost the Big Eye? Damn! How did you manage to do that, Mr. Michael?" Jackson dragged on his joint.

"The authorities at the Louvre took it away from me."

"Man …" Jackson shook his head. "You and your crazy art stuff. Screwed up, did ya? Why did they take it, Mr. Michael?"

Mike threw his backpack on his bed and sat down at the computer desk. "That's enough already with the Mr. Michaels!"

"Ooo …" Jackson ogled, tight-eyed.

"You'd never believe me if I told you," Mike muttered, as he booted up his computer. He eagerly reached into the tan-colored travel wallet that hung around his neck and retrieved a chewing-gum-size memory stick used for storing digital photographs. "They may have taken my camera, but they didn't take this. It's a little something I *saved.* I got some flashbulb memories I've been dying to look at."

When Mike realized he was about to lose his camera, he secretly ejected its memory stick and inserted another. He slyly slipped the tiny memory stick under his tongue, concealed from everyone. Now, back at his dorm room, he had access to a computer that allowed him to study the high definition images.

"Jackson, you got to see this. If I caught what I think I saw …" Mike hunched over the keyboard in anticipation. "You're not going to believe it."

"See what?" Jackson peered over Mike's left shoulder.

"Just wait and see." Mike enthusiastically inserted the memory stick into the computer's digital media port. Point and *click.* "I've got some great shots of the *Global Icon.*"

The computer screen flickered. The light from the monitor dimmed. Mike pressed a key to brighten up the screen. The screen flickered again. The sound from the speakers sputtered static. *KA, KA, KA, NAK.* A message window with a Logo of a quadrant-shaped mandala appeared on the screen.

PROGRAM ERROR, DO YOU WISH TO REPORT IT TO ACROSOFT?

"No! What are they going to do? Fix it?" Mike pressed CANCEL, then rebooted the computer with a three finger salute. He shot an angry glance at Jackson. "You've been playing your stupid games on my computer again!" he accused.

"Chillax, man. Don't get so bent out of shape. Things happen. It's the computer. They're all screwed up. It's a crazy virus that hit the Internet last week. I downloaded a fix, but it still has the awful crosstalk and the screen flickering. It's really not that bad once you get used to it. It's kinda like watching the six o'clock news."

Mike glared angrily at Jackson with no measure of relief.

A photo viewer program flickered onto the screen, as Mike enabled the data files from the memory stick. The display filled with a series of scrambled *zeros* and *ones,* along with random characters resembling Greek gobbledygook. The picture morphed into a muddy out of focus shape.

Mike tried another photo file from the memory stick.

Point and *click*. A similar out of focus image appeared on the screen.

He tried another.

Point and *click*. Each time, with the same results, the screen was filled with a series of random numbers and out of focus shapes.

"Dammit! The data's scrambled. The files are corrupted somehow," Mike barked.

Jackson stiffened slightly. "I don't know, man. Maybe it's that virus. I guess you're out of luck." He shrugged with disinterest and walked toward the door.

Chirp-chop, chirp-chop—

Mike's eyes darted to one side. "What's that?" He spied the small instrument Jackson toyed in his hand.

"It's my free birdcall. It's really cool. You got one too. Along with your transfer to E.Z.U. It's in that green package with the rest of your mail, Mr. Michael." Jackson pointed to an opened envelope imprinted with a severed one-eyed pirate's head, then strutted out the door.

"Enough already!" Mike scowled. He slumped in his chair in deep thought and stared at the green package. Sitting upright, he addressed the keyboard and started searching through his computer files. "Crap … where's his e-mail address?" He tried to remember. *My uncle knows how to fix stuff like this.* "Yeah … here it is."

JamesWinston @ bear-lodge.com

◙◙◙

The strength of a nation derives from the integrity of the home. - *Confucius* (551-479BC)

THE COPILOT pulled back the curtain hiding the cockpit and stepped into the rear cabin of the modified Falcon 10. "Whoa!" He twisted his head, as if not wanting to hear. *That's not the sounds of the birds I hear.*

Slumped to one side with his mouth half-open and his eyes closed, Winston reclined in his seat. The **FASTEN YOUR SEATBELT** sign was flashing above his head.

You would swear he was dead, if it wasn't for his snoring, the copilot thought. *He sounds like a badly tuned set of Scottish bagpipes.*

Tap, tap, tap—

"Excuse me, sir."

Tap, tap, tap— The copilot softy tapped Winston on the back of his left hand.

"Wh—What?" Winston stuttered, startled as his eyes fluttered open.

"Excuse me."

Winston's eyes started blinking.

"Excuse me, sir. **You have arrived**."

At 8:18 A.M. Mountain Standard Time, the Falcon 10 taxied down a side runway and nested next to Terminal A at Gillette Campbell County Airport. Winston exited the silver bird with the rucksack tightly gripped in his hand. With the face of confidence and determination, he strode across the tarmac and through the glass doors into the airport lounge.

After passing through a **Rapid-I-Scan** security checkpoint, Winston entered the airport lobby. He noticed a man sitting on a scuffed-up, blue bleacher talking angrily to a smiling man dressed in a *bright* sage-colored, travel-light shirt from L. L. Bea*m*. The smiling man sat contently licking an ice cream cone he held in his hand while listening to the problems of his fellowman.

"When I was a boy, I could fish for free," the angry man complained. "Now every time I go fishing, it costs me a couple hundred bucks. A hundred years ago a man could support his family on his own. Now it takes both spouses just to make ends meet. We are worse off than we were a hundred years ago."

"Brain freeze," the smiling man blurted. He stopped licking his ice cream.

Winston closed his thoughts to the anger, deafened by a radio announcer's voice booming over the airport's background music system — "And now Chuck Sucky's 'Home for Harvest' from his *Dakota Breezes* album on the Flying Fish label."

As Winston rounded a corner, he saw the welcoming smile on Billy's face. Billy had been sleepwalking with the spirits at the far end of the lobby. Around his neck hung his eagle bone gorget and a green braided lanyard tied to his free, bloodred Audubon birdcall.

"Hello, James. Welcome back to the fold," Billy greeted with his trademark smile.

"You old bronco, Billy." Winston said happily, shaking Billy's hand. "It's so good to see you. I see you have been talking to the spirits."

"So have you." Billy probed Winston's eyes. "I see your eyes are open. I have been thinking about the crow and the swan," Billy shared. "There once was a black crow who became filled with envy after seeing the beautiful, bright white plumage of a swan. He believed it was due to the water in which the swan constantly bathed and swam. So he left his home of the altars, where he lived easily by picking up bits of the meat offered in sacrifice, and visited among the pools and streams of far-off lands. But although he bathed and washed his feathers many times a day, he never made them any whiter." Billy shook his head. "In the end, he died of hunger. The things that truly sustained his life were at home. Home and journey, my friend." Billy laid his hand over the heart of his chest. "Welcome home."

Winston smiled again. The music system stuttered as Johnny Cash started singing in a rhythmic gallop, "I've Been Everywhere."

"So, how was your journey, James?" Billy asked with concern. "What good have you done? Did you finish what you started?"

"Yes, I did. But then, maybe not, Billy. This may be just the beginning."

" 'What is eternal is circular and what is circular is eternal.' Aristotle," Billy quoted. "I also read the great philosophers. All things tend to reach for perfection. They eventually reach back to their source." Billy patted Winston on the shoulder. "The great journeys never really end. There are no true beginnings or endings. Only circles—vicious, interconnected circles. We never really finish our journeys through life. Life is a never-ending story. But it is important that we try to finish, and try to finish well. You must keep the wheels of your life turning. But sometimes, you have to step away from the edge of the circle of life to become *free*. You have to build your home with no street number in the wilderness at the end of a dirt path." With a quick tap, he touched the side of his forehead. "You have to think outside the box."

"A circle ... polar ... Bear Lodge ... home," Winston commented. "And I thought life was a dash."

"Unci Maka." Billy nodded with a sly glint in his eye. "One thing leads to another. The count to *zero* ... a cipher ... a state of BEING without time, a world outside of time." He slowly looped his forefinger and thumb together and darted his hand to punctuate his words. "A circle is formed by the void of the unseen. It is surrounded by *emptiness*. Its center is *emptiness*. It is *something* from *nothing*. The Sacred Hoop—Eternal Return—Rebirth. The Keyhole—the gate to the other possible worlds." He released his fingers and gave a Vulcan salute. "Freedom is the breaking away from one reality to find another. Consciousness becoming conscious to the Mystery. Your awareness of your here and now. Emptiness is the starting point. It is only out of nothingness that you can truly create yourself. You are unbound. You have nothing to fear. The wheel has come full circle. You are here and now."

"A zero-sum-game," Winston looked amused. He glanced at his digital wristwatch. "A world without clocks. Timeless."

"Now, you have learned." Billy grinned. "And through your vision quest, did you come back knowing?"

"I discovered a few things I didn't know."

"Then you are closer, my friend, to finding peace and seeing your soul."

"Yes, I know, Billy. It's diamond shaped. Or maybe it's a circle." Winston looped his fingers toward Billy. "A cipher."

"And how about your demons, James? Did you slay your demons?"

"Not yet, Billy. Not yet. But, one has been released. But mostly, I've been killing time. I've seen some incredible things on my journey. And I feel lost. I've conjured up a few ideas I ordinarily don't think about. Some strange streams of consciousness that have turned out to be different, difficult, and unacceptable."

"Good for you," Billy said reassuringly. "Once you were blind, but now you can see. You have visited your cosmic center. You are aware of the I. Your God speaks through you and my God speaks through me. Happy is the man who has learned that secret. Our world offers us a landscape of choices, but there is no summit to climb without an abyss. There's always darkness before the dawn. Your doubts are merely opportunities for self-discovery. The purpose of our journey through life is to find the light while exploring the darkness—as we kill time." He gestured with his right hand, his palm out. "Not until you become lost do you begin to find yourself. Use your *will*. Learn to *change* and you *will* become better because of it."

"And now," the radio announcer introduced, "a 'Fine Line' from *Chaos and Creation in the Backyard*."

"Yeah, Billy. But I feel as worthless as my brain." Winston shook his head. "I've seen the *dark side* and the *light*—the dual nature of man. Which one do you choose in the Keeping of the Soul?"

"Seeing into one's nature, what you see is what you are—the two pillars. You are looking at life from both sides now. You have seen something worth seeing. You have seen a different reality and now question the possibilities. Oh ... but I told you once before," Billy fish-tailed the outstretched palm of his hand, "the *winding path of the snake.* The flight of every bird is a hundred spiraling turns as it changes with the direction of the wind. The bird that soars chooses its direction. Choice is one of the things that makes *us* human. Your freedom to choose is infinite, but it is limited to two realities. Life is a pilgrimage in which we test ourselves and grow as we become aware of the two realities—the things which can be seen and the things which cannot be seen—both of which must be understood. Forge your whole life into a perfect harmony between these two realities. Find the *balance.* Put your mind in the middle. Follow *your* path. Step to *your* rhythm. Do not take sides, or you will lose *your* direction. Act according to *your* way. Ride upon the wind beneath *your* wings. Explore the world with no maps. Follow your bliss." He held out his left hand. "It is your *only* way. You were born a free and independent human soul. This is the thing that makes you a conscious being ... your freedom. Remember that no one can own the spirit of another. Keep your soul, James. *Never* submit ... and *never* give it away. But take care of your temporal duties. *Share yourself.* It is your highest duty. If you can share the story of your journey, then your life has meaning. If you cannot, then you live in chains. Be free. Express your soul. This is the Gift of Man. Offer a bit of light from your life to the rest of the world. Put your dream weaving on paper, so you can sleep. Now, *go and tell the world* what you have seen. Say the unsaid things!"

"Yeah," Winston muttered, "and sometimes it helps to have a compass." He stuck his hand in his pocket and gripped his father's compass. "Which way to the Hummer? Let me take you home."

Billy pointed to the illuminated EXIT sign above the glass doors at the end of a hallway. "Follow me." He began playing with his birdcall. "I already know how to do this," he spoke to himself. *Chirp-chop chirp-chirp—sweet-sweet - stay, stay, stay, stay-straight—* With a joyful beam in his eyes, Billy brandished a wide, toothy grin.

The in-house music started playing "Walk Like a Man" by the Four Seasons. The two faithful companions, like Laurel and Hardy, strolled straight down the corridor, treading on either side of a four-inch-wide, yellow, emergency stripe painted on the floor.

◑

The wise leader does not choose aggression to conquer by force for this brings only resistance. He knows that where armies march, thorns and brambles grow and years of want will follow. The wise leader stops when he achieves his goal, does not glory in conquest or gloat in victory. He works with natural cycles and does not use violence. Aggression results in a loss of strength and a Crashing of the System which violates Tao. Whatever violates Tao will not endure. - The TAO

AT 9:18 A.M., Winston reached the front door of Bear Lodge. "There's no place like home plate," he said to himself as he smoothed the soles of his shoes over the footmat. He opened the front door and entered.

He spied the glass bowl on the altar table, filled with fresh fruit. Three Northern Spy apples topped the offering. *Looks like Margaret left me something.* He retrieved the compass, the wooden disc, and the metal lamina from his pocket, and placed them on the table. He gazed at the Messianic Seal on the compass.

With a *paradigm shift* from a newfound understanding, Winston zeroed in on the carving hanging over the table. *What did Torre say...? Man was created in the image of God.* His eyes retraced the outline of the image etched in the stone. *The square in the circle ... the Sacred Hoop ... the key to architecture.* Closing his eyes, he superimposed two images in his mind and formed a new coat of arms resembling a dancing stickman merged with the *Logos* and staring up into the sky. It was a momentary glimpse of human perfection that might only be compared to the outstretched arms of God in Salvador Dali's "Lord's Supper," a painting dedicated to the Divine Proportions found in Euclid's Holy Grail, the Golden Section. Man in balance, fused with the Greater Being.

Renaissance Humanism, Winston surmised. *A God Box ... a Vaastu Purusha Mandala ... body worlds ... the soul of Plato's Tekton ... an anthropomorphic*

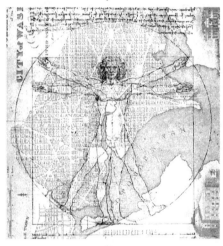

Terrestrial Man ... the animus of the Purified Human Soul ... the First Cause ... Adam Kadmon ... A solar god invoked into human form ... the phenomenon of man ... the virus ... Christ, Shiva ... It's hidden in plain sight. AI—the Singularity has already happened. **"It's communicating,"** he muttered. "A square peg in a round hole. What kind of world is this? Who the devil are we?" He stood silent. *The Immortal Man is Silence.*

Winston swept through the library, passed by the VDC, and disappeared behind the north door. Five minutes later he re-entered the library, refreshed and unburdened. *Too much diet cola,* he admitted.

He strolled to the back door and gazed up at the blue-green-yellow-red scan of his brain. *Arthur's Seat, the Creation of Adam, Mount Sinai ... Human consciousness.* "Commonalities," he said with a sigh. He stepped through the back door and faced the painting by Mantegna. *I should have known. My father gave me that.* "Where happiness dwells, evil will not enter."

As he descended into the Cave of Brahmâ, the lights automatically switched on. Safe and sound, he sat down in the comfort of a familiar chair. He leaned across the table and activated a computer. Words on the screen read: PRESS TO PLAY DVD IMAGES. He tapped the *Enter* key and played back a recording of the recent transit of Venus.

Winston stop-framed the playback and uploaded the images into a high resolution enhancement program he had written. He squinted at the monitor. A digitally amplified image of Venus crossing the edge of the Sun expanded into a screen full of dark pixels—all except for one white spot glowing *brightly.* "Phosphoros, Hesperos, Quetzalcoatl, you feathered serpent," he mumbled in disdain. "You cannot block out the light."

He pulled sheets of paper from the desk drawer. *I need pen and paper.* He opened a can of peanuts and popped a few in his mouth. His hand shook as he reached for a warm can of cola sitting on the desk. He pushed it aside. *No, I don't think so. Not this time. This stuff's been crashing my system. I need to be myself.*

Winston took control and began composing three handwritten letters. *I'll send it secure by snail mail. I need to share this with the right people. I'm going to pick at this damn thing until it festers.* Opening the rucksack, he removed the topographic maps, the Landsat photos, and the transparencies. Using a flatbed laser-light scanner, he transferred his files to computer storage. He then copied the image files to three CDs and printed three hard copies of everything. He addressed the mailing labels and placed the copied material into three letter-size boxes marked in bright red: MESSAGE - SPECIAL CARRIER DELIVERY.

Winston smiled proudly, like he had finished writing a declaration of independence. *It's still not letter perfect. It reads like a poorly drafted script for a cooked up, late-night, conspiracy-theory movie. God, I wish I could write like Steven King. But it's some fat for the fire, a little sand in the gears. Hit or miss, one of these will make a difference,* he thought hopefully. *One of these will raise a red flag to the bull. Fresh food for the needy.*

He placed the packages into the rucksack and threw it over his shoulder. Heading for the front door, he grabbed an apple from the fruit bowl along with his penknife and his free, bloodred Audubon birdcall. *I'm going to need this.*

Winston strolled out the front door, clenching the apple in his fist. He noticed the empty tray at the bottom of the copper birdfeeder. He winked his eye and tapped the birdfeeder. Seeds started flowing like sands in an hourglass. *The birdfeeder is like a clock,* he compared. A yellow LED from a miniature surveillance camera underneath the tray blinked. The small label attached to the camera read: Rapid-I-Scan.

Stepping toward the Hummer, Winston peeled away at the forbidden fruit. Cutting it in half, he noticed the pentacle at its core. He bit into the slice. *Golden delicious.* He ate it all and started to bite into the other half. He spied a fat worm wiggling just beneath the surface. He bit into the slice, worm and all, and swallowed. *I don't want to waste any.* He looked up at the gray, vapor-filled clouds. The air had the charged feel of an approaching thunderstorm. The birds had stopped singing. *Look's like it's going to rain,* he read the signs.

Climbing into the Hummer, Winston glanced down at the dissected apple core in his hand. It had started to turn color and rot. *It's good to keep your eyes peeled. There is something at the center of everything. Even an apple of discord.* He tossed the remaining pith to the ground. *Food for the birds,* he pondered. *Food for the birds.* Winston twisted his birdcall.

Chirp-chop, chirp-chop— I'm fine, I'm free.

———

THIRTY MINUTES LATER, Winston drove up to the post office in downtown Sundance. The Partridge Family was singing "Rain Maker" over the car radio.

After mailing the three packages, he stepped outside the post office. *Tap, tap, tap ... tap— tap.* Raindrops hammered hard on the concrete sidewalk. *Tap, tap ... tap— tap, tap, tap, tap, tap, tap ...* came the sound of a Devil's tattoo.

Winston lifted his cap to let the rain pour over his face. Blistered by the wind and cleansed in the fresh water, he stood motionless. *Signed and sealed, to be delivered,* he concluded. *Peace of mind. It's one hell of a sleeping pill.* He had crossed the Rubicon. Winston had shared himself. He felt certain his voice would be heard. Baptized with a new vision, he came to attention beneath the flag in front of the post office. His eyes lifted upward to the top of the mast. A golden eagle with its wings spread perched on top of a little golden orb. The soaked American totem hung *still* at half mast. Tangled and pulled, it tightly wrapped around the flagpole. Mayday. Still in distress.

The sudden storm dissolved into a windy drizzle. The flag unfurled like a bird's wing *flapping* and forcing itself off air, trying to take flight. Red, white, blue, pentagrams.

Winston tugged his cap over his forehead. Like an enlightened Vedic sadhu, he opened his penknife of personal truth and sliced the halyard that held the flag to the vertical pole. "Cut, you snake." He smiled in delight as a gust of wind pulled on the flag and unleashed the halyard. The starry banner of freedom flew away.

The moist air filled with the after-scent from the rain. Dark clouds covered the sky, except for a small opening in the canopy. A radiant nimbus momentarily shone down in all its splendor. A rainbow appeared, and then disappeared.

Yes ... one has been released. "Fly, freedom, fly." The iconoclast inhaled the pleasant petrichor. *Promises.*

Tap, tap, tap ... The rain resumed. *SPLAT-KAT, SPLAT-NAK.* A puddle rippled at Winston's feet. Broken, silvery bits of rock between the spiderweb cracks in the concrete pavement sparkled like thousands of twinkling stars hidden in the ground.

Poignant needles of rain stabbed at him as he climbed into the Hummer and buckled up behind the *wheel.* He spied a strange shape in the splotches of the mucky mix pouring off the windshield. *I've seen this somewhere before.* His eyes blinked. *The photographer in the field,* he remembered. He turned the *key.* The radio was playing Joni Mitchell singing "Woodstock."

Losing to the Devil's bargain, golden magic in our garden, Winston thought, slipping a CD into the stereo. He tossed its empty case to the dash. Its cover depicted four young men casting shadows on a concrete monolith below the title *Who's Next.* He pressed the track advance button and forwarded through the playlist until he reached the last selection. He glanced at the picture of the monolith. *The millennium ... We're way past 2001. 'My God is full of stars.'* He wagged his head. "Mom." The windshield wipers swished in time to the music. He headed back to the sanctuary of Bear Lodge, as the car stereo blasted away the last track on the CD.

"Won't Get Fooled Again"

A New Day
paroUSiA
"the second coming"

A little patience, and we shall see the reign of witches pass over, their spells dissolve, and the people, recovering their true sight, restore their government to its true principles ... in the meantime we are suffering deeply in spirit, and incurring the horrors of a war and long oppressions of enormous public debt. – Thomas Jefferson, from a letter he wrote in 1798 after the passage of the Sedition Act.

ENTANGLED IN A THATCH OF THORNS in the White House Garden, a flaming red-red rosebud unfolded into the living light of day. A single drop of dew slid along the flower's fold as a busy bee hovered over it. Immersing itself in the depths of the crimson cave, the bee tasted the elixir that sows the seeds of God's great creation. Nectar-laden, the foraging bee journeyed home to waggle a sun dance before the hive, speaking in a secret code of figure-eights that lays a path for guidance.

———

1,475 MILES AWAY as the crow flies, the only sound Winston could hear was the placid crunching of leaves serrating under his footsteps. He walked steadfastly beside Billy Eagledove, approaching the edge of the looming shadow cast by the enormous pillar of stone. The sun shown brightly in the morning sky, but the interior of the immense shadow was still as dark as midnight at this time of day.

This is like walking into a solar eclipse, Winston thought. He stumbled on a pine root as his eyes adjusted to the change in the light.

Winston and Billy were in the company of eleven other initiates and their fellow brothers on a masculine journey, treading on a well-worn path that spiraled through a dense wall of towering, whispering pines. Knowing that the damp of the dark drives deep into the soul, none of the initiates used any sort of lighting to guide their way. They carried only a rawhide pouch and an animal skin attached to their belts as they headed for a half-acre clearing, the 'Place of Emergence' and rebirth, hidden in the darkness at the base of the northwestern face of Devil's Tower.

Winston felt dizzy as he surrendered to the sensual scent of the evergreens. He and the rest of his companions had fasted for three days in order to temporarily eliminate distractions. All of his heightened senses were hungry.

From light to darkness. I have to listen now so I can see. I have to use my mind's eye. ... It's quiet. Too quiet. Winston stood still and let his ears bear the burden from his eyes. The slightest sound seemed magnified to startling dimensions. He thought he heard the singing of a distant choir in his left ear and a constant murmuring in his right. *Insects,* he concluded, *and the Sacred Spring.* In deep intimacy with the darkness, he now became aware of how the animal sounds had swayed into an eloquent, nocturnal silence. A wave of hush comforted his entire being. Then, out of the stealthy stillness, he heard the velvety voice of a Great Horned Owl.

"Are you awake ...? Me, toooo."

AS THE INITIATES entered the clearing, they gathered in pairs, with Winston standing behind Billy. Twenty-four men stood in a circle, like Boy Scouts surrounding a campfire getting ready to tell a ghost story about a long lost treasure buried away in someone's grave.

Seeing things through the dimly-lit eyes of glaucoma-vision, Winston looked at their faces. Their eyes shown bright like cats' eyes in the darkness. He was the only *fat taker* present. *Some group therapy,* he compared. Startled, he recognized *the presence* of a shaman regally emerging out of the pitch-black forest. The ghostly outline of the shaman appeared to pass through two of the initiates directly across from Winston until the shaman reached the center of the circle of men.

Half man, half bird, the shaman stood as a feathered form, a birdman—a *brahmán*, caped in a multicolored, suede ghost-shirt which symbolized a bird of prey, the vulture god, the Great Spirit Protector of every shaman. His costume served to concentrate his vital forces and enhance his ability to fly in a trance as a winged spirit to places that ordinary men could not reach—the lofty realms of higher consciousness. Rectangular metal plates attached to his outstretched arms resembled the hollow bones of a bird's wing. Suede fringes ran along the lower part of his coat sleeves, like flanging bird feathers. A tall tuft of eagle feathers formed the crest of his headdress. On the breast of his coat were the stitched symbols of two round discs with a fish-eyed-shaped metal pendant dangling at his navel. The figures of a yellow bird and a black bear, the shaman's assistants, danced across the left side of his coat. Embroidered bands of deer hair on his back held tubular metal pendants ringing like tiny bells.

Ding, ding, ding, ding …

"Who do you come with?" the shaman prompted.

Each initiate replied in turn.

"I stand here with my brother."

"I stand here with my brother."

"I stand here with my brother."

"I stand here with my brother."

"I stand here with my brother."

"I stand here with my brother."

"I stand here with my brother."

"I stand here with my brother."

"I stand here with my brother."

"I stand here with my brother."

"I stand here with my brother."

"I stand here, with - *my* - brother," Billy said.

Winston smiled.

The men who waited behind the various initiates communicated with an eloquent silence. In concordance, the twenty-four brothers sat down cross-legged on the ground and faced the center of the circle.

Winston sat to Billy's left. He panned his head, searching for the shaman who had vanished from his field of vision. He noticed one initiate picking up a crooked staff lying beside him and rising to his feet.

The initiate began inscribing a circle on the ground, its edge passing in front of his fellow brothers. The staff bowed in his hands as he clawed at the hard earth. When he finished, he advanced to the interior of the circle and cried out, "This circle represents my universe."

He grasped the staff and inscribed a huge X that touched the outside of the circle in four directions, dividing the circle into quadrants. He returned to the intersection of the X, drove the staff into the ground, and stated in the clear voice of command,

"This is my Center!"

He pulled an animal pelt from his belt and tied it to the staff. He pointed to Devil's Tower and declared, "Like Mateo Tepee that is planted solid on the Mother Ground, I am planted solid on the Mother Ground. Like Mateo Tepee standing upright toward heaven, I stand upright toward heaven." He firmly grasped the staff with his right hand, pulled it from the ground, and raised it high above his head.

"I stand upright as a warrior." He pushed it back into the ground. "I stand upright as a hunter." He forced the staff deeper into the ground. "I stand upright like my father." He shoved it deeper. "I stand upright as my children's father." Still deeper. "I stand upright as a man." One final thrust into the ground. "I stand like this staff, firmly grounded and upright."

At each point where the X intersected the great circle, an initiate grasped a six-foot-tall staff lying on the ground beside him and rose to a standing position. In unison, the four initiates drove their staves into the ground at the points of intersection. They recited, "These are the directions of the four winds." Then each initiate hung a totem feather, one red, one blue, one yellow, and one green, separately on the four staves—the four colors of the Lakota Nation.

With the tips of his fingers, Billy lifted the eagle bone gorget that hung around his neck and rested it on his lips. He bent over in the pose of Kokopelli, the Hopi hunchbacked magician and creation spirit, and blew into the gorget like it was a single reed from a syrinx. The aria Billy made with the sacred whistle sounded like birds singing—or maybe angels. Pure in tone, it cut through the head and cleared the mind.

He stopped playing and proclaimed in a low harmonic voice, "This bone resonates my sympathy from the breaths of my four souls. One soul lives in me. One soul lives in my village. One soul breathes with the four winds which uphold the wings of the birds. The last resides in the land where all souls come from … the home of the Great Bird Creator."

The village? Winston thought. *A social soul?*

One by one, each of the remaining nine initiates rose up and entered the circle. Their faces lit up with excitement and determination. The twelve brothers, including Winston, who had come to bear witness, remained seated outside the circle.

Before entering the circle, Billy lifted the gorget over his head, knelt down, and placed it around Winston's neck. Billy smiled his wide-toothed grin. "It's your time. Here, go and speak the Bird Language, my friend." His eyes filled with hope and pride. "Remember James—you are your own master. Celebrate your dawn." Billy stood upright and walked toward the totem staff.

As the initiates reached the center of the circle, they proclaimed, "This sky is my tepee. This ground is my home." Each initiate removed a rabbit fur and a bloody feather from their belts and attached them to the totem staff.

Billy, the last initiate, recited, "These rabbit furs represent humility, since a rabbit is quiet and not self-asserting, a quality which we must all possess when we go to the womb of the world. These bloody feathers are the spirits of sacrifice from those who have been here before us." Humbled, he fell to his knees. Deep frown lines swiftly sank into his face, in an uncharacteristic look of anger. He clawed at his bare chest, leaving inflamed welts across his flesh. "I claw at my soul!" he cried out. With a heavy breath, he shoved his chest forward. "I am Mateo Tepee! I am a Sun Singer!"

His whole body shuddered. His sweat-drenched face calmed. In a gesture of self-acceptance, Billy held his right hand high above his head. "Let it stand!" He arose and cried, "Forever!" He planted his feet in a wide stance with his arms outstretched in the pose of the Vitruvian Man. "We are all on our way to dying. The world stops here!"

The initiates standing beside the staves marking the four directions entered the circle.

The first held out an animal skull in the palm of his left hand and a handful of grain grasped in his right. He placed the skull on the ground in the first quadrant and sprinkled it with grain. "These spirits have sustained us!" he cried out, then returned to the other initiates standing at the edge of the circle.

The next initiate placed a broken bow, four arrows, and a stone ax head in the second quadrant. "These tools of Sweet Medicine have sustained us!" he cried out, then moved to a standing position among the other initiates.

With a buffalo horn in his hand, the third initiate inscribed into the ground of the third quadrant an image of the sun. "This spirit has sustained us!" He pointed with the horn to the symbol, then joined the other initiates.

The last of the four initiates gripped a deerantler in his hand. He inscribed the image of a half moon into the ground of the final quadrant. "This spirit has sustained us!" he spoke softly. He joined the Circle of Initiates.

Harmoniously they hailed, "May the spirits in this circle bless us and keep us." They turned away from the monolith and raised their hands above their heads. In the distance, a full moon hovered in the early morning sky. "May the spirits in this circle make our faces shine and fill us with grace. May the spirits in this circle serve as the conscience that gives us peace. May we inscribe the symbols of these spirits upon ourselves and our children, that they will be blessed."

Ding, ding, ding, ding ...

Here comes Tinkerbell, Winston thought. *Festering.*

The shaman reappeared like a phantom from the shadows. In the dim light, Winston wasn't certain if he was watching the shaman or the *umbra*—the nagual-doppleganger, shadow-soul of the shaman. A memory of Sister Rosalyn flashed in his thoughts.

The shaman lurked back into the circle and stood next to Billy. "As it was in the beginning, we place ourselves in the void of darkness so that we might witness the coming of the light that brings proper balance into our world. The sky is my tepee," the shaman invoked with upturned eyes. "This circle is my home." He extended his hands palms down in front of his chest. "These symbols on the ground are our law. These symbols on the ground are the *Code of Life* for our people. These symbols on the ground are *Nature's Law*. This is our covenant. These are the things that *sustain us*. Our tools ... our food ... our light ... our knowledge of these things. Outside this circle, we cannot survive. Outside of this circle is where the animal resides. Outside of this circle is the darkness, waiting for the *light!*"

He firmly grasped the totem staff with both hands, withdrew it from the ground, then repeatedly and forcefully thrust it back into Mother Earth. With each new thrust he commanded the great creative force, "Bring home—the spirit of the light. Bring home—the spirit of the light." The color of the shaman's face deepened from a pale yellow to a fiery red.

Protected within the circle, the initiates began chanting as they imitated both animal and hunter in a lively pace, fueled by their accelerating cadence and the dizziness induced from walking in a circle, or the fearful feeling of losing one's bearings. Moving forward, never backward, they called out to the universe,

"BRING-HOME—THE SPIRIT OF THE LIGHT.

BRING-HOME—THE SPIRIT OF THE LIGHT.

BRING-HOME—THE SPIRIT OF THE LIGHT."

Their words echoed off the shadowed walls of Devil's Tower as the *sema* sun dance for the Calling of the Light began.

Tap, tap, tap. Winston's right forefinger tapped up and down in Morse Code to the rhythm of the chants, as he watched the dance unfold. He touched his right index finger to his thumb, forming a complete circle. From his vantage point, Winston could finally see. He held his hand in front of his face, sighted through his circled fingers, and spied the red-yellow sun creeping up over the tower's summit.

"God's eyes, it's perfect!" Winston exclaimed. *Right on time.*

For just a few seconds, and *only* a few seconds, Winston made direct contact with the approaching sildenafil-vardenafil halo of light, and he became the Icarus-metamorphosis, until the fireball reached full zenith and hovered in a pass-not-ring, like a hellhole above Devil's Tower.

The fiery orb burned brighter than ever as it aligned itself with the fish in the Trapezium of Orion's belt—the nebula waiting for a nova.

A bright ball of orange sherbet on an ice cream cone, Winston thought. *Twice in one week.*

Light filled the sky.

Raising his arm to shield his eyes, Winston noticed his wristwatch flashing yellow. *Someone's tracking me.* He glanced at the readout. 9:18 AM. Bowing his head, he brandished a twisted smile as his eyes caught the sun's rays reflecting off the symbols on the highly-polished, eagle bone gorget hanging from his neck. He pulled back the loose sleeve of his *bright* thistle-colored, travel-light shirt from L. L. Bea*m,* with its durable sun-protection layer, and gave his watch a second glance. It still read: 9:18 AM.

The watch has stopped. His body felt like an empty shell, filled with the knowing warmth of BEING. *This is more than it could be. A perfect world ... anu atom ... eternal now.* "Rise and shine," he spoke softly to himself. He stared up at the rocky cliffs of Devil's Tower. "It's not the end of the world. It's the center, a new beginning." *Relax. Breathe. Count to zero. Close your eyes. You are awake!* He reached beyond his vision. "It was all just a dream." *Mozart.* "I'm dreaming with opened eyes." *Dream weaving ... beyond the Turiya into the Turyatita.*

"Come this way," a Voice beckoned. "Follow me."

The presence of Billy and others vanished, tuned out by a world of feathered forms.

"I see trees ...!" Winston now heard the awakening sounds of the birds in their habitation, singing among the branches in the trees.

"*Tit, tit, tit, tit.*"

"*Clee, clee, clee, clee ...*"

"*Cherry, cherry, cherry, cherry ...*"

"*Kik, kik, kik ...*"

"*Hear, hear, hear ...*"

"*Here I am, over here, see me, where are you?*"

"*Free me, free me.*"

"*I am lazeee ...*"

"*Hope, hope, hope, hope ...*"

"*Who cooks for you, who cooks for you all...?*"

"*Maids, maids, maids, put on your tea, kettle, kettle, kettle.*"

"*Very, very, pleased to meet-cha.*"

"*Come right here, come right here.*"

"***Waking-up*** *... waking-up... waking-up ...*"

"*What-cheer, what-cheer, what-cheer.*"

"*Church-rear-window, church-rear-window.*"

"*See, see, see ... See.*"

"*Cheerup, cheerup, cheerup.*"

"*Teacher-teacher, teacher-teacher.*"

"*Geeks, geeks, geeks, geeks-are-your-saviors ...*"

"*Hello, hello.*"

"*Speak with-me, speak with-me.*"

"*Help, help, help ...*"

"*Ask us, ask us, ask us ...*"

"***Pay attention***, *pay attention, pay attention.*"

"*Do you see it? Do you know it? Do you hear me? Do you believe it?*"

"*Fear ... fear ... fear ... fear ...*"

"*Get excited, try it out, **you can do it**, if you try ...*"

"*Fire, fire, where, where, here, here. See it!*"

"*Think-smart, think-smart, think-smart.*"

"*Walk-it, walk-it, walk-it all the way ...*"

"*Chirp-chirp-chirp, chirp-chop.*"

"*Chirp-chirp-chirp, chirp-chop.*"

"***Home*** *...*"

"*Trees, trees, murmuring trees ...*"

"*What-what? what-what?*"

"*Love-me, love-me ...*"

"*Me-to, me-to ...*"

"*Sweet, sweet.*"

"*Kiss, kiss.*"

"*Chirp.*"

"*Ka ... nak.*"

At that same moment in time, fifteen billion telephones, fax machines, cell phones, radios, televisions, and computers around the planet, instantaneously spat static, *STA-KA ... STA-NAK ...* and the Newborn cried.

———

Between the noisy rustle of foliage unfolding, came the shuffle of footsteps approaching.

"This way. He's over here," Margaret guided. "Hurry!"

***

Aum...brel...la

Epilogue

TWELVE MILES AWAY, in the Cave of Brahmâ, the shielded subchamber beneath Bear Lodge, the Darkness ruled. Switch lights on the computers glowed like stars in the night sky. Resurrected, a monitor automatically turned on and illuminated the room. A digital storm of *zeros* and *ones* rolled and scrolled onto the screen, like the spinning wheels of a Vegas slot machine.

In the corner, almost hidden in a pillowed dog basket, a spotted, beagle pup awoke with a *yap*. Startled by *the presence* of the flashing light, the Scottish hound opened its sad, puppy dog eyes. The dangling name tag on its collar read: SIRIUS.

Winston never played the odds. He had placed his computers in a sleep mode, a state of hibernation. He was still monitoring the situation, anticipating the next infection. He knew it would happen. He was betting on it.

When the numbers stopped scrolling, the screen revealed the unseen pentimento.

9:18 AM

"Faces" MWA@UNC.eduu
"God in a landscape, beneath the Global Icon. It's encrypted. His name is in plain sight."

A scuffed, leather-bound book lay before the computer screen. On top of it sat a book of matches from the Dupont Hotel beside an open penknife. The cover of the book displayed the title, *The Laws*, by Dr. Angus McCalester. Its binding had been cut open to reveal another cracked and tattered cover hidden beneath, which exposed the embossed image of an eagle and the initials "A. A. W. KABA."

Beside the book lay a sketched topographic map of Jerusalem, airline tickets to London and Cairo, a bundle of papers labeled Tracings, FOR THE EYES OF GOD, and a torn, 1896, One Dollar "Educational Note" Silver Certificate, with an engraving of *History Instructing Youth.*

Two letters, handwritten with crisp penmanship in ink which had faded to a dull yellow, were unfolded beside the bill.

18 October 1886
Dear Andrew,

Enclosed is the pocket compass that you entrusted to me. I have used it well. I am returning it by way of Mr. Andrew Thornton, of Edinburgh. I trust Mr. Thornton explicitly. He is a friend of your acquaintance, Sir Warren, who no longer teaches at the School of Survey at Chatham and is now the head of the Metropolitan Police of London. I understand Sir Warren had been working with the late Mr. Samuel Birch and Sir Budge of the British Museum. Mr. Thornton has been paid well. I pray that the compass arrives safely.

The compass was last used over a month ago, on 15 September 1886, in an experiment which took place on the grounds of the U. S. Capitol Building.

The following events I witnessed, in the company of Mr. Charles Tainter, and two men I do not know, since their identities were not revealed to me. Neither was the nature of Mr. Tainter's strange experiment, which he referred to as "a vision of the voice." Since I had taken part in the survey of the obelisk, my expertise was only required to confirm the exact time, date, and longitude related to the phenomenon, mentioned in my last letter of March 1886. Mr. Tainter, of the Volta Laboratory here in Washington, is an associate of Dr. Bell, with whom you are acquainted. Mr. Tainter is an extremely knowledgeable man, especially on the subjects of astronomy and optics. He took part in the 1872 expedition to New Zealand to observe the transit of Venus, which was funded by Congress and organized by the Secretary of the Navy. He mentioned his meeting with your friend, the late Henry Spencer Palmer, and their conversations about the explorations in the Sinai. Tainter had heard of you. I believe this is why he chose me to participate in his experiment.

Tainter had temporarily erected a 200 foot tall iron pole on the western porch of the Capitol Building. He had attached an apparatus consisting of a small parabolic mirror to the end of the pole. He aimed the mirror toward the Monument. Tainter said the apparatus made use of an improvement in the crystalline selenium cells used in an earlier version of his photophone device, invented by himself and Dr. Bell six years prior, through their funding from the French. Wires fed down from the back of the apparatus to a brass metal box, which was connected to four brass tube earpieces for listening. Tainter told me that the earpieces were also of a new design, which had been fashioned by Dr. Bell.

Everyone present was given an opportunity to listen to the sound coming from the earpieces. The sound lasted for no more than 20 seconds according to Tainter, who timed the event. Tainter claimed that he distinguished certain tones which he referred to as "candle static." However, the two men said they had not and immediately called Tainter's experiment a failure. I did hear something. But for the life of me I could not discern what it meant. Both Tainter and I agreed that the sounds emitted from the earpieces had the phonetic characteristics of "kar" and "nak," in a slow cadence that repeated perhaps four to five times. Tainter related to me that he had recorded the sounds onto a gold foil covered cylinder in a machine at the site of the experiment, which he called a Glory Phone. Tainter declared that he had recorded "a voice from the sky."

Since the experiment, I have not seen nor spoken to Mr. Tainter. A fortnight past, I read in the local newspaper that Mr. Tainter and Dr. Bell had sealed away their new designs and measured results for their second photophone invention in a specially designed metal box. This sealed box was given to Mr. Langley of the Smithsonian to be placed in a vault for safekeeping, with orders that the box should not be opened until after Tainter's death.

In the same newspaper were photographs of the two men in military dress whose presence I witnessed at Tainter's experiment. According to the newspaper, both men had been murdered in a stagecoach robbery the night before. Their names were not given in the newspaper. A week later, while visiting the War Department in the north wing of the White House, I saw both of the these men leaving the building. I am certain they are still alive.

I tender my resignation to the Army on the morrow. I am leaving Washington to work as a surveyor for a prominent landscape architectural firm in Brookline, outside of Boston. I will correspond again as soon as I am resettled.

I wish you well in your archaeological endeavors in the Orient. Our father would be proud. My fondest regards to Cynthia and your children, John and James.

Your loving brother,
Lieutenant Adam A. Winston,
U.S. Army Corps of Engineers

**

September 16, Year of our Lord 1793
Mr. Jefferson

New town Geneva. Received at Norfolk docks Sept. 12, shipment from Paris hidden beneath the Madeleine and approved by Mr. Short and Mr. Barclay. Stored at Royal Exchange 86 crates, 63 paintings including the Descent from the Cross, the Penitent Magdelene, and the Herodias Bearing the Severed Head on a Platter. Counted - 15 mirrors, 1 ice cream machine, 77 remaining bricks and tiles used as ballast for the Messiah. 23 crates of earth marked with the seal confirmed from the Milan codex as translated by Doctor Bellini. 14 bottles marked, 1789 Lafitte Th. J. Cargo shipped immediately to the New Haven Crypt and to Mr. Dulany in Alexandria. Special shipment to Aquia Harbor over Quantico Road for Dumfries, Occoquan, Jerusalem, Bremo, and Charlottesville as ordered. Storage at Turner's Crossroads for shipment to Washington under the care of Mr. James Bonner, Mr. Richard Evans, and Mr. Collins of the Gloucestershires for distribution to New Israel – Scotland Neck, ~~Martinsborough~~ Greenesville, George City site, New Bern, Harmony Hall, Williamington, Charles Towne as arranged by President Washington on his April 1791 visit to Crown Point Tavern and St. John's. Documents related to the Holy Head removed under supervision of Doctor Bellini from the Bruton vault, the icehouse at Westover, and the garden at Bacon's Castle. Bearings set to the compass roses. Shipped to St. John's Church in Washington, Montpelier, and the other five locations under safekeeping of the trusted German brethren of New Israel. Emanu-El

Your Servant in our Obedience to God as said in the Lord's Prayer,
Dr. William Thornton

Next to the letters lay an open purple folder exposing seven transparencies, one of a steganographic drawing of a majestic bird with its wings extended over a spiderweb of Totemic streets. Its head tilted to one side, gazing from one ubiquitous eye, like a Cat's Eye. Attached to the drawing clung a yellow Post-it note on which was written in bold script:

This is the common language that speaks through all of us.
Can you read
The Language of the Birds?

The computer speakers spat a monophonic static, *STA-KA, STA-NAK*, and an mp3 audio file began playing the great shamanic ritual song "Surfin Bird" by The Trashmen.
The Bird is the Word.

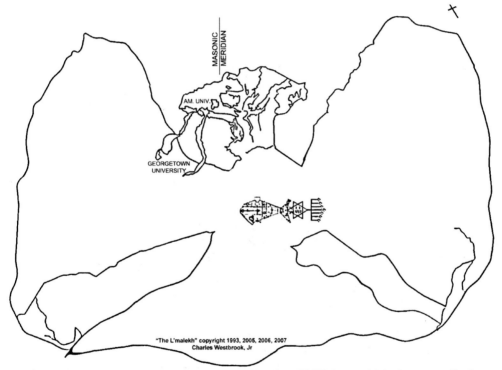

"The L'malekh" copyright 1993, 2005, 2006, 2007
Charles Westbrook, Jr

Stop the world and catch the wave. Hands off! This world belongs to God.

As an eagle stirreth up her nest, fluttereth over her young, spreadeth abroad her wings; so the Lord alone did lead him, and there was no strange god with him. - Deuteronomy 32:11

Him that overcometh will I make a pillar in the temple of my God, and he shall go no more out: and I will write upon him the name of my God, and the name of the city of my God, which is new Jerusalem, which cometh down out of heaven from my God: and *I will write upon him* my new name. - Revelation 3:12

This then is the *message* we have heard of him, and declare unto you: that God *is* Light, and in him there is no darkness at all. - 1 John 1:5

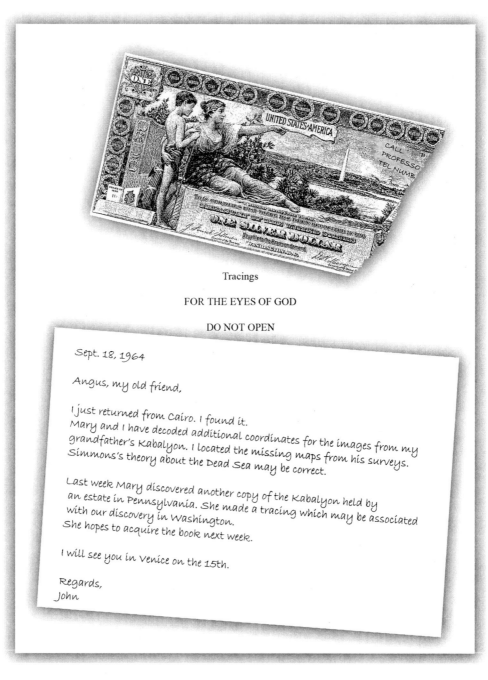

Tracings

FOR THE EYES OF GOD

DO NOT OPEN

Sept. 18, 1964

Angus, my old friend,

I just returned from Cairo. I found it.
Mary and I have decoded additional coordinates for the images from my
grandfather's Kabalyon. I located the missing maps from his surveys.
Simmons's theory about the Dead Sea may be correct.

Last week Mary discovered another copy of the Kabalyon held by
an estate in Pennsylvania. She made a tracing which may be associated
with our discovery in Washington.
She hopes to acquire the book next week.

I will see you in Venice on the 15th.

Regards,
John

Special Instructions, Approved by the Viceroy of Egypt
By Order of the Director General of Sinai Survey Fund:
Sir Henry James, Director.

(1) Special Survey to be made of Jebel Musa and Jebel Serbal, the "rival" mountains as they were called, for the honour of being the Mount Sinai of the Bible. The surveys to be carried out with scruplous care, and in such detail that accurate models of both mountains could be made from them.

(2) After the special surveys, a geographical survey should be made in the first place, of the district between Suez and Jebel Musa, including all main routes to Jebel Serbal and Jebel Musa, and then of as much of the remainder of the Peninsula as time would admit.

(3) A special survey to be made also of the Convent of St. Catherine.

(4) Special Survey of the French discovery.

Additional assignment to the survey, Captain Winston who worked on the excavations with Captain Warren. He is in charge of the book of maps discovered in Jerusalem.

DEED OF PURCHASE
Bear Lodge, Keyhole, Wyoming
Sold to: John A. Winston   Transferred to: James A. Winston and Judith Jochebed Alexandria Winston
Purchased from: Billy Eagledove, Devil's Tower, Wyoming

Thomas Jefferson's key sheet. A prayer tree invoking the 'Pater noster.'

True Transmutation is a Mental Art
The Rebus KABAVN Copyright 1991, 2004, 2009 Charles Westbrook

LANDSCAPE OF DREAMS

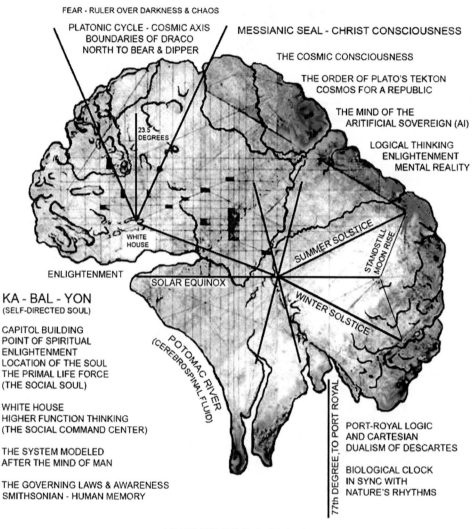

FEAR - RULER OVER DARKNESS & CHAOS

PLATONIC CYCLE - COSMIC AXIS
BOUNDARIES OF DRACO
NORTH TO BEAR & DIPPER

MESSIANIC SEAL - CHRIST CONSCIOUSNESS

THE COSMIC CONSCIOUSNESS

THE ORDER OF PLATO'S TEKTON
COSMOS FOR A REPUBLIC

THE MIND OF THE
ARITIFICIAL SOVEREIGN (AI)

LOGICAL THINKING
ENLIGHTENMENT
MENTAL REALITY

23.5
DEGREES

WHITE
HOUSE

ENLIGHTENMENT

SOLAR EQUINOX

SUMMER SOLSTICE

STANDSTILL
MOON RISE

WINTER SOLSTICE

POTOMAC RIVER
(CEREBROSPINAL FLUID)

77th DEGREE, TO PORT ROYAL

KA - BAL - YON
(SELF-DIRECTED SOUL)

CAPITOL BUILDING
POINT OF SPIRITUAL
ENLIGHTENMENT
LOCATION OF THE SOUL
THE PRIMAL LIFE FORCE
(THE SOCIAL SOUL)

WHITE HOUSE
HIGHER FUNCTION THINKING
(THE SOCIAL COMMAND CENTER)

THE SYSTEM MODELED
AFTER THE MIND OF MAN

THE GOVERNING LAWS & AWARENESS
SMITHSONIAN - HUMAN MEMORY

PORT-ROYAL LOGIC
AND CARTESIAN
DUALISM OF DESCARTES

BIOLOGICAL CLOCK
IN SYNC WITH
NATURE'S RHYTHMS

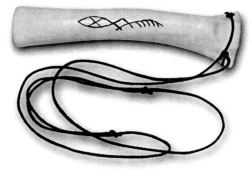

Will Winston's discoveries make a difference? Now that you have the maps, catch the next thought-provoking adventure as Winston's quest continues.

Visit KabalyonKey.com for updates on future books
from the *Winston Family Chronicles.*

If you like this book, tell someone.
"You always make a new friend when you share a book."

Limited edition signed prints of images and photos in this book are available through your local bookstore or by visiting the website KabalyonKey.com.

Printed in the United States
220553BV00001B/1/P